AMAZON/Print VERSION ONLY

Ebook/Print Cover: Carol Marques Design
Editing, Proofing, backgrounds, & Formatting: Dirty Sexy Words/ Storm shield Editing/Little Tailfeather Publishing
Cassandra's logos: Pretty in Ink Creations/Artlogo
Goosebusters Alpha team: Kat Silver, Becky Ross, Erica Taryn
Duckhunters Proofers: Jackie H
Sensitivity Readers: Brit Mason, Gail Jericho
Legal Services: Joshua Farley, esq.
Images/Fonts: Creative Fabrica, Depositphotos, Shutterstock, & Photoshop

No GenAI was used within this book. All errors and greatness are by an ADHD muppet.

CONTENT INFORMATION

This is a *paranormal whychoose romance with poly elements*—our FMC, Delores, will not have to choose between love interests.

There are many situations included that are intended for mature audiences (18+).

In this book, there may be instances/references (be they small or lengthy) that could trigger some individuals such as:

- liberal use of appropriate consent
- biting
- BDSM and intro to BDSM
- primal play
- raw sex
- shifted sex
- traumatic childhood
- MFM, MF, MM, and more
- super heinous puns (seriously, lots)
- underage drinking
- drug use
- unhealthy coping mechanisms

- body parts in jars
- neurospicy MMC
- death
- body modifications
- fancy genitalia
- mate knots/barbs
- slightly unhinged MMC
- bullying (in person and on social media)
- PTSD
- blood
- emotional abuse from parents and friends
- alcohol abuse
- domestic violence
- implied child abuse
- body dysmorphia
- Adult language
- emotional manipulation
- power play
- adorable nicknames
- physical intimidation
- coercive emotional abuse by authority figures (not in poly group)
- voyeurism
- rough sex
- biting
- masturbation
- sex with wings and tails
- attempted/successful kidnappings
- marking
- lawyers (ugh.)
- professors/student (above 18+)
- age gap (from 17 yrs to almost 2000 yrs)
- use of sex toys
- family dysfunction
- sensory deprivation
- talk of pegging

- betrayal (non-poly group)
- absolute disrespect for shitty parents
- pop culture references (so many)
- brief mentions of non-body positive dieting culture
- brief mentions of parental death
- mention of drug sales and distribution
- very liberal re-imagining of history
- discussion of other species as lower
- official corruption
- name calling
- occasional misogyny
- inappropriate use of a library
- exhibitionism
- hand necklaces
- adult bullying
- magical kinks
- impact play
- abusive bosses
- elitism
- bribery
- corpses
- fat shaming (not by MCs)
- drama
- physical threats to FMC and others
- species-ism
- discussion of shifter trafficking
- discussion of trafficking auctions
- suspicion of brainwashing

No sexual practices in this book should be taken as safe or appropriate for real life application.

Content information is important and I don't ever want to harm a reader with inaccurate information.

Stalk Cassandra Featherstone in the Dark Corners of the Web

Join my Facebook group and follow me everywhere!

Want More?

Sign up for
my bi-weekly manifesto for a
free series sampler:

AUTHOR RAMBLINGS

Readers,

As I said in the re-release of *Come Out & Prey*, this re-write was cathartic for me.

Not only did I have the chance to correct errors and topics readers gave feedback about, I could also explore storylines and character development I couldn't previously. It freed me in ways I cannot describe, and I enjoyed every minute.

The circumstances of the re-branding are not something I'm comfortable discussing, but despite the constant flow of obstacles and abuse, I was determined to give my readers what they deserved. I may write in a non-linear fashion, jumping from series to series to keep my muse satisfied, but I refuse to cultivate a fanbase and drop them cold turkey because of things they had nothing to do with.

It's not fair, nor professional, and I took the brunt of that decision on personally because *I love my readers and this world.*

Dolly learned a lesson in the last book—actually, quite a few, and *they're all applicable.*

Many times in life, even when you are not as sheltered as her, you will meet people who are excellent at hiding behind masks. They will seem like the most amazing person and the more you get to know them, the more you feel you've met your true match—in love, friendship, and even at work.

Eventually, that mask will slip and though you see it (like Todd or the Heathers), you rationalize their behavior. As time goes on and you get deeper into that relationship, the slips happen more often, but you forgive it because they'd never treat you that way and maybe those other people deserve it.

When the first flags pop up, RUN.

My great-grandpa used to say 'when people show you who they are, believe them' and though that's not a unique saying, it's always been dead accurate.

Dolly saw her friends and even Todd not acting like good people, but because she was afraid to have that power turned on her, she let it go. She didn't prevent them from treating others like garbage when she saw it, and she didn't distance herself from them for fear of being alone and ostracized.

Her struggle is all our struggles—even in our writing/reading community.

Hearing or reading people tearing others down, watching a group snicker over triumphs or failures, letting someone spread information they have no actual proof of… is tacit approval of their behavior. Unfortunately, it's no less prevalent in adult spaces than it is in those of children or teenagers.

If you can't stand up to a bully by telling them to knock it off, you have other options. Distance yourself from them, even if you worry you'll miss out or not be included. Approach the people being harmed and get their side of the story. Refuse to be part of conversations or groups that allow this behavior. Stop supporting the person who behaves this way publicly or privately.

But even Dolly learned that her lack of action allowed terrible people to thrive and grow more powerful—and then they turned on her. The abuse her so-called friends piled on others became her nightmare, and she had no one in her corner to help her fight it.

After the past year, I'm not afraid of those types of people's power or influence anymore. They've done what they could to destroy me, and I survived.

I will not be silent.

It feels amazing to say that, by the way, and while I'm not saying I'll jump on the train and spread vile BS like they do, I will answer questions about bad actors, scammers, and their ilk more honestly than I have in the past. Being quiet didn't stop them; it only kept me from feeling safe in my own spaces.

So, here's to our girl Dolly, and me, setting healthy boundaries, guarding our peace, and not letting the bastards grind us down.

Blood and guts,

Cassandra Featherstone

QUEEN OF SMART, SASSY SPICE

READER'S NOTE
A FEW THINGS YOU SHOULD KNOW…

Come Out & Prey should be read *before* this book, *Let Us Prey.*

This is a multi-book series, so *everything will not be revealed in the first book.* Some plot lines will continue through the series in a larger arc and not get resolved in the first or even the next book. I promise it will all get tied up and have a HEA; don't worry!

Let Us Prey is a why choose/poly romance, which means our FMC will not have to choose.

I would consider it a medium burn, slow build family group. It will get spicier in the following books. If you're looking for porn with little to no plot, no judgment, but this isn't the series for you. It's also not closed door or FTB, so I believe the spice will be worth the wait. I realize spice scales are subjective and everyone has different opinions on it, so forgive me if mine and yours aren't totally aligned.

There are some characters and creatures that speak in other languages. I made the *translations clickable end-of-chapter notes* to help.

Just an FYI: There are a *lot of puns*—they are intentionally bad and writing them made me giggle. If you don't like silly, world-specific humor like that, it may annoy you.

Note: In the South (where I'm from), it is fairly common to call people by their full names when you're being condescending to dressing someone down. It's not just family, and if they don't know your middle name, sometimes they even make one up! It's an authority flex to do so. This happens in my books a lot—even if they are not set in the South—so I'm just giving you a heads up that it's stylistic and purposeful.

There are some characters and creatures that speak in other languages. I made the *translations clickable end of chapter notes* to help.

There are some words that are slang, jargon, or foreign that may seem to be spelled wrong—*please email the author or find her on social media rather than report to Amazon* if you find a typo. This has been proofed and edited *several* times, so the error could be a stylistic or dialect choice. Every effort is made to find these pre-publication and since the publishing industry standard is below two percent of word count (and my books are almost always over 100K), I promise what you find is not out of the accepted range for the editors and teams who have reviewed it.

Please do not email critical feedback that is not a simple typo or formatting issue—this book is written and released. It will not be changed after publication to suit personal requests.

If you see this book *anywhere besides Kindle Unlimited in ebook format,* please reach out to me via social media or email. Pirating kills my ability to write full time and I am so grateful for your help.

Contact my team for typos or to report piracy: teamcassandrafeatherstone@cassandrafeatherstone.com

We are all constantly evolving… exiting our chrysalis as someone new in each stage of life.

Growing into our power shouldn't prevent us from finding love, friends, and, most of all, smoking hot professors who want devour us from head to tail.

*"Pretty and nice are not the rent you pay to
exist in this world as a woman."*

LET US PREY PLAYLIST

CHAPTER TITLE SONGS

Let Us Prey Chapter Playlist

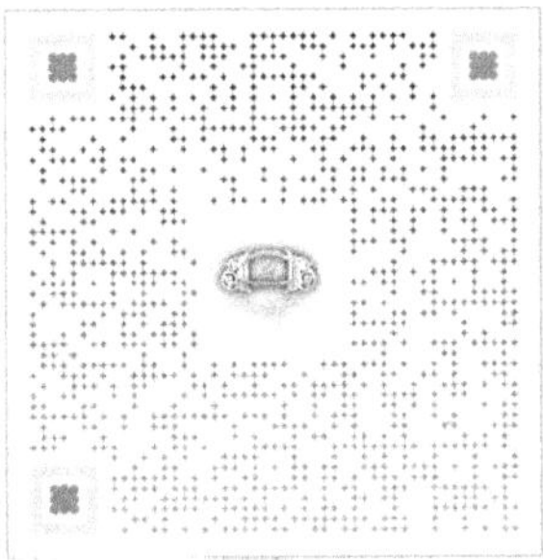

BONUS PLAYLIST

Rufus and Cori's Dance Break Playlist

Previously On Come Out & Prey...

When we met Delores in *Come Out & Prey*, she was tethered to a douche-y boyfriend and a couple frenemies.

Her drunken, abusive parents sent her to tour Apex Academy where she's meant to attend the next year—but education wasn't the only thing on her mind.

After ditching the snarky BFFs and immature guys, she stumbles on two hotties, giving a peep show that leaves her hot and bothered. By the time she catches back up to her group, she's had her fill of the campus.

Despite making the best impression she could, her evil mother berates her, and she invites her friends over to soothe the sting. That proves to be a mistake—one she pays for dearly the next day.

Her prom gets moved to Apex and after an unfortunate issue with the punch, she takes off with her boyfriend for a little 'alone time'. It goes poorly, and she ends up meeting one of the professors from earlier for a little pep talk about not being ashamed of who she is.

The betrayal of her boyfriend and ex-friends is nothing compared to her parents' wrath, especially when they declare she will still have to attend Apex despite a significant disadvantage.

That's when Delores vows revenge on the people who hurt her and starts a quest to find herself.

And now, to the beginning of her first year at Apex…

Bad Reputation

Delores

I crank the music up to max volume as I speed down the highway. My hands drum on the steering wheel of my vintage Mustang as I dance along, hair whipping in the breeze as the convertible takes the curves far better than a car of this age should. It's my first day at Apex Academy, and I need every ounce of encouragement I can get.

This is the place I'm supposed to die.

After the events at prom in the spring, when I emerged as a bunny instead of a predator, I was a pariah at Shifter Secondary. My former besties and ex-boyfriend filled my days with cruel pranks, dangerous threats, and promises that, once I got to Apex, the ban on killing underclassmen would lift.

You'd think that would have me running as far away from Apex Academy as my thumpers could carry me. Unfortunately, given the Council's decree that I attend Apex rather than get killed for emerging as prey, I don't have a choice in the matter, and my classmates know it. I deleted every speck of social media to keep the maniacal look in their eyes out of my head when I didn't have to be at school, and the absolute rage that lack of contact unleashed in the Heathers was terrifying.

Regardless, I kept my head down and endured the trauma of my last month of school by counting the hours to summer. My home life was even worse, however. If my mother wasn't calling me into her drawing room so she could spend half the evening drinking and berating me, my father was licking his chops as if he'd prefer to eat me and get it over with. The Council decreed I could fight for my life at the Academy. That didn't keep Bruno from eying me like a ribeye every single time he had to tolerate my presence.

I suppose it didn't help that I spent the entire summer defying every single edict they've handed down my entire life.

My text to Monsieur Growlvinchy secured a job at his fashion house for the duration of the break, and Lucille couldn't do a damned thing to stop me. Politics in the fashion world are as treacherous as they are in the Capital, and he assured Lucille that if she denied him the first apprentice he'd chosen in decades, he'd make certain she was at the bottom of every Fall Line preview list. She backed off immediately and allowed me to accept the position, which was the only thing that kept me sane.

Working got me out of the house for long stretches, gave me real money of my own rather than scraps of change, and allowed me to hide from my bullies. They would never take a job—even an internship as prestigious as this—so I could avoid contact with the people I wanted to see the least.

I had one small run-in with douchebag Todd, but luckily, it was outside of the underground goth club I was hanging out at. He threatened me and I wanted to break out the mace my summer friends had me buy, but a gorgeous feral tiger leaped out of the darkness to save me. I thought I recognized the look in its eye when I petted its head, but the fingers that appeared on my windowsill later confirmed it.

My flirty professor friend from Apex was watching me and he continued to leave presents and notes so I'd feel safe. I'd never had that before and it melted my frozen heart a little.

Wrinkling my nose, I sigh as the track changes on my playlist. That night at the club underlined a few things I'd been wrestling with for months. While it would be easier to associate with prey animals as much as possible because that's what I am, it won't work. I came back from the incident outside to find friends cowering along the back wall as the preds circled the dance floor looking for weak ones to cull.

I could never do that. Besides the danger of provoking more vengeful preds by simply socializing with them, Bruno and Lucille brought me up to act like a pred. I couldn't stomach hiding along the wall for the rest of my life; it's not in me, especially after I spent the entire break reclaiming my agency.

Okay, that's a super fancy way of saying 'finding myself', but I read a lot of psych and self-help books at night.

I had countless hours to fill once I came home from my job, since I had few people to talk to. I texted with my work friends, but since I had to escape from social media to keep my inboxes from filling with death threats, they excluded me from group chats. I wrote songs, but a girl can only write so many sappy betrayal songs or hate filled anthems before it gets depressing. So I buried my nose in books of all kinds to keep busy. I tried to keep my reading preferences a secret from Lucille, so I bought e-books instead of going anywhere with Bruiser to buy them.

After devouring everything I could on how to 'reignite my fire' and why I should just 'wash my fur', I finally realized that the key to surviving this year at Apex was to grab my future by the balls and squeeze.

That led to a flood of fantasies about hot professors featuring library stacks, gym mats, and art tables. That led to buying another boatload of books with the professor/students trope. I even found some books where the guys *shared* the girl—man, did that do it for me. Todd was a dud, and I didn't have the slightest interest in dating anyone my age, so more Amazon orders were necessary for fueling my book boyfriend fantasies. I hope that will hold me over until I get out of this hellhole Academy, and after that, I'll have to re-assess.

I mean, no way I could date a prey animal—not after being immersed in the world I lived in for eighteen years. But how could I ever trust some salivating pred dickhead not to chow down on me like I was the goddamn Cadbury Bunny?

Ugh.

Like I said, I've accepted that dating is off the menu. That's why I have a box full of distractions to hide under my bed in my dorm. We're lucky enough to have singles at Apex because the alumni are so wealthy. Given that so many mated pairs meet at Apex and form alliances, you'd hardly know single people exist by the time graduation rolls around.

At least, that's what my Google searches revealed.

Hundreds of message boards have sections dedicated to preds finding their mates between the different secondary academies via video chat and messaging apps. I carefully avoided using anything that could be traced back to me, but I had to know what I was walking into. My skunk friend, Clotilda, worked in a cafe nearby and she made sure we cleaned my phone of tracking and spyware. Unsurprisingly, it had malware on it from both my parents and my bitchy ex-friends.

Trust Gold—of the tech-giant Erickson family—to know absolutely everything about everyone so she can spread her venom. The girl has no life outside of maliciously bullying others or trying desperately to get validation through her circle of dimwits. I still can't believe I put up with those nasty girls for as long as I did. I'm still a salty Sally about my exes—friends and otherwise—and the way everyone cast me aside. I don't want to be in their circle again, but I want them to pay for treating me like a used Kleenex.

My rage at a lifetime of betrayal fueled me in a way nothing ever has before. I worked long hours for the first month, earning enough to buy myself a car so that I didn't have Bruiser lurking about like a shark in blood-filled waters. Lucille was furious, but Luc walked me through the paperwork. I'm eighteen, so there was nothing she could do to stop me—especially since I didn't keep it parked at the house. I paid for it in bruises and blood, and it was my first taste of freedom.

Since that day, I've physically transformed myself into the person I've always wanted to be.

I'm still blonde—because it's natural—but as soon as I had enough money, I started altering my body and style in ways that felt more genuine than Botox and French tips. My friends at the boutique used remnants to make me an entirely new wardrobe—a sort of goth/punk mash-up that makes me feel rebellious and hot. I snuck out late one night with my Flamingoth friends to get a tattoo—one I'll probably show no one because of its location. It reminds me of who I want to be and I love it. I traded my kitten heels for knee-high combat boots, and my dusting of neutral makeup for black liner and smoky eyes.

Yeah, I know. It's pretty basic to go from good girl to bad bunny, but I spent far too long being squeezed into a box I didn't want to be in. It's only fair that I get to rebel now that I'm free.

Frowning, I think about the prey friends I'm leaving behind. At Apex, I won't have any support nearby—even Luc will be an hour away. Preds'll surround me, and I'm fairly certain the Heathers— like their parents before them—will take over the social hierarchy of Apex Academy as quickly as possible. That means the likelihood of me making any actual friends or allies is nil.

As the music changes, I roll my head on my shoulders to get the tension out of my neck and think about the surprise 'gift' someone left on my doorstep last night. Todd's fingers showed up on my window about two a.m., and while I'm concerned about retaliation, I suspect the responsible party will help me. The necklace I lost on prom night appeared not long after, along with various other 'presents'.

Right now, there's only one pred in the entire world who could stalk me like that without tripping my fear response. I don't know how Fitz figured out who I was and where I live, but as soon as the tiger pounced, I knew it was him. Something deep in my gut told me he wouldn't hurt me that night after Todd or when he appeared again outside of the club. I lost my necklace in the ring when Todd took my virginity under false pretenses, but I still don't know how he knew it was mine and I needed it returned.

Why would he defend me? Why follow me at all?

The unanswered questions in my life are getting more complicated, and I don't know how I'm going to deal with keeping myself alive at the most cutthroat pred academy in the world, on top of my daily uncertainty.

"Nothing worth having comes easy," I mutter to myself.

Quoting the first human president secretly to hide their shifter side is probably not as helpful as an actual plan, but I'm exhausted. I've been stressing about this day for weeks, and Bruno was furious despite the necklace being unharmed. The ensuing family fight lasted long into the wee hours of the morning, and I couldn't pack my shit to get out of their house fast enough.

I might not belong here at Apex—or survive—but I sure as hell can't hang around where I'm not wanted.

The driveway to the school comes into view, and I crank the volume, letting Joan Jett blast from my speakers as a warning: *this bunny doesn't give a damn about her bad reputation.*

Like Fitz said on prom night—"Fuck 'em."

When Good Girls Go Bad

Delores

There were exactly zero staff members available to drive me from the parking lot to my dorm. I watched the owl shifters in Admissions flutter and adjust their glasses, fluffing up in a way that made it easy to identify their animals as they tried to locate the inconveniently absent concierges. After waiting for over thirty minutes while they made calls, I finally excused myself to go to the restroom.

As I thought, a facilities office was just down the hall from the admin area, and now I'm standing outside, watching five literal weasels yell at a rugby game on TV while the phone rings. Seems like the directive to treat me like scum upon arrival made it as far as the lower tiers of the Apex staff, even if the kindly office ladies didn't get the memo. I watch them for a few minutes until I notice a rack with numbered golf cart keys just inside the doorway.

Bingo was his name-o.

I snake my fingers through the crack in the door, fishing with my nails until I can grasp one set of keys. Carefully palming it in my hand, I stride down the hall, past the still fussing admin ladies, to the side parking lot. The golf carts have numbers on the back bumper and when I see number eight, I do a little fist pump. I retrieve my Yves St. Leopard luggage set from the back of my car —covered in stickers and band logos that decrease its value to zero —and prepare myself for my foray into grand theft auto.

Okay, Dolly, you can do this.

All I have to do is lug my shit to the cart, start it up, and take off. What are they going to do—expel me? *Fucking doubtful.* The Council would eat the headmistress alive if she dared to contradict their stupid edict of allowing me to attend and survive on my own. Ironically, their piddly rules made me untouchable in some ways; I could set the place on fire and the administration couldn't do more than give me detention.

Grinning to myself, I gather my bags, loading myself down like an actual pack mule. Once I find my balance, I grab the handles of the rolling suitcases and trunk and grunt my way over to the cart. I wasn't very strong when I started at Luc's shop, but after a summer of carrying heavy fabric rolls, restocking, and moving large boxes, I'm tighter and leaner than I was when I first set foot on this wretched campus.

Oh, and I quit letting people call me DD. That nickname reminds me of people who mocked me behind my back and ditched me the second I couldn't further their social status.

Who the fuck makes fun of someone's bra size, anyway?

Luc started calling me Dolly, and for the first time in my life, I felt like someone was actually seeing *me*. I mean, who wouldn't like to be called the same thing as the kindest-hearted woman in human music? So I embraced it, even though the edgy Flamingoth said it wasn't 'hardcore' enough. I said I wasn't ever going to let others influence my behavior, and that includes new friends, too.

Once I load my shit in the back of the cart, I take one more fortifying breath and climb into the driver's seat. I fire it up and look over my shoulder to back out. It'd be nice if Todd's or one of the Heathers' cars were around to 'accidentally' back into, but alas, that's revenge for another day. When I'm clear, I spin the wheel and floor it, careening over the hills in the grassy meadows separating the buildings.

To my left, I see the Erickson Staff Housing Complex. It looks like a chintzy little township that's trying too hard to look 'ye olde' timey. That doesn't surprise me—the Erickson patriarch is as obsessed with old-fashioned things as he is tech and women way too young for him. He probably insisted on approving every single brick and lamp in the entire place. Meanwhile, the quarters are likely substandard and bare bones because most of the money for the construction went to his idiotic vision on the exterior.

They probably installed listening devices in the rooms, too.

Clotilda helped me do more than de-spyware my phone—the skunk spent hours helping me compile dirt files on every one of my ex-friends, including Todd, his dude-bros, and their Council families. I'm not sure what I plan to do with all of it, but I know it will come in handy someday. I haven't had the wherewithal to look into my own parents yet. It feels like a can of worms I don't have the spoons to deal with now.

A wistful thought flutters through my mind as I watch the staff quarters go by—I wonder if my hottie professors live there? They have to, right? No one lives off campus.

The idea of the scary gargoyle bunking down in those tiny cottage style houses is kind of funny. My lips curve as I again think about the psycho tiger and his gift of Todd's fingers. It's nice to imagine he was looking out for me all summer, protecting me from the shadows. I wouldn't mind him or his sexy boyfriend dropping by the dorms for a late-night offer of more… protection.

Ack. Now I'm bouncing up and down over this damn landscape, with my thighs rubbing together and my vagina throbbing. *Great job, Dolly.* You're officially a horny teenage idiot with no options outside of your box of toys and late-night visits to PredHub.

I need to play it safe here anyway—and that means keeping to myself.

The facade of the Barrington Dorms finally comes into view, and I sigh in relief, eager to get a locked door between me and the rest of the students. Skidding to an abrupt stop at the front door, I reach into my tote and pull out the welcome packet the owls in Admissions handed me before the concierge debacle. The keycard with the Apex logo glints in the sun, and I turn it over. No sign of what room it opens, which, as someone with people hunting her, I appreciate. I shuffle my paper around until I find a paper with a description of amenities in my dorm building. I peruse the information about a gym, indoor pool, common rooms, and rehearsal rooms in the underground levels until I reach a line that says 'Gazelle 666' and I nearly fall out of the cart.

Oh, right. Gazelle is a building and apparently, the room was hand-picked for me, since the number is the sign of Satan. Just fucking great. I'll never have anyone over living in the goddamn *demon* suite.

I leave the golf cart keys in the ignition because I honestly don't care if another student takes it on a drunken joyride. Hefting my bags again, I maneuver up the ramp to the furthest building at the end. Not convenient for lifting and carrying large items, but its location makes it pretty defensible. I turn to the area just past the elegant windows and smooth bricks, and see the next closest building is the Leonidas Gym, which makes my stomach flip-flop.

Sexy tiger man Fitz was in the gym that day. Maybe he works there?

Oh, stop it, Dolly.

I'm a fool to think much older, super fucking hot professors are going to come anywhere near my almost virgin ass—even if it is pretty juicy after all that heavy lifting this summer at work.

Get your shit together and get into your room before someone comes along and pushes you into a fountain.

I sigh, using the card to swipe myself in at the main doors to Gazelle. The common area is empty, which suits me fine. As I head towards the elevator, I note all the potential places some asshole could corner me, trying to make a name for themselves with the Council heirs. It sucks that I have to do it, but my safety has been my responsibility for a while now, and my parents won't care if anyone hurts me while I'm here. When there are no consequences for inappropriate behavior, it encourages the vicious to be as horrible as they can.

The ding of the elevator brings me out of my reverie, and I step on, pushing the number six button. It's the top floor and I can't decide whether that's strategically useful or imminently dangerous. There are stairs at either end, supposedly, and that adds two more escape routes if I need them. I may have to invest in some sort of rope ladder I can toss out the window for emergencies. Chewing my lower lip as I scroll through the options on Amazon, I almost miss the doors opening.

So much for being cautious.

I grumble under my breath as I haul my shit to the room at the end of the hall, swiping my card in the reader, and breathing a sigh when it beeps green. My relief is short-lived. When I open the door, I find the entire room trashed—from furniture to broken glassware—including a scrawled message across the glass balcony in what I suspect is blood.

"Welcome to Apex. Run, rabbit, RUN!"

Dropping everything, I simply gape at the destruction in front of me. I have no idea who to call or how to deal with this, much less what I'll do about my accommodations for the evening beyond sleeping on the floor. I'll need a broom, trash bags, replacement linens, cleaning supplies and…

A feeling of hopelessness creeps over me. I lean my head against the doorframe, closing my eyes as I remember what it was like to have a bright future ahead of me, to be so full of blissful ignorance about the world I was living in. Everything was so much simpler, even when I was under the thumb of the malevolent queen Lucille. I didn't have to worry about the nearest exit or who else is rooming on this floor, or how I'm going to get the smell of rancid urine out of the carpets in my bedroom.

Does this mean someone else has keys to my room?!

How am I going to trust my food in the cafeteria or my clothes going to the laundry service? I'll have to do everything myself. I'm not lazy, but I have no idea how much schoolwork I'll get in my classes or how difficult my courses will be. I'll be the only freshman—no, the only student—who will dart around campus with laundry bags, brown bag lunches, and an umbrella to prevent random aerial attacks.

That might sound paranoid, but they covered my room in piss, so it's justified.

I sink to the ground with my skirt splayed over my thighs and my combat boots pushed against the opposite door frame. I spent my whole vacation shoring myself up for this day, this moment, but look at me.

Why am I such a fucking failure?

All I had to do was roll up to this place like a badass and kick in the door, but here I am, crumbling like a graham cracker at the first sign of trouble.

The unexpected arrival of my stupid moontime delight last night isn't helping—the implant Lucille had put in years ago is *supposed* to control this. Unfortunately, it isn't and my hormones are all over the place, making me a weird combination of angry, weepy, and horny. Being a girl and a shifter sucks hairy grizzly balls, and I'll be damned if I let anyone say any differently in my presence.

"Oh, well. It's not like I was getting laid soon, anyway," I mutter to myself as I wipe the snot off my face with the sleeve of my hoodie.

It's just me and my toys, probably sleeping in my car together.

How romantic.

Somebody's Watching Me

Fitz

Fitz

After I left the necklace on her windowsill this summer, the temptation was too great. If I hadn't known where my baby girl lived, I might have been able to control myself more. Unfortunately, self-control has never been one of my marketable skills. So I spent the rest of the summer sneaking away to leave special gifts for her, so she'd know she has one ally when she arrives.

How did I know nothing changed? Easy… bribes.

The nerdy owls in the office adore Chess, and he used that to help me keep tabs on her admission file. I *needed* to make sure Delores Drew shows up for the campus move-in day today without having to ask her. We haven't spoken since the prom, so I don't know if she realizes the tiger who saved her sweet cheeks was me. I'd rather tell her that myself if she doesn't, because I'll have to smooth over my uncontrollable urge to stalk her all summer long when I do. Some women consider that a turnoff and I have to explain that it was to keep her safe.

She'll get that, right?

Of course she will. The girl seemed pretty smart even if her previous taste in men was tragic. Plus, scores of women would give their dew claws to have the enforcer of the Khan ambush watching over them. Chess and I are catches, even in exile at this bullshit school. Once I figure out how to throw in the three grumpy ass kings, it will be even more impressive.

All I have to do is show them how fucking cool this chick is and we'll have a cozy little polyamorous ambush that will make everyone in the universe seethe with jealousy. Even my asshole father will have to bow to our royal fuck nest… and I'm looking forward to that shit.

But she has to *get* here before I can enact my master plan. I've been waiting all morning in the clock tower, my eyes trained on the road leading up to Apex like I expect her to appear simply by sheer force of will. Renard bitched I was disrupting his broody perch time, but I don't care. We let him stew out here like an emo singer all the time and no one bothers him. I need this vantage point today and if he isn't vibing with my energy, he can fly off to wherever the hell he and the lizard boy go to eat.

Everything's a state secret with those two—where they eat, what they eat, where they sleep.

You'd think they were drinking Elvis' blood to stay fucking immortal or some shit. Whenever I try to get it out of the dragon, he grunts and belches fire. Our sentient pigeon roost is no more helpful—he lectures me about 'boundaries' and 'privacy' as if I give a furry mutt's ass. We're a group of misfits who banded together in the home of misfits; if we don't look out for one another, no one will. And secrets fuck *everything* up without a doubt.

"Fitz, are you still drooling off the balcony? Come over here and look at the email I finally received from the Department of Health and Shifter Services. They got that idiot you tracked down to give a statement, as well as the other morons who spiked the punch. It was fucking peppermint schnapps, of all things, and no one has a clue why it kept the poison from killing everyone who drank it." The dragon scratches his chin, picking up an old dusty book as thick as my forearm to flip through it.

My idea of hell, but whatever gets his flag waving, I suppose.

"We assume it was poison, but couldn't it just as easily have been venom, man? I've known some shifter chicks in my time who threatened to take fangs to my cock and their juice would have done serious damage." I shudder, then hold up a finger. "Pro tip: Never piss off a pit of gorgons by sleeping with their sisters."

Aubrey turns his head so slowly you'd think he was Linda Blair and his expression is horrified. "You betrayed fucking gorgons? Multiple? And lived?"

I shrug, winking at him. "I convinced them another round of my disco stick was worth forgoing their vengeance. The longest week of my life, man. Those chicks have *stamina.*"

He puts his hands over his face, drawing in a deep breath and blowing it out as if I'm the most trying thing this side of a hang-nail. The dragon opens his mouth like he's going to speak, then shakes his head and goes back to the tome in his lap.

I don't see why my explanation was so irksome—it was one hundred percent true.

"Crazy snake haired women aside, man, I wish you'd come out to see Baby Girl this summer. All of you douches, even Chessie, refused to join me and when she shows up today, you're going to regret being so damn stubborn." I sigh, imagining her sleeping in that ridiculously pink princess room her mother probably deco-rated. It looked like someone spilled Pepto all over it, but she ignored the assault on good taste with aplomb.

Aubrey looks up at me with a reproachful glare. "None of us felt it was appropriate to borderline *stalk* an incoming *student*, Fitz."

"Definitely not borderline. I'm owning that shit and I'll even tell her. I'm positive my baby girl will understand." Whistling under my breath, I walk back to the railing of the gargoyle's perch, itching to see her arrive.

Suddenly, I hear the roar of her slick as fuck old school Mustang coming to the gates. I'd watched as one of her pseudo-friends helped her soup the engine up one afternoon and I'd know that purr anywhere. I had to find a better spot to ogle her from because seeing her bent over the hood in those tiny shorts made it impossible not to stroke my crankshaft, if you know what I mean. As she gets closer, I hear the sounds of 80s rock blasting from the open windows like a siren's song.

Delores Drew is so fucking perfect it hurts my goddamned soul.

BY THE TIME I SPEED RACE DOWN EIGHT FLIGHTS OF SHITTY OLD stairs in the Tower and across the green to Admin, she's disappeared. I should have shifted, but the dragon told me it was too much. *Bullshit, because I'm* much *faster in tiger form.* Now I have to track her down so I can lay eyes on her soft smile and kind eyes that feel like they hit me in the gut. Growling to myself, I pace the lot for a moment before I pull my phone out and text Chess.

> TigerWoody: Where the fuck is her dorm?

> CSpot: She's in Gazelle. That's where freshmen always are, Fitz.

> TigerWoody: Don't be so sour, baby. We've been waiting for this day.

> CSpot: I'm not sour about her. We've been here a fucking decade and you still don't know where anything is. It's embarrassing, Fitz.

TigerWoody: When love blinds me, you're my seeing eye cat, Chessie. See you at home.

CSpot: *grumble*

Tucking my phone away, I grin as I head to Gazelle. Lucky for me, it's right next to the Leonidas gym where Felix's office is located. That means I can peep out his window anytime I want to glimpse my baby girl walking through the common rooms and maybe even in her room! With that thought in mind, I pick up my pace as I pass the clock tower again, then veer left towards the dorm block.

Sneering at a few of the newbs as they enter, I chuckle when they give me a wide berth. I enjoy putting the fresh meat on edge and even though I'll filet anyone who comes near baby girl, it's in my nature to enforce the Darwinistic atmosphere here. The smaller preds have to learn to make their way in a world that is very much like the one at Apex or they won't survive past graduation—if they make it that far.

"Out of the way," I snarl at the mass of students gathered in front of the elevator like a herd of cattle. They stare at me like they're stuck on stupid until I bare my fangs, then wisely clear a path just as the doors open with a ding. This shit is exactly what I mean—stronger shifters are using the stairs or, if they're rich enough, their staff are. These kids are clumped like they're holding still for a massacre and it's going to get their asses beaten.

With a jaunty wave, I push the button to close the doors before anyone joins me. My phone buzzes right as I realize I don't know what goddamn floor Delores is on and I smile when I see Chess has texted me her room info. I couldn't love that cheetah more if I tried—he knows me almost as well as my twin. I hit six, pondering both the advantages and disadvantages of my girl being on the top floor.

It makes it easy to fortify, but hard to get out. Good thing we have a dragon.

I wrinkle my nose at that thought. That cranky fucker doesn't let anyone ride him, but if Delores is in danger and he refuses, I'll stab him right in his fiery ballsack. I don't give a single fuck if he roasts my fur afterward—there are some things you have to take a stand on.

When I exit, I can feel the blood thrumming in my veins and my tiger pacing in anticipation of seeing her. That night at the club, she ruffled his fur, and he's been a royal asshole about staying close to her ever since. If I hadn't agreed, the summer would have been a shitshow of epic proportions because his insistence is part of why I left so many offerings at her window.

I wonder if she knows the fingers were from her ex-fuck boy?

A pungent odor slaps me in the face as I head down the hallway and when I get to the last suite, my excitement has faded to fury.

The door is open and Baby Girl is sitting just inside of it with her face buried in her palms as she growls softly. Her shoulders shake as the tiny sound increases from that baby snarl to a full-on scream of fury that makes my ears hurt. She lifts her hands and makes fists, pounding on the floor with her eyes closed as the howl of indignance continues. It's all I can do to hold my cat back as I watch the pain and anger roil in front of me and fat tears run down her lovely features.

"Who. The Fuck. Did. This!" I roar as I take in the decimated dorm room full of shredded, piss-soaked uniforms, furniture, and surfaces. Claws pop free on my hands as I look around, noting that not one inch of the damn place isn't completely fucked beyond repair.

Her eyes pop open and she scrambles backwards at first, putting distance between us until she recognizes me. Heaving a huge breath, she straightens her shoulders and wipes her face before she plasters on a fake smile. "Hey, Fitz. Sorry about the mess. And the screaming. It's been kind of a day."

Hell no.

Striding over to her, I hold my hand out, hauling her up and into my arms. It's hard to push back my need to murder someone, but I can wait for revenge. Right now, what my baby girl needs is someone to let her get it out. No one can function if they tuck all their shit in a box and pretend—I should know, because it's what I've been telling Felix for almost a decade.

Her arms go around me tentatively, and I sit my chin on her head. "Delores, don't pretend around me. You don't have to be anyone but who you are when I'm here. Got it?" A small nod and a sniffle are my answer, so I go on. "I don't care if you scream the fucking roof down, but be real. Get that shit out so you don't end up carrying a wound that will cripple you. No one here will show mercy if you have a sore spot."

"Thanks," she whispers hoarsely. "At home, letting people see they upset you leads to bad things. I've learned to lock it down."

Boy, does that sound familiar.

"Yeah, that's how it was at my home, too. Lucky for me, I had Chess and Felix to help me figure out how *not* to be an emotionless psycho."

Delores lifts her head, and I'm delighted when she lets out a tinkling laugh. "Fitz, you left me severed fingers with a note that said 'thinking of you' written in sparkly purple marker."

"See? Not emotionless." I give her a proud grin.

That makes her smile again, and she pulls away, looking around the room with a frustrated sigh. "This is a nightmare. No flowers or air freshener in the world will cover up this stench."

Frowning, I scratch my head. "Should I have bought you flowers? I have to admit, I'm a bit out of my depth with this whole courting shit."

Her laugh erases my worry, and she shakes her head. "I can buy my own flowers, buddy. Don't worry."

I snort at the reference, liking the sass she's picked up since we talked last. My eyes rake over her, taking in the short pleated skirt, ripped fishnets, baby doll tee, and tall combat boots. She doesn't say anything as I look at the fruits of her visits to that tattoo parlor —multiple shiny earrings, a tiny silver nose stud, and a sparkling diamond Playboy bunny hanging from her belly button like a siren song.

I will not make it through this if she gets any hotter.

Pushing the image of her with her legs flipped over my shoulders as I feast out of my brain, I arch a brow at her. "What kind of girl *are* you, Delores Drew?"

"The kind who gets tingly when psychos leave me severed fingers with *XOXO* at the bottom."

Her bravado falters for a moment, and I see the uncertainty cloud her features. That jackhole did a number on my girl and she's obviously still healing. She's covered herself in armor to force people to think she's got a hard shell, but underneath, she's still forming steel in her spine.

Not surprising given Aubrey, and I figured out the prom was right after her eighteenth birthday.

"Good. Because I promise you, I'll do my best to figure out the boyfriend thing. I'm a quick learner," I say with a playful wink.

Her brows furrow, and she looks away, glancing at the state of her dorm again. "I don't know what it should look like, either, to be honest."

I suspected the walking corpse was her first and only boyfriend, but her reaction now confirms it. That stupid motherfucker dated her, took her virginity, and dumped her on her goddamned prom night. The urge to find out if you can actually kill someone more than once pumps in my veins, but I don't want to upset her again. If I find out the canine scent of piss in here belongs to him and his friends, I'm going to rip his cock off and shove it up his ass so he can truly go fuck himself.

But Delores doesn't need to know that right now.

"Baby Girl, I give you my word: if your ex so much as sniffs in your direction, I'll take the rest of his fucking fingers and let you feed them to the shark shifters." I see the tiny shiver run through her and the scent of arousal floods my senses. *How is a man supposed to keep his dick in his pants when she smells like fucking honeysuckle?* "I'm coming for the idiots who trashed your room, too. I don't care who it is—they're going to suffer when I find them."

Her expression tightens, and she waves a hand dismissively. "I know who did it. They're Council heirs and it's not worth the punishment they'd mete out for you to get involved. I'll deal with this in my own way eventually, but it will take some planning."

Blinking at the change in her attitude, I tilt my head to look at her again. Where she'd been at the edge of hysteria or shyness before, now she's got a cool, calculated look on her face. Her back is straight and her shoulders are squared as if she's preparing for battle—something I know a hell of a lot about. Being a Khan and Pred Games champion, I'd call this 'game face' and my gorgeous girl has it in spades as she glares at the mess. She *needs* to handle this problem herself or she won't get closure.

"Okay, baby girl. You take care of the snooty heirs and I'll hold off my baser instincts—for a while." Her impish grin makes me happy, and I wave at the pile of shredded shit. "But first, we have to find you a place to stay because this shit reeks. You're *not* sleeping here until it's clean and *safe.*"

That earns me a pointed look as she says, "Where exactly do you propose I go, Fitz? The owls in the office said the dorms are full when I asked if I could have a ground floor back corner instead of this bird's nest."

Smart, smart girl. She was planning escape routes.

As much as I'd like to throw her over my shoulder and take her home, I know Felix isn't ready for a house guest this alluring. He'll want her there eventually, but he's not on the bus to Pound Town yet and I don't want to piss him off. That only leaves…

I groan inwardly and rub my palm over my face. There's plenty of room in the fucking Tower and she'd be a hell of a lot safer than in these stupid dorms with their flimsy doors and lack of cameras. The only problem is the Tower is the nesting place of the two grouchiest and solitary preds on the damn campus. They have rooms *somewhere* in the building, but neither of them will admit to their location. The rule is simply that no one is allowed on any floor except the top one and if you step one toe off the stairs else-where, it's like Renard's super spy tech gear sets off alarms.

He always knows, and last time, he threatened to drop me from the balcony.

"I think I have a place, but I need to make a call. Can you gather everything that's salvageable you want to take, baby girl? I'm going to walk down the hall a little and plan."

She looks unsure again as she chews her lip, but finally nods. "Okay, Fitz."

I don't know what deity decided I'm the one asshole Delores trusts in this shit-hole, but I refuse to let her down.

A Place Called Home

Delores

The only things not destroyed by what was certainly an opening salvo from the Heathers and my ex's crew of clowns are the things I brought with me in the car. Anything sent ahead or purchased for the school year by my parents is a lost cause. So I load up the cart given to me at the admin building, piling it high with the boxes containing my most important personal shit while Fitz paces at the end of the hall.

He seems agitated because he's raking his hand through his long locks and his shoulders are tense. Whomever he's contacting about finding me a temporary space must not be eager to have guests. I don't want to put anyone out; it will make people hate me even more. However, I have little in the way of options. I wasn't lying when I said the snippy admin women told me everything was full in a tone that said 'get fucked' as politely as possible.

Honestly, I don't know what I would have done after my tantrum if Fitz hadn't shown up. This nasty welcome was the ketchup on the shit sandwich that's been my life since the night I emerged and I'm at my wits' end. I was so fortunate that Luc gave me the job this summer, so I had an escape from the hell house, but even that didn't make the rest of it easy. Lucille and Bruno were in rare form every time I saw them and my cadre of bitchy friends worked hard to make sure I wasn't safe anywhere preds gather.

That's why I stayed around the prey from work despite always feeling like I didn't fit—I didn't have anywhere else to go.

Being ostracized gave me a few gifts, though. I had more free time than I've ever had in my entire life, so I spent every second figuring out who I am and what I'm going to do with my life. Obviously, I'm not marrying Todd and there's no chance I'm sitting in the seat Lucille wanted me to. That meant for the first time, I could think about what *I* wanted to do—and it wasn't an English major, so I could run communications for my rich husband on the Council.

I also spent hours pouring over the social media of the Heathers in secret via the VPN Gold so kindly provided me with last year. She didn't remember to cut off my access and since I created entirely new accounts to watch their exploits, no one was the wiser. Being an excellent student paid off in spades while I gathered copious amounts of intel on every shady thing they were involved in and every boundary they crossed. I'm still not sure if I'm going to attack them outright unless shit like the piss room keeps happening or if I'm holding onto it for the right moment, but if they knew what dirt I've compiled, they'd fuck all the way off.

Some people have no sense of self preservation and it's always their downfall.

"...don't care if you dislike visitors, you overgrown gnat!"

Fitz's words make me cringe a little. This place he wants to stash me sounds less and less appealing with every shout. I've lived in a house where I wasn't cawanted for most of my life, but I hoped to have a safe space when I got to Apex. *Well, as safe as it can be in a pred versus pred academy.* If he forces someone to take me in, I'll have people glaring at me every time I emerge from my room, just like at the mansion. I don't know if I can handle that when I know

I'm going to have to fight my way through *everything* every day here.

"Fitz…" He doesn't hear me and I don't want to interrupt, so I turn away.

Licking my lips, I pull the paper out of my pocket, looking at the names of the people I'm going to teach a fucking lesson. It's a big ask, even with the data I gathered this summer, and I'm not sure I can do it on my own. Some people, like my parents, will be impossible to deal with until I find a replacement for my hacker friend, Clotilda, from the Growlvinchy shop. She could get a decent amount of rumors and gossip from the dark web, but we could never crack their systems to find *real* intel on whatever illegal crap makes them buckets of cash.

I stare at the words for a few moments, willing myself to hold on to the strength I found when I wrote this. It will not be a pleasure cruise here and I know that, but I can't let basic bullying shit like peeing on my furniture make me lose the plot. The Heathers are dead set on making my life miserable because… fuck, I don't even actually know why.

Maybe because I'm different? Or because I don't fit into their perfect plastic world anymore?

Their fury was more puzzling than Todd's from the start. He felt lied to and betrayed—join the club, asshole—but the Heathers had *nothing* to fear from me once they labeled me prey. In fact, it made their standing higher because it lessened the pools of heirs eventually joining the Council. Why spend all their time dragging me through the mud instead of letting me fade into obscurity?

I don't have answers to that question except the Heathers have often launched vicious campaigns against people for reasons I didn't understand. Because of our parents, they grouped us as friends from babies whether or not we liked it. It was fine until we hit middle school and emerging came up. They changed over the summer between elementary and secondary school—so much so that they were unrecognizable, both in physicality and personality.

Lucille told me to stop being a baby when I complained, then offered me similar plastic surgery to fit in better.

Maybe their behavior isn't really that puzzling. They've always had their eyes squarely on getting ahead, marrying rich, and taking over their family businesses to the detriment of anything else. If they think I'm still a threat despite my handicap, they'll stop at nothing to take me out. People shunning me for my species only makes that easier; I have to be more cautious while I work to take them down.

Fitz walks over, grinning ear to ear as he interrupts my musings. "Come on, Baby Girl. I'll help you roll this shit to your new nest."

I blink. It didn't sound like he was going to be successful, but here he was. "Okay."

Beggars can't be choosers, I suppose.

As we approach the looming tower, I look over at him nervously. "Are you sure this place is safe? It looks kind of… not."

Fitz barks a laugh. "That's on purpose. The occupants of this overcompensating monstrosity do *not* want visitors."

I frown. "What the hell are you bringing me here for, then?"

"The Tower is without a doubt the most secure place on campus. Unless you want to come home with me, Baby Girl?" He bobs his brows and my face flushes bright red.

I am not *ready for that.*

"Um, no thank you. I wouldn't want to intrude. I mean, you have your… and uh, your brother.. and…"

This time he practically howls, then leans in to press a kiss to the top of my head. "It's funny you think either of them would end up regretting me putting you in a room down the hall. You're so cute I could eat you up."

His eyes flash with a hint of the tiger I saw the night douchebag Todd tried to attack me, but it's very clear he doesn't mean for dinner. *Or maybe he does…* Desire sparks in my belly and I have to shake my head to clear the haze that forms over my vision. "You wouldn't be upset by that?"

It's a fair question. There aren't many polyamorous families in the Council families anymore.

"Baby Girl, I'm game for anything you are when you're ready." His lips curve as he leans in to whisper, "But I'm well aware you've only played in the minors, so I'll let you set the pace."

That makes me blush harder and I swat his arm. "Stop flirting and help me get my shit inside. Classes start tomorrow and I've lost most of the day already. I don't have a clue what I'm going to do about my goddamned uniforms and books that got ruined. This is a complete clusterfuck."

"As you wish, Delores." Fitz rolls the cart and shoulders most of my bags without breaking a sweat as we approach the front door. He pauses at the keypad, putting a finger to his lips and cutting his eyes to it. When I look down, he inputs a short code that he wanted me to see but not say out loud. "Too many pred ears."

"Got it," I reply as he pulls open the heavy metal door. The ground floor was open, and they covered most of the furniture in dusty sheets. It seems like *no one* lives here, which is confusing.

"The Tower has eight floors and I've secured the second floor quarters for you, baby girl. You'll enter the front and use this set of stairs to the right." He points at the opening right next to us.

"Do not come in the back, go up the back staircase or even go on any floor that is not yours. My friends are grouchy ass loners and even I'm only allowed on the top floor—well, until now."

I give him a suspicious look. "Again, you are absolutely *certain* they didn't say 'no'? I heard a little of your side of the argument."

Snorting, he shakes his head. "Despite their dickish need for total mystery surrounding their rooms and their diet, the guys aren't awful. They were sympathetic to your plight; I just had to make them see it from my point of view."

"Which is?"

"I'll make their lives miserable if they tell me no and mean it," he says with a shrug. "Now let's get all this stuff upstairs so I can make a list of what you need to survive living in Castle Cockwaffle."

That makes me giggle, and he looks thrilled.

Maybe this won't be so bad, after all.

Hot For Teacher

Felix

Shifter Basics is my least favorite class and always will be.

I don't disagree that new shifters need to learn how to master their forms, especially those who are destined for ranked positions in their families or groups.

No, I hate it because the wealthy dipshits who send their kids here leave most of the actual raising of their children to staff members. That means they come to Apex emerged early with terrible habits we have to break before they hurt themselves or they don't know *dick* about their species' needs. It makes it very difficult to help them and since they're all entitled little shits, they resist critiques at every turn.

You can be ignorant for a multitude of reasons and students here choose it purposefully every day of the week.

At home, we have a ceremony for emergence and though the content of it is… controversial, at least our children know what their tigers need and how to function as a shifter. No one makes it as far as post secondary without a good grip on their cat and the kids here come to college full of misinformation. It's bullshit, and I want to punch their idiotic parents in their faces.

Obviously, I'm not the person they send people to visit on tour days or for visits. My inability to hold my tongue about the lack of responsibility the Council members and their ilk take with their progeny would likely get me fired. Also not something I give a single fuck about, but I know Chess enjoys what he does here. Upsetting him would send my twin over the deep end, so I keep to myself.

It's what I deserve, anyway. I chose my fate and now I must endure it.

Fitz is much angrier that our father and one of my weaker brothers are ruling our ambush back home. I was at first, but after a few years, I concluded that he and I would not have ruled the way my sadistic patriarch wanted. We would have been fighting off coup after coup with his secret blessing and that life is exhausting. Our father wrested control from his brother and until he put the iron fisted rules in place that exist now, he fought off assassins and hostile takeovers for decades. We lost our mother to one when Fitz and I were babies, so I know how vicious Bloodstone can be.

I wipe my hand down my face as I watch the new crop of snooty little assholes filter in. It's clear there are alliances already formed or forming, because no one is entering alone. None of them look special, though I'm sure quite a few have royal or Council blood. My nose tells me there are canines, felines, ursine, and more in this group. I like when it's varied because then I can pair them off with animals they're unused to training with. It sharpens their skills to face the unexpected.

Not that any of them will understand or appreciate my talent for assessing weak points.

The scent of something different catches me and I whip my head around, squinting across the gym to see where it's coming from. I drop the dry erase marker on the tray of my mobile whiteboard, walking closer to the bleachers where students are seating themselves in their stupid cliques. I'll change this almost immediately when they're all present, but for now, I want to see why I scent something that should *never* be at Apex Academy: *prey*.

When I see her, my jaw almost drops. The curvy blond has her hair in a high ponytail with wisps around her round face. Unlike most of the females here, she doesn't have a lot of makeup on and she's not dripping with expensive jewelry. She's got hardware, sure, but it's understated. Her eyes dart to the stands and she scrambles up to the highest row she can get to without being obvious, perching on the edge of the wooden bench with her shapely legs crossed. I notice she's not wearing the ridiculous knee socks like the others; instead, she's got on ripped white fishnets and her uniform seems a little baggy.

I should violate her for the tights and the tall combat boots, but I can't find it in me to do so. How very odd.

I redirect my attention as a group of boys come in playing at fighting like a rowdy bunch of fools. The girls who follow them are everything I'd expect at Apex, so I think I've found the Council heirs. They're all together, moving in a group, and they entered the latest of all. When I flick my gaze back to the gorgeous loner, I can tell she's tense from head to toe now that these students are present. One girl grins like she's found dinner and directs her makeshift pack to the stairs as they're going to head for the loner.

Growling under my breath, I stride over to block their way as they try to go up the stairs. "Late comers sit in the front. Get your asses down to the front row before I send you packing with slips for the Headmistress."

"Who does he think he *is?*" one girl stage-whispers as she looks at her friends. She has a purple ribbon in her hair, but otherwise she looks like a carbon copy of the other three. The ones with the pink and silver ribbons titter to themselves, and I feel the rage forming in my gut.

"He's the fucking professor, and he gave you an order," I snarl, flashing my fangs in irritation. The nerve of these 'heir apparent' kids makes me want to show them how *actual* rulers teach their children to fight. But I won't—I don't agree with most of my father's methods and that's simply a reflex from years of brain-washing as a cub.

A girl with a gold ribbon steps forward and I know for certain this is their self-appointed head witch. She stares at me expectantly, trying to pull a power move by keeping quiet until I speak first. Unfortunately for her, she's fucking with the wrong goddamn tiger. I tilt my head, letting my cat bleed into my eyes and push the will of a true Raj out into the air. Words aren't even necessary; I use my royal influence to make it known what I expect these idiots to do.

The boys with them drop as quickly as many of their classmates, keeping their eyes below my sight line. One by one, the ribbon girls falter as I keep pushing until the silver, purple, and finally, pink give in as well. Gold is holding up, but I can tell she's going to give up the ghost soon. Her hands are shaking as she grips her books and struggles to make eye contact. After a few more moments of silence, she can't fight it anymore and hits the ground with a grunt of pain.

There. Now that I've shown them all what a true alpha tier predator can do, they'll back off.

Except for the one wide-eyed girl in the back row, who's looking at me with a cute little pout that makes me want to bite her lip. I stare at her from my spot in front of all the bowing morons, trying to figure out why she's not cowering with the others. That's when it hits me: this *has* to be the girl Fitz is losing his goddamn mind over. She arches a brow at me as I scratch the stubble I didn't bother with this morning, assessing me while I assess her.

It's clear she has no idea what it means to be immune to my power because her lips quirk and she finally looks down at her lap, picking up her phone to check the screen. Fitz's 'baby girl' also doesn't know I don't tolerate fucking cell phones in my classroom, either. Shaking my head, I try to break the spell she has on me so I can deal with the rest of the dipshits.

"Everyone, up! Group of dumbasses who came in late to the front." Sucking in a deep breath, I decide my twin's favorite student needs to learn a little humility as well. "Barbie in the back, no fucking cell phones in my class. *Capiche?*"

The cackling fools make their way to the front row without another word—apparently forcing them to kneel did the trick—and the blond doll in the back stows her phone as she blushes a delectable shade of crimson. I finally feel like I have control of this damn situation again, so I walk over to the board and grab the marker. Clearing my throat, I look out at the rows of preds in disgust.

"Professor! I would like to lodge a complaint. It's against the rules for any pred to—"

I glare at the bobblehead with the pink ribbon as I stalk forward slowly. "Who are you going to complain to, girl? The Shifter Training Arena out there bears the name of *my* family. There is no one in this wretched dump more qualified to teach you pampered twits how to master your shift, learn to fight, and become the preds your parents expect you to be. There isn't one person at this school who can best me in that arena—the only person who comes close is my twin."

Back row Barbie brightens, and that's all I need to fully confirm she's the subject of Fitz's summer obsession. There were rumblings last night about him bullying his way into Renard's creepy clock tower because someone trashed her room. I don't blame my brother for being furious; pissing on her clothes is as good as marking her, and that had to feel like a direct challenge to his animal.

"That means you're a Khan," the popped collar douchebag says. "You don't look like one."

Oh, these fuckers want to die.

Anyone with our hearing could easily make out Barbie's barely muttered words, "He looks like the one I know."

I can't decide if I'm angry or impressed, but something in my gut wants me to push her. "Anyone with a pussy knows my brother, Barbie. But unlike Fitz, I'm not so easily distracted."

The chorus of morons snickers when I come at her, which tells me these might be some of the assholes who destroyed her shit and left me to finish a bottle of bourbon while Renard and Aubrey bitched last night. I make a mental note to pass that info on to Fitz; I owe them for destroying my last night of freedom with the never-ending whining of my grouchy friends.

My words must have struck a chord in her because her spine stiffens, and she lifts her chin. "My name is Delores Drew, Professor, *not* Barbie."

Ignoring the gasps and whispers at her gumption, I smile slowly and continue to walk closer to the stairs. I only make it up two before the powerful scent of prey fills my senses and yet again, I feel the need to push her. "I'll call you whatever I want, *Barbie*, and you can call me *Sir*. Unless you'd like to be the first up in the ring?"

Her eyes widen in terror and she shakes her head at me, expression pleading. "No. No, sir. I would not like that."

Motherfucker. That was a mistake.

Now all I can think about is her pouty lips as she formed the word 'Sir' and it's making my tiger—and my dick—rise to the occasion. *Fuck, I want to see her squirm.* Turning on my heel, I head back down to the floor, approaching the whiteboard so I can hide the evidence of the effect she has on me.

"If you haven't picked it up yet, this is Shifter Basics 101 and I won't put up with any of your typical whining and bullshit. I don't care if you're injured, on your moon time, have a strained dick muscle, or cannot sweat because of a glandular condition. Whatever lame ass excuses they let you use in high school are *over*. You will come to class *on time*, put away your *phones*, and do *exactly* what I say without fail or I will make you regret the day your parents' condoms broke. Do you understand?"

One bimbette—the silver one this time—raises her hand. "Sir?"

Her nasally whine makes my balls shrivel and I shake my head. "Professor to you, mutt. What do you want?"

"DD talked back to you. If you really mean what you said, she should get punished." She looks at her friends who all nod with smug smiles and the boys sitting with them hoot in agreement.

I look at the girl with a narrowed gaze. "And you think I enjoy bitchy little tattletales more?"

She swallows hard and I grin fangily. "Up. You, your little friend, and those morons who came in late with you. Thirty laps around the gym… *now!*" They look at me in shock and this time, I put my coercion behind it. "*Now!*"

As they scramble to do as instructed, I tilt my head at the girl in the back. She's caused quite a stir for the first day and I can't help feeling that this won't be the last time. So I smirk at her as I ask, "Do *you* believe you deserve punishment, DD?"

Her reaction to the nickname is visceral, and I file it away. Fitz should be able to find out what shit I stepped on by repeating it, but for now, she needs to learn to lock it down. I stare at her, crossing my arms over my chest as I wait for her response. I watch as the indignance makes her posture change again and have to keep myself from grinning as her physical demeanor adjusts.

"If I do, *you* won't be the one to administer it, Professor."

Goddamnit, Barbie. I'd fucking clap if it wouldn't make me look weak.

The remaining students look at one another in awe, then back at her as she glares at me. Delores doesn't back down until I nod, which makes them all start whispering like they're in elementary school. Rolling my eyes, I walk to the whiteboard and write the names of the Pred Games fight videos I want them to watch before the next class.

"That's *enough!*" I shout when I finish writing. "Since today has been a shit show of epic proportions, and all I want to do is drink away the stench of failure wafting from you. These are the videos you will need to discuss on Monday. I've never understood why the fuck they have one day of classes after move-in, but I *assure* you if you choose to party all weekend and come unprepared on Monday, you *will* run this gym until you fall down."

With that, I chuck the marker back onto the tray and give them all one last sneer before I bark, "Dismissed!"

Then I watch the goddess sway her hips as she wiggles out the door of my gym with her head held high.

Suddenly Seymour
Delores

Delores

FITZ'S TWIN IS AN ASSHOLE; THAT'S ALL THERE IS TO IT.

I can't believe I have to deal with his moody horseshit all year, especially once he figures out I'm not a pred. Choosing not to let Fitz move me into his place was a damn excellent decision and I'm patting myself on the back for making it, despite the vigorous protests of my lady bits. Being where I could watch Fitz and Chess in *any* capacity sounded fantastic. But it felt wrong to invade their private space, when I hadn't even *met* the top kitty in their litter.

Way to be an adult, Dolly; good choices make happy bunnies.

Sighing, I look at the schedule I took a picture of on my phone. There's a gap between Shifter Basics and lunch, but I'm not hungry yet. Because of the stupid pee-pee incident, I didn't have time to explore the campus after I moved in, so I'm limited to a handful of known areas to hang out until I feel like eating. I chew on my fingernail as I look at the map and finally decide I want to go to the Shirdal Arts Center so I can change my major. The email I received during the summer said I needed a signature to join an art major and they'd only process my request if I got it.

This is as good a time as any to look for the prowling professor that cuddles up with Fitz.

At least this member of his family won't bark at me like I'm a fool.

My irritation at being underestimated by one of the Khan twins manifests in a speedy walk across the green and throwing open the doors of the theater once I'm inside. If one more person acts like I'm worthless today, I'm going on a rampage. That's all there is to it. I stalk down the aisle on a mission when I see Rufus, Cori, and the gorgeous Chess standing in very similar spots to the last time I left this room.

"Look what the cat dragged in… our adorable visitor from last spring," Rufus says as he slides his eyes to the professor with a smirk. Chess is facing a backdrop, studiously working on adding detail to it. He doesn't turn at the joyful exclamation, but I see his shoulders tense a little. "Get up here, doll face. Cori and I were hoping you'd drop by once you got here."

I smile, happy to feel welcomed by someone other than Fitz. Not that he isn't important, but he can't be by my side twenty-four hours a day. He might *want* to be, but I need other friends, even if I'm scared to death to make them. The Heathers emotional abuse after prom was no joke, but I refuse to let the terrorists win. All the internal work I did to heal from my trauma only goes so far until I resume living my life like a normal person.

So I comply with his request, taking the stairs on the side of the stage to meet the punk rock looking honey badger. I felt an odd sense of belonging as I saw that Rufus, like me, was wearing the Apex uniform as required, but he had his pants cuffed to show off matching Doc Martens and the sleeves of his shirt were rolled up to show off a myriad of interesting tattoos. He barely ties his tie, and he put a white chunk in his raven locks, making him look related to an X-Man. Even his hardware and eyeliner are chosen to amplify his 'rude boy' look.

I understand using unique style as armor against the automatons in a place like Apex.

As soon as I get on stage, Cori lets out a high-pitched squeal, bouncing over and giving me a bone-crushing hug. She's dyed her tumble of curls in a pastel rainbow that would make any little girl scream, and she's similarly decked out. Her style is the complete *opposite* of Rufus—more waifu than e-boy—but her smile rivals the sun as she pulls back. "I'm so happy you're here!"

Her words make my chest hurt, but my brain tells me I have to be cautious. Letting Fitz in after he helped me on prom night was dangerous enough, but he's proved himself over and over since then. Rufus and Cori were kind, but I don't know them well enough yet to trust they won't betray me. They seem like good people, but a lot of crazy bitches are good at hiding their insanity until you're hooked. Ignoring possible red flags is how I ended up staying with the Heathers for as long as I did. In the end, they showed their true faces and I'll never allow myself to be treated that way again.

I'm no longer the wide-eyed idealist I was before I emerged; people have to earn my trust now.

"I have some free time before my afternoon classes and I thought I'd come visit. Thank you for being so welcoming," I reply as I step back. My heart is racing from the proximity to a predator I don't know if I can trust, and I need the space to calm down. "Whoever put Shifter Basics at seven a.m. is a sadist, by the way."

Rufus howls with laughter. "No wonder you stomped in here like you were storming the beach at Normandy! You had Professor Felix snarl at you at the crack of dawn. Freshman Shifter Basics are the *worst*, especially in the first month. I enjoyed staring at his sexy ass, but his bedside manner leaves a *lot* to be desired."

"You *wish* you knew what his bedside manner is like," Cori giggles as she winks at me. "Don't worry, Delores. Felix hates all of us, though he'll pick some he hates more than others and those people should drop out. I doubt you'll end up on that list, though. You don't put on airs like the students he despises the most."

That information makes me feel a shit ton better. I thought he was focused on me because of Fitz, but he's just an asshole to everyone. Now I'm not worried I should avoid their house like the plague if my tiger friend asks me to visit. "Holy shit. I thought it was me. You have *no idea* how much better I feel knowing he's simply a dickhead."

Chess turns and looks at us, frowning. "Felix isn't really a dickhead. He's got a lot of issues, and anger is the way he deals with them. Don't write him off like everyone else."

"I wouldn't if he hadn't started calling me Barbie," I grumble to myself. "I'm not a dumb blonde like my ex-friends."

That gets a frown from the cute cheetah, and he shakes his head. "Sometimes he doesn't think before he speaks. Especially when he's dealing with new students. Fear is the way he keeps the spoiled kids in line."

"That's kinda true," Cori says with an apologetic smile. "He didn't turn into a ray of sunshine, but once everyone in my class calmed down enough to listen, Professor Felix mellowed a little last year."

"Exactly," Chess calls over his shoulder. "Give it time."

I roll my eyes and sigh. They might be right, but that doesn't make dealing with his derision any easier. "Fine. I'll try, but that's not why I came here, anyway."

Rufus looks up from the notes he's making on a score book, his lips curving into a wicked smirk. He rolls to his feet and walks close, eyeing me with a predatory stare. "Then why are you here? Tell me more, tell me more, girl."

I chuckle, enjoying his playful response. If I had any doubts about this change before, I definitely don't when I hear Cori snicker, and even Chess huff a laugh. Lucille always wanted me to get a job where I couldn't screw anything up and I chose English because I could work in communications, a library, or somewhere my mother wouldn't be caught dead. Back then, Todd wanted to intern in D.C. with the Council and I thought I could follow him during the summers. There were plenty of places an English major could work there and eventually, we might even have escaped my fucking parents.

Even I'm shocked at how naïve I was a few months ago.

I'll never get rid of Lucille and Bruno—not completely. My dream of a job in the capital is gone now that I've emerged as prey and Todd's been revealed as a total wanker. Everything I *thought* I wanted went up in a puff of smoke and it's time to grab the bull by the horns if I want to make a life for myself. Licking my lips, I prepare to give my mother the biggest finger yet—pursuing a career in the arts.

"I came here to get Professor Chess to sign my form so I can switch my major to performing arts." That gets everyone's attention and I smile shyly as I wait.

The cheetah grins a little, wiping his hands on a rag and putting his brush down. "Apex requires a singing audition for this program. Would you be able to do that… now?"

"Dolly, you have to. You'll love our program. We'd get to see you every Tuesday and Thursday," Cori gushes as she squeezes my arm.

I give her a tiny smile, my nervousness making it hard to match her excitement. I've never played piano in front of anyone before. I didn't even show Todd my songs on paper because he and our 'friends' openly mocked all the theater kids at Shifter Secondary. My love of music and singing was my dirty little secret, and even though my keyboard wasn't hidden when the Heathers came over, they never once asked about it.

Yet another red flag I ignored.

If I'm being honest, they barely asked about anything I did unless it directly affected them. I should have seen the ugliness beneath their facade sooner, but I was too wrapped up in dreams of running away to the big city with my douche-y ex to pay attention to their glaring self-centeredness.

"Uh-oh, Coco. I can see the little frown lines forming as we speak. Are you scared to audition? How can we help?" Rufus asks as he drops his book on the piano.

Chewing on my lower lip, I look between them, taking in the earnest expressions on their faces. I haven't had the greatest experiences lately with showing people my underbelly, and outside of Fitz, I haven't considered giving anyone the opportunity to get close enough to hurt me. I know the crazy tiger is an odd choice to place my shaky trust in, but his obsessive protectiveness has made me feel safer. Not that we won't have a conversation about his family—because they're known murderers with ties to my parents —but he hasn't asked for a single thing in return, besides the kiss, which I was happy to give. He's pervy, but I kind of like it, and he seems to be the only person in this hellhole who gives a shit about my safety.

Cori's eyes soften as she watches my internal struggle. "Ru-Ru, she's terrified. I recognize that look—someone's done a real number on our girl." She holds her hand out, clasping mine when I tentatively take hers. "I don't know who hurt you or why, but I swear on my Meemaw's peanut butter pie recipe that we won't do you dirty."

Her pretty words are pleasant, but I've heard them before. It's hard to accept anything at face value after you've grown up in a viper's nest, and lost every ally you thought you had in an instant. "I..."

"I second that, sister. Give us a chance to help you through this, and we'll prove we're not the enemy," Rufus cajoles.

"Okay," I murmur, taking a deep breath. "I never performed in public. All of my experience with singing, dancing, or acting has been in front of my mirror, with a YouTube video behind me. I don't know if I actually suck or not."

Their eyes widen as they share a look. Twisting my lips, I drop Cori's hand and stare at the marble floor beneath my feet, wondering if they're going to take back their offer to help. After a few quiet moments, I look up to find them both grinning at me.

Since I have no way of knowing what's going through their heads, I hesitantly add, "I might embarrass the hell out of all of you."

Rufus snorts, cutting me off. "You won't embarrass us, babe. The people we have to accept just to fill a production or show here at Apex are *not* professionals. Preds here *despise* this building because it teaches 'soft studies'. Those of us who have the *cajones* to major in the arts among ruthless business-types have pretty thick skin. You'll develop one, too."

"Let me call the other professors so we can get it done," Chess says softly. "You'll only get *more* nervous if you wait."

This time, my answering smile is genuine. If I can survive the horror of my prom night, I can survive a train wreck audition, right?

"WHAT EXPERIENCE DO YOU HAVE... DOLLY?" THE TALL, imposing woman glares at me as if I've wronged her ancestors by setting foot on the stage. Her willowy frame, fluid movements and the tiny remnant of sibilance in words with 's' sounds gave away Professor Bindi Sarabhai's species immediately.

I'd told everyone what I prefer to be called now when they arrived. My mother calls me Delores and my ex-friends called me

DD, neither of which I really want my new friends or professors to use.

"Uh, well. I don't have *formal* training or experience outside of the required dance electives at Shifter Secondary," I reply, discreetly rubbing my sweaty hands on my skirt. I feel like she's going to ask me to show her something impressive, and if Professor Sarabhai asks me to do some complicated step combo, I might flash lacy undies at the world.

As a rabbit, I have no interest in pissing this woman off enough that she shifts into a King Cobra, that's for damned sure!

"Hmph," she scoffs, shuffling the papers in front of her.

I frown as she wrinkles the pile of sheets I just spent thirty minutes neatly completing. The professor wouldn't even come downstairs to speak with me until I had a tree's worth of paperwork finished. Now she's crumpling it like a burger wrapper. "Is there something you would like me to show you?"

"No. This is not an appropriate venue or time for a trial. You will report to Dance and Movement at the Leonidas Gym on Thursday at seven a.m. sharp for our first class. We'll see if you measure up then."

The hissing makes everything she says even more threatening, and I wonder if she's stressing it on purpose. Are there any professors at this school who don't torture their students for shits and giggles? I haven't met one yet who hasn't harassed me—physically or verbally. Shifter Secondary wasn't like this at all, which makes me glad I didn't get to attend the Apex Lower School. I don't know if I would have survived teachers who scared the hell out of me every day during my younger years.

"O-okay. Thank you. I'll do my best not to disappoint you," I reply, turning to Cori and Rufus. They roll their eyes and I hold back a smile. Maybe Professor Sarabhai is less intimidating once she gets to know you. Neither of them seems overly concerned.

"I highly doubt you'll accomplish that feat, but we shall see," Bindi says before slinking off the stage.

"Annabella, you may proceed!"

A massive woman comes trundling out from behind the curtain like the prima in a production of Figaro. Her skin is shiny like patent leather, and her snow white hair flows down her back like a waterfall. "I am *la prima* of this school. My name is *Professoressa* Annabella Balena and unlike my colleague who is content to wait, for me, you will *sing!*"

Panic grips my chest as I look at my new friends with wild eyes. A little warning that the vocal professor prefers to walk around in her half-shifted orca form dressed like some sort of valkyrie from an opera would have been nice. This woman has a personality that could fill a canyon, and I do not feel ready for her. Rufus winks and gives me the hint of a smirk—he definitely knew she'd wig me out, but I suspect he's not being mean. He wanted to see if I could handle it.

And maybe... prove to myself I could, too.

I appreciate his blind faith in me, but I also think he needs to pay for his little ploy. "*Professoressa?* I didn't prepare for an audition today, so my chords aren't fully warmed up. Would it be permissible to sing a duet with Rufus to help showcase my abilities without risking nodes?"

Her face lights up like a jolly orca giant as she makes an excited whale sound. "*Bellissima!* Rufus, *alzati qui*[1]*!*"

Cori covers her mouth with her hand, shoulders shaking as she tries not to laugh. Rufus leaps over the two rows of seats in front of the proscenium and pulls himself up to climb on stage. He stops to whisper to the tiny raven shifter who took a seat at the baby grand upon Balena's entrance, before walking to me with an expression full of both mischief and approval.

"Since Dolly pulled a fast one, I get to pick the song. Only fair, if you ask me," he bares his teeth with a grin. "I hope you're warm enough to keep up, cottontail."

The opening bars of a familiar song start, and when he opens his mouth, I blink. I'll be damned. Rufus can definitely sing, and he knows his theater. I didn't expect to have to pull off Audrey to his Seymour for this song without so much as a warmup, but it doesn't look like I have a choice. I put him on the spot, and he returned the volley, so now I have to show them what I've got.

Time to sparkle, Dolly.

Closing my eyes, I let the world fall away, feeling the music flow through me like blood in my veins. The harmonies and rhythm are the only things in my head as we sing through the Broadway classic ballad from *Little Shop of Horrors* together, and when I finish, my whole body is trembling a little. I don't have a clue if we sounded good or not—I've never had a partner before—but I felt the performance in my soul.

"*Perfetta!* [2] You little blond girl will join my program. We will make beautiful *musica* this year!" Her large hands clap together—the thunderous sound enhanced by the theater acoustics, making me wince.

"Good job," Cori mouths at me from the audience.

Rufus sighs, dropping his mic on the piano with a bored look. "Yes, yes. We're fabulous, teach. Is it time for lunch yet?"

I let out an enormous sigh of relief when I look around the room and see only smiling faces. Even Professor Sarabhai seems pleased, in her grumpy way.

Maybe my time here won't be so terrible after all?

Dirty Little Secret

Chess

I almost swallowed my tongue when she walked in today.

Fitz warned me she might drop by the Shird. After he convinced Aubrey and Renard to let her take up residence on the second floor of the Tower, he looked over her schedule for today. He threatened the staff of the Apex bookstore so they'd deliver her replacement uniforms before her first class. The rest of the shit she needs replaced or bought will arrive throughout the day, but he didn't want her to get demerits. And Felix definitely would have punished her, even though he was present to see Fitz raging last night. His leniency is hard earned and Dolly hasn't earned it yet.

Hearing her sing and seeing the joy on her face when Balena accepted her was an absolute gift. Delores felt so sad and lonely when she was here in the spring, and when Fitz told me about his encounter with her at that foul prom, I was sick. I don't know her at all, really, beyond her accidental voyeurism and the brief chat we had. But something about her calls to me and I can't stand knowing the people who hurt her before are still doing it now.

Signing the paper to allow Delores Drew to become a permanent member of the arts department is a bad idea.

Once I watched her celebrate with my two most dedicated and erratic students, I ceased to give a shit. Sure, she makes my dick hard and my cat pace like it wants to pounce. She may have seen Fitz topping me in a way no one else ever has. I might have even backed her into a corner to inhale her honeysuckle scent like an addict. None of that makes a damn bit of difference if I get to see her smile like this almost every day.

I'm officially a complete tool.

"Is this all you need me to do to sign off on my change of major, Professor?"

Whirling around, I look at the blue-eyed minx holding a paper from the admin office out to me. I don't know how long I zoned out for because the last time I remember seeing her; she was on stage with Rufus and Cori doing some kind of victory booty dance. I knew better than to watch *that* with other professors in the room, and apparently, while I distracted myself, everything changed. "Uh…"

Delores looks up through her lashes at me, her expression tinged with shyness. It's a huge contrast to the hard exterior shell she's created with her clothing and makeup since the night of the pukey prom, but I like it. The opposition of sweetness and strength makes my inner muse want to write sonnets or paint something in striking color. I can't guarantee it would be good, of course, but I know how it would make me feel and that's where the genuine joy lives.

"Chess? Is something wrong? Do you… not want me to study here? Because of Fitz?" She whispers the last part as if her two friends aren't predators with excellent hearing, who are no doubt hanging on every word.

Shaking my head, I take the paper. "No, no. Of course not, an… Delores. I'm happy to see you pursuing your dream rather than something you were told you should do."

I had to curb my instinct to use the pet name I gave her when we were alone in my studio. My cat didn't like it and it felt weird as hell to do it, but Rufus and Cori are still here. There's no life-altering laws about students and teachers dating here, but the rumor mill is brutal. If Delores has issues with her classmates already, gossips finding out about her dating a professor—or in this case, several—will make her life infinitely tougher. She has enough bullshit to deal with as it is; I don't want to add to it.

Once I've signed the form, she gives me a tiny grin that says she knows what I almost said. The playfulness of her expression makes the cheetah flash behind my eyes, and she gasps softly. "Thank you for the support, Professor. I'm really excited to be working under you."

Holy shit.

She chose her words purposefully and my cat almost demands to be let free. I've never felt it so keenly in my entire life, even when we were still living on Bloodstone. Felix and Fitz were often involved in dangerous and bloody fights, so my instinct to protect the only family I've ever known was high. Still, I could control my shift, as they taught us all on that godforsaken rock. But right now, hearing her tease me with a twinkle in her eye, I'm going to lose it like a young cub.

"Yes, well… very good to see you again." I look at my meddling students, gesturing to the backdrop I'd been working on. "Can you two finish this? I have other plans to go over for classes. I'll be in my studio if you need me."

I barely wait for them to nod before I take off down the backstage hallway. Even when I'm not shifted, I move quickly because of my animal's genetics. It's not like I'm The Flash or anything, but I'm fast and I appreciate it more at the moment than I have in the past. Taking the stairs two at a time, I heave a sigh of relief when I see the door to my sanctuary. Yanking it open and scurrying inside, I dump my shit on the desk and lean on my hands as I take deep, calming breaths.

"Hey, baby. Miss me?"

My eyes pop open and I look at Fitz as he smirks from where he's sitting on the counter. He's sculpting something obscene with my clay and I roll my eyes as he makes rude gestures with it. "Always, but what are you doing here?"

"I don't know, honestly. I had this super weird feeling that you needed me and so I told my first years to fuck off. I wanted to send them to the library to piss old Smoky off, but it's only the first day. Besides, with my baby girl in residence, I don't want him tearing their fucking bat belfry down with tantrums. But regardless, I came as soon as I could get loose."

"You didn't have to do that," I mumble. Most of the time, I forget how Felix and Fitz were raised because it's not relevant to our life here. But when Fitz does shit like this, it hits me like a brick in the face. He can be a selfish, idiotic twatwaffle with the emotional depth of a jizz puddle.

That's sure as hell how the Khans wanted the enforcer of the ambush to behave, so no one would have batted a lash if he treated me like shit. Even Felix wouldn't have been surprised if his twin treated me like a temporary hook-up, while keeping me from anyone else. Consorts aren't given rights like mates, so he'd be within his rights to act like a total fuck boy and I'd have to take it. But luckily for me, Fitzgerald Khan is a psycho with a soft spot for the people he cares about. He doesn't give a single fuck that he pissed off his students or who might be mad that he's missing now —he only cares that I needed him. This is why I fell in love with him and why I would *never* have abandoned the twins when Felix was exiled.

Like Tolkein said, 'Faithless is he that says farewell when the road darkens'.

I don't care how dark it gets, I'll never leave Fitz and if my cheetah has anything to say about it, we may add the beautiful Ms. Drew to that statement.

Fitz tilts his head, studying me until his face lights up with a knowing grin. "Ah-ha! She came to visit, didn't she? I'd know that awestruck look anywhere, dude. Totally same."

"Yes," I sigh as he walks over and wraps his arms around me. "She's transferring to the arts department, for fuck's sake!"

Fitz arches a brow as he looks down at me. "How is that possibly bad? You'll get to see her *all the time*."

"That's the problem, Fitz!" I give him a frustrated look as I pull back. "Don't you think having the two of us linked to her is going to make her problem with the other students worse? Especially since… you know."

"Since we're bi?"

Rolling my eyes so far back I feel like I can see the inside of my skull, I growl softly. "No, dummy. Because we're Khans. Because we're teachers. Because we're older. Because she's obviously fucking prey and she shouldn't even *be* here!"

He blinks, looking at me with deadly serious eyes. "Don't say that so loud, man."

I frown. "Why the hell not? No one with a working nose at the stupid place will be unaware within the first thirty seconds they meet the girl. She can't hide it, Fitz."

"Yeah, but the walls have ears here. She's had one class and Felix said she sat far downwind and away from the rest of them like she was avoiding something. Her stupid friends tried to make trouble, but he quashed it. If she can keep it quiet for a couple days, we can get her living situation settled before more preds come for her."

I wiggle out of his grasp, walking over to pick up my bag and stuff a few things into it to work on at home. "I don't see why she can't stay exactly where she is. Those stubborn fuckers use like *two floors* out of eight. As long as she doesn't go walkabout in their haven, there's no reason to move her at all. And she's *much* safer than we could ever make her dorm."

Fitz grins as he holds his arm out for me. Sometimes his goofy shit kills me, so I take it. "Well, Chessie, that's my long-term plan, but I'm going to need some help to convince the two winged weenies. Do you think you might help?"

"Maybe Felix can talk to them. He's as much a king as they are and though ambushes work differently than clashes or clutches, they respect that he told your father to get fucked over Minerva. Not that either of them would ever *say* that because they keep more secrets than a spy agency, but I can tell by the way they listen to him."

"Mmmmm."

That's the noise he makes when he's thinking, so I follow him out the door and towards the staircase. Both of our attentions are captured when the sound of giggles and laughter echoes off the marble of the atrium. Fitz perks up and I can tell he's going to leap the rail to go after the object of our affection.

"Don't." He looks at me curiously and I shrug. "She needs friends who aren't trying to fuck her."

My lover blinks, then beams as he claps me on the back. "Excellent point, Chessie. We don't want to lock her away in that Tower because she isn't allowed to see anyone but us. We just want her to be safe. If I come on too strong, she'll feel cornered like a little birdie."

Blinking, I nod slowly. "Exactly. Let her hang out with Rufus and Cori. We'll find her later, maybe."

Who am I kidding? He'll definitely be creeping into the Tower to watch her sleep and no one will stop him.

It's Strange

Aubrey

Music streams from my DiePhone as I relax on my throne—one of the few things I like about the cursed device.

This is one of my least favorite times of year, and I need the calming influence of EDM to keep from losing my shit as my Smackbook dings with a regularity that defies logic. Giving my newest mochi a squeeze, I inhale deeply, counting to ten slowly. My new stress ball is courtesy of Fitz, as are the new breathing techniques. He's been strangely helpful in sharing stress relief techniques lately—something I would have never predicted nor believed if you'd told me it would happen.

Of course, until a few years ago, I would have called you stupid if you said I'd be friends with a tiger ambush, much less those from the Khan clan. That family is full of crooked, bloodthirsty criminals, and the entire shifter world knows it. Running Bloodstone for the Council is merely a side hustle that gives them unwilling victims to play with whenever they choose. No pred in their right mind goes anywhere near that wasp's nest if they can avoid it.

When the three of them first came crashing into Apex, full of resentment and righteous anger, they differed from who they are now. Felix is almost tolerable—when he's not trying to boss around two royals older than his family line—and Chess has come out of his shell nicely. Fitz is still Fitz, but he's a lot less overtly psychotic than he was when they first arrived.

Lately, though, he's been almost… tame.

The start of the school year is a chaotic nightmare for most of us, but he usually spends the first month screwing his way through the first-years like he's trying to win a contest. Renard actually makes us play 'Fist, Fang, Claw, Bite' to decide who has to applaud his conquests, but not this year. It's very odd, especially paired with his happy-go-lucky helpfulness over the break. Every time we needed anything, Fitz volunteered to run errands or grab supplies in town, jumping on his bike so fast you'd think they were giving away pred-stasy samples.

If it was anyone else, I wouldn't ponder their motives, but Fitz…

The near silent creak of the main doors rouses me from my musings, and I leap to my feet. Betsy, my ostrich assistant, is working in Admissions this week, helping with passwords and other shit I'd never touch, so the intruder can't be her. No one should be in my haven right now but me. I'm long past thinking my clan would send someone after me—my detractors have gotten what they wanted over the centuries, be it land, power, or wealth.

However, Apex is still a dangerous place on any day, and after the poisoning of students at the Shifter Secondary prom, I refuse to be surprised.

I know they cloaked the upper level in shadows, so I fold my wings in and quietly creep towards the balcony. Much like my gargoyle companion, I prefer the dark, and my night vision is superb. Whoever is invading my library won't be able to see me until I—

"Um, hello? Is anyone here? I'm supposed to be an aide? Hello?"

Who in the hell signed up to be a library aide and why in Anubis' name wasn't I consulted?

Rage bubbles up in my gut as I stalk to the railing, forgetting my half-shifted form as I jump over it and crash to the oak floor far below. Shaking my foot out of the hole I created for what might be the hundredth time, I let out a roar of frustration. I hate being unprepared as much as I hate having these idiotic rich prats in my beautiful sanctuary of knowledge.

"I did not consent to having some vapid twit lounging around my—"

The insult catches in my throat as my gaze lands on the girl standing in front of the main doors. It's the Botticelli-esque cherub from the prom, clad in the ridiculously sexy school uniforms they insist on putting the girls in. I didn't get to speak with her that night because some slavering hyena was dragging her around like an accessory, but I've thought about her all summer long. *Purely intellectually, of course, because she was one of the few students who didn't barf all over the ballroom like they were trying to recreate the Nile.* I've been working with the nursing staff and the scientists at the DHHS to identify the toxin and what specific properties of the laced punch counteracted it, so her input would be valuable to our studies.

I'm interested in her for research purposes, that's all.

Fitz talked Renard and me into letting her reside in one of the lowest floors of the Tower because of an 'emergency', but surprisingly, she hasn't broken our boundaries. Her respectful behavior means this is the first time I've spoken to her directly since she got here and I don't know why that makes me so angry. It's not like she's looking up Felix or my gargoyle friend, either.

"Um… are you the librarian?"

Her question startles me out of yet another twisted train of thought that hasn't fully formed, and I rumble in frustration. It would be much easier to find answers if there weren't so many blasted people trying to speak to me all the time. "I am the care-taker of the Draconis Memorial Library, yes. Who are you?"

A slight furrowing of her brow and a pout forming around her cupid's bow mouth tells me she's getting upset. "I'm Delores Drew, sir. When I visited last spring on my tour, they signed me up to be a library aide three days a week, in the evening. That's why I'm here." Her blue eyes widen as she looks up at me. "Didn't anyone... tell you?"

Of fucking course they didn't tell me.

Our not-so-esteemed dean, Henrietta, is so focused on pleasing the fucking Council and the wealthy donors that she barely sees the inside of a classroom, let alone the library. The Admissions staff is a flock of overworked birds with little concern for anything outside of completing their tasks, with enough time left over to keep the gossip mill churning. And with the volume of goddamn password reset requests from new students and staff—all of which I forward to Betsy before deleting—I haven't been able to look at my email for a week without wanting to poke my eyes out. Even if they sent a message, I wouldn't have seen it in the deluge of bull-shit I have flooding my inbox.

I suddenly realize the Botticelli-esque girl is patiently waiting for my reply, so I take a breath to calm my dragon.

"No."

"Oh. That's why you're..." She gestures at me with an airy ease, as if being charged at by a half-shifted predator in a mindless fury is completely normal. "No worries. I can come back on Wednesday if this is a bad time. I just wanted to get everything sorted before my classes start up."

I frown, tilting my head as I observe her more closely. Her gaze is steady and her posture is almost combative, but the scent of prey emanates from every pore. Someone like her shouldn't even be here at Apex; it's damned near a death sentence. But here she is, flitting into my library without a care in the world, and looking me straight in the eyes despite my scales and snout.

It occurs to me that no prey animal would *willingly* enroll here as a student, so there must be more to her story. Not for the first time, I wish I had interrogated her—find out what makes her tick. She's different from the girl I saw at the Vom Prom, and it's not just her emerged animal.

Delores Drew is idiotic or very brave, and I find myself curious to find out which.

Walking closer, I let my wings spread and my claws dig deeper into the wood. I'll have to replace the fucking floor again anyway, so why not see how this Council heir reacts to the full display? She maintains eye contact as I approach, though I can sense her heart rate speeding up. Towering over her, I don't see a sniveling rabbit like I should. Instead, there's a fire in her blue-eyed gaze that makes my breath catch. She gives me a haughty look that all rich girls seem to master before they can even walk, and I have to suppress a chuckle.

Brave it is, then.

No wonder this slip of a girl, barely alive long enough to be a good scotch, has been dominating the conversation in Renard's Tower all summer long. Most of that talk has been from Fitz, because out of our band of outcasts, he had the most one-on-one contact with her on prom night. Chess met her the day of the tour, but he's been noticeably close mouthed about that encounter. I'd find it weird if I wasn't sure he's in love with the effusive tiger.

"Does my dragon worry you?" I ask, deciding to test the mettle Delores is showing. My dragon seems interested in her, and since that's only happened one other time, I'm curious about what her reaction will be to him in return.

She snorts, covering her mouth with her hand. "Are you going to crisp me if I say no?"

I shake my head, wondering again what the hell they made this girl of as I stare at her. "No. I'm unused to people being so… at ease with this form. It is not how I present myself in public. Most shifters are raised to fear or covet those unlike them—nefarious intentions motivate both. I, however, am rare and unused to people being so at ease with this form."

"I'm not like most shifters; I was raised not to fear anyone." She lifts her chin defiantly, and suddenly, I can *see* who she is—who she came from.

This is the daughter of Bruno and Lucille Drew, a shipping magnate and the undisputed queen of Apex society. No wonder Delores isn't scared by my dragon; her father is known for eating business rivals during negotiations, and her mother is a drunken sociopath. Despite being an heiress, her home life must be hell on earth, especially now that she's emerged as anything but an apex predator, although it gave her the backbone to not be terrified by any of our beasts.

Even those of us with uncommon shifted forms.

"That's good, because it would be hard to instruct you in the care and keeping of my books if you couldn't be near me without fainting," I reply as I shift into full human form again. "There are many delicate texts here that require frequent monitoring in the basement, and part of your duties will be to assist me with these archives."

Her mouth drops open, and I frown. I expected her to be excited that I wasn't forcing her to be nothing but a shelving monkey—which I could, given she's only a first-year—but she seemed more dumbstruck than anything.

Did I break her brain or something?

Finally, she swallows hard and nods at me. "Yes, I imagine it would be… hard. I'd like to take care of that. Your books, I mean. I want to learn the books."

Her rapid babble makes me take a step back, unsure if I've somehow hit a switch and turned her into the bobblehead who come in here looking for the latest copy of *Fifty Shades of Grey-wolves*, as if I don't know what it's about. The sound of her heart jackhammering in her chest again makes me wonder if I've somehow triggered a response from her past, and I hold up my hand to stop the flow of jabber.

"Delores, it's getting late. I'm sure you need to get to the cafeteria before the bigger preds scarf up all the good food. But come back on Wednesday and I will instruct you on the different parts of the library. Deal?"

"Yes. You're right. It's late and I need to eat because I haven't had a bite all day and..." She takes a breath and shifts the bag on her shoulder, her knotted oxford riding up to showcase a diamond bunny decorating her navel. "I'm famished. I'm sure you are, too. So, um, have a good dinner, and I'll be back on Wednesday. Thank you." Before I can respond, she turns on her heel and practically runs out of the library like she has hellhounds on her tail.

I track the bounce of her hair and flutter of her skirt, considering the walking contradiction that just invaded my space. I'm not sure what whim of Horus or Bast or even Set put this girl on my path, but encounters like this are rarely a coincidence. The wheel of fate turns slowly, but it is always turning. Even a being as old as I am knows that the gods wrote our destinies in the stars long before we were born, and Delores Drew has flounced her way into mine like a fluffy-tailed wrecking ball.

Hmmm. Dinner it is—and I'm starving.

Joke's On You

Delores

Delores

For the love of everything holy, why are all the goddess-blessed male professors here so fucking hot?

I barely made it out of that library with my dignity intact, not helped by the fact I arrived flustered. After my nerve wracking audition, I had to quickly stop by Admissions and rearrange my schedule to accommodate switching my major last minute. They packed the office with impatient—and probably hungry—preds, and I thanked Cori and Rufus for coming with me at least ten times. I wouldn't have felt safe without them, and despite Fitz's constant barrage of flirty texts, he wasn't nearby to help if someone cornered me while the owls were busy hooting and screeching about password resets.

The entire scene set my teeth on edge, and when my new friends dropped me off in front of the library, I felt eyes on me, like I was being watched, but I couldn't pinpoint where it was coming from. I knew it wasn't my tiger stalker; Fitz told me he was busy humiliating freshman in basic coding classes then he was headed to the gym to 'destroy the bag'.

I may have to ask him to teach me to box because if I don't learn some offensive shit, I won't be able to defend myself when he's not around. Here at Apex, I need to strike offensively or I'm done for. Preds don't respect anyone who responds like prey, and even if I am one of them, I wasn't lying when I told hunky dragon man I was raised not to let anyone scare me.

I'll have to dust off the irritating lessons about commanding a room Lucille drilled into my head over the years. The giant midnight blue dragon who confronted me in the library seemed pleased I didn't cower at his half-shifted form, but if he knew just how often Bruno came after me in a similar state, he'd know why. I mean, a Nile croc isn't as frightening as an eight-foot tall fire breather, but the dragon wasn't advancing with a raised fist. I'll take a winged dominance display over an abusive drunk any day. The whole thing still made my heart feel like it was going to jump out of my chest and head for the hills, but I think that was for other reasons.

Like sexy dragon man reasons.

I approach the back doors of the Honeywell building, a dark mood falling over me as thoughts of my ex-friends flood my mind. The only place I've seen them so far is my Shifter Basics class with Professor Felix, but I know they're lurking around like stupid... what did he call them? Mutts. His insult makes me giggle, and even if he raises my blood pressure, I'll be forever in his debt for not letting them bully me on the first day.

Stopping for a moment, I take out my phone and pull up the picture I took of the campus map. They folded in it my Admissions packet, and again, I wonder how a school that gets so much money from tech giants has no interactive apps.

I see that the Charles Family Dining Hall is in the underground level of Honeywell, so I'll have to risk stairwells or elevators to get to it. I chew my lip, trying to decide which one seems riskier when someone bumps into my shoulder from behind, knocking my phone to the ground.

What in the actual fuck?

I scramble to grab it, looking up in time to see the retreating blazer of a scrawny-looking asshole with blond hair. It could be one of a hundred different d-bags who attend this school, but the scent tells me it's one of Todd's hyena friends. The size is right for Chad, and that kind of casual violence against a female isn't surprising, coming from him. Standing, I brush off my knees and look around, weighing how hungry I'll be if I skip eating to avoid a possibly worse version of this situation inside.

Damnit. I'll be starving. I have barely anything to eat in my room yet, and even if I did, I don't have a clue what to do in that tiny kitchen. Our cooks at home wouldn't allow me in there even on a good day, and Lucille certainly didn't pass on any 'motherly' knowledge about meal preparation. She's usually on a liquid diet anyway, so I doubt she would have cooked, even if she knew how. I'm going to have to hit YouTube for some cooking shows if this situation escalates.

Taking a deep breath, I search for the sass and bravery I summoned when I was clashing with Professor Felix and Professor... dragon man. Aubrey, I think the sheet said. Regardless, right now, I need it to get through this meal—hopefully with no scars.

It's okay, Dolly, you can do this.

I find Fitz in my phone contacts, and make certain his number is on the screen before I head down the stairs to the cafeteria with my head held high.

I've got this. I am a Drew, after all.

AFTER GETTING LOST NO LESS THAN THREE TIMES IN THE underground maze they call the 'student services' floor, I finally find an enormous set of cherry wood doors set into the natural rock wall of the building. It has donor names on plaques on either side, which seems strange for a place that's hidden this far from the view of outsiders.

I yank the door open, and my jaw nearly hits the floor. The moment I beheld the opulent room, I discarded my plan to make myself feel better by snickering about Purple's hillbilly agri-giant family sponsoring the dining hall in the basement.

Mother of Zeus, this is... astounding.

They set the sprawling room so far back into the bedrock of the campus that it reaches the lake. Windows and vacuum pressure doors at the opposite end of the room allow water shifters to come and go as they please, or simply watch their classmates as they eat. Whoever decorated this room had a rich person's idea of a mermaid's grotto in mind—vibrant jewel tones, platinum leaf, with real gemstones and mother-of-pearl inlays. The food is being served by a contingent of the pirate raccoons I saw on my tour—I don't see their Captain, but I assume this might be the less aggressive members of his crew.

I guess I won't be eating shitty walking tacos or frozen pizza in this joint.

Neither Cori's shock of unicorn hair nor Rufus's skunk-like coif are to be found, so I look for a table against a wall where I can easily see the entire room. There are too many unknowns in here and since the only exit—outside of the ones requiring gills—is the door I entered through, I have to make certain I have a snowball's chance in Hades of escaping if something happens. Warily watching the students in their various colored jackets, I keep close to the wall as I head for a table near the door and drop my bag on a chair. It's hard to concentrate with all the people milling around, so when a friendly raccoon approaches with a menu, it barely registers.

"Miss? Miss? Would you like something to drink?"

Blinking, I look down at the sharply dressed shifter in surprise. The sheer variety of chi-chi foods on the menu widens my eyes further. "I'm sorry. I didn't mean to be rude. Yes, I'd like a diet vanilla Dr. Pepper if you have it. Is this how dinner is every day..." I pause, looking for a name tag, "... Raina?"

It's the raccoon's turn to widen her eyes, and she titters into her hand before looking around as if expecting someone to yell at her. "Yes, miss. The academy serves full course meals, three times a day during the week and has buffets on the weekend for those who remain on campus."

I sigh. No surprise there, but it seems like a wasteful way to spend their money when students are likely to order in, especially on the weekend. Hopefully, they don't chuck the leftover food in the trash rather than donate it or something. "Well, Raina, I have had nothing since this morning, and am so hungry I could eat a dump truck full of food. What do you recommend?"

"Oh! I've never been asked that before, miss, especially not by a student of your... standing. Most of the ladies order salads or fruit, and they barely finish it at that."

"I see. Well, I'm not like the other ladies here in a lot of ways. I'd love for you to call me Dolly, and I really want to know what you think I should order," I say, smiling at her nervous but friendly chatter.

"Oh, dear, Oh, my. Call you... Dolly? Are you certain, miss? We're not supposed to be familiar, except with the Professor in the Tower. I don't want—"

"Raina, please call me Dolly. I give you my express permission. Now, before I die of hunger, what should I get to eat?" I ponder the information about a professor in a tower and realize it must be the enormous gargoyle I saw defend the raccoons during my tour. He seemed otherworldly and frightening as fuck, but if the small prey like Raina like him, he must be a good person.

I wonder what he teaches?

Her delighted gasp brings me out of my head and I wait for her to look at the menu closely. "It's not on here tonight, but I know the macaques who run the kitchen. I will ask them to make my favorite for you. It's not as fancy as the items on the menu, but I think you will enjoy it, miss… Dolly."

"Okay. I trust your experience, Raina. Thank you for helping me," I murmur, watching her smile in that weirdly mischievous raccoon way before she scampers off.

"Well, well, well. Look who was stupid enough to show her skanky mug in my cafeteria," the voice says loudly enough that every speck of sound gets sucked out of the room instantaneously. Hoots follow the declaration, then howls, and growls that echo off the walls as I look up at the face of my former friend.

"I don't think your family donating money to have this place built means you *own* it," I reply flatly, my fingers hovering over the call button on my phone under the table.

"But it does, little rabbit. We declare this cafeteria a 'Loser-Free' zone, so gather your crap and move on," she snarls, her tiny piranha teeth showing as she loses control of her animal.

Typical. The Heathers had 'zones' at Shifter Secondary as well; they even had Pink's parents launch an amended map in the school app to show where certain lower classes of pred shouldn't go unless they had class. I never kicked anyone out of an area or stole a table, but I know the Heathers and Todd and the boys frequently sent people packing. Now that I'm on the receiving end, I can see just how arbitrary this brand of bullshit is.

All I want to do is eat in peace, you know?

"Girls, I think DD didn't learn her lesson well enough after prom. Somehow, she got the idea that she still belongs with a higher class of animal than she does," Gold grins toothily.

"We should show her what happens when the food gets uppity," Pink chimes in, holding her phone up to record.

I have to fight off an eye roll. They're dangerous—simply because they're predators and I'm not—but their 90s bullying schtick is tired. Not one of them has an original insult, and even though my heart is thumping with the possibility of more preds joining their attacks, I will not let them see how their antics affect me.

"C'mon, DD. Show us that fluffy little tail so we can start the chase," Gold taunts, flipping her hair.

Silver leans in, whispering to Purple for a moment before she skips to her table and comes back with a large plate of steaming spaghetti and meatballs. My gaze narrows as I work out her obvious plan, and I push the button on the phone, leaving the line open as I covertly slip my arm through my bag. Pink straightens her ridiculous hipster glasses as she chats into the livestream, and I wait for Gold to turn her back to take the plate of pasta from her minion.

When she does, I leap to my feet and take off for the door, pushing through it like a freight train as I run towards the maze leading to the stairs. It was stupid of me not to map this out the first time, but there's no time for that now. I hear a panicked voice from the open phone line, and I raise it to my ear as I race through the confusing halls. I can hear some sort of large preds behind me, but I don't know if it's Todd and his boys or some other schmucks the Heathers commandeered.

All I know is that I have to get out of here before they catch me.

"Dolly? Dolly? Is that you?!"

The voice echoing out of the line isn't Fitz's, and I realize I called Cori by mistake. My stomach knots, because not only do I not know if the cutesy polar bear is close enough to get here in time, she may not even be able to help me navigate this place at all.

"Cori! I called you… by mistake. But… I need… your help. Where… hide… in the Honeywell underground?" I gasp out, trying to talk while I run for my life.

Miraculously, she understands the situation immediately. "Keep running!" she shouts, encouragingly. "Last left before the stairs. Take two rights, head down another set of stairs, and keep going to the end of the hall. The infirmary will never let a bunch of assholes follow you in; trust me."

With a sinking feeling in my gut, I realize I have to trust her. If I don't, I'm pred-bait.

Here's hoping my instincts about her and Rufus were good.

Running

Delores

Delores

By the time I reach the end of the hall, my lungs are burning. Before this summer, I wouldn't have been able to make this temple run, but hanging with prey was beneficial in a lot of ways. Not only did the Flamingoths and various shifters we mingled with from fashion row teach me about defensive weapons like the mace buried in my backpack, but we met at dawn every morning to run the huge park downtown together. My endurance is far better than it was when I believed I could rely on sharp teeth or fangs to save me if something threatened my safety after emergence.

I can hear the slavering idiots catching up as I stare at the reinforced steel door in front of me, and now they're close enough for me to know they're dingoes. I can only hope the infirmary will be secure—Apex is a dangerous place and the welcome packet said they have a full hospital and surgical suite on site—so I desperately dig in my pocket for my keycard, praying it will grant me access.

When I find it, I swipe quickly, my heart nearly pounding its way out of my chest as I leap inside and slam the door just in time. For a second, I tense, wondering if my pursuers will simply swipe *their* cards, but they must not have had them handy, as I hear them grumble and shuffle away.

I'm safe.

Pressing my back against the door in the darkness, I gulp in air in huge gasps as the voice on the phone echoes in the blessed silence.

"Dolly? *Dolly!* Did you make it? *Dolly, talk to me!* Rufus, get your ass away from my closet and come with me! We have to find her!"

Cori is panicking on the line, and I know I need to respond, but my animal is flickering over my skin like a staticky old TV, resulting in a crazy sci-fi movie, half-shift. A slow roll of my head confirms that I have long ears flopping about, and I raise a shaky hand, running my palm over one as the smell of antiseptic and bleach invades my senses. I may not see well enough in the darkness to verify that my new friend steered me true, but the clues are mounting up—this definitely is the infirmary.

"Can we help you, miss?"

The sudden voice scares the hell out of me, and I drop my phone on the floor as I peer around for the source. My eyes refuse to adjust to the darkness—as I would expect, being a rabbit—and I give the air a delicate sniff instinctively. Scents I vaguely recognize fills my nostrils as completely as fresh cookies in a bakery, and I inhale again as my mind works to identify the shapeless blobs in the shadows. It takes a moment to calm myself enough to really focus, but I finally pinpoint who I'm trapped in here with: a skunk, an opossum, and a hedgehog. Another sniff tells me they may have roommates of the mongoose variety, but they aren't here. The important part of this equation is that there are no preds in this room, so I breathe easier.

"Um, I... I... Cori sent me here because..."

I feel a small hand on mine, and I wince, but it doesn't pull away. "Unlike most of the students here, that lovely girl is not a heartless monster. She sent you here because we will let no harm come to you."

"Oh, Bettina, don't be so dramatic! Miss Cori sent this girl to us because she's *clearly* one of us and hasn't the slightest idea what the hell she's doing. She'll be dog food by the end of next week," grumbles the one that smells like a skunk.

"Hey!" I yank my hand back, bending to feel around for my phone by touch alone. The line is dead now, and I hope Cori knows I'm okay. "I didn't ask you to teach me how to survive; I can do that on my own, thank you very much. I just need a place to hide until those jackals leave the building."

I illuminate my DiePhone's screen so I can turn on the flashlight. Shining the light toward the voices, I find three small females dressed in nurse uniforms looking at me curiously. The hedgehog must be Bettina because she's glaring at the skunk, and the opossum is watching them both with an exasperated expression. Finally, Bettina looks at me with a smile, waving her hand dismissively at the other two.

"You are welcome to hide here, but given that you are attending a school full of preds who will want to re-enact this scene over and over until they get their desired result, you may want our help eventually, child."

A snort follows her statement. "She's going to need to get control of that nonsense going on with her animal, too. Can't you get the bunny to settle, girl? Talk it down, or you'll go into cardiac arrest. Rabbits have a resting heart rate of 140-180 BPM, and you're off the charts. I can hear it. Skunks have excellent hearing, you know."

"Argyle, please be more considerate," the quiet opossum finally speaks. "This girl needs our help, and we all took the Hippocratic Oath. I will also mention she was at the puke party, and I do not recall any of us treating her. She must have some sort of natural immunity that we could use to further study that unknown toxin for the Council. Does *that* make her worthy of our attention?"

The skunk fluffs her tail and my eyes widen, hoping she will not rat me out—or worse, spray us—for irritating her. "Fine. I suppose I can trust your sense of smell to be accurate enough to remember who was at the prom, Clarice. But if you're wrong, I'm going to let her handle the slavering meatheads on her own next time."

I'm uncertain what I should do at this point. These ladies will not let the canines chasing me get in—I think—but I don't know why they're arguing about helping me. My whole body is still shaking, and I hate to admit it, but the one they call Argyle is probably right. If I were to guess, my heart was beating way over 180 BPM —it feels like it's trying to escape via my throat. "Um, so... when it's safe, I can just go..."

"No, no," tuts Bettina. "If Miss Cori sent you, she would want us to help prepare you for when this happens again. She must be very fond of you to ask us to share secrets only prey animals know on this campus."

Blinking, I watch Clarice toddle over to the wall and flick on the fluorescent lights. She gestures to what looks like an intake table with chairs around it. "Come here. Bring up your Apex app so we can help you drop pins in the places you should avoid, and also mark where we prey have escape routes."

"Apex app? There isn't an app. All my paperwork is on... well, *paper,*" I frown, walking over and dropping my bag. I pull out the welcome folder, spreading all of my documents on the table for them to see.

"Oh, no. Oh, dear," gasps Bettina. "You have powerful enemies, Miss. These are *old* welcome kits. I haven't seen a student with a folder of printed materials in more than a decade. Didn't you notice no one else was carrying this?"

Come to think of it, I did, but I was so busy being distracted by the hot professors, a trashed room, and a wild hunt from the cafeteria that I never analyzed it. I didn't assume it was because I was being set up to fail from the moment I stepped into the office, but it tracks. The lengths my bullies—or possibly my parents—will go to endanger me just got infinitely more terrifying.

"I did, but it's been... a rough first few days," I whisper. "Is that how they knew I was in the dining hall?"

Argyle snorts. "Students can only see people who have accepted friend requests. Your enemies have staff on their side if they are locating you without having to put effort in."

Horror dawns on me. "I can't block staff members, right? So even if I download this thing and block the people I need to, their staff connections can find me."

Clarice nods, patting my hand. "Yes. But there are very few staff members who have access to the prey areas, and we shielded them from tracking to protect us from hungry predators—either students or staff making... an error in judgment. So if we teach you how to hide and safely get from place to place, it may protect you a fraction more."

"I don't like it. What if she tells her predator classmates? What if she puts us all in danger?" Argyle asks, flicking her tail in agitation.

"I promise I won't!" I insist. "I worked all summer with prey at the House of Growlvinchy, and would never put prey in danger," I turn the flashlight off on my phone and open the lock screen, bringing up pictures of me with my friends over the past few months. "See? Flamingoes and pangolins and peacocks and chinchillas and..."

"Okay, okay!" grumbles the skunk before turning to the others. "But if she betrays us, I'm going on record as a protest vote."

A loud bang at the door makes us all jump, and I dip my chin as I look at the similarly skittish nurses. We all sit in silence, waiting to see who it is as we collectively hold our breath.

"Open up, nightingales! Cori and I are here to pick up our bunny," calls a familiar voice.

"It's okay, Bettina. Rufus and I are here with—" Cori's voice fades as she whispers something I can't hear, then she starts again. "We're here with Raina. She found us when we stopped to check the dining hall for your bag 'cause we weren't sure if you had it. She has food for you."

My stomach rumbles and the nurses at the table narrow their eyes at me. I hope whatever Raina has for me isn't heavy on the meat because it might cost me some of the goodwill I've been granted. "That is very nice of her," I call back. "I've barely eaten anything all day."

"Well, I don't know how you earned special treatment, but I want to learn your tricks, boo. Spaghetti and moleballs were not on the menu today, but you seem to have a large, fresh container of the best dish this joint serves being delivered," Rufus grumbles. "So open this door before I steal it, girl."

I look at the nurses, and they nod, so I walk over and open the door. "You saved me, Cori," I croak. "I don't even know those dingoes, but they were… definitely… going…" Before I can stop it, my shoulders are shaking, tears flooding my eyes as I cry into my palms.

"Oh, sweetie," Cori says. She put her hand on my shoulder, gently pushing me back inside so we can close the door. "It's okay. My friends and I are going to help you stay safe. You seem like good people, sis, and those are limited in this hellhole."

"Amen," Rufus says, leaning in to sniff. "Now break open that food and share while we get you squared away. If we're lucky, we'll be done in time to catch The Real Housewolves of New York. I cannot wait to see if Rowena and Fenti are going to have a battle royale over Barnabas. He's a total d-o-g, but he's got an ass that just won't quit."

I look around the table, immediately grateful for the support system that seems to have adopted me, even if it's difficult for me to accept it. For now, I can take their help and use it to stay alive, but at some point, I'll have to distance myself from them again. I can't have anyone else getting hurt because of me when the fur really starts flying, but until then, I can enjoy the brief respite from my loneliness.

When I finally get in a position to take my vengeance, though, that will all change. The 'Fuck 'Em Up, Sis' list tucked inside my shoe is a constant reminder of what I came here to do, and every time something bad happens; I feel it like a telltale heart. It may take me the entire time I'm stuck in this deathtrap masquerading as a school, but I will teach those who crossed me who the real predator is—even if it damn near kills me.

That's a promise I intend to keep.

The Girl with The Flaxen Hair

Renard

Shuffling the papers on my desk, I look around the classroom I had constructed when I first arrived at Apex. I am the only professor who has an outdoor classroom for non-physical subjects, but the administration was so excited to have one of the few gargoyles living outside of our clutch on staff that they caved to my demands with little resistance. Thus, my literature classroom is in a garden extending from the recessed wall at the back of my Tower. Our view is of the lake so I can monitor my prey friends lest rowdy students give them trouble.

Over the years, I've made additions to my private oasis, including a wood-burning stove, hand carved chairs, lounges with pillows filled with ultra-plush goose down from a flock that migrates past the school, and a throne befitting a king that will support my weight whether I'm humanoid or fully shifted. Two years ago, I turned the foliage on top of the canopy into a self-sustaining biome, and the hanging vines and flowers allow students to enter, but also protect us from elements while inside.

This garden is one of my greatest joys, and if mouthy heirs mess with it, I simply shift and dump their asses in the middle of the lake. No one misbehaves in my classes—my wrath is not a well-kept secret. I wouldn't have to worry about it being incurred if Henrietta would allow me to have first refusal for students signing up for my first and second-year classes, but since they are open to all, I haven't won that battle. Yet. I hand-select the students who can attend the advanced portions and the two electives I teach for nocturnal and winged shifters.

Being the rarest shifter at Apex has its perks, and I am not above exerting my dominion to get my way. No other secondary academy in the world—not the Capital Prep, *Académie des crocs et des griffes*[1], *Zhuǎnxíng* U & M, or even Bloodstone—can boast one of my kind on their staff. It buys me a lot of leeway for getting what I want, including my private Tower and adjacent outdoor classroom, and forgiveness for my fury when crossed.

Of course, my quiet clock tower sanctuary stopped being entirely mine once Aubrey and I adopted the pack of Khan castoffs a few years ago. I've mostly grown accustomed to their loud, bickering presence, and my old friend typically helps keep the shenanigans at bay, especially if he knows I'm in a brooding mood. The seasons affect how I relate to the world, and when the right moment strikes, I'm quite difficult to be around. We have shared some of our deepest secrets over brandy and late night hunts over the centuries. The others couldn't possibly comprehend what beings as old as us have been through—they are still perturbed about being exiled for ten measly years.

I haven't seen one of my kind in centuries, and Aubrey only attempts to reconnect with other dragons once every quarter of a millennia. *We* know what true banishment is. Felix and I may have similar sins to pay for in the eyes of our respective families, but he hasn't had to endure the loss of his people entirely. His brother Fitzgerald and his consort, Chester, came with him and he's still in occasional contact with the true Khan head in India—Draconis and I did not have that luxury. We've spent many years forging our friendship by the light of his fire and the dark of my night. It's why I so often concede to his diplomatic efforts when I lose my temper with the group—unless he suggests that jealousy is perhaps what's fueling my short fuse.

Gargoyles do not get jealous of mere tigers and a cheetah; it's undignified.

"Hello? Is this… uh, Gothic Literature? I'm early, but I didn't know there was a classroom here… oooh!"

My wings pop free and before I can stop it, I half-shift at the intrusion. Frustration hums through my veins as I gape at the beautiful girl rushing through the vines to look out over the lake full of exercising aquatic shifters. I am not normally so on edge, and half-shifting like a teenage boy popping a boner isn't my style.

However, the external threats we are currently assessing at this school have me on a razor's edge. Before I came to Apex, I was hunted, both for my rarity and by those who still sought revenge for my poor decision making in the past. I have not seen a poacher or a huntsman in many, many years, but poison is a favored method of their kind—so the events of the prom were triggering. I am not as convinced as my scaly companion that the situation at the dance was an attempt on Council heirs alone.

"Oh, my! This view is beautiful! And the flowers and the scent… I've never seen such a lovely space to learn in." The girl turns towards me and the faint scent of honeysuckle finally catches my nostrils. "I'm Delores Drew, by the way."

Aine, give me strength.

This is the girl Fitz has been droning on about all summer, and now I see the reason he's been like a tiger cub with the zoomies for the past few days.

Delores Drew is as stunning as he and Aubrey have described.

She has a classical beauty that normally wouldn't lend itself to the rebellious body modifications she's sporting. However, the tiny sparkles of diamonds and flower-shaped jewels only add to the picturesque roundness of her face and blonde waves that spill over her shoulders. I was loath to believe them when they both insisted that, unlike almost every single female pred stepping through the gates of this school, she's not enhanced, but they are certainly correct.

Something about her is stirring urges I haven't felt in a very long time.

The irritatingly sexualized uniform doesn't hang on a malnourished frame, but drapes over supple hips and thighs. She's tied her blouse at her waist—a uniform violation I'll bet not one male professor has bothered to correct—and her slightly rounded belly is decorated with… oh, no wonder Fitz loves this girl so much. Her damn belly ring is a diamond Playboy Bunny symbol. Delores has the required kitten heels on, but she's swapped the knee-highs for white fishnet stockings and her plaid skirt is rolled just enough that I can see bows at the tops of her garters.

Where in the courts of night and spring did this temptation come from?

I've been here since this school opened, and not once have I ever encountered a student who floated across the grass as ethereally as her. Of course, I've never had a student who is obviously prey with no business attending this school enter my classroom before, either.

"Professor? Did you hear me?"

I blink, shaking my head and flexing my wings in both embarrassment and irritation. I can't decide if I'm angry at being interrupted, or embarrassed that I must have been staring at her like a full grown bat with a head injury. "Monsieur Renard, if you please. I've heard much about you, Delores Drew."

Her brow furrows and she stomps her foot, her entire body transforming with rage. "Why does everyone keep saying that? Is there some sort of nasty flier up somewhere? I swear, I'll put my fist through someone's teeth if I have to! I barely made it out of that stupid cafeteria alive, and if it wasn't for the ladies in the infirmary, some asshole dingo would have eaten me!"

That fire is intoxicating! Aubrey is going to love her smart mouth.

I wonder if I can lure him into a bet…

She keeps looking at me and I wait, unsure of what I should say. That would have been unfortunate and quite humiliating, even if she didn't survive her first week, but some don't in a place like this.

"Can you imagine? A *Drew* eaten by a measly *dingo*. Lucille would have a vodka-soaked aneurysm. Bruno would probably let Bruiser eat my corpse so the family shame wouldn't get publicized. Then they'd all win, because even though I have no control over how the hell I was born a goddamn *bunny rabbit* when my parents are a crocodile and a leopard, somehow they blame it all on me!"

I don't think this rant is going to end soon, and since it's amusing me, I drop into my throne and sit with my chin in my hand, settling in for the show. This girl reminds me of someone, and the memory is creating a warmth in my gut. The talisman at my neck pulses briefly, and I roll my eyes. I have plenty of time before nightfall to fully shift, but the damned thing likes to send me little reminders throughout the day.

"You know what sucks the most? Everyone abandoned me after I emerged. Not one of my so-called friends or family has tried to help me learn to stay alive. They *want* me dead. The only people who have tried to help me are prey animals—both here and in the fashion community this summer. Even though I'm prey, I don't belong with them and we all know it, but at least they tried. Luc also tried. And Fitz."

Leaning forward, I eagerly await more information about *that* budding relationship. Fitzgerald isn't known for doing much to be helpful beyond getting someone off, and while he'd surely offer those services here, I feel that's not all he's doing with this girl. I'm curious to find out why her name seems to come up every time he invades my tower, so getting the tea from the other side is tantalizing.

"Fitz is the only one who's made me feel safe. And I don't understand why because I mean, clearly he's a player and I'm just a silly rabbit with a small-dicked hyena for an ex and a bunch of bitchy dogs chasing me. What exactly could I offer him, or an artist, or even a grumpy… Oh, frosty goat balls, why am I saying this to a professor I just met?" she gasps, her eyes finally meeting mine from across the room.

Chuckling, I shrug. "My kind are excellent listeners, Miss Drew. We're accustomed to perching while people make long dramatic speeches. Most of the time, you wouldn't even know we're there." I wink, enjoying the squirming she's doing as she approaches. "It's the whole statuary thing."

Her eyes widen before she squints at me as if trying to figure something out. "Rock? So it's true? Like head to toe? I mean, I've never met a gargoyle before."

That's a question she's probably not ready for me to answer truthfully.

I roll to my feet, stretching my wings out as I approach her. "Well, yes. Obsidian is my form, and others vary, but you're not likely to see another soon. Gargoyles keep to themselves for a multitude of reasons, Delores."

"It's Dolly," she replies distractedly, as her eyes rake over my bare chest. "How come you're not like the dragon or the wolves or lions or whatever? They all have to strip or risk tearing their clothes. It looked like yours just... shooooooop!" Her hands make a vague gesture as the sound effect echoes off the stones.

"That, my dear, is not a secret I am comfortable sharing with someone I just met, even if she spilled half of her diary in one continuous monologue," I reply, giving her a gentle smile.

Her face reddens, and she ducks her head. "I'm sorry about that. I'm trying not to let what happened get to me, but it's been a very difficult couple of months and I have no one to talk to. All I've learned is you can't trust anyone, even if you're in love with them, you know?"

Ouch.

I absolutely know about the dangers of trusting those who don't deserve it, and she hit me right in the Achilles' heel with that sentence. "Yes, I do," I sigh, turning away from her for a moment. "I understand being betrayed by those you love very well."

"But being betrayed by a stupid, idiotic boyfriend who made a stupid video when he was the one who—just trust me, it's so much worse," she mutters, kicking a rock before she plops down on a lounge as if I made it for her.

Arching a brow, I don't correct her naïve assumption that an embarrassing video is the worst thing that could happen to her. After all, she's young, and has much to learn about love and loss. Instead, I murmur one of my favorite poems softly. "*She left the web, she left the loom, She made three paces thro' the room, She saw the water-lily bloom, She saw the helmet and the plume, She look'd down to Camelot. Out flew the web and floated wide; The mirror crack'd from side to side—*"

Delores rolls her eyes as if I've given her advice from a teen magazine, holding up her hand as she finishes my verse, "*The curse is come upon me!* Yes, yes, any lit student or teenage Goth knows the *Lady of Shallot*, Renard. Sheesh. Next, you'll try to comfort me with *The Raven* or something." Her head tilts, and a smile creeps over her lips. "Though if you don't shift back, I suppose the black wings would be fitting."

My mouth drops open, both at her familiar use of dropping the Professor title from my name and her intelligence. I didn't expect this side of the girl in front of me at all. She's beautiful, and that's all Fitz needs. Aubrey said she was sassy and liked books, so that explains why he's been grumpy. Chester has been awkwardly quiet on the subject, which I don't get because it sounds like she also has an affinity for the arts and poetry.

I'm uncertain what the standoffish tiger Raj thinks, but if I believed a girl on this planet existed that could capture the attention of *all* the outcasts in our little family, here she is. As I watch her swing her legs over my handmade chairs like she belongs here, I doubt I have any hope of resisting her pull, either.

I am incredibly, unequivocally fucked.

Bad Decisions

Aubrey

The library doors swing open at precisely three p.m. and I watch as the infamous Delores Drew sashays into my lair once again. The flurry of gossip surrounding this girl in the minuscule time she's been on campus is both annoying and intriguing, but I so rarely engage in such trivial matters. The only matter I'm giving my attention to is that she's infuriated, inflamed, and piqued the curiosity of my entire social circle with her behavior, both in class and out.

I, however, am not as sentimental or horny as the others, so I refuse to allow myself to get caught in her youthful drama. She's not the first shifter with a tragic backstory to grace our halls and she won't be the last. If they assigned her to assist me in the library, I will train her to the best of my abilities and see her to the door when her time is up—nothing more, nothing less.

I'll be damned if I let Rennie win yet another bet. His smugness is already out of control.

Her bag drops on the table with a resounding thud as she looks around, no doubt checking for hidden dangers. As the only prey animal to attend Apex as a student, she must be on high alert.

She'd be a fool not to be, and she doesn't strike me as stupid, although perhaps a little naïve. I don't even have to shift to scent the fear and doubt emanating from her as she walks towards me full of faux confidence.

It's almost like she's wearing a mask.

"My friends say you're ancient. Is that true?" she asks, blowing a bubble and popping it with a smirk.

I snort, seeing everything I need to know about her mental state from the way she's presenting herself compared to her last visit. This is a girl desperately trying to make people believe she has everything under control, and she's using that bravado to counter the prey instincts of an animal she doesn't yet understand. "I am the eldest shifter on campus, yes. That is why I do not suffer fools or games, Miss Drew. There is no need to pretend within these walls."

Her brow furrows, and she studies me for a moment before defiance flares in her gaze. "Who says I'm playing games? I'm here for my work study, Professor Draconis."

Renard was right—she's got a temper—and despite her occasional bouts of insecurity, there's strength in her.

She's definitely bright, although judging by the quality of company she kept at prom, she's spent a lot of time hiding her true self to keep from threatening the insecurities of those around her. The idiot who dragged her away during the vomit incident didn't look as though he could play Memory with a two card deck, so it's doubtful she's accustomed to someone treating her as if she has value besides being arm candy.

That will change during our time together.

"Indeed. While you are a guest in my library, you will drop the act and behave like a student that scored just shy of perfect on her ACTs." Her jaw drops and I smirk at her in satisfaction. "You are not the only one who can research their coworker, Miss Drew. I could not in good conscience allow an imbecile to assist me with the most valuable artifacts in our possession, if you were not up to the task."

She crosses her arms over her chest, raising her chin as she glares at me. When I don't respond to her bratty posture, she rolls her eyes and sighs as if I'm the most tiresome shifter she's ever encountered. "Look, Professor, I have my reasons for being the way I am and I'm not about to explain myself to you. I don't owe you my story."

An actual smile ghosts over my lips at her keen observation. I spent many exhausting centuries draining my resources to help people understand my past, and it never led to the enlightenment I'd hoped for. Giving curious bystanders weapons to use against you will never make the shame or helplessness fade—it's a subject my old companion Renard and I have discussed at length over the years.

If she's going to survive the gauntlet that is Apex Academy, Delores needs to stop basing her worth on the opinions of shifters unworthy of such a boon. Acceptance of her true self—fluffy cottontail and all—is the only way she'll be strong enough to rise above the inconsequential judgements of her peers.

"That is true, and I applaud you for saying so," I reply. "Differing from everyone else is both a blessing and curse, but only *you* get to decide which one to give weight to. Now, if you're ready to drop the mask enough to learn something new, we can begin."

A flash of fear vibrates from her, but she forces her shoulders to relax as she walks over to my table with a guarded expression. "What will I be learning today?"

The myriad of scents clinging to her slam into me, and I have to pause as my delicate olfactory nerves identify them. There's a hint of oleander, magnolia, and gardenia that tells me she's been in Renard's oasis. Earthy tiger scents mixed with expensive cologne mark her as part of both twins' days today. I don't smell the cheetah, but I can catch hints of her friends, the badger and the polar bear.

Prey… she doesn't smell solely of her own species, but of several. She's been in the dining hall and the infirmary. Has someone already tried to harm her? It's only her third day on campus!

I'll kill them all…

A low growl rumbles out of my chest, and she gasps, backing away quickly with downcast eyes. Her hands clasp together, wringing, as she cowers against a table. "I'm sorry! Did I do something wrong?"

Fuck. My dragon's response triggered her goddamn PTSD.

"No, no," I explain, making certain to keep my voice level and my hand gestures small. "I haven't eaten in a few hours, but not to worry… bunnies aren't on my menu."

Her lips quirk for a second, and she tilts her head. "Really? I mean, I never thought about it but, what *do* dragons eat? Meat, I'd guess, and maybe… coal? No one ever talks about your people, even in school."

I arch a brow. "You haven't earned my story, either, Miss Drew. I am uninterested in a rabbit sampler platter."

At least, not for sustenance…

That thought surprises the hell out of me, and I scramble to school my expression so she doesn't see.

A laugh bubbles out of her before she can stop it, and she covers her mouth. The sound is admittedly delightful, and I reach into my pocket to squeeze the shiny dragon mochi to stave off my typical reaction to something so cute. Delores doesn't need me to coddle her as others might, nor allow her to wear the false face of confidence she doesn't feel. Outside of teaching her a fraction of my vast knowledge this semester, I get the sense she needs someone to allow her to simply exist and become comfortable in her own skin.

"They didn't say you were funny. I mean, they didn't say you were *not* funny, but humor wasn't something I expected. The other night you were different..."

I shrug. "Very few people at Apex know me as more than the grumpy librarian, who won't allow them to destroy texts or violate my realm with their childish chatter. You won't find many who can give you the information you're looking for on my kind—you'll have to earn it."

She narrows her gaze, giving me a suspicious look. "Earn it?"

"Be on time, be yourself, and be eager to learn. That is all I ask." I stand, towering over her as I raise a brow. "Is that fair?"

She nods, chewing her lip as she considers my words. "I think so. What are we going to do first?"

This time, I do smile. "We're going to the archives, little one. Keep your hands and arms inside the ride at all times."

WHEN THE ANCIENT LIFT SYSTEM TO THE ARCHIVES REACHES THE lowest level, she turns to look at me with wide eyes. "You neglected to mention the 'ride' was a dragon sized boulder with no railings that shoots through a dark cave at warp speed!"

"Did I? Careless of me. I did caution you to keep to the middle."

I seem to enjoy riling her up. Perhaps this is what my gargoyle friend means when he says he enjoys creating chaos.

Her glare is full of vengeance, and because I think she means it, I let her have her moment before I walk to the edge and leap to the west platform. She stays rooted to the spot, looking at the gap warily. I wait, pulling my DiePhone out of my pocket to check my email as she hems and haws over what is an exceedingly easy jump. After a few moments in silence, she walks over, peering at the darkness below.

"How am I supposed to follow you?" she shouts, putting her hands on her hips in indignation.

"Don't be a simpleton. Jump," I answer as I go back to checking my email. "You are a rabbit, are you not?"

"I... I... well, yes!"

Shrugging at her sputtering, I toss a few emails from Fitz in the trash. He's still demanding answers for loopholes in the Khan decree, but it's simply not high on *my* list of priorities. "Rabbits can jump. Get over here so we can get to work."

A frustrated screech echoes through the cavern, and I chuckle as I walk away, leaving her to ponder her predicament. The security installed in the outer lobby of my archives is infinitely more advanced than the elevator, but I have to protect the documents and books down here from thieves and grubby hands alike. I lean in, using the Erickson-branded biometrics to gain access, and step back as the airlock whooshes open.

She's going to be shit out of luck once I'm inside, although I will probably need to add her face to the approved visitors list, which currently only includes me and Renard. I stop to listen for a moment and when I don't hear the click of school issued heels, I sigh. Well, at least she'll learn *something* this evening, even if it's how to confront her own fear. I step into the small lobby and gather the gloves, tweezers, and various implements I'll need to handle the texts I'm examining tonight.

The family from Europe submitted five books for admission to the collection this month and claimed them to be written around the time Apex and Bloodstone were founded. I don't know yet if they're originals or excellent forgeries, so I'll have to read through them carefully in order to catch physical or lexical tells that would give away provenance.

I could explain this to a certain student aide if she'd pull up her big bunny panties and get over here.

Cursing under my breath, I try to avoid thinking about panties and focus on the first book. It's a history of the Council, and the texture of the pages gives away the discrepancy with the copyright date. I set it aside, marking it as a forgery on my forms. The next book has severe water damage, and it cannot be in contact with the other collection items. Another mark on the sheet, and I pick up the third book. Maybe it's better the scaredy rabbit isn't here because this batch may be a total dud.

A History of the Honorable Academy of Apex Predators has the feel of a centuries old book, so I place it on the table carefully. The spine is fragile and the pages are faded in a manner consistent with the purported age. I'm about to start the first chapter when a loud crash against the outer doors startles me and I drop the tweezers.

"What in the name of Anubis are you doing?" I roar.

A snort follows another bang. "We have already established that your dragon bellow doesn't scare me! If I'm supposed to learn something before the time is up, let me the hell in, you jerk!"

Well, I'll be damned.

I stand, walking over to the internal keypad and punching in the code to get the doors to slide open. "I suppose you've earned entry… it took you a while."

Delores stomps in, her uniform slightly askew from her efforts. "You were testing me on purpose; don't even try to deny it. But don't worry—I made the leap without a scratch and snooped around your stupid cave before coming here."

"Miss Drew, your curiosity will get you in trouble if you are not cautious. Dragons do not take kindly to uninvited guests in their lair."

Her lips curve. "That would apply only if that sad little bedroom that smells like detergent was actually your lair."

I blink. No one has ever caught on before that I have a false lair set up like a red herring. How does this fucking girl get into the heads of shifters far older and wiser than her so easily? "I thought you knew little about dragons."

"I don't. I just guessed. It's super obvious you spend like zero time there, big guy. Few dudes have rooms that smell that clean." She bats her lashes, giving me a smirk. "So unless you want to reveal where you actually sleep, let's talk about dusty old books."

The fire in my belly sparks for a moment and I close my eyes, counting backwards from a hundred in Greek until I have it under control. "Fine. But stay away from my room—any room—and stop poking around, bite size. Deal?" I hold my breath, wondering if this is the moment of truth or truce.

"Deal."

You Can't Always Get What You Want

Felix

This is the worst first week of classes I've had since we arrived at this cursed school.

Unlike previous years, Fitz isn't spending his time dedicated to nailing the new staff or older transfer preds like his dick is going to fall off if he stops. No, instead, he's trailing along behind the blonde bombshell like a puppy, screwing Chess into the ground loudly enough to wake the dead, or babbling *incessantly* about his new obsession. My twin has *never* been this into anyone besides his consort, and it's blowing my fucking mind. His entire demeanor has changed and I don't know how to deal with it.

"...so I brought all the shit upstairs to the second floor and set up the little kitchenette in the outer suite, but she admitted—without sounding like an uppity bitch—that she doesn't have a *clue* how to cook anything that isn't microwaved! I'm going to look into some kind of meal service because she's adamant about not going to the dining hall and I can't seem to get it out of her why… something had to have happened…"

Rubbing my face, I let out a long, suffering sigh. My brother is the most loyal, stubborn individual I'd ever met until we moved here.

The loyal part is still true, but he's definitely eclipsed in the stubborn department by the two fools who haunt the Tower we love to relax in. Yet he somehow convinced them to house his newest hyper fixation on one of their *many* unused floors and was in and out of the place with more frequency than ever. Even Chess is squirrely when we visit the top floor now, as if he wants to investigate the place Fitz feels perfectly at home in, but isn't sure what to do or say.

Delores Drew is severely fucking the dynamics of my ambush and our friend group—but I don't have a clue what to do about it.

Her presence on the campus has started a cascading wave of bullshit that affects *everything* in my world, and it's making my tiger extremely restless. Students seem to be divided between not wanting to be near her, wanting to harm her, or wanting to side with the group of bullies who target her. Whispers amongst the staff are angry that she's here or determined to punish her to please the Council. Even my own nemeses in the professor pool are making snide comments and looking at me sideways because Fitz doesn't give a single fuck who hears him ramble on about her.

That concerns me because Fitz and I made a lot of enemies when we first arrived, but being Khans, we had to establish dominance over the lesser preds. I may be an exiled royal, but allowing the rest of these assholes to defy me wouldn't go over well at home. All three members of my family had to enter the ring week after week to show the fools who sat at the top of the pile at Apex, otherwise my father might have sent the Shadow Ambush to take us out. His pride wouldn't allow for *any* of his sons to seem weak, even the ones he's disowned.

Being attached to Fitz will paint another target on Barbie's back, and my cat doesn't like that one bit.

At least I figured out that our grouchy bastards have finally encountered her in class and can weigh in on the topic. Aubrey spent a good deal of the night huffing smoke rings while he angrily read some ridiculous old book with gloves on, like a butler. All he would share is that they assigned her to be an aide in his library without his permission, but he'd decided she could stay to help with his special archives. That asshole won't let *anyone* down there, so we assume it's where he truly sleeps. He won't confirm it, but I'd bet a hundred bucks he curls up down there like a fucking weirdo, surrounded by old books as if it's his golden horde.

As for Renard, he refused to discuss it at all beyond saying she has him for a class in the magical greenhouse. Fitz tried to pry more information out of him when he started brooding on the balcony earlier than normal that day, but he puffed up like a giant winged puffer fish and took off into the sky without a word. The lizard rolled his eyes and took off after him, leaving the rest of us *non-winged* preds feeling like dicks as we waited for them to return from his tantrum.

Those two were lucky that we all have our flaws, and we were all raised to be part of entitled rich royal families. None of us handle shit as well as we should for our age and we make exceptions for stupid ass behavior like that. The two of them barely complained when I returned from the fighting ring night after night, drunk and bloody, for the first three years of our tenure here. They wouldn't give me the same leniency for messiness *now*, but until I got my shit under control, they gave me space to be a stupid ass motherfucker.

I appreciate that—we all do.

Leaning back in my chair, I stare at the ceiling. My friend group is experiencing growing pains because of her presence, but that's nothing compared to the bullshit I have to endure while I'm trying to teach. My focus is shot to hell and back the second she walks in, especially once my animal senses her in the hallway. The nasty little shits who seem to know her snark, prod, and bait her at every turn, even when she's being quiet as a mouse in the back row. I have to give menacing looks at the hyenas who sit with that pack at least once a class for some filthy commentary about her bedroom skills or virtue—a feat which is difficult because my tiger wants to fuck them up something fierce.

But Delores simply sits in her seat in the back, her eyes observing the room for danger in between taking diligent notes. She doesn't give them the time of day while she works; instead, she focuses on me with an intent I suppose is borne of my resemblance to my twin. It's like she's risen above the childish behavior of her peers and she will not respond unless she truly feels threatened. It's an impressive display of control and exactly what I try to teach the new shifters regarding their animals in my class.

I wonder what happened to her to give her the ability to mask her emotions so well at such a young age.

Fitz might know. He seems to have the inside track to all things Delores Drew because he's been stalking her, with permission, I might add, all summer long. He's recounted every trial and triumph he saw while she navigated the changes in her life, so it's not a stretch to assume she might confide in him about what's going on behind closed doors at the Drew mansion. The rumors about her father aren't great, but her mother is a whole other enchilada. I know for a fact she has dealings with my asshole patriarch and nothing about that is good. Delores grew up amongst vicious, greedy adults who likely fobbed her off on the staff more often than they paid attention to her. Yet she seems more grounded than I would have expected from that kind of upbringing, so her nanny must be a fucking miracle worker.

Why do I care so much about this? It's ridiculous!

Frustrated beyond belief, I stand, walking over to the bar to pour myself another bourbon. I toss it back and pour another immediately, uncomfortable with the conflicting emotions warring in my mind. Our girl is in constant danger at Apex—in class, walking around, eating... everywhere is a potential death sentence. But she walks around with her head held high, ponytail bouncing as she moves from place to place confidently. It's as if *she's* the biggest pred around, not the only prey animal not employed as maintenance staff. She does it without being escorted by Fitz everywhere, which he hates, and without asking the friends Chess says she has in the drama program, either. Delores Drew moves through her days like she doesn't give one single fuck if people try to kill her, and that bothers the hell out of me.

And she's not 'our' girl, I remind myself.

"... I wish I knew what her animal is, you know? I feel like I could protect her better if I at least knew if it was big or small, had hooves or horns, or even if she had any defense mechanisms. But it's rude as fuck to ask and she hasn't offered it up. Felix hasn't forced them to shift yet, so I can't even cheat..."

Aubrey lumbers up next to me, giving me a 'help us' look as he pours his scotch. I grin a little, shrugging at the large lizard man. I might be Fitz's Raj, but I've never used that power over my twin unless he's doing something that puts us all in danger. Flexing the 'alpha' influence over your siblings and friends *never* works how you think it will and I watched my father turn his loyal soldiers and counselors into sniveling worms who lied and betrayed him constantly because he did that. I won't do it to people I care about and *especially* not to my brother.

Suddenly, an obnoxious sound rings out in the high-ceilinged living area, blasting *Short Skirt/Long Jacket* by Cake, and I arch a brow. It's an odd choice for my brother—who prefers rap for its fast beats and lyrics that fit his ADHD like a glove—and it's even more odd for him to have his ringer on.

I mean, I haven't had mine on since the early 2000s, for fuck's sake.

"Oh, hi, baby girl! I was just talking about you. No, nothing bad. Of course, I wasn't making fun of you. I'm upstairs with the guys relaxing... Well, I can. Do you have that book still? I mean, I know you told me not to hack your Amazon account, but I had to so I could find what you needed replaced. *Yes,* I know it violates privacy, but I replaced all your dirty books, didn't I? You have fresh spank bank mater—ow! Don't yell!"

Every single head in the living room turns to watch him stalk away to take the rest of the call in the stairwell with wide eyes. Obviously, we're glad it distracted his incessant prattle, but even Chess looks a little shocked at what we just overheard. Fitz Khan invading someone's privacy is no surprise, but *apologizing* for it is another thing entirely. And doing it simply to replace some creature comforts and maybe personal items to make her happy? He hasn't even touched her yet! I say that with certainty because he wouldn't be able to keep his fat mouth shut about it for sure; he can't even shut up about what she eats for breakfast.

"So, did anyone else find that weird?" Chess says from where he's curled up on the fat loveseat he and Fitz usually share.

Aubrey huffs and rolls his eyes. "Fitz is eternally baffling, Chess. I choose not to indulge his hyper-fixations because they often fade within a few weeks."

I nod, agreeing with his premise on the surface. Delores Drew may not prove to work similarly—and I believe she won't—but my twin gets obsessed with shit and drops it pretty often. "It's strange, Chess, but we all know how Fitz is."

"Instead, I'd like to point out that I've found something interesting in my research." The dragon leans back in his chair, sipping his expensive single malt with relish. "They amended the current laws of the Khan ambush when your father was a child. Codicils about the role of the consort to the king were added, and it allowed for a vast overreach in the power of the current ruler regarding their heirs."

My eyebrows shoot up and I lean forward, resting my forearms on my knees as my eyes flash golden. "Tell me more, Aubrey."

"The change gave your father the power to demand you follow the wishes of your intended wife or be stripped of your status. I haven't been able to figure out *why* this was added because, according to the history, that was never something your people gave a shit about. Males or females wanting to marry into the ambush's royal line were made aware of existing relationships and had the choice to accept it or walk away." His expression is puzzled and I know it must conflict with how dragons work, but Aubrey shares nothing with us he doesn't want to.

I ponder that for a moment. A great deal about my father's rise to power is under royal seal. He doesn't discuss how the power switched from the Rajah, who was my great grandmother—who now lives in Thailand in some massive estate—to my grandfather and ultimately, my father. No one says a bad word about the old gal, but our history books and education gloss over the period as if it just magically took place in a single night with a ceremony handing over the crown. Never mind that in every other transfer of power, it occurred because they killed the former royal in battle or died of natural causes. No one seemed to question it, but it always bothered me to have a living relative on my mother's side we couldn't contact.

I just chalked it up to my father being a fucking sociopath and let it go.

"What my scaly friend is trying to convey is that something very sketchy went on during that time and someone is helping your father conceal it—even to the level of altering *very* secure archives at the main library in D.C. If we can find out what it is and why he's hiding this information, you may challenge your exile," Renard adds from where he's perched on his throne.

I blink, looking at my friends in amazement. Fitz's determination to find a loophole in the Khan law never seemed like it would pan out, so I didn't take it seriously. But here we are, amidst two ancients who believe they might thwart my father's will with a technicality. The only question is… do I even want that anymore? That's not a sentiment I can share publicly right now, so I nod at them.

"That would work if I had a consort or a potential mate, but that ship sailed long ago." Lifting my hand, I scrub it down my face as

I sigh. "I'd rather stab myself in the gut than present Zhenga as the next queen, guys. She's the only person I've been anywhere near in years and the only person with the balls to go on this kamikaze mission."

"Unless…" Chess whispers softly.

Aubrey and I whip our heads around to look at him in disbelief. He can't possibly be suggesting… My eyes dart to the gargoyle sitting back on his throne like he wishes he had popcorn and a red leather jacket. *Fuck, that guy loves chaos.* When I turn to my twin's consort, he looks like he regrets saying anything. I've never treated Chess like he wasn't good enough to have an opinion—toxic alphas make my skin crawl and it's not how I planned to rule my people.

"Unless what, Chess?" I say, hoping it will spur him to untangle his tongue.

He ducks his head and shrugs. "It seems to me we have an excellent option from an acceptable family who needs a little training, but… You'd have to share her."

I'll be a cereal eating cartoon kitty… Chess never *asserts himself like this. What is* with *this fucking girl?*

"Talk about a good time to have a birds and bunnies and bees discussion with the young one," Renard says with a snort. "Fuck knows Fitz hasn't done it yet, despite sticking his dick in him every chance he gets."

Whirling around, I glare at the winged asshat, then snarl at his partner in crime who's also guffawing. "Leave him alone, you clowns. What would you know about it, anyway? Neither of you have even *approached* a woman in the decade we've been here. You're experts on celibacy, not the birds and the bees."

Renard quirks a brow at me, his lips curling lazily as he swings the leg draped over the arm of his throne. "Oh, Felix. It's like you don't know me at all."

A loud snort comes from the dragon as he continues fiddling with his book, and I frown.

Ever since Delores Drew rolled into the parking lot of this place, my mini ambush has lost its collective mind.

I can't decide if that's good or bad.

You Don't Own Me
Delores

My first week at Apex is little more than halfway over, but I'm still meeting obstacles at every turn. Monday I had to deal with the gruff Professor Felix, the last-minute audition, and my work study with the oddly attractive book dragon. On Tuesday, I attended classes in the Shird with Cori and Rufus, but afterward, I stayed cloistered in my room, snacking on vending machine fare, and memorizing all the secret prey information the infirmary staff shared with us. There are days I won't be able to depend on my friends to protect me, and I can't let Fitz see me as a weak little girl.

He's already doing far more for me than he should have to.

Yesterday, I had an annoying class before I stumbled into the resident gargoyle's haven. He's different from the others, but something about Professor Renard intrigues me. Since I don't have as many classes today, I have time to find food to squirrel away to take back to my room for tonight—anything to make attempting the cafeteria again unnecessary.

I may have to order some provisions on Amazon, to be honest, and learn how to cook. The dining hall is beautiful, but with the

Heathers and their followers circling it, I don't know if I'll ever feel safe going in there alone. It's too enclosed, and I'm too easy a target when I don't have backup.

I can't ask Cori and Rufus to babysit me.

A quick stop at the mirror has me checking my high ponytail, and my gaze drops to the Apex Academy issued black sweatsuit. The email Professor Sarabhai sent Monday evening said we would focus on ballet, jazz, and tap in the first semester. I don't have the correct shoes yet, but I got them ordered. I can dance barefoot until they arrive if I have to, but I cobbled together tights, booty shorts, and a sports bra to wear. I won't look fancy, but I'll survive.

Sighing, I stuff my uniform into my bag on top of my stupid, school-issued kitten heels before loosely tying my preferred combat boots. It's not cold yet, so I can head over to the gym in my dance gear without worrying about freezing my cottontail off.

Eventually, I'll have to get the right attire, but if I play my cards right, I can get Lucille to send it. She's due to check in with the Headmistress within the next few days—if I know her, and I do— so once she hears that I'm competing against some of her rivals' kids in dance wearing nothing but booty shorts, the floodgates will open. I just have to play to her obsession with image and a veritable cornucopia of gear will arrive, lickety-split.

If not, I'll figure it out. Luc paid me well this summer, and I've been saving as much as possible to help support myself if my parents ever decide to cut me off completely. So far, I'm only annoying them with my 'plebeian rebellions', but there may come a time when they strike back.

I have to be ready to make it on my own.

Picking up my bag, I open my phone, looking at the newly installed map app carefully. If I take the east stairs to the west lobby, and exit from the fire door that's never armed, I should pop out right by the side door to the Leonidas Gym offices. Fitz hangs in Felix's office there, and if I text him, he'll be at the window in a nanosecond to watch me enter the Leo safely. That covers my journey to dance in the morning. All I need to do is remember how Clarice told me to get from the gym to the library, and from there to the Shird to meet Cori and Rufus.

After that, I'm home free, except for Shifter History.

That's a future Dolly problem.

Maybe my friends can advise me on the history professor, to help mitigate the fact absolutely none of my allies will be with me in that course.

Hera, help me. I'm going to need all the advice I can get.

"I SUPPOSE YOU CAN CONVINCE ME TO ALLOW YOU TO CONTINUE with this class, Ms. Drew. If you acquire the attire and equipment by next Thursday," Professor Sarabhai adds, looking over her elegant shoulder at me, as if I'm contaminating her studio with my non-compliant clothing.

This isn't the hill to die on today, so I simply nod. "Yes, Professor. I'll make certain I have everything I need next week. Thank you."

She stalks off, leaving me to finish packing up my bag. I made certain to take as long as possible after class, allowing the older students to head for the locker room before me. Neither Cori nor Rufus are in this section of the class, and it surprised me when I found myself amongst mostly second and third-year students, rather than beginners. That means there isn't a Heather in sight, so once the rest of the girls are gone, I can try to slink in and change before I head to the Shird.

Fitz doesn't have a class during this block, and I know he's here somewhere. Professor Sarabhai had to kick him out of the room when we lined up at the barre to stretch, and even though he snarled, the cobra didn't back down. She may not like me very much, but she's a tough old bitch, and didn't want someone creeping on her class, regardless of who it was.

I have the feeling few people stand up to my erstwhile stalker and live to tell the tale.

Pushing the door to the locker room open, I step inside and head for the benches. I would never be stupid enough to leave my belongings in a space I can't control, but I do need privacy to strip off my sweaty clothes and freshen up. After a quick sweep around the banks of lockers to make sure I don't see anyone lurking, I set my bag down and begin.

Keeping my hair in the ponytail so it doesn't get wet, I peel off my sports bra and booty shorts and head to the showers to rinse off quickly. It might make me late, but since Professor Chess seems to be absent every time I'm in the Shird, I might get lucky and still get to my costuming class with him before he does.

When I return to the lockers, my mouth drops open.

For the love of Dionysus' wine breath!

My bag is on the bench, but every piece of clothing is missing—my uniform, heels, and knee socks, even my stinky dance clothes, are completely gone. Panicking, I zip around the room, nose twitching as I look for clues. All I can smell is a... civet and a bearcat.

Motherfucker! Those bitches were in my dance class.

How did they hide in here and why, in Hades' name, would they take my clothes? Neither of them even glanced in my direction during the class. Hell, no one did save the Professor. What am I going to do? I can't stalk across campus in the buff, and I definitely won't make it back to my room without clothes, either.

Taking a slow, deep breath, I work to calm my racing heart as the bunny flickers over my skin again. Instead of tears, rage wells up in my gut. This *has* to be a half-baked Pink plan. She *loves* old 80s and 90s bully girl movies, and she's always trying to pull outrageous stunts to get people's attention. I swear, if her daddy looked at her as anything but a meal ticket, she might like herself enough to let people see who she really is. Strike that—the real her *is* a conniving, scheming, attention-grabber with serious self-image issues. No one wants to be friends with someone who so clearly hates themselves as much as she does.

Which brings me back to my current problem: a buck-naked run across campus to my room for new clothes or a calculated play so I don't burn a bridge with the hottie cheetah I've been waiting to see all week by being late to his class.

Duh, Dolly. Plan B for the fucking win.

I pull my phone out of the hidden compartment at the bottom of my gym bag, my fingers trailing over the 'Fuck 'Em Up, Sis' list I stashed there with it. I was paranoid enough to hide the two things I can't live without from anyone who wanted to make trouble. I wish I'd thought to hide my damn clothes somewhere as well, but lesson learned. Fishing around in my bag, I locate a pen and unfold the piece of paper, storing the sins I'm owed penance for.

Fuck 'Em Up, Sis List

Lucille (existing, shaming me, throwing goddamned glasses)

Bruno (everything, including threatening to send me to Bloodstone, fists, plus Bruiser)

Todd (lying, cheating, hunting me, shitty sex)

Gold (nicknaming me DD, "run rabbit," being a twat, dosing me)

Pink (videos, sleazy dad, ordering my execution)
Purple (liar, behavior on stripper bus, hypocrite)
Silver (follower, didn't help me)
Chaz, Chad, Brett (not knowing my name, hunting me,
stripper bus)

With a level of rage that's almost frightening, I add a few more to my list:

The dingoes who hunted me at the cafeteria (find out
exactly who they were)
The civet and the bearcat from dance class who stole my
clothes (names to follow)
The fuckers who pissed in my dorm room (all the above
are suspect)
Anyone else who gets in my damn way.

I frown down at my list. I haven't crossed any names off yet—in fact, I've only added more. You can't make an omelet without breaking eggs, though, and I'm bound to run across more people who deserve my wrath as I navigate this nightmare. I take a picture of the paper, just in case it ever gets discovered and destroyed, and fold it carefully before slipping it back into the secret compartment.

Now, it's time to execute Plan B.

Tapping the first contact on my favorites list, I wait for the call to connect. Fitz answers in less than two rings, and I chew my lip as he goes through his usual flirty banter before I interject. "Um, Fitz? I have a problem." My lips curve as he suggests a solution that will *not* help me get dressed—the opposite, in fact. "See, that's the thing. I'm already naked and—NO! I don't need *that*, what I need is clothes. Some bitches swiped mine while I showered and I can't be late for Professor Chess' class…"

An angry growl rumbles over the line, and before I can finish my sentence, he's hung up. I'm pretty sure that means he's on his way, but while I'm waiting, I'll see if I can at least find a way to—

"Open up, Baby Girl!"

Sweet baby Hermes, that was fast.

I walk over to the door, cracking it enough to glare suspiciously through the slit. "How did you get here so fast? Did you even bring me any clothes?"

"Of course I did!" he huffs, not-so-subtly attempting to wedge himself through the cracked door. "You think I'm going to ignore your request to get in my pants?"

Opening the door a little further, I snatch the pile he's holding, ignoring his protests when I shut myself in for privacy. His black Apex sweatpants are baggy on me, so I tug the strings tight and roll the waist on my hips. The same goes for the white tee, which I have to knot at my waist before covering myself with the giant zip hoodie. I'm not sure if the tennis shoes he brought will fit, but I plop onto a bench and give them a whirl, anyway.

I'll be damned.

Fitz and I have almost the same size feet. Mine are big as hell and Lucille always complained I was disproportionate. She was rumored to have considered trying to bind them when I was a child. I don't know who stopped her, but luck has to go my way at least once in a blue moon, right? I leave the laces loose and tuck the sweats in, knowing I look like a reject from a Run DMC video, but, hey—at least I'm not naked. Grabbing my phone and near-empty gym bag, I walk over to the door and pull it open, coming nose to nose with my tiger savior.

"Thank you, Fitz. I don't know what I would have done if you weren't here. I don't think I'm ready for a naked walk to the

Tower, even if it *would* show whoever pulled this shit that they can't shame me."

Fitz's hooded gaze sweeps over my baggy outfit, and a low growl rumbles in his chest. Only this time, it has a different tone. "As tempting as it is to watch you take a naked stride of pride across campus, I do like seeing you in my clothes..."

My nose scrunches as I flush under his gaze, feeling my body heat as he watches me. I have to get out of here before I do something stupid. I'm standing in the gym, completely commando, with a professor's clothes on, and I definitely need to go before someone notices how close we are.

Okay, Dolly, get a grip on yourself.

"I have to get to set design, but um... I'll see you later?"

"You bet," he chuckles, and despite his promise sounding a bit like a threat, I warm all the same. Once again, I'm surprised by how comfortable I am with an actual Khan having me in their sights, but I'm not going to question it.

Before I round the corner, a wolfish whistle pierces the air, causing me to glance back over my shoulder. "What can I say?" he shrugs with faux innocence. "I hate to see you go, but I love to watch you leave."

Rolling my eyes, I turn and head out of the Leo, toward whatever challenge awaits me next.

Lonely Girl

Delores

Delores

CLASS CANCELED

My jaw drops as I stare at the sign on the door to the backstage area. I risked having my ass and the secret tattoo I got over the summer flashed all over campus to make sure I didn't miss seeing this professor, and he fucking ditched!

Of all the bullshit…

I look around in frustration. My tardiness means Cori and Rufus are long gone, but I'll have to stay to make certain whether the set design block—also taught by Professor Chess—suffers the same fate. If I head back to my room, I'll just have to haul cottontail back here again in… damn. Forty minutes. I'm really fucking late. I'll need to remember next week that I can't shower or change after Dance & Movement before I book it to the Shird.

Live and learn, I suppose. It's not like I can't dash some perfume on as I hop between buildings, but I hate thinking I'll be stinky when I'm working around the adorably shy cheetah. He's wary enough as it is; I don't need to repel him with my stench, too.

Ugh.

What am I going to do? I can't hang around in the hallway; it's too exposed. I don't think the Heathers would be caught dead in this building, and the Todd bros are too stupid to attack without instructions. Unfortunately, with what happened in the gym earlier, I can't trust that *anyone* in the student body, regardless of their year, isn't working for my enemies. I'll be a sitting... *rabbit...* everywhere I go.

I wrinkle my nose as I pull out my phone and look at the Apex app. The prey modifications the nurses helped me add show a lot of options if I want to sneak away without being seen. Since that's not what I want at the moment, I have to find a place in the building to hole up in until I can confirm Professor Chess is avoiding me like a severe case of the clap.

He won't cancel class for the entire year, will he?

I tense as I hear footsteps approaching, waffling for only a second before I sprint down the hall toward the closest stairwell. Once I'm through the door, I hop onto the railing, sliding down in my borrowed joggers like a frat boy at a kegger. Three minutes and a few close calls with gravity later, I'm at the bottom adjusting my enormous boy-clothes wedgie.

Not the most graceful exit, but it'll do in a pinch.

Scampering across the lobby, I ignore the gaudy Angry Bird statue in the center and slip into the brightly lit Shirdal Memorial Theater. There aren't any students or professors in here, but there's an enormous amount of space. There are at least ten hidden exits; the nurses had me mark them on my app. The best part is the piano, which makes me smile. I can work on my songs while I wait and won't need to worry about being trapped like a rat. It's the best option, given the circumstances.

Plus, I haven't had a lot of time to practice since I arrived. I'm not ready to share my compositions with my friends, and while I know Fitz would listen, I don't want him to feel obligated to praise me if

I suck. Lucille was so critical of my music that I learned to keep this piece of my heart sheltered because, if it broke, I don't know if I'd have survived it. I can't imagine how bad it would hurt to have someone I'm coming to value tell me I'm terrible—or worse, pretend I'm *not* just to save my feelings.

If that happened, I'd have to enter the Predation Protection Program like a stool pigeon, so I could start an entirely new identity. I couldn't bear having the one creative outlet I've used to combat my loneliness and depression become the thing that drives anyone else away.

My vision narrows as the bunny fights its way to the surface again, and I groan. I just don't have the spoons to figure out what the hell it wants with me. I'm still coming to grips with being here at Apex with a campus full of enemies. Closing my eyes, I give in briefly, using the ingrained senses of my inner prey animal to listen, scent, and feel if there's a presence in the theater I can't see. When it passes muster, I push the bunny back in the box and head to the piano on stage.

My eyes take in the majesty of the instrument like a child in a toy store. The Steinway D-274 concert grand is one of the most expensive models they could purchase, and it glistens like a crown jewel in the bright stage lighting. I've never played something so rich and luxurious looking, and I'm a little intimidated, to be honest. I slowly walk around the curve of the piano, trailing my fingertips over the lacquer case as I go.

Am I worthy of something so valuable?

I don't know, but nothing good comes from being scared. I learned that lesson the hard way last spring. If I'd made a stand with Lucille, the Heathers, or even Todd sooner, maybe my emergence wouldn't have been the catastrophe it was. Maybe I would have found someone who actually gave a shit about me before my animal appeared, rather than a bunch of assholes who used the event to destroy me.

Maybe I'm not that girl anymore…

Deciding not to let a beautiful hunk of sugar pine, maple, spruce, and Swedish steel scare me, I plop down on the bench and use my phone to pull up my sheet music. I'd rather have my notebook since this screen is small and I won't be able to make notations, but I didn't bring my messenger bag to the Leo this morning. That's probably good, because I bet those bitches who stole my clothes would have done worse with my personal items.

I lift the cover off the keyboard, gliding my fingers over the enameled spruce lovingly as I do. One day, I'll own something as beautiful as this, even if I suck rocks at songwriting. When I'm in a proper home, no one will care if I stink or if I'm a T. Swift in the making. That's how real love works, right?

Geez, Dolly. Get a grip.

Me and my infinite sadness will attract none of the sexy professors I'm lusting after. No one likes a bitter bunny, I tell myself as I stretch my fingers. A few more internal admonishments and warm-up exercises later, and I have the feel of the strikes and the balance rail—ready to play more complex pieces now that I've got the mechanics of this baby down.

The intro to my latest piece is a lilting sonata, and I close my eyes, my body swaying while I follow the rhythm of the prelude. When I reach the first verse, I sing softly along with the rich sounds of the piano echoing off the acoustics.

Torrents and waves crash every day
carrying me out to sea
Don't know the way
Don't know what to say
For you to be kind to me

I sigh as I play through the pre-chorus, sadness enveloping my heart again. I hate them all, but can't help wondering why it was so easy to cast me aside. Am I so worthless that even the people who are supposed to love me—like my own parents—can't? Is *that* why I was cursed to be prey?

My heart is my guide. I wear it outside,
but I hide what you do to me
The words you say
The thoughts they convey
Pain makes it hard to breathe

If that's true, if I'm truly such a burden to bear, then why did Luc help me by giving me a job and financial freedom? Why did Mattie always try to protect me? Why was I able to make friends this summer and why has Fitz followed me around since I arrived at Apex? Some obviously think I'm worthy of their attention, so why couldn't my former friends and family?

Apologies sweet, the cycle complete
I'm drowning in misery
You bruise and you scrape
There is no escape
I don't know why you can't see

I don't understand what I did to deserve the chaos my life has become, but I know I can't wallow in my own tears forever. I have to stand up for myself, and that starts with making the people who hurt me pay for their misdeeds. It doesn't matter why they treated me poorly or what reasons they thought they had—there's always a choice, and they chose wrong. Even if it destroys me, I'm going to make every single person who has broken my heart into pieces pay for their crimes.

I'm floating away… floating above the fray…
The only way I can grieve…

The ache in my lyrics echoes that of my soul as I finally release my desire to change the past. As always, my music helps me process my overwhelming emotions, and I breathe a little easier as the melancholy notes of the outro ring through the empty theater. I think I might have this song almost finished—it needs only a little more work before I can add the chorus.

Just like me.

DEFYING GRAVITY
RENARD

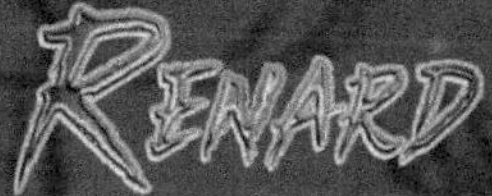

I'M FOREVER GRATEFUL I'VE MENACED THE OFFICE STAFF ENOUGH over the years to keep my teaching schedule light after mid-day. My species needs nighttime shifting when we hunt. Having others present when the itch to transform begins is irritating, and except for my adopted pack and closest companion, I am uncomfortable with the curiosity my shifted form engenders. I'm able to do things other shifters can't, and the vow of secrecy my clutch took around those abilities remains deeply ingrained in me, even though I'm no longer living among them.

There are some species you do not want to start a war with.

Henrietta uses my less-than-friendly demands to force me to teach one class of her choosing each semester. This fall, it's an advanced placement course for fourth and fifth-years about the evolution of shifter politics and governments. Despite Aubrey's imminently longer lifespan, she insisted *my* knowledge of the relationship between pred and prey was invaluable to the understanding of students with a career path in leadership.

She told me to present a carefully curated version of interspecies relations, told from the viewpoint of someone who's been alive long enough to remember how it was used as propaganda. Unfortunately for the Council, I have no need of their favor, and I'll teach the damned class however I see fit. That's going to make for some very interesting phone calls from angry parents to the Headmistress, but gargoyles are stubborn as fuck by nature and she shouldn't have backed me into a corner.

The classes I offered this year are far more interesting and useful, if you ask me. My fall schedule—besides the interminable year-long Henny course—comprises Gothic Literature, Shakespeare in Reality, and Music of the Night.

Reading has always been one of my vices, and that love of literature and knowledge is another reason my scaly companion and I bonded so easily. I teach many things to the students here based on how much my clutch moved around—languages, history, culture—but English courses are by far my favorite. I've also occasionally taken Chess on in independent study, but both our schedules are often hectic, so these private lessons are sporadic. My secret love of Gaston Leroux and Andrew Lloyd Webber is the reason I named my nocturnal predation course the way I did, and if anyone besides the book wyrm knew that, I'd have to murder them on the spot.

Obsidian is supposed to be hard and unyielding: the depth of my emotions is not something I wish to advertise.

In the spring, I'll teach botany, Romantic Lit, and poetry, but I prefer to do that when my garden is in bloom. The imagery flows so much better, and I'm able to use the lifecycle of nature to enhance the themes I emphasize. The beginning of the wheel of the year is a good time to show the beauty and ferocity of nature as it ebbs and flows.

Turning to the single Rothschild's slipper orchid sitting on the pedestal by the bookcase in my Tower, I close my eyes. Like me, it has survived out of its natural habitat for far longer than anyone would have believed. Memories of transplanting that flower into the crystalline container where it still grows flash through my mind, and I shake my head to clear it. The pain that comes with ruminating on the origin of my most prized possession feels fresh, despite the passage of time. I've considered getting rid of the orchid countless times over the years, knowing it's a masochistic symbol of a wound that cannot heal. Each time, I place it back in its suspended reality with its heat lamp and humidifier, unable to bring myself to cut the ties to my past.

Now that a certain bunny showed up in my classroom, I wonder if perhaps it's time.

"If you want it gone, I can take care of it for you."

I roll my eyes as the dragon stomps in, offering the same solution he's voiced a hundred times before. "Have I ever taken you up on that, Flames?"

His eyes narrow, and he glares at my choice of moniker. It's a game we've played for many years, and probably will continue long after those with shorter lifespans are gone. The more our respective days get filled with irritating students and posturing colleagues, the more we rib one another until something amusing enough to break the tension sticks. Our ability to find humor in the petty grievances of day-to-day life keeps us sane, and our grumpy old shifter routine is one of my favorite ways to pass the time.

"Listen up, granite-for-brains. You keep telling me to let go of the past, but you moon over this flower like Viola and the Duke. You're the poster shifter for handing out sage advice you don't take," Aubrey muses. He drops a stack of texts I requested from the library on the end table, running a hand through his short hair, and when I don't respond, I can smell the sulfur threatening to turn into irritated smoke rings.

So predictable.

Ignoring his insult and unnecessary commentary, I walk over to the balcony outside of the bedroom, climbing up to look out into the starry sky. It's almost dark enough for us to head out on the hunt. Neither of us needs to go every day—the bland groceries we ingest to seem more like the rest of the population sustains us well enough in between larger kills—but the start of the school year and one chaos-inducing student seems to have shaken up the entire campus, including us.

Aubrey's destroyed at least ten squishies since she arrived.

Something about Delores Drew has both of our preds in a knot, and I'll be damned if I know what it is. Even my meeting with her in the garden left me with questions I couldn't answer and thoughts I can't escape, so I can't blame the others for being similarly distracted. Her presence has thrown our comfortable routine into unmanageable entropy, and I don't know how I feel about it.

"If you lurk there, staring at the sky long enough, some idiot first-year is going to think you're Batman when you shift. It happens every year, you morose asshole."

My eyes narrow as I look over my shoulder at the bulky librarian as he fussily sheds his accouterments to prepare for our nocturnal feeding. He's one to talk about being a sulky old grump—when I came to Apex, it took him fifty years to even *speak* to me. Even after thousands of years, my scaly companion was so immersed in his shame and misery, he barely talked to anyone unless the Headmaster at the time forced him to.

After the first decade, I almost taught myself sign language because I thought he might be deaf; that's how anti-social he was.

"I'd rather the dimwits think I'm the morally gray, winged billionaire than a roided-out Indiana Jones. Elbow patches have never been hot, and your wardrobe needs serious attention that doesn't involve folding it into origami because you're so obsessive," I reply.

His snort makes me grin, and I give in, half-shifting so I can stretch out my wings. I don't know what it feels like to shift for other species, but for winged shifters like Flames and I, letting your wings out is like stretching your legs after they've been in a cramped space for a long time. If the two of us weren't such fucking novelties at Apex, we'd probably stay half-shifted most of the time.

Alas, neither of us enjoys feeling the weight of explaining our entire species to looky-loos and exotic shifter buffs.

"I see you had the appetizer in class yesterday," the dragon remarks, tapping his finger on my notes as he sets his glasses down. "She's working in my lair as an aide—Thoth only knows why someone in the office thought I would want an intruder there multiple days a week..."

The look I give him is skeptical, and it doesn't take a polymath like him to decipher it. "We're all aware you let her ride the dragon coaster down to your special collection, Flames. Out of our small circle, I'm the least likely to believe that's out of the goodness of your black heart. Sell it to someone who's buying."

Before he answers, Aubrey half-shifts, his wings stretching out behind him and his tail whipping back-and-forth in agitation. His multi-colored eyes find mine as he flexes his bulk, walking out onto my balcony. "Are you asking or *asking?*"

Pissing him off is always so easy and so worth it.

I rise to my feet, tilting my head back as the moonlight washes over me and the transformation that comes with a full shift occurs. The light glints off of the obsidian now surrounding my skin as my size multiplies until I'm towering over the massive man beside me. To his credit, Aubrey has never once commented on either my diminutive human body or my massively intimidating shifted form. Once he finally spoke to me, our similarities were far more important than our differences.

"I believe you know the answer to that question." Tossing him a wink, I launch myself into the air, my wings catching on the slipstream as he curses below.

"Cheater! Charlatan! Crook!"

I knew he wasn't ready for our usual race to the buffet, but that's a future Renard problem. Right now, I'm in the lead and he'll have to give chase if he wants to harangue me further, whether about the ingenue bunny rabbit or my dastardly ways. My wings stretch as I make a sharp turn into a gust of wind, using tailwinds and windshear to soar to a higher altitude and pick up speed.

My scaly friend is in an exceptionally playful mood tonight—despite his cranky exterior—and I know him well enough to recognize the extra 'spring in his wings'. If his interactions with Delores have affected him so much, maybe I should prepare myself for similar emotions.

Perhaps it really is time to put the past in the past.

A dinosaur-like scream echoes over the hills as my companion goes full Smaug before appearing at my side, one jewel-toned eye glaring. I knew he'd catch up eventually—gargoyles have high aspect ratio wings and do more gliding and soaring. Dragons like Aubrey have larger wings, with a shape that reduces drag and doesn't require nearly as much vertical thrust or horizontal taxi space to take off and gain speed. On any day, one or the other of us pretends we don't actually understand the physics of our flight and lets the other win, even when the odds are unfair.

After hundreds of years together, it's easy to compromise, so we both feel like we can come out on top.

"You didn't say I had to count down," I growl into the wind, knowing that will irritate the shit out of him.

An unmanly squawk escapes my throat when his answer is to yank the pointed end of my tail with the spiked end of his, causing me to hit the wrong wind gradient and spiral into a dive.

And he says I cheat?

I barely turn downwind fast enough to catch another shear before I end up with a face full of trees. It's a close call, but I get lucky when the slope shoots me up into the air, higher than he can match until he banks along the ridge. Spying a good place to start our hunt, I take a sharp left toward an open-air campsite with dots of firelight and smoke billowing from several points.

Like items on the menu...

I glance at Aubrey before gesturing to a lone campfire isolated from the others, but he simply gives me a noncommittal shrug in return, which makes me smile. People like to talk a lot about dragons and their tempers over their hordes of gold, but as a long-time member of the 'crisped by a pissy lizard' club, I know there's not a single thing they treasure more dearly than their bloody pride. You can take that little tidbit of trivia to the bank—that is, if you're like me and can survive being roasted alive.

Hopefully, Little Miss Cottontail is worth the effort.

IDGAF

Delores

Shifter History is my least favorite class. You'd think it would be Professor Felix's Shifting Basics, but I get to look at *him* the entire time, so it makes the time go faster. I could do without him attempting to goad me in front of the idiots who used to be my friends, and I have no idea why he seems determined to push my buttons, but it doesn't bother me as much as I thought it would.

This class, however…

I walk into the traditional-style classroom in the Rostoff Scholastic Complex—gag me—and drop into the seat in the furthest corner of the room. After my stint in the cafeteria, I make certain to sit where I can not only watch my back, but every entrance, exit, and potential threat when I enter a room. I don't trust the preds in this place as far as I could throw them; too many people have parents whose businesses and wealth are tied to the Heathers' families, so they could have allies everywhere.

The voicemail Lucille left this morning rings in my head as I wait for the rest of the class to arrive. She was especially ruthless, probably because the phone didn't wake me at four a.m. as she intended.

Delores Diamond Drew!

I don't know what those weak-minded prey friends of yours filled your head with this summer, and I don't care. You will represent the family appropriately, including excelling in your classes and dressing appropriately. I don't want to hear about you running around looking like a ragpicker, even if you insist on indulging your ridiculous dreams of humiliating us on some rinky-dink dinner theater stage.

I've sent satisfactory attire for the dance classes you joined without my permission and you will otherwise dress in a manner befitting your stature, even if you don't deserve to be associated with us.

Your father and I have high standards, and you will represent the family in public and in private.

If by some miracle you find an acceptable suitor who tolerates your… failings, we will not be pleased if you look like trash while on the town with another shifter.

Any further nonsense will be dealt with severely and swiftly.

Do you understand?

I expect an answer before cocktail hour, or so help me…

Shuddering, I shake off my rabbit's instinctual fear. I can't exude any weakness with the rest of my classmates filtering in. The scent will pique their interest and the nasty asshole who teaches this class won't put them in their place like my guys would.

My guys. What a silly, naïve idea.

As if men with decades, or centuries, of experience would have the slightest interest in *me*. I'm a social reject and barely more than a virgin, experience-wise. What could I possibly offer to any of these guys? Everything I know—and admittedly, it's not a lot—comes from watching videos on PredHub that can't be realistic. I mean, the *size* of… things is clearly possible, given what I spied in the fighting ring during my campus tour, but there's no way everything else is accurate. Movie magic, right?

Argh! What is wrong with me?

I avoided even *thinking* about dating most of the summer, and I was perfectly fine. Why am I now in this lust fog that I can't shake? Is it these specific men or am I finally healed enough from my moronic ex that I can see guys as potential partners again? Is it hormonal? I wish I knew, because it's really fucking with my focus and it's far too dangerous at Apex to be unaware of my surroundings while spraying out pheromones.

"Oh, look. It's the appetizer," Gold snarks as she sashays into the classroom with her troop of ass-suckers.

That nickname is a lot less endearing when it's not coming from a grumpy book dragon muttering it under his breath. I glare at Gold, stretching my legs under the desk to reveal my shit kickers. Hopefully, she gets the point that I wouldn't mind shoving one up her entitled ass, but I doubt she's capable of making the leap. When the random girls with her snicker in chorus, I roll my eyes and open my DiePad, pointedly ignoring her as I get ready for class.

Pink strolls up with eyes full of malice, thrusting her phone in my face. "Looks like some lucky doggy caught your little scamper through the tunnels on video. I have uploaded it to all my channels, so everyone knows what a cowardly little rodent you are, DD. So sad."

Something in my gut reacts, but I refrain from outwardly reacting. I've had a little self-defense training, but not enough to start a fight in a classroom that's slowly filling with curious preds. I look around, hoping to find anyone who might step in, but the closest I get is a dude in the corner who gives me a sympathetic look. He holds my gaze for a second, but quickly drops his head and stares at his desk. I don't know what kind of animal he is, but it must be a smaller pred. He's not willing to intervene, even though he seems to recognize what's happening is wrong.

"I don't care what people on social media think, B. Honestly, we all just pretended to be interested in your shallow vids and blogs to keep you happy. Even E. used to say you and your creepy dad were barely rich enough to be included as Council members," I reply, leaning back in my seat as if I don't have a care in the world.

It's an act, because I'm more than outnumbered, and I definitely have my hand in my pocket hovering over the speed dial for Fitz, just in case. But I also can't keep allowing them to make me their bitch in public or it'll never stop. If I cower or simply ignore them, it seems to just encourage them to up their terror tactics. This year has barely started—I don't want to imagine what it's going to be like if I let their venom fester.

"Oh, DD," Purple says, clicking her tongue and shaking her head. "We know who you are now and it doesn't matter if you're a weak little bunny or another small pred, we're coming for you. There's nothing you can do to stop it."

Before I can retort, the squat professor waddles in with his brief-case tucked under his short arms. Professor Abel doesn't *look* threatening in his bad suits, tiny spectacles and balding head, but his scent alone is enough to send you running. He's a Tasmanian devil shifter, and they're known for being stinky-ass carrion eaters. That puts him at the bottom of the totem pole in size, even if they eat in a frenzy only comparable to sharks. But he's been enjoying the hell out of exercising his meager authority over me.

"Miss Drew, I will not spend the entire semester allowing you to disrupt my class with your self-centered antics. The rest of the students are here for an education, not to make a mockery of our hallowed traditions."

My eyes narrow and I swear, for a half a second, I feel like I've channeled Lucille. Outrage at his audacity—blaming me for the bullshit my ex-friends are pulling—rushes through me at breakneck speed. Something deep inside of me longs to put this inferior shit in his place. I've never felt the 'Rostoff Rage' as Lucille calls it, but then again, I've never been the type to designate other preds as 'beneath me' until this moment.

"I beg to differ, Professor, but I arrived early, have my materials ready, and am seated as per class rules. You certainly can't say that for most of the others right now." I incline my head to the Heathers and the crowd of hangers-on standing around them.

The weaselly little jerk strokes his pencil thin douchestache, harrumphing as he toddles over to my desk. His sharp fangs aren't enormous, so unlike Bruno, he doesn't set off my prey instincts. I blink up at him with an innocent yet knowing expression, knowing if they catch this on camera, I'll look like any other Council heir asserting dominance.

That should placate Lucille for a bit.

"Your mother and father aren't here to save you, Miss Drew. Although, I have it on good authority they wouldn't be inclined to even if they were," Abel sneers. "Therefore, you will sit quietly and allow your betters to receive the education they are entitled to. Unlike you, they are destined for great things."

I'm on my feet before I know it, peering down at the runt with every ounce of courage and imperiousness I can muster. My bones ache as I push the bunny back, only allowing the indignation of a wealthy Council heir to fuel my response. "I don't care what gossip you've heard. Lucille would not appreciate knowing that I allowed you to speak to a member of her family this way, regardless of my current position. Try me again, Professor, and I'll make certain she knows what an insolent toad you are."

Professor Abel gives me a look that screams murder, but I know he can't be sure if I'm bluffing or not. Stepping away from me, he huffs again and turns to trundle up to the front of the classroom. "All of you, be seated! We've had enough dramatics—this isn't a joke of a class in the Shird."

My lips curve in distaste as I sit at my desk again, leaning back as the twat starts up the smart board. I definitely put him in his place, but it doesn't feel good to behave in such an entitled way. I'm not like my parents and I won't allow myself to become them deep down, but surviving Apex means I'll have to use more of their lessons than I thought.

A spitball hits my face, and I turn in the direction it came from to find Todd's idiot friends guffawing like the hyenas they are. I've seen little of my ex since I arrived, and I'm perfectly fine with it. But his lackeys trail behind the Heathers like their pussies are made of solid gold, and I have to endure two classes of their bull-shit. Professor Abel grins as he watches me pull the loogie soaked paper off my face and I groan inwardly.

The likelihood of him interfering with their grade school tactics is nil. Putting him in his place only goes so far if he can use these petty assholes to do his dirty work for him. I'm not sure what I'll do if it escalates further than this kind of crap, but I know one thing for sure: I don't have a single ally in this class, so I'm going to have to make sure I hightail it out of here the second the bell rings.

Ignoring their laughter, I try to focus on the lecture. It's about the formation of the pred government a hundred years ago, but my textbook starts earlier than this, and I read ahead. Professor Abel's not bothering to discuss the differences between various shifter clans, or how shifters interacted before the Council was formed. That's very telling about who's writing the curriculum, if you ask me, but I'm in no position to question it. I don't plan to go into politics—Lucille's made it clear she no longer sees me as her Council heir since my emergence, even if only in private.

The next object to strike me is a crudely folded note, and I sigh as I unfold it, scanning the immature handwriting on the paper in annoyance. The loopy scrawl dotted with skulls and crossbones tells me Purple wrote it, but I don't need to look to imagine the expression on her pinched face.

I wonder if the piss smell in your room makes it hard to sleep at night. I can smell it on you from here, so you must not have figured out how to get your laundry done, loser.

How original.

Now they've confirmed they wrecked my room, and I don't think they get how dangerous that is. If I let Fitz see this, I'm fairly certain her fake nails will only be the first thing to go when he gets a hold of her. Crumpling the note, I shove it in my bag for later, deciding that I'm not sure if I want to start a war that involves the Khan ambush.

Fitz makes me smile, and I enjoy having him on my side, but I still feel like I want to deal with these petty assholes on my own—at least until I feel more secure about my place at Apex. Channeling my mother may be the only way I survive for the next couple of weeks, even though it makes me feel all kinds of gross.

Now I smell a stench, and it's coming from my soul.

Revenge

Delores

This week has been fucking exhausting. I knew coming to Apex would be awful, but I didn't expect the onslaught of bullshit I'm dealing with. The only reason I'm sleeping soundly is that I'm ensconced in the Tower, where I know the assholes hunting me aren't able to get to me. Everything else is a damn toss-up, depending on who's around to walk with me or if I can find the right tunnels.

Arriving at Shifter Basics before the door shuts is a minor miracle given the route I chose, but I'll take it. I can't deal with another verbal smack down if I cause problems here again.

Looking around, I see other preds, but no canines, so I try to relax a little. Maybe this period won't be so b—

"Miss Drew, you'll be assisting me today." The tiger smirks at me in a challenge, then adds, "Unless you aren't up for it?"

There's no way I can say 'no' without letting him win, so I sigh and roll my gaze up to the ceiling in supplication. Once I've calmed my nerves, I look Fitz's brother square in the eye. "I'm game if you are, Professor."

Take that, you domineering shithead. I won't let you make me cower.

His lips quirk up and he rises from his chair, stalking over to stand close enough to make me look up at him. "I'd advise thinking about it long and hard before you accept a challenge from a Khan. You might not like the result."

I snort, shaking my head as I push my desk back a little to give myself space. "I'm pretty sure saying 'no' isn't an option here, Sir."

My retort makes him frown, and he says softly, "Withdrawal of consent is always an option, Delores. I may be a Khan, but I'm not a scumbag."

It feels like we're talking about something else entirely right now, and I'm not sure if Fitz filled him in on my shitty prom night or not. Regardless, I nod, studying his conflicted features as I consider what I'm going to say. "Then I accept your challenge, Professor. Give it to me good."

His eyes widen, and I know I got to him when he turns on his heel to stalk to his desk. Big, bad Felix Khan is speechless, and I caused it. I lean back in my chair and stack my hands behind my head, feeling satisfied. That is until he comes thundering back over and yanks me out of the chair with a dark grin.

"Hell yes! Professor Khan is teaching DD a lesson," Gold crows as she walks in at the exact moment he tugs me away from the safety of my seat. Her acolytes titter as they follow her to their places, and I roll my eyes.

My pulse is pounding from surprise, but I don't believe Fitz's twin will hurt me. He seems demanding and arrogant, but not cruel. He probably wants to make me an example because I snarked back at him previously. If so, I'll have to take my medicine like anyone else. After all, I earned it despite what I told him in front of everyone.

Relax, Dolly. You can handle this; it's not Lucille.

"Sit down and shut up, plebs!" Felix looks at the students straggling in as he plants me in front of the whiteboard with a dark glare. "Miss Drew is going to take notes while we discuss why predators dominate prey."

Arching a brow at him, I turn to the board and pick up a marker, gripping in my hand. "You mean besides being petty tyrants?"

He barks a laugh, looking out at the other students. "None of you, including Miss Drew, have seen petty yet. I suggest you never find out. Now one of you dipshits tell me why we're dominant and the prey animals aren't."

"Wealth and fame," Purple says with a big, shit-eating grin. "We have it; they don't."

Professor Khan makes a sound like a buzzer and shakes his head. "Wrong, mutt. Plenty of prey families make good money servicing prey specific needs, and some of them are skilled enough to work for preds in highly skilled areas. You'd be surprised how many extremely rich and sought after prey species there are. Try again."

I shrug and write 'Try again' on the board dutifully. It's no surprise that my ex friends have zero clue about how the world works outside of their cushy bubbles. Working for Luc opened up a whole new world for me, even if the prey species didn't all accept me. For instance, most preds can't do the fine detail work the pangolins do for him or construct the miniature computer chips the Ericksons put in all their devices. That's all done by different prey species—their economy is vastly ignored, but super important.

Not that I'm telling Purple that.

Felix hides a smile as he nods at me, then looks expectantly at the class again. "Next?"

"We're bigger and stronger," a random kid in the third row ventures.

The tiger buzzes again, shaking his head. "Wrong again. Elephants are bigger than many apex predators, and so are hippos. If you'd ever seen a hippopotamus fighting a crocodile, you'd question that little theory. Prey species have the same instinct to survive as we do, except they have to use it to save their necks far more often than us."

I write 'pampered and complacent' on the board, which makes a couple of the dipshits gasp, but Felix smiles.

"She's right. By sheer numbers alone, if the prey animals concocted a revolution and spent a considerable amount of time planning, they could overtake preds. We win in toe-to-toe battles, but many of us are no longer in fighting trim or even very smart. In comparison, the prey species have had to use their brains constantly to avoid being killed." The professor tilts his head, looking at me again. "Why do you think we're still dominant?"

The Heathers look at me with disdain and Todd's crew snickers behind their hands as I think about it for a moment. The disgust on my ex's face makes my gut clench and I curse internally, unable to forgive myself for missing what an absolute twit he is. Giving that weak little shit my virginity was a stupid move and I'll never forgive him for the shit he pulled afterward.

My bunny pushes against my skin, outraged at how we were treated. I blink in surprise because bunnies aren't known for being angry or aggressive. However, mine is ready to tear the eyes out of my ex-boyfriend for daring to look at us.

Fucking weird, man.

"Barbie, answer my question." Felix's voice brings me out of my trance and I shake my head to clear it.

He seems to know something's up with me because he's pushing that stupid alpha thing at me. It makes my skin itch and I wrinkle my nose in irritation. If he's so big on consent, he needs to back the fuck off with that shit. "The only reason preds still dominate is because they are allowed to. With enough support, it could change at any moment."

That makes the room explode in indignant shouts, people waving fists and baring fangs as they yell. I catch his satisfied expression for a second before the tiger turns to the class and lets out a bone rattling roar. It stops the riotous noise completely and some students even freeze in place. When he sees they're done, he points at the board. "Add that. It's technically correct, though I'd challenge your premise unless you provide proof."

I scribble my words, and when I'm done, I look at him smugly. "Power is about perception, Professor. If you allow disrespect or lose face, you can't control the masses. All it takes is one voice of dissension to start a coup."

The look on his face is resigned as he replies, "Quite so, Miss Drew. Controlling the narrative often leads to controlling the people."

It's the only reason anyone pays attention to Pink—that's for sure.

After that, he lets the rest of the students offer reasons, knocking down the stupid ones about jobs or titles that can disappear at a moment's notice. I write whatever he tells me, putting my spin on the idiotic shit they throw out. It's fairly obvious his point about intelligence is well met, because I can't understand how any of these people would have gotten into such an elite university if they weren't loaded.

By the end of class, even my brain hurts from listening to it.

Felix dismisses the class at the bell, tilting his head as he watches me. "Don't bother with erasing it. I'd like it to marinate in this bullshit before I get any of them in a ring."

I shrug, heading over to the spot I left my stuff to gather it. Once I'm ready, I pause. "Is that everything you need today, Sir?"

Okay, I'm not above torturing the asshole professor a little. Sue me.

He stalks closer as I descend the steps. "You seemed to have a control issue earlier, Barbie."

"It won't happen again. I promise, Sir," I reply automatically.

The tiger frowns and shakes his head. "Something tells me that isn't true and perhaps isn't the right answer, anyway. You will need to let your animal out and learn to control it in this class, but it shouldn't be because those idiots who hate you got under your skin. Never let shitheads like that win; if you do, you'll never be rid of them."

I watch him as he stands in front of me, looking up because I'm poised two steps above the ground. It's probably the only way I'd be taller because while Fitz is buff and bulky, Felix is tall, lean and muscled in a way that isn't as obvious. His tiger is probably faster and more vicious because he seems to have brains. I lick my lips as I consider that, remembering how sexy Fitz was in tiger form.

Suddenly, Felix's eyes flash with his animal and I feel the primal ripple over him. "Hit the bunny trail, Miss Drew. I won't be giving you a note to excuse tardiness for your other professors—no matter what the reason is."

"Understood, Captain Asshat," I grumble under my breath as I push past him, hoping the slickness coating my thighs isn't as noticeable to him as it is for me. I hear his deep chuckle echoing behind me as I haul ass out of the gym to get to Gothic Lit on time.

* * *

"… so you'll need to visit the library before you head home tonight, unless you're using an app to read along." The gargoyle pauses by my desk, his brows drawing together as he looks at me. He seems to be unsure what to say next and I duck my head, not wanting to draw attention to his staring.

"Professor Renard? The librarian won't let us in without appointments. What are we supposed to do?"

I cover my mouth, hiding a snort at the whiny voice of the small shifter from my Shifter History class. He transferred in after the first week, and I don't have a clue why. It's obvious he doesn't give a shit about literature and is woefully unprepared for the curriculum.

Though, he's not wrong about Professor Draconis…

"Get on the Apex application and set up an appointment, Craig. It's easy and though Professor Draconis will probably lose his mind at the amount of last-minute requests, I'm sure he has assistants who will be happy to help him."

Lifting my head, I turn it slowly to look at the now smirking gargoyle in horror. I don't have to work there tonight, but after a very frustrating day, I was planning to go home and have a little 'me time'. He's just guaranteed I'll be summoned to the library instead, because Betsy doesn't work after dark.

That son of a warthog!

"Payback's a bitch when people know where you live," I mutter just loud enough for him to hear.

Coughing, he leans down and whispers, "Sure would suck to be hunted and homeless."

I laugh softly, giving him a sweet smile. "Felix will love dealing with you when Fitz moves me into their townhouse without asking."

He groans and looks around before admitting, "You win this one, *petite.*"

Fuck, the French gets me every time. This guy is determined to torture me.

Now I'm Following You

Fitz

Fitz

No one would believe I've had my girl on campus over a week without making a move. But those fuckers wouldn't realize that she's been through a lot and even though I'm banging the shit out of Chess, I'm dealing with my blue balls.

Why?

I'm not a fucking animal—at least, not entirely. The night we met, she was brokenhearted and destroyed. When I finally revealed myself this summer, she was healing, and that fuckwit re-traumatized her. Now she's trying to adjust to a world that wants to kill her for funsies. My baby girl isn't quite ready to dive into the deep end of the relationship pool yet.

And taking Chess and I on definitely means something, so I don't want to push her before she's capable of handling us.

She doesn't seem to mind me meandering down to her little enclave in the Tower at night or even showing up in the morning. No, the lovely Dolly laughs and continues getting ready while I putz about her room and jabber. It's kind of comfortable and besides Chess, I don't think I've been that close to anyone that's not my twin before. I like it, though I'd like it a hell of a lot more if it followed sexy morning time.

Being a good guy is a pain in my tight ass.

That's why I'm not worried about dropping by her room without texting. She knows I'm keyed to her floor and hasn't once complained that I come and go as I please. Occasionally I catch her in a delicious state of undress—which I'm hoping to now—and she turns a shade of pink I'm sure matches her nipples.

Dear Bast, please let her nipples be that rosy shade and I'll try not to scare the sheep for at least a week.

Seems like a good deal, right?

Smirking to myself, I whistle as I enter the Tower from the front, following the path the two ancients prescribed for my girl to her floor. It's likely the rest of my friends are upstairs grouching about the day, but I'm eager to see my girl. I'll pop upstairs to check in after I've taken a dive in her sweet scent for a bit. They won't miss me, anyway. Chess can hold down the fort.

The room is dark when I fling open the door, and I frown. It's dinnertime; where the hell is she? Pulling out my phone, I prepare to fire off a concerned text whether or not I'm over my daily limit. It's not overbearing when it's out of concern, right?

Fuck it, I don't care. I'm doing it.

That's when I hear laughter. Not in her room, but filtering through the drafty old structure's vents. I move down the hall to the staircase, knowing the acoustics are better in the long, empty stone paths.

"… so I told them all to go to the library to get the books they'd need for the reading. He's going to explode!"

My lips curve when I realize it's Renard. Since the target of his joke has to be the spicy lizard, my brother and Chess must be upstairs. I grin a little because I enjoy poking at the dragon, but his OG BFF Renard is the tits at it. He knows how to get that scaly asshole going like no one I know, and he doesn't even get his tail fried off for it. Normally, I'd head up to join their tête-à-tête, but I really wanted to see my baby girl first.

Wait a tick.

If the winged wonder set Aubrey up to have a library filled with students after classes, he'd need help. He's not good with crowds anyway and that skinny chicken who works for him doesn't stay after dark. Now I know why my girl's not here—fucking Aubrey has her running her tail off because of Renard.

My eyes narrow and I ponder stomping upstairs to kick the gargoyle's ass. That won't work because he's goddamn enormous if he shifts. I could go beat the dragon's ass, but he'd roast me like a pig on a spit. Not that I'd ever in a million years admit that either of those senior shifters could best the entire staff at Apex without breaking a sweat on their stupid wings.

Being able to fly and having other badass abilities is cheating.

Growling under my breath, I stalk back to my girl's room and yank open the door. If I can't get satisfaction through violence, I'll have to satisfy my needs in other ways.

I bet if I hunt long enough, I'll find her diary.

That would definitely tell me where she is on the ready to get freaky scale. Chicks always confide in their journals and shit, right? That's how I'll know if I can make my move.

Fitz Khan is on the hunt.

HAVING FELINE NIGHT VISION IS RAD. I LEAVE THE LIGHTS OFF AS I let my tiger guide me by scent, rifling through my woman's drawers and smirking at some of the decidedly not innocent garments in them. She may not be ready for everything we can offer—yet—but she's thinking about it. Otherwise, she wouldn't have scraps of lace and strappy shit that makes my cock throb.

Once I finish examining her clothes, I move to the bathroom. She has the usual assortment of chick shit, including a massive amount of beauty products that I'm not sure she uses. Dolly does dramatic eye makeup, but she doesn't cake it on, so some of these look superfluous? Hell if I know. I doubt anything would make her look less pretty, and if she used all of it, who am I to judge?

I prefer women who make their own decisions, not ones who want to please assholes like me.

The selection of shampoos and body washes smell heavenly, but none of them carries the honeysuckle that emanates from her like it's calling to me. That must be all her, and when I noticed the toy stuck to the back wall of the shower, I almost lose it. It's not small, though if I had to guess, it's about Chess sized. He's average but nice and thick, but she's going to have to get used to me and Felix being bigger.

I shudder to think what those winged fuckers are packing. They don't shift in front of us because of their weird secretive shit.

Grinning to myself, I leave the bathroom with a raging hard-on and a bounce in my step. That discovery makes me want to do a little more 'research' as I look for an old-fashioned diary in her shit. My eyes scan the room and I saunter past her desk and book-shelves—too obvious for secrets or dirty stuff. Moving to the closet, I open the door, poking through sexy clothes, the new fitted uniforms I had delivered, and various shoes.

No hidden compartments or stowed boxes with delightful contents in here.

I glare in frustration. There's no way I'm wrong about this— according to Felix, her ex-friends are super bitches and everyone knows what tools her parents are. I highly doubt a girl as smart as ours would store her thoughts in a hackable digital format. No, she definitely poured her soul out on paper and she's skillfully hidden it because she's always had to. The keyboard catches my gaze and a lightbulb goes off.

Chess said she's definitely been a singer for a long time, though no one nurtured it. Maybe she keeps her heart in lyric books? Her parents would never look at that, nor would nosy little shits pretending to be her friend. I stalk to the bench in front of the instrument, lifting the lid to see a plethora of sheet music with scribbled melodies and lyrics. It only takes a glance to confirm these are full of her feelings about shit, so I snap pictures for later before I close it.

My baby girl can't fault me for wanting to get to know her, right?

I mean, obviously I'm right. I'm Fitzgerald Khan, enforcer of the Khan ambush. No one would dare to correct me or I'll—I pause for a minute when a noise in the Tower catches my sensitive ears. Probably just the guys arriving upstairs from wherever those two asswads have been hiding.

The lid closes with a snap, and I prowl over to the bed. I left it for last because it's the most likely place she's hiding the sin bin. Who wouldn't want their box of orgasm assistance close enough to grab without leaving the comfort of your pillows? Bending down, I look under the tall bed frame, frowning when I only see slippers. I squint, pulling open the bottom drawer of the nightstand and growl when I see nothing.

It has to be here.

Before I can explore more, the sound of stomping boots and cursing echoes in the hallway. That's her coming home, and she sounds all lathered up. I don't know if that benefits me or not, but perhaps surprising her will make her giggle. She teases me about my stalking anyway and it sounds like she could use a laugh.

To the closet, I go…

Settling into the tight squeeze of her clothes and shit, I wait with a smirk. I'm going to pop out after she has her little tantrum, and she'll immediately be happy again. After all, who wouldn't love finding me in their room? I know preds who would sell their souls to find me creeping around their private chambers, and I never gave a fuck enough to do it to them.

I watch through the slats as she stomps in, turns on the low light lamps instead of the overhead ones, and kicks off her boots. Her tiny skirt bounces against her upper thighs as she walks to the bathroom, humming something under her breath and shaking her booty a bit. It occurs to me I should have been doing this before I curse myself for missing shows the previous week. The sound of water tells me she's washing up and I stroke my pulsing cock lightly, hoping it will calm down a bit.

Seems to be a lost cause since I met this girl, but a guy can try, right?

"Giant fucking bat asshole using us to torture the other big dick-whistle like we're his personal serfs. I mean, honestly… grown fucking men… ancient ones… and I get called in on a day I don't work to help morons find poems. I should invade their stupid off-limits Tower spaces and move everything around to teach them a fucking lesson…"

Oh, I like vengeful on my girl; it's sexy as fuck.

"… not going to add them to the list, though. That's for evil fuckers and this is just jerky shit. But I'm definitely getting them back," Dolly mutters and then I see her plop on the bed.

She peels the blouse off, tossing it towards a hamper with a perfect arc that lands it in the opening. I'd be impressed, but I can't take my eyes off the white lace contraption she's wearing now. It's got lace and straps and some sort of rings… hell, if I know what it's called, but I want to remove it with my teeth—slowly.

I'm about to give myself up so I can see it better when she flops back on the bed, wiggling until her whole body is horizontal on the giant mattress. It gives me a perfect view of her boobs and I squeeze my dick as they rise and fall with her breaths.

"Stupid hot know-it-all dragon," she mutters as she stretches deliciously. "And after that freaking torture whispered in Lit..." Her hands drift down her body to her abs and my eyes widen.

If I was a cartoon character, my tongue would loll out and roll over the floor. I think she's going to...

Those perfect pink fingernails slide down to toy with her belly ring for a minute and I have to bite back a groan. "How the hell am I supposed to focus on anything when that asshole tiger keeps throwing out sexy innuendo during class? Calling him 'Sir' is hard enough because it reminds me of all those crusty old farts that are friends with my parents. But maybe if he changed it to..."

Changed it to what?!! Felix is going to die when I tell him about this.

I should be jealous because her hand is sliding lower into the strappy white matching panties while thinking of my brother. But who the fuck cares? My plan has always been to share her with my ambush and hearing she's distracted by the others is utter perfection.

All I need now is for her to say the magic words...

I Want You To Want Me

Delores

Delores

I didn't plan this when I got home tonight, but fuck if it doesn't feel good.

All day smoke show men have surrounded me, giving me smoldering looks and rough, raspy orders. I'm not experienced enough to know if my bunny or I have kinks, but I don't have to think twice about enjoying their praise. Given the grumpy librarian and shy cheetah also float my boat, so maybe I'm somewhere in the middle? Times like this are when I wish I'd paid more attention to all the shit my ex-friends were looking up on their unfettered internet searches. I'm not sure I know all the terminology, much less what the rules are.

Letting out a groan of relief as I flick my clit, I imagine the last two participants in my mental orgy. Chess is worshiping Fitz, both of them watching as my sexy French growling gargoyle licks me and the enormous dragon holds me in place. Felix is directing the show with his arms crossed over his chest and a hungry grin on his face as he strokes himself. The scene is way beyond my skill level, but it's making my pussy throb with need.

Good thing I believe Hera helps those who help themselves.

I withdraw my hand from my thong, pushing it down so I can use my feet to kick it away. Next, I wiggle out of the bra, tossing it as well, and then I crawl over to the edge of the bed. I look around as if someone's going to see me, and dangle my head and arms over the side of the bed to pop the latch. This hidden under bed compartment is probably a remnant of history like everything else in this dusty palace, but if you don't know it's here, it's perfect for shit you don't want found. Pondering for a moment as I wiggle my hips, I finally select the dual vibe with the sucking motion.

It matches my fantasy, after all.

I consider the lube, but honestly, I don't need it at this point. My underwear has been a lost cause most of the evening because Mr. Scalypants kept peering over my shoulder while I worked. His hot breath and intensity being that close made my nipples hard enough to cut glass. I could barely conceal it when I left, though I feel like he knew. Otherwise, why the hell was he hovering so fucking close?

Pressing the button to start it, I feel my core clench in anticipation and I sigh the names of the last two professors haunting my dreams when I slide it inside of me.

"Oh, hell no!"

My eyes pop open and I drop the toy, leaving it hanging half out of me as I roll to see who in Hecate's name caught me masturbating. I'm not ashamed; it's totally natural and I'm a teenager, but it's not normal to fucking spy on someone while they take care of their needs. In fact, yelling at me makes the violation worse.

I open my mouth to scream for help when Fitz comes into view, looking very much like that proverbial cat. He seems to think I'm his canary because I swear to Freya, he's licking his goddamned chops like he's about to devour something.

Or someone. If I'm lucky.

"Fitz, this is unacceptable!" I shout as I grab a pillow. I forget about the semi-lodged vibrator, and it hits a sensitive spot, making me clench my teeth so I don't moan. "You can't hide in my closet while I… relieve my tension."

His grin only widens, and he shrugs as if this is the most normal thing on earth. "Baby Girl, I was going to pop out and scare you, but when you moaned people's names… How's a man supposed to make smart choices then?"

Scowling at him, I cross my arms over my chest and he pouts when it hides my breasts. "You should have come out when I first came in the room, you creeper. Boundaries are important."

Gold flashes in his eyes, and I see the tiger beneath his skin prowling. Fitz places his hands on either side of my legs, using powerful forearms to hold himself up as he crawls onto the bed to hover over me. "They are, baby girl, but I don't want boundaries with you. For the first time since finding Chessie, I want to storm your gates and kidnap you so only we can have you."

I frown, tilting my head at him. That's very serious and I'm not sure I know exactly what I want yet. He can't just lay claim to me like some feudal lord. "Fitz, I don't know if I'm ready to settle down yet. I just got away from a long-term thing that wasn't good and even if you mean you and Chess…"

That makes him laugh, and he dips his head to lick my nose. "Don't be silly. They'd all be furious if Chess and I hogged you to ourselves. You, baby girl, are going to be the center of our… Well, I don't know what those other assholes call it, but for tigers, it's an ambush. Just wait and see."

My mouth opens to argue, and he places a finger against my lips. Shaking his head, Fitz reaches down and tugs the buzzing vibrator out, making me gasp. The low hum touching me while we talked made everything tingle and my clit throbs at the loss. He winks, slipping a hand between us until he gets to my belly button.

"Now, baby girl, I'm going to give you a little preview since I took away your release. But then you're going to curl up with me like a good girl and let me stay until I know you're fast asleep. Understand?"

Clearly, I don't have a choice in the matter and that makes it easy to nod.

Looking satisfied, Fitz moves down my body, spreading my thighs and burying his face in my pussy before I can blink. A ragged gasp escapes my lips and my hips buck as he suckles my aching clit, then slips two fingers inside of me. I clutch the linens under me as his fingers slide in and out and he flicks the tip of his rough tongue over the sensitive nerves.

He's not playing around.

His other fingers slip through the moisture between my legs and when his pinky presses at the other entrance, I tense up. I haven't done that, though I have toys made to try it. I figured it would give Todd another new experience and now I'm mad at myself. Fitz looks up at me with a wicked grin as he presses the wet tip of his fingers against the hole.

"Relax, baby. It's only one little finger. Just wait till I put my cock here. Unclench for me and let me teach you."

Ooooh, that did it for me. Fuuuuuck.

I spread my legs more, and he goes back to alternating between slow licks and drawing designs around my tight bud with his agile tongue. Within a moment, he's got his pinky worked inside of me, and I moan at the sensation. Rocking into his face and hand, I pant as his speed increases and the pinnacle I've never reached with a real person comes rushing at me.

When my orgasm crests, I squeeze him with everything, my body holding on as shudders ripple through me in the best possible way. It takes a moment for me to come back to reality and I squeak when I realize I have his head crushed between my thighs.

"Oh, Fitz! I'm sorry!" This time I blush, feeling like a complete idiot who almost smothered her new lover.

He lifts his head and winks. "Baby Girl, you squeeze as hard as you want. If I die, I die, baby."

Picking up a pillow with a limp hand, I smack him with it. "Don't be a cheesy asshole."

"Sorry. Just how I'm built." He rolls to his feet and my eyes widen as I watch the evidence of his arousal bob in his sweats as he heads to the bathroom. When he comes back with a towel, he cleans me up and moves the discarded vibe to the nightstand. "Now, I believe you owe me cuddles."

"What about…"

"Not tonight, baby girl. This one was for you. We'll get to me next time."

I'm a little stunned as I do what he says, slipping under my covers and waiting until he joins me.

Fitz just made himself the little spoon and I think I'm in serious trouble.

I wake up a couple of hours later, and he's gone. There's a warm spot where he was when I fell asleep, but I guess I can't expect him to leave Chess alone. He said he wanted to stay until I was sleeping and I can't fault him for being honest.

What I can fault him on is hiding in my damn closet and scaring the piss out of me, but right now, I can't bring myself to object more than I did earlier. My body is humming with satisfaction and I feel amazing.

Anyone who tells you there's not a difference between a boy and a man is a filthy liar.

My basis for comparison is not extensive, but Todd couldn't even find my goddamn clit and Fitz went for it like it had a neon sign flashing at him. Everything he did was geared to making me feel good, even though I'm woefully inexperienced compared to the other women he's been with.

Rolling over, I wrap myself around the pillow his head rested on and inhale. I know it's not illegal to be involved with professors at Apex, and shifters don't have the same weird hang-ups about age gaps that humans do. I'm not underage and I definitely can make my own decisions, so I'm not about to worry what a bunch of bitches who already called me a whore all summer think.

Making an irritated face, I consider what will happen if Fitz is right and the others actually want more than just flirting with the pretty co-ed. That will paint an even bigger target on my back because that's… a lot of guys and they're all hot enough to burn down a freezer factory.

I might even have staff members after me.

Merciful Frigg, I might have Khans after me!

That thought has me burying my face in my pillow and letting out a frustrated growl into the stuffing.

Good going, Dolly. Take the hardest route possible every time.

I clutch the pillow and chew my lip before I mutter, "It's not like you know for sure yet. Maybe they have no interest in you at all and this is all… sound and fury."

The quote makes me think of Renard and I thump my head against the pillows again, cursing my brain as it races through all the possibilities. I can't seem to stop thinking about this now that Fitz made it crystal clear what he wants to happen. It was surprising, but the tiger has taken care of me from the second he met me. I bet he was the same way when he found Chess and, if so, he looks at his family group the same way.

Odd that he's younger than Felix; with that behavior, you'd think he was a Raj, not an enforcer.

Shaking my head, I blow out a breath. I'm going to need to walk off all these thoughts or I'm never getting back to sleep. I have dance in the morning and I can't fall over, so I'm going to take a stroll around the second floor until I get sleepy.

That should help me get some fucking rest.

Detective

Delores

Delores

This place is drafty as hell. I'm glad I pulled my giant bunny snuggie thing on before I explored in the middle of the night. There wasn't much in the rooms at the other end of the hall near the back stairs—boxes, dusty furniture, paintings, and a bunch of stuff that looks like it's being used as storage space.

So much for finding something to occupy my brain until I get tired again.

I turn around, marching down my hallway to the stone steps they have given me permission to use. Technically, I'm only supposed to go down, but I'm not leaving the safety of this place at three a.m. It'd be risking my life and I'm sure as hell not that bored.

Tapping my fingers against my lips, I look around for a second before I take one tentative step up toward the third floor. No alarms go off as far as I can tell, so I grin to myself and start the hike up the spiral staircase excitedly. I wondered what the hell else was in this place from the minute Fitz moved me in and the whole 'don't go anywhere outside of your room' shit was way too Beauty & the Beast for me.

Telling me where I can't go is like begging me to go there, for fuck's sake!

When I reach the landing, I tiptoe up to the entry arch to the floor, scoping it out before I walk in. Nothing pops out at me or starts blaring a loud noise, so I pad into the hallway of the floor above mine. The layout is similar, though it appears to have fewer doors. I wonder if they have knocked walls out to make bigger areas for something… like a library.

Oh, quit thinking about Beauty & the Beast, Dolly! There's an amazing library next door; it'd be silly.

But why would each side of the hall only have one door? There's only one way to find out, and my curiosity will not get sated until I do. So I quietly slip down the cold stone floors on silent bare feet, only stopping when I'm in front of two opposing doors. I wrinkle my nose—if either has security, I'll only get to see one before I'm caught. It's a literal Catch-22 and I don't have the patience to weigh this out.

So I do what every mature adult in the universe does to decide between two options: eenie-meenie-miney-mo.

'Mo' turns out to be the door on my right, so I open it carefully, listening for movement. It's still quiet, so I squeeze into the room and shut the door slowly. When I turn around, I cover my mouth with my hand. I'm standing in a huge formal dining room with a table for ten, cabinets full of fancy dinnerware, and a set of double doors at the back that I'd bet leads to a kitchen.

And I've been ordering out and microwaving noodles in my room because I can't go to the dining room!

Sneering at the bullshit involved in not letting me come up here and use the executive chef level shit to nourish myself, I poke around the room looking for clues. I doubt the two loners have ever used this place, so I can't figure out why it would have even gotten built.

Did they build this tower before the oldest pred still on campus arrived? If so, what was this Tower used for before? Is that what the prey tunnels were originally for? They do all connect under this building and spiral out, so it's possible.

The nerd in me is having a field day, as I imagine preds in here over a millennium ago, using this building before it was even a damn school. Maybe it was an old church or part of one… how cool would that be?

A glint catches my eye and I walk over to the corner where I saw it, admiring the filigree on the mirror that takes up most of this wall. My reflection is messy as hell in it despite the layer of dirt and dust. It's a gorgeous piece, and it feels weird that it's in a dining room, not one of the bedrooms that I assume are plentiful in this mini-stronghold.

Though truthfully, men live here and they have very little use for shit like this, I guess.

I'm definitely cleaning this place up when I have some time. It's wasteful to let it sit and not use all the beautiful stuff in here, especially that kitchen. And I'm fucking tired of ramen, so there's that, too. Even if I set the place on fire, I'm going to teach myself to cook shit so I don't have to depend on anyone else to take care of me.

Faces flash through my brain, and I growl under my breath. "Stop it, brain. I don't need them to take care of me just…"

I don't know how to finish that sentence and I throw my hands up in frustration at my own treacherous mind.

"Time to explore across the hall," I mutter under my breath. "Otherwise, I'll stand here and talk to myself all night."

IT DIDN'T LOOK LIKE THEY HAD USED THE ROOM FOR LONG enough to make me sneeze for three minutes straight. After I poked around, looking at the weird symbols and paintings on the walls, I left fairly quickly. Unfortunately, I'm still keyed up, so I made my way back to the front staircase. Exploring further into the Tower is the only thing I can do if I don't want to head back to my room, so I climb to the fourth floor on quiet feet.

When I enter the archway to this floor, a myriad of scents hit my nose and I grin. Finally, I've found signs of life and my curiosity ramps up as I look at the two doors on either side. I started with right last time and this time, I'll go with door number two first. Tiptoeing to the door, I note the smell of incense—heavy, fragrant scents I can't put my finger on, but they definitely seem familiar. I put my ear to the large metal door, listening with the added skill of my bunny to ensure it's empty.

Score—silent as a tomb.

There's one glitch, though. This damn door has no knob—only large ornate knockers and a gentle push verifies that it isn't unlocked. Puzzles are my jam, though, and I assume this either has a hidden latch somewhere or a particular order of operation to open the locks. I drop to the ground, feeling around the frame and lines of rivets, hoping to find buttons or spring catches I can use to get in. The stone below my knees is warm but not comfortable, so I fiddle a bit more, then rise to my feet again to look at the knockers.

What the hell—I doubt this will work, but it's worth a try.

Taking a deep breath, I lift one knocker and tap out the most basic rhythm I can think of:—'shave and a haircut'—and echo the second line with the other one. To my complete astonishment, the damn doors swing open to reveal an enormous room packed to the gills with books, cute stuffed animals, hundreds of squishies, and a giant bed covered in pillows. There's a huge armchair in one corner with a lamp and piles of books around it and a door that I assume leads to an ensuite like mine.

I inhale again as I step inside, and my lips curve up in victory. This place is one I've been looking for and now that I'm here, nothing about it surprises me in the least. The furnishings are sturdy and look expensive, including various non-adorable arti-facts and paintings that confirm my suspicions. Everything in this room screams who its owner is and I'm going to milk this for all its worth.

I, Delores Drew, have located the true horde of Apex's one and only dragon.

And he's a total simp for shit so pastel and cute that it looks like a Hello Kitty cafe in Japan.

Frowning, I walk around inspecting the fancier pieces, noting jeweled eggs and statues that must remind him of home. I never considered how much the exiled professors here could be missing their families or even their kind, but being in Aubrey's space high-lights how devastating it must be to be disconnected from those you care about. He's obviously attached to them and he had no choice to come here; it must hurt his heart more than he let on.

However, the big question about this place, other than why he hides so much of himself from the others, is: where the hell is he if he doesn't sleep here or in the cave under the library?

I walk over to the bed, noting it's definitely custom made and would fit a small army of people. I'm sure he's huge as a fully shifted dragon, but it's not big enough for that. From what I gath-ered from my new friends, the grumpy book lover isn't known for having any dalliances, either. Why is this so big? Maybe he's just one of those bed hogs and splays himself out like a beached whale.

The picture in my head makes me giggle softly and I lean in to look at the small pile of stuffies in the middle of the bed. Based on my own proclivities, I'd guess these are favorites and my eyes pop open when I see a snow white bunny sitting at the top of the heap like royalty.

Oh. Oh...

Putting my hand to my mouth, I feel my cheeks get hot and back away, suddenly feeling like I'm being an absolute bitch for invading his space like this. I shouldn't be here and even though they've been assholes about allowing me to roam this place, I'm violating that trust.

I back out of the room quickly, chewing on my nail as the doors shut on the lair of the serpent. My brain and my heart are warring about what I saw, but deep in my gut, another voice is screaming at me to climb the stairs and explore one more level before I give up for the night.

Is that intuition, or am I being horridly invasive?

The questions ping around in my mind as I walk back to the front stairs, and by the time I get to them, my bunny answers.

I need to find out what's on the fifth floor.

A feeling of unease crawls through me as I climb the steps, and I don't know why. Whether it's because I'm snooping and I shouldn't or something bad is hiding here, I don't know. I haven't learned to read the whims of my animal yet, despite the efforts of my prey friends this summer. Prey instincts differ greatly from the ones they taught me to expect as a pred, and I just don't know how to read them yet.

Everything comes across as danger, and that's not accurate.

Looking at the doorway to the new hallway, I square my shoulders and take a deep breath.

Whatever my rabbit thinks I need to find up here is important, and if I have to put myself in danger to find it, I'll do it.

Lucille Drew didn't raise a coward.

Of course, she didn't really raise me at all. It was more Mattie, but…

Stop it, Dolly. Get your shit together and walk down the corridor until you sense what room you have to enter. You can do this.

My eyes burn as I feel a slight shift from my bunny and the top of my head aches briefly. Blinking, I notice my night vision has worsened, but my hearing is amplified so much that I feel like I can hear dust settling.

Perfect timing, rabbit. Confuse the fuck out of me while I'm worried about running into something scary.

When I reach the middle of the hall, I look at both doors, squinting until the gentle noises of breath call to me on the right side.

This is where I need to go.

I put my hand on the wood, hesitating before I finally give it a soft push and it opens.

The sight that greets me shocks me once more, and I have to cover my mouth.

I'll be a monkey's uncle. I've hit the mother lode.

Secret

Renard

RENARD

BEING A NOCTURNAL CREATURE, IT'S DIFFICULT TO ALTER MY sleeping schedule to accommodate the diurnal nature of a mixed shifter population academy. When I first arrived, I spent months finding the delicate balance between my nature and the require- ments of my position. My concern didn't lie with being able to socialize or finding compatriots as much as giving the students my best, so I slowly shifted from a completely night time waking period to a swing shift.

It took a long time to rewire my circadian rhythms, but once I did, it became second nature.

Lucking into another shifter with similar inclinations and back- ground as myself was a surprise—especially given how vocifer- ously the dragon fought my attempts to get to know him.

My lips curl as I burrow deeper into my nest, soaking in the warmth and familiarity with a sigh of pleasure. The safety of my huge, hollowed out space filled with soft cushions, blankets, pillows and other comfort items is not something I share with hardly anyone—except the shifter who became the center of my world so slowly I didn't register it until it was done.

We move between our respective nests depending on the day, and our connection is a well-kept secret. Much like the targets of our hunts, we choose not to share private aspects of ourselves, even with our friends. After all, we have been together for centuries and our new friends' decade at Apex is a blip on our radar.

I have shoes older than their tenure here.

Thoughts of youth lead me back to the enchanting new student who seems to have captured the attention of everyone in our little clutch. Despite her naïveté, Dolly is the first woman to make Fitz act like a fucking normal man, and though he's clearly nervous as hell, she also intrigues Chess. Felix grumbles about her as if he's angry, but I can tell it's a cover for not comprehending his feelings.

And Aubrey…

Flames struggles with accepting affection because of his past. His emotions about the girl confuse and irritate him, making his temperament volatile. But I know from personal experience he needs to deal with it in his own time—even if it's not the best way to handle the situation. Dragons cannot be forced to confront anything; it's not in their nature.

My attraction is easier to parse. She's intelligent, kind, and reminds me of someone I knew long ago. For that reason, I have to keep a suitable distance—the last time I indulged in such feelings led to my exile. Outside of Aubrey and now the tiger ambush, I have much precedent from distrusting people who catch my interest. Until I came to Apex, no one I loved showed me the loyalty these men have, even my species.

A noise so faint it's almost not there pricks my hearing, and one of my eyes pops open to look through the darkness of my suite. The outline of the shifter I was just thinking about, clad in some ridiculously huge blanket dress, is as clear as day with my enhanced vision. She looks shocked to find herself in my room and more so to find me curled around the hulking body of the grouchy librarian.

Obviously, we've done a bang-up job of keeping our relationship a secret.

I watch her wander around the room, looking at my treasures and keepsakes from my long life. She doesn't seem to have ill-intent, though she's definitely violating both our privacy and the edict we gave the tiger when we agreed to allow her refuge in my tower. My body tenses when she pauses at the magical orchid, her hand stopping short of touching it, but wonder is clear in her expression.

It's a relic and reminder of my painful past, and I don't allow anyone to see it. My brow furrows, but I can't find anger at her being here to look at it, and that confuses me. The tigers nor Chess have ever been down here; Aubrey and I keep everyone away from our personal areas in the Tower. They think he sleeps in his cavernous space at the library, as does everyone else. The only person who's ever guessed he doesn't live there is currently creeping through my room like a terrible spy in a comedy.

She turns to come closer to my nest and I narrow the open eye to a slit. I can see her, but I don't want her to know I'm awake yet. Perhaps if I continue faking, she'll give away a clue as to why she's up here snooping rather than curled up in her bed like a good little bunny rabbit. I don't get the feeling they sent her here to spy for her awful parents or the Council, but I don't trust anyone until they give me reason.

Even if Fitz is so obsessed with her, he can barely make it through the day without constant contact.

Her voice is hardly even a breath as she mutters, "Son of a badger, I didn't expect this at all."

I have to fight not to smile at her incredulity.

"Why are they all so fucking hot? It's not fair," she grumbles. "Watching Fitz with Chess and now this? No wonder Fitz keeps saying shit about 'all of us', like they're going to adopt me as a group. I'm a total professor slut and I'm going to make a fool of myself. How could any of them really be interested in me? I'm a total failure at everything, even emerging as a pred."

The sadness in her tone awakens my gargoyle, and he doesn't like it at all. Since he rarely gives a fuck about anything other than hunting and our dragon, I'm a little shocked. A ripple of his power pushes against my skin and I push back in shock—he never tries to do this shit. Or at least, he hasn't since I was a wee pup learning to work with my inner beast rather than being controlled by it.

My gargoyle wants me to comfort her, make her feel better—now.

That revelation makes my gut clench, and I have to fight off the urge to jump up and run away in fear. Adding people to my tiny circle of trust is always terrifying, and this girl caught the attention of the one part of me who will not be denied. He asks for very little and aids me in protecting those I do not wish to see harmed. I can't deny him the few indulgences he demands.

So I open both of my eyes, letting the blue glow of my gargoyle's gaze find Dolly in the dark. Her hand flies to her mouth when she sees it, and I smile gently. Before she can speak, I scoot back a bit, making room in between myself and my grumpy love.

Whispering low, I hold my hand out. "Come. We will help you feel safe, *petite*."

Her expression is unsure, and I watch her struggle with the concept and her own fears. She chews on a fingernail for a moment, probably realizing I heard her talking to herself, but eventually starts padding forward.

"Snacksize, for the love of everything holy, get in here so he goes back to sleep. I have an early class in my fucking library tomorrow."

Aubrey's grumble makes both of us blanch and we exchange a sheepish look as she climbs into the recessed space. Dolly crawls over, placing herself between us in the fluffy sleepwear that dwarfs her frame. I note the bunny ears on the hood and let out a soft huff of amusement.

"What did I say about going to sleep?" the dragon rumbles as he reaches back to grab my hand and yank my arm across both of them.

"Sorry," I say quietly, pressing close to the nervous bunny as I place my hand back on my love's hip.

Dolly's body eventually relaxes, and I smile to myself as the breaths of both the people sharing my nest even out. Something about this feels right and my gargoyle is almost purring with happiness inside of me. It worries me, but at the moment, I can't find it in myself to care.

I haven't had a real clutch for hundreds of years and much like Aubrey, our kind live in polyamorous groups centered on our females. Neither of us ever expected to find one another, much less a woman that might fill that hole in our beasts' desires.

Delores Drew may be the answer to everything all of us have ever wanted, and that terrifies the hell out of me.

Aubrey is going to lose his shit when we wake up and he realizes what he did in his sleep.

Did I forget to mention he sleep talks and rarely remembers it in the morning?

It's going to be hysterical when he wakes.

I can't wait.

The Bitch Is Back

Lucille

Lucille

"I didn't say I wanted excuses; I said make it happen, or I'll have you mounted and stuffed for the servants' quarters!"

Blindly pitching the phone across the room, I snort to myself when I hear the resulting pained squawk from my vapid avian assistant. I can only hope it knocked some sense into her—Matilda has been useless since the greatest disappointment of my life packed her things for Apex Academy. It's amusing to me when lesser preds get attached to their betters the way they do, and only fitting.

We are to be emulated, adored, and, most of all, feared.

Delores, however, deserves none of those reactions. Emerging not only as a prey animal, but one of the weakest kinds has sullied our family name in a way I cannot forgive. The Council's decision to force her to attend Apex chafed at first. If I'd had my way, Bruiser would have dealt with her, and I could have spread the rumor she disappeared into the night after we threatened to disown her. If she dies at Apex, they will treat it as a routine event, and they won't examine her scandalous heritage as closely. It's still a satisfactory outcome, either way, so there was no need to meddle from the shadows.

I keep my paws clean and even though some will question why I didn't save my only heir from the Council's decision, they won't be able to whisper behind my back about suspicious 'accidents'. Back in the old country, my father preferred we handle our business swiftly and without remorse, which is how he built the impressive empire he did.

Yes, the skin trade is lucrative, indeed.

Shifters live all over the world, but the rarest breeds are notoriously difficult to locate. I've been working with my father's traders and runners to find them. Their women and children fetch astronomical prices on the black market for everything from delicacies to breeding, to sales to private collectors. I'm not picky about who buys my products; their money is all green, and the Society has no qualms about where their cut comes from. My only concern is maintaining my family's legacy, even if Dmitri Rostoff rarely acknowledges my invaluable contributions.

His approval is more difficult to locate than a dragon's clash.

Unfortunately, even with the occasional rare shifter being exiled—including to teach at Society-run academies—none of their ilk has been furious enough to reveal locations of their homes. I have spies working on it, but given how insular most of their cultures are, it's almost impossible to get them to socialize, much less spill secrets.

However, with my simpleton daughter at Apex, I might have an 'in'. Her own pathetic sob story may entice the few living there to take pity on her, especially if I can further exploit her weaknesses. Those nitwit heirs should be able to continue their harassment, but they're too soft to inspire true terror, so I need to gather additional allies on campus. Delores may not be a predator, but she is a Rostoff, and she won't break easily. Bruno and I made certain she learned how to survive as part of her upbringing, before she turned out to be a waste of our efforts.

"Mattie, if I finish this glass before a new one appears, I will assign you to Bruiser for a month!" I say, turning to glare at the useless bird with feline eyes.

The diminutive shifter looks as if she's going to molt on the spot, and she rushes to fix another martini before I shift further. The abilities of a true alpha female vary by species, but I learned at a very young age to control my shift precisely—something no other female could. My father left me in the care of his lieutenants until I could shift every part of my body at will in order to intimidate people more effectively. It was a lesson I'd yet to teach our erstwhile daughter because she took her sweet time emerging, and Bruno's mother wouldn't allow me to send her to a shifter group who still practiced the old ways, like the Khans.

Perhaps if she hadn't interfered with my plans, we wouldn't be in the situation we are now—heirless.

All because of a twist of fate resulting from a physical issue, we paid heavily to keep secret for many years. This entire mess is because of a superstitious old Cajun gator who interfered with my plans to get rid of an unpredictable genetic result. Delores resulted from a solution I sought decades ago, after I could not find a believable stand-in to play my heir. The past is the past, but if I cannot resolve the rabbit situation in a manner befitting my family's name soon, I will have to endure a future visit from my father.

That rusty old jaguar is the last thing I need right now.

No, the solution to my problems lies in my disappointing offspring. If I can back her into a corner, Delores will either get herself killed, or she'll end up finding an idiot mate who will hopefully have rare shifter connections I can use to my advantage. Once that happens, I'll be able to ferret out the information I need to weasel my way into profitable shifter settlements.

Either way, I win.

The martini is cold, and I swirl it in the glass as I muse. In order for my scheme to work, I'll need to pinpoint the most important exiles at Apex, in hopes the tactics of the other heirs drive my blonde bimbo of a daughter straight into their arms. The only way to do that is to… ah, yes.

That will do.

"Phone!" I bark, whipping my head around to glare toward my birdbrained assistant.

She comes running over with the object I threw not ten minutes ago, and I grin fangily when I note she has a similarly shaped red mark on her temple. Papa always said I had deadly aim, even when I wasn't paying a bit of attention to my target. Using a clawed finger to scroll through my contacts, I find the one I need and press the call button. It rings several times, and by the time the bumbling headmistress answers, I'm seething.

No one keeps me waiting.

"Henrietta, I was unaware you'd developed a suicidal streak. Shall I send someone to fetch you, since you seem eager to bleed out on my carpet?" The squawks and flutters on her end are so intense, I can actually hear her panicking despite the lack of intelligible words coming over the line. Her fear sates my hunger for the moment, and I wait until she gathers herself enough to respond. Breaking the silence is a sign of weakness, and I won't give this fool any ammunition.

"M-M-M-Madame L-L-L-Lucille… I… my phone… I was not…. I would never…" the eagle babbles, her words interspersed with screeches and beak chattering sounds.

As much as I enjoy her terror, this is getting tiresome, so I cut her off. "If you are eager to prove your allegiance, I am a reasonable feline. I will allow you penance for your grievous breach of protocol, headmistress."

"How-how may I serve you, Madame Councilwoman?" Henrietta's breaths slow, and I can sense her trying to calm her nerves.

This is why her own family—the Shirdals—excommunicated her to Apex. Henrietta may be an apex predator by birth and by lineage, but nothing they did could instill the spirit of ferocity necessary to survive as a Council heir. They sent her to replace the elder Headmaster once she emerged at nineteen, and she's remained on campus since. Unlike the Drews, the Shirdals had several spares waiting in the wings, and their next heir stepped in with a vicious reign of terror.

If only I was as lucky…

Alas, I mistakenly chose not to gamble with the risks of creating extra heirs, and focused on beating our family expectations into the one I had. Annoyed, I snarl into the phone, taking out my frustration at my own choices on the frail eagle. "You will do precisely as I instruct, no deviation, and you will tell absolutely no one what we discuss when I contact you. Swear it, and know—if you break this oath, I will ship you to Bloodstone to be dinner for the ferals in their little jungle course."

A sharp inhale tells me she understands perfectly, for once. "Y-Yes, Madame. I swear. I will not break the oaths of the Council."

No, I don't think you will, feather duster.

Even Henrietta isn't cut off enough to have missed stories of the blood-soaked orgies and hunts that take place on Bloodstone. Criminals, spies, traitors, political prisoners, and various inconvenient innocents end up as fodder for their ambush's ceremonies and sacrifices. The myths about what goes on at their prison and reform school are more than enough to keep not only our children in line, but the less ferocious adults as well.

That moron Barrington would have taken his wife there to have a little 'accident' so he could upcycle her for a new one, but his vapid daughter caused that scandal in the media, and now he's stuck with her.

That's what happens when you allow children to believe they aren't replaceable. They grow up and think they may breathe the air on this planet without you allowing it.

"You'd better not, Shirdal. Your family won't mind if you went permanently missing, and a new headmaster or mistress won't be hard to find. Killing you wouldn't make a blip on my schedule; remember that," I purr, sipping my martini slowly while she digests that statement. "Now, take notes. This is what I need from you."

I can hear her clicking away at a keyboard as I list the internal documents I want copied and sent via foot messenger. Given the prevalence of hackers, I trust nothing important to be transmitted electronically; even Erickson does most of his personal business on specially manufactured flash paper, like an old school bookie. If the Council's own tech mogul knows there's a threat, I will not question the methods.

Waiting for the idiot to catch up, I stress I want every single professor and adjunct's personnel file, plus every map and blueprint, dating back to before they created the Apex app. The class schedules of every student in her classes will allow me to know not only where my dimwit is at all times, but who she may associate with—especially which staff will lay eyes on her.

Once I have all of this data, I can compile a dossier of her life at the school. Delores may not be useful as an heir, but until some lucky predator gets their claws into her, I can use her as bait—a means to an end. That's what all the weaklings around me are, and I'll be damned if I ignore one of the most easily manipulated students on campus, simply because she embarrassed me.

That wouldn't be strategic, and I'm not arrogant enough to ignore the opportunity.

"Henrietta, I want every single scrap of information or gossip you can find. Talk to those twits in your admissions office, scare the prey staff into spilling things they've seen, and get me answers—

preferably immediately. I won't tolerate a second failure. Do you understand? Get. Me. What. I. Want."

The eagle shifter vomits apologies, praise, and fealty for another few moments, until I finally grow tired of the noise. I don't bother with the niceties. I simply hang up the call and pitch my phone over my shoulder. A muffled squeak of pain makes my fangs grow, and I lean back on the chaise, closing my eyes in satisfaction as I sip my drink again.

I probably should keep my feathered dipshit of an assistant. She makes an excellent martini, and an even better target.

Hmmm.

Start A War

Felix

Felix

This is the day I've been dreading for the past week.

Apex requires me to put the students in the ring to test their base fighting skill set and control over their shifts, so that I can develop my plans for all incoming freshmen accordingly. Henrietta implemented that rule shortly after I arrived because I started my lessons with Bloodstone style free-for-alls.

Unfortunately, these pampered fools couldn't hack it and it flooded the infirmary with near fatal injuries. My hand got slapped and the 'Khan test' was born. I despise having to coddle my students almost as much as I do having a preventative rule named after me.

Somewhere, my father is probably laughing his furry ass off every time one of the ambush gets sent here and the materials for guardians arrive. They highlighted the goddamn rule in the section about Shifter Basics like a Vegas billboard.

Letting out a deep, long-suffering sigh, I watch the first section of freshman tromp through the grass in completely ridiculous attire. I warned them we would be out here and this would be a physical activity, yet many of the females wore designer bullshit and heels. Likewise, their male counterparts are clad in expensive preppy shit that's going to get absolutely wrecked in the ring.

What about physical activity said 'ditch your uniforms, but don't wear gym clothes?' Fucking ridiculous.

"This is torture, Professor. My vintage heels are getting ruined!"

Tension spirals up my spine at the whiny, high-pitched voice of a random member of Delores' bully club. I still can't tell them apart —which I know is by design—so I refer to them by their colors in my head. Out loud, I usually find the name of a random dog character since they're all canines. My tiger enjoys their twisted expressions of distaste when I do it and I know the one student I can't help but focus on does as well.

"Perhaps when your professor advises there will be physical activity, you'll make better choices in the future," I reply as I trudge toward the round ring. "Regardless, that's a 'you' problem, Muttley."

"Such an asshole," one of her compatriots mutters in a tone meant to be heard by everyone, including me.

My tiger rears his head, demanding I show her the penalty for insulting a Khan, especially the rightful Raj. I squeeze my hands into fists, letting the claw tips cut my palms to distract me. I could get away with killing Council heirs—my family is too powerful to make enemies and those rich dipshits need us to take their rotten apples—but the amount of red tape and paperwork involved makes my dick shrivel.

Instead of letting the bitchy little shits get to me, I stomp into the middle of the ring, looking at everyone as they pile into the stone bleachers like the king I am. "Welcome to the Khan Ambush Training Ring, losers. In class I'm the last word, but in this ring, I am your king."

That gets their attention and more than a few uncomfortable looks. I can see the need to correct me crawling over some of the more entitled students, especially the bully group. When my eyes land on the one student I truly want to test, she jerks her chin up and gives me a level stare. Unsurprisingly, she's the only fucking person dressed for the occasion.

Of course, the curves and skin displayed in the tight sports bra, leggings with peek-a-boo panels and matching shoes don't help with my inability to keep my damn eyes off her. It'll be worse when she's fighting, given that she wrapped her hands in matching colored tape, I'd bet my throne this ensemble is courtesy of my meddling twin.

I'm giving that fucker a piece of my mind tonight.

"Today, we will focus on sparring in humanoid forms. I can't trust most of you to can fight after your shift, plus there are some that will require special locations, such as the lake, to show me their animals. This lesson doubles as a test of what physical abilities you have—both innate and trained—so I can make an individual plan for each one of you for your tenure at Apex. That plan will be adjusted if your progress speeds up or slows for any reason."

"I know kung-fu," the same smart mouthed gold bow girl blurts out. "My Daddy hired a master panda to come train me."

I arch a brow, refraining from commenting that she wants us to believe a... kung-fu panda has trained her. Once I keep from laughing at the stupidity, I give her an unimpressed look. "Be that as it may, I will pair you up with another student to assess your skills. I have a female professor with fighting experience coming to assist because it's well known that I make no exceptions for gender in my tests."

That's when Zhenga rolls up and I almost lose my shit again. Her fighting gear is just as skimpy as the girl in the back row, but unlike Barbie, I want nothing to do with touching her exposed skin. The lioness is gorgeous and built like a brick house—I just have no interest in her. The males in my class, however, look like they're about to jizz all over themselves.

Better put a stop to that before Z does—she's not very subtle, either.

"Get your shit together," I roar at the boys, making googly eyes at her. "This is Professor Zhenga, and she teaches… well, you'll find that out next semester depending on what your family has told you about our biology. Her other skill set is being a top competitor in the female Pred Games. She will gladly chop your cock off and feed it to the sharks in the lake if you get fresh with her."

Zhenga's laugh is sultry and I notice Barbie making a sour face as she listens. "Felix is correct. If they have not forced you to control your baser instincts in your cushy home lives, you will learn to behave at Apex. There are many places you will get away with acting like spoiled twats, but this ring isn't one of them."

Her words cause a buzz of conversations in the stands, and I roll my eyes. I'm sure they're all contemplating calling their parents or fucking lawyers, but it won't help them. This is a required program and if they don't complete it, their asses get booted from the Academy. No parent will want their darlings labeled as drop-outs from the premier pred school in the country. Each one of them will find that out eventually, but not right now.

"Enough!" I reach down and tug my shirt off, tossing it aside as I back away from the lioness. "We will demonstrate first, then call on pairs of you until we're done."

That almost gets a purr out of Zhenga and she mutters something about the last time we got naked together that makes me shoot her a dirty look. It earns me a pout, but she drops into position anyway, nodding when she's ready to begin. "At your word, Raj."

Her words draw another gasp out of the crowd and I roll my eyes. "Only the basics, Z. No shifting, no funny business. This is not a staff event."

"As long as I get to wrestle with you, I'm game," she replies tauntingly. Before I can correct her on her bullshit again, she darts forward with the speed of her animal.

I've fought Zhenga enough times to know her strength is in her speed and willingness to play dirty. She's aiming for my knees, so I allow her to get close before I pivot out of her path. Her forward momentum works against her and she can't stop quickly enough to veer off her path. With a wink at the crowd, I dance backwards as she charges past. I wait for her to wheel around, springing forward to knock her off balance. Once she's on the ground, I use my body weight to pin her in place.

Normally, she'd fight her way free, but that would entail much more violence than I've asked her to display. She purrs as she looks up at me, clearly enjoying her position under me despite my repeated warnings.

My ears catch a tiny growl in the air and when I lift my eyes to find it, I'm surprised to see Barbie sitting so rigidly you'd think she was about to lift off. Her fists are clenched on her lap and a dark expression is playing about her features.

Is she… jealous?

The thought makes my tiger rumble in pleasure, and Zhenga gives me a sultry smile. Blinking, I give her a stern look, lifting off her body to dust myself off. I could have shown them more captive positions, but I'm not interested in giving her the wrong idea if Barbie's ire arouses my beast more.

Which it shouldn't, but fuck me if it's not.

I can feel the weight of her stare as Zhenga rises from the ground and tilts her head at my students.

"I allowed Felix to pin me so you might see how a fight should end —domination. When we fight with no limits, there is more blood, more ferocity, and it takes far longer because we are close to evenly matched." A snarl rips from me, and she gives me a suspicious look before adding, "His tiger takes umbrage to my claim and since his lineage trumps mine, I will yield."

She drops to her knees, head bowed, and I sigh in irritation. It calms my cat, but I'm not fond of overt displays like this in public. "Get up, Zhenga. No need for this shit."

"But I love being on my knees for you," she says with a mischievous expression. The growl sounds again and her grin gets bigger as she gets up, looking for its source. "However, it sounds like there's another person eager to jump in the ring. Perhaps we should allow her to have her turn?"

Barbie's eyes go wide and a look of fear comes over her. "With… one of you?"

Zhenga laughs and I shake my head. It's clear she's not even certain which one of us she'd be more terrified to take on—though, obviously for different reasons. "No, Barbie. With one of the other students. I'm feeling generous, so I'll even let you pick which one."

Her gaze narrows as she stands, putting her hands on her hips. I don't know why I thought she'd back down or cower; the girl has stood her ground every time I'm around. She finally points at the head bully with the gold bow, her lips curving as she looks to me for approval.

Fucking hell. Bravery looks as good on her as everything else.

The snooty Heather stands, tottering a little on the sky high heels she foolishly wore to class. Kicking them off, she watches as one of the idiotic hyenas picks them up and flips her hair over her shoulder. "DD, you'll never learn your place. Just like before and until the day you die… I'll make you snivel in fear and defeat in front of everyone."

"Prom wasn't a fair fight, E. You rarely give your enemies one and that's why you think you're hot shit." A feral grin spreads over her face as she calmly walks to the stairs and makes her way to the ring. "This time, it's just you and me. No minions, no flunkies, and no cheating."

You could drop a pin in the dirt and hear it, as the previously quiet Barbie steps into the center of the ring and turns to face the crowd with her arms spread in 'come at me, bro' position. An acrid scent fills my nostrils and I realize its fear radiating off Gold Bow as she stares at her opponent.

"I don't have to do this, right? I'm not even dressed for it, Professor. And if I get hurt—"

Zhenga smirks, cutting her off. "That's your fault, honey. I know Felix didn't bring fresh meat to the pit without telling them to be prepared. It's not his style. If you didn't listen, that's on you."

"Agreed," I respond with a satisfied grin. "I offered to let Barbie pick, and you made yourself a target by acting like a fucking fool at every turn last week. Let it be a lesson for all of you—if you wave a flag at a bull, you eventually get the horns."

Barbie holds her hand out, crooking a finger at the griping dog. "Afraid a wittle bunny is going to beat you, E? What would Daddy say then? Gosh, I can't imagine!"

Ouch. She's going for blood and we all know where that attitude came from.

The acolytes around the whiner whisper, and she rolls her eyes, finally stomping to the center of the ring with Barbie. Losing face must be more important than fear because she drops into a basic fighting stance with a small growl of annoyance. I watch as her challenger stands loosely, eyeing her from head to toe.

"Ground rules are no shifting, no eye damage, no permanent disfigurement, no crippling—"

I don't get to finish because the adorable girl my brother loves bum rushes her bully with a speed I didn't know she had. When her attack knocks the girl off balance, she counters with an uppercut and a swift punch in the kidneys that doubles the bleached bimbo over. Screams of fury and pain fill the air and the crowd goes wild as Z and I scramble to get out of the way.

The rage in the air makes my tiger pace and I feel Zhenga's lion ripple over her as well. We have to watch this closely because if we're not careful, it's going to force a shift of every pred in the training area.

Bloodlust always does.

A leg sweeps out, catching the canine as she's stumbling around trying to catch her breath, and the dipshit in gold hits the ground with a solid thud. Barbie leaps forward with a snarl of anger, pinning her down with her thighs as she rains punches on the prone Heather over and over. I almost step in, afraid she might kill the bitch, but suddenly, she yanks the blond ponytail hard enough to make her opponent scream. Exposing her neck as if going for the final blow, Barbie looks up at me with a dark satisfaction before turning back to her foe.

"You pretended to be my friend. You used my loyalty to keep me quiet about all the evil shit you said and did. You lied to me about everything to keep me compliant. And when I wasn't useful anymore, when you'd drained every ounce of narcissistic supply you needed, you threw me to dogs to make yourself look better."

That draws gasps from the other students and even Z looks a little sympathetic.

I, however, am having trouble keeping my dick from bursting through my goddamned pants so I can fuck the shit out of this little warrior.

"Listen up, E. Your reign of terror is over. You can come after me as much as you want; you may even knock me down a time or two. But… Every. Single. Time. I will get up and hit you back exponentially harder than you hit me. If you keep pushing me, I'll be the one standing over your corpse in the end. Do you understand me, you two-faced moron? I. Will. End. You."

Holy fucking Odin on a tricycle.

Z leans in and whispers in my ear softly enough that no one else will hear it. "I don't blame you, Raj. Even I want to fuck the shit out of her now."

My head whips around and I look at the lioness in panic as she laughs. "I…"

"Put a stop to this before the dumb whore mouths off or your girl is going to kill her," Zhenga says drily. "Arguing with me won't make it less true, though it explains a lot."

Swallowing hard, I adjust myself surreptitiously and stomp into the center, tapping Barbie on the shoulder. "That's enough. Clearly, we have a winner. Class is dismissed and I advise all of you to work on your shit, lest I make you fight the boxing bunny here next time!"

It takes another tap to get Barbie to come back to reality, and she finally rises, letting go of the bimbette on the ground. She doesn't look at me as she walks to the stands, avoiding the other students while she grabs her things. Before she leaves, she tosses one triumphant look at me. Her lips curve in a smirk as she jogs to the edge of the ring. She's obviously heading to the main campus and I should talk to her before she goes.

"Professor!" The gold bowed Heather is screeching as her friends try to help her up unsuccessfully. "You'll be hearing from my parents and my attorneys. You let her purposely injure me and—"

Sighing, I stalk back to her and get right in her rapidly bruising face. "Your parents signed paperwork stating attending Apex, particularly Shifter Basics, could cause a serious injury, up to and including death. You do what you want, Scrappy Dipshit, but I promise you won't win the favor you think you will. Hell, if it were my father, he'd have me killed for losing. What about yours?"

That said, I grin and turn to Zhenga. "Shall we join the rest of the staff for drinks in the lounge? I feel like being one of the bourbon lunch people."

"As you wish, Raj," she says. This time it's without her usual innuendo, and I give her a grateful look. "I know when I'm fighting a losing battle, Felix. Don't act surprised."

Well, isn't that wonderful—Zhenga's become a shipper.

POISON
AUBREY

THE TOWER IS EMPTY WHEN I STEP INTO THE OUTER SANCTUM.

It's unusual, to be sure, but the others have later classes or duties to attend to today that leave me with a rare opportunity to escape to the relative quiet of our meeting place. This is preferable to remaining in my library, where students and staff alike could bother me while I'm reviewing the information I received today.

I've begged Henny to close the library earlier, and more often—given that students rarely stay in my lair long—but she refuses. 'The library is a place for all to find knowledge and comfort' is her favorite way of saying she would rather they are under *my* surveillance, than hanging out where the likelihood of shenanigans is higher.

Plus, I'm the least likely person to tell her to fuck off when she insists I man the building like a sentry. My sense of honor and duty prevent me from calling her on her bullshit—dragons are bound to their calling, and the books are mine.

Taking advantage of that species-specific trait is not ethical, but nothing at Apex is ever ethical, so why should this be any different?

I drop into my handcrafted 'throne' in the sitting room, sinking into the comfort of one of the few things I've spent a great deal of money on.

Yes, yes, dragons hoard, and I'm old enough to be so wealthy that such frugality is completely unnecessary, but old habits die hard, as they say.

I dislike spending recklessly by nature—unlike the Khans—so when I do, it's for things I cannot live without. Comfortable furniture, stress relievers, quality clothes, and books are the extent of my vices. I had all three of my thrones for the library and the Tower built to my specifications to ensure I can relax in luxury. Non-corporate craftsmen struggle in the technology age, and it bothers me to think skilled trade will go the way of the dodo shifters if the Council assholes get their way.

With a sigh of discontent, I open the app on my DiePhone, accessing the Bluetooth surround sound system Renard finally consented to having installed. He resisted at first, preferring the gramophone in the bedroom, but since introducing the game system and virtual assistant, he's been a bit more flexible about the 'infernal spread of technology'. I think he's secretly enjoying being able to access information when he wants, rather than moving from his brooding perch to look it up in the library, but that's more fodder for me to poke him with, so I let it go.

Which is more than I can say for him—he's eternally riling me up on purpose, like inviting the snacklet to our nest the other night. I don't care if he swears I told her she could. I know he was involved somehow because he's a meddler like Fitz.

The soothing sounds of my music fill the air, and I pull my Smackbook out of my briefcase. The folders of organized research and first-hand reports get placed on the side table, and my notebook is the last thing I balance on the arm of the chair. I want to go over my own conclusions and evidence about what happened on prom night, while I wait on the Council's results from testing the blood samples. I don't trust them to provide us with the full picture—it would be entirely uncharacteristic for them to give us unredacted, undoctored reports—but I plan to fill in the blanks when I combine their shit with the files Renard's friends in the nurse's office have shared.

I click on the email icon, growling under my breath as I sort through the various missives I've received throughout the day. Many of them are from students and staff regarding passwords, which I forward to Betsy. She can resolve those issues without me, and I'm never in the mood to deal with idiots who can't memorize their shit and constantly lock themselves out of the Apex app or the Blackboard system for their classes.

The email from the Council lab finally appears at the top of my unread messages, and I open it, waiting for the extensive file to extract itself. Interestingly enough, the results seem to be straight-forward. The toxin did not match any natural or synthetic poison in their database, nor does it match that of any venomous shifter species—including rare species and those thought to be extinct or so endangered that we rarely see them outside of their own communities. Nothing on file, even at the Library of Congress, matches the chemical composition of the substance found in the punch.

That still doesn't explain why the dimwits attending Vom Prom were unfazed. Henny and the nursing staff got some of them to admit to the consumption of pred-stasy and various kinds of alcohol, but nothing in their samples is consistent enough to create a controlled group. It's a puzzle, and I can't help wondering if that ridiculous alcohol is the key, but without a toxin identified, it will be near impossible to confirm.

The results of Delores' blood test, sent to an independent lab by the nurses, haven't come back yet. I expect little to come from that, as the nurses told Rennie she didn't drink the punch or imbibe anything on the foolish party bus.

That means she's not an anomaly; she just avoided the contaminant.

I have to admit; the girl is still fascinating and having her between us wasn't uncomfortable in the slightest. That surprised me.

Her work in my archives is articulate and impeccable, despite her clear lack of true self-confidence. She doesn't fawn or simper like most of the idiotic women here—students and staff alike—because while I believe she craves positive reinforcement, she actually wants to *earn* the praise. Her upbringing must have been rough; she doesn't talk about home or friends before Apex at all. In fact, she seems content to work alongside me, asking questions and occasionally poking at *me* until I divulge crumbs of information about myself.

Her effect on me is truly baffling. I've never met anyone quite like Delores Drew, especially given her background. The librarian in me finds her wit, organization, and professionalism extremely appealing.

My dragon… has his own ideas.

I understand why she's wormed her way under the skin of my friends, and it's a bit unsettling to find she's crawling under my scales as well.

Fitz is damned near obsessed with her. He's been blind to Rennie and me for a decade, yet he notices if this girl changes her fucking nail polish. Chess is a little out of sorts as he figures out how to handle his attraction to her, but he's coming around. Hell, even Felix had a bounce in his step yesterday when he stomped in, smelling of bourbon and regaling us with the tale of the killer rabbit.

There may be hope for him yet.

Rennie and I have avoided addressing his struggle with being exiled, because his self pity was simply exacerbating the toxic masculinity programmed into alphas of many species. The gargoyle and I both came of age with powerful royals and clan leaders—which we would have been ourselves, if not for our own debacles—and these leaders did not always rule with an iron fist. His behavior since Delores arrived has been more befitting a king than anything *he's* done in the past.

An angry teenager is affecting men several times her age simply by existing in our stratosphere.

I can't decide if that's a good thing.

"A-dog! Fuck am I glad you're here! My baby girl is studying and Chess is working on knitting, so I'm bored. I bet I can whoop your scaly ass in Smash Bros."

As usual, Fitz's entrance is a cacophony of disturbance in my precious thinking time. I glare at him over my glasses, hoping to convey my wish to focus on the task at hand without words. When he doesn't take the hint, I snap the Smackbook closed, watching him fire up the video game in annoyance. If he'd amuse himself, I wouldn't mind his presence, but Fitz is like a hopped up rave kid 24/7 because of his ADHD. His inability to focus becomes everyone's problem when he's like this, and it makes my head hurt.

"I'm reviewing the files and results from the prom disaster. I fear it's nowhere near being resolved and we all agreed this was bigger than an attempt on Council heirs."

The tiger tilts his head to the side, tapping his fingers on his legs as if he's itching to wrap his hands around either a controller or someone's neck. "Is my baby girl in danger? Who do I need to kill? I dealt with that little shit who broke her heart already, and I have ideas for when I find out who trashed her room. Hint: it involves hooks."

Pinching the bridge of my nose to push away thoughts of roasted preds, I breathe deeply. Of course, his concern is limited to the immediate people he gives a shit about. He's not one for looking at the big picture and he revels in punishing the people who violate his rather interesting moral code. "I don't know yet. The Council labs couldn't ID the toxin in any of their vast databases, and that points to a more skilled opponent than a lackey or an idiotic teenager."

"Ok, so what the fuck are we all gonna do about that?" he asks, fiddling with his controller in agitation, surprising me with his ability to hold the thread of our conversation.

"Again, the course of action is still unclear. At the moment, it's a single incident with too many variables and not enough hard evidence to point in a specific direction." I arch a brow, watching him fidget. "You seem more concerned with this than you normally would be."

"Hell yes, I am! And the same goes for you too, you spicy lizard. The rest of you assholes might think you're immune, but I see more than you know, dude." He drops the controller, leaning back against the couch and clasping his hands behind his head with a smirk.

I fucking highly doubt that.

Snorting smoke, I shift in my throne, putting my work aside as I huff. "What are you hinting at, Fitz?"

"My Baby Girl, duh." His grin widens as he watches me shift in my seat. "As you know, Felix got thrashed at lunch after her spectacular fight and told the entire staff she's under Khan protection. We both know that's getting around before the weekend and probably spreading further within weeks. Once she's ready, Chessie wants her to join us. You're spending time on technology—which you *hate*—researching something that's been over for months. Fuck, even the rock man is brooding more than normal. You all need to get with the program."

What in the seven wonders of the world is he babbling about?

I'm simply doing due diligence in investigating a threat that might affect our home and our group. Unfortunately, tech is a necessary component of that search. There's no hidden meaning behind it.

"Miss Drew is a student, and she's quite intriguing, but I'm not working on this because of her. Apex is the only home I've known for many years, and if there's some jackass out there trying to harm students, we could lose our jobs and our residence," I protest. My frustration escalates as I talk, causing puffs of smoke to escape as the fire burns inside.

Dragons are not good liars, for reasons that should be obvious.

"Yeah, yeah. Keep tragically lying to yourself, Smoky. I don't know why I'm the only one in this crew who sees it, but Delores Drew is the best thing to hit this place since *I* arrived." He winks and shrugs, his eyes dancing. "And I'm pretty sure she'd be down with giving us *all* a little lovin'."

Having Fitz Khan read my thoughts was not on my to do list. This has to stop.

My eyes widen and I sputter, unable to form coherent thoughts as his implication sinks in. I'm not one to share the intimate details of my people with others, so Fitz can't know dragons are some of the few shifters that live in polyamorous communities. The strength of our people lies within the bonds of the mated groups, but I didn't expect to find something like that after being exiled. In fact, for more years than I can count, I believed I'd spend the rest of my life alone.

That may have changed, but it doesn't mean Fitz's vision of the five of us sharing a Council heir is coming to fruition, either.

Not that I have any desire to—the girl is young, traumatized, and so sheltered that she barely recognizes her own desires, much less those of men exponentially older than her. My horn dog friend is biting off more than he can chew with his horny train of thought, and I don't know how he expects me to react.

We're an island of broken toys, and she's badly damaged—what possible good could come from entertaining his little fantasy?

"Dude, chill. You look like your brain is going to explode. I'm not saying the kitty pile needs to happen tomorrow. Baby Girl isn't ready for a dragon-sized dick… or your teeny weenie, either."

Narrowing my eyes, I rise from the chair and stalk over to the chuckling tiger. "You don't know shit, Fitz Khan—not what I'm thinking or what a dragon dick looks like. Give me the other controller, so I can kick your furry ass."

I Ship It

Delores

Delores

"I feel like half the teachers in this stupid school are giving me suspicious or dirty looks. I really am cursed," I mutter.

The books in front of us on the stage are full of musicals we can license for this year, and the professors left us to our own devices while we looked. I'm sure they've fucked off to a teacher's lounge or in Professor Sarabhai's case, smoking one of those weird clove pipe things she likes.

Rufus snorts, shaking his head. "Girl, you've got it twisted. Yes, that snivel-y bitch in Shifter History probably hates you, but it's probably because you're an heir he can't suck up to, so he sided with those doppelgänger girls. Professor Short Dick has been schmoozing heirs for *years*; you're not special."

"What about *Fame?*" Cori asks, her brightly colored hair popping up from behind a big songbook. "It feels appropriate."

"Fuck, no, Coco. Where are we going to get that many dancers who don't look like water buffalo galloping around the stage?" Rufus shakes his head, leaning back on the stage as he stares up at the lighting rig. "There is a serious lack of talent and eligible, non-closeted dick on this campus. I can't wait until they finally start letting us out on the weekends."

Cori snickers, ducking back behind her book as he rambles. I pretend to focus on our task for a minute before I finally give in and ask, "What about everyone else? Felix glares at me like I offended his ancestors now and Chess keeps hiding from me. How am I going to survive the semester? The dudes are all bent out of shape, which means I'm fucked because my only female professors are from this program. Artemis knows they won't go easy on me grade-wise."

"Dolly, you told us you've always been an outstanding student. I'm sure, regardless of a professor's personal conflicts, you don't need to worry about—" Cori stops, looking at Rufus and I staring at her with our mouths open. "Right. I forget what an unregulated hellhole this place is. Yes, I suppose it *is* possible a few rotten apples could wreck your GPA and make your bitch mother go bonkers."

I nod, chewing on my lip. "It's like Fitz and the cranky crew are the only ones besides you guys who give a shit if I survive. But that doesn't even help, because only Fitz is willing to really get involved."

"Oh, honey. Fitzgerald Khan may care, but that will only continue until you give up what he's hunting. At least, that's been the buzz in the beehive since I arrived." Rufus holds up his finger and pauses. "Speaking of which, *Best Little Whorehouse*, anyone? We have ourselves a Dolly."

Even though I'm not worried about Fitz—he's with me so much he can't be fucking around with anyone else—I smack Rufus with my book. "You asshole! I have enough people calling me a whore; I don't need to star in a show where it's accurate!" The two of them giggle as I cross my arms over my chest, huffing. I may be a blonde, but I'm not *that* blonde. Painting that target on my ass would be as bad as the stupid bunny tail already there.

Cori reaches over and pets my hair, her expression rueful. "Aw, Dolly Bear. We didn't mean to make you pissy. Rufus was just being… well, Rufus. He's a grade-A bitch."

I roll my eyes at her, giving up a smile. "I know that. I'm not mad at either of you—the joke was funny, but the people after me aren't. If it weren't for you picking up the phone when I ran to the nurse's office, I might not be here to choose the musical."

That's when I see the change in my friends for the first time—the preds they keep underneath. Rufus' face morphs under the tattoos, somehow looking even scarier than he already does, and Cori's bulk grows as white fur sprouts on her limbs. I back away, not because I'm afraid of them, but I'm aware my scent might provoke their animals. Within seconds, a giant polar bear and a half-shifted honey badger are sitting amongst Broadway song-books and notebooks as if it's perfectly normal.

"Um, guys? Guys? I didn't mean..." My butt scoots along the wooden stage slowly, wanting to be ready to run if need be.

My friends aren't first-years like me, but that doesn't mean they have full control over their shifting. It takes years for that to happen, which is why Shifter Basics is a five-year class. People need years to master their animal and their emotions. Or at least, that's what Professor Felix says when he's not purposely riling me up.

Rufus morphs back to human first, plopping back down on the boards like nothing happened. "Shit, girl. I haven't lost my cool like that for non-business reasons for months. You really have the damsel in distress thing on lock."

The enormous bear heavily sits on its haunches next to me, leaning in to lick my hair. I blink. "Uh..."

"Don't worry. It'll take Coco a mo'. She's not an alpha/pack leader/what have you. Shift control is much harder to learn when you're not destined to take the throne. I, however, already look fabulous in a crown," Rufus drawls, winking at me.

I turn to look at the polar bear, blinking again when she places a paw on my shoulder like she's comforting me. "Ooookay. That's not weird at all." We go back to paging through the books in silence, and after a few minutes, our curvy friend is back to normal. Of course, that's when I realize they're both naked and my eyes widen. "Um, guys… clothes?"

Cori laughs, her rainbow curls shaking as she clutches her chest. "You were definitely raised by weird shifters, Dolly. It's perfectly normal for us to be naked after we shift. Most of us learned that the hard way as kids, when our parents hulked out and went 'animal' when we were bad."

I feel like the dumbest person in the room.

Lucille and Bruno shift all the time—though usually what people here call 'half-shift,' so it never causes a clothing problem. Their control must be superb, which matches up with their claims of importance within their families. The Heathers never invited me over to their homes, so I have no baseline to judge other shifter households. My new friends are telling me full shifts and nudity are basically so normal they're blasé, and I had no idea.

Hera, help me, I've been so sheltered I may never fit into this society—bunny or not.

Frowning, I wonder what other parts of 'normal' life I've missed, and how stupid I'm going to look as they get revealed. My confusion will be prime gossip material if the Heathers figure out I don't have a clue what 'real' shifters do when they're not in public.

"Dollface, whatever you're sweating about, stop. Every clan, pack, or whatever does things differently. You don't have to know everything right away—that's what classes are for. The curriculum may be half-bullshit and half-reality, but you'll figure it out. Stop making a face like Coco murdered your yappy dog."

Great. Now they think I'm a cloistered little rich girl with a pocket Yorkie.

So much for being a badass at Apex.

I sigh, reminding myself that Rufus and Cori are just looking out for me. "Thank you for sharing, but I'm really concerned the tiny sphere Lucille kept me in will hurt me. I don't even know what things might get me in trouble."

"Eh, we'll help you learn. Besides, you can't look any stupider than the dimwits you used to hang out with. They're barely able to string five words together without their brains melting, and I heard they all joined the school paper yesterday," Cori says, her eyes dancing with mirth. "Can you imagine? Trust me, Professor Cormac will not let them get away with whatever they have planned. That platypus is fierce."

A giggle escapes before I know it. She might be a social justice warrior, but Cori can be as catty as the rest of us when she's not in public. "I know! I was going to major in English first, so I visited the paper during my tour and her spurs were no joke. That's why I used the office for the change of major form; I was afraid she'd come after me!"

What Cori doesn't realize is Pink doesn't need the school paper to spread rumors and lies—her father owns the legitimate news outlets and most of the social media platforms. She can spew her venom anytime, anywhere, without fear of reprisal. Their plans for the paper have to be Apex-specific, and I'm not sure what would warrant making it one of their extracurriculars. They can't be cheer-monkeys because post-secondary Pred Games don't have squads. Professional ones do, but none of the Heathers are good enough dancers or tumblers to get picked for that level of performance, no matter how much money their parents throw at the Leonidas family.

Why the school newspaper? What am I missing?

I look over at my friends, giving them a shrug. "It's hard to predict what those girls are planning. They aren't book smart, but their cunning lies in being raised to be so ruthlessly ambitious that they'll do anything and everything to win. They don't care if you're not playing their games; their parents expect them to be victorious, so they will *make* you play so you can lose. Their drive to prove they deserve their Council seats is completely ingrained in their personalities; hell, it might *be* their personalities."

"They don't scare me a bit," Rufus says, leaning back on his hands again. "They might play rich girl games, but in my family, the games aren't so civilized. Let them show their hand. I won't hesitate to show them how real gangsters operate."

The toothy smirk would make me shiver if I wasn't beginning to trust him. I don't doubt that whatever his family does, Rufus is tattooed-neck deep in it. Still, I nibble my lip in concern. "If we're waiting for them to make a move, what do you suggest we do in the meantime?"

"Maybe we should talk about why you think all of your professors hate you when five of them clearly want to chase your fluffy cottontail," he replies. "Outside of Abel, the Asexual Asshole, you've got all the hotties trying to peek at your panties."

"What?" I blurt. "*Rufus!* Don't say that kind of stuff where people can hear. What if someone told them I'm crushing? It would be humiliating."

Cori looks at us for a moment before dissolving into giggles. "Shit, Ruf, she doesn't know!"

His head tilts as his smirk grows wider. "Oh, now that's adorable! Dolly Bear thinks they're being mean to her because they don't like her."

I smack my foot on the ground next to him. "They don't! I mean, okay, except for Fitz—he's clearly being a perv. A sweet perv, but a perv. You can't possibly think Felix or Renard or Aubrey...?" They look at one another and burst into laughter again, making me crinkle my nose.

What in the hell is goddamn funny?

"Dollface, you don't realize because you're new here. Big kitty's brother is known for being allergic to students—period. That he put you under Khan protection in front of the entire staff is shaking the grapevine something fierce."

"And, and... " Cori cuts in excitedly. "The other two never let students call them anything but professor or… well, to be honest, people don't call the librarian anything because he roars and kicks them out before they can open their mouths. His assistant handles everything because his temper is like… *legendary.* There's never been a student aide that made it through their first week in the library. They always get kicked out with bellows and flames."

What? Are they serious?

They have to be pulling my leg. I mean, yeah, the guys are all pretty stand-offish, but it's not like I've worried they're going to roast me or anything. And Felix probably said the Khan protection thing because Fitz would lose his shit if people messed with me. After I kicked Gold's ass in the ring, her family might have bribed people to hurt me, and he knew that.

Right?

Rufus bats his lashes, sighing as he clasps his hands near his cheek. "Methinks the blonde bunny has suitors. However, will she choose?"

That makes me scowl even more. Not only do I not know what to do with their claims of a goddamn harem lining up for me, I also don't like the insinuation I'd have to *choose* one of them. It's putting the cart before the horse, I know, but it bothers me to hear Rufus say it.

"Oh, shut up, Ru-Ru," I mutter, pulling out my phone to look up the ranges of the last show I spotted in the book in front of me.

"Touchy, touchy. Guess I won't suggest *Seven Brides for Seven Brothers,*" he snarks, picking up his book and flipping the pages.

"Clearly, our Dolly would put a hit on six of them. Greedy, greedy."

Narrowing my eyes, I pointedly ignore him while researching on my phone. I'm not greedy; I just refuse to be pigeonholed into the antiquated idea that monogamy is the only option. I'm a feminist.

Yeah, that's it.

So Am I

Delores

After my classes are over, I trudge back to the Tower via one of the 'safe routes' the ladies in the infirmary marked for me. There are quite a few, depending on where I'm coming from and where I'm headed, which is comforting.

I marked emergency-only routes in bright red on my Apex app—those are underground and only to be used in the most dire situations. The nurses told me if we use them and a pred sees us, it could give away the location of prey housing if someone looks hard enough. I don't want to get a bunch of people who have been kind to me killed, so I won't even consider using these tunnels unless I have absolutely no other choice.

The Shird is close to the Tower, but the roundabout path I'm taking doubles the time to get home. I don't have work study with Aubrey tonight, but I have homework in nearly every class. Most of it is lengthy essays, because I've read so far ahead of the curriculum at this point I could probably take a final and pass.

Simply passing isn't good enough for Lucille, so I have to buckle down and get some work done over the weekend. The twenty-page paper on the 'Glorious Formation of the Apex Council' is looming over me like the sword of Damocles and I have no idea how I'm going to pretend to kiss those wrinkly old farts' asses for that many pages.

When I emerge from the tunnel just inside the walls of the Tower, it occurs to me I don't have a damned thing to eat. I've run through the small order I received from Amazon last week, and I didn't have time to place another. Sighing, I remember the vending machines in the Shird with a frown of displeasure. Tasteless health bars and bits of freeze-dried meat sounds unappetizing as fuck, but I have neither the supplies nor the space to do much else.

I can't bother Fitz by asking him to help me, either. He's done enough to take care of me since I arrived. It feels like I'm a kept woman and this summer I vowed to let no one 'own' me ever again.

Delivery it is, I suppose.

Walking out of the stairway, I head to my room, dropping my things before I look up menus. My phone buzzes, distracting me from my mission, and I curse under my breath. *Having an entire student body hunting you really puts a goddamn crimp in your fucking life, let me tell you.* Things would be so much easier if I could go to the damn cafeteria.

"Go for Dolly," I mutter when I answer.

"Is that how you answer your phone for your two bestest friends in the entire world?" Rufus tsks.

I can imagine him shaking his badger-striped head as if disappointed, and it brings a small smile to my lips. "Only when I'm trying to dig up dinner. I just left you guys. What could have happened in the past thirty minutes that's so urgent?"

"Is that her? Dolly, we miss yoooooooou!" Cori squeals in the background, and I immediately realize I'm on speaker.

If only they understood they're my only friends, and trusting them is taking me some time. I'm having trouble accepting they only want to talk to me because they like me, not because they want something.

That sounds a bit 'wah wah, poor little rich girl', but it's true.

There are people helping me, but it puts them in danger and doesn't really protect me. The nurses and the raccoons can't defend me if a pack of dingoes breaks down this door. My guys' positions as staff limit them. It's not *forbidden* for Fitz or any of them to be with me, but I don't want them to lose their jobs, either. The Council instructed my parents to send me here to either fight or die, and I have no idea what they get out of that. I was a blip on their radar before, besides being the Drew heir apparent, but they're eager to see my life end at Apex now.

I'm convinced all preds over fifty are assholes who take pleasure in routinely destroying everything good to keep their power.

It's hard, but I finally decide to trust Rufus and Cori enough to show my underbelly. "You guys might be the only ones who give a shit—save Fitz. Everyone else wants to serve me up as stew," I grumble. "Besides the dickhead in Shifter History, my other professors tolerate me more than anything."

"We covered this earlier, hot sauce. You've got your hooks in more than the playboy and his softie boyfriend. What about Mr. Big Bad Tiger? 'She belongs to us' is a helluva statement, girl. Methinks Professor Felix has more than *protecting* your fluffy butt in mind."

Rolling my eyes at the honey badger's eager matchmaking, I consider his words. I'm sure it is a big deal to 'claim' me as under their protection, but he did that for Fitz. I mean, all Felix ever does is smirk and call me Barbie—which I *hate*. Lucille's insistence on my perfect image has always limited my hair color choices, and even though I'm doing my thing now, I've been hesitant to step over that last line.

But nothing's stopping me now, is it?

Sure, someone might tell Lucille, but that's different. She's not within arm's reach and neither are Bruno nor Bruiser. They wouldn't be able to take their vengeance with a wild pair of scissors. I pause for a moment, turning the idea over in my mind. They never discovered the tattoos I got over the summer, but those are covered unless I'm in the shower. This is a much bigger statement of independence—one I can't hide under clothing.

"Dollface, you still there?"

I squeeze my hands into fists, trying to psych myself up. Rufus and Cori both have amazing hair, but if this gets fucked up, I'll never hear the end. My enemies are already dinging on me for my supposed flaws every time they see me. But who gives a shit, right?

Okay, Dolly, woman up and ask. You can do this. Your parents can't control you anymore.

"Well… I was thinking… Felix is such a dick to me in class—always calling me out and using weird tactics to force me to be tougher. He protected me in public, but in class, it's like he's… hell, it doesn't matter."

"Dolly, did he do anything to hurt you?" Cori's worried voice chimes over the line, and I groan inwardly.

I didn't mean to suggest that.

Felix has never harmed me, and something deep inside of me believes he wouldn't. But his constant picking puts me on edge, and I feel like I don't live up to his standards as—either as a student or as his brother's… friend? Obviously, he's far from perfect, because he's here at Apex, instead of being a Raj with the other Khan psychos, but I can't say that to his face. I'm pretty sure it wouldn't end well.

"No Cori, he didn't hurt me. He gave me a scare a time or two, but I think that was *testing* me. Maybe. But I hate when he calls me Barbie—it's so demeaning!"

"Let's teach him a lesson, bombshell." I can almost hear Rufus' smirk over the phone as he chuckles. "He's old enough to know that pulling a girl's pigtails isn't how you tell her you like her. Whatever shall we do to frost his cookies?"

My lips curve up as I think about his constant focus on my hair, and how someone as controlling as Felix would get infuriated with a major change. If I have Rufus and Cori dye my hair a completely wild color, I can stick it to him *and* Lucille in one fell swoop. Plus, I can reclaim another piece of myself.

I decide what I want to look like, not them.

"I need to study first, but… maybe later you could come over and we could order a pizza and scheme? I think I have the perfect plan to vex him and all the people who think they can tell me who to be," I say quietly, hoping they won't decline.

Even if I place an order on Amazon, I don't know if I can do this on my own. I need steady hands and moral support to do something as big as this. After all, over the summer, my friend Clotilda had to hold my hand the entire time I was getting tattooed and pierced.

"Are you asking us to have… a slumber party?" Cori squeals into the receiver.

"Um, I guess I am." I smile to myself, realizing this is the first sleepover I've had that didn't involve the Heathers coming in drunk or high and spending the night trying to 'fix' me.

Rufus barks a laugh. "Oh, sweetheart. You have no idea what you've started. Tell us what we need to bring."

Hopefully, this doesn't get me evicted by the secret couple upstairs. I don't know where else I would go.

"Guys? Are you sure you know how to do something this complex?"

"Pfft," Cori replies, picking through strands of my hair to wrap another foil. "I've been coloring hair since I could reach the shelves. I can't even remember what my natural hair color is at this point."

Rufus hums his agreement, working on the opposite side of her. "Yeah, my aunt Brandine had me help at her salon when I wasn't delivering product as a kid. I know my way around forty volume, Dolly bear. Don't worry your cute little nose over it."

My eyes drift to the mirror and I feel the butterflies start again. Every rebellion this summer started with those nervous buggers, and I can't imagine it will stop soon. The last big decision I made before then ended with finding out I'm prey and being excommunicated, so it's not surprising. I'm still working on the damage prom night did to my shaky self-esteem, but I hope this will help.

"The picture was so complicated looking, but I trust you guys know what you're doing."

"Oh, Coco and I have been doing one another since we got to this hellhole. Our hair, of course," he smirks, winking at me in the mirror as he uses a stinky brush full of dye to paint a section of hair carefully. "Sometimes, preds even pay us. It's a convenient side hustle."

I blink.

Should I be paying for this? Oh, fuck, Dolly! You didn't even ask if they wanted money for the color or materials or anything. What a fucking idiot.

"If you want me to pay you, I'm happy to. I can pull money out of the ATM in Honeywell tomorrow..."

"Hush your mouth!" Cori comes back around to face me, her expression irritated. "We would never charge *you*—only the bobble headed morons. They have more money than sense, and it tickles us to get them to part with their parents' coin, only to get in trouble for doing it."

"I love me some drama," Rufus coos. "It's almost as much fun as fucking the uber-jocks with 'I'm not gay' complexes, although, lately, the field has been barren. Maybe you should tell us about your adventures in sausage-slapping, Dolly. Give the parched a sip."

Oh, no.

I don't... how am I supposed to talk with them about what Fitz and I did together? I know they won't judge me, but I've never engaged in this type of 'girl talk' before. Will they want... details? "Um... well... I don't know if I should..."

Cori bursts into laughter, covering her mouth with her hand. When she finally gets herself under control, she gives me a serious look. "We are a *vault*, Dolly. Your secrets stay with us and vice versa. If you're too nervous to talk about whatever... *sandwiches* you're dining on, we understand. But damn, girl. Your face is a dead giveaway."

My eyes widen. I*t is? Oh, shit. What if someone ever tries to interrogate me?*

I cover my face with my hands, trying not to disturb them as they continue circling me with dye bowls and foil. "Guys, I have no experience with lying. I mean, I got away with little white lies occasionally, but Lucille can damned near smell deception, so I didn't try it often. What if I need to lie to protect Fitz or one of the guys? You're going to have to teach me."

"Did I hear sweet little Dolly ask us to corrupt her?" Rufus crows. "I have been waiting for this! Coco, we're going to need a sound-track for this. Please?"

Cori skips to the counter and pairs her phone with my Bluetooth speaker before clapping her hands. "Okay, Ru-Ru. Let the corruption begin."

I blink as Taylor Swift blares out of the speaker, and Rufus waves his dye brush at me playfully.

Sweet Hermes, what in the hell did I just agree to?

Look What You Made Me Do

Delores

Strolling up to the lake in a school issued one piece and shorts, I smile to myself when I feel the heat of Felix's gaze on me. My recently colored hair is in a perky ponytail to keep it out of my face and I have on my new tennis shoes. Despite his irritating demeanor, the ability to get out of my uniform on some days is making this and dancing my favorite sections.

I like that he's staring, but I'd cut my tongue out before I admit it out loud.

Unlike last time, the other students are filtering into the makeshift classroom dressed appropriately. The email said we'd likely get wet and might shift, so we should wear appropriate gear from our academy kit. I'm not excited about getting my fresh dye wet, but as usual, this asshole waited until the last minute to send the message. I think he gets off on inconveniencing students as much as possible—especially me.

"Oh, look. We have Rainbow Magic Barbie now; how cute," Felix says as he saunters past. His smirk makes me want to snarl, and I realize Fitz probably tattled on me.

Having a stalker does fuck with your privacy somewhat.

I turn my nose up at him and walk over to the chairs someone placed in rows next to the lake. If he thinks he can intimidate me, he's dead wrong. I don't care how sexy and muscled he is in that tank top and low-slung board shorts. Though...

Fuck me if he isn't goddamn mouth watering.

"Put your worthless asses in these seats and listen up!" Felix stands in front of the chairs, glaring at everyone again. "Last week, we watched Barbie and her counterfeit copy go at it like it was their time of the month. Fairy Magic back there destroyed her prey, but I'm not confident that will always be the case. Fighting based on rage will only get you so far, especially if your opponent is better trained than the Golden Puppy was by her karate panda."

My hand flies to my mouth, and I stifle the laugh that almost escapes. I think he might hate the Heathers as much as I do. Though, honestly, Felix seems to hate damn near all the students, so maybe I'm overthinking it.

Gold looks furious in her non-regulation two-piece and booty shorts in sparkling gold. The others wore the same bikinis in their respective colors, along with the shorts and slip-on shoes. "My lawyer is drafting a motion as we speak. You should be ready, Professor."

That makes him throw his head back and roar with mirth. When he finally stops, he arches a brow at her. "You should send him to meet with my father if he's suing me. Say your goodbyes first, though. While he enjoyed the piece in the Predator Press about the 'unnamed professor' who encourages violence between students, he wasn't happy about the accompanying suggestion that the Khans don't have control of their heirs."

My eyes pop open. Holy shit. I didn't see the piece because the minute Cori said my ex-friends were taking over the paper; I knew to avoid it. It was likely Pink's idea, and she conferred with her Daddy about it without mentioning what their plans were.

Who is stupid enough to print something negative about the Khan Raj and expect to live?

All four of the Heathers pale under their spray tans as Felix crosses his arms over his chest, grinning. "When I explained myself to his assistant over the phone, my father ordered him to send Fitz and I bonuses next month. He may not want us around, but he applauds our representation of the fierce Khan name."

Man, did that gambit backfire.

Not only did they fail to get Felix in trouble, they drew the ire of the former king of Bloodstone. They have to be shitting their pants right now. None of their parents will enjoy being on his bad side. The tiger in question walks over to me and winks, looking pleased with himself. Even though his declaration helps him and his twin, the other one does not help me and I intend to find out what he was thinking.

"Why did you tell the staff I'm under Khan protection? You had to realize that would hurt me more than help, Sir." I put a hard emphasis on the word, feeling just irritable enough to rankle him.

His eyes narrow and he cracks his neck, giving me a look I can't decipher before walking back to the front of the class. "Today we're working on shifting, hence the proximity to the water for those of you who are aquatic. A select few of you will display the ability to half-shift—something only possible if you are top tier bloodlines like Council heirs, some powerful seconds, and royalty —but don't worry if you're unable. It means you're average and I expect that to be the case for most of you."

The silence that falls over the crowd is eerie and a brave shifter in the middle raises their hand. "Would we know if we can do this naturally or—?"

Felix looks surprised and strokes the light stubble on his chin thoughtfully. "As the future Raj and enforcer, Fitz and I could do so from a young age, though learning precision control was the struggle. Many don't master it, they simply can go 'whole hog' or nothing at all. If you have the innate ability but have not done it yet, focusing on shifting partially will hopefully lead you to the skill. Those who know, should be able to achieve this based on heritage. Step into the appropriate space for your kind."

I chew my lip nervously. Bruno can half-shift and Lucille has razor-sharp control over every part of her shift.

Technically, I should head for the ground or lake, but since I turned out to be prey, I doubt that bloodline extends to me. *Who the hell has ever heard of alpha prey?* No one, so I'm not going down there only to humiliate myself.

Todd and one of his idiot friends stand. Then the Heathers, a wolf, two smaller feline preds, and some bears join them. The three aquatic shifters follow and my nose twitches as I try to identify them by their scent, like Fitz has been teaching me. I can tell who's pred and prey well enough now, but defining the danger to me based on species is in development.

I'm game to learn everything I can while I'm forced to attend Apex because if I survive, I'll need it. Lucille might put up with me during my school years, but she'll cut me off the minute I graduate just for thwarting their plans. I have to support and defend myself when the time comes. I don't want to end up beholden to people I can't trust ever again.

Watching the candidates line up, I frown. In truth, I'm still not fully connected with my bunny. My ingrained training to be a pred conflicts with her natural ones, though not as much as I expected, so I feel divided. The desire to rip into those who wrong me and the fear of being attacked doesn't mesh. I often have to choose which side I want to listen to and it involves more brain work than anyone told me my animal would require. My bunny rages when she feels cornered more often than she wants to flee— something that could get me in trouble with preds more formidable than my ex-BFFs.

I have no idea what to do about any of it.

"Why are you still sitting there like a lump, Rainbow?" Felix arches a brow at me, motioning with his hand. "Get down here with the other heirs, as instructed."

By Hermes' winged feet, this dude won't give me a break—ever.

"I've been disowned, Professor. You're aware of that; everyone is. I don't belong down there since my… problem," I reply quietly. Making me admit that in front of everyone was shitty and I'm tired of people making me feel shitty because they can. I thought he was demanding, not cruel, but I may have to re-evaluate.

Snorting, he shakes his head. "Council bloodlines are the strongest in their respective areas. Removing a title from someone doesn't change what's running through their veins, whether your parents would prefer it or not. You were born into the power and I won't let you waste it; get down here."

Something about his tone holds a disdain that seems to be about more than my situation, and I make a note to ask Fitz why this would piss his brother off so much. I can't imagine he's truly angry at my parents—not at this level, at least. We barely know one another. I finally meet his eyes as I rise from the metal chair, kicking off my shoes so I don't ruin them. His approval washes over me and I have to clear my throat as a spark of desire lights in my chest.

I'm not sure if my damage causes the sexiness of his love-hate shit or not, but I can't find the wherewithal to care.

By the time I join the other students, Felix has pulled his shirt off and is addressing the class. "Full shifts are deeply linked to our animal sides; you will learn to control your human brain during them eventually, but at first, it will be hard. During a half-shift, you can transform a part or parts of your body while your mind remains normal. This is a normal level of half-shift."

His body changes within seconds, showing feline features, fur, claws, and fangs, but in a shape that is more akin to a were-animal than a shifter. It's dangerous and hotter than hell, so I press my thighs together to avoid letting my scent travel to the smirking tiger. I've seen my parents do more specific things, but Lucille is far better at it than Bruno. Like Felix, she's seamless from form to form in a blink.

I'll never be able to do that shit; hell, I'm lucky I can hear my animal.

"Of course, very few of you will have the ability to do this," he says casually and my eyes widen at the seductive rumble of his words coming out of the feline form. "Speaking while half-shifted is only for the most powerful and well-bred lines, like the Khans."

Todd snorts and I hear his stage whisper to the Heathers. "He means it's only possible with families full of forcibly bred relatives like the Khans."

"Oh, good. Maybe the half-breed boobalicious bunny can do it, too," Pink snarks in return.

That's when a wave of fury that dwarfs all the previous ones fills me from head to toe. I feel the animal within stretch, spread, and push against me hard enough to shove my consciousness aside. My hands ache as they curl into fists and my gums feel like they're on fire. I have to grit my teeth as I turn my burning stare on the two idiots who used to be part of my life.

"Man, she's even uglier angry than she was giving head," Todd says in a guffaw.

Bad move, asshole.

Power surges inside me and I leap forward from my position, knocking into the hyena with the force of my strong rabbit legs. Once he's on the ground, I wrap clawed fingers around his throat, keeping one point on his jugular and placing another by his eyeball. "Say shit like that again and we'll find out if you look good with an eyepatch, Captain Short Dick."

Laughter echoes around me and my prey struggles, but finds he can't move with muscular legs and arms pinning him in place. Hate twists his once adorable features, and I blink as I realize I spoke in a partially shifted form. My grip tightens on the lying jackass beneath me, wanting to punish him for spreading rumors about me in public. Before I can make good on that desire, a hand clamps down on my shoulder. I look up to see an amused tiger man with lust fogging his golden eyes as he stares at me.

"You can't kill him for being a lying douchebag, Barbie. That's not within the rules," Felix says as he holds his hand out. "His words made you angry enough to show your potential, so we'll take that as enough revenge for today."

Licking my lips, I note the sharpened teeth in my mouth in surprise. This is more shifted than I've been since prom, but I don't feel weak and scared like I did then. Now I feel in control and powerful—ready to take on anyone who tries to hurt me or the people I care about. It's a good feeling, so I loosen my grip on the sputtering hyena and move off him.

"Frigid bitch," Todd splutters as he gasps for breath.

Felix whirls around, growling low as he moves me aside. "You'll have to choose one or the other, Deputy Dog. She's a frigid bitch or a whore who gives bad blowjobs. Choose wisely."

Gold lets out a loud, nasty laugh as she looks at the crowd. "Now we know she's fucking him for sure. Tell your parents everyone— they won't put up with favoritism at Apex."

I arch a brow, leaving Felix with my ex as I walk towards her with a fangy, buck-toothed grin. "I think favoritism is one of the primary advantages of Apex for Council heirs. Ask any of the other preds in this circle if they think people with certain last names get treated better."

My words stir up a cacophony of shouts and protests, making Gold and Pink whirl to calm the masses down before they lose their pedestals. The distraction gives me time to get back to Felix, who's now dangling the hyena by the scruff of his neck. Todd is almost in tears as he tries to get free and I sense as much as I needed an intervention earlier, my professor needs one now.

"Of course, he could just admit we only had sex once—on prom night when I emerged—and he couldn't find my clit with a map and two hands. Then I shifted for the first time, which was unlucky because his fumbling tore up all my clothes. When he saw I was a bunny, he and his idiot friends tried to eat me. I can only assume he'd be bad at that, too—in any version."

Felix blinks at me, logic returning to his expression as he drops my ex on the ground and doubles over, laughing. Once he breaks the silence, the rest of the students join in and I grin to myself. I won't win any of them over right away, but if I can get one less person to bother me, it's worth the bullshit I just had to deal with.

"We're out of here. The atmosphere sucks," Purple says, looking at Gold for reassurance. Gold nods and waits for Todd's friends to scoop him up before they all stomp away from class in a huff.

"Mmm. Since the trash took itself out, let's work on shifting in a bigger group. Steer clear of Rainbow, though. She's in a mood today."

Felix winks at me, and I let out a sigh of relief.

Maybe I'll survive in this class, after all.

She Makes Me Feel Like

Chess

Fitz is gleefully hopping up the steps to the first floor of the Tower, his enthusiasm buzzing over me like fine champagne. Ever since he got his hands on her the other night, he's barely been in control of his hyperactivity. I don't know how in Fenrir his students are dealing with him; Felix and I are at our wits' end.

He insisted we come visit her because, according to him, 'you've been avoiding my baby girl and I know it upsets her'. I can't correct him, unfortunately; my struggle with accepting my attraction to Delores is making me too nervous to be around her. Fitz always knows when I'm having trouble with shit, and I suppose he gave me two weeks to sort it out on my own. Now, he's pushing the envelope because he can.

If I didn't love him, I'd throttle him.

"What if she's… indisposed, Fitz? We can't just bust into her room," I protest weakly.

My lover claps a hand on my shoulder, grinning broadly. "I do it every day, babe. My girl expects me to visit her after class and she enjoyed my visit when she was indisposed the other night."

I roll my eyes, sighing at his typical cluelessness. While I'm sure he took care of our angel, I'm less certain she wants him showing up without notice constantly. If we weren't so secure in our relationship, I'd be jealous, but I know Fitz would never let me go. His fury at his father's edict with Felix told me everything I needed to know about my place with him.

He yanks the door to the room open, calling out to her as we walk in. "Baby Girl, I'm here! By all means, stay undressed if you're naked. Chess is dying to see."

Heat travels to my face so fast I get a head rush and I glare at the tiger. "I... I..."

Luckily, she's not standing starkers in the outer room. It takes a moment, but I hear water in the en suite and her lilting soprano singing a pop song. It makes me smile broadly; encouraging her to pursue her genuine passion is one of the best things I've done since we came to this place. I'm still patting myself on the back when I realize Fitz is opening the door to the occupied bathroom. A muffled admonishment follows a squeak of surprise and he swaggers back out with a satisfied grin.

"She'll be out soon," he tells me before he flops on her bed. "Come sit with me."

I give him a doubtful look, eyeing the bed. "I don't know if I should climb onto Delores' bed without her giving me permission, Fitz."

"Aw, Chessie, don't be so tight-assed. Our girl thinks you're hot, too. She won't mind, I promise." He bats his lashes, sprawling out in a delicious pose that makes his shirt ride up over his chiseled abs. His hand pats the spot next to him again and I take a step closer, tentatively.

Shifters who live in groups like ours, particularly canines and felines, enjoy contact. Fitz has never been good with respecting people's space—something that likely comes from being part of the royal family. No one tells the Raj's family 'no',though I know for sure Fitz would accept it if they did. Neither he nor Felix have ever had to work for companionship, and they definitely didn't need to force it. If Dolly had told him to fuck off and meant it, he'd be pouting like a child, but he'd do it.

That tells me she's allowing him to virtually stalk her; he's got her consent.

Instead of joining him, I walk over to the bookshelves she's filling. My lips curve as I see the usual assortment of romance novels, fantasy, and mysteries I'd expect. I bet she has overflowing cases at home because there are stacks of songbooks and sheet music covering her piano bench. Between her love of singing and theater, I see a dreamer in this girl. Reading was likely an escape from her home life and I understand that. My hobbies are all how I kept myself occupied when all I had at Bloodstone was Fitz.

"Do you think we should invite her on our trip to town? She'd love it, and I'm sure she needs more supplies food-wise by now." Fitz's eyes light up and he whispers, "If we get her proper food, she'll have to come to our place to cook it!"

That makes my cat purr happily. He likes the idea of us caring for the girl, especially if I get to cook for her. I've always done the meals for the three Khan refugees and it makes me giddy to think Dolly might join us. My brow furrows for a second when I consider whether Felix will be okay with it, but from the look on Fitz's face, that will not matter.

My enforcer plans to brute force this girl into all our lives if it kills him, it seems.

I give into Fitz as my feline rumbles in my chest, walking over and dropping next to him to curl up. He knows I enjoy taking care of people, especially those I care about, and I know he's stroking my cheetah in perfect time to his plans. His arms wrap around me and he presses a kiss to my temple. "I had a good plan, didn't I, baby?"

"Yes," I admit with a sigh. "I would like that very much."

The door to the bathroom opens, letting steam out as the lovely Dolly exits wrapped in a big, fluffy towel. "Hey, Chess! I haven't seen you in forever. I'm glad Fitz brought you to see the room that he helped me commandeer."

My eyes widen at the array of tattoos visible on her pale skin. She definitely went buck wild this summer, like Fitz told us. I hadn't gotten a good look at the ones crawling up her legs because of her fishnets and she has one on her left bicep of a goth-styled cartoon bunny that's adorable as hell. I take a moment to find my voice to reply, and when I do, it's rough. "You got ink over the summer, huh?"

Her smile brightens before she walks over to her dresser, pulling out lingerie that makes me gulp, and Fitz squeezes me to his side. "Sure did. My friends talked me into it and I'm a little addicted. I'd love to get more, but I have to wait for the right ideas to strike me."

"We could take you, baby girl. I've got plenty of my own, but I'm always game to add more," the tiger says before giving me an excited look. "Chessie doesn't have much—maybe you can talk him into more? I mean, all three of us have the required Khan ink and brands, but he's never gone past that."

She turns quickly, holding onto the towel to keep it from falling. "I'd love to! We could have a big outing. Maybe even the other grumpy pusses would come. I mean, since I discovered that amazing kitchen, I want to get food I can make like a normal person. Delivery is getting boring."

I cock a brow at her with a shy smile. "Do you know how to cook?"

"Well, no." She wrinkles her nose and walks over to the bathroom with her clothes, talking to us from just inside the door as she dresses. "But I'm a fast learner. I can use YouTube and with that setup, I should be good."

Fitz's lack of movement when she didn't close the door was distracting, but after a moment, I catch what she actually said. "Did you say… you discovered a kitchen? Where?"

That gets my lover's attention and his eyes get wide as saucers. "Here?"

Dolly pops her head out as she braids her gorgeous sherbet colored locks. "Yes, here, you goons. I couldn't sleep the other night and I kind of went on a walkabout… I found out that the second floor is a big dining room and kitchen with so much cool shit. It's ridiculous for it to sit empty."

Renard and Aubrey do not let people explore their domain.

"Uh, Angel? What… What happened when you were wandering? Did you… run into anyone?" I ask carefully. Neither of the winged members of our group mentioned this, and I'm astounded.

"Duh," she replies as she walks out in a pair of skintight ripped jeans and a cropped black hoodie with strategic cuts in the arms. "But it's okay. I'm allowed to clean up the second floor and get the kitchen working. Scout's honor."

My mouth hangs open in shock as she makes the gesture everyone recognizes for pledging, and I turn to look at Fitz. He's in a similar state of shock and even shakes his head as if trying to make sure he heard correctly. "Aubrey or Renard… gave you permission to use another floor? Alone?"

She rolls her eyes at me and plops on the bench to pull on her boots. "Yes. In fact, I'm free to roam wherever I want. So ha!"

That revelation is paired with her sticking her tongue out at us, and I laugh softly. Fitz was right for once; this girl has literally wrapped all five of us in some weird web. Not even the grouchy book dragon is immune to her charms. They don't allow us free rein in their Tower, and we've been friends for over a decade. Yet

Delores Drew waltzed in with the sound of punk rock and her middle finger raised… only to enchant every single one of us.

She really might be an angel.

"Are you ready to go, Angel?" I ask with a soft smile. She nods and I roll to my feet, holding a hand out to Fitz.

"We can take Felix's Jag since there's three of us. His bike only seats two safely."

She snorts, covering her mouth as her sapphire eyes dance. "You don't want to ride on the handlebars, Chess? It'd be dangerous, but fun as shit if it isn't far."

"No, no," I blurt. "We can take the convertible. No need for danger."

Both my wicked tiger and the smoky eyed temptress look at me with similar teasing smiles on their face. It occurs to me that I have a thing for bad boys—and girls—who push my boundaries. Dolly was teasing, but I know she would have tried that stunt if I'd said yes. Fitz absolutely would have let her and I'm going to be the voice of reason in this little triad, for sure.

I can live with that.

"Now that we've established Chessie is a wet blanket, can we go? I can't wait for you to feel that engine purr for you, baby girl." She gives Fitz a reproving look and I rub my hand over my face. "What? She likes vibration and we both know it! I'm being considerate of her needs."

"I'd rather take my Mustang and let you feel my girl purr," Dolly interjects. "Both of you."

My face flames as I look at Fitz for help, but he's just giving her a dreamy look. He finally snaps out of it and replies with a smirk. "I'd love to see how you handle a stick, and so would Chess. Lead the way."

Merciful Bast, I hope these two don't get worse while we're out or I will not survive this trip—and we'll get kicked out of the store for certain.

Everybody Wants to Rule the World
Lucille

Lucille

Lucille

"Matilda! Get your feathered ass in here!"

I rise from the Queen Anne desk in my study, heels clicking on the Amazonian Ipe wood floor. I'd prefer Italian marble, but Bruno insists on flexing his manhood by filling the house with endangered pelts and materials. As if anyone assumes *he's* in charge of this family simply because we've decorated our home with expensive trophies—the idea is laughable.

He's little more than a crocodile handbag I drag out for special occasions, but I don't mind the false front. The right people see him strut and posture, and I'm able to conceal my activities for the Society without scrutiny. The general population of predators has no idea how much of their day-to-day lives are decided by a select group of elites led by a woman, and I prefer to keep it that way.

Despite the *survival of the fittest* atmosphere of pred life, they don't give females equal credit for their abilities. Our men are no more enlightened than human ones, and I don't have the patience to justify my decisions simply because my balls are on the inside of my body. Knowing that the revelation of who they bow to would horrify and emasculate them certainly improves my day.

After all, isn't secretly wielding the bigger stick more satisfying?

"Yes, Madame? How can I be of service?"

The sound of my dingbat assistant rushing in abruptly jerks me out of my ruminations, reminding me I'd called for her. "Where were you?" I scowl.

"I—I was downstairs taking a meal with the kitchen staff. You asked me to get out of your sight. I..."

For the love of Hera's peacocks, this dimwit is going to ruin my day simply by breathing the same air as me. "Matilda. Stop. Talking. Now."

Her stature shrinks even more and her hands fidget with her glasses shakily, clearly unable to execute even the most basic of responses. A sharp jerk of her head shows she understands me, and I let out a sigh of irritation as I roll my eyes. The wounded dove act is worse than her stammering idiocy.

"Get my drink and give me the weekly report. I have four meetings today and I cannot attend them without the information I tasked you with locating." I glare at her as I walk to the large lounge by the window, dropping onto it with feline grace.

"Y-Yes, Madame," she stammers as she hurries to the sideboard to pour my martini. She's still trembling as she stirs the vodka gingerly, making certain not to bruise it with incorrect technique. I've drilled that into her numb skull over time, and the care she takes not to fuck up makes my leopard snarl in satisfaction. Fear is the most intoxicating scent in the world.

And I bask in its musk as often as possible.

"Start with my daughter. The last message I left her did its job—she's terrified of disappointing me or besmirching our family name."

The hawk shifter stares at me behind her horn-rimmed glasses as she hands me my glass. "Yes, Madame. From everything I could gather, she has adjusted well to her environment. There have been a few unfortunate incidents with fellow students, but her grades so far are excellent."

Eyes narrowing, I bare my fangs at her. While I've forbidden Matilda from having direct contact with Delores since she left for Apex—since her failed emergence, really—I still expect intel. "I could have found that out myself. Tell me who she is keeping company with and pray you don't disappoint me again. I'm sure Bruiser would love to escort you home this evening."

Feathers flutter through the air as she loses control of her animal for a moment, stammering, "I... she... Miss Delores has two friends, both second-year students in her arts program. Their names are Rufus and Cori. I have not yet traced their heritage, but once I do, I will prepare a dossier for you."

Hmmm.

That's not the company I wanted to hear about, but information about other families with ties to Apex is never a bad thing. "What about men? I've heard whispers of a professor following her around. Delores is not unattractive, and some preds prefer their meat fattened."

The look of horror on her face makes me throw my head back and laugh. Oh, I adore shocking the diminutive moron I employ to deal with shit beneath my pay grade, although none of what I said should have been surprising. It's no secret I have little maternal instinct outside of amassing more power through my hcir's marriage. That I birthed the ungrateful bitch means less to me than her value on the open market.

"She... she... Well, there are rumors from the main office that your spy has frequently seen her with the younger of the Khan twins. She has the other as a professor, as well as the consort. And —and she has a work study with the Draconis' exiled heir. That is all I know because... something happened to her dorm room and she hasn't been living there. Your surveillance is not of use at the moment."

Her stammering admission makes my face light up. While this isn't enough to advance my plans, the knowledge that my chunky offspring is cozying up to some of the most well-connected and rare exiles in the entire school is quite pleasing. Sipping my drink, I consider how I can use this to my advantage.

I need to speak with the other birdbrain I have under my thumb.

"Hand me my phone, Matilda. If Henrietta can confirm what you've told me, I will spare you Bruiser's company for another day," I reply absently. My mind is spinning with the possibility of having dirt on the Khan ambush to use as leverage in future nego-tiations.

Delicious is the word that comes to mind.

When she scuttles over with my DiePhone, I snatch it out of her hand and flick through my contacts impatiently. The sound of multiple rings makes my animal pace, and I roar into the speaker when the Headmistress finally answers. "When I call, you answer immediately, Henrietta Shirdal, or so help me…"

A flurry of squawking and excuses echo in my office as she tries to apologize for her insolence. I hold my glass up for Matilda, watching her fetch my refill as the eagle continues to babble inanities.

When I tire of it, I snap, "Henrietta, if you don't shut the hell up, I will eat you myself." She finally shuts her beak, and the silence is blissful. "Is my daughter consorting with your staff? Don't you dare lie to me."

"I—I don't know if she's… I do not know about intimate acts. But she… the rumor is Felix Khan declared her under Khan protec-tion. I believe it because she moved to another room without office help and I'm not sure where she's living. Plus, Fitzgerald follows her around campus like a cat in heat. I am sorry, Madame; that's all I know."

A laugh bubbles out of my lips and the pure joy of knowing I have ammunition against those feline fools floods my veins. Oh, how I hate having to work with those filthy mobsters on Bloodstone, but I've never had a choice. The Society's illegal activities are inextricably entwined with the empires of both my father and those mangy felines, but now…

Now I have a direct line to their fallen Raj via my disappointing progeny, and I couldn't have planned this better if I had schemed it myself.

Everyone in our world knows about the shame of Felix Khan and his exile to Apex with his playboy brother and their orphan companion. Clearly, his preference for rare meat hasn't lessened, and my daughter bedding the three of them couldn't be a more convenient blackmail tool. If she whores herself out to the two rarest shifters in the place as well, I'll have a royal flush.

Who knew the blonde dipshit would ever make herself useful?

"Madame Lucille? Are you there?" Henrietta asks carefully.

I glare at the phone, unamused by the interruption. "Of course I'm here, you twit. I was considering my options."

"Yes, Madame. Forgive me," she squawks.

"Shut up, you Kentucky Fried idiot. You should have called me the second you heard that rumor. Here's what you're going to do to make up for your lapse in judgment." I pause for a moment, waiting for her to gather materials to record my instructions. "I want you to throw a huge celebration for Halloween. Spare no expense, and make attendance mandatory—costumes as well."

"Even for the staff?"

"Of course for the staff, you fucking idiot! I want every single body on that campus in attendance, or *your* head will roll. Remember, your father cast you out years ago, Henrietta. He won't lift a wing if I decide to end your life. I want my daughter and her suitors there so I can gather more information, so make it happen. Do you understand?" The last part is a snarl, and I have to calm my leopard down before I shift on the spot.

More babbling and apologies follow, but I hang up. I've made my point, and set the wheels in motion. What I need to do next is convene a meeting of the Society so we can discuss how to use Delores' new position to our advantage. Our quarterly meeting is overdue—the postponement because of my child emerging as prey, adding to my humiliation. With the plans I've conceived today, I can sit proudly at the head of the table once more.

Delores Diamond Drew's purpose has always been to facilitate my control of the Society. I didn't envision it happening in this exact manner, but the latest twist makes me once again pleased I sought… alternative methods of providing an heir for our family.

"Matilda!"

"Yes, Madame. Another drink?"

I roll my eyes and hand her the glass, letting the gears in my head turn. Delores' emergence as prey threw a wrench in my plot to use her spouse for consolidation of power, but now I have other plans for *her*. I thought she would be nothing but a thorn in my side until they killed her. What a stroke of luck she endeared herself to *three* Khans and is working for one of the most cloistered shifter species in the world. If she finds out where the dragon clash's nest is, my father's sales will quadruple. Even one female dragon would be worth more than the rest of Dimitri Rostoff's stable combined.

"Get lost," I mutter when Matilda brings the next refill. "I will call you when I'm ready to head to the salon."

She nods, pushing her glasses up her nose as she scurries out the door. I wait until I hear her footsteps fade down the hall before I check the time on my limited edition Patek Philippe watch. It's 8 a.m. here, which makes it 4 p.m. in Moscow. Dmitri should sit for his afternoon tea right about now, which makes it the perfect time to share my news.

"Dobryy den',[1] papa. I have news to report."

The harsh laughter on the other end is familiar—Dmitri Rostoff vacillates between finding me satisfactory and useless on any day. Unlike my whiny brat, I've never complained that I have to work to earn his praise. I pride myself on exceeding his low expectations at every turn, and now I head the most powerful group of preds in America. My father still isn't impressed by my position, but I can live with that for now.

"Speak."

"Delores isn't dead yet. However, she may prove useful even while she's still breathing. She's bedding the fallen Khan heirs, and has formed a close connection with a dragon."

For the first time since my erstwhile offspring humiliated us, my father's tone was filled with interest rather than scorn. I let him interrogate me, pausing for effect in all the right places. As we discuss my plans for the academy, he grows more and more excited. The possibility of locating not one but two hidden shifter species has him salivating. If it works, we may expand to scour the other academies around the world for vulnerable exiles to exploit.

When he disconnects the call, I feel the glow of my father's pride for the first time since I sold my sister at the auctions.

Perhaps Delores isn't entirely worthless after all.

Bully

Delores

We're getting close to midterms, and all the professors are buckling down to prepare for what I assume will be a grueling exam in every subject. My only saving grace is that Fitz bought enough lingerie to keep me wearing new things for the entirety of October and insists on playing 'hot or cold' guessing games about my daily choices. His texts are bright spots in the drudgery of my long, exam prep-filled days.

I'm not worried about passing most of my classes. In fact, I'm even excelling in dance now that I have the right equipment.

The only question mark in my GPA is the class I'm headed to right now—Shifter History. The grubby little jackhole who teaches it has been grading every assignment, no matter how thorough, as low as he can without being outright dishonest. I have to double- and triple-check each paper I hand in to make certain there aren't any typos, extra spaces, or grammatical errors, as if I'm submitting a piece to the fucking New York Times. Otherwise,

Professor Abel dings me like he's some goddamn Oxford scholar instead of a random teacher assigning college essays.

I'd love to know how people get the absolute *chutzpah* to rip apart the work of others when they're not qualified to do so. He gets off on being rude and condescending, and except for the heirs he sucks up to, everyone hates him, even other professors. It's not surprising he's the only professor on campus to be voted off the island and exiled from staff housing.

Even Felix seemed surprised by how closely I have to weigh every word and phrase to ensure I don't fall into a syntax pitfall that will earn me another point subtracted from my grade. If my guys didn't already dislike Professor Abel, I'm pretty sure they hate him now. My laptop crashed one night, and I lost an entire section of my paper. Crying like a baby the first time I appeared on their porch wasn't on my to-do list, but I was so overwhelmed by everything, I couldn't hold back.

It took all three of us to stop Fitz from stomping out of the house to hunt the Tasmanian devil shifter down so he could kill him.

The compromise we settled on is arriving later in the week, and I'm torn between being excited and frustrated.

I'm trying to be as independent as possible, and while I can't control Lucille sending me shit I'm ordered to accept, Fitz is determined to solve all my problems with Khan blood money. The nefarious provenance of his cash isn't the issue, truthfully, because I'm pretty sure my parents are no cleaner than his family is. It's *depending* on someone that's bothering me. I've learned you can't trust people to be who they say they are—when you do, you inevitably get disappointed. If I don't learn to take care of myself, I'll be as useless as my ex-friends.

My declaration of independence would have a lot more credence if I hadn't bargained Fitz out of murder by allowing him to buy me an egregiously expensive replacement Smackbook. Even Chess was cajoling me into letting them help by the end, and I couldn't hold out any longer. After all, it will be a hell of a lot more useful to not have to worry about my old crappy laptop crashing again rather than accepting thousands of dollars of lace scraps, right?

Ugh. Not good, Dolly. Stop letting the hot tiger spoil you 24/7. Remember—people leave.

I want to argue with myself further, but I'm at the doorway of the lecture hall. If I don't get inside, I'll miss my chance to claim the best location for a rapid escape. Shaking my head, I scramble into the room and drop into the seat I chose on the first day. The hall is usually empty when I arrive, but I notice the scrawny fisher cat in the back corner. He meets my gaze briefly, then goes back to drawing in his notebook, as if he's worried someone will walk in and see him looking at me.

How have the Heathers terrified the student body so thoroughly that they either attack me or avoid me like I'm contagious?

I know they ruled the roost at Shifter Secondary, but Apex has five times as many students, most of them older than us. My phone dings and I sigh, deciding whether I should unlock it to see what fresh hell is being posted on the app message boards. They can't get to me via social media anymore—I deleted my old accounts and had my skunk hacker friend Clotilda set up untraceable ones to keep the harpies off my case. Once Gold figured out I gained access to the Apex app, my former besties started using the student message boards to spread lies and venom instead.

Too bad no one in this fucking place monitors student internet activity, right?

Except there *is* someone whose job it is to watch over digital student domains, but she's a six-foot tall ostrich shifter who barely gets home without some testosterone-laden asshole trying to make her dinner. Betsy sure as hell can't confront the heirs about their nasty cyberbullying—if she did, she'd be lucky if all she lost was her job.

That's how the elites win here; they control who is in charge of what, and their pawns won't fight back.

Finally giving in, swiping my DiePhone open and typing in my encryption key quickly. I discover the sound wasn't from the Apex app—instead it's an alert from the web crawlers I have on search terms that might relate to me. My eyes close as I open the video montage on YouTube—it includes clips from the run for my life, my walk of shame at the Vom Prom, my trudge across campus in Fitz's borrowed clothes, and a laugh track over my battle in the shifter circle.

Unsurprisingly, that bit has got edited to look as though Gold got the drop on me.

Just. Fucking. Great. They've threatened the A/V kids, I see.

A gasp from the back makes me turn my head and I give the fence-riding fisher cat a narrowed-eyed glare. If he thinks this video shows me being treated poorly, maybe he should grow a pair of fuzzy ones the next time the assholes in this class are torturing me. Otherwise, I don't have time for his faux outrage.

"Oh, look! It's the village bicycle, and she's parked right in the front for easy access!" Silver crows as she walks in. She's followed by Gold—who's acting like she needs the support of Pink and Purple to walk. All four of them have gotten their asses trounced in Shifter Basics in the past two weeks and Gold thinks she's going to win a court case.

I almost ask how she plays both the victim *and* the bully at the same time without her head exploding, but I don't want to give her the satisfaction of engaging with me. Instead, I flip my rainbow hair over my shoulder and pointedly close my screen. With an imperious arch of my brow, I grab my headphones and put them in my ears, hoping to end the conversation.

"Awfully dangerous to cut off one of your senses when you're on the menu, pork chop," Pink hisses as she guides her leader past me.

Continuing to pretend I can't hear is more effective than reminding her I'm a goddamned bunny, not a pig, but that doesn't mean the constant commentary about my animal isn't frustrating. Refocusing, I open my textbook, checking over my notes for the practice exam we're taking today. I spent hours last night pouring over the chapters full of pred propaganda. I'm aware my professor will deduct points on any open-ended questions, so I'm determined to get every single multiple-choice question correct.

"Good afternoon, class! I presume you are all ready for the practice exam," Professor Abel says, bustling to the desk at the front of the hall. "I know I promised to split the exam into equal parts closed and open questions, but I hate to remain stagnant. So, I wrote an entirely new exam consisting only of essay questions, so I can really assess your depth of knowledge."

My jaw drops. If there aren't any strictly fact-based sections on the exam, I will certainly fail. This weasly little asshole will mark everything I say as incorrect or ding me on every possible pedantic point he can.

I have to say something.

"Professor?"

His beady eyes find me, a sneer crossing his lips as he replies. "Yes, Miss Drew? Is there a complaint from the prey gallery?"

"You had us study for an exam that no longer resembles the one we will be taking. It isn't fair to penalize us simply because you changed your mind at the last minute," I say, choosing each word carefully.

A bark of nasally laughter erupts from his throat for far longer than is professional. When he stops mocking me, he slams a stack of test packets on the desk. "Life is rarely fair, Miss Drew. As the professor, it is within my purview to change my test anytime I wish. However, since you feel unprepared, I'm going to insist you leave class for the day. You may return in our next session, to learn from your more studious classmates' results."

What? Is he fucking serious? He's kicking me out of class?

"That's hardly a surprise, Professor. There are two reasons we've always called her Double D," Gold interjects with a smug grin.

I whip my head around, digging my nails into the desk to keep from losing control of the bunny simmering in my veins. "I wouldn't run my fat mouth if I was the one who thought the sinking of the Titanic was a made-up story in a movie. You based your entire theory on the fact that 'cameras weren't even invented back then', you moron."

A low gasp followed by a chorus of laughter makes her shoot out of her seat, but Professor Abel raps his knuckle on the desk. "Despite Miss Erickson's lack of human history knowledge, she's at the top of the class in *our* history. Miss Drew, you need to exit so the students who *want* to learn may take their exams. Run along, little bunny. Take your 'F' like an obedient afternoon snack."

I grab my book and my bag, head held high, and stomp to the door. Before I leave, I look at the pudgy Tasmanian devil with anger radiating from my being. My voice is steady as I get in a parting shot. "You may think you're safe because you suck up to the heirs in this class, but I'm *still* a Drew heir. *They* have also claimed me as a Khan protectee. Neither of our families forgives those who cross them. Think about that when you're trying to sleep tonight."

His face turns as white as a snow leopard, and a feral smirk crosses my face. This is what Felix meant by me still being a worthy opponent. The look of fear on this shrimp-dicked pissant is making every cell in my body hungry for more. I'm enjoying his discomfort and the scent is making my skin tingle.

I've never heard of prey responding like this before.

But I can't think about that right now. I have one chance to assert my dominance, so I wink and blow a kiss at the professor, tossing my hair over my shoulder as I slam my way out the door. My sensitive bunny ears catch whispers of incredulity from the classroom as I go, and it only makes me smile wider.

I'll still fail this exam, but when the story of why I failed gets around, I won't be in trouble. It will please Lucille, that I didn't allow him to talk down to a member of our family, even if I dragged the wolves into it. Her taste for blood is unparalleled, and striking the first blow against a lesser pred is exactly her style.

With a sigh, I trudge towards the library to start my work study early. Maybe the grumpy book hottie will make us do something so strenuous, he'll be forced to take his shirt off. That would make up for this pisser of a day.

One can hope, right?

SONATA NO. 14 "MOONLIGHT"

RENARD

EVEN THOUGH THE MOON IS HIGH, THE LIGHTS ARE STILL ON IN the library, and waiting is making me restless.

It's not as though the recalcitrant dragon and I have a specific schedule of when we meet to hunt, but it has been over a week. We've known one another long enough to sense the need to feast, and it's overdue by several days. However, Aubrey's drive to solve the riddle of the poison used at prom has him pushing himself far beyond his typical obsessions.

It's almost like he's worried about something other than general student safety.

The Khans aren't gathered upstairs for once. I hear they are having dinner at their place with the fascinating Delores Drew. Usually I'm pleased to have my roost to myself, but tonight I pace the lower balcony outside my bedroom. My impatience has nothing to do with the silence; that's a ludicrous proposition and I won't entertain it. She's not even that loud downstairs.

Except…

Stomping over to the gramophone, I lower the needle and close my eyes as the haunting strains echo off the stone. Music always calms the beast inside of me, even when I'm hungry. My wings pop free, and I groan with pleasure as I walk onto the balcony again. Unlike most royals or alphas, a gargoyle lord can do more than simply half-shift—we can all shift specific parts at will. It's a closely guarded secret that is rarely shared outside of our clans, and at times like this, it's a blessing. I don't want to transform enough that the rumbling allows my monster free.

He's far too on edge to allow him free rein until we land on our hunting grounds.

The talisman around my neck flashes briefly, and I roll my eyes in irritation. It's not late enough in the evening for it to matter that I haven't shifted yet, so my magical watchdog is being overzealous. I brace my arms on the railing, inhaling the night air with a sigh.

Then I hear it—a soft humming coming from below. It's so soft it barely registers, but the notes match the sonata playing in my room. I lean forward, trying to determine who it is, but all I can determine is that it's a female, and she's in the library courtyard.

Who would lurk there at night? What are they up to? Does Aubrey know someone is there?

Panic sets in. My scaly friend has been so concerned about someone trying to harm one of us, and a random person hanging around his library at night is suspicious. I need to find out who it is and what their intentions are… immediately. *If people are breaching our perimeter, they could get inside and hurt the bunny hiding on our lower floors.*

I jump onto the railing, flexing my wings as I look down at the courtyard. As soon as I home in on a landing spot, I leap and let my wings expand when I dive. My feet hit the soft earth with a thud, causing a gasp to interrupt the melodic humming I came to investigate. I walk further into the small space, accessing my enhanced night vision to see the figure in the shadows.

"Professor Renard!"

Oh, *mon coeur*[1]. I thought Delores was eating at the tigers' townhouse this evening, but here she is, walking through the courtyard like Annabel Lee.

No, I'm not exaggerating for dramatic effect—Delores is wandering under the tree in a long white nightgown and bare feet, humming along with my Beethoven. It's like Byron's poetry is leaping off the page and into my world.

"You—you dyed your hair," I stutter, so entranced by her spell I can't think of anything better to say.

Oh, this is going well, Renard. Way to show you've barely spoken to women since before the humans crossed the ocean to settle here.

Her cheeks flush with a color that matches one layer of her hair, but she still twirls a little to show it off. "I did! I've always wanted to express myself in this way and… now I can."

The twinkle in her eyes is infectious, and I smile as she flits around under the enormous tree. Moonlight is shining through the branches and hitting her in a way that, once again, reminds me of long ago. I rub my hand over my chest, feeling the familiar ache this memory brings, though somehow, it's a little less sharp than usual.

"Isn't it dangerous to be out here alone? I'm surprised Fitz isn't hiding in the bushes, monitoring you." I watch her face screw up in what I'd almost call a pout, and I have to hold back laughter.

She stomps over and pokes me in the chest, frowning at the hard obsidian her finger meets. "Listen, you. He is not my keeper. My enemies could kill me every time I step out of my room, but I can't live my life in fear. I'm eighteen and I should be able to run around after curfew and let my hair down. It's not fair that I have to stay locked up like Rapunzel."

A flare of overprotectiveness from my gargoyle replaces the dull ache—after all, watching over those we care about is in our nature. Despite my inclination to chastise her for being reckless, I also understand what she's feeling. When I was her age, my desire to break free from the shackles of responsibility was just as strong. Unfortunately, the consequences were dire.

I don't want her to suffer like I did.

"Dolly, I don't believe anyone wants to lock you up." She gives me a wry look and I grimace. "Okay, maybe *Fitz* does, but that's because it terrifies him to think someone might hurt you. Sure, they tasked him with protecting his Raj, but Felix is more than capable of handling himself. And Chess grew up with them in a dangerous environment. He can fight if he has to. But you… Even wi*th* the amazing performances in Felix's classes, it's easy to worry someone will get the drop on you."

Her long lashes flutter as she looks away, expression serious as she considers my words. When she looks up again, she places a small hand on my chest. "You're not as aloof as you'd like everyone to believe, are you, Renard?"

I swallow hard, pretending I don't like how astute she is, or the way my name rolls off of her tongue. Her skin is warm on mine, and she's standing far too close, but I don't know what to say that won't betray the effect she has on me.

I hope the feeling is mutual because the night she slept with Aubrey and I was the best slumber I've had in centuries.

Everything seems so *familiar,* but as much as I'd love to immerse myself in those memories, Dolly isn't *her* and I'm not the gargoyle I used to be. It wouldn't be fair to either of us to indulge in nostalgia. Although, a waltz in the moonlight might soothe the irritable git inside of me while I wait for my companion to arrive for dinner.

My mouth opens before my brain catches up, and I blurt out, "Would you like to dance?"

Okay, not the smoothest line in the world, but Delores is making me nervous with her moonlight fairy singing and sassy mouth.

"I suppose I could allow you to lead, Monsieur Renard, if you promise not to step on my toes. I have a dance midterm in two weeks and I can't be hobbling around," she teases, her lips curving into an adorably mischievous grin.

She takes my hand, letting me lead her into a two-step waltz to the sounds of Beethoven wafting from my room. Once we make a few circuits around the grass, I arch a brow at her playfully. "Am I leading satisfactorily, or do you have a critique, *il prima?*"

She chokes back a laugh, shaking her head. "I am far from a *prima*. However, you'll do as a partner."

I widened my eyes, and she gasped when she realized how her words could be misinterpreted. Her face flushes that rosy color again, and I spin her around, dipping her backwards to dispel the awkward moment. I know what she meant, but the ingenue blushes and natural shyness are making my chest tight. I don't know how to handle her intriguing combination of charming innocence and worldly sarcasm. It makes every nerve in my body fire, which only riles up my gargoyle.

Must. Keep. Animal. Brain. Quiet.

"Good to know, as I don't make a habit of waltzing with people in the moonlight." The gentle tease makes her giggle again, and I see exactly why Fitz has been running around like a lovesick cartoon character for months.

Delores Drew's appeal lies in her depth, not just in her surface-level pouty lips or soft curves. Their exile hardens the women at this school, or they have no personality outside of the personas their families molded for them. This girl is unapologetically discovering her *own* identity and watching her fumble and fire back is endearing as hell.

"You don't? I mean, there's enough room out here for Fitz to teach you to grind or Chess to waltz with you…" She throws her head back and laughs when my eyes narrow. Once her giggles are under control again, she raises a sassy brow and continues.

"Maybe Felix then? He seems like a foot stomper, though, and putting you and Aubrey together in this tight space might be a squeeze. One of his grumpy belches might toast you, but I bet he's lighter on his feet than he looks."

I snort, the imagery finally getting to me. She's not afraid of anything, it seems. Most of the shifters she just poked fun at would kill someone on the spot if they heard these musings, but I know none of them would harm a hair on her cotton candy head. I lift my hand and let her twirl again, watching the moonlight hit the voluminous gown as she spins a few times. It's been such a long time since I had this much fun with someone who is not my ancient companion, and she paints the prettiest picture, inside and out. When she stops spinning, she rewards me with a brilliant smile that hits me in the chest like a cannonball.

Romance will not be enough with this girl.

"Renard, are you okay?" she asks worriedly. "Your necklace thing is… *glowing.*"

Nodding, I rub my chest again and send her a reassuring look. I'm about to give her my go-to explanation of the talisman, but before I can, the very book dragon she mentioned before lands in front of us. He's half-shifted as usual, and a knowing smirk is playing over his lips as he eyes the two of us.

"I looked for you on the balcony, but imagine my surprise when I heard you down here instead," Aubrey drawls, his eyes dancing with mischief.

He can smell how this is affecting me—and he'd better keep his damn mouth shut about it.

Delores' eyes light up. "We were dancing, you old fuddy duddy. Don't be grouchy just because I made him late for whatever the hell you two get up to when no one is looking."

I blink, rushing to stop her from asking too many questions. "I was worried because she was down here alone and defenseless, Aubrey. Plus, you were late and didn't even send a text. Again."

"Oooh. Five points to the rock man," Dolly whispers, tilting her head at the scaly librarian as she awaits his response.

His eyes narrow for a moment before his lips curve into a grin that means nothing but trouble. I've been his friend long enough to know he's returning the favor of causing chaos. "Well, lunchable, I suppose if you're here... " My eyes widen and I shake my head, knowing where this is going. It's like watching a train wreck about to happen. "... perhaps you should come with us. We both require a hunt."

Holy Bridget in the bathwater, is he fucking serious? We take no one with us.

"Oooooooh, can I?!!" Her nightgown bounces as she jumps up and down, clapping her hands like a little kid. Compared to us, I suppose she is, but the analogy is damned near perfect.

Sighing, I pinch the bridge of my nose. Aubrey isn't trying to screw up our relationships—whatever they are—with this girl. He's testing her covertly to find out if she can handle the aspects of our animals that very few know about. If she can't, the question of her presence in our life is answered before either of us gets too invested. The mere act of inviting her tells me he is more interested in her than he will probably admit to anyone—including me.

Sly dragon.

When I don't protest, he turns back to her. "You may join us, little one. But Rennie here isn't meant to carry even a girl as small as you for too much of a distance. You'll have to ride me." Her eyes pop open and I choke, making him howl and puff smoke as he laughs. "Meaning I'll fully shift; both of you read far too much smutty romance from my stacks." Delores flushes, then scowls, pointing at me as if it were *my* fault.

Feeling playful, I point back at her, and Aubrey snorts again. "You look like two-thirds of the Spiderman meme Fitz sent me the other day. Own your word porn addiction so we can get moving."

I shrug. "I've been alive a long time. It's hard to find a mystery I haven't solved yet and I don't care for blue aliens. It seems a little farfetched."

Dolly looks at me, partially shifted and obsidian, then at Aubrey in his winged, scaly, half-shifted form. "Oh, yes, totally unbelievable. I can see how you'd have to suspend your disbelief, Rennie."

Aubrey rolls his eyes and huffs. "Stop flirting. We need to get going if we want to return with enough time for you to get decent sleep, bite size." With that, he turns and allows her to climb onto his back, grunting as she finds a hold. "I'll finish my shift as we gain altitude, so hold on to my neck tightly if you don't want to fall to your death."

"Thanks for the warning," she mutters, right before he leaps into the air and flaps his large wings to propel them higher, tearing a scream of half-terror, half-elation from her throat.

I grumble. I'll have to catch up with them after I hike back up the Tower for altitude. After all, I'm a glider, and that asshole damn well knows it.

Cheater. He's a goddamn cheater.

Hail to the King

Fitz

Fitz

Closing my eyes, I breathe deeply through my nose. My tiger is ready and raring to go, riled up by the knowledge that this is the first staff Pred Games match of the year. Chess would tell me this is the point of Apex holding these games—helping the more violent residents get some of their aggression out in a controlled setting, so that we don't tear into their little darlings. This one is the first of six held throughout the year and the winners take home both the glory and the women.

I should know; I've won six of them since we arrived.

Felix won the first three years, of course. He needed that outlet more than anyone and plenty of staff met their end when my exiled Raj took his anger at our asshole patriarch out on whatever pred he could prod into getting in the ring with him.

Oddly, Zhenga's the only one who's survived him all these years, and that tells me she should be in charge of her people, not her dimwit siblings. That woman was not made to be married off and sentenced to raising cubs she doesn't want. She's annoying, but she's a force of nature and the Leonidas' are as stupid as the other fuckwits on our esteemed Council.

The swimmers and winged preds have already headed to their own fighting spaces. I'm sure the gargoyle's prey friends are wrangling the ring they place in the lake for that arena and who the fuck knows what the fliers do. My focus is the ground game here in my family's arena—this is my space and I refuse to do anything but dominate it.

Sadly, we're not supposed to kill people here.

On Bloodstone, death matches were how they settled damn near every conflict. My father and the rest of the family sat on high in our boxes like the emperors of old, watching the players go at one another until one paid the ultimate sacrifice. Felix and I watched tigers, rejects, criminals, and more tear each other to pieces from the time we could walk. Violence is not only in our blood, but such a part of lives that we breathe it.

Khoon mein, ham bandhate hain; mrtyu mein, ham vijayee hain. [1]

The Khan motto is branded on every feline in our ambush at birth and we're expected to live it every moment of every day. Our Pred Games team is the dirtiest, bloodiest opponents in the entire league, and I used to lead them. When Felix and my father started fighting over his consort, I quit the team and came home to show them Felix would have a strong enforcer to back him up. I thought it might change things, but it didn't.

I don't regret it for a fucking second, though.

Walking away from the trees, I approach the stands, watching one of the male lions go after a grizzly bear. I'm fairly certain the lion will win—bears are vicious when cornered, but slow and easy to wound if you know the right spots to hit, then dart away. I do and I'd be willing to bet any cat trained by Z knows that as well. She's thorough as hell and won't let one of her pride make the family look bad.

I squint at the smarmy looking fennec foxes running around taking bets as usual. Foxes make up for being some of the smallest preds at Apex by being criminals. They run sports betting, bootlegging, black markets, and even procure skin for the right price. Something about them makes my fur itch, but I recognize their place in our ecosystem. Adults trapped with teenagers have needs and their vices are being tended to by a species who would otherwise make a good snack.

Que sera and all that shit.

The bell clangs when the bear finally taps out and I smile as Zhenga runs over to check out her fighter. He's a little torn up, but not bad, so she'll have someone run him to the infirmary. This fight was the last one before the intermission and after that, comes the ultimate battles. The biggest, baddest preds take these two slots and it's where Felix and I usually dominate the field.

My eyes roam to the crowd, drifting back to where Chess is sitting with my woman and her two weird friends. I like that she has them, but I set the spicy lizard on checking them out despite Chess' vouching for them. The gangster badger worries me a little because his reputation with the students is like mine and he looks like three miles of dangerous road. The colorful polar bear is less worrisome and I enjoy the way my girl giggles when she's talking with the curly haired thespian.

I lift a hand, nodding at Chess. He smiles broadly, elbowing Dolly so she looks over at me. I see her cheeks flush and it makes my dick jump in my pants. I can't believe one brief trip to town to grab shit helped my cheetah get comfortable with her, but since it did, I can put my master plan in effect. If I can get my darling feline on board, I can get my brother on board, and then the two ancient assholes.

Then we're one big banging family and everything I want will be in place.

Chess says I miss having the whole ambush to curl up in more than I want to admit and this is 'transference', but he's wrong. I love being in the enormous pile and sometimes Felix will let Chess and I do it with him as long as I behave.

What I really want is a family—one I choose who won't drop one of us for some bullshit 'flaw' or a disagreement. The Khan ambush is the antithesis of that, but if getting his throne back will make my twin happy again, I'll do anything to make it happen. At least, I thought I would until this leggy bunny walked into our lives and changed everything.

Now I'm not sure and that makes me irritable.

Using that, I bounce on my feet as I keep my adrenaline flowing through the break. I don't want to lose momentum because after Felix told me about all the trouble those idiots on the far side of the stands have caused my girl; I knew I had to show them what happens when you piss off a Khan. He said she held her own, but I don't give a fuck. They tried to hurt my baby girl and I will make sure every single one of them pays dearly.

Especially that little shit from prom night who dared to mouth off in Felix's class.

"Eager to fight the snow leopard, enforcer?" Zhenga walks over to me, arching her brow as her grizzly friend Raquel follows behind as usual.

I snort. "Barely worth my time. I'll have him tapping within a minute. You can put money with the slimy bastards on it."

The lioness laughs throatily, nodding at the dim-witted bear. "Go do that. And make sure you put a grand on the Raj. He's fighting Gregor and you know how much the canines and the cats hate one another."

"The alpha will win," Raquel says as she shakes her head. "Felix is too soft to do what it will take to beat him. Alpha Gregor is dominant in every way—just look at him."

Her words draw a snarl out of me and Z has to push me back so I don't go for her throat. "That mangey, flea-bitten mutt beats the females and acts like an assault should turn them on. Felix has wanted to get in the ring with him since he arrived late last year. This will be a bloodbath."

"He fights dirty. Felix shouldn't pull his punches," Zhenga comments.

As if we summoned him, I grin at my twin when he rocks up with an expression of pure fury on his face. I tilt my head, curious why the sudden flip in his demeanor. He's never Sally Sunshine, but he seems particularly enraged at the moment. I follow his gaze and find he's not looking at his moronic opponent—no, he's looking at my baby girl laughing with Chess and her friends like she's a flank steak and he's starving.

I couldn't have planned this more perfectly myself.

The wolf is enormous and I'm not sure all of it is natural. Rumors spread like wildfire around Apex, even amongst the staff, and the word is the wolf pack expects a particular look he couldn't achieve without chemical assistance. He must spend a small fortune on his habit because shifters process drugs differently than humans and whatever he's doping with is not made by our kind. I eye him carefully, knowing Felix is next to me, doing the same. His size is an advantage, but given Felix's speed when shifted, it will probably work against him.

"Dibs on this fucker next round if he survives," I mutter, and Felix chuckles darkly. My penchant for picking the dirtiest, bloodiest fights is well known amongst the participants in this league. I feel like Felix requested a change in the card on purpose, so I'll let it slide.

Felix listens as they announce the wolf, his expression getting darker by the second as Zhenga's shit-stirring grizzly friend gushes over his past wins. When the muscle-bound douche finally walks into the ring, my twin stands taller, disguising his fury with a nonchalant look. The rightful Raj of Bloodstone never lets the sheep see his actual feelings. They get the disinterested mask now that he's no longer on his bender.

Tearing his shirt off, he smirks when the crowd roars as he saunters into the ring. My brother is leaner than me, but every inch is hard muscle. The strength of our entire ambush flows in his veins and he looks at the rowdy on-lookers with a regal tilt to his chin. This ring is nothing compared to the trials arena at Bloodstone and Felix is used to looking up at an entire island worth of hungry fans.

When the noise dies down a little, the contenders take their places and I sneak a look over at my baby girl. Her mouth is hanging open, and she looks like she's contemplating jumping into the ring to climb him like a tree. My lips curve as I consider what's going to happen when he shifts and no longer has clothes for his human form. Felix's dick is going to make her lose her goddamn mind and it will be on display when he knocks the snot out of this mutt.

What? My dick is no slouch, but my twin is terrifying—even I know that.

I finally drag my eyes away from her curves to note Felix and Gregor circling one another. The wolf looks smug, and I can't fathom why. This idiot has never beaten anyone of our caliber, and I don't know why he's not scared. There's a little crazy in those yellow orbs and for a moment, I wonder if he's doing more than juicing. If so, I hope my twin sees it because it will change Gregor's reaction times.

The alpha runs his mouth as they move—bullshit trash talk that wouldn't distract me from finding his weaknesses and certainly won't fool Felix. It's dumb shit and while he's spouting it, I notice him favoring his left arm. Something about it is off and I'm sure my twin sees it, too. That's a perfect opening, especially if that's an old injury.

Felix's tiger ripples under his skin and I think he's going to make his move when Gregor says something in a lower tone. In a blink, I feel my brother's tiger bust loose, forcing a half-shift as the idiot in the ring points towards…

Oh, shit. Bad move, dawg.

Gregor's lips are hitched in a slimy sneer, and his finger is pointing directly at my baby girl. The depth of fury I feel is making it hard not to react, but I know Felix has to handle this. That one gesture is a direct challenge to his authority, both at Apex and as the heir to Bloodstone. If he doesn't meet it with severe punishment, our father will get word. The last thing we need is for him to decide our girl is another weak spot for his exiled son.

One set of enemies on campus is enough for now, thanks.

The ref hits the bell and Felix leaps through the air like he has fucking wings.

I swear to hell, I've never seen my twin move like this, but he's on the dumb motherfucker so fast it barely registers. His claws are tearing into the wolf and everything from fur to skin goes flying. The scent of blood is heavy, amping up the crowd as they watch what a true king can do in battle. Gregor is definitely high because he's scrambling for better purchase, but not tapping out. His eyes flash as he shifts to full wolf form, scampering out of Felix's range.

The sound of a bone-rattling roar echoes off the buildings when my brother's tiger enters the game. When he shifted, Felix is ten feet and almost eight hundred pounds of cat. He's the biggest member of our ambush at home and I'm sure that played a part in my father's ludicrous decree. He can take six tigers in the ring without breaking a sweat; that kind of threat had to be neutralized somehow. I watch him stalk towards Gregor, his prowl slow and intent.

Shit. Okay, I might have to tap in, or he'll kill the flea-bitten shit.

Moving to the ref, I tap him, letting him know I want to sub in for my brother. He blasts an air horn and I almost tear into the dopey looking Komodo when it rings in my ears. The spectators boo, having sensed this fight was about to become a bloodbath. I don't give a shit about their disappointment; I'm worried about Felix losing his coveted control publicly. He's already so close to the edge—if he kills Gregor, no one will care, but it will make him punish himself even more.

I walk up to the hulking cat advancing on the wolf, regardless of the horn. "Felix, my Raj. I will make him suffer for insulting our name. Let me do my job, brother."

His feline eyes dart to me and I shift quickly, revealing my white tiger form before nuzzling against him. Our cats stare at one another for a moment and I think he knows why I'm interrupting. Silence hangs in the air for another moment, then he shifts to human, looking down at me with a hidden, but grateful expression. All the people behind him see is a terse nod as he stalks out of the ring.

Now it's my turn and I never play fair.

Huge paws slap the ground as I circle my prey, looking at it through my cat's eyes this time. Every sense is heightened in this form and I can smell and hear things I couldn't before. Gregor's wolf backs away, and he ripples to a stupid looking half-shift that makes me think he's not a full-blooded alpha. Information for later, but it highlights his weakness in other ways as well. He won't be able to use 'alpha push' on me—or try to, at least.

"Awww. Did I scare your brother? He sent the psycho to play instead of fighting his own battles?"

Giving him the tiger version of a snort, I keep watching him as he dances around the circle. I could shift to answer, but I'm not wasting energy. This fool will talk himself into a pine box soon enough.

My hackles raise when he stops, looking at me with a smug grin full of fangs. "Maybe he couldn't take hearing your little pet will be pinned under me as I fuck the shit of her pert ass after I tear her throat out. Do you think that upset him, Fitzy?"

Rage. Red, hot fury.

That's all that goes through my mind before I shoot across the ring and knock the ugly son of a bitch to the ground. My tiger takes up where Felix left off, tearing and shredding at him like he's dinner. Whistles sound and the bell clangs, but it's all in the distance as I pound the living fuck out of this asshole who not only insulted my Raj, but threatened my baby girl with rape.

It would have to be—Delores Drew belongs to my ambush, even if she doesn't know it yet, and she's not letting anyone outside of my family touch her. My animal lifts its head and roars into the night in pure domination as Gregor wriggles out of my grasp after taking a dirty swipe at my cock. That's a banned area and if he'd connected, I would have torn his off. As it is, I might do it anyway.

Rules be damned.

"Finish it, Fitz."

Felix's voice rings in the air and I feel the atmosphere shift as he stalks off—likely to sulk. My anger at Gregor for baiting him, for the threat, and for using my fucking nickname flows through me like lava. If my Raj wants me to finish this asshole, I will.

With another roar, my blood-stained body darts through the air like a white flash and I knock the wolf into the ground so hard he chokes on his own spit. Opening my giant maw, I look directly at Chess and my baby girl, wanting them both to see what I'm about to do. My fangs clamp down on his head, making him scream bloody murder right before I rip it clean off of his body. Tossing my head as blood drips from my mouth, I rear up on my back paws and my tiger declares its own victory.

The applause is deafening, and I sniff as I walk over, lifting my leg to piss on the severed head as one final 'fuck you'.

I feel lighter than I have in forever when Chess helps our girl stand and make her way through the raucous spectators as they freak the hell out. When she approaches, I consider shifting back, but then Delores Drew drops her hand to ruffle the fur of my gory head. Her lips are quirked in a mischievous grin and I see the heat in her gaze, despite touching my bloody face.

"Here, kitty, kitty. Let's go get you some cream to celebrate."

Chess pales and fidgets, acting like he's going to pass out on the spot. "I, uh, I'm going to check on Felix."

He takes off like a hellhound is after him and I let out a big ass tiger huff.

"Yeah, I don't get it, either," Delores says. "But that's okay. He'll come around. You're all mine tonight, warrior kitty."

How the fuck am I supposed to argue with that?!

Take Me To Church

Delores

Fitz doesn't bother changing into his non-tiger form, and I find myself surprised my bunny doesn't seem perturbed by it. In fact, nothing that happened tonight made me afraid—quite the opposite. Cori and Rufus warned me that the last few fights would get pretty gruesome and Chess offered to escort me back to the Tower before it got bad, but something in my gut told me to stay.

Or maybe it was my crotch, because the second I saw Felix and Fitz's bare skin, I knew I wasn't going anywhere.

Cori was a little worse for the wear by the time Fitz took over for Felix—something I still don't understand—and I know Rufus had to hold her hair after the beheading. She's as weird a pred as I am prey, so I know she didn't judge me perching on the edge of my seat thirstily.

I wanted to jump in and join them.

Shaking my head ruefully, I look over at the massive beast trotting alongside me as we head to the stony landmark. A scent drifts through the air and I look up, noting the curling smoke I can see in the distance. Aubrey and Renard are up in their little boys' club; the smoke from either the dragon's pipe or his temper gave them away. Fitz nudges my hand with his gigantic head and I laugh.

"Don't be a jealous kitty. I see them, but I'm not going to ask them to come down and join us." He gives me a huge tiger huff, and it makes me smile broadly. I'm not worried about his current possessive streak; it's the animal in him driving that bus. Fitz has made it clear over and over he wants to share me with his friends. I'm not so sure about that concept, but he has not been shy about it.

It should surprise me that seeing all those bigger preds fight in front of me didn't make my bunny wig out, but it doesn't. After Aubrey and Rennie took me flying on their hunt, I realized the way my psycho parents raised me had one benefit: I have more control over my fear reflex than most people and definitely more than normal prey. Once I could commune with my rabbit inside, I figured out how to let her know I'm safe rather than in danger. Since then, I can hide amongst the trees while my winged friends chow down on baddies and not end up a quivering mess.

Though I highly doubt they want me blabbing about their species' preferred dinner in front of everyone—that would leave them vulnerable to pitchforks and waves of hunters of the non-shifter variety. The Council would love to use the information about dragons and gargoyles to set the race of beings we largely ignore on the rich, powerful ancients, if only to steal their kingdoms and wealth. I won't be the idiot to trigger a freaking genocide, that's for damned sure.

Besides, they pick the evil ones, so who cares?

A soft growl gets my attention and I look down at the enormous cat waiting for me to enter the Tower. If I didn't know better, I'd think Fitz was nervous. He's purposely stayed shifted and is letting me lead the way like I'm in charge—though of what, I don't have a clue. I've only done this shit once, and it was not an educational experience. In fact, it was about as remedial as possible without having to draw a damn map for the dumbass. I may have seen and read about better experiences, and that little treat he gave me the other night was amazing, but I'm still an amateur with sex.

I doubt Fitz will let that stand for long after tonight, but it doesn't mean I'm not a little worried.

When I open the door to my room, he finally shifts back, kicking it closed in all his naked glory. My eyes roam over his lithe form, taking in the cut muscles, scars, tattoos, and a painful-looking brand on his ass. It's obviously a Khan mark, because the paw with slashes is burned in deeply, along with some flourishes and a script-y 'K' with a crown. There's also an ugly-looking claw scar under his ribs that I'd wager almost killed him, and my gaze softens as he turns back to me with hungry eyes.

"Did someone try to kill you?" I ask, my voice breathier than intended. He nods, walking towards me slowly. I'm trying not to look down, but the anticipation is killing me. My pussy is throbbing with excitement and a hunger that matches his is curled in my gut. "If I meet them, they're dead."

His eyebrows fly up as he stops within mere centimeters of me. "Why?"

"Because…" I fumble for a minute, not knowing why that threat jumped out of my mouth unbidden. His hand comes up, a knuckle tracing down my cheek, and I shiver. Then it hits me and I look him dead in the eyes. "Because you're mine, Fitz Khan, and no one touches what belongs to me."

That stops him dead in his tracks, and his chest rumbles with a growl. I don't know if it's good or bad, so I reach out and trace my fingertips over the scar on his ribs. My voice is soft as I give him a smile much shier than my words. "Except Chess, obviously. But if someone comes for you, they're going through me first."

Fitz doesn't laugh or ask how I'm going to defend him against other preds as a bunny. He doesn't look amused or condescending. Instead, he yanks me to his body and buries his face in my neck as he mumbles, "Fuck, yeah, I am, baby girl."

Oh, I'm full of heady confidence now.

My hands wrap around him, palms smoothing up his back and then down to the dimples I saw at the base of his spine. He seems to like it, so I dip lower to squeeze his ridiculously tight ass and he moans. I shift, lining my body up with his, swallowing hard at the press of the cock that is definitely as big as his twin's. I may bite off more than I can chew, but hell if I'm not going to enjoy every second.

"Fitz..." I mumble. "You know I'm not... experienced, right?"

His grin is almost feral when he lifts his head to look at me. "I'm going to love being your teacher. And if you tell Felix I said that, I'll spank your ass scarlet."

Laughing, I let him back me towards the bed, my expression playful. "Oh, but I think he'd enjoy a little schoolgirl over the desk action."

"Uh, hell yes, he would, but this is my night, baby girl," he rumbles as my knees hit the mattress. "Now, be a good girl and get those clothes off."

Good Goddess, I think I almost had an orgasm at those words.

Sucking in a breath, I force my liquid limbs to move, pulling off my clothes until I hit the racy lingerie he ordered when he replaced my stuff. I chose a pale pink, lacy set today and I can tell he likes it... and so does his dick. It bobs in front of him as he looks at me and I reach out, running my fingertips over him.

"Ah, ah, naughty girl," Fitz growls. "No making me lose my damn head before you lose yours. Put your hands above your head and keep them there."

This is a new game and though I'm nervous, I do as he says. I know Fitz wouldn't hurt me and nothing he's done so far has been bad. His eyes get little flecks of gold in them when I cross my wrists above my head and let him run his enormous hands over me without moving. Fingertips run over my curves and hips as if he's memorizing my shape. I flush a little; I know I'm not built like most of the women here. I'm a little thicker and have more to hold on to than the average Apex female.

"Beautiful," he rumbles. "The dragon said some shit about an Italian guy, but I think you're built like a pin-up." His hands squeeze my hips and he gives me a wicked smirk before lowering his head to bury his face in my boobs.

I guess he doesn't mind after all.

His mouth moves over the mounds of my breasts, nipping and suckling at the skin hard enough to leave marks. I know he's doing it on purpose, but I can't find it in myself to care. If Fitz wants to mark me from head to toe, I'll writhe around while he does it and be a happy bunny.

"You will, huh?"

No. I. Didn't.

Lifting my head a little, I look down at him with wide eyes. "Out loud again?"

His chuckle is dark as he goes back to removing the fragile pink lace, preventing him from getting to my nipples. When he tosses it aside, he groans and wiggles on top of me like he's in pain. "I fucking knew it. Same fucking color."

"Do you have a bet with someone about my nipples?" My face turns bright red as the blood rushes from every part of my body to my cheeks.

"No. Well, maybe with myself," he mumbles before he wraps his lips around one and steals my breath away.

Well, okay then.

His mouth moves over me until I'm squirming with need, arching my back to press against the hard length jutting into my stomach greedily. I keep my arms in place, but damn, it's getting difficult with the scrape of his teeth and the hard suckling. My blood is thrumming in my veins and I feel my bunny shimmering under my skin as if she wants out. But I can't do that… can I?

No. I need this to be me and Fitz, just us coming together for the first time.

When the stubble on his chin has me so sensitive I can barely stand it, I gasp, "Fitz, please."

The growl that escapes against my skin tells me he liked that, so I repeat it until he moves lower. His tongue dips into my belly button, flicking the jewel there before he bites a hip bone firmly. That's going to leave a mark and I whine with pleasure. I don't know if it's a pred thing for teeth to flood my basement or if it's just me, but I can't control myself when I feel the sting. I may have a biting fetish and I completely blame vampire shows on TV for it.

Sink them in, dear Goddess, do it…

Chuckling darkly as I writhe, the tiger prowls lower, blowing over my bare skin and raising goosebumps. He plants soft kisses all over me, tongue swiping over tender skin to soothe it after he makes mark after mark. My limbs are trembling and I know I'm leaking like a faucet all over the bedspread. I feel the clenching inside as my body desperately seeks something to fill it and I'm ready to explode.

By the time he lowers his mouth to me, I'm almost vibrating with need. His tongue traces around my clit in a way that a toy can't replicate and I can't control the whimpers as I buck into him. Panting softly, I fight the urge to bury my fingers in his hair and hold him in place. My tiger teases and tortures me right to the edge and when he pushes me over, I let out a wail they probably heard across the fucking campus.

I don't even want to contemplate where he learned that, but I'd send the bitch a fruit basket if I could.

It takes a few minutes before the stars in front of my eyes recede and when I go boneless, Fitz lifts his head to reveal an expression of pure satisfaction.

"Baby girl, I'm lucky I didn't blow my load when you made that sound. You'd better be ready."

Gulping in a deep breath, I nod, moving my hips to encourage him. "Now, Fitz. Do it now."

His body is covering mine and his dick is poised at my entrance before I can finish my sentence. When he shifts, pressing in a little, I let out another throaty whine. That snaps his control, and he buries himself inside of me as far as he can in one swift stroke. I shudder as my body adjusts to his size, muscles squeezing him eagerly.

"You're going to want to hold on for this," he growls low.

I sigh happily, raising my arms to hook them around his neck and pull my thighs up on his hips since he gave permission. He gives me a feral grin and pulls out, then slams into me hard enough that I see stars again. His pace is furious and I hold on tight, muttering stupid shit under my breath because I can't focus my brain on anything but the searing pleasure every time he rubs the right spot.

The louder I get, the rougher he is, his eyes full of golden heat. "Not going to let the kitty loose this time, babe, because that's a discussion for everyone, but… you're making it tough."

I'm not sure what that means exactly, but I nod. "Just fuck me until I can't walk. I want to feel you all day tomorrow."

His eyes widen, and he lets out a dark snarl. I almost cry when he pulls out, but he flips me over and drives into me from behind. That lights up a whole new scoreboard and I bury my face in the comforter to muffle the screams as he hammers into my pussy like he's trying to crawl inside me. I feel a burning sensation at the base of my spine and dig my fingers into the bed hard, unable to hold back any longer.

The orgasm that rips through me is big enough to make my vision blurry again and I melt into the material as he pumps a few more times, then fills me with cum for so long I'm sure I've broken him. When he finally stops, I feel him cover me completely, panting in my ear like he ran a marathon.

"Holy fuck, baby girl. That was…"

"Perfect," I groan as my body gives out.

His chuckle is dark, and his hands move from the tight grip on my hips to my back. "I knew when I first saw you I'd be chasing you, but I didn't realize you'd have a fluffy cottontail to play with."

I suck in a breath, unable to form words when he's touching the appendage I've never manifested outside of a full shift before. "Uhhhhhhh…"

"Shit, now you're strangling my cock again, babe." He rolls off of me, pulling out and turning me to face him as he slips fingers into the mess we made. It's almost like he's pushing it all back into me, and I look at him in confusion. "What can I say? I don't want a drop wasted."

My brows furrow and I feel heat flush up from my chest to my face. I whisper softly, "You know I have an implant, right? Like Lucille made me get one when I turned thirteen."

Fitz winks playfully. "Even better, though maybe someday…"

I narrow my eyes at him. "Fitzgerald Khan, you get that out of your cave tiger brain immediately! I'll cut your balls off myself. I'm eighteen years old, creep."

He shrugs, looking completely unfazed. "I've got forever to talk you into cubs, baby girl. For now, I'm obsessed with your pussy for other reasons." His eyes twinkle as he looks at me. "And if you think I'm moving from this spot until morning, you're out of your cute, fluffy mind."

"I'm too tired to argue," I mumble as my eyes flutter closed. "Don't make me late for your brother's class or he'll make me suffer."

"I suspect he'll do that anyway when he smells you," he rumbles as he reaches for the lights. "Lucky you."

Mmmm. Lucky me, indeed.

BROTHER

CHESS

CHESS

FELIX WAS BESIDE HIMSELF WHEN WE GOT HOME LAST NIGHT.

It took me several hours worth of cat contact and listening to him grumble and growl in single syllables before he could stay still. Usually, Fitz does this, but there was an unspoken agreement that passed between us after he decimated that idiot Gregor. He needed to be alone with our angel and I was happy to allow them that time.

After all, I've had Fitz's sexy after-match horniness many times and Dolly has yet to experience it — it only seemed fair to share.

I didn't expect Fitz to come home, but I also didn't expect to wake up with Felix curled up beside me like he needs to be watched over. Our Raj guards his emotions carefully, and he doesn't enjoy appearing weak, even to his family. But right now, the anger and confusion radiating from his sleeping form is almost more than I've ever sensed from him.

At least when he's sober.

The first few years we lived at Apex, he was a ticking time bomb of fury and unchecked rage. He drank constantly, tore up the rings in fights, and screwed Zhenga as if she could erase the memory of Minerva from his brain. It didn't work and eventually, his tightly coiled control came back with a vengeance. Neither is healthy, if you ask me, but Felix has always supported Fitz and me, so I will not judge him.

I just wish I could help him.

Lying on my back, I stare up at the ceiling while Felix snoozes. I wish Fitz was here and honestly, I wish our angel was, too. I've spent the past few months adjusting to my desire for her and when I saw her glee at the gore in the fights, I knew my tiger was right. This girl is perfect for the twins and me—maybe even for all of us, like I suggested in the Tower. She's smart, caring, strong, and undaunted by life handing her shit every day as if it's her job to shovel it.

She even puts up with Felix's asshat behavior in class with spunk and has the two ancient grouches wrapped around her finger. That's something none of us have done in over a decade of friendship.

"Stop thinking so hard," Felix rumbles over his shoulder. "I can feel it."

I blink. *Felix doesn't leave our ambush link open anymore—not since we left Bloodstone.*

"I'm sorry, Raj. It's hard not to turn all this change over in my head," I murmur in reply.

He snorts and rolls over, looking at me with fondness. "You're not wrong. I've never seen Fitz act like this before, either. And you, Chester… you seem to get more confident by the day."

My eyes narrow. "Don't call me that."

His laugh is deep, and the vibration slides over my skin. "Then don't call me Raj. You know I hate that formal shit."

"Mmm, unless you're making a certain bunny call you 'Sir', I hear." I grin broadly, enjoying the back and forth with the tiger who's always been like a big brother to me.

Another irritable huff and Felix flops on his back. He looks up at the fan quietly for a few moments, then finally speaks. "I don't know how to handle her. I have conflicting feelings about our ambush, our family, our friends, and myself. I try to push her and she shoves back harder. No one shoves back at me, Chessie, except Fitz."

I grin. "Maybe it's time someone did? I mean, besides your ex-booty call. She can stay a respectable distance."

"Z actually backed off in class the other day and made some weird comment about my interest lying elsewhere. It was like she knew. How do women do that shit?"

"Hell if I know. My experience with them is limited to pleasantries and family, Felix. And what Fitz says, though I know that's mostly bullshit."

Felix coughs, choking on air as he laughs again. "Very astute of you to notice."

I haven't seen our king laugh this much in years; it's making my chest hurt. Fitz will hate missing this, though I suppose what he's getting in return is worth it. Knowing our angel is sparking this kind of emotion in my brothers makes me even more sure she's the one we need to rally around. I look at Felix with a shy smile. "But he's right about Delores, brother. He's said from the second we laid eyes on her she was perfect for us. He meant for me and him at first, but after that stupid dance and the summer, he's been downright certain she's like the center of our wheel."

The king looks thoughtful for a moment, crossing his arms over his chest as he considers my words. "I hate any sentence that starts out with admitting my twin is right about anything."

Huffing another laugh, I shrug. "I know. We can't tell him or his head will get so big he won't get into the Tower without it being greased."

"I'll think about it, Chess. Now go to sleep or I won't be able to get up to torture the woman of the hour in class. Since my shit-head brother isn't home yet, I assume I'm going to enjoy making her pay for her night of debauchery."

"That's cold, Felix. Ice cold."

As usual, I rise first and head downstairs to our small kitchen to start breakfast.

We could eat in the fancy ass cafeteria, but Felix hates being around most of the staff in the lounge. Fitz never minded, but he was also fucking half of them. Personally, I've always sided with Felix on that account, so I learned to cook fairly soon after we arrived. Being able to take care of the brothers who have been my family since I was a cub makes me happy and I don't have to endure the hungry stares of the female staff members picturing a Fitz-Chess sandwich.

Though, given the way Fitz acts about our angel and Felix's admission last night, I have the feeling Zhenga may warn them off.

I never thought I'd be grateful for anything that clingy lioness might do, but if she can back the women off our dicks, it would make me a hell of a lot more comfortable. And it might save someone's life too, because Felix declared her off-limits and I feel his Hulk out last night in the ring had something to do with Delores. His eyes cut to us before he went nuclear and I know Fitz tapped in before Felix did something he couldn't walk back.

Of course, then my love did something ridiculous, but everyone expects it from him.

The door slams and my eyes widen as a rumpled, limping tiger comes sneaking in through the back. His smile is shining like the sun and it makes my breath catch to see him so damned happy. Turning the heat down on the eggs, I walk over and comb my fingers through his long locks, trying to untangle them for him.

"I take it you had a good night, my love?" I murmur as he buries his face in my neck.

His voice is muffled as he nips my mark lightly. "Fucking amazing, Chessie. I cannot goddamn wait for you to join us. Baby Girl damn near killed me."

Chuckling, I tip his chin up and kiss his lips, noting the lingering taste of sweetness on them. "I will when she's ready. I think… I think I'm ready for it."

The look on his face is pure delight, and he squeezes me to him, lifting me off my feet. "Directing the two of you is gonna be so. fucking. hot. Sweet Bast, I didn't think my dick could get hard again after last night, but there he is, ready to rock!"

I shake my head, waiting until he puts me down to go over to the stove. "Sit down, Fitzy, and you can tell me all about it—at least until Felix comes down to yell at you."

He snorts, rolling his eyes as he lowers himself into a chair gingerly. "Man, Saint Felix of Unfulfilled is going to give baby girl hell when he sees how wobbly she is today. I wonder if I should hide somewhere so I can watch."

Walking over to the table with his plate, I arch a brow. "If you do, you better have improved upon your skills since the last time I saw you stalking someone. You got caught because you couldn't stop snickering in the fucking bushes, dude."

Fitz shrugs and gives me his million watt grin. "Maybe, but I saw a lot of sexy shit before Elektra caught me, man. That tigress was fiery as hell and fifteen-year-old me was ready to make her my Mrs. Robinson in a red hot minute."

Somehow, that doesn't make me feel any more confident.

Family
Aubrey

"It was quite enjoyable when Delores went hunting with us," Rennie remarks off-handedly.

He's much less broody tonight, and I'd chalk it up to feeding recently, but even the music in the Tower is lighter in tone. His classical doesn't calm my dragon as much as house music, but it doesn't require as much soothing in our sanctuary as opposed to when I'm forced to interact with the general population.

I watch him meander around the room, futzing with things, the restless energy making me chuckle. "If you don't stop buzzing around like a giant hummingbird, I'm going to call you Fitz."

The gargoyle turns to pin me with a glare, flicking his tail in annoyance. It's not unusual for him to strut about the lower level of the Tower in varying degrees of his shifted form, but when the tail comes out, he means business. "Flames, she didn't run away."

No shit, she didn't, and it was hotter than hell when she licked her lips as we fed.

"She seemed to enjoy it," I sigh, closing the book on my lap when

I realize I won't be learning anything tonight about synthetic poisons.

"Yes!" The tail snakes over to wrap around his glass of port, and he sips it quietly before speaking again in a low whisper. "I think so too. At least, I *hope* so."

I don't know why he's acting unsure—he could also smell what the hunt was doing to her.

Smoke rings escape my nose as I cross my arms over my chest. "A notoriously vicious predator family raised Delores, Rennie. I doubt it's the first time she's witnessed death. Besides, the whole campus knows she strolled off with Fitz after he ripped the head off that overgrown pooch."

"Not like we couldn't hear that," Renard grumbles, running his hand through his hair, as he reconciles his thoughts. "This place needs sound-proofing."

My stony companion has more baggage than me, and that's saying something. His infamy may trump his broken heart, but his actions since his exile make me question if his scars are worse. Over the centuries, I've forgiven myself for the mistake I made as a child—despite occasionally getting triggered—but Renard is still bleeding inside.

I've never been able to get him to share what happened to him, and it drives me crazy.

But maybe… maybe Delores can?

I don't know the entire tale, but that ridiculous orchid he treats like Fang Dynasty china is part of the story; there's magic in it, but he won't tell me where it originated from. Enchanted objects like the flower, or the talisman he never removes from his neck, have become rare in our world since the Middle Ages. I'd give a broken claw to study it, but he's quite stubborn on the subject.

"She's so naïve—and I don't mean compared only to us," the irritable shifter mutters as he stalks past me. Now he has his wings out, folded around his arms like he's hugging himself, and I groan.

This is going to lead to brooding on the balcony for hours; I can feel it in my scales.

"Yo, Smoky! Where is everyone?"

Fitz's voice echoes off the walls as he climbs the back stairs. Loud is his typical entrance, and I throw a concerned glance at the pacing man in front of me. Renard halted, raising his eyes to the ceiling as Fitz's voice disrupts his focus, and I snicker.

Leave it to the brash tiger to interrupt the gargoyle's slide into a good funk.

"Come on, Ren. Let's go see what our furry friend has to say," I coax, rising to my feet. "I can't guarantee it will be interesting, but at the very least, Fitz will be amusing."

With an annoyed growl, he walks over to the railing around the shaft of the Tower and jumps. I watch him leap from side to side, climbing up towards the belfry, where the main sitting area is located.

So dramatic. He could have used the stairs.

Picking up my scotch and his port, I head up the back stairs to where I can hear the younger twin jabbering like a tour guide. When I round the corner at the top, I gape like a beached orca. I almost can't believe my eyes, but I know I'm wearing my glasses.

Delores Drew is standing in the middle of our sanctuary, listening to him describe his Super Smash Brothers victories while Chess smiles at them fondly.

What in the seven hells of Dante?

"Aubrey! This place is amazing!" Delores cries, rushing over to greet us. She frowns when she sees the gargoyle perched on the railing by the bell. "Renard, why are you lurking over there like a creeper? It's not like I haven't been—"

"Stop!" we shout in unison.

She knows enough of our secrets now to get the others digging and the look I give her reminds her of the promise she made when she invaded our privacy the other night. Delores' cheeks heat and she drops her head to let her hair fall in front of her face. It's adorable, but I don't want her to forget we're not ready for everyone to know the secrets she's keeping.

Chess' brow furrows, and Fitz stares daggers at us when Delores wilts.

She looks up with a disappointed expression, but shrugs it off quickly. "Fine. I thought we were friends after what the three of us did the other night."

That statement changes the tenor of the room immediately and I rush to correct her typically innuendo-filled word choice before Fitz zeroes in on the intel. "Renard found her wandering the courtyard—alone—a few nights ago."

The tiger turns to the pastel-haired girl between them with an arched brow. He growls playfully and Chess tickles her sides. Their reactions make Delores laugh, which makes me smile as well.

Interesting.

"Did they at least take care of you, baby girl?"

"That's a good question." All eyes turn to the stairs, where Felix is leaning against the wall with a quirked brow.

Isn't this a full fucking house?

"We did—eventually," Renard says as he leaps off the rail and stalks over to take his drink from me. "Calm down, testosterone trio."

"Who pissed in your port tonight?" Fitz snorts, dropping her hand to walk to the kitchen area. "I'm getting a beer. Bro? Chess? Baby Girl?"

"Ew," Delores says, wrinkling her nose. "Do you have Dr. Pepper?"

Felix nods at Fitz before crossing the room to find his favorite armchair. "Define eventually."

I arch a brow at him as I walk over to my chair and settle in. "In this case, eventually is an adverb meaning in due time."

"Don't be an assface," Delores says as she sashays into our circle of chairs. Chess follows her like a lost cub, and she waits for him to choose his seat before plopping onto his lap. His expression is surprised, but he holds her in place. "They took me flying, and I got to watch—"

Oh, shit. She's going to spill what we've kept secret for a decade. I thought I was clear about it being between us.

Renard surprises me by joining us instead of claiming his spot on the balcony for the evening. He perches on his damned near unused throne, his eyes focusing on our visitor as his tail flicks in agitation like a cat. "Shhhhh. You remember the terms *petite lapin.*"

Oh, she's got him extra twisted. He only reverts to French when the gargoyle is riding him hard.

The Raj arches his brow and suddenly, there's a staring match between all the dominant shifters in the room. Delores frowns at us and crosses her arms under her chest—which, I'll admit, distracts everyone long enough to break the spell.

"Why are you all glaring at each other like a bunch of fuck knuckles?" Fitz hands Chess a beer as he passes and then turns to Delores. "Here you go—a Dr. Pepper for the lady. I'm surprised we had it. Who filled the fridge?"

No one owns up to it, and again, I turn a knowing smirk to my winged companion as he remembers how to sit comfortably on the throne he rarely uses. Rennie is a fixer at heart, and I don't know where he picked up the information that our girl likes that soda, or how he knew she'd end up here eventually, but he was ready for her. Despite his grumpy attitude about her sudden presence, he clearly expected this scenario to occur.

He's such a fucking mother hen.

"I said they took me for a ride the other night and now everyone's boxers are in a knot." Delores scrunches her nose in a very bunny-like fashion as she shrugs. "I don't know why that's such a big deal, but apparently, it's very hush-hush."

Fitz smirks, turning to look at me like a goddamn pervy asshole. "Please, Baby Girl, enlighten us about how you went soaring because that privilege has always been a *bone* of contention." He snickers at his own pun like a teenager, and we could play marbles with all the eyes that roll simultaneously.

I'm annoyed by his nosey probing, but Delores beams at him before clapping her hands and bouncing on Chess' lap. His pained expression makes me cover a chuckle with a cough, but I stay silent to see what she's going to say.

"I got to ride Aubrey! We went suuuuper high and Rennie had to chase us because he doesn't fly the same. It was so cool because how many people can say they got to live Game of Preds like the dragon queen! Draconis!"

Fuck. Now she's done it. I can't decide whether I'm aroused by her words or irritated that she's going to get Fitz started on his dragon rider bullshit.

Her excited cry and wiggling are almost killing the cheetah she's seated on, and the amusement I get from watching him struggle is worth the impending aggravation once her story sinks in with the others. Hell, I'm even feeling kindly enough to forgive her bringing up that travesty of a show.

They didn't take the time to properly research my people.

Felix's brows disappear into his hairline as he realizes what she means, and Renard snorts. It takes another full minute before Fitz leaps from his chair to point at me accusingly.

"You let her ride the fucking lizard? Not cool, man. I thought we were bros."

Sighing heavily, I take my glasses off and look at them, moving my eyes between him and Delores pointedly. "First, it was Renard's fault. He was late to meet me because he was waltzing in the moonlight. Second, who would you rather have on *your* back? A sweaty cat or a sweet bunny?"

That coaxes a giggle out of our girl, and a round of laughs from the rest of the guys. Fitz pouts and Delores rises with a sigh, walking down to the couch to drop onto his lap. She runs her fingers through his hair, giving him a fond smile, turning his grumpy frown into a self-satisfied smirk.

If she keeps spoiling him like that, he'll be intolerable.

"Fine. Point taken, spicy lizard. But I'm going to want this story at some point, capiche?" Fitz waggles his finger, first in her face, then at the rest of us. "Flying is cool and all, but *I* bit that fucker's head off for insulting her. That's gotta count for something, right, baby girl?"

Her eyes widen, and she turns beet red, squirming on his lap. The other Khan didn't react, so Felix wasn't angry that Fitz broke the 'no killing' rules at the Games. Delores turns to Renard and me and mutters, "He did. I mean, I didn't hear what he said or anything, but I'm sure it was *awful*. That's the stuff they're doing all over social media and in class every day."

Rage fills me, and I count to ten in Arabic in my head. My hand slips into my pocket to squeeze the new—annoyingly adorable— bunny stress ball Fitz brought me. Smoke puffs out of my nose as I work to regain control over the dragon as he writhes in anger in my gut.

He wants to fry the motherfuckers who are torturing her, but I have a better plan.

Before I can lose my cool, Felix shoots me an amused look. "If it's bothering you so much, old man, we can look into it."

"Yeah, we can," Fitz mutters, tugging the girl on his lap tighter against his chest. "Just wait until I unleash hell on those bitches' devices. The Winged Wonder over there will help me, I bet."

"Guys, it's okay. Don't get yourselves in trouble just because those rich bitches and their pawns are determined to fuck with me. I can handle it." Delores' words sound more confident than the look in her eyes conveys, but I nod.

I'm still seething, but her kind heart doesn't need to worry about shifters as old and crafty as the five of us. She may dissuade Fitz from seeking his retribution with pretty words, but based on the expression on the others' faces, he's not the only one who is eager to hand out much deserved punishment.

All our bunny needs to do is say the word, and we'll swoop in like knights—dragons—in shining armor.

Dragons are especially excellent at settling scores—the painful, crispy way.

TROUBLE

DELORES

"YOU DIDN'T TELL US HOW YOUR NEW PASTEL HAIR WENT OVER with Professor GrumpyPants," Cori says as she threads her needle. My polar bear friend is impressively adept at sewing, which is why she's the head costume designer for the entire theater program, while Chess only occasionally oversees—so we can say a professor is running things. Her eyes flick to the skirt she's working on as she mutters, "Definitely a blind hem stitch here. The idiot who made this doesn't know their ass from their elbow."

Rufus snorts. "Look at the blush on Dolly's cheeks! Woooo, girl, I think it went very well."

Tucking my hair behind my ears, I pick at the buttons on the dress I'm holding. "I've had an enjoyable week, yes."

The two of them howl with laughter, stopping their work completely to give me pointed looks. My face flushes hotter and I squirm under their gaze. Neither of them looks away, determined to drag juicy gossip out of me at all costs.

"Okay, okay. I spent the night at the townhouse after Pred Games. Things got… really hot." I put my hands over my eyes, feeling exposed and unsure. "After prom, I didn't have the chance to talk about losing my virginity with friends, like a normal teen—even with how terrible it was. I don't exactly know how to do this."

Cori scoots over and pats my shoulder. Her mouth is full of pins as she tries to comfort me. "Is oh-kay Dowwy. Don' be shy."

"We won't tell a soul, Dollypop. You can share all the nasty details —especially if it's about hot dicks," Rufus whispers conspiratorially as he plucks buttons out of the jar to study them.

I wrinkle my nose and grin a little. "Ok. So, I spent the night... with Fitz."

"Woooo-weeee! Our girl landed herself a big kitty dick to swing from! You know, I hear they have these insane hook things on them when they're with a mate." The badger waggles his brows and his hips, making him look ridiculous. "Coco, we have to up our game. Dolly's making us look dull."

Leaning in, I swat him playfully until he stops making sex sounds at me like a pervert. "Rufus! Someone will hear you! Stahhhhhp!"

My other friend picks up her sewing again, scrutinizing the fabric intently as the two of us battle. Once she finishes a section, she looks up with a raised brow. "That's it, though? Just a little fun with the tiger? No other smoking hot profs getting a glimpse of your new La Perla?"

Oh, damn.

I thought my tidbit would be enough to satisfy their need for vicarious thrills. Rufus looks at me expectantly and I sigh, trying to figure out what I'm allowed to share. I don't want to blab everyone's secrets; they trust me. But I also desperately want to have friends I can share my life with who actually care what I have to say.

Can I trust them? Ugh. I think so.

"I went on a late-night outing with Renard and Aubrey. We… took a quick trip together, after I danced with the gargoyle in the moonlight."

Their eyes pop open, and Rufus holds his hand up for a high five. I smack his palm sheepishly, knowing that I'm blushing again as they crack up. Cori holds up the bias cut skirt she's working on with a satisfied grin and tilts her head.

"You realize this means you have to go to the Halloween dance with *all* of them, right? It's only a few weeks away and we need costumes. It's mandatory."

"What?" I practically screech. "We *have* to wear costumes? Everyone? Where am I going to get a Halloween costume better than the cheesy ones on Amazon? We have exams and I have to study and we're not allowed off campus…"

Rufus grins, stacking his hand behind his head as he lays down on the floor to lounge. "That's right, Dolly Bear. Why do you think Coco is practicing her herringbone stitch? She's gonna help us get fancy."

I must look like someone has smacked me in the face with a brick, because Cori stops sewing to pat my hand. "We can all work on the costumes together—even for your guys. There's plenty of time, and since we haven't decided on the musical yet, I'm sure Professor Chess will allow you to work with us on a large costume project like this for midterms instead. Just bat your lashes a little..."

Snorting, Rufus nods his agreement. "Find out what your men want and we'll help. It's not like I haven't had to sew up people after fight night at home. I can't do fancy shit like Coco, but I'm handy with a pair of scissors."

The way he says that both creeps me out *and* relieves any fear of making a fool of myself from building in my chest. I pull out my phone to start a group chat on Predbook. I've never messaged anyone but Fitz before, but he made sure I had all of them friended, just in case I got cornered somewhere.

Oh, great. He preset nicknames for everyone. I'm gonna pay for this; I'm sure of it.

          BabyGirl: Um, hi, everyone.

CSpot: Delores? Is something wrong?

TigerKing: Who picked these names?

LustyLibrarian: It had to be Fitz.

EmoBatMan: Where am I???

CSpot: Delores, tell us you're okay.

      BabyGirl: I'm fine, Chess. Don't worry—
      there's no emergency.

TigerWoody: Baby Girl, are you naked?
That's def an emergency.

      BabyGirl: No! I'm in class. But I have a
      question.

TigerWoody: Yes, my dick is the biggest.

TigerKing: Fitz…

TigerWoody: Okay, okay. What's up, baby
girl?

      BabyGirl: My friends say everyone has to
      go to the Halloween Ball, including
      teachers… in costume. Did you know?

LustyLibrarian: What??!!!

EmoBatMan: Uh-oh.

CSpot: I must have missed the email.

> BabyGirl: Well, Rufus and Cori said they
> would help make yours, but I don't know
> what you want.

EmoBatMan: That's very kind of them,
petite lapin.

TigerWoody: If you need sizes, I'm an extra
large.

TigerKing: For fuck's sake, Fitz.

CSpot: Why don't I gather our sizes for you
and you can have full creative freedom?

TigerWoody: I'll give you something to
measure, Chessie.

LustyLibrarian: Costumes?!!

EmoBatMan: We've broken Flames. It will
take a while to talk him off a ledge. I agree;
we trust you to choose.

TigerKing: I don't, but fine.

TigerWoody: I'm all yours, baby girl. Make
me something sexy. No, wait. Make YOU
something sexy.

> BabyGirl: Okay. But I don't want to hear
> any complaints from the peanut gallery.

TigerWoody: Yes, ma'am! Ooh… how
about you go as a dominatrix—

"What's the word, Dollybear? Are we making like a Fashion Week strike team or what?" Rufus asks. He's got his Smackbook out and is already cruising the internet for group costumes as they wait for me to finish.

I give them a sheepish look. "They said we can pick. Chess is going to take measurements so we can get started."

Cori's eyes widen, and she covers her mouth with her hand. "Oh my gawd. They said… you… can pick?!!"

My brow furrows in confusion as I nod. "Well, yes. Why is that such a big deal?"

"It's a big deal because with no input, we can completely flip the script on your alpha assholes," Rufus replies with a fancy grin.

"Mmmhmm," Cori hums, scooting over to look at the costume websites. "Halloween costumes are disproportionately skewed to make women look like overly sexualized versions of everything. Who the hell fights ghosts in a goddamn thong? No one, that's who!"

Smothering a giggle at her indignation, I study the pictures of the group costumes with a fresh eye. She's right; everything from a sexy firefighter to a slutty pumpkin is represented, and it's more than a little gross. I scrunch my face, thinking about what Fitz demanded. I'm not opposed to looking hot; if I'm honest with myself, I enjoy the hungry looks I get from my professors, even if they think I don't notice. But that doesn't mean I can't have some fun with a little role reversal.

Five slutty dude costumes coming up.

"Okay, I'm in. What do you guys have in mind?"

Rufus whoops, the dark flash of mischief in his eyes simultaneously frightening and appealing. "You'll have to give us the inside scoop, cutie. We need to hit 'em where it hurts."

I arch a brow. "Inside scoop?"

"Tell us their soft spots, Dolly. You know, like what would irritate the hell out of them, and we'll plan the costumes around that," Cori responds as she clicks the trackpad to advance the page.

"I don't think Fitz is ashamed of anything, guys." My lips curve up as I consider for a second. "But we can make him look silly, regardless. It won't bother him, but his antics will drive the others nuts."

"Sexy nurse it is!" Rufus declares, scribbling on a notepad. "The hardest part will be shoes for these giant dudes, but don't worry. I know a place."

"Didn't you say Fitz has big old feet like yours, Dolly? You had to wear his shoes that time, right?"

I nod at Cori, ducking my head. "The big ass feet make sense now that I know about the bunny part, I guess. Lucille always made fun of me."

"They made you exactly how you needed to be; that's what my mama says. I wasn't meant to be a skinny-mini 'cause polar bears are self-insulating, and you have big tootsies because you gotta hop away. Now, let's plan how to bring these alpha doggies to heel."

I ponder for a moment, considering her words. Perhaps she's right that I'm built exactly how I needed to be to support my animal when it emerged.

Maybe all I needed was a shift in how I was looking at it.

As for what to do with the guys—I already have ideas. This will be a perfect opportunity to teach them a lesson, I think. "Whatever we do for Felix has to be girly. He'll flip his lid because he's so 'I'm a big, bad king. I'm the strongest shifter ever'. Blah, blah, blah."

"Oooh, if we do that, maybe he'll get annoyed enough to turn you over his knee!"

Her excited clapping makes my eyes widen and I trip over my words for a few minutes before I can even plan an answer to that. I mean, I'm definitely not *averse* to that scenario, but I don't think I'm quite ready for it, or to discuss it with anyone out loud. The best I can do is hiss at her. "Cori!"

The ongoing cackling from my friends makes my cheeks flame red as I add a few ideas to Rufus' notepad. I can't even look at them as Rufus smacks his ass and squeals like a girl on purpose before Cori follows up with a well-placed spank of her own.

Hera, help me, I'm going to die on the spot.

"Dollypop, loosen up! You're never going to fill 'er up with five dudes if you can't even take us handing out spankies in front of you." Rufus snorts and turns his attention back to the website, pinning me with a look. "Time out—let's talk about *our* costumes for a moment."

Cori grabs the list and scribbles a few things on it as she mutters to herself. When she finishes, she gives me a bright smile. "Just making some notes on materials. Rufus and I are doing 80s cartoon characters."

I look at the pink metallic material, finally understanding what she's been hemming while we talked. "Ooooh! I wanna be a cartoon character. Can I do it with you?"

A slow grin creeps over Rufus' face. "Oh, definitely. That'll get their goats; you won't match *their* sexy vibes. Good idea!"

My brows furrow and I pout. "I wanna look cute. Lucille never let me dress as hot as the Heathers—not that I wanted to go as far as *they* did—but now that I can, I *want* to be sexy!"

A flash of multi-colored hair is all I see before Cori barrels into me with a laugh, squeezing me into a tight hug. "I don't know if you could be any damned cuter, but we will make sure you look both sweet and smoking hot, Dolly. Trust me. I'll come up with something perfect."

"Okay, now back to torturing your harem. Tell us what evil schemes are in that cute wittle head of yours and we'll start ordering the supplies, stat. We'll have to bust our fabulous asses to get all of this done in time," the badger tilts his head, looking at me expectantly.

I grin broadly, thinking about what I can put each guy in that will make him squirm—besides Fitz, of course. The Halloween party sounded like a nightmare when they first brought it up, but now I'm actually looking forward to it. Maybe it will erase the memory of the shitty prom I attended here in the spring.

I can finally move on as I was meant to.

Love Her Madly

Fitz

Fitz

I want to go inside that damn auditorium and see what she's doing, but Chess told me not to. Being stuck out here in the shadow of this dumbass eagle statue is making me antsy, but I'll endure. If I didn't know it would end up being a problem for my consort, I'd defile it because whichever Shirdal commissioned this piece of crap deserves the comeuppance.

As if eagles are worth something this grandiose in the pred world.

Baby Girl is in rehearsal until five thirty and my brother had the brilliant idea I should meet her afterward to give her some hand-to-hand lessons in the gym. I was all in until I figured out he meant actual self-defense, not the fun hand-to-hand.

He should do it himself, but I don't think he trusts his tiger alone and sweaty with our girl.

Mores the pity for him, because I intend to have a fucking great time pinning her to the floor after she gets all violent with me. My cock's hard just thinking about it, and it feels nothing like a punishment for either of us. Though, I'm more the light BDSM type compared to my control freak twin, so he's probably misjudging my kinks again.

My eyes narrow as I realize yet again that I have no idea what those overgrown moths do for a good time. They don't share a fucking thing and it's not fair. But it seemed like Dolly got under their thick ass armor a little because she's hiding something big they let her know about. Her fumbling over what she knows in the Tower didn't fool anyone, least of all me.

I can smell liars, and she was fibbing.

Chess says we'll find out eventually, and he's probably right, but I want to know now, damn it!

Does the giant gecko wear frilly thongs? Is that obsidian asshole sporting a multi-headed, sentient dick?

Inquiring minds want to know, and I'm going to find out if it kills me.

I'd settle for knowing what the hell they eat besides the smattering of normal food they occasionally consume in front of us. I mean, we're all preds—who cares if they eat roaches or cute kittens? We'd get over it; just quit hiding it.

Grumbling under my breath, I hop onto the statue, throwing a leg over it like I'm riding a giant bird that should have been the transport to Mordor in that long ass shit Renard made us watch.

The blond elf was a smokeshow, though, and so was the chick, so I guess all those hours weren't totally wasted.

I lean back on my hands, propping myself until the bell rings. My smartwatch says it's close and I only have to be patient a little longer. Not my strong suit, but the more of my baby girl I get, the more willing I am to do out of the ordinary shit to keep her happy and safe. She's more addictive than the catnip pred-stasy I love so much and I'm helpless to her pull.

The doors finally swing open and I see her come out with her two odd friends in tow. They give her weird looks where it seems like they're talking with only their eyebrows and I frown. Is there some fucking eyebrow language I need to learn to be hip? Why the hell didn't anyone tell me? I'm definitely putting Chessie on that shit so I can learn.

"What the... Fitz!" she says in a loud, harsh whisper. "What are you doing riding the Shirdal eagle?"

Grinning, I lift one hand and wave it, rolling my hips like I'm riding a bucking bronco as I smirk. "Yeehaw, baby girl."

The punk rock badger puts his hand to his chest like he's going to faint and the colorful bear giggles like a madwoman as my girl scrambles up to tug on my sleeve. "Get down! You'll get us all in trouble if any professor besides Chess sees you."

"Highly doubtful," I reply as I bare my canines. "There's not a snake, whale, platypus, or bird who would dare attempt to challenge me. You're rolling with the big guns, baby girl."

She gives me a look full of exasperation and puts her hands on hips. It makes her breasts fill that button down, so I stop clowning to stare at that sight instead. After all, where Felix is an ass man, I'm a tit lover, so I can't resist. That makes her gaze narrow more, and she reaches up, yanking on my arm.

"Come on, you perv. Dismount and tell me why you're here before I end up in detention all night."

That simply won't do—I have plans, so many plans...

I hop down as instructed and sweep her off her feet, spinning us in a circle as I talk. "His Royal Crab Ass wants me to give you self-defense lessons starting tonight. He thinks he's punishing me, but he's wrong. You're hot as fuck when you get bloodthirsty, baby girl."

The bear clears her throat, doing another round of eyebrow gymnastics, then grabs the gaping punk next to her. "Well, we need to get to the cafeteria before the line gets too long. Have fun, Dolly!"

"But, but…" her friend sputters as he watches me pull my girl close.

"Now, Rufus!"

Once they leave, my girl gives me a sheepish smile. "Sorry. They're the first friends I've ever had who really wanted to know what's going on with me, and I guess I let them go on a bit."

I shake my head. "Don't apologize. I've seen who your old 'friends' were, Dolly. These seem to be infinitely better, especially since they have Chessie's approval. You need to have normal shit in your life sometimes."

Holy shit, I actually mean that. Bast wept, I want her to have fun with people who aren't me!

That's some fucking growth, right there. Chess will be proud of me—I deserve two blowjobs for that shit.

She smiles broadly, grabbing my hand and I'm surprised to find I don't mind a bit. "Thanks, Fitz. That's really sweet of you."

Blinking, I formulate how to respond. Women don't call me sweet and I don't know how to take it. Words fail me, so I tug her out the door and down the steps to the green outside. She pops a pair of adorable sunglasses on and I pause for a second. "Wait. I should text Chess and let him know Felix gave me a mission. Otherwise, he'll hold dinner and he hates when we're late without calling."

"Ooh! What's he making?"

Her expression is curious and hungry, so I make a note to have her over for dinner soon. Chess is a fucking amazeballs cook and Felix will just have to take the stick out of his ass long enough to sit across the table from her without flipping out.

"Some Asian beef thing. He experiments a lot because he's addicted to cooking shows. Ask him about the Great British Bake Off at your own risk," I reply with a chuckle. "It's sort of our thing to get the others to watch human shit without being dicks. I find their lifestyle amusingly simple and everything they have to do to live without animal instincts fascinates Chess. The others act like we're making them eat bugs."

"I have to see that," Delores murmurs, her eyes dancing. "I bet Aubrey is the worst. He gets so angry when things aren't researched properly. The romance section in the library makes him lose it on the daily."

I boop her nose after I shoot the text off, winking playfully. "You'd be right. Freya help us if there's any fucking dragons in the show or movie—he rants for days on end."

"Speaking of the sourpuss, I need to stop and leave him the files I put together on these old books he has me verifying. This one seems way older than the others and it has all these really familiar drawings I can't place. It's like I've seen these places and symbols, but I can't access the memory."

"Now you're speaking my language, baby girl. Error 404, right?" I arch a brow as we head towards the library. It's on the way to the gym anyway, plus I'll get to fuck with the spicy lizard, so I'm totally game. "Maybe it's something from when you were a kid?"

She snorts. "I doubt it. Lucille and Bruno weren't around much when I was a kid, only Mattie. They were too busy with the Council and their flavors of the week to show me anything."

As I expected, I hate her parents more every time she talks about them.

"Do you want to show me? I'm not a scholar like Emo Batman or Scaly Shakespeare, but Felix and I had to learn shit in order to take over. Not just fighting and ruthless shit, but actual history and politics—though he's infinitely better at it than me." I tilt my head, feeling nervous as I offer.

No one ever asks me about this kind of shit and I get why, but just because I'm a hyper, jokey motherfucker doesn't mean I'm stupid.

Her eyes widen and she squeezes my hand excitedly. "Do you mind? I'd love to show you. I mean, every perspective helps and your viewpoint will be so different from Aubrey's. We can use all the help we can get puzzling out why this makes both of us feel so edgy. It's like the book has mojo or something."

My heart grows five sizes like that green dude in the cartoon. My baby girl wants my opinion on book stuff and she thinks I can fucking help with something that isn't beating the snot out of someone. This shit is why Delores Drew is goddamn special. It's not that she's different from others; it's that her heart is enormous despite going through the massive amount of crap life has thrown at her.

I might rock the boyfriend stuff, but my baby girl puts us all to shame in the good person category.

As we approach the front door, I notice the sign flipped and sigh. "Dragon Master is off with the Rock Man. They locked up this place tight, babe."

She reaches between her breasts and I'm distracted again until she pulls a key out of her bra. "Voila!"

I've never been jealous of a key before, but fuck it, here we are.

"You have a key? What the hell did you do, lick his sooty balls?" I snark in amazement.

Dolly rolls her eyes, huffing at me indignantly. "I most certainly did not. I am, however, pretty good at the tasks I'm assigned, so I'm allowed to come in to work when I want."

That damn near floors me because El Fuego doesn't let anyone in his stupid library without supervision.

"You must be fucking outstanding, baby girl. Now let's get inside to see what you've got before he comes swooping in and toasts my ass for setting foot in here."

Giggling, she guides me into the main area on the first floor, humming under her breath as she deftly avoids every obstacle in the dark. She really knows this place and I can see why the spiky tailed asshole is creaming his tweed over her. When my eyes adjust, I realize she's leading us to a back corner out of the sight line of the open tables.

"What's the story, morning glory? I can't believe Aubrey is keeping something valuable back here, even if it is a delightful spot to get it on." Squinting, I look at the shelves and laugh when I realize this is a non-fiction section on religious history—probably never used in the slightest.

My girl goes on her tiptoes, looking delicious in the short skirt as she does so, her fingers skating over books one by one like she's looking for something. When she finds it, she yells in victory. "Ah-ha!"

I'm about to chastise her for drawing attention to us, but I'm too stunned to get words out when the fucking bookcase swings out like we're in Clue. She grabs my hand and tugs me towards the darkness behind it with a mischievous grin.

"Come on, Fitz. We have to take the elevator thingy to get to the archives."

What the actual fucking fuck?! The archives? The ones where sooty balls hides all his good shit?!

"I'm definitely not allowed in here, baby girl. Our dragon buddy barely lets me in the regular library because I might damage shit. I don't know if—"

She snorts. "Just do what I say, and I promise it will be fine. Can you be a good boy, Fitzy?"

Shit. Shit. Shit.

She used Chessie's name for me and she said those words.

My cock is ready to tear out of my pants to get to her. I blink, licking my lips. Dolly bobs her brows, and I wonder where she learned that tidbit. Our girl is full of surprises today, and hell if I don't want to see what they all are. "Uh, well, I probably could have until you said that."

"Don't worry. I'm going to love being your teacher," she replies, her ass swaying as she leads me into the void and the shelf clicks shut.

Spitting my words back at me? Fuck, this girl is my goddamn queen.

Raiders March

Delores

I had no idea Aubrey kept his archives so secret. He gave me the key to get in unbidden and I occasionally pop in when I can't sleep. It's never been an issue, but the way Fitz is acting, I'm fairly certain not even Chess gets to access the parts of the library I've been granted leave to work in.

Does that mean the dragon likes me? He was pretty pissed when he woke up with me sandwiched between him and Rennie that morning.

Sadly, I haven't gotten an invitation back yet. Maybe that's why he gave me the key—he was distracting me, so I didn't bother them again. That thought makes my heart ache a bit, so I take a deep breath and let it out. Fitz is following me and he wants me around; if the stodgy old coot wants me to be far away, I'll stay there because other people want me.

Like Chess. And maybe Felix.

I come to a stop in front of the torch I need to light before we get on that deathtrap. Pulling a lighter out of my bag, I flick it and touch the flame to the main torch, then watch it spread along the walls until the room is lit up enough to see. "Pretty cool, right? Like the adventure movies human watch."

His eyes narrow. "Oh, it is. I know exactly where that asshole got this idea from. What's next, a rolling boulder?"

"No, silly. We have to take the elevator down." I guide him onto the platform, relishing in my decision not to tell him what this will be like, just as Aubrey did to me. "Brace yourself."

The floor drops underneath us, rocketing down to the bottom of the cavernous lair of Apex's one and only book dragon.

"Holy fuck!" Fitz gives me a wide-eyed look, like he might have pissed his pants, and I giggle.

"You get used to it," I say nonchalantly. His gaze narrows again, and he follows me out into the next challenge. I drop his hand and gesture at the glass enclosure on the other side of the chasm, winking as he gapes. "This is where we have to jump."

"I'm sorry. You'll have to repeat that, baby girl. It sounded like you told me to jump over this fucking chasm."

I grin, crouching down for a moment before I leap into the air, springing over it like its child's play. He groans and I watch his dick jump from my new perch. I bet it is going to be much harder with a fucking erection.

Oh, well.

"Fitz, get your ass over here!"

Turning on my heel, I leave him to figure it out as I walk into the archival chamber to wait. I hear the rustle of clothes and a grunt and raise my fingers to pinch the bridge of my nose. I did not tell him to get naked and shift. The low growl followed by a curse lets me know he changed back, so I whirl around with a stern expression.

The smirking shifter saunters over to the air locked doors in all his glory. "As the lady wishes."

"I didn't say get naked; I said jump!" I hiss at him in annoyance like a damn cat. His dick notices that, too, and I growl. "Aubrey will lose his shit!"

"It's not my fault I'm bare assed in Charcoal Cock's lair. Serves him right for making it a goddamn obstacle course. I'm rubbing my balls on everything, just so you know."

I look up at the ceiling, praying for the patience to get into this room and show him the damn book I want before I kill him. My fingers fly over the keypad without looking, because I've been in here often enough.

When I look back at Fitz, he's eyeing me with a gleam in his eye I don't trust.

"What?"

"This entire trip is very Sexy Spy shit and I think we should role-play 009 inches later on. I haven't seen this side of you before, baby girl. You're totally Moneypenny in that skirt and if I get you nerd glasses like Chessie, it will be hot. as. Fuck."

Note to self: Fitz has a thing for nerds.

Second note to self: Chess and I should definitely take advantage of that together.

But I just wink at him, needing to keep him focused on our actual reason for being here rather than what his cock wants. "Maybe later. Get in here and check this out with me. And I can't believe I have to say this out loud, but... do not rub your balls on everything."

He pouts as I lead him to the table where I've been working. I pull on a pair of the white archivist gloves before handing him his own set. A thought occurs to me and I whirl around, glaring. "Also, do not put the gloves on your dick."

"Aw, baby girl! How did you know?"

"Dick-tuition," I mutter with a snort. He laughs as well and I pick up the tweezers on the table to turn the pages of the fat tome until I reach the section that's bugging me. "Here, look at this map."

He steps closer, looking at the book curiously. "This looks familiar. Are there more?"

"Yep." I turn the page, showing him the next map, then the three following those two. "There's five of them and something about the placement is tickling my brain. Like, they're definitely in a fantasy style, but the outline makes me think of something familiar. I just can't figure out what."

Fitz nods, looking at the last one for a moment before he taps my bag. "Hold it flat. I want to get scans with your phone because the rest of the guys should see this, and old cranky shorts will never let us all in here."

I nod, pulling my phone out of the side pocket and unlocking it one handed for him. "And what the hell is the Apex Society? The Council is one thing, but is that some old name or…?"

I frown as he snaps one picture after another. My eyes cut to the symbols on the maps, something still just outside of my conscious mind. I have a pretty good visual memory and that last map in particular really seems like something I've seen before.

Maybe at home… though I don't know where. I wasn't lying when I said my parents don't share shit with me except their disdain. It must be something I saw that I shouldn't have.

Suddenly, my eyes widen and I turn my head slowly, looking up at the camera in the room's corner. Oh, we're both dead. Aubrey will definitely know we've been in here by the pictures and when he looks at the footage, he's going to go all Targaryen on our asses. Not that I'd dare call his tantrums that to his face, especially after what Fitz just said.

"Fitz," I whisper, while he continues to get a few more angles of the very first map. "I forgot something important."

He looks up and smirks again. "To pat my bum for being such a good boy? Don't worry, baby girl. You still have time."

"No!" Inching closer to him, I make sure not to look up at the security camera as I murmur, "Aubrey has a camera in here just in case something gets stolen. I don't think he watches it unless he needs to, and when we pull these pictures out, he won't be able to stop himself from checking."

That makes him stop completely and look at me with wild eyes. Before I can grab his arm, Fitz pulls the big chair out from under the table and plops into it, wriggling around with a shit-eating grin on his face. He scoots back and forth in it, then makes a show of getting up and facing me with his naked ass pointed right at the camera. For a finale, my smug troublemaker does a few toe touches, still aimed at the video feed, and then stalks around the table with his dick touching the edges the entire time.

We're so fucking dead.

"I cannot believe you. You promised," I say as I close the book and ditch my gloves. "Aubrey might take my key back."

He snorts and shakes his head. "Oh, I highly doubt that. Felix might have to peel us apart when he comes for me, but honestly? I've never sent someone one of my turds covered in the ashes of their kin. That fucker has, and it's not the worst thing his grumpy ass has ever done."

I blink. That doesn't seem like the dragon I see at all. He collects stuffies and squishy stress balls in cute shapes. Aubrey's growly, but that gross? "Are you sure that wasn't… you?"

"Oh, baby girl. Men are disgusting no matter how wise and ancient and refined they are. Try stealing some of the poetry reading prince's special flowers in the garden just once… Kablooey! You find your beer full of some liquid that makes you crap your bed for a week."

Covering my mouth with my hand, I try very hard not to laugh and fail. I can only imagine the sneaky shit the troublemaking gargoyle gets up to and since I know things Fitz doesn't, I recognize his stamp on the dragon's vengeance plots. "Oh, Fitz."

"You'll learn to get fun, slightly illegal revenge on those you can't murder, too. We can teach you," he says with a wink.

I see how it is.

The professor thing isn't his jam, but this 'I'll teach you' bit is our little game. I can dig it.

"Okay, baby girl. Let's blow this popsicle stand and get you home before you turn into a pumpkin."

I snort. "The bunny was shocking enough, thanks."

"Ouch. That was bad."

WE R WHO WE R
DELORES

Delores

"READY FOR OUR DAILY GRIND, DOLLY?" CORI CALLS FROM THE stage.

I smile, feeling sore from dance class but excited to see my friends again. We're nearly done with the tap unit—the routine being the entirety of our exam—and then I'll be able to ditch the tiny, ass-baring tap shorts and sports bra I'm still wearing. I haven't changed yet, because Fitz helpfully pointed out it would convince Chess to allow us to work on the Halloween costumes during our design periods until after exams. Even I'm self-aware enough to realize that I'm wearing little more than a bikini in this dance gear, and I agree it will distract the fuck out of anyone who sees it.

I still didn't sprint across campus wearing nothing but this shit. I'm not suicidal.

Waving hello to my friends, I walk to where they have piles of fabrics, sequins, lace, sewing baskets, and pattern pieces strewn about like a fabric store exploded, unzipping the giant hoodie I've decided Fitz is never getting back. As comfy as it is, it gets boiling in here because of the lighting, and I'd rather not be sweating, no matter how much I love the feeling of safety wearing it brings me.

Todd was a mannerless ass-pig who never *once* offered me his jacket, even if it was twenty below. I want to experience *real* boyfriend stuff, even if it's only in my head.

Dropping my bag on the wooden boards, I frown. No one has actually said I'm their girlfriend—not even Fitz. I sort of assumed they were serious about me, but… that might be my naïveté showing again. Dickhead Todd simply *told* people I was his, and I went along with it because I was a young, swoony idiot. These professors are men; and I don't know if I'm delusional in thinking things are more official than they are.

What future could they possibly see with me?

Frowning, I plop down in front of the pile of sample pieces Cori is using to teach me to sew. I told her I didn't know a whip stitch from a whip-it, but she assured me she could teach anyone. I can feel eyes on me as I thread my needle with the day-glow thread I'm using for the hem of this dress, and when I can't take it anymore, I look up from my project and wrinkle my nose at my friends.

"Why are you staring at me like I have a big bug on my face?" I pause, eyes widening. "I don't, do I?"

Rufus snorts and shakes his head. "Chill the fuck out, Dollypop. You're insect free, but you look like someone drowned your pussy and not in a good way. What's got those skimpy knickers in a twist?"

"Rufus! Be nice," Cori chides as she tugs a piece of thread with her teeth. "You know she's shy about that shit. Talking about her Penis Flytrap won't make that any better."

I choke, sputtering incoherently as my face flushes bright red. "My-my… what?!"

Howling as he falls backward onto the floor, Rufus clutches his stomach. It's several minutes before he's able to sit up again—meanwhile, my face is getting increasingly hotter. "Oh, Dollybear, your face was priceless."

Cori smirks, trying to hide her mirth by focusing on the sequins she's applying to the bodice of the costume she's working on. Rufus stares at her until she throws a hand up. "Fine. She looked like I pissed on her LaPerla, and it was fucking hysterical. Happy now, you bitch?"

His smug smile is affirmative, and he turns back to me. "We are going to have to desensitize you to dirty talk. No way those naughty professors are going to spout poetry when you fuck. Well, maybe the morose gargoyle will. You've gotta quit blushing like you're losing your V-Card all over again."

"Fitz talks dirty all the time and I do just fine!" I retort indignantly.

Rufus' smile is even craftier than before. "Do tell, girl. "

Cori smacks him right in the chest as she snorts. "Stop baiting her, Ru-Ru. She'll tell us deets when she's comfortable. Besides, she didn't look embarrassed when she came in; she looked sad. Maybe we could focus on *that* rather than gathering material for your spank bank?"

I give her a relieved look before realizing now I'm expected to spill what's making me sad. That's no more comfortable than discussing details of my burgeoning sex life, so I shrug. "I dunno. Just a heavy morning, I suppose. Mid-semester blues, maybe."

"If you think I'm buying that, my uncle Sal has a swamp he'd like to sell you. It's in a hot real estate market and that's just as true as what we just got from you." Rufus arches his brow and I narrow my eyes at him.

"Okay, okay. I'm feeling a little insecure about the lack of definition in my relationships. Well, okay, maybe not all of them because some have barely started, but…"

"Aw, the whittle tiger hasn't asked you to wear his pin yet?" Rufus bats his lashes and chuckles. "Cori, help me out with this, so I don't sound like an asshole."

The polar bear looks up, clearly surprised. "Um… well, I think he means dudes suck at defining that shit because they're raised to pretend they don't have emotions. Hence, why I'm a vagitarian with a love for the clambake. But your guys are probably caught up in something even more complex—they're much older, your teachers, and none of them have a reputation for their dating skills. In fact, most of them are known for barely acknowledging women, while the tigers are known for playboy shit."

I take a moment to ponder that, rolling around the idea in my mind. Their reluctance to start a discussion about what our various relationships mean might be nothing more than *their* level of inexperience, despite their age or track records. Aphrodite knows the tiger group is clueless about Rennie and Aubrey—and once I knew it was super obvious. Maybe they're just as dumb about me.

I'm certainly not eager to put myself out there, either, am I?

"You percolate on that, sweetness. I, however, would prefer to work the gloomies out in other ways." Rufus holds his hand out and I take it. He pulls me to my feet and then helps Cori up. When we're all standing, he leans over and digs a bluetooth speaker out of his bag with a triumphant look. "Ah-ha!"

"Are you going to play some sort of relationship audiobook? *Preds Are from Mars, Prey Are from Venus?*" I give him a perplexed look as he fusses to pair his DiePhone with the speaker.

Cori snorts. "Hell no. Ru-Ru finds dancing meditative. That's how we solve all our deep-seated traumas. Dance it out." She thinks for a moment. "Maybe we should write a book about it…"

"Far too much work, Coco. Plus, I'm not sharing my family's therapy methods with the world. Between the mosh pit and drinking moonshine until you puke, I'm keeping those secrets to myself, thanks." He winks as he fiddles with a playlist and finally, Ke$ha is blasting at full volume. "Now, *dance*, ladies."

I'm still limber from my earlier class, and this is significantly better than tap, which has never been my favorite. I kick off my shoes, giving them both a mischievous look as I wiggle to the beat. Rufus claps, shaking his hips obscenely, and Cori joins us with some impressive booty shaking. The beat is electric, and we take turns singing the lyrics as we dance around the stage like crazy.

Rufus smirks as he pulls off a ridiculous breakdancing move, and I hoot as he flips and turns. To my surprise, Cori waits for him to finish and starts a 2-step hip hop routine that he follows along with easily. I should have known they'd be decent dancers, given that theater folk have to learn damn near every art form to be successful. They finish with a high five as the song changes to '*Good Girls Go Bad*'—a favorite of mine—and gesture at me to take center stage.

I'm definitely not used to doing this in front of anyone beside my reflection in the mirror, but I wait for the bridge before starting a series of *fouettes* across the stages. Ballet is what I'm most comfortable doing, because Lucille allowed me to take those lessons, along with ballroom. The break hits as I stop at upstage left, and I wink at my friends as they holler and whistle. Their encouragement makes me feel brave. Since they're the only other shifters here, I raise my hands, do a quick run to gain speed, and bust out my cartwheels and handsprings. When I land just shy of the lip of the stage, I turn towards them with a shit-eating grin, only to find them gaping at me like landed trout.

This is awkward.

"What?" I shrug, cringing as I worry my rickety gymnastics looked stupid.

"Dolly, that was amazing! If you can do stuff like that, we can pick something cool as hell, like *Newsies!*" Cori gushes, as she claps her hands in excitement.

Rufus is oddly serious, tilting his head at me thoughtfully. "Do it again. Flip that ass back this way, Dollypop."

Wrinkling my nose, I give him a confused look. "Why?"

"I just wanna see it again. Can you do the splits at the end?"

He crosses his arms over his chest as if he's challenging me, and I feel my bunny rearing her head, as if to say, 'how dare you?'. That's interesting. Since I started working on mindfully harnessing my animal in Shifter Basics, I have noticed she gets her back up when she senses any potential threat. Is there such a thing as an *alpha* prey animal?

Hell if I know, but I'm thinking I might be one.

Taking a deep breath, I channel all the energetic fury she's stirring up and funnel it into the lead-up run. My palms hit the wood as I execute the first cartwheel, each subsequent flip and twist getting more complex. The last move I do before I run out of stage is a back handspring, and as my feet hit the floor, I let the front one slide out until I'm in a full split.

Holy Shit, I did it!

Not bad for a self-taught klutzy bunny, eh? Lucille has always sworn that I was so clumsy as a child that they thought I had a balance problem, but here I am doing my best impression of Simone Biles and everyone is clapping and cheering!

Wait a minute. Everyone?

I squint at my friends in puzzlement when I hear an echo of their applause coming from behind me in the theater. Rufus does a little shimmy, clearly pleased with himself.

"Angel, that was incredible! What are you wearing?"

My eyes widen as I turn to find Chess standing at the edge of the stage with a box of sewing supplies for the costumes at his feet. Cori's requested order must have arrived and now he… Oh, dear. I'm never going to live this down. I give him a sheepish smile as I wiggle my fingers in an awkward wave. "Oh, um, hi, Che… *Professor.* We were uh… just dancing. You know, to uh… burn off energy."

Cori snorts and I whip my head around to glare at her, finding her studying her fingernails as if they hold the answers to the universe. The bitchy honey badger keeps grinning like the *Joker,* clearly enjoying the show. Great. Neither of them is going to lift a finger to get me out of the mess *they* created!

"This exercise required *that* outfit?" Chess quirks a brow, his lips curving. My nose twitches as I pick up on pheromones I've never noticed before, and I realize the pred trapped inside him must be trying to claw its way to the surface.

Why is that so hot?

I shoot him a bratty look, crossing my arms over my chest in a way I know stresses my boobs. "I'm wearing the required uniform for dance, which was my last block, and the schedule here doesn't exactly allow for much time between classes. We were making costumes until we took a dance break, so it's a good thing I didn't change."

The struggle in his expression is real as I pop my hip out, and I almost giggle, enjoying the effect I have on him. We stare at each other in tense silence until Rufus finally hops off the stage, strutting to our professor and grabbing the box from him.

"Thanks, teach. This will help us continue to work on costumes, while taking sexy dance breaks." Rufus bats his lashes and waves his hand. "Now shoo, so we can work on the *surprise.* Go on now. Ogle your *girlfriend* after class."

My mouth drops open, and Chess pales before he nods and turns on his heel like he's running from a plague of locusts. As he disappears, I hiss at the badger. "What was the point of that?"

Rufus drops to the stage and starts tearing open the box as he cackles like a madman. Cori sighs and joins him, giving me a 'sorry, not sorry' look. As much as I want to be mad at my friends—or possibly kill them slowly—I realize they may have just done me a favor by moving things along.

I guess I'll let them live.

Wicked Games
Renard

My eyes sweep over the students in my garden as they gather their books to leave. I rarely end class early, but I'm sending them en masse to the library to research their papers on the impact of Gothic literature on modern works of literature and film. Twenty unplanned student visitors eager to Google vampires and werewolves ought to drive a dragon to distraction, which brings me no shortage of chaotic pleasure. Chuckling under my breath, I sort my lecture notes into a neat stack and move to slide them into my bag.

That's when I notice Delores is still standing at the edge of the classroom, staring out into the lake.

The thumping in my chest feels like one of the rave DJ's Aubrey listens to is in control of the muscle there. I watch her silently for another moment, unsure what to do. We've been alone many times now, and each time it gets a little easier, but it still makes me nervous. She's wormed her way into our routine seamlessly—something I would have declared impossible a month ago. Her presence makes all of my misfit cohorts smile, and she doesn't seem to want us for our inheritance or titles—in fact, Fitz has to beg her to allow him to buy things for her.

Ugh. I feel like I'm inadvertently giving an old literary cliche to her: she's not like other girls.

I'm better than that drivel, but Delores Drew differs from the women at Apex Academy—students and faculty alike. She's smart, kind, and completely unconcerned with anyone's bank account or family provenance. Despite all the difficulties she's had, she seems interested in spending time with various members of our outcast clan not to help her claw her way back into society, but because she *enjoys* our company.

It's fascinating and terrifying how she affects all of me so completely.

None of my friends are without trauma, most resulting in why we're now living at Apex, instead of within our communities. Family and friends have damaged each of us in their own way, so it's a struggle not to be naturally suspicious of the ingenue walking amongst us. If she betrayed any of us, I believe it would irreparably harm the broken men that gather in my Tower most evenings.

"Renard?"

Her voice draws me out of my musings, and I blink, feeling sheepish because she's caught me staring like a fool... *again.* "Yes, Dolly?" I respond without tripping over my tongue. Her eyes are wide when they meet mine and a strange sensation zings between us. I've felt nothing like it before, but the pull towards her in that moment is undeniable. Making a mental note to ask Aubrey if he's felt it around her, I watch her closely to see if she's experiencing it as well.

Delores bites her lip, fiddling with her notebook, but I swear, her scent has changed. "I was wondering if I could ask you a few questions? I'm sure I can tackle my research project during work study in the library, so it won't affect my paper if I don't go there now."

Mon Dieu, this can't be good. Is she going to ask about hunting? What am I getting myself into if I say 'yes'? Before I can come to my senses, I'm nodding at her.

Merciful Lugh, I can't control myself around this girl!

"Great!"

She beams, and my heart trips again while she rifles through a bunch of papers in her bag until she pulls out a small black journal. My eyes widen and panic sets in—she cannot be considering reading things from her diary! The stream of consciousness that escaped her lips the last time she confided in me was enough to do me in; what am I going to do if she confesses anything else?

"So, I'm working on an authentication project for Aubrey, and the other day, I saw pictures in the book that seemed weirdly familiar, but I can't place them." She shimmies a bit as she pulls out her phone to show me a picture of the book cover, her eyes sparkling with the excitement of the hunt—in this case, the hunt for knowledge.

This is why my fiery companion is so taken with her.

How many students—or women—would wiggle their bums about a dusty old book from his creepy cave? That explains his willingness to invite her to hunt earlier in the month. Old Sparky is positively smitten with the book-loving bunny, and I fully plan on teasing him mercilessly about it.

If only to draw attention away from me.

However, I see one problem. "You took… *pictures?* In Aubrey's archives?" I ask carefully, unable to stop my face from scrunching in a wince.

Aubrey is fanatical about the archives—that's not an exaggeration. It took me a decade to get the grumpy fuck to speak to me when I arrived at Apex, but it was a solid *century* before he allowed me to enter his precious book hoard. His meticulous care of the priceless tomes and scrolls down there includes temperature and light controls to keep the ancient texts from turning to dust.

Hopefully, she didn't damage the text…

Delores nods, biting her lip again as she whispers, "I may have… gotten over excited—but I didn't use flash, I promise! When I realized they were something I'd seen before, I dragged Fitz along with me to investigate. Of course, he was being a dork, so I got distracted for a tiny second. But anyway, I took the picture because he said I should ask *you* about the Society since you're so old…" Her eyes widen and she grimaces when she realizes what she just said.

Oh, she does like to play with fire, doesn't she?

I decide to go the mischievous route because her reactions enchant me. "Well, you'd be right about my age, though Aubrey has a millennium on me. Speaking of that easily angered dragon, did you just admit to letting Fitzgerald Khan into his beloved lair?"

"Oh my gawd, don't tell me he isn't allowed in there! He didn't say anything," she groans, covering her face with her hands. "Am I in trouble?"

The laughter tumbles out of me and I clutch my stomach. 'Is she in trouble' is the best question I've been asked all week. When I finally gain control of myself, she's glaring at me, tapping her foot in irritation. I wipe my eyes and shrug, deciding to tease. "That depends. Do you own a fireproof suit?"

"Fuck," she mutters as she scuffs her combat boot on the ground. Her face brightens when she looks up. "Maybe *you* could help break the news? I'm sure Aubrey wouldn't be as mad, since you guys are so close…"

I arch a brow at her, then shake my head. "No way, *petit lapin*. I never come between the scaly man and his books. You're going to have to brave the fire on your own this time."

Wrinkling her nose, she makes an adorable pouty face at me that almost breaks my resolve. "Fine. If you won't help me keep the dragon from frying my bits, then you have to help me figure out what this 'Apex Society' is. I mean, everyone knows about the Council, but this book is talking about a *Society*. Does that sound familiar to you?"

I pause, deciding it's best to err on the side of caution with my young ingenue—she has enough enemies chasing her fluffy tail as it is. While there were whispers of such a thing, long before I came to Apex—from a time before shifters broke contact with the other magical communities, and well before the predators reigned supreme—I was too young to be certain of what I heard.

I would hate to lead her astray.

"Unfortunately, no." I shake my head, sighing for effect. "Throughout most of my lifetime, I've only heard about the Apex Council. The Society must be some long-forgotten remnant of ancient times. I'm sure it was just a blip in our long, tumultuous history."

"Hmmm," she says, staring at the pictures on her phone. "I wish I could ask that twatwaffle Shifter History professor, but I can't risk him kicking me out of class again since there's another quiz tomorrow. I have to do everything perfect to make up for the fact he *flunked* me on one of the four tests this semester simply because I dared to criticize him."

The rumble from my gargoyle startles me, but I tamp him down in favor of being reasonable.

"Some professors take criticism poorly..." I start, determined to play devil's advocate and not just jump to her aid without giving my colleague the benefit of the doubt—despite how odious Professor Abel is.

"I didn't criticize him to be a bitch, Renard! He walked in and told us he changed the entire exam to a completely different one than we studied for! I'd bet my last dollar everyone else in that fucking class but me got a heads up!" Her eyes fill with fat tears and I freeze.

Holy fuck, what in the name of Aed do I do now?

Fighting the urge to flee from this display of emotions, I step closer. The floodgates are open now, and I bet she hasn't let this out for a while. The snotty sniffles aren't delicate, but the despair and anger radiating from her is real—changing her scent again in a way I'm having trouble pinpointing. My internal response to her current situation, and the ongoing torment she's endured, courses through my veins like lava. My skin hardens and my tail drops, swishing in agitation, indicating the gargoyle inside of me is extremely pissed.

Sigh.

Delores looks up at me with a watery smile as I gather her in my arms, allowing her to rest her wet cheek on my chest. "I'm-I'm sorry. I'm always a m-mess around you. I don't know why."

Another chuckle rumbles out. "It's the effect I have, *petit lapin*. Gargoyles are… Well, we differ from most shifters. The members of the clan I was born in have been around as long as our dragon friend, and we have… adapted into superb listeners. It is easy to bare your soul to one of my people when we sit there like statues."

Sniffling, she buries her face deeper into my chest, holding on like a koala bear. "I suppose that's true, if I'm any sign. I babble like an idiot every time I'm alone with you, and now I'm leaking all over your shirt. Plus, I made you get all 'grr' at me."

She gestures at my shifted parts, which makes me laugh again, and I squeeze her—involuntarily, of course. Mostly because she's shaky. "Not at you. I'm discovering that I particularly dislike seeing you so distraught. I'm quite vexed about it."

She lifts her head and narrows her eyes at me. "Vexed? That's all? Hmph."

That adorable tantrum should have been followed by the stomping of a foot, but she seems far too comfortable teasing me while nestled in my arms. "Yes, vexed. I'm well aware you know what that word means. You have an excellent vocabulary, Dolly."

"I do," she admits with a sigh. "But I was hoping for something a little less… Victorian."

If only she knew how very Victorian my thoughts actually are…

I snort, leaning my cheek on the top of her head, purely to rest my neck. "The Victorians were pretentious assholes."

"Duh. Are you going to tell me anything I don't know?"

Clever girl.

"Okay, fine, it pisses me the fuck off people are torturing you," I expel, in a rush, before I change my mind. "Aubrey says you can take care of yourself, and Fitz says he has it handled, but I worry that one of us won't be around the next time someone tries to hurt you."

That seems to satisfy her for the moment, because she nestles closer before softly replying, "My turn for a truth: I worry about that, too. But I can't hide from the world, or depend on everyone to take care of me—that's how I ended up cluelessly losing my virginity to a tiny-dicked, douche canoe ex-boyfriend and getting the surprise of my life, emerging as a *bunny.*"

She really can't help herself, can she?

"The real secret is that most people's first time is a nightmare, *petit lapin.* Everyone pretends it's moonlight and roses, but it's usually awkward and silly and not at all what it will be like later on, even for us ancients. It's a lot like learning to fly, I suppose. Those of us with wings all looked like idiots while we learned to use them," I muse, proud of how I steered the conversation to safer territory.

I don't know how my gargoyle will react if we keep talking about sex.

Luckily, my redirection worked. "Flying was amazing! It was the biggest rush. I'm so glad you guys took me. Can we go again sometime? I don't mind if it's at dinnertime." Delores babbles, gazing up at me with so much excitement, my heart skips a beat again.

Son of a bitch.

"Yes, we can, Dolly. Anytime you wish," I murmur, knowing in my stony heart it's the truth.

She sighs and rests her head against my chest again. "Thank you, Renard."

I guess we're staying like this for a while. I don't mind that much—not really.

King of Pain

Felix

I'm still mad at Chess for allowing that little smart ass bunny to pick the costumes for this ridiculous event. Apex always has a big Halloween bash, but it's never been mandatory for staff or students to attend. That's suspicious, much like the dance last spring, and Aubrey has been going bonkers meeting with the prey working the event to ensure we don't have a repeat of students projectile vomiting like out-of-control fire hoses. Renard provided the nursing staff with a variety of herbs to brew up antidotes to common poisons and anti-venom, but since we haven't figured out what the hell they used last time, it's like shooting in the dark.

The whole thing makes my fangs twitch and stinks of Council intervention.

Those fuckers won't be in attendance, but Bast knows they orchestrated the affair. Henrietta is far too eager to please them and too chicken shit to say 'no', even when it's not safe for the kids she's supposed to be caring for. I almost sent a missive to some of the few allies I have left within Bloodstone and their satellite locations to see if they've heard anything, but I'd rather save that for a genuine emergency.

Favors are never free in the Khan ambush and I don't want to spend capital that I don't need to.

My current frustration is fueled by that impotence, but it's also tinged with fear. Since my exile, I don't allow anyone to have power over me. Chess giving Barbie free rein to outfit us for this event took away some of my tightly held control and if I didn't love him like a brother, I'd find a suitable punishment for his little gambit. Nothing violent or harmful, but he wouldn't be comfortable in public for a short time.

I don't hurt the ones I care about if I can avoid it, but I also have to maintain order in our ambush.

Looking at the bored expression on the face of the raccoons delivering our boxes, I sigh internally. The damn things require a signature and I can't fathom why in the fuck that would be. As if anyone would dare touch something addressed to Khans without permission—the idea is outrageous. Even the staff know better than to cross the shifters living in this townhouse, so making me stand here and put my name on this cutesy paper is a flex our little bunny is probably giddy with glee over.

That girl needs a spanking something fierce.

I haul the pile of boxes inside, dumping them in the middle of our living room with a growl of irritation. I don't know why I let this girl get under my skin so badly, but she's a genius at riling my tiger up like no one I've ever known except my twin. The outside of the damn things are full of drawings and designs and sparkles that make the contents feel even more suspect.

"Hell yeah, baby! Our shit is here," Fitz says, as he leaps over the couch in a graceful arc. He's been buzzing with anticipation all day and luckily for me, Chess kept him busy. "I can't wait to see what my baby girl made for me."

"Made?" I ask as I look to Chess for confirmation.

He nods, a small smile flitting across his lips. "Yes. Delores and her friends used my measurements to make our costumes—including Aubrey and Renard—as their mid-term projects. I wasn't allowed to watch them create, so I'll have to grade them mentally as they are revealed."

Pfft. He's going to give them perfect scores no matter what, but I hope to hell they actually had enough skill to create costumes that don't look like kids at a craft fair.

"Great," I reply, rolling my eyes at both of them. "This is going to be a nightmare; I know it."

Fitz grabs a paper taped to the top of his box and laughs. "She created an adorable little manifest for the box."

Our girl is nothing if not thorough.

Not your girl, Felix, I remind myself as I flick out a claw and slice the tape on the top of my package. It's bigger than Chess and Fitz's boxes and that makes me worried, too. What if she put me in some weird inflatable dinosaur monstrosity? I didn't buy anything and I'll be forced to admit to Henrietta that I don't have a costume.

If I end up monitoring detention for a month because of her, I'm tanning that girl's hide even if she isn't mine.

My phone buzzes, startling me as I pull out a mass of tulle and sequins that have my eyes almost bugging out of my head. I drop the bundle back in the box, sucking in a calming breath when I realize what she dressed me as. The screen shows a message in the group chat and I roll my eyes to the ceiling for patience when I see it.

BabyGirl: You got the boxes!

TigerKing: We did.

I groan when I remember fucking Fitz picked out the names for this damn thing. As if the costumes weren't humiliating enough.

BabyGirl: Tell me, tell me! We worked really hard on them and I can barely contain my excitement. I'm bouncing off the walls like Fitz when he has too much caffeine. My friends and I spent a lot of time picking out the different themes and our grade is kind of riding on this so…

HER NEED FOR REASSURANCE MAKES MY DICK TWITCH IN MY sweats. I can tell by the way she looks at me in class and the tone in her voice now that she'll respond so well to praise. Letting her show me what a good girl she can be when she's not being a petulant brat would set both of us on fire; I know it. But that's not my place and it can't be. I can't allow her to charm me with her cotton candy hair and big blue eyes like she has Chess and Fitz.

I have to be strong.

But it couldn't hurt to give just a little so she doesn't get hurt, right? The way she talks about her home life with the others doesn't sound like she'. given much encouragement. Her parents' dismissal of her performing talent particularly irritated Chess, and he's usually very easygoing.

Praising her for working hard wouldn't be out of line, right?

I look over at Fitz as he holds up the sexy nurse outfit that glitters with sparkling accents and appears to be cut perfectly for his body. He's waving it at Chess, not perturbed by the matching fishnets, cap, and heels in the slightest. My twin is adaptable as fuck, and I think he'd wear a banana hammock and flip-flops if Delores sent it for him. When he offers to take Chess' temperature with his meat thermometer, I shake my head and go back to my package.

Lifting the enormous pile of gossamer and sparkling fabric, I chuckle to myself. I suppose I deserve to wear a Rainbow Magic fairy dress after giving her hell about her hair in class. I'm sure she thinks I'll balk at the yards of material, crown, wings, and matching shoes, but I could give a fuck. So far, her choices seem to coincide with things she associates with each of us: Fitz making her feel better and my pushing her boundaries.

It makes me super curious to see what she's picked for everyone else.

"Fitz, stop trying to play with his ass and let Chess show us what she picked for him," I growl in annoyance.

Chess gives me a red-faced, apologetic look, but I wink at him. He and my brother are good for one another; I give Fitz hell because he's my brother, not because I actually give a shit they're fucking. "Give me a second to unwrap it, Felix."

My twin is on it before his consort can finish the sentence, ripping into the tape and paper like a toddler stealing someone else's Christmas present. He yanks the garment out of the box, his eyes full of delight. "Chessie! You're a can-can dancer!"

The dress looks like something out of that French musical thing Renard made us watch one night and I scratch my head, wondering what that's supposed to mean. "He'll look pretty, but I'm not sure I get it."

"I told her she could follow her dreams, and dance is part of that," Chess says with a soft smile. "I think it's a pun."

Chuckling as the realization hits, I shake my head and pick my phone up to text the smart assed little cottontail. She texted again while I was inspecting the goods and I turn away from the other two as they playfully snark.

> BabyGirl: Did I do a good job, Sir?

Son of a bitch, she's going to fucking kill me.

> TigerKing: You did well, princess.

The little dots appear, and I watch as she types, erases, and types again. I don't have the patience for this shit usually, but I'm interested to see how she reacts.

> BabyGirl: Thank you. *heart emojis*

My eyes widen and I click the screen off, stalking over to my mini-ambush. I clear my throat and they stop wrestling with one another, looking at me expectantly. "What the hell do you think she sent the winged assholes?"

Fitz gives me a broad, wicked grin. "I don't know, but I'm dying to see what sexy fuckery she sent Old Pepper Pecker. He'll lose his mind no matter what because he was pissed as hell that we had to go and more so about the costumes."

I grin to myself. *Maybe a trip to the Tower is in order.*

"KNOCK, KNOCK, STONE COCK!" FITZ CALLS AS WE TRUDGE UP the backstairs to the top floor.

He's so hyper, even Chess is having trouble dealing with him. The poor cheetah is trudging up behind my twin as he bounces like a sugared up human toddler. I don't know how we're going to keep him in check until this damn party tonight. I may have to fucking slip him some of that catnip pred-stasy shit, so he chills the fuck out.

Aubrey ambles into the main living area with a book in his hand. The look he gives me is accusatory, and I shrug sheepishly.

I'm aware bringing cracked out Fitz here is a dick move.

"We received a special delivery this morning and even though it wasn't the package I prefer in the morning, it was divine!"

"Zeus's beard, Fitz!" Chess mutters. He looks over at Renard as he comes in off of his brooding perch and shrugs. "He's out of control. Dolly sent our costumes, and he's barely able to contain himself."

The gargoyle arches a brow, his expression smug as he replies. "Perhaps you should send him downstairs? If she did this, she should be the one to deal with the fallout."

"Actions have consequences," the dragon rumbles with a matching look of glee.

I don't disagree, but Fitz's ADHD isn't the princess' fault.

"She's probably getting ready with her friends. We should let her have that time," Chess says as he pushes his glasses up. "Those two seem to make her feel accepted and normal. I think she needs that."

"She's gonna be maaaaad all you fuck knuckles are talking about her like she's not an adult capable of making her own decisions," Fitz interjects. "My baby girl has enough people trying to control her."

My snort hurts; that's how hard it is. "Fitz, you track her like you're hunting her—on the app, in person, in her room—how are you any better?"

Crossing his arms over his chest, he gives us a very knowing look. "She knows I'm trailing her. If she told me to fuck off, she knows I'd try. And I let her make every decision I can without acting like she's a kid because she's younger than us. Stop trying to be her daddies and be her Daddy, dumbass."

His words hit me like a giant whale dick slapping me in the face. I've never known Fitzgerald Khan to drop wisdom like that, but I'll be damned if he's not right. We're acting like overprotective parents, not… whatever we should act like. Despite his psychotic tendencies, Fitz has given her the most freedom possible, even though it has to be killing him.

I'm not touching the 'Daddy' thing with a ten-foot pole—because it made my dick feel like it grew that fucking big.

Adjusting myself as discreetly as I can, I scratch my chin and nod at my brother. "He's right. Even if she gains a little experience and wants to try out advanced kinky shit with those two, we can't boss her around when we're not in class. That girl has a brat streak a mile wide, and she'll do stupid shit just to teach us a lesson."

"Oh, for shit's sake, Felix!" We all turn our heads to look at Chess. He's rolling his eyes hard enough to pop them out of the sockets. "Let's all take a moment to admit, even silently, that I'm right. We're all interested in her, whether or not it's smart, and we can quit dancing around semantics."

"He's not wrong," Renard says with a smirk as he lounges on his throne. "You are constantly correcting yourself, Raj. You can't win the prize if you're not on the board."

This isn't the time to argue about this crap.

Luckily for me, my twin jumps in as if he just found the thread again. "Aren't you asshats going to show us your costumes?"

Saved by his inability to focus yet again.

"No!" Aubrey snarls, as he crosses his arms over his chest like a child.

I'm surprised when the lazing gargoyle leaps to his feet, grinning a little as he walks over to retrieve two boxes from behind their chairs. His eyes are dancing with merriment, and I assume he must like what the snarky rabbit sent. He drops them, bending to pull out a sexy version of a Batsuit.

I'll be damned.

Fitz howls with laughter and even Chess is snickering as he looks at the short skirt and heeled boots. "Oh, baby girl, I'm giving you the best orgasm ever for this. I can't wait to see what the hot tamale is going to be."

The dragon hunches further into his seat, his iridescent eyes glittering with promised vengeance. Renard winks at him before he pulls out a wildly colored rave girl outfit complete with short tutu, a unicorn horn that lights up, furry boot covers, fishnets, gloves and a bikini top. It looks like the 80s threw up over the clothes and it only takes a moment before we're all howling again.

Oh, she got him good. That damn EDM and cute shit… he's not mad because it's sexy or colorful. He's mad because it's adorable and he doesn't want us to know how much he's enjoying the cuteness of his costume.

And they say I don't notice shit.

Chess looks over at me with a smug smile and mouths, "She's perfect."

I'm starting to see that, little brother.

I Know You Want Me

Delores

"Hold still, Dolly," Cori says through the bobby pins in her teeth.

She's working on my hair, and I swear to Hades, she might pull it out at the roots.

According to her, our costumes are 'loosely based' on the 80s cartoon characters we chose, which is why instead of the traditional primary color palette of Rainbow Brite, I'm in a pastel version. The polar bear is currently busy gathering my matching locks into twin ponytails on top of my head and clearly, she was never taught the gentle hand Mattie used when she did my hair when I was younger. I tried complaining, but Cori told me 'Hold still—beauty is pain, baby.'

Hmmph. I guess being scalped is beautiful in her family.

"I *am* holding still," I grumble, wincing as she yanks the brush through my hair again. "Anyway, so like I was saying, I stayed behind after class with Professor Renard, and spewed word vomit again until I cried like an idiot, and he humored me until I had to leave for my next class. I'm a total waste at this shit."

Rufus tsks as he works on ratting up his freshly dyed blood red hair for his Lion-O costume. "Oh, I doubt that. You're collecting them like Pokémon—got to catch all of 'em, Dollybear. What did this talk entail?"

"Stuff about my pathetic ex, and my Shifter History professor being a douche—that's why I cried—but then he calmed me down. It was cool to hear a little about his people, even if he's still cagey about his history. Both Rennie and Aubrey are kind of touchy with sharing." I trail off, as I realize I'm one to talk about withholding information about my past.

Awareness is half the battle.

Cori reaches for her curling iron, and I flinch because of an incident when I was young—the one time Lucille pretended to be a mother during an on-camera interview. Let's just say her skills were lacking and I'm pretty sure all evidence was destroyed, including the reporter.

"I won't burn you, silly. Quit shrinking away," Cori mutters as she rolls the hair up tightly and sprays it. "Of course, they're tight-lipped about their past, D. All the teachers here were given the boot by their families. That's how the administration keeps them under their thumb."

I blink. It's not what I meant, but I file away that useful tidbit for later. My friends will think I'm even more sheltered than they already do if I admit I didn't know teaching at Apex is a *punishment.* "No, I mean about their species. I had no idea that gargoyles can all shift *parts* at a time, not just the royalty like Felix taught us."

"*STOP. THE. FUCKIN'. PRESSES,*" Rufus practically yells. "Coco, you can take this one. I don't even know where to start with this shit."

He walks over and takes the curling iron to manipulate my other ponytail while Cori shimmies her metallic fishnets on, giving me a pointed look. "What Ru-Ru is failing to communicate is that your entire statement is… well, shocking doesn't cover it. If we ignore the part where Felix Khan taught half-shifts to a first-year class—which is unheard of—there's still the whole 'shifting only parts' thing. Dolly, *no one* shifts one appendage at a time!"

My brows furrow. Renard said it was rare, but he didn't say *no* other shifters did it. Oh, fuck, did I spill something I shouldn't have? Anxiety creeps in until it's replaced by confusion. Lucille can shift parts of her as well; it can't be that rare. Cori must be mistaken, and I haven't told them a big secret. It's fine.

It's totally fine.

"Um, well… When he gets agitated, Rennie's tail shifts and flicks like a cat. And he can pop out just his wings, too. I asked him about it, and he said his family has done it since, like, a thousand years ago before they moved from the Carpathian mountains to France. But it can't be that big of a deal, guys. My bitchy mother can do it." They gape at me in unison and I turn bright red. "What?"

"Dollypop, that's not normal."

Cori nods as she pulls on her JEM dress, adjusting it fussily and fluffing her adorable curls in the mirror. "He's right; it's not, even for leopards. Maybe it's genetic? Didn't you say your mom is a Rostoff? They come from a similar part of the world, right?"

"Um, her family's in Moscow now, but when Mattie was tutoring me as a kid, she said Lucille's family moved to Moscow when their import business expanded. Something about buying up more territory for crops? But I think they came from somewhere in those same mountains originally—a long time ago. Like pre-Council, maybe?" I stand up and walk over to the costume pieces that are mine, tugging on my thigh highs while Cori is getting dressed.

Rufus snorts so hard he messes up his eyeliner. "Crops. Right." When I give him a confused look, he mutters, "Okay. Crops it is, then."

"Rufus," Cori says reproachfully. She turns to me, tilting her head. "So it was your nanny who taught you about your family and shifter history? Mattie?"

"Yeah, I mean, I took it in school, too, and that asshole Professor Abel is teaching it now. Sort of."

Why is she asking me this? Am I missing something important?

"Dollybear, the Council only lets professors teach a sanitized version of history—post-Council takeover—so Mattie sharing this with you was a big no-no. Did Renard mention *why* his people moved? While we're getting the tea, you might as well spill." The badger pauses, his application of the white liner on his eyes, arching a brow at me in the mirror.

"He said… something about a disagreement with their neighbors. They moved to Paris when Notre Dame was built in the 1200s, but then moved again around 1780. I think it was because the humans had that nasty war." I slip on my iridescent dress, smiling at how gorgeous it is. Cori made it a little short for my taste, but when I balked, she added a matching fluffy petticoat that I absolutely love.

"The humans?" Cori chokes, wiping a bit of her soda off her mouth. "Um… Dolly. Are you *sure* Mattie taught you shifter history?"

I frown, feeling totally clueless once again. "Yes, *and* human history. Lucille insisted I learn things at home because of the role I would play when I got older."

"There is no way to break this gently, Dolly," Rufus sighs, turning around to face us. "Girl, they lied to you, and I have no idea why, since you're supposed to be an heir, and would need to have all the facts. Shifters and other supernatural species used to have treaties. When the Council came along, those treaties were broken, and that's why we don't get along with other supes anymore. Rare shifters like your boys hide because their women and children are worth money on the black market, and without the more powerful species, they don't have the magic needed to cloak their groups out in the open."

My eyes widen, and I gasp, looking over at Cori for confirmation. She nods, rubbing her arms, almost as if she's comforting herself. "Brave shifter families teach their kids the *actual* stories at home—despite the risk of doing so. After the Council took over, shifters became more vicious. All the human wars were shifter territory wars. To limit the casualties, the Council finally made a treaty with *humans* that included partnering with the Khan ambush to send lawbreakers to Bloodstone. It's why humans pretend we don't exist now."

What. In. The. Actual. Fucking. Fuck.

"Are you telling me that Aubrey and Renard won't talk about their people because they don't want them to be hunted down and sold? And I blabbed like an idiot?" I shriek.

"Yup," Rufus says, popping the 'p', like the brat he is. "Also, I'm dying to know if your momma passed on that little trick you mentioned—the partial shift. Lucille's from that part of the world, so maybe someone already has a little gargoyle in them. Hehehehe."

"Oh my gawd, Rufus! Why can't you ever behave?" Cori grimaces, putting her hand on her face. "Dolly, don't listen to him."

I tilt my head, thinking about it for a moment. It's a pleasant distraction from my complete lack of knowledge, and I only extended my fangs during my fight with Gold in Shifter Studies. Maybe it *is* some rare hereditary thing coming from that part of Europe. I don't know what the hell that would mean, but it feels pretty goddamned amazing to do something those bitches tormenting me can't. "I can try? But if I do, I can't guarantee I can... put the bunny away... before we leave. Or at all. I don't have excellent control over my shift yet."

Cori's face lights up as she gives me a sly grin. "Oh, girl. Come here and let me do that makeup, and you can give it a go while I do. If you get stuck, Auntie Coco can fix that costume for you right quick. How about you focus on something small like… your fluffy little tail?"

Rufus' eyes glitter with mischief, and I feel the exhilarating zing of a challenge rocket through me, encouraging my bunny to come out and play. "Tail it is, then. Talk me through this, guys."

By the time the guys arrive at the party, I'm nervous as hell. I thought Cori, Rufus, and I had arrived fashionably late, but they didn't show until at least ten p.m.

Maybe they had to wait for Aubrey and Renard to get back from dinner?

That's probably it… not that anyone had to be manhandled into the cheeky costumes I sent, right? My texts with Felix made me feel a little better, but since I have a—*ahem*—surprise of my own, I've been on pins and needles while I wait.

I see them sneaking in as I dance with Rufus and Cori in the middle of the Khan training ring. Apex's ridiculously extravagant Halloween party is being held outside, but luckily, the weather didn't throw a wrench into everything. They set the DJ up where the judges for Pred Games would normally be, and tables of food and drink line the path to the circle. They even set up a bar in a roped off announcer section. A bored-looking vulture is pretending to check IDs and Fitz growls at him, howling in amusement when the frightened bird drops his wrist bands all over the ground.

Who the fuck is stupid enough to card a Khan?

Covering my mouth as I snort, I peek at their costumes while the song changes, thrilled that they all humored me. Felix in his huge fairy dress, arm in arm with Fitz in the sexy nurse outfit—they're both strutting like they own the place, and it makes me shiver. Chess is gesturing animatedly as he talks to Renard, both of them looking unconcerned with their 'feminine' attire as well. My gaze lands on the last of my guys, trying not to laugh as I watch Aubrey stomp in, like he's going to open a crack in the Earth with his feet. Rufus helped me cut the raver girl outfit suit so it would be adorable, but not obscene.

After all, who the hell knows how well-versed a 2000-year-old dragon is about making sure fishnets don't ride up your ass?

"Dollybear, you got a handful of beautiful guys watching you like a flank steak. You gonna put them out of their misery?"

I'm about to answer when the weasel from my Shifter History class randomly walks up to us. He's dressed as a zombie from the Walking Dead, and I snort. I've definitely seen better blood and gore in person, especially lately. Squinting at him, I cross my arms over my chest, unimpressed. "What do you want?"

He shifts from foot to foot, looking around as if he's worried someone might see him with me. "I… can we dance? I need to talk to you."

"Oh, now you want to speak to me? Well, since I haven't been good enough for you to defend in the past, I don't think I—" Cori elbows me and I see every one of the guys straighten and pretend they're *not* watching this interaction like a kettle of hawks. My lips curve up as I get a very bratty idea. Maybe Felix is right. I do like to poke the proverbial bear with a tiny stick. Turning back to the weasel, I sniff. "Fine. One dance and if you have nothing inter-esting to say, it's going to be a short one."

"It probably will be, regardless," Rufus smirks as he glances at my guys again. "C'mon, Coco. Let's grab a drink while our bunny beards the lion, so to speak."

When did I start calling them my *guys?*

I follow the weasel nervously, a slight flashback to losing my V-card at this exact spot making me falter. When the slower song starts, I groan and let him take my hands as I try to ensure there's enough space to keep anyone who sees us from yelling 'slut' comments. I'm not in the mood, and frankly, Fitz might kill them if I don't do it first. The small pred tries to lead in some sort of 2-step for a moment, and I sigh. He has no idea what he's doing, so I take over, leading him as I impatiently wait for him to spill whatever information was so pertinent that he had to approach me at a dance, of all things.

"Thanks for hearing me out. I mean, I know I haven't…"

I shake my head, in no mood for a false show of support. "Cut to the chase."

"You're in danger at Apex!" he says, then ducks his head as if he's expecting me to hit him. To be honest, I'm ready to hit him with the world's most sarcastic 'duh' when he's yanked away from me and dangled in the air, like a fish on a hook.

Fitz's eyes are golden as he snarls at the terrified mammal. *"What. In The. Fuck. Do You Think. You're Doing. Dancing With My Girl?"*

Oh, shit.

Dead Man's Party

Delores

"Fitz!" I lay my hand on his other arm as he shakes the shivering weasel like he's trying to make the loot drop. It's hard to take him seriously in the short vinyl dress, but if anyone can look like they're going to murder someone while wearing four-inch Leopartins, it's definitely Fitz Khan. "Put him down," I hiss. "Everyone is watching!"

His growl makes my thighs clench as he grinds out, "What the fuck do I care? He had his hands on you."

Rufus is damned near ecstatic as he walks over with our drinks, with a wincing Cori close behind. Neither of them gets too close to my furious… *boyfriend?* Fuck, I still don't know and now isn't the time. We're all going to get tossed out of this party if I don't calm Fitz down quickly, and I have no idea how Lucille would react to that. She seemed pleased to learn I've been seen with one of the Khan brothers, but since she's also a total psycho, I have no idea how pissed she'll be if I get suspended.

"Fitz!" I hiss, tugging on his arm again. "If we get kicked out, I might get suspended, and then I'll get in trouble with my parents!"

His head whips around, and the amber in his eyes fades. He drops the weasel in an unceremonious heap, holding his hands out for me with a sheepish grin. "Sorry, Baby Girl. What can I say? I can't control the tiger around you."

Squirming in place, I take his hands and let him tuck me into his side possessively. My irritation disappears like mist when he growls in my ear playfully and I giggle. "You can't just attack people at a party!"

Rufus walks over and gives me an eye roll as he hands me my Dr. Pepper. "Oh, that'll show him, Dollypop. Crack that whip."

The big cat side-eyes my besties for a moment, then shrugs dismissively. "No one asked you, little gangster." I glare at him and he mutters, "Thanks for keeping my girl company until we arrived."

"Your girl, huh?" Cori says, her eyes full of reproach. "That's *her* decision, Professor, and I don't think anyone has asked her yet."

My face turns bright red and I sputter into my cup, turning my glare on my meddling friends. Fitz looks confused, and I have no idea what I'm going to do about it. I sure as fuck don't know how to bring this shit up without getting triggered. The last time I tried committing to someone, they chased me down and tried to eat me —and not in a good way.

What in the hell am I supposed to say to lock down Fitzgerald Khan, playboy extraordinaire?

"C'mon, Baby Girl. I heard about this awesome game people are playing, away from the noise. That's really why I came over." Fitz gives me a less-than-subtle grin, and I snort at his lack of finesse.

The idiot from history slunk away while we were having our 'protective BFF vs. protective maybe-boyfriend', standoff. I nod at Fitz, assuming the warning the smaller pred gave me was all he needed to say. "All right. I can go see this *game* for a few minutes, I guess, but then I have to come back and hang with my friends."

"Go have fun with your temperamental suitor, girl. Coco and I are on the prowl for ourselves. I smell drunk athletes and have a hankering for beefsteak," Rufus says, waving his hand with a wink. Cori laughs and takes his arm, her grin enough confirmation that they'll be fine without me.

"I'm all yours, Fitz," I say, feeling better than I have in a while. His eyes dance mischievously and he drags me off the dance floor, toward whatever naughty surprise awaits.

"IT SHOULD BE RIGHT THIS WAY."

I nod as he leads me into the forest surrounding the training ring, smiling secretively to myself. The way Cori cut my dress allows my fluffy bunny tail to poke out, but the petticoats and dress hide it a little in the folds. It's almost invisible in the darkness outside of the training ring, so none of the guys have noticed it yet. Luckily, Fitz has his arm around my shoulders, so my secret is still safe.

I'm kind of excited to see what they think.

It only took me an hour to even get it to pop out enough to peek out of the slit Cori created in the dress. Both of my friends were stoked that I managed a partial shift, and Rufus started taking bets on which one of the guys was going to lose their shit when they saw it. I don't know why he thinks it will be such a big deal, but he's dead certain it's going to get me flipped over a goddamn table —possibly by *all* of my guys.

I will not lie; as exciting as it is, the idea of all of them is intimidating. I don't know if I'm ready for *sex* with more than one person at a time. I'm struggling to keep asshat Todd's memory out of my head when Fitz touches me.

Regardless, I'm really fucking proud that I pulled off a partial shift.

At the very least, I'd better get some praise.

My cheeks heat when I think of Felix's last message to me on Predbook. 'You did well, princess' wouldn't be that big of a deal to most people, but to me, it's more than I usually get. From the grumpy taskmaster, it makes my skin tingle, and I can't wait for him to see my shifting accomplishment. He's been encouraging in class, in an intensely overbearing way, and I bet he's going to be impressed.

"We're almost there," Fitz whispers in my ear and for a moment, I feel embarrassed that I was thinking about his brother while he's sort of cuddling me. Is that a party foul or something? That's not the right word, but hell if I know how to date five guys who are decades older than me.

There you go, grouping them all as 'yours' again, Dolly.

"What is this place?" I ask the tiger, deciding to get out of my head as I look around the thick foliage of the surrounding forest appraisingly. I've never ventured this far into the woods of Apex before, although I know there are some prey escape routes that run through this area.

"It's not like the enchanted wizard forest in the movies, if that's what you're worried about," Aubrey rumbles from behind us, surprising me with his appearance. I can't even look at the dragon in that flashing unicorn headband without giggling, so I don't answer.

Rufus' source for accessories made for big guys was this amazing store called the Cubby Holer. We had a blast on a video chat with the owner as we ordered everything we needed to complete the costumes, especially the pieces for the growly librarian.

Fitz snorts and turns his head to give the dragon a nod of acknowledgment. "Nice one, Smoky. No, baby girl, it's not full of trees that will beat you up and throw apples at you. It's just… private."

"Uh-huh," I reply, practically *hearing* his suggestive eyebrow waggle as I peer into the darkness. My vision isn't great in the dark—thanks, rabbit genes—but the guys seem to navigate okay. I don't want to trip over a branch and make an ass out of myself before we get to what I'm suspecting is *not* a game. In fact, I'm pretty sure this is an invitation-only party, and I've been hornswoggled by the resident horndog.

The scent of cheetah precedes Chess as he sidles up on my other side. "You look lovely tonight, angel. I suppose I have you to thank for the fact that I'm traipsing through the forest in this historically accurate period dress? Excellent bead work, by the way—I'll put in a good word with your professor."

I giggle just as a shout echoes from the back of the group. "Ooh-la-la, Chess!" That was definitely Aubrey, and he's snickering along with Renard as they bring up the rear. Chess flushes as red as his Moulin Rouge dress, then growls, which gets a snort from Fitz. I wrinkle my nose at the group antics.

Boys. They're so fucking goofy, even when they're like… older than the internet.

"Actually, you have Fitz to thank for being out here," I counter. "He's the one leading us on this *Lord of the Flies*-style hike. He swore there's some sort of cool game out here, but I'm thinking he's full of—oh my god!"

We hit a clearing, and right out in the open, slumped against an oddly shaped tree, is a dead body. I'm pretty sure it's dead because it's got blood all over—oh, shit. The blood *might* be makeup, because I just realized it's the weasel who was trying to talk to me before Fitz lost the plot. He was dressed as a zombie, so maybe…

I shrug the tiger off and rush over to the collapsed predator, drop-ping to my knees so I can feel for a pulse in his neck. When I can't find one and my fingers come back bloody, I realize the mess isn't his costume, and this is *not* a prank.

"Holy fuck, Baby Girl! You have a fluffy tail!"

Of course, Fitz would notice that now.

There's a loud growl from behind us and Felix comes stomping through in his shimmering gown, as if he's expecting the killer to jump out at any moment. "You didn't disappear after you hassled this kid out in the open, right?"

Hera help me. His wings are fluttering behind him as he walks over and the glittering shimmer of his dress is making it impossible to take him seriously.

His twin shakes his head. "Hell, no. I didn't want anyone else sneaking up to mack on our girl!"

"Fitz, he's trying to protect you. Everyone saw you threaten this kid tonight," Renard says as he gazes at the treetops, inhaling deeply. His voice goes soft as he murmurs, "Something in this place feels familiar."

Aubrey walks over to look at the body, sighing heavily. Rainbow-colored irises flick to my rear end briefly and he arches a brow, but says nothing more. I turn away as goosebumps crawl over my skin, pretending to look at the dead student in front of me as I try to figure out if I'm feeling a prey instinct or something else. A puff of smoke spirals through the air from over my shoulder before I hear him growl, "I'm going to check the view from above."

One powerful jump later, the half-shifted dragon is flapping his wings and taking flight. I've never seen a seven-foot-tall lizard in a tutu and fishnets before, but I'm never going to forget this image until the day I die.

Renard watches him fly off, shaking his head. "Dragons are always so dramatic. Aubrey's probably bitching about the paper-work being a nightmare."

Felix grimaces, nodding at the gargoyle. "He'd be right. We'll be up all night dealing with this mess." His gaze finally lands on my tail, and he looks almost… wary. "That's what we get for following something small and fluffy into the forest." He awkwardly clears his throat and pointedly looks away.

I open my mouth to shoot back a retort when something sparkly catches my eye. Brushing off my knees as I stand, I walk over to where the moonlight is shining on something metallic on the ground beneath the leaf litter. It takes a second to kick off the brush, but once I do, I find a small plaque embedded in the ground.

"Guys! Come here!" I yell, way more excited than I should be, considering there's an actual dead body a few feet away. Dropping to the ground again, I work to finish clearing the leaves and sticks off until it's fully revealed. I hear them approaching and turn to face the group, grinning wildly. "Look at this! It's a marker. Do you think it leads to a secret door? Maybe it's how the killer escaped."

Renard frowns, crouching beside me. His cape flutters out when he does, and it takes everything in me not to snort. "That's the symbol for the secret prey tunnels."

"I know! And the prey tunnels go all over campus, so it has to be how the murderer got away. We have to find the door… I mean, this kid doesn't look like he's been dead long, right?" I ask, as I trace my fingers over the design. The silence is deafening, and I turn to look at my guys, finding them staring at me in return. "What? Do I have something in my hair?"

"Uh, no, angel. You're… awfully calm about finding a dead body, given that you're… you know." Chess trails off and I roll my eyes.

Why. Are. Men.

"Prey. You can say it; it's not an insult," I snipe back, irritated that they're underestimating me because some kid I barely knew got killed. "It's not the first dead body I've ever seen—even this close —and I'm sure it won't be the last one I see at Apex."

The tiger king gives me an amused look. "No, I suppose that's true."

The ground shakes a little as Aubrey lands behind them, smoke curling around his face. Oh, he's all worked up about something. "I didn't see anyone, but I stopped by the circle and asked Zhenga to call Henny, so we should have company soon. None of us have our phones because of our... attire." His gaze turns to me and I grin, satisfied with my petty refusal to give them pockets in their dresses.

Welcome to my world, dudes.

"I think we should explore this door another time," Renard murmurs as he moves to stand. He holds his hand out and I take it, moving out of the way so he can kick the brush back over the marker, clearly deciding we should keep its discovery to ourselves, at least for now.

After a minute, it hits me, and I squint at the spicy Dark Knight, pointing an accusing finger at him. "You're only speaking in iambic pentameter. I knew you sounded weird!"

"For fuck's sake, don't encourage him," Felix mutters, shaking his head at us.

"Sir, yes, Sir!" I say sarcastically, giving the tiger a salute. His eyes narrow, and I feel a sizzle of satisfaction zing up my spine at the thought of getting him riled up—and what that might mean for me.

"Baby Girl, quit trying to give him a woody," Fitz snorts, throwing his arm around me. "We're gonna have an audience soon."

I tilt my head, listening intently, and realize he's right. There's definitely people coming—Headmistress Henrietta and some of the administration staff. Of course, I feel awful that a student is dead, but attacks like this are usually random, and I'm always watching my back.

Plus, maybe I now have others watching it, too.

Stupid Feelings

Aubrey

Tugging on my bowtie, I watch the room as parents drift in well past the time Henny set for this wretched meeting to begin. They're all dressed to the nines, casually gossiping like fools, and flanked by varying amounts of staff alternating between bored and psychotic. Despite the screeching outrage over the events of Halloween night, it took an entire week for the supposedly concerned guardians of the spoiled assholes who attend this school to make time in their busy schedules to gather here. Hell, the dead kid got buried days ago, but these self-important twits have suddenly given the untimely death the attention it deserves.

Considering all the paperwork I had to do, one could say I find it rude.

I sigh, sipping my scotch. Once again, I got elected to be a presence at an official function. None of us wanted to endure hours of whining, blustering elite families, and lurking Council members, but we all agreed we needed to have eyes on the scene. This was to not only discern what motive there could be for killing a random student, but also to experience the Drews in person. Their daughter has wormed her way into our homes, and a clinical assessment of what threat they are to her—and how that may translate to us—is necessary.

Of course, Fitz volunteered to come with me, because the last time we chaperoned an event here it was ' the night my baby girl fell in love with me', as if this was an enjoyable excursion. Felix overruled that fairly quickly—he knows his enforcer wouldn't be able to control his ire if her mother was as odious as her reputation. Honestly, I'm not sure how I'll react, either, but ironically, I was still the one everyone felt was most appropriate to represent our group.

There's a fucking first time for everything, I suppose.

Speak of the devils and they shall appear. The room goes silent and all heads turn as Lucille Rostoff Drew and her brutish husband, Bruno, enter. She's unironically dressed like the loyal daughter of a Russian mobster, with a garishly red designer dress, stilettos, and diamonds dripping from every available surface. Hell, the woman even has on a huge black hat, like she's going to a goddamn polo match. Conversely, her toothy husband is in a boxy pinstriped suit with slicked-back hair, no doubt attempting to emulate a rich businessman. Unfortunately, the croc looks more like a lumpy mafia enforcer than a Don, and it's immediately clear who is wearing the pants in this family.

"Henrietta Shirdal!"

The reigning leopard queen booms at the Headmistress as she glides across the floor, eyes disdainfully sweeping over every single shifter as she passes. They land on me for a moment, narrowing appraisingly before she turns to face the poor eagle running towards her like a frazzled chicken. When Henny stops, she adjusts her glasses to look up at the tall, vicious pred, and mutters a pathetic apology. Within seconds, she's taken off again towards the dais in a flurry of motion. Lucille Drew clearly wants this meeting to begin.

Too bad it could have started half an hour ago, if she and her thug spouse had been on time.

Henny taps on the mic to get everyone's attention, looking as if she'd rather get eaten by a bear than try to wrangle the parents' attention on her own. Moving from where I'm standing in the back, I walk to the front row and pointedly sit across two chairs in the aisle before turning to glare at the crowd. Murmurs and shuffling follow, and I nod up at the Headmistress. She needs to get this show on the road before these idiots get restless—or worse, drunk—and start shouting.

"Good afternoon, esteemed families, honored alumni, and Council members. In the wake of the tragedy that occurred at our hallowed academy last week—"

"How could you let a student get killed?! Are you incompetent?"

The shout comes from the back, and I whip my head around to identify the source. Everyone looks smug, but no one owns up to the interruption. Delores' mother is staunchly facing forward, ignoring the rabble, but I spy a slimy bodyguard type, leaning against the wall in the back who wasn't here before. He looks to be reptilian, and apparently shops at the same suit warehouse as Bruno, so he's probably the Drews' eyes on the crowd, so they can look disinterested.

None of these elite pred dipshits would survive outside of the cushy bullshit they've surrounded themselves with. It's almost comical.

"Students have died at Apex every semester since it opened," Henrietta says, finally answering the heckler, her voice shaking as she fearfully gazes into the crowd. "However, this is an unusual circumstance as it occurred outside of the Pred Games or a shifting control issue where the animal needed to be put down."

"Cold-blooded murder isn't normal!"

This time I'm sure I'll catch the shouting twat, but it comes from a different direction, and suddenly, they're all yelling. Predators rise from their seats, shaking fists and waving their hands, some even half-shifting as their emotions—or liquor—get the better of them. *I'm never getting out of here if Henrietta doesn't get this shit under control*, and I'm about to go on stage to help when the evil queen herself rises to her feet. Lucille Drew gracefully strides up the steps of the dais, shoos Henny away from the mic, and gives the riotous parents a look so cold it could freeze the balls off a walrus.

"Silence, fools," Lucille snarls.

The low timbre of her voice is from her animal, but her composure is as steady as Renard when he's brooding on his balcony. She reaches up with one hand, removing her sunglasses to show the yellow eyes of her leopard and smiles with a hint of fang against her red lipstick. The roar of outrage dies instantly, and asses hit seats so fast, you'd think they were going to win an open-bar in Belize.

When the audiences' submission is deemed sufficient, the woman who supposedly gave birth to our fuzzy ball of sarcasm and babbles sweeps her gaze over everyone. "Apex Academy has *never* been a safe place for students. It exists to teach our heirs and future leaders the way of our world—that the strongest predator survives because he or she does whatever it takes to do so. We do not know why this… weasel… was murdered, but given his family's *unimpressive* standing, it is unlikely that it is an attack on the school or the Council. Since it was likely a personal grievance, we have decided to *not* provide any additional security on campus for the rest of the year. The Council expects their heirs to handle themselves in a manner befitting their status—to prove they can handle themselves."

Did… did this bitch just tell everyone that their kids are on their own with a murderer on campus?!

Henny looks like she's going to be ill, implying she wasn't aware of this decision, and I blink as I brace for the reaction from the angry parents.

"You don't have the authority to decide that!"

"Doesn't the Council accept appeals?"

"What does Bruno think? Shouldn't *he* be the one to make this decision?"

Oh, shit.

Delores' mother doesn't bat a lash before leaping off the stage, shifting mid-jump as she lands on the unfortunate dickwad in the second row, who thought to open his mouth about her husband. Before he can even respond, fangs rip his throat out, blood spraying to coat the screaming shifters on either side of him. Lucille shifts back to her mostly human form as she calmly turns to the crowd, a delicate finger wiping blood from the corner of her mouth. "We don't talk about Bruno."

I look away from her nakedness, feeling a shiver of disgust roll up my spine at the unnecessary display. I couldn't care less about the killing—it's the dictatorial dominance that makes me want to hurl.

This crazy bitch is definitely worse than our snack-sized girl is letting on, and I'm going to make certain Rennie, Felix, and the others know the full story. Growing up with two sociopaths as parents is no picnic, and it explains a hell of a lot about why Dolly seems to constantly struggle with self-confidence. Even if we can protect her at school, now I'm worried about what will happen when she goes home for breaks.

Perhaps she can stay here… with us.

Deciding I've seen enough, I rise, nodding at Henny as I make my way to the exit in the back. She knows I'll take care of alerting a clean-up crew. I don't know where those carrion-eaters are right now, but I'll email maintenance once I get back to the library. Dolly's in the archives finishing up a few tasks before the weekend, and I suddenly feel compelled to check up on her. Something about her mother and father being on campus with that sneaky looking bodyguard is putting my teeth on edge.

Squeezing the bunny mochi in my pocket, I grit my teeth and stomp out of the Admin building towards the library like a dragon on a mission.

Perhaps I am.

"WHY DIDN'T YOU TELL US YOUR MOTHER IS A RAGING PSYCHO?" I demand after I pound the panel to gain entrance to the archive room. I've worked myself into an infuriated froth on my journey from the Honeywell Admissions building, and it takes every ounce of self-control I have not to completely lose my shit at the girl hunched over in my workspace.

Dolly looks up, her blue eyes wide with concern. There's a slight tremble to her hands as she carefully puts down the tweezers she's holding a piece of parchment in, and she ducks her head for a moment. "I don't like to talk about my family," she mumbles.

Stomping over, I position a finger under her chin, forcing her to look up at me, searching for the truth in her eyes. What I find isn't dishonesty; it's shame. Whatever her parents have done or continue to do behind closed doors is painful enough that she doesn't trust *anyone* to know about it. The adorable spark of defiance and wit I've grown accustomed to has dimmed, because she doesn't even fight me as I yank her out of the chair to her feet.

"Why, Dolly? Tell me why you won't discuss something that obviously hurts you." I press her, even though she's squirming in place. This is important—if this girl has any hope of assimilating into our pack, we can't have secrets.

Ironic coming from me, I know. I have plenty of my own secrets, but they don't put any of us in danger.

"Because they fucking disowned me!" she shouts, finally looking up with a fiery glare. "They sent me here to survive on my own—to die—by order of the Council, because I'm not a predator. I'm a genetic fluke… a *failure!*"

I blink, watching her face screw up and before I can stop myself, I burst out laughing. Her expression goes from teary to murderous in a blink, and she lets a hand fly, punching me in the jaw. That only makes me laugh harder—I mean, fist vs. dragon—and despite the loud racing of her heart, she lets out a screech that would rival a goddamned pterodactyl.

"Why are you laughing at me?!"

It takes a moment to get my mirth under control, and when I do, I push her back into the wall with a smug grin. Pinning both her hands above her head with one of mine, I shrug, unable to keep from smirking down at the enraged bunny shifter. "Because, lunchable, you seemed to think any of us would give a chicken-fried gazelle you were exiled. Newsflash: *all* of us got exiled from our families for being fuck-ups."

She sucks in a shaky breath, sniffling a little, and I almost let go, but I sense she needs someone else in control right now. Dolly has been a mess since we found out about the parents' meeting, and working here in the archives was her idea. I assumed the thought of having to face her mother was distasteful enough to make her volunteer to do work study on a Friday night, ensuring no one could find her down here if they were looking. Of course, I'd never turn down her help, and she seemed determined to continue searching for clues about the mysterious maps.

I didn't realize she was doing it out of fear.

"How would I know that?" she shoots back, equaling me in fire. "Fitz and Chess hinted at the reason they left Bloodstone, but everyone else hasn't deemed me worthy of their story yet!" I smile as she fights against my hold, throwing my own words from our first meeting back at me.

Very clever, little dessert.

Snorting a smoke ring, I pause for a moment as the dragon lumbers inside, stretching and pushing against my skin. He likes her—who the fuck in their right mind wouldn't—and this proximity is making it difficult to focus on the conversation. Dolly seems to notice my quandary, and she softens a bit as she waits for me to answer.

"Touché. I'm used to everyone knowing my sordid tale of rejection from the throne of my clash. I promise I will elaborate at the proper time. But, for now, do you have questions, bite size?"

Her body bucks against mine rebelliously, trying my tenuous hold on my control. "Yeah, are you going to kiss me or what?"

That does it—the fire in my belly ignites, and my dragon takes the fucking wheel before I can blink. Our lips crash together in a blur of movement, and my body curls around hers as she tries again to wiggle her arms free.

It won't be that easy, bunny rabbit. I've been thinking about doing this since the moment you first sassed my dragon in the library.

Gently nipping her bottom lip, I growl low as my hand tightens on her wrists. Dolly gives me an adorably shy grin, almost making me give in as she pushes up on her tiptoes, presumably to kiss me again. The slide of her body against mine distracts the hell out of me, and I have to count to ten in Sumerian to hold back from delivering a harder bite. I know this girl is inexperienced—since Fitz won't shut up about it—and...

Holy fuck, the minx just bit me!

A roar escapes me as her sharp teeth dig into my neck, and I immediately let go of her wrists. Backing away with a shudder, I desperately try to maintain control of the flames bubbling up inside of me before I roast my entire goddamn collection and get myself banished from another library. Her lips curve up in a satisfied smirk that makes me want to teach her a lesson, but I can't. She doesn't know what she's doing.

"You..." I croak, straining to hold both my cock and my rampaging animal in check. "You can't... simply do that. Shifters... can't ..."

Her expression drops into despair, and I swear my heart hits the floor.

If I've hurt her...

"I thought you'd like it."

I clear my throat, still not able to move any closer to comfort her, without fear of losing control. "I.. It's not that I didn't. It's that... Oh, I can't do this. You need a shifter sex ed class. I'm sure we can get it added to your syllabus for the spring."

"Oh my god, I did it wrong again!" she wails.

Shaking my head, I rush over, fighting my animalistic urges so I can gather her in my arms. It aches to see her upset, and I don't have the slightest idea why. "No. But you need to understand what an action like that means, before you do something you didn't intend to."

Nodding against my chest, she sniffles pitifully. "Okay. If you promise I didn't mess everything up, I believe you."

"I promise. It's time to get you home now, anyway. It's getting late," I rumble as I run my hands over her back soothingly.

"Don't wanna go anywhere they can find me. Bruiser will be looking for me," Dolly mumbles as she looks up at me.

That must be the lizard from the back. Another growl escapes as I realize she fears the fucker. "I can escort you to the townhouse if you like. The tigers may still be awake."

"Can't I stay here with you?" She pauses for a moment and gives me a sly smile. "Or snuggle up with you and Rennie again?"

Horus, take the wheel of destiny, because I have definitely veered off course.

She keeps looking at me with big, teary eyes, and I crumble like a fucking cookie. I can't allow word to get out that I let her spend the night, or I will never hear the end of this.

"If you stop crying, I'll take you."

The satisfied smile she gives me does absolutely nothing to calm the situation in my fucking pants, but it makes the scaly bastard inside of me smug as hell.

"I make no promises, Professor, but I have a feeling being with you will make me happy."

May the odds be in my favor…

Fall in Line

Lucille

Lucille

"Madame Lucille, I wanted to discuss your speech…"

I accept the chilled martini from the nervous headmistress, flicking my eyes around the room briefly, looking for anything suspicious. Once I effectively ended that nuisance meeting, the Council and other supposedly important preds got ushered into a separate lounge so the clean-up crew could dispose of the carcass, and I could get a drink.

Worth it.

Elite gatherings are never wasted occasions—they always provide an opportunity for business to continue, no matter the circumstance. Those with the most power and influence customarily provide a secure location to solidify deals that should only be discussed in person. We cannot put some things in writing or risk a recorded line, and we cement these transactions at private cocktail hours such as this one.

"Henrietta, I have no interest in listening to your beak flap about the students being in danger. Fear keeps the sheep in line—and the sheep include smaller preds. If their sad progeny can't defend themselves, they do not belong at Apex."

The eagle fluffs up a bit, pushing her glasses up her nose as she no doubt tries to figure out how to protest without looking like she's questioning my decision. She's smarter than she looks, as finally, she nods, and I smile into my glass in triumph. I refuse to have the Council or its heirs looking weak by adding security to the campus.

May the strongest survive.

It's infuriating enough that my weasly informant got himself killed before he could provide much in the way of useful intel. Bruno and Bruiser paid a visit to the weasel's parents weeks ago in order to secure their cooperation in keeping tabs on my errant child, and now that effort has gone to waste. He was getting mouthy lately, so I suppose this isn't the worst outcome.

It saves me the trouble of having his family killed, one by one, for leverage.

Unfortunately, his death leaves a gaping hole in my ability to monitor Delores. Her pathetic ex-friends keep her beaten down and frightened, but none of them can provide undramatized information on the shifters she's cozying up to.

I need facts, not hysterics.

But I spied some intel of my own.

"Henrietta, why was the *ex*-heir of the Draconis clash allowed to leave the meeting before I was finished speaking?" I arch a brow at the sniveling Shirdal, making certain she can see how displeased I am at the disrespect.

"Aubrey… I mean, Professor Draconis… has lived at the Academy for longer than anyone. He frequently assists with administrative matters. I believe he left to locate our clean-up carrion," she squeaks out.

I scoff at her response—I'm familiar with more royals than her. His exit was one of disgust, not diplomacy. I haven't had the pleasure of dealing with a dragon, but my father despises them. He's complained about their hoarding of wealth and knowledge my whole life, and if I can locate where the largest clash has hidden themselves for all these centuries…

A victory such as that will more than make up for birthing a defective heir. It's vitally important that my wayward daughter befriends the surly librarian, perhaps even seduces him, but I will need more information to ensure she seals the deal.

Of course, this would be much easier if I could simply order her to do what I want, but she's far too stupid to understand how the real world works. If dragons weren't famous for being a bunch of judgmental inbred fools, I'd contact the Draconis clash and offer her in trade. Alas, even using her as a bartering chip isn't possible for my albatross of a child.

I hold my empty glass up, instantly annoyed when none of the roving waitstaff gets the hint. "You allow your staff far too much autonomy, Henrietta. Get them under control, or I'll find someone who can teach their underlings respect."

"Yes, Lucille," she replies, taking the glass and scurrying off. She did it to escape my wrath—my birdbrain assistant isn't here this evening, but Matilda does the same thing when she believes I'm going to lose my temper before I receive a fresh drink.

Works for me.

Surveying the room again, my gaze alights on Bruiser. He's standing near Bruno while my husband talks shop with Atticus Volkov. The Luna of the wolf pack has several nephews and nieces at Apex—both staff and students. One of them got killed in the staff Pred Games earlier in the month, so I can guess why she cornered my other weak link. She wants to demand the Council punish a Khan for a perfectly legitimate death in the Games, as if *Bruno* has any sway. Per usual, Felicia underestimated me for that conversation, but I've also made it clear I have no interest in whatever nonsense he's spouting. The Volkovs are useful because they have a firm grip on imports and exports. Other than that, they're dumb as a box of rocks and not worth the air they breathe.

When the eagle returns with my martini, I tilt my head, pretending to be curious. "The dragon isn't the only celebrity professor you employ, Henrietta. Tell me about the staffing here. I find myself curious about the quality of education my daughter is receiving. Outside of murders at holiday parties, that is."

"No, no. Death outside of the usual turf wars is not normal, Madame Luc—"

"Oh, stuff it, feather head. I know this event was unusual. Tell me about the rest of your staff before I lose my patience."

Gulping, she nods and clears her throat. "Yes. Well, we have Professor Abel in the history department—his family traces back to royalty in Europe, although he himself is far removed. Professor Sarabhai's family are world renowned dancers, and Professora Balena retired after many years as a *prima* for the Metropolitan Opera."

Not what I want to know, idiot. It's like pulling teeth with this moron, I swear.

I'm perfectly aware of the history and background of every single person on this campus. However, if the disgraced Shirdal keeps talking, she'll spill secrets that aren't in the files. If I can bear to listen to her ramble, I may glean gossip that will be useful when I need to properly… motivate Delores.

I may also need more alcohol.

A waiter finally walks by with a tray of wine and I pluck a glass off, handing it to the flustered avian with a deceptively friendly smile. "Henrietta, I can read their staff profiles anytime I choose. Are any of those people… *exotic* shifters? Dragons are a species

Delores would never meet if she were attending another institution, and I want to know what other perks you're hiding."

She takes the glass cautiously, as if I had time to poison it—or would waste the poison on her. "Yes, having Professor Draconis at Apex to curate our archives has been a great boon, and you are correct, Madame, in assuming he is not our only rarity. Professor Laveaux is a gargoyle—as you know, we rarely see them outside of their clans. He teaches botany and literature, depending on the season."

My eyes narrow and I give her another fake smile. "Does my daughter take any of his classes?"

"Absolutely! Delores is excelling in most of her classes, Madame. She has high marks in Professor Laveaux's class and good evaluations from her work study with Professor Draconis. That alone would be quite impressive, but she also did well on exams for Professors Balena, Sarabhai, and Chester in the areas of her arts major." She pauses for a moment and sips her wine, then holds a finger up. "Even Professor Khan has been impressed with her progress in Shifter Basics, and he's a very difficult tiger to please."

Oh, I'll bet he's impressed.

That predilection of his is infamous, and my dumb bunny is the perfect bait. I've always wondered how to bring the Khans to the table more often, and snaring their disgraced heir might be enough leverage to make it happen. The question is, how I'll achieve all of this without tipping anyone off.

"That's very interesting, Henrietta. I would think—given her unfortunate handicap—that Delores would be more of a hindrance in shifting studies class than a star student. Good thing you have a Khan in charge, or the poor thing might get eaten!"

Henrietta sputters into her glasses, nearly choking as she attempts to speak. "Oh, no, Madame! I can assure you we have taken every precaution to ensure the safety of your illustrious heir. I promise—"

If only I'd put my sunglasses back on when Bruiser brought my spare Yves St. Leopard dress after my shift. I could roll my eyes at this imbecile without killing the mood I'm creating. As if I care about our family's embarrassment getting killed on campus… I wouldn't have sent the little twat to this school if I was concerned with keeping her alive. "I'm sure you set the correct expectations. However, as we both know from our time at Apex, shifting is where those instinct-fueled 'accidents' are most likely to occur."

"Delores bested Heather Erickson in the ring a few weeks ago, Madame. The girl had to have another nose job to correct the damage. I spent a lot of time smoothing over the incident with Mr. Erickson. Oh, and I believe she sent Todd to the infirmary. Todd… I'm forgetting his family name, as there are so many Todds and Chads and… Either way, you should be proud," the eagle says as she nervously gulps down another sip, babbling, just as I'd hoped.

Interesting. Delores has grown a spine, has she?

I nod, pretending to look bored as I scan the room again. "That idiot Erickson should stick to his microchips, and his daughter deserves to be taken down a peg. Notice how he didn't request *my* input on the situation."

"No, Madame. He was most insistent that I *not* disturb you with something so trivial. He said he would speak to Mr. Drew at the next Council meeting."

Of course he did.

Bruno is so gullible that every male in that wretchedly ineffectual group thinks they can influence *me* by starting with him. It's laughable, if not deserving of a decisive slap during our next business negotiation. Perhaps I'll require a hefty donation of Erickson tablets to the school as an apology.

Yes, I believe that will be a worthy tribute for his insolence and a beneficial tool to spy on my disappointing progeny.

"Henrietta, I want copies of every assignment my daughter turns in to her professors forwarded to my assistant. We must monitor our heirs to ensure they are representing their families appropriately." She bobs her head and I turn to look at her. "I also want files on every student who attends classes with her, including their parents' information from Admissions. I need to know exactly who my daughter is cavorting with at all times."

As most of the students are not in the one percent of society, all I need to do is dangle the right carrots—either money or power. Eventually, my wayward rabbit will be the key to securing my spot at the top for good.

Carrot. Aren't I clever?

Family

Chess

Chess

The amount of time we spend sitting in this living room discussing my angel is getting ridiculous. Like Fitz said last time, we really need to just invite her up here to join us. She's smart and brave, so I don't think a group of men trying to decide her fate without her will sit well.

It's certainly not getting any of us closer to sampling what Fitz has.

His new feminist leanings make me chuckle; he's never been a misogynist, per se, but he's always been callous with his playboy attitude towards women. Delores Drew is subtly changing the bad boy of Bloodstone, and she doesn't even realize how powerful that influence is.

Looking around at my makeshift ambush, I smile to myself. She's having a similar effect on the others, too. Felix is more interested in the bigger picture at Apex than he ever has been—more like a true king. My book loving friend is still grumpy as fuck, but his smiles are more frequent and his humor less toothy. And the loner gargoyle joins us in the circle rather than grunt from his perch all the time.

My angel is turning us into a genuine family and it makes my heart squish because it's what I've always wanted.

I don't even mind that my cat is more demanding and present in my mind. His desire to protect her rides me constantly and though I'm the smallest pred in the room, I would charge a giant mother-fucker like Gregor to save her, just as I would with Fitz and Felix. The cheetah looks at her differently than Fitz, but I think eventually they will be equal in importance.

If I can figure out how to approach her, that is.

"None of you were there, but I watched Lucille Rostoff Drew rip someone's throat out in the middle of a meeting and no one did a damn thing. I can only imagine what she's been doing to the lunchable most of her life." Aubrey looks at each of us and though I know he's not one to be dramatic about death, he's trying to warn us of the danger my angel is in.

Renard snorts. "Don't tell me it made your stomach turn, old friend. I know better."

"Of course not. I'm not upset by the violence as much as her iron grip on everyone. You didn't see how Delores behaved when her family was on campus afterward. The confidence she's built up over the past few months dropped like a stone and she cowered like prey."

"She is prey," Felix reminds him. "But I understand your point. She may be capable of holding her own here against her old enemies and the students, but her parents are another level of fear she has yet to face. Their betrayal and decision to send her here to be killed must cut deeply, even for someone used to their abuse. I can relate to that."

Wisdom like that from Felix is unusual since we left Bloodstone, and I tilt my head to watch his reaction. "It's how you behave when your father or his minions reach out."

Fitz glares at me, opening his mouth to defend his twin, but Felix gives me an impressed look. "Yes, Chess. That's exactly what it's like. Being victimized isn't only for the weaker species; strong preds like me can have trauma that is triggered, too. My father definitely qualifies as one of those."

Suddenly, my lover frowns and whips his head around to look at the dragon with narrowed eyes. "Wait a minute. Where the hell did you find my baby girl on Friday? I couldn't find her anywhere and I even used the tracking shit I put on her phone. I checked with her nutty friends and even looked in on Three-Finger Todd to see if he needed a beating. But nada enchilada, man. The last location I saw on the network was your damn book dungeon, Lizard Lothario."

That gets the attention of both me and my king; our eyes snap to Aubrey, who shifts uncomfortably in his chair. "When I ran into her, she was in a very precarious mental state, Fitz. I recommended she allow me to walk her to the townhouse or the Tower and turn her phone off. She needed rest and comfort."

Renard snorts, shooting the dragon a knowing look, and I frown. He's usually quite eager to poke at things, but this topic has him tight-lipped. Felix arches a brow, leaning forward to rest his forearms on his knees as he watches the two of them.

"Ooh, tell me more, Hot Lips. Did your special brand of comfort include a paper cut inducing roll in the pages of dusty old books where she worshiped at the altar of your teeny dragon weenie?"

Fucking hell, Fitz. Get us all roasted like pigs on a spit, why don't you?

The dragon pops out of his chair, his wings spreading as he shifts while walking towards my big mouthed lover. Smoke billows from his nose as he glares fiery rings of promised pain at him and growls, "Fitzgerald Ulysses Castor Khan! That is none of your fucking business."

Holy shit, he came for the full name.

Fitzy hates that shit with a passion. This is going to be bad. I get ready to throw myself between them when Felix stands, holding his hands out to calm them. He gives me a nod and I rise slowly, just watching this play out.

"It is all of our business, dragon. Delores has aligned herself with each of us, and we have all been receptive in our own ways. As Fitz and Chess have repeatedly suggested, we are on the precipice of something bigger than one pred's pride or need for secrecy."

"Well said, kitty cat," Renard comments. He's still lazing in his chair, not perturbed for a second about the Shifter War about to start in his living room. "Especially since you publicly claimed her in the name of Spain in the faculty lounge. We know it got back to your dear old dictator, so that complicates everything."

"But—"

"He's right," I say as I look at the infuriated lizard. "Put your dicks away, both of you, and let's figure out what Delores needs from her ambush."

The two ancients glare at my word and I roll my eyes over to Felix, who sighs. "Whatever we want to call it. By Zeus' wandering dick, you're even touchier since she showed up than before."

I think about that for a moment and realize Felix is spot on. They've gotten even more secretive since Fitz stuffed our girl in this private oasis and she's been silent about everything to do with it and them. There must be something they have instructed her not to talk about because normally, she vomits info like she has the flu. Nothing to do with our winged companions comes up when Fitz verbally downloads their chats to me when he gets home.

"You took her flying while you hunted," I say as it slowly dawns on me. "And walked her home to this place when she was upset." Fitz and Felix look at me expectantly, and I grin when I get it. "She knows what you eat and where you sleep. Son of a bug-eating wombat!"

Aubrey lets out an annoyed huff and Renard shrugs nonchalantly. That neither will confirm nor deny the statement tells me everything, and I drop back onto the couch in amazement. I've been here a decade and not once have either of them given us even a hint about those topics.

"I'm sorry to disappoint your need for details, Fitz, but nothing happened when she came back to the Tower. There's no hanky panky to report." Felix stares at him and I feel my Raj knows something we don't. "Fine. She kissed me. That's all."

Fitz's eyes widen comically and he clasps his hands together with glee. "Salty Salamander, that's fucking great! I cannot wait until—"

"But I put a stop to it when she bit me," Aubrey adds with a grimace.

The room freezes as we all look at one another in panic. Biting is a very serious topic, and doing with intent is sacred to all shifters. For fated mates—something rarely seen anymore—intent isn't even required. If they break skin and share their kind's marking, it's done. The animals within us know, even if we aren't taught them by our parents.

"Yeah, she definitely loves when I give her teeth, man. And I know she's left a mark or two on me." He grins fangily. "My kitty likes it, and so does hers."

"Fucking hell, Fitz," Felix grumbles as he shakes his head. "While I'd think prey animals would be terrified of that, the princess isn't. It fits in well with my theory about her behavior in the ring. I wonder if she'll feel a push to be more dominating as she gets more accustomed to her animal."

Aubrey turns bright red and I flush a little as well. I guess she's been more forward with us than we expected.

Fitz snorts and shrugs. "I'd say that's possible. My baby girl is getting more comfortable and with that, sexy as fuck when she wants shit."

"With her fangs?" Felix asks.

Our stony friend sits up, tilting his head. "She has fangs? Not just big teeth?" Felix and Fitz nod simultaneously and he stands, walking over to stare at a woodland landscape hanging on the wall. "Interesting."

"Care to share, asshole?" Aubrey prods, aiming a stern look at the gargoyle.

"Tell us, fucker. I can't deal with all this mysterious bullshit going on. I feel like we're in the middle of some big fucking plot on a TV show and we missed two seasons. I'm not stupid, but I don't enjoy feeling out of the loop," Fitz growls as he looks around.

"I'm uncertain about my theories. The memories I'm recalling are much older and most of those tales are mere legends now. It wouldn't help to spout off and be wrong." Renard turns back to us and eyes Felix. "We should ensure *ma petit lapin* is taking Zhenga's Shifter Sex Ed class next semester. She's obviously a student whose parents didn't educate their child appropriately. No shifter with any sense bites another without knowing what it means."

"It's like some idiotic human with no knowledge of how any of this works in their shitty smut novels," Aubrey sneers. "I have to cull my library of that sort of nonsense all the time. Some of our kind will read anything if it gives them spank bank material."

I open my mouth to protest, but Renard beats me. "*Mon ami*, don't be such an elitist twat. There are many wonderful, yet steamy tales in that section. A few rotten apples don't spoil the bushel entirely. Besides, like every genre, the flash in the pan people will die out, eventually."

This is going nowhere.

"While this literary discussion is fascinating, the point is she needs to know about breeding and mating before accidents happen," I interject. "None of you would be happy with that."

I see the tension ratchet up in the room and it proves my point. Not everyone is ready to claim her out loud, much less permanently, but they sure as fuck don't want someone else treading on their territory without a discussion. It would cause a major rift in our evolving family and no one wants to cause it, least of all me. My cheetah being so interested in her is new and I've avoided her because I have no clue what he'll do when I actually get to touch my angel.

"We need to get on board with this—all of us—while she's learning. Take her out, show her a good time, and get her mind off murder and fucking bullies. That's how we can make sure everything develops honestly and with open communication," Fitz says with a shrug. "You assholes all need to up your game. I'll go first because I fucking earned it."

Glaring at him, I jerk my chin up, but his knowing look calms me. He's right, of course. I've run away at every turn unless he's there and my relationship with my angel has to be solid before it can include both of us. I don't want her to invite me because he said so.

I give my love a small nod, smiling a little in understanding, but I can't help noticing the brooding aerial preds also communicating without words.

What the hell are they on about?

And where does that leave Felix?

This is going to be a long night.

FIRST DATE

FITZ

Fitz

My suggestion about taking my baby girl out worked. I was a little shocked that the rest of them took it, but lately, they've been listening to me a lot fucking more. Maybe there's something to this being a mature adult shit?

Nah.

As convenient as it is to get my way, I don't want anyone assigning me a bunch of responsibilities because I'm growing up or whatever. I'll reserve my knowledge drops for when it benefits me the most and is least likely to earn me a bunch of mind-numbing work. That's much more me, anyway.

Pulling up to the front steps of the admissions building on my Vyrus Alyen, I sit back to watch for her. I wanted to visit with my baby girl while she got dressed, but Chess insisted that a proper date wouldn't happen if I did. He was probably right, but that doesn't lessen my excited tics as I do the one thing I truly suck at: waiting.

Patience may be a virtue, but it's one of the many I don't possess.

The one downside to winning the conversation the other night was my unwilling election to spokesperson. I've been telling our girl that I want to share her with the group forever, but she doesn't believe me. My one assignment for the evening is to convince her she should formally date all of us—a feat that won't be easy since those other morons have been holding out on her.

I don't know why my friends have such deep emotional shit going on inside of them and refuse to say it out loud. We're the tippity-top of Apex staff society and any of the females here would cut off a toe to be chosen as the center of our cream puff.

Why wouldn't Delores?

We're hot, rich, and eager to make her scream. Okay, I am, and the others need a little push to get past their hang-ups, but that doesn't make my statement less true. Growing up with Felix means I'm well aware of his skill in the bedroom and I can't imagine the other two are older than dirt with no fucking skills. Together, we make that three-fingered doucheweasel look like the participation prize in a school science fair.

"Ooh! We're taking your bike? Can I drive?"

The excited squeal of the girl in question pulls me out of my thoughts and I turn to look as she approaches. I purposely kept our transportation secret to see what ass-hugging outfit she'd wear and how hard it would make my dick to see it straddling my other baby.

Of course, she could wear a potato sack and my cock would salute, but who am I to quibble?

Both parts of me are pleased as fuck to see she's clad in an alluring mash-up of her usual tight leather or sinfully short skirts. Her rainbow locks are gathered in two space buns that pull half her hair off her face while the rest cascades over her shoulders onto the bad ass leather jacket she's sporting. Under it is a tiny black dress short enough to ruffle around her thick thighs in a tempting ripple.

Baby Girl has legs to her neck and the knee-high 'fuck me' raver boots only accentuate her assets.

I may fucking die of a boner before we get there, but if so, what a way to go.

"Do I look okay? Cori said I should still be me, but get a little fancy. Rufus suggested some crazy contraption that I was sure would get me kicked out of a nice restaurant and you said that's where we're going, so…"

Her nervousness is adorable, especially since it's taking every ounce of control I have not to bend her over this bike and fuck her until everyone on campus knows she's mine.

I blink as that thought makes my tiger push at my skin, shaking my head to clear it before I kick the stand out. Dismounting, I walk over and pick her up, spinning us around for a moment as I look at her sparkling eyes. That weird feeling of possession rears its head again and I whip my head around to snarl at two fifth-year assholes checking out her ass from the lawn. Those little shits will have to wait, though. My girl needs me.

"You look fucking fantastic, baby girl. In fact, I may have to take some eyeballs before the night is through, so make room on your body part souvenir shelf."

Hell if I know if she has one, but when in Rome…

Her eyes widen, and she smacks my chest lightly. "Shhhh. Todd's parents were furious about that, and no one knows about my trophies. If they find out, I'm even deader meat than before. Keeping them secret meant they couldn't get reattached, you know."

My jaw drops open as I set her on her feet. "You have a fucking severed body part collection shelf? For real?"

Every time I think she can't get any sexier, she surprises me.

"Well, not really a collection, because only the three fingers, but… I figured it's possible more will come. It's your M.O." Her cheeks turn bright pink and I have to count down from fifty to keep my animal in check.

I grab her hand, needing to put a little space between us to maintain control. Once I lead her to the bike, I throw a leg over and look at her with a feral smirk. "I'm falling down on the job, baby girl. I owe you some gruesome tokens of my affection."

Hand to Hera, her eyes goddamn sparkle at that.

She takes the helmet from me, mounting my bike like a pro as she asks, "Where are we going, anyway? Cori seemed to think it was fancy and I have to assume someone dropped her a hint."

Chuckling, I shrug. "Chess loves to gossip. We're going to The Jade Sceptre. It's one of the closest Khan owned places to us."

I feel her tense up and I rev the motor for a second before grinning over my shoulder. "Relax, baby girl. Being in public at a family place is a good thing. It will show the sheep we're serious."

"Okay, Fitz. I trust you," she replies as she wraps her arms around me.

Gunning the motor, I take off into the night as I realize how fucking painful this trip is going to be. Then I remember her bright smile, and it makes my gut flutter.

Worth it.

THE JADE SCEPTRE HAS A SIX MONTH WAITING LIST AND A LINE down the block.

Dolly bites her lip as I park my bike in front of it, tossing my keys to a valet with a snarl. I'm sure she thinks we're going to get turned away or challenged, but neither will happen unless someone wants to die. I'll walk into any of our places any fucking time I want or I'll send my father pieces of his henchmen in separate boxes for months.

Even he isn't stupid enough to cut Felix and me off from the family perks. That kind of anger breeds rebellion, and so far, his crooked shit hasn't been retaliated against. Pissing us off more would be foolish.

So I take her hand, walking up to the podium with a toothy grin at the small cat working it. It might be a caracal, but regardless, the flunky recognizes me immediately. His naturally lined eyes widen, and he gestures for the bouncer to lift the rope immediately.

"Prince Fitzgerald," he says in a hushed whisper.

My girl looks at me, giggling a little at the formal moniker. I narrow my eyes at the idiot and growl, "Enforcer to you, moron. And give us the royal table, even if you have to kick someone out."

"Aw, but I like Prince Fitzgerald. It makes you sound so…"

"Ridiculous?" I grumble. "My father has a thing for history and, being the oldest, Felix and I suffer for it."

She bats her lashes as she snuggles my arm against her breasts, whispering, "I want to know. Please?"

Shaking my head, I grin down at her as the snooty maitre'd leads us to a booth in the back that looks fit for a king. "Only if you tell me your middle name. I couldn't find it in your files."

"Fitz!" she hisses. "I'm not telling you; it's embarrassing."

I shrug and wink as I let her scoot into the booth before me, giving the host a glare when he seems like he's going to touch her. "Price of admission, baby girl. Show me yours and I'll show you mine."

Once the fox shifter slinks off, she gives me a little smirk. "We've already played that game."

Laughter escapes me before I can stop it and I throw an arm around her as I scope out the dining room. I see several local goons and quite a few mini-bosses, plus some tigers who would throw themselves in front of a tank to protect us. That eases my worry about having her away from the school when so many morons seem to think they can threaten what's mine without consequences.

"Fair, but let's play another one tonight, shall we?" I pause when a waiter steps up to take the drink order and after I get us drinks, I give her my best princely smile. "Truth for a truth."

Delores narrows her eyes at me suspiciously. "Where's the escape hatch?"

"No escape hatch unless you'd be breaching someone else's confidence. Deal?" I bat my lashes at her, trying like hell to look innocent. I probably look like a demon wearing a pie tin like a halo, but it's worth a shot.

Sipping the Dr. Pepper, the shifty vulpine slips in front of her. My girl thinks for a moment before nodding slowly. "Okay."

Brilliant job, Fitz!

"Tell me your middle name," I say. My eyes dance as I pick up my whiskey, waiting for her to complain.

With an adorable huff, she crosses her arms over her chest, giving me a spectacular view. "Diamond. My name is Delores Diamond Drew, and if you laugh at me, I'm punching you in the junk."

Not the boys! I wince a little, rubbing the back of my neck with my hand as I choke back laughter. She's right; it's stupid as hell, but she didn't choose it. Her dumbass mother did, and that's not her fault. "Your turn, baby girl."

"Now I want your full name, asshole. I know it must be bad because you get cranky when people use even your whole first name."

You have no idea, little bunny.

I sigh and lean in, looking into her eyes. "I'll whisper it, only for you to hear because it's ridiculous. I can't even get monogrammed shit because my dickface father wanted us to sound regal."

"Okay." Her face is full of glee, and it makes my chest hurt to look at her.

"Fitzgerald Ulysses Castor Khan."

It only takes her a minute, but she slaps her palm over her mouth before the giggles can escape. She looks at me with renewed softness, despite the laughter she can't quite control. When she finally locks it down, she lets out a long breath. "Oh, Fitz. I'm sorry."

"It could be Chester Cheetah or Felix Ivan Nestor Khan," I drawl with a satisfied smirk. "My brothers don't have it much easier, unfortunately."

That sends her into another round of laughter that has her wheezing, and although I'm going to get my ass kicked, I can't stop. I want to make my girl look like this all the fucking time, even when we're not naked. The pure joy on her features has my entire body buzzing with happiness; it's damn near intoxicating.

"Do the others know?" she asks when she has control again and I shake my head. "I mean, they know mine and Chess. Felix is fucking vicious in keeping his under wraps."

The mischievous look on her face tells me that information will probably get her a nicely warmed ass in the future, but that's a future Dolly problem. I'm merely a purveyor of information. "My turn."

"Yes. You get two because 'fuck' and 'fink' are worth it."

"Ooh. Fairness is sexy, baby girl." I take a deep breath, hoping the humor has warmed her up enough to broach this shit. "Do you like all of us? Like sexy times and such like us?"

Her eyes widen and her entire body tenses against mine. It's silent for a long time—or it feels like it—and she swallows hard. "All of you? Like you and Chess and Felix and Aubrey and Rennie?"

I nod, tilting my head as I run my fingers through her hair. "Yes, baby girl. All of us."

Dolly chews her lip for a minute, looking at her hands as she fiddles with the folded napkin in front of her. "I... I mean, I like everyone and um, I would like to get to know—"

Rolling my eyes, I grasp her chin and turn her face towards me. "No escape. Do you like all of us or not?"

"Yes," she whispers as her eyes meet mine. There's fear in them, as if admitting she desires more than one of us will get her in trouble with me.

No fucking way.

My hand slides down to her neck, pressing lightly as I smile. Her breath hitches as I hold her in place and I make a mental note that she might have a few darker kinks to explore when the time is right. "Good girl. See? That wasn't so hard, right?"

Felix will lose his goddamn mind when I tell him.

"What's the other question?"

This time I inhale slowly, hoping the important task they have assigned me won't freak her out. "Would you consent to dating all of us if we asked? Just us and just you, baby girl. No one else is invited."

Her pulse thumps under my hand and I brush a thumb over it lightly before tipping her head back more, so she has to keep looking at me. The question hangs in the air and I wait, allowing her to process it without pressure. Her tongue darts out to wet her lips and I bite back a groan.

I may not make it through this damn dinner. I hope there's a nice fucking bathroom.

"You're asking for… everyone? Even Felix?" she finally asks.

Nodding, I give her a gentle smile. "I know. Chess would have been a better choice because he's got the words, but he's so damn jumpy around you, baby girl. You make him feel shit he's never felt before and it's taken him a while to get a grip."

"Is this just because you want to protect me? I'm not a weakling, you know, and no one has to put their… claim… on me to keep me safe. I don't want that."

Shit. Now she thinks we're doing this out of pity, but little does she know none of us does anything for people we don't want to.

I shake my head and grin. "Trust me, baby girl. While we want to protect you, there's not an altruistic bone in most of our bodies. Boners, however, seem to be a different story since you hopped onto campus."

That earns me a little giggle and her cheeks heat as she looks at me again. "Then… okay, but I have conditions."

"Driving a hard bargain, eh? What are these conditions? I have to know before I agree to anything or my twin will murder me."

Bad Girl

Delores

I'm so nervous I can barely finish the delicious array of sweets the servers bring us. It's not even close to the first time I've been intimate with Fitz, but things have taken a serious turn. The playboy rumors about my tiger don't line up with the conversation we just had, and if I think about it, they don't match the way he's treated me from the moment I stepped on campus. But a guy who acted like he cared has burned me before, and even though I want to take this next step, I need a moment to wrap my head around it.

What should I do? I don't want to hurt his feelings with my mini-panic attack.

My body moves of its own volition as I stand, placing my napkin on the table with slow, controlled movements. I can see the confusion on Fitz's face, but he stands as well. "I have to go to the restroom. Can you point me in the right direction?"

A relieved expression comes over his handsome features, and he snaps his fingers, bringing a well-dressed giraffe scurrying to our table. "Take my girl to the ladies. I don't want her getting lost in this crowd."

I smile at the harried-looking server, whispering my thanks as he leads me across the room. The stares are hot on my back as I pass by tables full of big cats from all ends of the spectrum—wealthy to rough looking. I'm sure Fitz has brought dates here before, but I'd bet it's the first time a prey animal has been *seated,* not serving. Keeping my chin up, I thank the giraffe again before entering the large powder room leading to the ladies' bathroom.

Okay, Dolly. Just breathe.

My reflection is perfectly coiffed and primped, but the emotion in my eyes gives me away. I'm not scared of getting sexy with Fitz after this, but the dating part is freaking me out. I'm just… I don't know if my heart can take another blow like prom night, and I'm placing some serious trust in this tiger—and the others. Saying 'yes' to his… poly-posal… was easy until I realized I'm going to have to reciprocate the things I asked of them. I have to trust *them* —with my heart and my body—and that means I will need to share the good *and* bad parts of my past as well.

Stuff I've told no one, not even Mattie.

I sigh and shake my head. My nightmare childhood is a bridge to cross later; now I need to get my jitters under control before he thinks I fell in the fucking toilet. I reach under my skirt and pull my phone out of the little concealed pocket Cori cut into the side of my dress. Hitting the phone icon on my group chat with my friends, I tap my foot while I wait for them to pick up.

"Girrrrrrrrl. Why are you calling us instead of being twisted like a pretzel?"

Rufus' drawl helps to calm the knots in my stomach, and I let out a slow breath. "Guys. I can't talk long, but someone needs to help stop me from having an episode… because I just agreed to be the girlfriend of *five* dudes."

"Wooooohooooooo!" Cori whoops in the background.

I wince. Sensitive ears—I can't help it. "Yes, yes, it's very cool, but how do I keep my fucking hands from shaking?"

"Easy, Dollybear. Get out there and shake your bunnymaker so he'll dick you until you forget your name." Rufus snorts, clearly amusing the hell out of himself.

I hiss into the receiver, "Your advice is to get fucked and I won't worry anymore? I could have thought of that by myself."

"Just think, if you had, you'd already be naked and happy," Cori chimes in, her giggles tinkling over the line.

Son of a bitch, they're right.

"Hanging up now!" I sing-song as I end the call, and look in the mirror again. Tucking the phone back into my pocket, I walk out into the restaurant with my head held high once again.

It's time to rock Fitz Khan's world and the rest will fall into place on its own.

"This is the Khan suite. They keep these everywhere we do business, so family members have a place to stay," Fitz says, as he throws open the door to a room that's easily as big as the entire floor of my original dorm room.

I have to physically stop my mouth from gaping as I step inside, so I don't look like a rube. Sure, Lucille and Bruno are loaded, but they've never taken me anywhere like this. I should have known it was going to be ridiculous when he had to wave off an actual fucking *butler* that wanted to follow us onto the private elevator, but I don't know if I could have prepared myself for this place. There's a grand piano in the living room, multiple doors to Hera knows where, a full kitchen, and chandeliers. A panel on the wall, full of lights and buttons that must control this space shuttle, blinks at me as Fitz takes my coat and hangs it in the closet.

Holy Aphrodite, what in the hell have I gotten myself into?

The smug grin he gives me makes my thighs clench, and I wrinkle my nose. "I can't believe your family owns a royal suite at the Plaza. This is like… king shit."

"Baby Girl, your other boyfriends are kings—whether Raj or royals—or they *should* be. At least, most of them. Chessie and I don't need that kind of responsibility."

He winks at me like a jackass, and I cross my arms over my chest, suddenly self-conscious. I didn't make that connection, especially about Aubrey or Rennie, but hearing it out loud brings me back to reality. "Gods, Fitz. What in the hell do you guys want with a nearly virgin *outcast* with a truckload of baggage?"

The look in his eyes is downright predatory as he stalks over to me, yanking me against his body. His hand buries in my hair, tilting my head back so I'm gazing up at him, and my heart thumps like it's going to escape my ribcage. He must feel it because he leans in, his lips almost touching mine as he growls softly. "Never talk about yourself like that again, baby girl. I won't stand for it, and neither will the others."

To reiterate his point, his free hand squeezes my ass, pulling me against his erection. I almost ask 'why me' again, but he takes my open mouth as an invitation to kiss me like he's trying to crawl inside my body—which he probably is. My fingers inch up his chest and I loop my arms around his neck, returning the kiss eagerly. The hunger in the air is palpable, and I make a split second decision to simply let things happen.

When our mouths part, he pants, and I bite my lower lip, looking at him through my lashes. "Maybe we should look at the bedroom."

No point in being subtle with this guy.

"Fuck, yes," he snarls, letting go of my hair and using his other arm to lift me up with his huge muscles. My legs wrap around his waist, and he hums his approval as he carries me to the door, smacking a button on the frame to open it.

Isn't that handy?

"If you don't quit squeezing your thighs like that, I'm going to throw you on this bed and flip that skirt up before you even have time to look around."

Gathering my courage, I arch a brow. "What's stopping you?"

Before I know it, my back hits pillow-soft linens, and Fitz is diving between my legs like he's starving. I don't even get the chance to tell him not to rip the special lingerie I picked before they're ripped and flying over his shoulder. I try to say something, but the tiger fangs nipping their way up the tender skin of my thighs make my breath catch in my throat and my eyes close in ecstasy.

"How the fuck do you even *smell* like honeysuckle?" Fitz mumbles, as he hooks his hands under my legs and throws them over his shoulders.

I hope he doesn't expect me to answer, because his tongue is flicking over my clit, and all I can do is dig my nails into the bedspread. Until that night when he walked in on me, I'd felt *nothing* like this before, and even with my lack of experience, I know he's good at what he's doing. Two fingers slide along my slit as he continues to lick and nibble, and I let out a frustrated whine. "Fitzzzzzzz..."

His chuckle vibrates against me, and I whine again, moving my hips to get him to move faster. "Tell me what you want, little bunny rabbit. I want to hear you say it."

My eyes pop open, and I freeze in place. He wants me to... talk dirty?

I am so fucking out of my league.

"Stop overthinking. Just tell me," Fitz growls, turning his head to nip my thigh again. "Be a good girl, and you'll get a big reward."

Right. I can do this.

"I want… I want..." I take a deep breath and summon my inner vixen. "I want you to use your mouth and fingers until I come all over your face and then I want you to fuck me until I don't know which end is up."

"That's my girl!" he crows, squeezing my hips in encouragement. My answer is a long moan as he slides his thick fingers inside of me, curling the tips to rub that magical spot that makes my entire body tremble.

The rhythm of his fingers sliding in and out while he laps at my sensitive bud is a damned-near perfect combination. My hips lift and fall to grind against his chin, shuddering as he does *something* with his tongue that has to be illegal. I feel him slip another finger inside of me, and the stretch is intense, but good. The combination is overwhelming, and I'm so embarrassingly close that when he nips lightly; I explode.

"Fuuuuuuuuuck," I groan, melting into the bed as my limbs turn to jelly. My breaths are coming in harsh pants as he gives me a smug, glazed-looking grin. If it's possible, I flush even brighter.

Fitz crawls up my body with a hint of yellow in his eyes, stopping once he's nestled close. Even though a moment ago, I thought I couldn't move; I wiggle against him eagerly. "Have I mentioned how fucking stellar it is that I don't have to *worry* about rubbers with you?"

I chuckle throatily. "A time or two, yes."

"There are so many chicks trying to get a piece of our family. I've never once taken a dip in the pool without my trunks *before you, baby girl. It's a fucking gift.*"

I roll my eyes up at him, my expression teasing. "So, are we going to do it, or do I need to help myself?"

"Fuck yes, with my baby girl on top," he growls, before dipping his head to bite my lower lip.

Oh shit. I've definitely seen it being done before in movies, but we haven't done it yet. You can do this, Dolly.

Pushing on his chest, I wait for him to roll onto his back before I climb on, straddling his hips. When his cock slides against my wetness, I moan. I just came like my life depended on it, but something feels *extra* slick this time—almost like a natural lubricant. He holds onto my hips as I rock over him slowly, my head falling back when his crown bumps my clit.

Insecurity flares up, and I lean down, looking into Fitz's eyes with a fierce, pleading expression. "Don't you *dare* make fun of me if I'm bad at this."

The smile he gives me is probably aiming for angelic, but we both know that's not the case. "Cross my heart. Now grab the reins and show me how you ride 'em, cowgirl."

I ignore the persistent blush creeping over me and rise to my knees. Fitz grins wider as he helpfully holds his dick at the ready, and I close my eyes as I lower onto him, little by little. He's bigger than Todd, and this new angle is tighter. Once I'm settled, I gasp, holding perfectly still for a minute to get my bearings. "Holy fuck."

His hands grip my hipbones, squeezing hard for a moment before he grinds out, "Fuck is right."

Damn, this man is being patient with me.

The lack of action has to be killing him. I breathe deeply, gathering all of my courage as I move. Swiveling as I raise and lower myself on his cock, I close my eyes, letting my body mimic what I've seen without worrying that I might do it wrong. The satisfied sounds my tiger makes encourage me, and I rock faster, gasping again when he thrusts up to meet me hard.

Sweat trickles down my spine as our skin slaps, and I can feel the buzz of another orgasm rushing towards me as he repeatedly hits just right. Knowing I'll have bruises from his fingers makes something inside of me almost purr with satisfaction, and a deep hunger forces my eyes open, so I can look down at him as I bounce on his dick.

"I don't know where you learned this, but I'll buy you a fucking subscription. You're bucking like a seasoned bronco," Fitz grunts as he reaches up to flick my nipples, making me squeak in surprise.

When he pinches them, I snap, giving in to the urge that's been burning through me—to claim what's *mine*. Diving forward, I bite his shoulder, hard, squeezing around him as I do so.

"Holy shit!"

With a pleased grin, I bite harder and his hips slam into mine, throwing me over the edge into a climax that makes my entire body tremble. Our movements stutter as he shouts, his dick twitching as his orgasm chases mine. Collapsing onto his chest, I pant softly, feeling like every part of my body has melted.

This is what people talk about in books, Dolly.

"You're gonna have to give me a few, but we are *definitely* doing that again," he says as he runs a hand over my hair. "But first, let's hydrate."

"That sounds amazing," I mumble.

He chuckles and slides his hands under my thighs to raise me off of him—but I don't move.

"What the fuck?" Fitz frowns, his brows furrowed in confusion as he tries to lift me again, with no success. "I know your pussy likes my dick, but they have to part occasionally. Let go."

"Let *go?* I'm not doing anything! It's not my fault you're stuck!"

"It has to be you; this hasn't happened before!"

"It didn't happen any other time, either, Fitz!" Panic sets in as I frantically try to move, but can't. Fitz looks concerned, and my heart races.

Maybe there *is* something wrong with me, and I'm doomed to screw up everything with every guy I ever…

What in the name of Hades made me agree to date five of them?

I close my eyes as they fill with tears, not wanting him to see the shame building inside me as I replay all my faults. Lucille always said there was something wrong with me, and then I turned out to be prey. Todd sneered at me after our first time together and tried to eat me. Now I've broken Fitzgerald Khan's famous dick.

I'm never going to live this down.

That last thought completely wears down the confident façade I've been maintaining, and I slap my hand over my mouth to catch the sob before it escapes. I'm crying like a giant, cock-breaking baby and I can't stop as I shake from head to toe. Suddenly, I feel him move, sitting us up so I'm wrapped in his arms, despite still being impaled.

"Baby Girl, don't cry. You're making me want to kick *my* ass, and I can't do that while the key's stuck in the lock." Fitz's cheek rubs against mine while he emits a comforting, low growl against my ear.

He's trying to be sweet, but it's only making me cry harder. "I—I b-b-broke youuuuuu!"

His bark of laughter startles me, and he nips my earlobe lightly. "If anyone was going to break me, I'm glad it was you, Delores Drew. Don't you dare be ashamed."

I suck in a deep breath, trying to pull myself together. Fitz isn't mad at me; he was just surprised. It's okay—I didn't ruin anything. "I don't know why this happened, but I'm sorry. I… I'll try not to do it again."

"Oh, once we figure out how to undo this, doing it again is at the top of my list. How fucking awesome is the sex that we broke each other?! It was meant to be!"

The sniffles finally relent, and I laugh softly, wrapping my arms around him. "Okay, okay. Do you have any ideas about what we should do?"

"Well, let's just give it a minute… see if it fixes itself. Lucky for me, I'm trapped by a hot pussy with a fantastic pair of tits I haven't even paid attention to yet. Seems like a damned good way to pass the time for now."

I can get behind that plan.

"Fitz Khan, you're corrupting me."

"Fuck, I hope so."

Best Friend
Delores

"It sounds like you had a delightful time on your date," Cori grins.

She's standing on a block while I carefully pin the fabric around her, trying to follow the lines of her body the way she taught me to.

Our Halloween costumes earned us high marks for midterms, despite the professor being forced to wear one himself, but now we're practicing our skills on more formal wear until we decide on our talent show number. My curvy friend has asked for a full-on ball gown because, according to her, she's 'just extra enough to show up to class in a fucking pumpkin coach looking like *Cinderella*, if she feels like it.'

I spit out the pins I'm holding in my teeth so I can answer, as I haven't mastered Cori's ability to converse with sharp shit between my lips yet. "Yes, it was a fantastic date. You two are borderline obsessed with my sex life, you know. I don't ask about Rufus' scorecard or your secret chica."

Rufus pouts at me from where he's sorting through patterns. He's determined to match Cori, so he's trying to find patterns he can Frankenstein together to make a 'tuxgown'. "You don't need to ask about my hanger steaks because I *tell* you. But I'll give you that —Coco is *très* secretive about her fish tacos."

Cori glares at him, crossing her arms over her chest. "Don't be a bitch, Ru-Ru. Girls have it worse than boys at this place. We're expected to marry someone politically advantageous, and then pop out heirs like it's our job. The Council dipshits don't care where you *men* dip your wicks—ever—as long as you wrap it until you breed. Women don't get the same leeway, so the wallet often trumps the heart, unfortunately."

My brows furrow. It's not like Cori to be so irritable, but it sounds like whomever she was seeing chose money and power over love. I haven't been friends with them for long, but this scenario seems to happen to the polar bear pretty frequently. I don't envy her trying to find love outside of the norm in a society set up like ours.

"I have to be careful, too, Rufus," I add, backing her up. "It's not supposed to be a problem that I'm dating professors, but with my luck, some asshole will turn around and find some obscure bullshit rule to ding me for, and I'll be forced to choose."

"Would that upset you, Dollybear? Are we catching feelings for our sugar daddies?" He gasps as he holds up two designs. "This is what we need for my bespoke couture creation."

Sighing, I walk over and take the patterns from him, giving him a light smack on the back of the head. "Of course I have feelings, you big dummy. I wouldn't be so nervous if I didn't! And don't call them sugar daddies. If I cared about money that much, I would still play by my parents' rules."

The polar bear chuckles as I hand her his choices, before dropping to my knees to work on the gathers at her waist. "Dolly isn't like us, Ru. She's not a gold-digger; she's happy with exiled princes."

I stop pinning and look up at her with an arched brow, not believing a word of it. *"Us*, huh?"

Her face turns bright red as Rufus howls with laughter. "Coco, if she didn't say it, I would have. You pretend to keep things casual with your dates, but you always fall hard. It's your soft heart, and we love you for it." He strides over and plants a kiss on her cheek. "Now, do you think we can make this work?"

"Don't be daft. I can make anything work," she grumbles, although she's clearly soaking in the affection.

Covering my mouth with my hand, I chuckle, enjoying their banter. This is the friendship I didn't have with the Heathers, and everything I've experienced with Rufus and Cori only serves to shine a harsh light on the difference. I look up from the neatly pinned section and grin at my sewing teacher. "Did I get it right?"

She pauses, studying her pattern to beam at me as she takes in the row of pins. "Fuck, yes, Dolly! You're a goddamn natural apprentice—unlike Mr. Noseypants here. Let's get back to the subject of *your* love life!"

This time it's my turn to blush. I struggle with praise still—it's hard to accept it without expecting a smack down to follow. Lucille is an expert at backhanded compliments, and she always made sure I knew my worth was zero, no matter my accomplishments. However, I *am* getting better at opening up to my friends. "Okay, okay. No need to butter me up. I'm not gonna go into details about the bedroom antics, but I do have some interesting news."

"Well, tell us, Dollypop! You know there's nothing I love more than dick, but gossip is a close second." Rufus plops down on the floor behind me, fiddling with my hair as I continue to work.

I have no idea how to react to a friend randomly deciding to do something nice, like braiding my hair, so I forge ahead with my news. "Fitz dropped me off at my room the next day, and by the time I'd cleaned up, there was a text in the group chat asking if I would come to their Thanksgiving dinner."

"Ooooooo-wee! Girl, it sounds like *you're* about to be the feast to be thankful for," Rufus crows. He gets so excited that he accidentally pulls my hair too hard, but he doesn't dismissively snort when I hiss. Instead, he soothingly pats the spot, loosening his grip as he works through the sides.

I don't know what he's doing, but it seems very fancy.

"Don't be crude," I laugh before sobering. "There's actually something bothering me more than *that*... probable future scenario. Fitz asked me to date them all, and I agreed, but only if I was treated as an equal. I may have also demanded they all share more about themselves with me... which means *I* have to share more, too."

Cori bats my hands away from the dress and steps down from the block to join us, giving me a curious look. "Dolly, I love you, but you are tight-lipped about your life. I don't mean about sex; I understand you're still getting comfortable with that. But you're vague about *everything*—it's like you're worried we'll judge you for your past and who you are now. How are you going to open up to *them* if you won't be open with us to start?"

Damn. She's not wrong.

"Yeah, I promised him I'd share something new about me every day. Doesn't always have to be big, but... So, during breakfast at the hotel, I mentioned how Lucille said I shouldn't come home during breaks. I guess he told the others..." As Cori had observed, I feel very exposed sharing this—like I did with Fitz—so I pick at my nails, unable to move my head and look away while Rufus is doing his thing.

"Ohhhh," my friend breathes the word like it's an epiphany. "You think they sent you a pity invite."

Rufus snorts, gently tugging a strand to get my attention. "First, I'm pissed that you didn't tell *us* about what Lucille said. You know, either Cori or I would have taken you home for Thanksgiving rather than let you stay at this creepy old school. Second, if you think a pack of *men* are feeding you at a holiday dinner for any other reason than they like you, you are out of your fuckin' mind."

"Truth," Cori echoes. "Dudes don't give a flying fuck about whether you're a poor little orphan if they aren't interested in you. It's not in their DNA to be nurturing. My mama says if men had to raise the kids, all the species would be doomed."

I chuckle, feeling a little better about baring my soul. "Lucille isn't a sparkling example for women, either. She never even pretended to care about me, unless it benefited her."

"I say go have dinner with your little squad of admirers and screw your shitty parents. Better yet, screw your hot guys. Work up an appetite before the big meal." Rufus laughs at his own joke as he continues to fiddle with the other side of my hair.

I smack his leg. "You are such a thirsty bitch." Cori high-fives me and I grin wider, proud of my burn. "But I am glad I won't be alone during the break. With the dead body at the Halloween party and the weird decree about no extra security at school, I'd probably have locked myself in my room the whole time if it weren't for them."

"That murder shit was fucked up. I think the victim was in my web design class." Cori's rainbow curls bounce as she nods emphatically. "He was always leaving to take phone calls and the professor never said a word. It felt very skeevy."

I arch a brow. Now that I think about it, the weasel left my classes a few times, too. All of my professors—including the guys—are pretty strict about phones in class. A student leaving to take calls all the time is very odd, especially as he wasn't a Council heir or anything.

Who was that meek little shit connected to that earned him such VIP treatment?

"Maybe he was boffing Professor Marten in web design," Rufus says as he waggles his brows.

Cori reaches over and punches him on the thigh. "Not everything is about sex, Ru-Ru! Don't freak her out—professors here actually *don't* make a habit of sleeping with students, so it only goes to show how serious Dolly's guys are about her."

I give her a grateful smile. "Thank you, Coco."

"Hmph, I was just trying to make a joke!"

Since I still can't turn my head, I lightly pat the spot on Rufus' thigh where Cori punched him. "I know Ru-Ru. I appreciate your humor, and the invite to come home with you if I ever need to. I'd love to meet both of your families someday. I'm sorry… I'm still learning how to trust people, and I'm not holding things back on purpose. I guess I didn't realize how damaged I was by all the shit before I met you two."

Rufus holds his hand out to Cori, who seems to have some sort of mind meld with him because she has a twist tie ready. "We know that, Dollypop. That's why we adopted you when you showed up. Misfits like us need to stick together."

He lets go of my hair, and I dig in my bag for a mirror. Rufus rolls his eyes, pulling out his phone to take a picture of the masterpiece he's been working on, texting it to both of us.

"I look like a Viking!" I squeal in excitement. The intricate braid makes me look like a total badass, and I cannot wait to show Fitz. He's going to love this.

They all will…

"Dolly, come hang out in our room tonight. I'll show you how to preserve this look for your dinner. It's only a day or two—and your sexy professors will love it."

Thank Hera I found the two best friends a girl could have.

Somebody's Watching Me
Renard

"Stop messing me up, Fitz!" Delores' frustrated cry echoes through the Tower, but I know it's coming from the kitchen.

Despite her utter lack of cooking knowledge, she's determined to 'help' with our dinner preparation.

Chess tried to get her and Fitz—who is currently nipping at her heels like a lovesick puppy—to go play with the Slaystation, but she insisted, declaring she wasn't a charity case to be served. No one wanted to push the subject, as we all know she wasn't welcome in her childhood home over the holiday break. It's probably why Chess is allowing her in his sacred space at the moment, despite the added distraction of his lover, who is no doubt doing nothing but feeling her up.

"Aw, baby girl! How am I supposed to keep my paws to myself when you're wearing that frilly apron thingy?" the younger tiger whines.

How indeed.

Delores shrieks again before her giggles fill the air, and I shake my head, glancing at the dragon lounging on his throne with a large, dusty book. Aubrey senses my eyes on him, smirking knowingly as he carefully shuts the book. He's been feisty since the night of the parents' meeting.

Could it be that he's having as much trouble keeping his dragon calm around Dolly as I am with my gargoyle?

"You could go down and mediate," the dragon suggests, arching a brow at me. "Living in Paris for all of those years must have rubbed off on you a little. Surely you know how to cook?"

I snort. He damn well knows I love to learn things and frequently take up hobbies on a whim. I absolutely know how to cook. Aubrey and I had no need for that skill until the cats came along, and Chess does most of the cooking, but still. "I don't want to disturb Chess' workspace, as I had them renovate the kitchen to his specifications. Besides, there's already too many cooks in there, don't you think?"

"Fuck, yes, there are," Felix mutters as he gets up and walks towards the stairs. "I'll go handle my brother before Chess loses his mind."

Aubrey watches him go before smirking at me. "If he thinks we believe he's getting involved to wrangle Fitz and *not* to ogle the frilly apron and dress combo, he's in deeper denial than we thought."

"You know what they say about denial—it's not just a river in..."

"Stop it," the dragon huffs grumpily, shifting in his chair. "You're especially cheeky today. Is that because you agreed to let bite size come hunting with us after dinner?"

Since Fitz's 'date' with Dolly, she's become a frequent visitor in all levels of the Tower, even on the top floor. Whether she's plopped at my desk doing homework, playing Slaystation with Fitz, or even simply curled up on the couch with headphones and sheet music, I almost expect her presence at this point. And since Dolly doesn't like it when I brood on the ledge 'like emo Spiderman', I now make a habit of joining the circle.

Shrugging at the pointed question, I rise from my throne and walk to the sidebar, pouring us each a drink. "I promised she could join whenever she wanted. I couldn't very well take that back, now could I? Besides, you let her spend the night with you, big guy. Don't throw rocks in glass Towers."

Take that, you stubborn old lizard. If I have to admit things, you do, too.

Aubrey puffs a few smoke rings, always grumbly when he has to discuss things he's not ready to. I come back with scotch and I chuckle, wondering if he'll attempt to redirect. "She was scared, Rennie."

"She was crying, Flames."

This is a stand-off we've had many times over the years about various things. Furniture? Yes. Hobbies? Yes. His fucking books? Absolutely.

But never a girl.

We eye one another for a moment, and I drop onto my Gothic throne with a satisfied grin. He hates when I logic him out of being purposefully obtuse, and I know it. Our stand-off is broken when Felix comes stomping back into the room, covered in flour from head to toe. My eyes widen as I watch the alpha continue to the bathroom, cursing like a sailor on leave. When I look at my companion, we burst out laughing at the same time.

Felix Khan has met his match in Delores Drew.

"Twenty bucks says Fitz talked her into it," Aubrey snorts, leaning back on his throne with a grin. Now that someone else's hangups are in the spotlight, he's much more amenable.

I shake my head. "Fifty says our girl did that all on her own."

"You're on, poetry boy. Shall we go see what trouble the children have gotten into?"

Nodding, I rise again, taking my absinthe with me. "Chess' kitchen is probably a fucking mess. He'll be tearing his hair out."

"Word."

"Oh, sweet Aed, never say that again."

THE LIGHTS FROM THE CHANDELIER MAKE THE CRYSTAL GLISTEN, and I find myself amused as hell that Felix demanded we set the big table for dinner. We almost never use this room—I have no idea why it was even built. During the holidays, we typically all eat in the sitting room upstairs while drinking and grousing about the students and staff. But with Dolly here, we apparently need to roll out the red carpet.

We've definitely never used this china, nor the silver. I haven't opened the cabinet they're stored in since I moved in because I didn't see the need for the trappings of a king at a place like Apex.

Okay, outside of my chair and my private quarters, I suppose. But who likes to be uncomfortable in their own space?

Once the Raj comes out of the washroom, Aubrey and I could herd Dolly and Fitz so Chess has enough peace in the kitchen to finish. Dolly is relatively clean, and Fitz has stripped to his boxers to rid himself of the dust, although I bet that was his choice. It's all quite comical, but I know dinner will be burnt to a crisp by the jittery chef if we don't intervene.

"Does it look right, Rennie?"

I blink when Dolly comes bounding over to me, her full skirt bouncing. She's dressed in an outfit that could only have been picked by the fucker elected to discuss our… proposition with her. Fitz came back the next day smug as hell, crowing that she'd accepted all five of us, but beyond that, he's kept his mouth shut. I'd never tell him, but I actually respect him for letting everyone—including Dolly—get comfortable with the arrangement instead of running his big fat mouth about their escapades.

Besides, I'm not sure if I could take it.

Of course, he couldn't completely let it go, judging by how the bunny in question is dressed in a baby pink pin-up style dress that ties around her neck, and the entire delicious looking garment is cherry patterned.

No one ever accused Fitz Khan of being subtle.

Truthfully, Fitz seducing Delores first probably affects Felix more than any of us. It's usually the Raj who would take on that role in a poly tiger group, but neither he nor Chess are ready for that yet. Aubrey is notoriously slow to let people in, but allowing her in our *actual* bedroom was a big, flashing light that he's made some sort of decision, even if nothing scandalous happened. And I... benefit from all of their familiarity without having to define anything too closely just yet.

There's a safety in being the watchful one, and I've been quietly arranging things to show that I enjoy her presence in the Tower.

"Rennie?"

Oh, shit. I got lost in my head again.

I smile, tilting my head as I walk around the table slowly, admiring her work. Our girl may not cook, but her sharp mind knew how to set a formal table. "You set it European style."

Her face lights up and she wiggles a little, making the dress flounce invitingly. "I did! You can always tell by the salad fork."

Fitz walks up, re-dressed and looking pleased about his part in making his brother and the entire kitchen an absolute nightmare. "You can fork me anytime, baby girl."

"Preferably with a barbecue fork," Aubrey adds as he strides in with Felix in tow.

They share a chuckle, and I smile to myself. They've always been more alike than not, and not just because they're both grumpy alphas. Since Dolly arrived, the tiger is slowly becoming the leader his ambush needs, and Aubrey is coming out of his hard shell.

"Excellent burn, spicy lizard. I might enjoy being stabbed a little, but I don't think our girl's ready for that kind of play in the bedroom." Fitz pecks her cheek and trots over to the bar, leaving Dolly with eyes the size of the dinner plates.

Felix gives Dolly a once-over he thinks is subtle, as Aubrey slips his hand into his pocket, looking everywhere *except* at her.

Oh, this is delicious—they're both so fucking stubborn, they can't even admit how attracted to this girl they are. I'm going to have a ball during dinner.

Chess pops his head out of the kitchen, narrowing his eyes at the rest of us. That's an unusual look, but I suppose I can't blame him for being frazzled today. "It would be nice if you could all help bring the food in..."

Oh, that was definitely aggressive... I'm going to need some popcorn.

"Oooh! It smells amazing. I'm so hungry I could eat an entire cow," Dolly says, clapping her hands as she rushes over to help, earning her a smile from Chess that shows she wasn't the reason for his ire.

Aubrey and I look at the tigers, shock clear on our faces. Fitz snorts, elbowing his brother before smirking at us. "You didn't know my baby girl is a ravenous meat-eater? Man, you two are sooooo far behind. Tragic."

My brow furrows. I stocked snacks for Dolly upstairs for when she camped out here, but none with a carnivorous bunny in mind. I suppose this explains her lack of disgust when she joined us on our hunt. Fitz is still gloating about his insider knowledge, and

Aubrey puffs another smoke ring, clearly annoyed that he didn't know this little… eccentricity of hers.

Dolly pokes her head out of the kitchen, interrupting our stand-off with a haughty exclamation. "This isn't your palace, guys, and neither Chess nor I are June Cleaver. Come in here and help us!"

The enforcer opens his mouth, but Aubrey rolls his eyes, cutting him off before he can speak. "Yes, yes, Fitz. We're all aware you're happy to come for her anytime. Move your ass."

That catches the tiger off guard, and Felix bursts out laughing in a way I've never seen before. I'll be damned—Dolly's a goddamned miracle worker.

I grin at my companion, holding my fist up for a bump as I pass by him. Felix isn't the only one she's good for, and I enjoy seeing him have a little fun, too. Aubrey is far too tightly wound for his own good, especially with anyone who hasn't been around for centuries, like I have. Much like Felix does, my dragon punishes himself for mistakes of the past more than he'd like to admit.

We wait at the door, allowing Chess to walk through with the turkey, followed by Dolly, carrying an impressive amount of side dishes on her arms like a pro. The rest of us follow Felix into the kitchen, grabbing the various platters full of prime rib, venison, gazelle, and other savory meats. As we set our dishes on the table, Dolly bustles past, then returns with another multi-plate load of side dishes, and I finally give in, asking what I know we're all thinking.

"*Petite lapin*, where did you learn to carry dishes like that? Surely you didn't serve the food at home. Combined with the place setting—where did you pick that up?"

Aubrey snorts. "We know your mother didn't teach you." When he mentions her mother, she gives the dragon a look that could shrivel a lesser pred's balls, and I cover my mouth with my hand.

I bet she learned that *from her mother.*

"Over the summer," she says, sashaying over to the small ice bucket full of Dr. Pepper I left out for her. "I worked at House Growlvinchy for Luc, and it allowed me the freedom to experience real-world things. I made friends with a lot of prey animals who worked in the area, and one of the nicer ones was Clotilda. She's a skunk who worked in the coffeehouse nearby, but she also had experience catering for Council families. We got to know each other when I helped her cover busy shifts, and she helped me wipe all of Lucille's spy shit off my devices 'cause she's *also* a hacker."

No one seems to know what to do with that information. Fitz is looking a little cagey, and I wonder how closely he was stalking her during the break. I clear my throat, waiting for someone to speak, and when they don't, I sigh.

Not my forte, but okay…

"How did you end up working for… Luc, did you say?"

"I'll share that information with you, but only if you guys do what I do with Fitz." She grins, walking up to the table and plopping her cute butt right in the chair at the head.

Five sets of eyes stare at her with open mouths, though whether it's because of her statement or the chair she chose, I can't say.

"What… you… do… with Fitz?" Aubrey finally breaks the ice.

Chess snorts as he takes a chair one spot away from the grinning bunny.

Dolly rolls her eyes, sipping her soda as she gestures to the other chairs, implying we should all sit. "Yes. I tell you something about me and you then have to share something about you—something important, not some random factoid."

That gets everyone's attention, and Fitz shrugs. "Seemed like a fair trade when she was naked."

"Fitz!" she hisses, her face flushing as pink as her dress. He just smirks at her like an asshole, then drops into the seat between her and Chess.

To my absolute shock, Aubrey does not point out Delores' bold choice of seats, instead following suit on her other side, shaking his napkin out and putting it on his lap before he responds. "Seems fair. Is there an out for questions we cannot answer for various reasons? At least, not yet... "

Good question.

My gaze flits between Chess and Felix, both of whom do not look excited about this game. That means I'm the deciding vote, and since I enjoy the hell out of watching everyone cautiously dance around Dolly, I choose chaos. Giving her my most charming grin, I take the seat next to the dragon. "If there's a way to pass on questions we can't or won't answer yet, I'm game."

"What?!" Chess grumbles, but Fitz ignores him, reaching over the table to high five Aubrey and I.

"Fuck, yeah! Hey bro—come sit your brass balls at the sharing table with us!"

Felix narrows his eyes at his brother and stomps over to the remaining seat. His gaze locks with our girl's the second his ass hits the chair and she lifts her chin in a challenge.

This couldn't be more fascinating if it was an episode of The Good Life.

"Okay, baby. If you wanna play with the big preds, we'll play. What's your question?" His expression is knowing, as if he's already won, and he passes a basket of rolls to me while he waits.

Dolly gives him a feral grin as she thinks for a moment and then asks, "How did it fall on Fitz to ask me out on behalf of all you big baddies?"

Felix leans forward on his elbows as the rest of us fill our plates quietly, only the clinking of the silverware in the air as he grins.

"We thought you'd be most comfortable with Fitz, but I may have helped coach him with phrasing."

"Why would you do that?" Dolly sits back, the smug grin replaced by surprise.

"You owe us an answer first," Aubrey pipes up, and I turn to look at him again in shock. "How did you end up working for Luc Growlvinchy?"

What's gotten into him tonight? Spicy lizard, indeed.

She rolls her eyes, making a show of reaching for a gigantic piece of prime rib and slapping it on her plate. "I met him when I bought my dress for prom. He was kind during the fitting, and I think he sensed I needed an ally. He gave me his number, 'just in case' I had dress issues, so when I needed to earn money after everyone deserted me, I called him. He has a lot of prey animals working for him, and I knew he wouldn't mistreat me."

"Fair enough," Felix casually replies, although I notice his jaw tick as he no doubt tamps down the instinct to protect. "Who's next?"

Oh, we are going to need a lot more alcohol for this.

Heartbreaker

Felix

Being on trial at Bloodstone wasn't as nerve-wracking as being grilled by Delores Drew. If we'd raided a distillery, there would not have been enough alcohol for her sharp questions and fierce determination to get to know us. Fitz spent most of the time doing his typical over-sharing, which she allowed him to do with a soft smile that made my gut clench.

How did the former playboy of Apex worm his way so thoroughly into her graces, and how did this girl get my brother to settle in a way I never thought he would?

It's a fucking mystery.

Chess was quieter, offering information as she asked, but obviously still trying to come to grips with his feelings for her. He's much more vocal about her when we're all alone and I might have to take him aside to have a chat if he doesn't get it together soon. It will go much smoother if I do it rather than Fitz, and I want him to keep developing these sparks of confidence I've been seeing.

The three royals, including me, were less effusive because we have questionable pasts. My scandal might be well known, but trusting a Council heir with more information was difficult. Aubrey and Renard rarely speak about their past, even to us, and I could tell they were answering cautiously. I hoped that after ten years, I might find out exactly what they did to end up here, but no dice.

We'll all have to earn those tales, I suppose.

Luckily, our girl had enough sense to dance around things that shouldn't come up at a family meal. She didn't ask about my consort, despite Fitz sharing far too much with her on their date. No one asked about Aubrey and Ren's hunting or their weird inability to admit where they sleep. No one asked Chess his real name or about how he came to be with us.

That impressed me a bit because it felt like all of us were being sensitive to one another for once.

As Fitz pointed out, sharing our fuck-ups makes us look more sympathetic. Delores was horrified by what happened with my exile and it explained why I'm such a closed off asshole—according to my brother. I wanted to kick his ass when I found out he blabbed, but honestly? It's a relief that I don't have to relive that shit again. My ex's betrayal still smarts even though I don't love her anymore.

My father, however, can put on a cape and get super fucked.

Looking over at the gang of preds in the Tower kitchen cleaning, I smirk a little. The nefarious bunny is downstairs asleep in her gilded chamber, but I rousted the troops early to get this place cleaned up. If Delores is going to use it during the week to make herself food, it can't be filled with crusty dishes and leftover crap.

"Do you all feel like she was trying to crawl into our brains to pick them clean?" Aubrey asks grumpily.

He doesn't mind the early morning wake-up as much as his half-zombified companion, who's barely said a word since he ambled down to the third floor. However, the frilly pink apron he has tied around his neck and waist makes it hard to take anything he says seriously.

"Look, Betty Cocker," Fitz drawls as he pretends to dry a plate on his ass. His pantomime earns him a glare from the silent gargoyle, but he laughs, "all our girl wants is to feel like she really knows us. That jizzbag she dated before had her totally snowed and she's afraid of making the same mistake twice."

I snort, trying to get my shit together as I watch the dragon and my brother flick soap bubbles at one another. "Don't make a bigger mess, assholes. But yeah, I felt like I barely escaped with my life."

"I, too, felt a bit cornered. That was not *ma petite's* intent, I'm sure, but it's been a very long time since I've been interrogated so thoroughly." Renard finally speaks, and as usual, makes perfect sense.

"Do you think she realizes what things we did not share?" Aubrey asks, pushing his glasses up as he looks at me. "There are things we simply cannot share yet."

My brows furrow when I realize our stoic, scaly friend seems worried about upsetting her. He rarely cares what anyone thinks, and it's interesting that he's thought about what could happen if we aren't completely honest with Delores.

Yeah, we're a fucking mess.

"We did our best, given the skeletons in everyone's closets," Chess says as he walks in with two more steaming mugs of coffee. "I don't know everything about the two of you, nor do Fitz and Felix. Our angel is perceptive, but I think she realizes one night of 'truth for a truth' didn't reveal everything."

"I know you douches think you're protecting her by not spilling all your dirty beans, but Baby Girl wants to be treated like an equal partner in this. She can handle Felix's heartbreak, my womanizing, Chess' cheetah, and whatever the hell you fuckers are hiding from us. Stop treating her like a kid."

Again, Fitz is the voice of reason and it's freaking me the fuck out.

"Do you think we should tell her about the email we got this morning?" Chess says softly. "I don't know if telling her three students didn't show up to their families' homes after they supposedly left for Thanksgiving break is the best plan."

Fitz frowns. "Why the hell do any of us call it Thanksgiving? I get the humans—all that mythos about the indigenous people and their ancestors. Shifters have been here longer than the indigenous people, anyway. Us and the other creepy crawlies that go bump in the night, at least."

Aubrey takes off his glasses and pinches his nose in frustration. "Fucking hell, Fitzgerald. Could we please stay on topic?"

My brother pouts, and Chess leans in to whisper to him, "Because we enjoy having a big feast, dummy. It doesn't mean anything."

I roll my eyes and look over at the gargoyle as he polishes the glassware. "The question is still on the table—the real question, that is."

We all look at one another, our expressions belying how torn we are. I want to protect the newest member of our ambush and something inside of me says we shouldn't tell her. But I know my twin, and he's going to tell her no matter what any of us say. He's on this whole 'personal growth' kick with the rainbow Barbie and he won't give a single fuck if it rats the rest of us out.

What a time to grow a conscience.

"I'm worried about her safety," Renard admits quietly. "Aren't you?"

Aubrey snorts, smoke rings wafting through the air as he grips a plate hard enough to split it in half. "Of course we are. Even Felix looks as if he wants to tear someone to shreds. But we have to decide if telling her will make her safer or less so."

"Henrietta said not to tell the students," Chess says as he leans on the counter. "That's why I asked. If we tell her, she cannot tell anyone else, even her friends."

"Freya's tits, guys. All we have to do is let my baby girl know and that it has to be a secret. I'm pretty sure she's already keeping secrets from multiple people in this room." Fitz glares at our hosts and I frown. "So I know she can keep her twitchy nose in place."

The winged ancients share a look, then Aubrey sighs. "Yes, fine. I vote with Fitz. We'll tell her, but make sure she doesn't share the information. Maybe she'll notice more quickly if students disappear during the rest of the term than we would."

Actually, that's pretty fucking brilliant. I tell him so, and the dragon snorts again.

"Felix, you do not have to take on the responsibility for this entire group by yourself as you would at home. We are all capable of contributing and definitely willing when it comes to keeping bite size safe. Stop assuming you are the only one able to lead."

"Especially when we've been telling you for over a decade that women make far better leaders, anyway," Renard mutters as he continues shining crystal. "Gargoyles and dragons allow it in their kingdoms."

"Okay! We tell her." I sigh and rake my hand through my hair. "On to the next topic… what do we do about Yule break?"

They look at me in surprise. None of us has left Apex for any break since we arrived—most exiles don't.

Various species have their own traditions in the staff housing and many of them invite others to join, but usually the five of us hole up in the Tower with scotch and video games.

Bitter old recluses, that's us.

"We'll be here, I imagine," Aubrey says with a frown. "Why?"

Fitz blinks, looking at me as he finally catches on. "He's worried about Dolly. She might have to go home to the nuthouse, right?"

I nod, my expression grim as I remember what the dragon shared about her parents and their behavior at the meeting. "It concerns me, yes."

"Hell yeah, big bro is on the D train now!" He grabs Chess, spinning him around crazily before he gives us a bright smile. "Now we have to get you to quit swallowing your tongue around her and the Flying Fartknockers to dig their heads out of their asses. Then we can all do the bunny hop together!"

Every time I think Fitz is maturing, he follows it with something like this. Sigh.

"What have you found out about the prey tunnels and the symbols on that door? We haven't talked about it since you belched fire at everyone," I ask as I pick up a stack of clean dishes to put in the cabinets.

The dragon gives me a murderous look and, despite his frilly attire, I feel it in my bones. "I am having difficulty locating the information we need. Renard is talking with the prey about the inside of the tunnels, but we are hitting brick walls."

"Baby Girl found some map things in a book. Has she asked you?" Fitz flips a knife across the room and I catch it with an irritated growl.

Aubrey whirls around, looking at each of us until he hits the guilty expression on his Tower mate's face. "She asked you and not me?"

This kitchen might turn into an Easy Bake oven if he doesn't give the answer our friend wants.

"Yes. But she planned to ask you since she found the clues in one of the archive books she's been working on for you." He grins a little, winking at the angry librarian. "I'm fairly certain the dead body at the school party distracted her, Flames."

Just like that, Aubrey lets out a slow breath and nods. "You may be right. I'll speak to her after and together we can try to piece together what she believes she found."

"You have the fucking coolest lair, Lizard of Oz. I nearly pissed my sweats because our bad bunny didn't warn me, but I definitely want to ride it again."

And then the dragon puffs up again, wings and all.

I always knew my brother was going to be the death of me.

Under Pressure

Delores

My head is pounding as I walk out of my last exam of the semester. I should be excited because I'm finally free, but to be honest, I feel like I might keel over on the spot.

The weeks after Thanksgiving were a blur—mostly because every professor in the entire fucking school piled the students with projects, papers, and study guides that could double as bludgeons. I don't know why they were intent on making us study twenty-four hours a day, besides seeing if we'd crack, but it's been the most intense two weeks of school work I've ever experienced. I haven't even had a sleepover with Fitz lately, because I was so buried in work.

That would have helped me let off some steam…

I spent most of my nights in either Rufus or Cori's dorm room, all of us wearing headphones while we stuff our faces with pizza and clack away at keyboards. I wanted to work upstairs, but to be honest, this time of year is about cramming knowledge and bitching about your professors… over half of which are my boyfriends, so it seemed prudent to hunker in downstairs with my friends instead.

Lucille will definitely check on my grades, and although I'm not permitted to come home during Yule break, I'll surely receive a not-so-vaguely threatening phone call if my marks aren't up to snuff. I wouldn't put it past her to send Bruiser to 'remind' me how important it is to still positively represent the very family I've been shunned from, so the bags under my eyes and my shuffling gait of a zombie have been earned. I don't know if I've slept more than ten hours since Friday, to be honest.

I'm still a hundred percent likely to flunk my fucking Shifter History exam.

That shitty asshole Professor Abel changed the test—again— without notice, so everything I spent the weekend memorizing was damn near useless. The professor's smirk at my dismay, and that no one else in class seemed to freak out, makes me wonder if I'm not being given completely different material than everyone else.

My DiePhone vibrates in my pocket, and I pull it out, smiling for the first time in hours when I see who it is. "Hi Cori! I just got out. I'm headed to your room to—oh. I see." I stop in my tracks, looking across the campus in fear. The Honeywell Admissions building looms across the lake, and I can't repress the shiver that shoots down my spine as I listen to my friend explain why she and Rufus think I need to join them in the cafeteria.

"... besides, Dolly, you can't avoid the building entirely for the next three and a half years! Rufus and I are already inside, headed to claim a table. No one will mess with you when we're together; I promise. They have fish tacos tonight, and we want to spend the whole dinner giggling like idiots. Pleeeeeease?"

Swallowing hard, I put my free hand on my chest, feeling the rapid thump of my heart as the prey animal inside of me remembers the last time I was in there. Rufus and Cori don't understand how that chase made me feel—they can't.

They'll never be able to comprehend the desperation I felt trying to get to the infirmary before some dickwad dingoes I didn't even know tried to attack me. It's not something I can explain, because it's so far out of their experience as preds, especially ones who can hold their own. The invitation is still tempting because I don't want to keep running forever.

Chin up, Dolly. It's time to face your fears and kick their ass. That's what your guys would do.

Ugh. It's definitely what they'd do, while also encouraging me to do the same. "Okay, Coco. But no one gets to make fun of me if I'm a little jumpy at first. Tell Rufus not to be a bitch about it." Her laugh tinkles through the line, and before I know it, we've said goodbye.

My feet move again before I can think too hard about it, carrying me along the edge of the lake towards the Shird. The Captain and his crew are out in the middle, tossing things into the water—it must be aquatic shifter food. When I squint past them to the garden behind the Tower, it's empty, so I know Rennie has finished his last class of the day.

I miss spending my nights with them, and thinking about my guys makes my heart squeeze. After I celebrate with my friends tonight, I plan to plant myself in their space and dig my claws in, so I don't have to leave for a while.

As if they could hear my thoughts, my phone buzzes again, and I swipe it open to find new messages in the group chat.

> TigerWoody: Baby Girl, I have one more exam for you.

> LustyLibrarian: Don't say it, Fitz.

> TigerWoody: … you should exam-ine my balls!

> TigerKing: Why the fuck do I need to be in this chat again?

> EmoBatMan: Perhaps we could ask Dolly how her actual exams went?

CSpot: How did your exams go, angel?

LustyLibrarian: Yes, tell us, bite size.

SMILING TO MYSELF AS I WALK AROUND THE ARTS BUILDING, I consider how to respond. I could definitely tease the guys about their own classes, but I don't want them flying off the handle at any of my other professors if I complain—especially with my suspicions about Shifter History. It won't make me any friends, and since I don't know yet what my classes will be next semester, I have to tread lightly.

BabyGirl: I'm pretty sure I did okay in
Shifter Basics: :wink emoji:

TigerWoody: Bro, didn't give you a D? A
big D?

TigerKing: Fitz, fuck off.

TigerKing: You did great, princess.

BabyGirl: My solo and dance went well—at
least that's what Cori said.

TigerWoody: Chess should have watched!
You're going to like when he watches.

CSpot: Fitz…

LustyLibrarian: Do we get to see you
perform at some point?

TigerWoody: …

EmoBatMan: Keep it to yourself, Fitz.

TigerWoody: Baby Girl, tell them to stop
picking on me!

I pause for a moment in the space between the Shird and the Honeywell Admissions building. To be honest, I like Fitz's teasing even when it makes me blush—like now—but I also love the way they jump in to save me. I'm not used to so many people completely focused on me in a good way, and I'm not sure how to handle it.

What would Rufus say?

He'd tell me to give it to them good. I ponder for a moment and take a deep breath, feeling braver with the distance messaging offers.

> BabyGirl: Fitz, you're begging to be spanked. Don't cry to me.

The dots float on the screen for a few heart-stopping moments and I almost lose my nerve. But then I see typing, and I bite my lip as I wait for the response.

> LustyLibrarian: The lunchable has you pegged, Fitzgerald.
>
> EmoBatMan: Agreed.
>
> TigerWoody: Baby Girl, you're a traitor. :pout: Chess, tell them.
>
> CSpot: You're on your own.
>
> TigerWoody: Bro is being real quiet in the chat suddenly.
>
> TigerKing: I will end you, Fitz.
>
> TigerWoody: Well... let our girl spank me first....

A wide grin splits my face, and I do a little fist pump and shimmy before looking around to make sure no one saw me being an absolute dork.

Score one for Dolly.

> BabyGirl: I think I did well in everything else but Shifter History. But I have to go because I'm meeting Cori and Rufus in the caf for dinner and celebration. Can we message later?

CSpot: You're not coming to our spot tonight?

EmoBatMan: It's okay, petit lapin. Go have fun with your friends.

TigerWoody: No, it's not, my balls don't think it's ok…

LustyLibrarian: Ignore him, Dolly. You can celebrate with us tomorrow.

TigerWoody: …

LustyLibrarian: Yes, your balls. We know.

TigerKing: How the fuck do I get out of this chat?

> BabyGirl: Thanks, guys. I'll message later. Fitz, play with Chess. You can tell me about it later. :wink emoji:

Feeling good about my handling of five men, I look up at the Admin building and take a deep breath.

Okay, Dolly. Joking about sex helped pump you up. Now it's time to channel your inner badass.

I STRIDE INTO THE CAFETERIA WITH MY SPINE STEELED. AS I WALK to the table where Rufus is lounging, I can feel eyes on my back, but I don't let it bother me. These shitty assholes are just followers

—people who are too scared of the social caste system at Apex to stand up to the Heathers, even if they don't agree with what they're doing. I don't give a flying fuck about their judgment or their pity.

"Hi, Ru-Ru!" I say, making sure my voice carries even in the loud dining hall. "Where's Coco?"

He gives me a sly grin, catching on to my need for bravado immediately. "She's scoping out the menu while we waited for you. You know how she loves to sample all the different fish in her tacos."

Snorting, I plop down on the chair next to him, smiling when I see Raina the raccoon beeline for our table. I was so scared after what happened here, I never came back to thank her for bringing my food and bag to the infirmary the night they chased me down. Raina beams at me as she hands us our menus, and I give her a grateful smile in return. "Raina, I didn't get to thank you for your help at the beginning of the semester. I'm so happy to see you again."

"Miss Dolly, I'm thrilled to see you here. I'll grab you and Mr. Rufus' drinks while you decide what you're having. I can't wait to tell the kitchen staff you're back!"

The raccoon scurries off, and Rufus arches his brow at me. "What in RuPaul's name did you do to earn *that* kind of service? I thought you just got chased by the bottom feeding dingoes."

I shrug. "I did. But I was nice to her, and well, I'm sure she knows I'm prey. And Renard is really tight with all the prey staff, so... maybe it's a combo?"

"Dolly, queen of the downtrodden—it fits you, girl." He chuckles and waves at Cori, trying to get her to stop flirting with an artsy-looking aquatic shifter by the lake entrance. "Coco needs to shake a leg; I'm starving."

Before I can respond, a ridiculously realistic-looking newspaper is plopped on the table in front of me. I turn my head, and like a bad case of the clap, the Heathers are back.

As if I didn't have enough to deal with, my ex-friends seem determined to continue harassing me like creepy stalkers, even though I avoid them. Rufus picks up the paper, not even giving them the courtesy of looking in their direction. When he sees the headline, he hands it to me with a huff of annoyance.

SHOULD APEX ACADEMY ENACT A MORAL CLAUSE IN ITS HONOR CODE?

A Student Perspective by Heather Barrington

Apex Academy has a long tradition of excellence.

Its students are known for representing the school and their families with the utmost refinement and grace, whether in public or in private. When the administration allows unworthy students to not only attend our school but also flaunt their deviant behavior, it reflects poorly on all of us.

Our current honor code does not have a moral turpitude clause like many other honored institutions around the world; however, recent changes in the student body and their relations with multiple staff members calls that decision into question.

Closing my eyes, I pinch the bridge of my nose. It's getting easier to write these pathetic losers off because they're so incredibly off-base in their accusations that it's laughable. Between the four of them, they've slept with more guys than I have and I'm dating five. I don't care who they fuck, or even who they procreate with, but I'm getting mighty goddamn tired of being slut-shamed.

The least they could do is get it right if they're going to publicly call me out for my private life.

Cori glares at the Heathers as she approaches, hand on her hip and murder in her eyes. "You know, this article is already all over social media. Now it's in the school paper. This kind of accusation —made with school resources, no less—might constitute… bullying. Aren't there a few lines in the honor code about *that?*"

I nod. "There are more than a few lines, Coco. In fact, I'm fairly certain it's grounds for expulsion."

Gold crosses her arms over her chest, looking at her acolytes for confirmation before she speaks. "I believe you'll find nothing libelous in this article, DD. If you even know what that word means."

The smartest bitch in the room, right here.

Rufus barks a laugh, turning to her with bared fangs, morphing from fun-loving to gangster in the blink of an eye. "Oh, honey. You're going to want to trot your bleached-fried bobbleheads elsewhere with that legalese. My family doesn't worry much about the courts; we have our methods of meting out justice when necessary. Don't you winter in Vail? I have cousins out that way…"

"Skiing can be pretty dangerous," Cori says, tapping her lips with her sparkly nails. "I'd be fine stranded on a snowy mountain, but I don't think you hot-blooded canines would do too well."

Amusement quirks the corner of my lips, and I'm grateful once again for my new friends. Who else would threaten to murder my ex-besties as casually as they discuss *Grey's Anatomy?*

"That's a threat! I'm going to the Headmistress' office immediately!" Gold fumes.

"Good luck with that. Bye Felicia!" Rufus calls as they stalk off as a group. He looks at me and then at the paper. "Dollypop, you are a drama magnet and I am *here for it.* I haven't threatened anyone in days. I almost couldn't remember how."

Wiping my hands down my face, I groan. "I'm glad you enjoy it because I am beyond over it. We need to work on a plan to deal with them, because I'm sure they're not done, and I definitely cannot do four more years of that dance."

Leaning in, Cori gives me a crafty smile. "It's all about making them look bad and you look like the next big thing. I think we can come up with a plan."

Did I mention these guys are the best friends a bunny could have?

A Little Wicked

Lucille

Lucille

Lucille

"Matilda!"

Where in the name of Croco Clawnel is that useless bird?

"On my way, Madam!" The panicked squawk echoes through the house, and it makes my lips curve up.

I can imagine her huffing her way from whatever hole she was hiding in, while I completed my evening beauty regimen. That is a task I do not include my witless assistant in—no one needs to know what lengths I go to in order to maintain my flawless appearance.

Information like that would end up on PMZ in the blink of an eye.

The master bedroom is my domain, with every item placed for my convenience. Unlike some wives, I don't have to worry about my oafish husband stomping around my space, as Bruno hasn't slept on the same floor as me since Delores was conceived, which pleases me to no end. I only open the doors to my boudoir for those worthy of sharing my bed—young, fit shifters who haven't been coddled since birth.

"Matilda!" I shout again, my tone rising along with my annoyance. The hawk shifter's place in this household was more secure when my chubby child lived here. Now that Delores is out for good, I could replace this ninny with a snap of my manicured fingers.

The door flings open, and I blankly stare at the huffing bird as she catches her breath. "Apologies... madam. I was... in the east garden... supervising the rose garden renovation."

Rolling my eyes, I sigh. If she were in better shape, she would have arrived faster, and my glass wouldn't still be empty. "Drink."

Matilda's eyes widen and she scurries to the bar, locating the ingredients to make a fresh pitcher of martinis. "You look younger every day, madam."

I smirk, turning to the mirror to verify her words. "It's true; I do. Living well has its benefits." Swiveling in my seat, I look at her frumpy, frazzled attire and shake my head. "You'd do well to take a page from my book, Matilda. That outfit ages you ten years."

"I'll burn it, madam," she replies as she approaches with my drink. "I always appreciate your sage advice."

I'll bet you do.

My father taught me to read people at the auctions when I was very young, and I'm well aware Matilda is simply telling me what I want to hear. However, as long as she continues to show me the respect I deserve on the surface, I don't care what's going on in her little birdbrain. Forcing others to cower under your gaze is one of the most powerful tools a leader can possess, and I've got mine honed to perfection. Any shifter interested in survival knows if they don't properly cower under the weight of my stare, they face the wrath of my leopard.

Killing a few people here and there helps reinforce a healthy level of fear.

"Bring me my phone. I believe it's time to check in with my rebellious rabbit."

My assistant's brow furrows in concern, but she walks to the desk and hands me my DiePhone. "It's after dinner, Madame. She may be out with her friends since exams are over."

Eyes narrowing, I grab the phone, my tone dark as I snap, "Are you presuming to criticize when I contact my child? Or suggesting I'm unaware of what goes on at that school? I know better than *you*, as I have ordered you to no longer be in communication with Delores."

"No, no, no! I was attempting to make certain you had all the information you required for your phone call. Of course, I'm only making educated guesses based on my limited understanding of campus life." The hawk shifter backs away slightly, swallowing hard as she cautiously watches me.

Fool. As if she could outrun me if I went for her throat.

"If I require your help, I will demand it, you overgrown chicken. Until then, fetch me two slices of raw pheasant and keep your beak shut."

Turning my back to her, I swipe the screen and locate Delores' contact information. The brat had better answer my call, no matter what she's doing, or so help me… I'll send Bruiser to remind her who owns her. Nothing like a mild threat to herd the sheep where you need them.

Once Matilda rushes off to the kitchen, I call my daughter. The phone rings several times, and by the time she answers, I have to calm my leopard down. If I want the bunny to give me information, I have to at least *pretend* to give a fig over what she's babbling on about.

"Delores, it's your mother. No, I'm not calling to—" I roll my eyes in disgust as she begins a lengthy diatribe about why she didn't answer sooner—as if I care what sorry excuses she has, since none will be sufficient. Already annoyed, I interrupt. "Stop. Talking. Thank you. I simply called to inquire about your exams."

That inspires another rapid-fire marathon of insipid drivel, so I lean back in my chair and sip my drink to calm my ire. My patience for dealing with useless twits is usually stretched thin by mid-morning, and we are well past that deadline. However, if I tear into her too quickly, she'll curl up like the pathetic rabbit she turned out to be, so I have to tread carefully.

Pretending to care is exhausting.

"Yes, it sounds like you may not have humiliated us this semester. Well done. If your assumptions about your grades are accurate, I won't need to send Bruiser to remind you how I feel about failure." When she asks about our holiday plans, I hear the careful tone in her voice. I've already informed her she was no longer welcome in my house during breaks, but this almost sounds like she doesn't *want* to come home—like she's hoping I *won't* force her to.

Very interesting.

"Your father and I are headed to Ibiza for the winter holiday, so you'll be staying at Apex over break, as discussed," I reply, listening for the telltale exhale of relief, smugly pleased when my suspicions are proven correct.

My bumbling bunny has plans for Yule. Who in Hera's name invited her anywhere?

I pause while she pretends to be disappointed, trying not to laugh at her pathetic attempt at lying. This behavior is why it's a fucking miracle she's my offspring; Delores doesn't have a deceitful bone in her body. No Rostoff is this ridiculously inept at subterfuge.

When she finally takes a goddamn breath, I cut in. "Delores, dear, do you have *anyone* to spend the holiday with? I'd feel so much better knowing you're taken care of while your father and I are abroad, as we will be completely unreachable in case of an emergency."

I'm sure she doesn't realize I don't mean a single syllable of that sentence? Per usual.

My brow raises when she gets cagey—at least for her—and describes a meal in the cafeteria followed by a present swap with her friends. Intel from Henrietta confirmed that her gang-banger badger and the les-bear from the fishing family were both leaving campus for the entire break. That means Delores must have plans with one of the professors she's been seen in the company of—a revelation that is most fortuitous for my plans for gathering information from influential families.

But how do I get her to open up about her dating?

"I'm pleased you will have *friends* to keep you busy." I let my sentence hang for a moment, relishing in the fear I can almost taste over the phone line. "I should mention your father is seeking eligible suitors since your… handicap… lowered your betrothal value. Perhaps we could line up dates for you around your spring holiday to introduce you to some prospects?"

Silence. Oh, that's very good.

Her voice is wobbling when she protests, so I know the bulbs in her dim mind are flashing in panic. "Delores, if you can't locate a reasonable replacement for the hyena, it's our responsibility to see you're provided for." I wait again, my lips curving up as I sip the martini. "I encourage you to open a dialogue with whomever has piqued your interest, because if you have not announced a courtship by the end of the school year, we will do it for you."

Matilda walks in, and I know my machinations have ended. Even though I've cut off their communication, I know better than to trust anyone in overhearing my plans.

The walls have ears, as they say.

"Delores, stop babbling. I'm tired of this conversation, and you've heard my decree. Remember to beautify yourself before you go to bed; your looks don't have too long of a shelf-life, and on that note, I suggest you entice someone soon, or we're marrying you to the highest bidder."

Ending the call, I glare at my assistant, annoyed that she interrupted my threats, just as I was getting on a roll. "Bring that tray over immediately and freshen my drink while you're at it. Talking with my daughter dehydrates my fur."

"Yes, madam," she mumbles as she walks over to do my bidding. Her expression is crestfallen and I have to hide the smile on my face at her pathetic loyalty to my daughter.

"Don't get your wings in a twist, Matilda. I'm only looking out for Delores. She's not meant to succeed in our world, but she's been raised to be a part of it. Bruno and I have to ensure she finds a husband, so she won't be on her own."

She looks suspicious, and I don't blame her—I'm not one for compassion. However, I force my face into a mask of concern that eventually wears the hawk down. She nods and murmurs, "Miss Delores needs solid allies on her side, madam. As always, you are correct."

I almost snort; it takes monumental control not to. What my daughter needs is to be sold off to Augustus Khan, so I can make a profit off of her. Otherwise, our investment in her life has been a waste of capital.

We'll consider that Plan C.

"Of course I am, Matilda. Now leave me alone while I finish my maintenance routine. Your presence makes my eyes ache."

She curtsies, and I roll my eyes as I watch her leave. I wonder if I should allow her a relationship with Delores again, if only to have another way to gather intel. After all, what kind of leader would I be if I didn't use all the tools at my disposal?

And they are all *tools.*

Laughing at my joke, I sip my drink as I continue to scheme, having no intention of snoozing soon.

Sleep is for the weak.

Snowman

Aubrey

Aubrey

When I awoke to find the campus covered in snow, I sourly stomped to the sitting room with my coffee. My kind is more suited to hot weather, and winter chills make the Tower drafty. It occurred to me during my correspondence with several sister-school archivists in various climates that the cold might be just as difficult on Delores. Our girl isn't an Arctic hare, and from what I've seen of her fur, it won't be enough to keep her warm while she's here during the break.

Plus, it'd be harder to get her naked if she's…

Nope. That line of thought is off-limits for the moment.

It took a bit to rouse Rennie—he's not a morning person in the slightest—but once he was coherent, he agreed, and was more than happy to fly into town with me to purchase a myriad of space heaters for the frequently used spaces in the Tower.

He also insisted on purchasing an extra desk with materials for homework, about twenty cases of Dr. Pepper, and other household junk I've always talked him out of before. This time his excuse was it will make Dolly feel welcome, so I simply watched indulgently. It was good to see him throwing things into a cart like a kid in a candy store, and the smile on his face made it impossible to grump about spending a fortune on silly, decorative bullshit.

That bunny has us all wrapped around her little finger, and I doubt she has the slightest clue.

Since her mother called to confirm she was staying at Apex for Yule, our girl has seemed a tad… *pensive.*

I don't know if anyone else has noticed, because she's hidden it well, but there's something bothering her she doesn't seem to want to talk about. I tried using her truth game, but all I got out of her was that those bitchy ex-friends of hers had dosed her with pred-stasy one night last spring, and she's planning some brand of revenge with her new friends for the talent show in the spring.

"Flames, what else can we have delivered to the Tower? We've never really celebrated the holidays together before, and I want to make sure Dolly feels at home," Renard says as he thoughtfully looks around the vast store.

I snort, arching a brow at him. "I'm fairly certain anything we do will make her happy, especially if it doesn't resemble her parental home, Rennie. But I don't disagree—she deserves to have a pleasant holiday."

He wanders over to a nervous-looking tapir shifter, talking to him animatedly for a moment before returning. "I have plans."

Uh-oh. I've somehow activated mother hen Rennie.

"You realize Dolly can't… move in… anywhere, right? At least, not at the moment," I say carefully, remembering the last time he had 'plans' was when he upgraded his nest to fit me. I know he enjoyed having her snooze with us, but I doubt we're ready to go public to our entire group.

The gargoyle looks at me as if I've lost my marbles, scoffing. "Of course not. That is far too presumptuous. We're going to look at winter gear while that gentleman's staff makes arrangements for decorations to be delivered to the Tower, along with every pillow, blanket, and cushion they have in stock. Now, quit frowning and let's go!"

Vengeful Ra, the Tower is going to resemble a magazine spread from Martha Stewart Living.

"Whatever you think, Rennie, but… take a breath, okay? We don't want to crowd her; she's just getting used to having all of us… around." I give him a fond smile as he rolls his eyes and speeds off towards the clothing section. I can't even imagine what the hell he has up his sleeve to look so unusually *not*-emo, but whatever it is, I'm in.

TWO HOURS LATER, WE LAND ON THE BALCONY TO FIND THE Captain barking orders at both his crew and several unfortunate delivery men. I give Rennie a pointed look and he shrugs, grinning broadly as he walks over to the raccoon pirates to chat.

It's really fucking hard to be grumpy when he's acting like this. Hmmph.

"Aubrey! The clothes are here, too!" he shouts. "I'm calling Dolly; you call the cats!"

I nod, shaking my head as I make my way to the steps. My companion has already pulled his phone out, tapping his foot as he waits for our girl to answer. Apparently, all it took to unleash his enthusiasm was a shopping trip? That feels like a piece of knowledge to tuck away for the next time he gets into a weird funk about that stupid flower.

Sighing, I stab at the screen of my phone as I enter the private quarters. Rennie will be down once he's talked to Dolly and I'll have to don the ridiculous snow get-up he picked. My only comfort is that he picked outfits for everyone, so I won't be the only one dressed like a North Fox catalog model to go out and play in the snow.

He even bought fucking coal and carrots to make snow animals!

The sound of Fitz's voice on the phone line jolts me out of my head. As usual, he doesn't wait for me to speak, so I listen to him blather on for a few moments before finally deciding to bring the conversation back to why I called. "Fitz. Fitz. Fitz!"

"Whoa, spicy lizard, take a pill! What's got your tail crimped?"

Counting to five, I wait until my fire simmers down and answer him, "Fitz, you need to bring Chess and Felix to the Tower immediately."

"Is something wrong with my baby girl? Why isn't she answering my texts?"

I wince as my ears ring, despite holding the phone away from my face. He's as hopped up as Rennie today. Horus, save me. "Nothing is wrong, you *idiot*. We're..." I pause and heft a sigh, knowing he's going to whoop again. "... we're having everyone over to… play in the snow."

I'd like to immediately retract that statement and erase it from memory. I'll never live it down.

The sound he makes is awfully close to that animal-wannabe *Tarzan* he made me watch a cartoon about, and I have to wait until he gets himself under control before I can bring the phone to my ear again.

"You assholes are brilliant! Our snow bunny in a snowsuit? I'm in like Flint, baby!" The line rustles as he puts a hand over the phone —incorrectly—and yells. "Chess! Bro! Baby Girl's going to play with our balls… our *snowballs*, I mean." He snickers like a teenager, and I roll my eyes.

Felix has the patience of a fucking saint, I swear to Bast.

"Fitz, I'm hanging up now. Rennie bought everyone's snow gear, and now I have to get dressed. Get your furry ass over here before our appetizer arrives."

I don't even wait for him to answer before I end the call and plop down in my chair. Two overly enthusiastic shifters in one day are a bit much for me, but before I can consider how to handle Renard and Fitz together, the gargoyle in question rushes through the door with bags draped over his arms.

"We had a lot of snow in the mountains," he murmurs. "I used to play in it as a kid. That was before, of course, but..."

Well, shit. Now I feel like a fool. This is about sharing something with our girl—something that means something to him.

With that revelation, my irritation fades as quickly as my fire, and I walk over to take a couple of the bags out of his hands. "This was a wonderful idea, Rennie. Let's get dressed before everyone arrives, and you can tell me about it later, yeah?"

His smile brightens, and he nods. "I'd like that. I'm feeling unusually talkative today."

Knock me over with a fucking feather. Today really has knocked something loose.

I grab the big bag he holds out, leaning in to give him a matching grin as I do. "Then I'd be remiss not to take advantage of your good humor. Now, get dressed."

"Always the cheater!"

Snorting, I head into the bathroom to figure out what in unholy hell he's chosen for me to wear. Rennie has a wicked sense of humor and a taste for chaos, so I wouldn't put it past him to pick out the most ridiculous shit possible when I wasn't looking. I open the bag, pulling out a complete Underarmadillo compression set, socks, a sweatshirt, and gray sweatpants.

I really must keep him and Dolly out of the romance section of the goddamn library.

It could be worse, I suppose, and I have the feeling he's outfitted us all like a buffet of cock outlines on display for our bunny's benefit. Of course, that means bite size will turn bright pink and is likely to stay that way the entire day. The image makes my dick stiffen and I groan. She's so fucking adorable when she gets all shy about innuendos, and it's even hotter when she gets brave enough to snark back. Thankfully, it's cold as hell outside—which should help keep everyone's hormones under control for a while.

I'm not sure Dolly's ready for her fluffy tail to be chased by apex predators.

Fuck knows, Rennie loves the thrill of the hunt.

Since that's not an unappealing scenario, I take a minute to squeeze myself into the winter garb before looking in the mirror. The damned outfit fits perfectly, despite the style looking out of place on me.

Dragons aren't meant for sportswear. It's undignified.

"Flames, get out here!"

Smiling to myself, I walk into the room to find Rennie hopping around as he wiggles into his version of our 'team uniform'. The basic elements match, but his sweatshirt is black, where mine is a bright emerald. His tail is whipping back and forth, and I give him a knowing smirk. He refuses to confirm the talisman he wears allows his clothing to shift with him, but I'm neither naïve, nor stupid. Gargoyles have some sort of relationship with magic, and whatever it is must be forbidden to talk about.

But he is in a talkative mood…

"Look at the outfit I got for Dolly," he says once he gets situated, and I pinch the bridge of my nose.

For fuck's sake…

Rennie yanks a baby pink snowsuit with a fur-trimmed hood out of the bag, and I bark a laugh. I'm not sure what exactly flipped his switch with Dolly, but this form-fitting outfit makes it very clear where his brain is. My lips curve when I consider how our curvy rabbit will look in it—it's an adorable visual, and I curse under my breath when I realize I don't have a squishy in my jacket pocket.

Dropping Delores' suit on the wide nest in the middle of his bedroom, he winks and reaches into a drawer, tossing me a sparkly unicorn. "I take it you like it, huh?"

I narrow my eyes at him, huffing, but I accept the stupidly cute toy and I shrug. "I'm sure it will look good on her."

"Uh-huh," he replies with a smug smirk. "I'm sure it will."

"Fuck, Rennie, let's go downstairs before they drag Dolly up to the top floor and ruin the Yule surprise the Captain's working on."

His eyes widen, and he grabs the other bags. "Yes! We have to keep them from seeing it before it's ready. C'mon!"

Chuckling to myself, I follow my friend, closing the door behind us. I hope to hell that Dolly and the others are ready for manic Rennie.

It's going to be a very interesting day.

Crazy Train

Renard

I don't understand why they're all so damn grumpy.

Well, except for Fitz. He's easily as excited as me because he's bouncing on his toes as the lovely Dolly comes out of the Tower. Everyone changed into their snow clothes and it worked exactly how I predicted—extremely obvious how much they all appreciate my choice of attire for our bunny.

I've decided I'm #TeamFitzandChess on this topic. Both of them seem absolutely certain this love quadrilateral will work and since Chess is never this adamant about anything, I believe it's prudent to listen.

That's also why I lobbied to get him the next 'date' with her. It's time for those three to seal the deal and it will never happen if Chess doesn't have 'alone time' with her. Someone as inexperienced as *ma petite* won't feel comfortable with him and Fitz until our shy cheetah quits hiding from her.

My penchant for organized chaos will help everyone get on board or else.

This outing is definitely part of my plan—my friends seriously need playtime. While I had a decent childhood until I got exiled, they cast Flames out young and the Khans never got to be kids. I highly doubt Dolly was, either. A good, old-fashioned snowball fight is both fun and light, but competitive enough to interest all the alphas in the group.

I know; I'm a genius.

"What are we doing, Rennie?" The rabbit in question looks over at me with wide eyes and I feel that undeniable pull again.

Bending down, I scoop up a handful of snow and fashion it into a lumpy ball. "We're going to play in the snow, *ma petite*. There's enough to have a friendly snowball fight and we have an even amount of people."

Fitz lets out a whoop of joy. "I fucking love it, Pouty Poet. I pick Chessie 'cause he's fast as hell."

"That means I'm the other captain," Felix growls as he gives his brother a dark smile. "And I pick Aubrey. Flying projectiles and all."

Shit. Now it's become a Twin Terror competition and the odds of someone getting their ass handed to them are exponentially higher.

"We pick Renard," Chess pipes up. "No fair having two fliers."

Dolly's eyes narrow as she looks at each of us with obvious irritation. "I'm on Team Felix by default and don't think I'll forget being picked last, assholes."

Oh, that's much worse.

Felix watches her stomp over to us, murmuring something to her as she joins them. Her answering grin is vicious and yet again, I see the Drew in our girl as she turns back to rake her gaze over each one of my team members. It's cold, calculating, and absolutely the stare of a predator sizing up its prey.

How does anyone think this girl isn't one of us, regardless of her biology?

"We're in deep trouble, my friend," I murmur to Chess. "Dolly will go for the throat now that she feels underestimated, and you know how dragons love losing."

Chess grimaces. "The past fifty game controllers tell me what he'll do. And Felix and Fitz never pull punches when they go up against one another—stay light on your feet."

"I may have misjudged the 'fun' aspect of this activity," I mutter as Fitz comes over and gathers us into a huddle.

"Not at all, Rock Man. We're gonna crush them like bugs and then I'll kiss my girl's boo-boos until they're all better."

I blink. "You're going full force at Dolly? Are you crazy?"

He rolls his eyes and sighs. "How am I the only one who gets it? Look, you tools. Especially since she was picked last, we have to treat her like one of us—equal in every way except age. Other-wise, we're going to piss her the fuck off and you losers will have no chance with her."

This is going to be a nightmare.

SINCE WE'RE DAMN NEAR ALONE ON CAMPUS, FELIX AND FITZ agreed to expand the playing field to include from the Honeywell building to Shirdal. There are a lot of places to get pegged by a flying object in the open, but also a decent amount of places to build small arsenals as you run from section to section. The two of them even shook hands—as if either planned on playing fair.

If you believe that, I've got a couple of monuments in Europe to sell you.

"Chess, you're the fastest runner, so you should be the one who distracts attention. We only get ten hits before we're out and if you draw fire, Renard coming from high and me sneaking up from below will create a pincer move."

Fitz is plotting this out like we're in a war game, and I'd bet his twin is on the other side. I haven't seen hide nor hair of the others since we split up, which is surprising. Our girl is wearing bright pink and Flames should be in the sky, but neither has appeared.

Our team has strategically placed armories of snowballs in a side corner of Shirdal, on the back area of Honeywell, facing the staff housing, and near my garden by the Tower. I made sure they weren't completely obvious but easy enough to access that Chess could dart over to get more ammo if he needs it as he races around.

I can't help wondering why the others don't seem to be creating safe zones, though.

"Got it, Fitzy," Chess says with a smile. He's pulled his hair back in a little bun and looks ready to show off his major strength in front of the others.

The tiger winks at me, shifting to his animal, and I gape. He damn near blends in, though he has to be freezing. He is not a Siberian and this climate can't make him feel good. But winning is clearly more important to a Khan than freezing his nuts off.

"I'll go get some high ground," I say with a chuckle. "Don't get frostbite anywhere important, or Dolly will be very upset, Fitzgerald."

"Me, too," Chess scowls as he watches the tiger melt into the land-scape without a word. "Zeus' beard, he's such an over competitive idiot sometimes."

I nod and clap him on the shoulder. "Agreed. Now go show off for the girl and I'll watch your back."

The cheetah gives me a boyish grin and zips off with a speed that's impressive, even in humanoid form. I'll be damned; he really is like the damn Flash.

Looking around, I squint at the high areas. Flames will expect me to take to my Tower out of habit, so I can't go there. But Shirdal has a very nice dome and a spot I can try to blend in with statuary. If I dive right, my speed will eclipse him because of wing structure. That's where I need to be. It's a lovely day for a climb, anyway.

FROM THE TOP OF THE ARTS BUILDING, I HAVE A PERFECT VIEW OF the large playing field. I can see movement zipping from zone to zone that I know is Chess—no one else is that fast. There's something on the ground by Honeywell, but it's hard to make out what. That might be Fitz covered in snow and blending like a guerrilla fighter, but I'm unsure.

A loud roar comes from the ground and I see Flames diving in from out of nowhere to pelt Chess with three snowballs that knock him off his feet. My eyes widen and I push off the building, heading into a dive that brings me close enough to grab him as I glide by.

"What the hell?" I growl at him as I carry us towards the far lake behind Honeywell.

"Frozen. Someone froze the snowballs," he grunts as he works to catch his breath.

Oh, our girl is clever as hell. I guarantee that was her idea.

"Looks like Team Felix is playing dirty," I chuckle when my feet touch the ground. "They've got a mastermind coaching behind the scenes."

Chess wheezes a little and nods. "Hard as your ass, man. I've got seven left, but it's going to take a few for me to get back to speed."

I nod, looking around us for a ground assault. "I'll need to find high ground again. Where do you think Fitz is?"

My answer is a stream of fire shooting into the air by the opposite lakeside. I don't know if Fitz found my dragon or the opposite, but the burst of fire tells me something is afoot. Chess waves at me, letting me know to head in that direction while he recovers. I have to trust he'll find cover somewhere nearby until then, so I do a quick run and take off to glide over the ground. I'm not very high, but I'll be faster.

When I get to the shore behind my haven, I have to cover my mouth to stop the laughter. Fitz and Aubrey are in a standoff, just lobbing snowballs from small piles at one another over and over. Aubrey is covered in snow and his dragon is shimmering beneath his skin; I can feel it. Fitz is taking the hits from the ice balls like a champ, though I suspect he'll have bruises for a few hours. His tiger is batting the projectiles with the aim of an elvish prince regardless, so if I don't stop them, his chestnuts are definitely going to get roasted.

"Stop! You're both out, obviously." I smirk at them, giving the duo a wink as I take off on the wind over the lake before anyone can try to knock me out as well.

We still haven't seen the Day-Glo bunny in her suit or Fitz's cagey brother.

It makes my gargoyle rumble in suspicion.

"I know," I murmur to myself. "It's almost as though they've planned for the hotheads to take one another out. This plan is craftier than I expected and we've all made a grave error in underestimating the fluffy cottontail."

Banking left off the water, I glide towards the staff housing. A sudden burst of rock hard snowballs bounce off my wings, throwing me completely off balance. The ground approaches fast and I tuck, then roll, so I don't injure myself on impact. When I pull my wings in, there are five circular marks on the left one, clear as day.

What in the curve of Loki's horns was that?

Felix's head crests a defensive bank built of snow and he unleashes another rapid fire round of the damned things that flatten me immediately.

I blink as I look up at the sky, catching my breath. Chess was right; the damn things hurt like a bitch.

The tiger appears above me, smirking as he sing-songs, "Strike ten and you're out, old man."

I accept the hand he offers, glaring. "How did you manage the Gatling effect with snowballs?"

His rumble is low. "Trade secret, man."

"I rigged a slingshot with multiple load capacity."

The voice comes from behind us and I watch in awe as Delores struts into the middle of the field holding Chess by his collar. His face is red, though I doubt it's from the cold. I watch her sit him down in front of Felix, noting she covered her suit in snow to camouflage it.

"Bras are good for more than keeping your boobs in place, Rennie," she says with a giggle. "And men need to understand that female adversaries think totally differently than them. Luckily, Felix the Grump let me lead this one."

Aubrey and Fitz stomp up, both grumbling about being taken out first, and my smile stretches. Even though Dolly got Chess, it was good for him to last almost as long as she and Felix. He needed that win, and I doubt he's truly upset by being snared by our vicious little bunny.

She's a force to be reckoned with and everyone at Apex should be on guard—Delores Drew is playing to win.

Santa Baby

Delores

Waking up in the Yule Village decor of the Tower is surreal.

Lucille always had professionals tastefully decorate the house for the holidays, but she and Bruno typically did exactly what they're doing this year—yeeted themselves to whatever resort was in vogue. I always stayed home with Mattie, opening the presents Lucille made her pick out, pretending I didn't realize my parents preferred being photographed by the paparazzi to spending time with me on Christmas.

I know, I know. Poor little rich girl, right? It still hurt knowing I was little more than a walking, talking accessory.

"Psssst, baby girl, are you awake? If you could wiggle a little more to the left… I have a big present for you."

A big forearm flies over Chess and smacks Fitz on the back of the head. I giggle, feeling brave in the makeshift nest Aubrey made in the middle of the sitting room last night. I grab the hand quickly, giving it a squeeze. To my delight, Felix squeezes back before he pulls away.

It's a Yule miracle.

"Not cool, bro. Chessie, tell them to quit picking on me!"

The rumpled cheetah stretches, his bare chest making my tummy flutter. When he opens his eyes, he gives his consort a shrug. "You deserve it."

Fitz pouts at me, and I shake my head as well. Finally, he glares past me at the other two. "C'mon, spicy lizard, rock man… back me up."

"Perhaps you'd find more support if you weren't always running your mouth," Aubrey says as he looks over at the tiger.

Renard pops his head up from the other side of him, nodding. "It's true. You make it very difficult."

"Fine! Whatever."

I smile at his petulance, stretching to place a light kiss on his lips. "Don't pout—it's Christmas. There are presents…"

His face lights up, and he damn near springs out of the pile of blankets and pillows, like a kid on, well, Christmas morning. "What the hell are we waiting for, then?"

Taking his hand, I let him pull me to my feet. Fitz grins wickedly, and I look down, realizing my pajama pants are in danger of falling down. Flushing, I roll the waist so they stay put, covering the skimpy thong straps so I don't look like a dancer in a hip hop video. "Perv," I mutter, smacking his chest lightly before padding over to the gigantic tree.

"You know I like it when you're violent," he croons.

Ignoring him, I gaze at the tree that magically appeared yesterday. Aubrey told me Rennie had the raccoons help with decorating, but some lights seem awfully high for them to reach. My fingertips brush a tiny rabbit-shaped ornament and I grin. All the decor is bunny-themed, and the tree is a rainbow ombre, like my hair.

I think someone has a crush on me.

"I don't know how you made this happen, but I love it," I say, turning back to look at them all, with my gaze lingering on Renard. "I've never had a tree that wasn't designed to impress rich guests before. This feels like… *me.* Thank you."

Even the grumpiest of my men look pleased with my response, and it makes my heart squeeze. I walk over and place a light kiss on each of their lips, making sure they can see the appreciation shining in my eyes. I've been conditioned not to expect much from the people around me, but so far, they've all proven it's possible to have people who care about you—who don't crush your heart for shits and giggles.

It's helping me believe I deserve it.

"Okay, let's open presents!" I clap my hands, excited for them to see the special gifts I commissioned for each of them.

Hoisting up the hems of my oversized pants, I scurry closer to the tree and pick up my stack of packages. After the guys brought me up here to see the decorations last night, I got Fitz and Chess to come downstairs with me to grab my loot to put under the tree. I probably should have grabbed more appropriate PJs while I was there, but I didn't expect the Christmas Eve Slaystation tournament to last so late that we'd all end up sacking out up here.

Aubrey's blanket nest was a pleasant surprise, that's for *sure.*

"You didn't have to get us anything, angel," Chess says as he heads over to the bar. That's funny coming from him, since the quiet cheetah takes care of everyone without being asked.

I smile fondly as he starts a coffee maker that mysteriously appeared right before I started cramming for exams, then I turn to the group. "I *wanted* to, and I'm excited for you to see what I got, so scoot back over here," I reply as I plop into the nest area. Aubrey tries to hide a grin, but I see it and crook my finger. "Come on, guys—all of you!"

They finally move, some of them stopping off at the tree to pick up a present, and my eyes widen.

Holy shit, did they actually get me something? Like… picked it out themselves?

Unsure how to process that, I set out the gifts in a half circle as I wait for them to join me.

Fitz is first, skidding to a stop inches from my face as he places a large box in front of my crossed legs. He then positions himself behind me, pulling me onto his lap. "Sit on Santa's lap and tell me what you want, little girl."

"Ew!" I pretend to cringe, swatting him playfully as he laughs.

My gargoyle is next, placing a medium-sized square box carefully next to Fitz's before he sprawls out on his side. Until I started spending so much time here, I would have never expected a gargoyle to behave so much like a giant cat shifter, but Rennie is forever draping himself over things. His tail flicks out behind him and I reach over to catch it in my hand, enjoying the surprised look on his face.

Bull by the horns—or gargoyle by the tail—Rufus would be proud.

The stoic tiger king is next, his box is smaller but wrapped in sparkly paper with an enormous unicorn-printed bow, which is kind of adorable. I run my fingers over the ribbon with a shy smile, and he dips his chin as he sits across from us.

"Don't move. The coffee is hot as hell," Chess says as he walks over with a tray of steaming mugs.

The guys all grunt in acknowledgement, which I suppose passes for 'thank you' in dude.

I take the mug he hands me, squealing in happiness. He's put everything I like in here: French vanilla creamer, whipped cream, and a drizzle of white chocolate, and I take a sip with a low groan of pleasure. "Thank you, Chess."

When I look up, all five sets of eyes are riveted to me, and I duck my head in embarrassment. The room fills with masculine laughter, and I burrow a little deeper into Fitz's arms as my face turns bright red.

I wasn't trying to be sexy or anything; it was really good!

Chess sets the tray on an end table before joining us in the nest, placing a tiny box on top of Fitz's. I look at the haul with wide eyes, and a throat clears.

"I'll go last, if you don't mind," the dragon says as he perches on the arm of the couch.

What on earth is he *hiding?*

"Okay," I agree as I look at them. "How does this work?"

Felix frowns. "How does what work, princess?"

"Um… you know. Do we do it all at the same time or one at a time?" I feel a bit exposed, but my family didn't exchange presents and now that I think about it, I never once swapped gifts with the Heathers.

I didn't realize how sheltered I was until I came to Apex.

Fitz nips at my ear, growling low. "Let's all do it together, hehe."

My face turns red again, and I pinch his side, making him laugh. "Okay. You guys all go and then I'll do each of you, one by one." This statement inspires another round of laughter, and I sigh heavily, although my annoyance is half-hearted.

I can't seem to avoid verbal pitfalls in this company.

The guys rip into their boxes, throwing paper and ribbon aside with reckless abandon, and I wiggle with excitement. All at once, they pull the specially made *Kigurumi* suits I had made for them, based on their animals. Felix's tiger is orange bengal striped, and the head on the hood has fierce fangs. Aubrey and Rennie have stuffed wings that stand up in the back, and Chess' cheetah has a fluffy tail. The white tiger I had made for Fitz has a bit of blood dyed on its fangs and fur, and he picks me up with a hoot of approval, standing with me in his arms like I weigh less than nothing.

"I love it!" Fitz spins me around before setting me back on my feet so he can quickly shimmy into his suit. Holding the hood in place, he throws his head back, letting out a loud roar, making me laugh.

"The quality is amazing," Rennie murmurs, examining the onyx color. "When did you make these?"

I shake my head. "Oh, no. I'm not this good yet. Not by a long shot. I had some friends from my summer job at the fashion house whip these up."

Felix strokes his chin, tilting his head as he studies his suit. "It's perfect, but when do you see us wearing these?"

My eyes dance as I grin at them. "During our future slumber parties."

That got their attention. Ha!

A hand tugs me back down to the floor, and Chess places a kiss on my jaw. I lean into him, loving the soft growl he emits. "I love mine, angel. Thank you for making my cheetah so sleek and fierce."

Fitz barrels over to the nest, having zoomed around the room in his for the past five minutes, and puts me back on his lap. I pull the tiger's hood up, and he growls again before he looks over at Aubrey. "Put yours on, you adorable reptile! I want to see!"

I have to cover my mouth as the grumpy dragon glares daggers at him. Taking pity on him, I pick up the smallest gift. "Maybe I should open these first?" He gives me a barely perceptible nod, and I take that as my cue to begin.

Chess' box contains a stack of songbooks, novels, and a beginner knitting set that makes me feel all squishy inside. He wants to share hobbies with me and it's so cute I can't stand it.

Inside the biggest package is a slinky black Ostrich de La Renta dress and matching LaPerla to go underneath. As always, Fitz found exactly the right size.

It's his superpower.

Renard unveils a gorgeous wild orchid that seems to sparkle in the twinkling lights, and I smile at my botany loving professor, wondering if it will remain perfect like the one he keeps under glass.

With only one package left, I rip into the paper, furrowing my brow at the heavy, flat stone. Felix gives me a grin, allowing a single claw to emerge from his finger before scraping it over the stone, and suddenly, I get it—it's a whetstone for sharpening my claws.

It's like each of them gave me a little piece of themselves, except for…

Aubrey rises from the arm of the couch, disappearing from view as he descends the stairs. He must be going to Rennie's room, but why did he hide his present there? The Khans all look at each other in confusion, but the gargoyle looks like he has a secret. When Aubrey returns, he's carrying an unwrapped brown box that's…. *moving?*

"I had to keep this downstairs, or it would have spoiled the surprise," he explains as he walks over and joins us on the floor. "But a colleague in Morocco found a litter whose mother died, and I thought…"

The lid pops open and a small, golden cat jumps out, looking at us with wide eyes. It has abnormally large ears, stripes, and looks certain we're going to eat it.

I mean, for some of us, that might be fair.

"Is this a domestic cat?" I ask, reaching out carefully, so I don't scare it.

The dragon shakes his head. "No, it's a sand cat. They do best in the wild, but this one has been living with foster families since it was born."

"You got me… a kitten?"

Fitz's face splits into a huge grin as he looks at me. "I hate to say it, but lizard man wins this one, guys. You can't beat a fluffy cat."

"And she's so, so cute," I murmur, as the small feline butts her head against my fingers. "I think I'll call her Jinx." When I look up, I swear Aubrey's eyes are twinkling.

He has a soft spot for cute things, and this is killing him.

"Where is it going to live? Here, right?" Felix says, eyeing the kitten as if he's terrified I'll send it home with him.

Rennie waves his hand. "There's plenty of room here, and we're all here often enough to help take care of it together. Dolly has free rein of the building, so should her pet."

My eyes fill with grateful tears as the little ball of fur jumps into my lap and starts purring like an outboard motor. I look down at her with a soft smile and say, "Well, I'd say this has been the Merriest Christmas I've ever had."

When I look up, all of my guys are giving me fond expressions and my heart swells all over again.

Merry Christmas, indeed.

Angel Eyes

Chess

CHESS

The time between our lovely Yule celebration and the night of my date with my angel was excruciating. Fitz insisted I spend New Year's Eve with her because, according to him, 'what better time to lose your lady cherry than ringing in a New Year?'

His logic was hard to argue with, especially when Dolly made that adorable shy expression as she agreed with him.

I've been working off my nervous energy with endless projects in my studio—suffice to say, no one needs a scarf for the winter weather anymore. Felix has rolled his eyes so much at Fitz's eager advice that I thought he might get them stuck facing the back of his skull. Renard and Aubrey are more amused than anything, so they rib me gently when I get flustered.

It's given me such a feeling of family that my chest aches when I slip into slumber at night. I doubt the rest of them understand how incredible the formation of this small, tight-knit group is to an orphan who always felt like a 'plus one' to the royal twins.

Not that Fitz or Felix ever made me feel like that, but children are sensitive and

I overheard a lot of nasty commentary from adults at Bloodstone when I was a cub.

Sighing, I finish the last couple lines of the piece I'm working on, and look at the clock on the wall. I know my brothers will be at the townhouse when I go back and Fitz will be bouncing off the damn furniture, waiting for me to get ready for my date. He wanted me to take her to one of the Khan businesses like he did, get all dressed up in fancy clothes and show her a better time than she had at that wretched prom.

It's more the twins' style than mine, but the idea of replacing that awful night with a more pleasant memory appealed to my cheetah. He practically purred with approval when I let Fitz make the reservation at *Le Joyau de la Couronne*[1]—his father's ritziest spot in the area. Knowing where we were going made me even more nervous because I know Khan flunkies, Council members, and other species leaders might be there on a night like New Year's Eve.

My angel would be safer going to that tiger's den with one of my brothers or the ancients.

As that thought echoes in my mind, I lock the door of my oasis behind me. My cheetah pushes at me, not appreciating my dismissal of his ability to take care of our girl if we need to. I swallow hard, placating him as I walk down the hall of the Shird. My cat has never been as present in me as he is since we met Delores Drew and despite my efforts to manage his sudden dominant behavior, he refuses to listen.

That's probably because he's certain she's our mate.

I have no idea what to do with that information because I didn't think we could have more than one mate—and Fitz sealed that deal not long after we came to Apex. He'd talked about it before, but once we were away from the protection of Bloodstone and the crown, my tiger was determined to ensure I stayed safe. His father is an evil, old bastard obsessed with power, so he might well have sent someone after the disposable orphan to teach his sons a lesson.

Fitz never once hid me from his family, nor did he entertain going anywhere without me—even if they forced him to get married for political reasons. I haven't ever questioned my place in his life because he tells everyone everything in an endless stream of consciousness that isn't unlike our fluffy rabbit.

Maybe that's why she's entranced him so easily? They're cut from a very similar cloth.

My lips curl up as I cross the lawn and head towards the staff housing. If I'm correct, the vicious streak in my angel is much bigger than frozen snowballs and ass kicking in Felix's classroom. The more time she spends with my morally translucent mate, the more of her natural tendencies will come out.

I'm not sure the world is ready for Fitzgerald Khan to have a twin and a soulmate.

If it is true, tonight is my night to find out where I fit in with our girl and why she makes my animal want to burst free every time we see her. I don't know if his whispers about her also being our mate are true, but I'm excited to see what the evening brings.

Even if that means getting my nerves under control in a room full of the biggest preds in town.

It's my turn to wait in front of the admissions building, though I'm leaning against Felix's Jag. The sleek convertible is as similar to its owner as Fitz's bike is to him. My brothers picked out a ridiculously expensive tux for me and I yank at the bottom of the jacket nervously.

I'm not the flashy type and I definitely don't wear couture almost as expensive as a normal car, but they insisted.

Fitz bought my angel a gorgeous designer gown for Yule and he declared our date the perfect occasion for her to show off her curves in the slinky Ostrich De La Renta. That meant he and Felix trussed me up in the latest winter fashion for New Year's: a black satin leopard print tuxedo with a dark bronze shirt and matching bow tie. I tied my curls up into the messy bun I prefer, but chose not to struggle with contacts.

Of course, my love almost mauled me before I got to the door and that would have made us late. Felix winked and assured me it meant I looked good before he rushed to the kitchen. When he returned, he was holding a black velvet box and a stunning bouquet of pastel roses.

Now I'm sitting on his car as I wait, my nerves jangling from all the trappings around me, including that blasted box containing one of the fucking Khan tiaras. Between it, the car, and this outfit, you could pay two professors for years. It's making me twitchy, but neither of them looked even concerned when I waltzed out the door.

I'll never get used to the way the most elite preds operate, no matter how long I live among them.

A scent catches my nostrils and my head jerks up to gaze at the woman crossing the parking lot. Suddenly, I'm very glad we're on break and the other students haven't returned yet. If anyone gave my angel shit right now, I'd probably kill them myself.

How odd.

Delores is a vision in the long black dress that appears to be cut to fit her form perfectly. I know my lover bought it for her, and his precision impresses me. The De La Renta gown dips low between her breasts, exposing the luscious curves, and it has slits from hem to waist on both sides to reveal her long legs and thighs. I guarantee it has little to no back—Fitz planned to show off as much of her skin as possible without being totally indecent.

I pick my jaw up long enough to smile at her glossy pink lips, artfully messy up do, and smoky eyes. She's been learning quite a bit from her two friends during classes—everything from costuming to makeup and hair—and it shows. Everything about my angel looks grown up and sophisticated tonight, right down to the sky-high 'fuck me' pumps. She's rocking it all with confidence.

No one would mistake the woman walking towards me with the girl who toured our school last spring.

"Angel, you look luminous," I say when she reaches me. I open the car door with an exaggerated flourish, loving her giggle as she lowers herself to get in.

When I round the car and hop in, Dolly smiles shyly. "Thank you, Chess. You look rather handsome yourself. Did Fitz coordinate us?"

I chuckle and nod. "Of course he did. I've never seen my consort so invested in playing Cupid, but he's definitely jumped into the role with both feet."

She wiggles in her seat, then frowns and reaches under her bum. "Hey, what's this, handsome?"

My cheeks flush bright red at her words, and I cough to clear my throat. "Felix sent some bling to complete your outfit. If it's too much, let me know and I'll lock it in Felix's box in the trunk."

"His box in the trunk?" Her brow arches, but she opens the jewelry box anyway, letting out a loud gasp when the pink diamond encrusted tiara is revealed. "Holy fuck, Chess! This thing is… expensive looking."

"I try not to question the price tags on shit the twins do, angel. It makes my blood pressure rise. But yes, it's a Khan heirloom, so I'm certain it's damn near priceless, anyway. Want me to help you put it on?"

Her lips purse as she takes all of that information in, but the siren song of sparkly bling gets the best of her. "Yes. Make me a princess as intended, Chessie."

Oh, that sneaky son of a bitch. Well played, Raj.

I smile, taking the tiara from her and wait for her to bend a little so I can settle it on her head. When she raises up, the picture takes my breath away. She truly looks like they made it for her and I reach for my phone quickly. "Let me take a quick picture to send to the guys and we'll be off, angel."

Biting her lower lip impishly, Dolly mocks a couple adorable poses while I snap and once I hit send, she buckles her belt. "Okay, let's hit the road, handsome. I'm ready for snooty people and weird fancy-ass food."

"It's good to have accurate expectations," I say, winking at her as I put the convertible in drive. "Good thing I didn't put the top down."

* * *

Le Joyau de la Couronne is further out than Fitz's date location. It's halfway between Apex and Cambridge, nestled at the front of a sprawling piece of land owned by the ambush. Patrons not part of the Khan family would be shocked to know that the Khan family uses the rest of the land for various training, deals, and extractions to Bloodstone. The fanciest restaurant around is sitting on the same land as a landing strip to transport Eastern seaboard prisoners and train future staff for the reform school.

The current Raj loves the irony and I wonder if the Council even knows what he's doing under their noses.

Regardless, we won't be heading anywhere besides the top of the Khan Tower to our reservation. I don't even want to get off on another floor in this place without having the twins along, much less take our girl there. We haven't heard from their father or her parents since break started, which makes my fangs twitch. I don't like not knowing what those evil fuckers are doing.

"This place is so modern looking," Dolly says as we hand the keys to the valet. "I wouldn't have expected that based on the decor of *The Jade Sceptre* or the pictures I've seen of Bloodstone in our history books."

My eyes dance. "Bloodstone looks a little like the Temple of Doom, I admit it. But *Sceptre* is more of a mid to lower-level joint —it's not geared towards attracting the rich and powerful in the supe world. Khan Tower houses more than our destination."

Her eyes widen, and she leans into me as I guide her inside. "You mean Khan business happens on some of these floors?"

"Yes, but don't think you're going all Nancy Drew here, angel. Fitz designed their security, and it's nothing to shake your finger at. After we were exiled, they likely revoked all his access, so it would take a lot of preparation to get to anything incriminating."

"Mmm. But it's good to know for future escapades, Chessie. I wasn't joking when I told Fitz I'd take down the entire fucking lot of them if they threaten my guys."

Delores pauses as we stand in front of the elevator, and I can see the ferocity in her gaze. She means it; she'll take on the entire Khan ambush if they come for us. It makes my heart skip to see the determination in her gaze and I take her hand, squeezing it with a soft smile.

"Let's hope it doesn't come to that, angel. But thank you for caring about us," I murmur as I pull her closer.

She shrugs, her eyes flashing with a red tint for a moment as she practically growls, "We take care of our own."

Fuck the princess thing; this girl is going to be our queen.

The bell dings and I feel emotions swamp me as we head into the tiger's den—literally.

New Love
Delores

Delores

The way Chess looks at me makes my skin tingle. It's like he's discovered the most precious thing on the planet and wants to wrap himself around it forever. He looks at Fitz with adoration, too, but it's different when he's watching me.

I could almost feel the change in his confidence when I said I'd protect them from the Khans if need be. It didn't matter that I didn't have a clue how I'd do that, but voicing it seemed to help my nerdy cheetah break free of his fears. He's been laughing, talking, and sharing delicious food with me all evening without ducking his head once.

Perhaps he needed the reassurance that I wanted him? If so, I wish I'd known sooner.

The twins dressed him in that smooth, suave suit, but as wisps of his floppy curls escape his bun and he gestures animatedly when talking about geeky shows and books with me, the real Chess peeks out. I ignored Fitz's warning from before and asked about the baking show; it started him on a detailed rant about cooking shows and the superiority of his favorite in comparison. That led to other shows we enjoyed and after that, everything was easy.

I see exactly why Fitz fell for the quiet cat and his habit of needing to push his glasses up after he gets too excited is making me squishy as hell.

Of course, when he took the suit jacket off during dinner, I got a good gander at his lithe muscles and tight ass, so my lady bits are standing at attention, too. Chess is the complete package and I can't help but give him starry-eyed looks as we hold hands and wait for the desserts to be served.

"Do you think their pastry chef will pass muster?" I ask him teasingly. "You have awfully discerning opinions about filo dough."

His chuckle rumbles over me as he shrugs. "If not, I'm sure Fitz will spill the beans to someone and they'll find a new one. He hates for people he loves to be disappointed."

I'm about to question that gem when a huff of anger sounds behind me. My spine stiffens and the hairs on my entire body stand on end as I recognize the sound. Swallowing hard, I will my hands not to shake as the clack-clack of Leopardtins moving across the marble comes closer.

Lucille is in the house.

"Delores Diamond Drew! What on earth are you doing here?" Her tone is full of acid and disbelief, as if they should have cast me out with the riff-raff before my feet hit the pavement out front.

I give Chess a pleading expression, hoping he understands. I lick my lips, letting go of his hand and turning in my seat to look at the woman standing just outside of my peripheral vision. That's one of her tricks to make you come to her, so I'm resisting standing up defiantly.

"Happy New Year, Lucille. I thought you were in Ibiza for the holidays," I reply in a mild, unperturbed voice. I school my features to keep her from knowing how much seeing her affects me.

"I'm surprised to see you here, of all places, Delores. You've never shown the slightest interest in attending events such as this." The woman who gave birth to me rakes her eyes over me briefly, then looks at Chess with a narrowed gaze. "Stand up and introduce your friend. I can't abide rudeness and you know it."

Chess rumbles a little as I push to my feet, moving away from him to allow Lucille full access to inspect me. He rises as well, pushing our chairs in so he can step forward and meet the most dangerous woman on the Council's stare evenly.

Being raised by Khans has its benefits.

"Lucille, this is Chess. He's my date this evening." I smile politely as I turn to my cheetah. "Chess, this is Lucille Rostoff Drew, head of the Council, heir to the Rostoff empire, and my mother."

The words taste like acid on my tongue, but I was taught the proper way to introduce my parents from a very young age. They each have rules that must be followed, and any deviation led to severe punishments. Hera forbid a seven-year-old forget a title or important lineage declaration at a school function.

"Interesting. Someone enticed a designer to alter couture to fit your ample frame—they must have impeccable assistants. I don't remember selecting that gown, though," Lucille ignores Chess for the moment, too busy tossing barbs about my appearance to notice the animal shimmering under his skin. "And that diadem is not one of ours; your father wouldn't allow you to sully my family's heirlooms in that ridiculous hair."

I can feel the growl before I hear it and I reach out to take Chess' arm, pretending to use it for balance. "No, Lucille. The dress was a Yule gift, and the tiara was loaned to me so I would be suitably attired for this auspicious occasion. I thought it would please you if they photographed us in public."

"Loaned to you? Delores Diamond Drew, we are not peasants! Drews do not need to borrow accessories!" Her tone gets sharper and I sense her leopard rising to the surface as well.

Before I can attempt to repair the damage, Chess steps forward, a hard look on his face. "The Panther Princess tiara has been a Khan family heirloom since my grandmother was a child. Are you implying the crown of the Khan matriarch is not good enough?"

Oh, snap.

Chessie just trapped her into choosing between humiliating me and insulting the Khans. I press my thighs together, hoping my immediate reaction to the normally submissive cat dominating the conversation like a fucking boss isn't obvious. That kitty just earned himself a very happy ending when we get out of here.

The horror on Lucille's face only lasts a second before she locks it down, arching a brow as she eyes my date critically. "Since you're not the heir or the spare, you must be the orphan. Interesting to find you here with Delores rather than your... brothers. Of course, she's always had a soft spot for inferior preds. I've never been able to teach her how to separate the wheat from the chaff, so to speak."

Shit, shit, shit. This is getting out of hand.

"It was kind of Felix to send the tiara for me to wear, though, wasn't it? The future Raj is one of my professors and he's been extremely helpful to my studies. This boon is a fitting tribute to our name, is it not?" I squeeze Chess' bicep, wordlessly begging him to let me end this before blood is shed.

"Mmm," Lucile says as she looks at me again. "Yes, those bird-brains informed me of your schedule. I wasn't aware being his student afforded you such a close relationship with the princes. I should visit campus soon and meet the men who hold your... education... in their hands."

My cheetah looks like he's going to lose it again at her implication, but thank the gods, a waiter with a large tray full of desserts arrives. Lucille looks at it in horror, as if she'll gain weight by seeing the items on it, and waves her hand at me dismissively.

"Enjoy your calories, Delores. You'll want to keep track of them if you're going to prove useful to me in a long-term fashion." With that grenade lobbed, she stalks off towards the other half of the restaurant. I see Bruiser materialize behind her, but not my father.

Where the hell is Bruno and why is Lucille at a Khan business instead of in Ibiza, as she told me?

I turn to Chess, and he cups my face in his hands gently. "Don't worry, angel. She can't hurt you; you have protectors now."

Shaking my head, I feel the sting of her verbal cracks more deeply than if she'd used her fists. I don't want to be a needy, broken doll, but Lucille knows exactly where to land the punches to make me feel the worst.

Narcissists always do and they purposely aim for the weakest spot so they can maintain their control over you.

"Shhh." Chess says as he kisses my eyelids. "I'll get all the treats boxed, and we'll head home to finish our date in much better company, angel. How about that?"

I nod, giving him a watery smile. "I'd like that a lot, my spotted knight. In fact, I'd like it as much as I did you wanting to tear apart the most powerful woman in the room because she was mean to me."

"You could feel that?"

Shrugging, I give him a look. "Women always know, Chessie. Now take me home."

"Anything for you, angel."

THE RIDE HOME WAS UNEVENTFUL, BUT CHESS INSISTED ON carrying the to-go bag and me across the campus to the Tower. When we reached the door, he let me enter my code and lead him up the front stairs to my room without even asking. I know all the Khans are fascinated with the freedom Aubrey and Rennie have granted me in their lair, but I'm not giving up the ghost until they tell me I can.

"Come on, knight. We're going to get these beautiful, but highly uncomfortable, clothes off and pig out."

His eyes crinkle at the corners as I pull open my door and kick off my shoes the second I get inside. "Leaving your door unlocked is a recipe for disaster, angel."

"I don't care what Fitz rifles through," I say as I tug the gown up and over my head to leave me in the tiny thong and nothing else as I root through a drawer for jammies. "He's welcome to sniff my undies if it makes him happy."

"You really are an angel," he says as he drops the bag on the floor and kicks the door shut.

A soft growl echoes out of his chest and I feel the animal in him. Turning to face the adorable cheetah, I smirk. "When I want to be, Chessie. But maybe tonight, I'd rather be bad."

He moves with a speed I haven't seen before and suddenly, his arms are around me, pulling me tight to his body. The rumble of his cat and the erection pushing against my belly tell me he's excited, but I see the uncertainty in his eyes. This is a first for my knight, and having been there not so long ago myself, I want him to have a far better experience than I did.

Reaching up, I cup his face and smile softly at him. "Hold on there, cowboy. Let's take this to bed so we can explore."

The blush on his face is so cute I can barely stand it, so I grab his hand and pull him over to my bed, toppling us onto the large mattress the moment we're close enough. His hands coast over my skin as I wiggle on top of him and bracket his legs with my thighs. I sit up, pulling the pins from my hair until it tumbles over us, then do the same for him.

"Much better, don't you think?" I whisper as I place his hands on my hips. Amazingly, I'm not nervous about Chess; in fact, since Fitz and I have been exploring every position possible for weeks, I actually feel confident.

"Oh, yes. Much," he says with a hungry look. "But it could be better."

I nod, rocking my hips over him slowly. The friction pulls a moan from me and I watch his eyes bleed amber as the cat within makes itself known. "You have too many clothes on."

His eyes widen and he practically tears at the buttons on his shirt, wriggling and bumping my pussy as he fights to get it off. Laughing softly, I rise a little to let him do the same with his pants and boxers, then settle on top of him again. His cock rubs against the lace of my panties and I growl softly.

"I'm going to tell you something I told Fitz," I murmur as I roll my hips against his, letting the head of his dick bump my clit through the fabric. He blinks, eyes hazy, as he looks at me. "I have an implant and since I know you're clean because he is, we're going to do this the fun way."

Chess swallows hard, blinking at me. "Holy shit, angel."

I shrug and smile as I lift again, stretching down his body to kiss him hungrily before I speak. "What can I say? You're lucky boys. Now help me with this before we both explode."

His lips curve and the sound of ripping lingerie fills the air, followed by the scrap flying across the room. "Angel, you're going to fucking kill me."

Winking playfully, I lower again, sliding my wetness over his throbbing cock slowly. "Hopefully not, because I'm looking forward to this. Are you ready, my sweet knight?"

A gasp rips from my lips when my nerdy cheetah grabs my hips, lines up, and thrusts into me like a seasoned pro. He's thicker than Fitz and I'm shocked as hell to feel something pressing inside of me, stroking a spot that makes me quiver.

"What the hell, Chessie?" I breathe as I lift and drop to feel it again.

Oh, my fucking stars and garters—that is amazing.

"Didn't Fitzy tell you? I'm pierced, angel. Can you feel it?"

I bob my head, swallowing hard as I keep moving over him to ride the sensation building in my gut. "Uh… noooo… he didn't. Fuck, Chess, that's…"

"I should have asked if you were ready," he teases as he grips my hips. "Are you?"

Digging my nails into his shoulders, I use the leverage to speed up, riding him like my life depends on it. The hardware bumps the spot in me over and over and before long, I feel the beginning of my orgasm rocketing toward me. My eyes open and I look down, loving the look of pure delight on his features as we move together.

His hand creeps up my thigh, fingertips feathering over my pussy until his thumb finds my clit, and that does it.

I scream his name, shivers running over me as my walls contract and squeeze his dick until he explodes as well. It feels like we're suspended in time for a moment as we gently coast down from the high and I finally collapse on his chest.

"Holy shit," I pant. "That was fucking hot."

The laughter makes his chest vibrate under my cheek and I sense the grin on his face. "Just give me a few and we'll be ready for round two, angel."

I push up a little, swiping my hair out of my face as I blink. "Why, Mr. Chester, I think you might be an addict."

Let's Talk About Sex

Delores

I WALK INTO THE NEW CLASSROOM, DETERMINED TO FIND THE MOST strategic place to sit. Freezing in place as I look around, I notice it's smaller than most of the classrooms at Apex, and there are no desks. Instead, armchairs, beanbags, and a multitude of comfy pieces of furniture are spread throughout the room. I'm already on edge, and that feeling only increases as I look around.

How many people are going to be packed in here while we discuss a very personal topic?

"Choose any seat you want, Miss Drew. My classroom is a safe space for all the students at Apex. I will watch your back."

I turn to look at the gorgeous lioness who 'assisted' Felix in the ring during Shifter Basics, remembering the way she spoke to my grumpy tiger when he pinned her down. She's definitely slept with him, probably more than once. Hell, maybe Fitz, too. She's curvy and oozes sensuality—a bombshell with the brawn to take on any alpha—and she's my new Shifter Sex Ed teacher.

Just. Fucking. Great.

"Thank you, ma'am," I mutter as I find a large cushy chair near the door. I don't care what she says; a scorned ex is a hard person to trust, and I don't have it in me to fight with a new professor every day.

Her laugh is a deep, throaty purr as she gives me an amused look. "We're going to have a lot of fun in class, I can see."

I highly doubt that.

The rest of the class filters in, finding seats of their own. There are less than twenty other first-years here, and most of them are people I don't even recognize. There's not a Heather or a Todd-bro in sight, which is odd, considering they can't seem to leave me alone. Frowning, I pull out a notebook and pen and situate myself, wondering what the hell is going to happen.

"Good afternoon, everyone. My name is Zhenga Leonidas, and I'm the lucky lady who gets to teach you about shifter sexual behavior."

No wonder she was game to fight in the ring; she's a Leonidas. They're the most competitive Council family—and the most physical because they own the Pred Games.

Before she can continue, a jaguar in the back raises his hand. He doesn't wait to be called on, which makes her sneer. "I don't see why I'm in this class, nor do I get why I have a woman teaching me about sex."

In a move that would make Lucille proud, the lioness pounces, pinning him to the bean bag he's sitting on.

"Every semester, I have a shriveled little asshole like you who thinks his shit doesn't stink. I'll tell you what I've told all of them —you're here because your parents or a professor have determined you do not understand the basics of shifter sexuality. Regardless of where you've been dipping your wick..." Her eyes slide to me and she smirks. "... or who's been dipping it into you, you've shown a complete lack of knowledge about traditions, safety precautions, or breeding that must be corrected before you endanger yourselves or others."

Crap. Now I know why this class is small… we're the remedial sex dummies.

"Fine!" the jaguar says as he struggles beneath her. "So my parents punished me for what happened over Christmas break—it's still bullshit."

Zhenga snorts as she rolls to her feet lithely, slinking back to the front of the room as if nothing happened. "You wouldn't be the first rich boy to earn a spot in my class for getting caught with sex workers. Don't take it personally; I'm an equal opportunity bitch."

"I'll bet," he mutters.

This moron wants to die, I swear.

Deciding I might as well learn something if I have to be in this embarrassing situation, I raise my hand. "Will we be learning about… rare shifter behavior as well?"

The lioness tilts her head, and I can see the wheels turning as she considers her answer. "Yes, I believe we might need to, Miss Drew."

I let out a sigh of relief as she moves to a table to collect some papers. A sheaf of syllabi makes its way from person to person, and I wait for mine while Zhenga walks over to the light switch by the door.

"The first thing we're going to do is watch a film about the traditions of canine and feline shifters. This information may also apply to other shifter types who behave similarly to these larger groups. You will need to take notes, because I expect a five-page paper on an animal of your choosing by next Monday."

My eyes adjust to the screen and I watch intently, taking notes as the narrator explains how the two classes of animals find and identify others they want to mate with. A vibration in my pocket gives me pause, and I look around, hoping I'll be able to at least read the message without getting in trouble. I almost laugh when I see the professor stretched out on her own bean bag, texting away like a pro. She's not going to notice if I get up and start dancing a rhumba.

> Ru-ru: How's the birds and the bees going, Dollypop?

> Coco: I've heard the teacher is a grade-A bitch.

I put my hand over my mouth, trying not to make a sound. Cori doesn't mince words about people she doesn't like, and I have a feeling my leonine professor is on her list.

> Dollybear: She's… something, that's for sure.

> Ru-Ru: You'd be cranky, too, if you should be the heir to the Leonidas empire, but your daddy won't hand it over until you find a suitable mate.

> Coco: Another reason the patriarchy needs to die off.

> Dollybear: That would explain why she seems like she's stalking the royal men.

> Coco: It better not be yours, or I'll…

> Ru-Ru: Coco, even Dollybear has to know she's done the horizontal mambo with the tiger king. It's no secret on campus. But the past is the past.

> Coco: I'm just saying I'll… cut a bitch.

> Dollybear: Cori!

> Coco: Well, I will.

> Ru-Ru: What else is going on? We haven't
> seen you since we got back.

I chew my lip. While I'm dying to tell my friends all about break and my date with Chess, there's a more pressing issue they need to know about.

> Dollybear: Something weird happened this
> morning… right before class, actually.

> Ru-Ru: Tell me!

> Dollybear: I got this weird letter… from the
> murdered weasel. He must have arranged
> for it to be delivered after his death,
> because someone slipped it under my
> door before I was awake.

> Coco: I don't like the sound of that. Letters
> from dead people are no bueno.

> Ru-Ru: Call us immediately after class. I
> don't like that, either.

"Miss Drew, put your phone away!" Tearing my eyes off the screen, I find Zhenga Leonidas glaring at me as if she'd like to flay me alive. "You, in particular, need this information. Don't be a fool."

I open my mouth to respond, but the door to the classroom opens and a new girl strides in. She walks up to Zhenga, handing her a slip of paper, and turns to the class with a sneer of disdain.

"My name is Heather Mac Lachlan, and I just transferred from Bloodstone Academy."

Oh, shit.

Zhenga rolls her eyes and mutters something about idiocy running in the family before she points to an open armchair, blessedly across the room from me. "Thank you for the information, Miss Mac Lachlan. Unless you have something else you'd like to dramatically declare, I suggest you sit down and start taking notes. Being late to my class doesn't mean you won't have to catch up with the information you missed."

Ducking my head, I scribble notes through the rest of the class, but I can feel the new Heather's eyes on me. I'll have to find out why she's here, and how she's related to my guys—and why her name is freaking Heather.

Something about this feels like a set-up, and I've got enough enemies at Apex as it is. With a name like that, you know she's going to be trouble. The last thing I need is some fucking Khan spy helping my ex-besties with their campaign of terror, but I have enough on my plate as it is.

Shaking my head, I continue watching the video, marking down different aspects of mating and hunting that seem important. Zhenga's right—which I hate to admit—but I need to know how things work with my guys.

The surprise appearance of my period twice this semester prob-ably means I need to make time tomorrow to visit with the nurses in the infirmary. According to Google, that means my implant needs to be replaced; after all, Lucille had it put in when I was thirteen and the internet says they have a shelf life of five years.

Another detail it might have been helpful to have before I got naughty with two brand new boyfriends recently—thanks, Lucille.

I'm still bitterly griping in my head when the voice on the screen describes sex with big cats, which makes my face turn bright red. Curiously, it doesn't say a fucking thing about dicks getting stuck, and I frown. Did that happen because I'm prey? Fitz was such a player—he had to have fucked another prey animal at some point. Maybe it's because I'm a rabbit?

Fuck, I don't know, but it wigged both him and Chess out big time.

Chewing on my fingernail, I warily eye the lioness texting on her phone, knowing there's only one way to find out for sure. I'm going to have to talk to her at the end of class and hope it doesn't result in a literal cat fight with a teacher.

Hera help me, because if I get kicked out of this school for taking on a Leonidas, I don't know if Lucille will be angry or proud.

THAT MIGHT BE THE MOST UNCOMFORTABLE CONVERSATION I'VE HAD in a long time.

Talking with Zhenga about the 'difficulty' I experienced during sex, without disclosing which breed of shifter I was with, was a dance unto itself. The lioness is sharp as hell, and I could see the suspicion in her expression as she listened to my description. I doubt I could keep as much concealed as I wanted to, because when she promised to do some 'research', I saw the almost gleeful look in her eyes.

But I can't worry about that now. My life is a ridiculous mess of secrets and threats, and I promised Rufus I'd call them about this letter as soon as I got out of class.

"Hellooooooooo, Dolly!" he sings at the top of his lungs.

I wrinkle my nose, glaring at the phone as if he can see me. "I hate Badgers & Hammershark, Ru-Ru."

A scuffle ensues, and finally, Cori takes the phone and turns it on speaker. "He's being an ass, Dolly. Tell us about this letter. I'm really worried, not gonna lie."

I quickly glance around to make sure no one's close enough to overhear, especially given what I'm about to tell them. "Like I said, I found it on my room floor when I was leaving for class. Someone must have shoved it underneath early this morning. The postmark is recent, but that asshole's been dead since Halloween. Maybe he had someone send it on his behalf if something happened to him? I don't know. The whole thing is super weird. I barely knew him."

"We need to see what it says ASAP, Dollypop. Meet us at my dorm after your last class so we can comb through it and try to analyze what that sneaky little shit's game was."

I nod, even though he can't see me, although I'm worried about the fact I haven't told the guys yet. They'll be twice as concerned about me as they already are, and I don't want to be treated like a ceramic vase. "Okay, Ru-Ru. I'll see you both after classes and we'll figure out how to puzzle through this mystery without raising the alarms."

Why can't I be a normal girl and spend my time drooling over my five hot professor boyfriends?

"THIS PART IS PRETTY OMINOUS... 'YOU CAN'T TRUST THE PEOPLE closest to you; they want to see you dead'. It gives me the willies," Cori says as she rubs her arms.

"I know. The Heathers and their groupies didn't make a secret of hating me last semester, but after I fought Gold in class, they've been more of a nuisance than an actual threat. So he must be talking about someone who isn't making their venom known."

As soon as the words leave my mouth, I realize I don't see the Heathers as much of a threat anymore. Maybe it's a part of growing up, or finding my own way, or the fact actual deaths are happening on campus, but I can't be bothered with their school-yard antics. I've even taken to leaving my 'Fuck 'Em Up, Sis' list in my room instead of carrying it around with me.

One less thing to worry about, that's for sure.

Rufus squints at the paper again. "Why do people do shit like this? If this was to be sent after he died, why not call out the motherfucker in question? It's not like they could kill him again. 'Dear Dolly, this specific asshole is trying to kill you. Sincerely, cowardly weasel.' That would be a lot more helpful."

Sighing, I fold the paper and tuck it into my bag. "I don't know, Rufus, but it sure as hell makes me feel like I'm in danger. Maybe that's all it was supposed to accomplish—to throw me off my game."

My friends and I exchange worried looks as I pack my things to head to the Tower.

Maybe I should call one of the guys before I leave…

Sucker for Pain

Felix

Felix

As I listen to Aubrey read the latest email from the administration, I marvel at their incompetence. Another five students are missing since they left their homes to return to Apex for the spring semester. It took a week for professors to raise the alarm because the entitled shits who attend school here frequently show up late, especially in the upper classes. The five are all fourth and fifth years, so no one spoke up until now—likely to keep from incurring the wrath of rich parents.

Fitz is sitting on the couch sipping a beer as I pace the floor in the middle of our circle. He's not showing it outwardly, but I know this disappearing act is making him worry for Delores. I can tell by the fury flooding our ambush bond as he idly runs his fingers through Chess' hair.

If he knew who was responsible, I know he'd tear them limb from limb to ensure her safety.

"Felix, when Henrietta told me we were at a missing count of ten, I requested to be part of the investigation. She's too worried about appearances and donors to push the various parties to solve this shit. We still don't know who tried to poison the heirs last spring or what they used. A student died on Halloween, and now we have people falling off the face of the planet; they need to call in the Sibbies."

Renard looks up from his book, squinting at Aubrey as if he just started paying attention. "The Supernatural Investigation Bureau? That witch leading the Council will never allow them inside Apex —not anymore than your father would Bloodstone, tiger."

"The Council may not have an option if too many more kids get snatched, Ren." I scratch my chin, pondering how irritating that turn of events would be. "None of the major families have lost anyone, but the second they do, it's going to be like an unpleasant episode of that dance parent show."

"Hey, good one, bro!" Fitz says, holding his hand out for a fist bump. "I'm going to pull you asshats into the modern era even if it kills me."

I roll my eyes at him, but I walk over and give him what he wants. He beams at me and in that moment, it hits me how carefree my twin is since the princess entered our lives. He's not out boozing and drugging it up every night. He pays attention to shit, and he's even less hyper unless he's really excited.

Score another goal for the cheeky rainbow bunny; she's made Fitz almost normal.

"Have we considered maybe the poison isn't poison, but magic?"

The abrupt change in topic catches me off guard, but my tiger isn't having it. "I don't care what the hell it is if we don't know who's doing it. They could use fucking phoenix shit and it wouldn't matter if we don't know where to find them!"

Chess blinks, looking thoughtful. "Either idea is about as likely as Aubrey joining the cheer squad, Raj. But I see your point."

"Magic is more prevalent in this world than the Council leads the supes they control to believe," Renard murmurs as he turns to pin us with a serious expression. "It may only thrive in rural areas of this country, but overseas, the people who wield it are simply keeping themselves hidden from the assholes governing us."

Aubrey frowns, taking his glasses off to clean them as he often does when he's perturbed. "That sounds plausible, old friend, but would any of them work with the people you claim they hate? Even for a promise of money or power?"

The gargoyle shakes his head. "No. Even rogues know better because the previous versions of the Council sought to exterminate them. Anyone caught doing so would be on their own, as the magical community would turn on them as a whole. But they might work for powerful magic users with less than honorable intentions—especially if there are factions working towards overturning the rule of our dictators."

"Aw, man," Fitz sighs as he leans against the cheetah. "Now I'd feel bad for fighting against them. Those fuckers need to be taken down and have for a long time, just like dear old dad. But killing our kids isn't the way to go about it. Fucking Catch-22."

"How do you even know that phrase?" Aubrey asks incredulously.

I agree; my brother isn't known for his literary prowess.

"Baby Girl is reading it for a project for that dickhead," my twin says as he hooks his thumb at Ren. "We like to read aloud. I can focus when it's auditory—I wish I'd known that years ago. Would have made school a hell of a lot easier."

Giving him a curious look, I can't help but ask, "Delores figured that out?"

"Yep. Our girl is a smart cookie and I love her creamy center," he says with a sigh that's almost dreamy.

"Fitz!" Chess admonishes him with a chuckle. "Can you behave for five minutes? While I'm a bit stunned that you're listening to classics and actually retaining the information, we're getting off topic again."

I nod, looking at the librarian and our host. "He's right. Ren, you may need to do some poking around in the magical world since you're the only one who believes it exists. Aubrey can help with the old texts that may refer to it."

"Thanks for your permission, Raj," the dragon grumbles as he shifts in the chair. I can tell his dragon is pushing at him as much as the animal in me is sliding through me.

They don't like the idea of our girl in danger, even if she shouldn't be our girl.

"The missing kids—as well as the dead one—are all smaller preds with lesser family ties. Does that help my angel or hurt her, do you think?"

"That's a good point, Chess. She's not defenseless, and I have proven it in public. Her family is the highest ranking at the school, so she's not from shifters without the means to hunt and destroy a kidnapper. But… Everyone knows she's been disowned and is prey. I don't know if it makes her more or less attractive to potential danger." I frown as I try to run the scenarios in my head, but it's useless because nothing has appeared to give us motivation for the awful shit on campus.

Without the why, we're floundering.

"She's defended herself against other heirs, but that doesn't mean shit. Most of them are soft and refuse to damage themselves in fights. It may not deter someone looking to cripple the Council." Aubrey gives me a pointed look before he continues. "You may need to pit her against more formidable foes. Is it time to revive the student games?"

Motherfucker. I ended those when I arrived because they were so pathetic.

The only person who can convince Henrietta to restart them would be me, and it would mean we'll have to enter competitions with the other schools worldwide again. Apex will have to have a real team or no one will fund it—which also means a long chat with my ex, Zhenga. The Leonidas pride will have to approve the re-entry to the league and fund the endeavor.

"Z will say 'yes', bro. She'll even help coach the girls' team. You know that chick is always looking for a way to shove it up her old man's ass," Fitz says helpfully. "I suppose I could help coach the boys."

Something about the way he says that makes me suspicious, but the dragon is right; if we don't get the princess known for kicking ass publicly, she might remain a target for her entire tenure here. That's especially true if the Council blocks Sibbie investigations, and they will until they don't have an option.

"Fine. I'll chat with Zhenga later this week, then Henny. What else is on our agenda before the princess shows up?" I rake a hand through my hair, considering purchasing a giant fucking whiteboard on wheels to manage all this shit.

There are too many fronts we have to wage war on to lose track.

As if he read my mind, Renard tilts his head and says, "Perhaps we need to track these leads and enemies, *mon ami*. Chess, you and I can look into finding something we can use, yes?"

"Yes, but we have to talk to Angel about being escorted when she's out and about. She won't like it, I know, but I think it's necessary," Chess says softly. "Her friends will want to help and I think if we all work together we can make sure her entire schedule is covered."

"Not it!" Fitz yells as he looks up from his phone. He's definitely texting with her while she's in class and I roll my eyes. "I took the hit for the group dating thing; it's someone else's turn."

"I'll do it," the broody gargoyle says as he crosses to drop onto his throne. His tail swishes, and I watch as he considers his words. "I want to take her out on the 14th and I can speak with her then. It's only a week away. We'll manage until then."

The book dragon snorts smoke rings as he laughs, looking at our host in amusement. "A date on Valentine's Day, huh? Should she expect French cuisine? Don't forget the red roses and beret, Monsieur Laveaux."

Chess and Fitz snicker and I can't help joining in. It's funny as fuck when the stodgy librarian goes after the broody botanist. The two of them rib each other in ways none of us could get away unsinged for.

"Simmer down, Flames. If you're worried she'll find me more entertaining than your usual bar-be-queue, you'll have to think of a better idea for your date."

Fitz stops texting for a moment to grin at me and I feel my stomach drop. "What about you, bro? Got big plans for our girl? You're going to have to outdo Chessie and me—we scored big points."

"I don't know," I admit as I pace back to the balcony. "I'm still working through all of this and I can't decide if I'm just not right for—"

"Stop it," Aubrey says in a low, dark voice. "We have all watched you torture yourself since you arrived, Felix. The past is the past, and the snack sized bunny seems to be our future. No one has said it before and it's time you hear it… *Get. Over. Yourself.*"

My eyes widen and my tiger leaps inside of me, ready to take the grumpy asshole out for impertinence. I step forward menacingly, only to hear a loud voice echoing off the walls as it approaches.

"Hey, assholes! Which one of you wants to tell me why your dumbasses haven't explained barbs and knotting to your goddamn girlfriend? You're all too damned old for this shit!"

Renard narrows his eyes. "Hello, Zhenga. Welcome to my home —uninvited." He shifts in the throne and mutters about the Captain's guards, likely deciding to increase their watch on our doors.

Z stalks up to me and stabs me in the chest with her finger. "You are supposed to be a Raj; act like it! If that Council heir had your dick stuck in her for any length of time, there should have been a conversation long before you chickened out and sent her to my remedial classes!"

Damn it, that's twice today someone has suggested I'm shirking my fucking duties and I'm going to…

"She told you?!" Chess chokes out with wide eyes. "Holy shit…"

Fitz jumps up, wagging his fingers at his lover. "You, too?! What the goddamned hell is in her pussy? I mean, it stopped but…"

Hades, strike me down, here and now. This is humiliating.

Zhenga looks at them, then me, and bursts out laughing. She laughs so hard she doubles over, holding herself up on her knees, and by the time she's caught her breath, the winged wankers are laughing, too.

Fuck my life.

"Just how many of you morons are chasing this bunny's tail?" Z asks curiously as she looks around.

"All of us!" Fitz yells before turning back to Chess. "And you should have told me, baby."

Before I can cut in, she shakes her head, "Then every single one of you dumbasses will be in my class on Wednesday. You obviously need the reminder of remedial level shifter sexuality if you failed to discuss the possibilities when top tier shifters fuck."

I frown. "I've never been told anything about it being different because of our lineage…"

"And I need Cliffs Notes, babe. What can Chessie and I look up? I refuse to look stupid in front of a bunch of newbs in that class…"

"That's because it almost never happens anymore, Raj. Most groups think it's an extinct fairy tale," Zhenga says smugly.

Aubrey tilts his head, looking at her in interest. "People think what is extinct, Leonidas?"

"Fated mates!" she says with a gleeful wink. Saluting us, she turns and stalks off, leaving us with that bomb ticking in the middle of the room.

Absolutely fuck. my. life.

Complicated

Delores

Delores

If only I could disappear off the face of the Earth, rather than come to this sex ed class…

Professor Zhenga focused the first half of today's class on reviewing the information from Monday's video. *That* I could handle; it's pretty straightforward information.

Heather M. interjecting with 'but that's sex with a worthy *pred*, right?' after every fucking statement was harder to manage, but I kept my cool. She's obviously a plant for someone and within a few weeks, she's integrated herself in with my ex-besties without a hitch. I'm calling her Yellow because of her weird fetish for a certain fruit that she has zero fucks about sharing with everyone.

This is sex ed, not kink camp, you dumb fuck. Show a little restraint.

That's what I want to say, but Yellow works her bullshit into every conversation as if she's a seasoned practitioner. Even Professor Z has told her to shut up about shit she has no clue about, but she doesn't listen. She keeps running her mouth and I'm honestly waiting to call her out on her lies in public. I catch our teacher looking at her the same way I do and I wonder which one of us will break first.

I can't tell if Zhenga is a rival or an ally, but she definitely has no patience for interruptions in her lectures. She told Yellow to 'fuck off Regina' at least three times before announcing her class would now have a points system. Every stupid question would earn a demerit on the board, and she would assign the person with the most demerits a cleaning task in the gym—starting with the men's bathrooms.

That shut Yellow's nasty ass up, praise Hera.

Now that the review is over, Zhenga has switched gears to mating in myths and legends. I'm confused because the syllabus she handed out last time said we wouldn't get into myths and legends until we'd covered basic biology and behavior for all the major shifter types. It's a pretty rapid switch, and I can't help but wonder if it's because of my conversation with her after class. She seemed disturbed when I described the situation, and although she promised to do some research, she certainly hasn't reported back to *me* about it.

I raise my hand, intent on asking about the one eighty in the curriculum so I can figure out how to work ahead, when the door swings open and my jaw hits the floor. All five of my boyfriends are making their way to the back of my *remedial* sex ed classroom with irritated looks on their faces. As if my inexperience isn't enough to make me insecure, they get to witness one of their exes *teach* me how fucking sex works!

I'd like to die here and now if it's convenient, thanks.

Scrunching down into my seat, I tuck my legs under me and pull up the hood on Fitz's stolen sweatshirt. I can't *actually* disappear, but I can keep the heat on my face from being as noticeable. My eyes are trained on the front of the classroom, waiting for a smirking Zhenga to continue with the lecture.

"Now that our guests have arrived, I have a special film to share. I dug through old lecture materials until I found lesson plans and films referencing certain types of folklore. This one is extremely old, so giggle away at the outdated shit. It's grainy and cheesy—the girls should also be prepared to be angry at the blatant misogyny. But in a pinch, this is the best I could do without being granted access to any *special archives*."

That dig was aimed right at my grumpy librarian, and I can hear his snort of irritation before I smell the smoke rings. I'm not sure whose side the lioness is on, but it's clear she has absolutely no fear, and maybe no sense of self-preservation. My dragon will *roast* her if she isn't careful, especially with the mood he's been in lately.

"I expect to see all of you taking notes. They have banned the information in this film in the past—it's rare to learn this at all since the Council took over. You may not get to see it again."

Frowning, I wonder why the Council would give a shit about legends and mating practices. What could be in this damned movie that's so scandalous? Maybe she's being dramatic because she figured out I was talking about a Khan when I asked her my questions, and this is her way of making me feel dumb.

That has to be it.

Zhenga turns the lights out and drops onto the bean bag she prefers, whipping out her phone. I can't complain, though. The benefit of her distraction is I can watch the guys out of the corner of my eye. What I see is giggle-worthy, but I don't want to draw attention to myself, so I bite my lip to hold it in.

The aforementioned dragon is seated in a large armchair with a frown on his face that looks more thoughtful than grumpy. His phone is out, and I think he might be recording the sound of the video rather than playing around like my actual professor. Rennie is perched on the arm of his chair, his expression unusually stormy as his tail flicks in sharp, angry beats. Fitz is sprawled on a beanbag next to Felix, focusing on the film more than I'd expect as his brother runs his fingers absently through his hair. It's like Felix is comforting him, but I don't know why. Chess is standing off to the side with his arms crossed as he leans against the wall, watching quietly.

Something is off with them, and I'd sure as hell like to know what it is.

Now isn't the time or place to ask, but it's making me nervous. I can't message them in such an open space, nor can I get caught slacking when this change in the curriculum was clearly prompted by *my* questions. I return my focus to the video, squinting when the word 'knotting' flashes on the screen.

What in the name of Aphrodite is that?

I don't have to wait long to find out because several *very* detailed diagrams appear on the screen, and I feel the color drain out of my face as I recognize exactly what happened—with both Fitz *and* Chess. The film explains that the phenomena differ from species to species, and can be called other things, but it's specific to sexual activity between 'fated mates'. Wincing at the weird hook thing that happens in felines, I struggle to keep up with my notes despite my shaking hands.

Fated mates—what does that even mean? Does it mean the guys don't really like me? Maybe Fitz and Chess didn't have a choice? What if it doesn't happen to the others? What if my stupid prey shit caused this?

The questions whirling through my head are overwhelming, and I don't know what to do. It feels like my world is being tossed into a blender, and it's set to high speed, but I can't turn it off before the lid goes flying. I put my pen down and close my eyes, desperately trying to calm myself. When I felt like this during the summer, I would go out and get a new piercing or a tattoo. The pain distracts me, and though I know it's not *technically* the healthiest way to deal, it helps.

I wonder if I can get Rufus and Cori to sneak off campus with me to a tattoo parlor.

When I open my eyes, I realize I'm white-knuckling my notebook. I'm feeling so insecure and naïve, but I need to get a hold of myself. My gaze cuts to the lioness again, but she's not looking at me or my guys. Maybe she really is doing this to be helpful? I'm not sure I'm ready to trust anyone else just yet—it's been hard enough to share my trauma with Rufus and Cori, and now I have to swap truths with my boyfriends in order to get the same from them. I'm still reconciling how exposed that makes me feel, but I know it has to happen.

Any good therapist would tell me I can't lock my heart in a vault forever because of a few assholes in high school.

Maybe that's what I need—*real* friend time. This is my last class of the day, and I could go have a 'therapy' session with Rufus and Cori. Their parents taught them a *fuckton* more about shifter life than Lucille allowed me to learn, so they might know about this 'knotting' and 'fated mate' stuff. If they explain it to me in layman's terms, I might feel less like an idiot.

I might stop wondering if the guys felt compelled to be with me.

That thought makes my heart ache, and I frown. I know my animal has been pushing me to bite them and is very receptive to the feel of their teeth on me. I don't think I can bring myself to ask Zhenga if that means my bunny wants to mate. When I have my implant changed, I should probably ask the nurses; they have to know a little about this, right?

Speaking of that, I need to do it soon because I'd like to have a sleepover with Fitz and Chess together—soon.

I pull out my phone quickly, making a note to ask Bettina about biting. Accidental mating seems like something I need to be wary of; Aubrey was very clear about that. A thought occurs to me, and I add another quick task for during my work study this evening… *visit the archives and look up fated mates.* Between that and my research on the Society, I have plenty to keep me busy.

When the movie ends and everyone stands, I scurry out of the room as quickly as possible. I can't bear to look at the guys until I have my head on straight, and I definitely can't let any of them touch me until I fix this damned birth control issue. Wanting to scream in frustration, I put my earbuds in and duck into a small corridor that leads to the prey tunnels.

I don't want anyone to see me freaking out, especially not that obvious spy, Yellow.

Using the modified prey version of the campus map, I follow a series of twists and turns until I arrive at a door that has a *caduceus* on it. The symbol for medicine makes me sigh with relief, and I push open the door slowly so I don't startle the three nurses when I emerge from their supply closet.

"Um, hello? Bettina? Clarice? Argyle? It's Dolly..." The three women are sitting at a table chowing down on lunch, not batting an eye when I appear out of nowhere. I give them a nervous smile as I shut the closet door and walk over. "I need your help again."

"Told you she'd be back!" snorts Argyle.

Clarice frowns, and Bettina glares at their colleague. "Stuff it, Argyle. What can we do for you, Dolly?"

"I need my implant refreshed and, um, I have some questions." They look at me curiously and I rush to add, "*Private* questions."

Bettina wipes her mouth with a napkin and stands, nodding. "Well, then girlie. Come lie down on the exam table and we'll get started."

"Oh, no! I'm interrupting your lunch," I reply, shaking my head.

"Nonsense, girl. Birth control is not something to *put off*." Argyle gets up and heads for their locked medicine cabinet in a huff. "I can forgo a full belly so *you* don't get a full belly."

Clarice sighs and leads me to the exam table. "Don't mind her. Being gruff is her love language. I promise she likes you."

"If she didn't *spray* you, she likes you," mutters Bettina.

Well, that's comforting.

"Don't fret, Dolly—we'll have you all fixed up in time for Valentine's Day," Clarice adds with a bright smile.

My eyes dart between the skunk, the hedgehog, and the possum.

Did she just say… Valentine's Day?

How in the hell am I going to handle that—eeney, meenie, miney, moe?

CASTLE

AUBREY

I WAS NOT HAPPY WITH DELORES TAKING UP RESIDENCE IN THE privacy of our Tower at first, I'll admit.

When Fitz called to bully Rennie into it, I made my frustration clear. He and I have shared our spaces for many years now and we've kept our secrets safe by only confiding in one another. That grew into something more well before the tigers arrived, but we chose not to elaborate on our relationship purposefully.

We have more similarities than differences, despite species, and are comfortable in our anonymity.

But my romance reading, poetry loving dreamer couldn't stand for this girl to be unsafe. So we gave her the second lowest floor and strict rules to abide by—which she promptly broke.

Again, my hopeless empath caved, and we comforted her when she needed it.

Now we're all entangled in her web, including me, and I have no idea how to handle it. Rennie is going on a date with her soon and I'm sure he'll enchant her with his Byron and 'ooh-la-la' self. I, however, am in a similar boat as Felix because I have no idea what I'll do when I'm expected to take my turn.

Fitz is… well, Fitz. He's out of his mind, but in a lovable psycho way. Our quiet cheetah is sweet and supportive, indulging her artistic visions and letting her go wild with her friends in his classes.

What the fuck am I going to do with her outside of the camaraderie we share in my archives?

I respect her sharp mind and fierce heart, as well as her refusal to let the world keep her down. Perhaps I need to find something we can share that will appeal to that? Fuck, I don't know. Rennie and I spent so much time together that our love sort of… happened. I didn't have to court him; we just knew.

Growling under my breath, I stalk away from the library for the night. I've been buried in old tomes trying to research the poison, magic, Societies, and all manner of intrigue. Delores had practice for the talent show, so I allowed her to move her work study to another night this week. I doubt she realized I'd still be working regardless, but I didn't want to make her feel bad by saying so.

I trudge up to the scanner on the door and enter my master code carefully. There's far too much danger not to be overly cautious and I don't want any intruders here with our girl asleep in her bed tonight.

Frowning, I look at the front staircase for a moment. Fitz learned about Dolly by stalking her and rifling through her shit—which she didn't seem to mind. That blows my mind because dragons are extremely protective of their spaces and hoard, but she barely even scolds him for it.

Is it possible I could take a page out of his crazy book so I can plan our future date?

My feet decide for me, and before I know it, I'm striding up the stairs, until I hit the second floor. When I walk into the hallway, I notice her door is cracked. That's not safe at all. What if someone sneaks in her room to hide and isn't Fitz?

The thumping of my heart forces me forward quickly and I listen carefully as I approach the partially open door, hoping to catch the asshole who is in our girl's room without permission.

But all I hear are soft sobs and sniffling.

What the hell? The lights are off; is someone hurting her?

I'll rip their fucking arms off and beat them to death with them before I sear their bones.

Pulling the door open, I stomp in, looking around with my dragon's eyes so I can see in the dark. I feel him spreading through my body, eager to break free and roast the person stupid enough to believe they can harm our mate.

Wait, what?

Shaking my head of that errant thought, I locate the source of the sounds I heard in the hallway. In the middle of the large mattress is Delores, curled around a pillow in the dark, crying as if her heart is breaking into pieces. She doesn't even move and I know her instincts have warned her she's not alone.

I lick my lips, unsure what to do. Fitz or Chess or Rennie would know—maybe I should call them? I have zero experience comforting a crying woman and though Dolly has over shared personal things with me before, I'm uncertain I'll be able to do what the more emotional members of our little group would. Hell, I'm not even sure what they'd do, so I know I can't emulate it.

A loud sniff distracts me and a tiny voice murmurs low enough that you'd have to be a supe to hear. "I just want to be alone."

Fuck. Whatever it is, it's bad.

The glow of a cell phone lights the room for a second, then fades. Delores growls low from her prone position, winging the damn thing in my direction. I catch it, frowning as I realize she didn't even open her eyes to look at it before she hurled the wretched tech across the room.

Whatever is upsetting her is online.

Lucky for me, the screen isn't locked, so I scroll through the notifications. There's a flood of vicious garbage from the Apex message boards—nasty comments and horrible accusations going back to what seems to be the beginning of the year. A few of them reference the damage done to her dorm room, and I tuck those names away to consult with Fitz. But I doubt that is what's making her sob in the dark, if it's been going on the whole time.

No, this is something recent because she's been stoically weathering this abuse from her peers without saying a word.

Finally, I hit the bottom of the list, and my eyes widen. My dragon's fury hits me before I can stop it and I half-shift in the middle of her room. Wings flex and smoke puffs out of my nose as I fight to rein in the fire and brimstone my animal wants to use to lay waste to everyone he can find who is involved with this.

Who am I kidding? He'd lay waste to this entire hellhole except for the few people I give a shit about.

"Aubrey, is that you?" Her voice is so small again. It makes my chest ache and the fire burn hot inside of me as my dragon rumbles about mates and enemies and murder. "Why are you down here puffing like a magic dragon?"

I snort, almost laughing at her ability to be adorable even when she's clearly in pain. "I… came to, uh, leave a note…but the lights were off and the door was open…"

She sniffles and shakes a bit on the bed for a second, then takes in a breath. "Did I hit you with the phone?"

"No." I pause for a moment, looking down at the email that has my wings, tail, and fangs twitching. "But my dragon needs to know *who. did. this. to. you?*"

She sighs and shrugs, looking more defeated than I've seen before. "One of the Heathers—she's bragging about it to her followers because apparently, it's completely okay for her and her cronies to get me kicked out of school. It's only my future they're messing with."

It takes a massive amount of control not to roar like a beast. The spoiled assholes who attend school here are rarely aware of anything beyond their own needs, but this reeks of a level of narcissism I'm not used to dealing with.

What kind of person gambles with someone else's future prospects over a petty squabble?

I know the answer to that—one with no moral compass and a troubled psyche. But my realization isn't helping my dragon calm down, nor is it helping our girl feel better. Fixing her problem will come after I comfort her, when she's ready to hear potential solutions. So despite my half-shifted form, I walk over, dropping onto the bed, and gather her in my arms.

Delores wraps herself around me like a spider monkey, clinging to my chest as she lets the water works out again. I assume this trivial problem is bothering her more than the murders and people hunting her because it's such an unnecessary addition to her already full plate. It didn't need to happen and the fact that she's stuck dealing with the machinations of vicious backbiting instead of more important things chafes.

"It's just so h-h-hard. I'm busting my ass to do well in classes and keep out of the line of fire, but every time I succeed, those bitches roll up to knock me down again," she says in a raspy voice.

Stroking her back gently, I nod as my wings wrap around her as well, forming a cocoon. "We all see how hard you're working, lunchable. Even Fitz knows, and getting him to pay attention to anything that doesn't involve you being naked is almost impossible."

That makes her giggle a little and I almost fist pump in excitement. Score one for the old ass grouch who has no idea what he's doing. Maybe I'm not the worst person for this situation, after all.

"He really has two modes—hyper-focused or off the rails." I feel her smile fondly against my neck. "It's endearing once you learn to work with it."

I blink. "You know how to get Fitz to flip the switch? Really?"

She shrugs, her fingers tracing patterns on my skin that leave fiery trails of sensation. "No, it's more like I've figured out how to work with him, no matter which mood he's in. I adapt instead of making him adapt, and it's much easier."

Son of a two-faced chaos god, she's brilliant.

"Well, if you're smart enough to figure out our resident psycho, you sure as hell don't need to plagiarize a fucking Shifter History paper." I growl softly, furious that no one brought this to my attention before they issued edicts. I certainly have the damn software to check for that shit and even if I didn't, I spend much of my time authenticating texts.

"That asshole hates me, anyway. He'd believe the fucking moon is made of green cheese if one of those girls told him so. I can't decide if he wants in their pants or in their parents' graces." She sighs heavily, a shudder rippling through her. "Either way, I'm the one getting screwed."

My smile is more of a grimace because I feel her heat against me and this is the absolutely wrong time for my body to agree with her declaration. Instead, I press a kiss to the top of her head, hoping that helps soothe her jagged edges. "Probably, if Fitz has his say, but I think if you give me a chance, I might help."

She looks up at me with teary eyes, her expression hopeful. "Really? How?"

"Fitz is quite skilled with nefarious online things and I believe if he can get definitive proof of their bragging, plus I can match the paper in question to someone else's work, we will have enough proof to present to Henrietta. She won't be able to ignore it if two professors show her powerful evidence." I pause and tilt my head. "I'll need a copy of the original paper you submitted as well."

"I can give you that. I mean, it's the one I worked on upstairs last week. All of you answered questions for me when I asked, even Fitzy. It's not like I didn't do the work." She sighs again and burrows her face against my chest before muttering, "But that didn't matter because some jizz stain must have switched them after I turned them in or something."

"It's possible—or the girl who accused you is crazy enough to have claimed your work is hers. I think it'd be just as easy for someone who isn't as smart or talented, but very petty, to have reported you with little proof and this happened as a knee jerk reaction. Henny despises conflict and bows to power to avoid it."

Dolly sits up, looking at me with disbelief. "You're saying she might have just taken this bitch at her word with nothing to back it up? Expulsion would ruin my future and the morons in charge might have just said 'okay, your word is good enough for me' before they sent that email?"

I nod, my expression rueful. "Possibly. You stood up to three of your tormentors so far, according to Felix. They may have gotten the message, but someone looking to get in their good graces wouldn't worry about it."

Her voice is dripping with bitterness as she mutters, "Fucking Yellow. I knew that simpering little twat was going to be trouble, especially after Professor Z started slapping her down."

My eyes narrow when my dragon hears its target. I lift her chin, looking at her as I ask carefully, "Who the fuck is Yellow?"

Eyes sparkling, she shrugs and says, "I call the Heathers by their color because it's easier. That one is Heather M. She's new this semester—a transfer from Bloodstone, she says. I doubt that, though, because I'd think she'd be... tougher? But she's not."

The beast inside of me roars in satisfaction now that we have a name. I'll help our girl work this out the right way first, but after that, this snooty rich girl is going to learn a very serious lesson. Renard and I will find out her game and end it; that is for certain.

"Fitz and I will look into her as well." I rise from the bed, still holding her as she clings to me. "For now, let me take you to the nest and we can find our broody friend. Some relaxed cuddle time would do you a world of good before tomorrow."

"Okay, Aubrey," she whispers. "Thank you for taking care of me."

As if I could choose to do anything else for my mate.

Don't Be Shy

Renard

After Dolly sprinted out of Zhenga's classroom, it feels fitting that I'm the one escorting her on the next date. Whereas the tigers and Flames can be overwhelming, I'm a soothing presence who allows her to spill all the worries she keeps bottled up.

Or, I would be, if my gargoyle wasn't on a rampage.

Her presence in our nest the other night was wonderful, but once my old friend relayed why she was curled up as if the world was ending, I had to put a leash on my beast. He's infuriated that our girl was so defeated, even in private, by a false claim that puts her in more danger. If they expel her, she'd be left with going home to those two nut jobs who gave birth to her.

That's less safe than being here for more reasons than I can count.

I assume her behavior after class was because there are so many intricacies to shifter sexual behavior that no one in her family saw fit to educate her on. The 'legend of the freaky cocks'—as the lioness so eloquently put it after the film on knotting—isn't helping her feel less ignorant. I sense she was keeping her distance as she tried to process everything, but then her idiot friends forced her to focus on other things.

Aubrey thinks I can broach her safety on campus while we're out without restarting her trauma. I have no idea how I'll bring up that topic during our outing without making her angry, but I promised I'd try.

That's a future Renard problem.

My current problem is figuring out what to wear tonight, and how I'll keep my… issues… under control.

I originally planned to take her to *La Belle Époque*, to dine under the stars. However, after recent events, I changed my mind. I'll save soaking in the moonlight for a time when my inner monster is calmer. He's been prowling under the surface for weeks, and though I know what happened isn't Dolly's fault, I'm having more difficulty controlling him than I ever have in the past.

Our version of Valentine's this year will have to be a bit… less traditional to soothe the beast.

"Did the Captain drop off my keys?" I yell. Flames is in the bedroom, reading in his chair, but he should be able to hear me from the depths of my closet. Tilting my head, I wait for the huff of irritation and grin when I hear it.

"Two hours ago. They're on the dresser. Take a chill pill!"

I cover my face with my hands, shaking my head at how ridiculous the dragon sounds when he spouts slang. Fitz is always teaching him that shit, and though it's funny, he gets touchy when it doesn't quite land. "I'm not hyper!"

That's probably not true. I am a little hyper.

His lack of response isn't unusual—despite how long it took for the grumpy book dragon to let me in, he's eerily aware of how to deal with my emotional states. I suppose knowing one another for centuries makes things smoother, but our easy companionship didn't take long to form. He calls me out on wanting to take care of people, but the nest he built on Christmas Eve got created because he knew it would make me happy. Gargoyles sleep in groups—similarly to wolves or cats—and unfortunately for me, exile stole that comfort. It made my first few decades at Apex a nightmare.

Aubrey figured it out within a week.

But he won't be with me tonight, and it makes me nervous.

It's been a long time since I've operated without a wingman, and even longer since my gargoyle has been this agitated. When I'm angry, even the hundreds of years of practice soothing my instincts fall to the wayside.

I walk through the closet, pawing through all of my clothes as I try not to panic. Delores reminds me so much of someone from long ago, and that ended in epic tragedy. What if my stars are aligning the same way? I'll ruin it for everyone if I scare her off because of my temper and…

"I can hear you freaking out from the bedroom. Why aren't you dressed yet?" Aubrey appears in the doorway, studying my face before he continues. "Are you brooding?"

I roll my eyes, turning to walk towards the casual wear end of the closet, so I don't have to face him. "I am not brooding; I'm considering my wardrobe."

He takes off his glasses, stuffing them in a shirt pocket—a sure sign he's frustrated and doesn't know how to address it. He, too, is pacifying his inner animal after the incident, and I know it's even harder for him to keep his fury under wraps. Flame spewing rage is his Achilles' heel, and even his squishy toys aren't helping of late. We've gone on far more hunts recently than necessary, but the carnage seems to cool him down for a bit.

Other extracurricular activities would help, as well.

"Rennie, the snacklet likes you. She likes all of us; that's why she agreed to this weird pentagram dating thing."

"I think you mean polyam," I chuckle.

Huffing, he shakes his head. "I didn't, but that works, too. The point is, she wants to date all of us and that includes you. Stop reliving whatever it is from your past that you still refuse to talk about, even with me."

Now I've done it. I've hit our sore spot.

I open my mouth to respond, but the tiny sand kitten he bought for Delores comes skittering into the closet. She immediately trots over to Aubrey, climbing up his leg to his arm, and then onto his shoulder. The tiniest 'mew' escapes, and I watch his face soften as he reaches up to scratch her ears.

Jinx to the rescue!

Arching a brow, I stare at him until he finally throws his hands up. "Fine! Something cute distracted me. But I'm not wrong—the past doesn't need to ruin the future, Rennie. Dolly might be your second chance."

"But who's counting?" I reply, turning back to the wall of clothes.

"For fuck's sake..." he mutters. "Wear the Farmani with the blue."

My lips twist as he stomps off with Jinx in tow. He's not mad; he's worried, and I understand why. Aubrey believes if I don't talk about my trauma, I'll never get over it. That's saying a lot, given his lack of detail about his own banishment, but we're men. It's in our DNA, I guess.

He's right about the outfit, too, damnit.

I pluck the sapphire silk Farmani shirt off its hanger and grab a pair of black slacks before heading down the hall to shower. When I walk into the living room, I can tell his crankiness has faded, because he smirks at my outfit as he pets the kitten on his lap.

Know-it-all.

"Don't forget your keys," he says as he nods at the dresser.

Turning back to face him before I head into the bathroom, I sigh. "Thank you. We use vehicles so infrequently…"

A snort is my answer as I close the door behind me, but I know he heard the unspoken apology for being on edge.

I'm not the only mother hen.

"I had no idea you had a car like this. You guys keep surprising me with sexy machines," Dolly exclaims as she runs her hand over the hood.

Shrugging, I round the side of the '62 Aston Martin. "I went through a car phase in the 60s. I learned to drive long before then, but it had been a long time. Plus, I got a wee bit obsessed with James Dean and so… There's a warehouse in the city where I store them; I have quite a collection—your Mustang would fit right in."

Her eyes widen, and she nods enthusiastically. "I love fancy cars. When I learned to drive, it made me feel free. I finally gained the freedom to drive during the summer, unlike all of my peers, and experienced the liberation of not having to rely on a creepy body-guard for transportation.

The joy on her face makes my heart squeeze a bit, and I tilt my head. "Is that why you enjoy flying so much?"

"Um, no," she replies quickly as her cheeks pinken. "I mean, yes, but I also like to share things with you and Aubrey. It's like our special thing." Ducking her head, she opens the car door before I can, and tucks in the long leather coat I bought her as she sits.

It helps immensely to have a small army of prey animals who will leave gifts on your girl's doorstep.

She's wearing the outfit I sent—a thought that makes the simmering beast inside preen with pleasure. I prefer this to his recent fury, so it's a win. Shutting her door, I head to the other side of the car and drop into the driver's side, looking over at her. "It is special, *petit lapin*. You're the only person here who knows where we go and what we do when we hunt."

I watch her wiggle in the seat, pressing her thighs together. Finally, she looks up at me, her eyes dark with promise. "I enjoy watching, you know."

"Oh, I know," I chuckle as I pull away from the Admission Building and head down the winding road leading off campus.

A pout crosses her lips, and she wrinkles her nose at me. "How could you tell?"

This time I laugh for real. For a girl raised by preds, Dolly has so little knowledge of how we work biologically. It's curious and adorable at the same time. Her frown deepens, and I take pity on her, tapping my nose with one finger. A hand flies to her mouth, and she turns redder than I've ever seen her as she squirms in the seat.

"Oh my gods, that's so embarrassing! That's why everyone keeps..."

I give her another amused look as I steer the car onto the highway, taking us away from town and towards Cambridge. "Of course it is. Predators hunt by scent—surely you realize that."

"Well, of course I do! I just didn't think... Ugh—men!" She huffs, crossing her arms over her chest in irritation.

"Hunting for partners isn't that different from hunting for food, *petit lapin*. It's a different hunger, but it's basically the same instinct."

And you are my new favorite prey.

THE PARKING LOT AT LIQUID ONYX IS PACKED, DESPITE THE HOUR. I've never been here before midnight, but even as early as ten, shifters are lined up at the door and around the block. Luckily for us, that won't be an issue. I pull up to the valet and hand him the keys before walking over to Dolly's side to open the door. She quirks a brow at me as I help her out of the sports car, curiosity written on her face as she looks at the long line of people in front.

"I should have guessed by the fancy outfit we were going somewhere nice, Rennie, but this is a surprise. You don't seem like the clubbing type."

"There are many things you don't know about me yet, ma petite. Experiencing loss when you are young can cause you to develop a thirst for living, and I enjoy many things that might shock you," I reply as I tuck her arm into mine. "Perhaps you will discover new things to enjoy as well tonight."

We approach the door, and the massive gorilla shifter grunts before lifting the ropes for us without so much as a word. Dolly gives me another look, and I smile when she murmurs, "I believe you."

Dance music pounds from the DJ booth as we make our way inside. I stop at the coat check, allowing her to peel the leather duster off and reveal the couture beneath.

My eyes start at the black patent leather platform boots, traveling up the wide fishnet stockings to the pleated black skirt—similar to the one she wears at Apex. The beavers in the laundry room were an excellent resource for sizing, and I'm glad I checked in with them before I ordered the outfit last month. Her glittering bunny belly ring is hanging just above the waistband, and I bite my lip as my gaze roams up to the tiny silver halter top. Her rainbow hair falls in waves, and I grin when I notice she's wearing the choker I sent, with the tiny locket dangling from the ring.

She's absolute perfection.

"Come with me; we'll get a drink," I rumble, offering my hand again as I work to get my reaction to her under control. "There's quite a selection to choose from."

"Are we going to… dance?" she asks, her eyes dancing with excitement as she looks over the crowded floor. "I've never been to a rave, but this definitely seems close."

"Raves are more Flames' thing, but we can add it to the list. I think he'd love to have another person to dress up like an electric light show with him." That's entirely true—I'm not a huge fan of the human-filled, fake furry festivals he loves so much, but I'd bet my last prey-so Dolly would bounce around with him until the sun rises.

Our dragon has such a soft spot for the cute and fluffy—and our girl fits that to a tee.

Dolly squeezes my hand as she looks at the neon menu above the bar, squealing. "Look at the drinks!"

"Uh, *petit lapin*, the fancy ones are all alcoholic. You don't drink, so I'll order you a—"

"Hell no! I am not my mother, but I also want to live a little, just like you said. Can't I have just one? That really pretty pink thing in the big fancy glass?" She turns to me and her expression is so sincere and bright that I groan.

Fuck. They're all going to murder me if I let her get tanked, but…

"Just one," I say carefully, motioning for the bartender. When the leggy flamingo comes over, she titters in excitement and I chuckle. "Dolly, this is Lucinda. She's one of the owners of Liquid Onyx. Lucinda, this is my… girlfriend, Dolly."

The bunny in questions flushes pink with pleasure, and Lucinda flaps her wings, feathers dropping in excitement. "Holy Hades in a wetsuit! Renard, you cradle-robbing dog!"

My eyes widen, but Dolly just smirks at her and tosses her hair over a bare shoulder. "Oh, he's not my dog. Three of my other boyfriends are felines, though."

Well, I'll be damned.

Clearing my throat, I give the flamingo a shrug. "She has a harem. It's a thing."

"Dammit! Why do you rare fuckers have all the fun?" Feathers fly again, and Lucinda sighs. "Okay, what do you and your adorable little girl want to drink?"

Dolly bristles at the 'little girl' remark, and I can see the Council heir magically appear in her bearing. Her spine stiffens, and her expression goes from sweet to regal in less than a second. The look she gives Lucinda is downright scary, because the way the flashing strobes hit her, it looks like her eyes turn red.

"I'm not a little girl, and Rennie hasn't fully introduced me yet. My full name is Delores Rostoff Drew." She waits for recognition to blossom on the flamingo's face before she gives her a slow, knowing smile. "And I'll have a Pink Bikini Martini."

I'm definitely in trouble now. Not only have I unlocked daring Dolly, but I also found 'possessive, scary heir' Dolly, in one fell swoop.

Lucinda gathers herself, nodding as she looks at me. "Your usual? I'll have someone bring it to the floor for you."

"Yes, please," I reply as Dolly stares her down. "Thank you, Lucinda."

Tugging on her hand, I finally get my girl to budge from her stand-off with the bartender. I find a nice dark corner of the dance floor and tug her into my arms, brushing a strand of hair off of her face. The tension in her form fades as I trail my fingers down her jaw to her neck.

"Sorry about that," she mutters. "I don't know what came over me."

I snort, leaning in to whisper in her ear. "That was the predator in you, *petit lapin.*"

Her hands land on my waist, and she sways her hips, moving to the pounding bass of the surrounding music. "Do you think there is a predator in me somewhere?"

"Oh, most certainly. Even without that display of dominance you put on for Lucinda, we've all seen you show others that being an apex predator isn't always about what animal you have inside of you. It's how you carry yourself, and that's something that can't be taught—you were born this way."

Her tinkling laughter vibrates through me, and my tail drops immediately. It's going to be damned near impossible to keep the gargoyle under control—all my pent-up frustration, rage, and heat paired with her bare skin are sending me into overdrive.

"You all still act like I'm too fragile to handle things, though."

The assignment the others gave me flits through my mind, and I frown. She's going to be irritated no matter what; I might as well rip the band-aid off now so we can enjoy the rest of the evening. "It's because we worry about you, and none of us have had anyone to worry about in a long time. With the recent problems on campus, we would like to take extra steps to ensure you're safe."

She rolls her eyes, giving me a look reminiscent of every surly teen to come through my classroom. "Fine. What do you have in mind, an escort everywhere I go?"

Well, that was easy.

I nod and she throws her hands up, growling, "That was sarcasm, Rennie! I'm not a child!"

Oops.

"We don't think you're a child, petite. But someone is attacking students, and none of us would forgive ourselves if you got hurt when we could have prevented it."

She considers my words for a moment and nods.

When I sigh in relief, she steps closer, looking into my eyes with a mischievous grin. Then she reaches down and wraps her fingers around the end of my tail, squeezing it lightly. "How about I show you what a big girl I am, and you can decide for yourself?"

Cue Renard losing his motherfucking shit in the middle of a club.

Closer

Delores

Delores

When Renard's eyes glow bright blue, I swallow hard. I was feeling bold after my confrontation with the disrespectful flamingo. So I didn't even think before I wrapped my hand around his swishing appendage and squeezed. I've only seen the fierce look on him a few times before, during his hunts with Aubrey, and I wonder if it's related.

I've awakened the beast.

The thought makes butterflies erupt in my stomach, and I grin at the blue-eyed man as an idea flits through my head. During the video in sex ed, the narrator mentioned how canine and feline shifters often enjoy 'stalking' their mates as foreplay. Zhenga said a lot of what those groups do can apply to other shifters…

Without giving myself time to overthink it, I pull back, crooking my finger as I whisper, "Come get me."

I take off down the nearest hallway, unsure where I'm going, but hearing him behind me in pursuit—just as I'd hoped. A tiny sliver of fear runs through me as I navigate the twists and turns of an unfamiliar place with a predator on my tail. Despite a similar circumstance triggering me earlier in the year, it's now giving me a thrill. My pussy clenches as I take turn after turn, claws out as I sprint in the heavy boots.

They did not build this outfit for stealth, but that's okay—I want to be caught.

I finally hit a dead end with nowhere to go, panting as I lean against the wall and wait.

A few moments later, I see Renard stalk around the corner. Gone is the lounging emo man: instead, there's a partially shifted, onyx warrior stomping toward me with a feral look on his face. My eyes run over his wings, short horns, and immense bulk as he fills the hallway. His tail is flicking rapidly, and as he comes closer, I realize two things. One, his talisman is glowing and two, his clothes are gone and holy mother of Zeus, he might actually break me in half with that thing.

Have I made a grievous error or a really brilliant decision? Fuck if I know, but I'm going to find out.

"You found me," I say, knowing I sound breathy and ridiculous.

The gargoyle taps his nose, winking at me. I laugh nervously, but I muster my confidence, propping one foot on the wall and stretching my arms above my head, hoping it looks inviting. His steps quicken, and before I can say anything else, his hands grasp my hips and haul me off my feet. I wrap my legs around his waist, gazing into his eyes as I touch the smooth, hard stone covering his face.

"You," he growls out between four very serious fangs, "... are in for it, little one."

Oooh. I like snarly Rennie. It's hotter than shit.

Deciding to up the ante, I lean in and bite his lower lip, tugging on it with my teeth. "I'd prefer it to be in me, to be honest."

"That can be arranged." A hand snakes under my skirt to my thong, and a loud ripping sound fills the air.

Son of a bitch! Those were brand new.

"I'll buy new ones," he mutters against my ear, as if he can hear my thoughts. "But for now..."

Tilting my hips up, I grind against the hard cock nestled between my thighs. The rumbling snarl that echoes out of him is scary and sexy, so I tilt my head, kissing him hungrily. Our tongues dance as he shifts his position. The head of his cock rubs against my clit enticingly, and I dig my fingers into his shoulders to hold on.

"Don't tease me, Rennie," I gasp when our lips break. "I want you now."

That sounded sexy, right?

It must have, because he leans his forehead against mine, that brilliant blue flashing in his gaze as he murmurs huskily, "I'll take it slow so I don't hurt you."

"You'd be amazed at what I can take. Don't hold back for me." I smirk as I grip his shoulders and push myself down on the smooth, hard cock at my entrance. Our little game of chase turned me on anyway, but just like with Fitz, my pussy is so slick and wet, it's like a goddamn slip-and-slide.

I'm not complaining, since I didn't bring any lube with me to the club.

Gasping as he fills me, I realize he might have been right about taking it slow, but I'll be damned if I'm backing down now. Renard may have centuries of experience on me, but I have a premium subscription to PredHub and a higher tolerance for pain than I've ever let on.

Plus, I'm stubborn as fuck.

Concern eclipses the lust on his face, but I wiggle to encourage him, and that snaps the leash he has on himself. His wings flare out behind him like a shield as he starts a hard rhythm. I lean back against the wall, using it as leverage to meet every thrust as it stretches me just shy of pain. The sting makes my pussy flood, and my bunny inside pushes against my skin like she wants out.

I guess she wants to play, too.

An idea flits through my sex-hazed mind, and I let go of his shoulders to grab his tail as it whips around. Curving my lips into a wicked grin, I bring the tip to my mouth and bite. A loud roar of pleasure is his response, so I do it again, and his hips piston me into the wall so hard, I might actually dent the drywall. However, the bunny inside seems to like it, and before I can stop it, I feel my fluffy tail and long ears bust free, followed by my fangs and claws.

"Ah, the vicious rabbit," he growls. "I was waiting for her, *petite*. Now, let yourself go..."

The dark rumble in his tone makes me shiver, and I ride the waves of sensation as our bodies move to the beat of the pumping bass of the club. When I feel the orgasm rushing towards me, I bite down on his tail again, and he throws his head back with another roar. Suddenly, something changes—as if his cock swells, rubbing spots it wasn't hitting before—and I explode.

When I can finally open my eyes, his electric blue ones stare back at me in what looks like surprise. His hips are moving, but...

Holy Aphrodite, he's my mate, too? But what if that's not what he wants?

The confidence I was projecting before deflates.

A soft expression crosses the fierce features of the gargoyle, and a clawed hand brushes the hair off my sweaty face as I dare to hold his gaze. "*Ma petite*, you're far too smart to have missed the reason all of us attended Zhenga's class that day."

"I... I know what the video said, but... I didn't think..." It's hard to form words when he's looking at me like this. I'm getting much better at expressing the sexy side of things—even if a lot of it is bravado—but the emotional stuff is still a struggle. "It's wild enough that two of you are my 'fated mates' already. I didn't expect it to happen again."

"Would it be so bad if it did?" he rumbles softly. "Are you frightened by the idea of five fated mates, Dolly?"

Ignoring the voice in my head screaming in fear, I whisper, "Truth for a truth?" I wait for him to nod and continue. "A little. I worry none of you have a choice—that this is all a fluke or something."

The impish grin that spreads over his face is adorable and makes my chest ache. "Fate doesn't always get to decide, *petite*. I was told what they wrote in my stars from an early age, and my current life wasn't in those predictions. Neither was my past pain." His lips brush my ear as he murmurs, "But I would live through it all again to be where I am now."

Be still my heart, poetry boy.

"You owe me that story," I say, hoping to lighten the mood before I turn into a rabbit-shaped puddle on the floor.

Suddenly, the feeling of fullness inside me lessens, just as it did with the others. He chuckles, letting my legs slide down his body slowly, holding on to me as I find my bearings with limbs that feel like jelly. The onyx skin melts away, and his clothes are back, though his wings and tail stay put.

"How… how do you do that?" I ask, still breathless, gesturing at his clothes as he hands me a cloth to clean up with. "Is it a gargoyle thing for your clothes to shift with you?"

"Ah. Perhaps I'm not the only one experiencing this benefit. Check yours?"

Frowning, I glance over my shoulder to discover that my damned tail is sticking out of the skirt, as if they designed it for me to shift in. "You are not a sorcerer, Renard Laveaux. Tell me how you did it!"

"Okay, okay, *ma petite*. The secret hides in this..." he says, pulling the glimmering talisman out of his shirt before pointing at the new necklace he gave me. "And that."

My hand comes up to the choker, touching the locket in confusion. "It's... magic?"

"Of a kind. But don't tell Flames. I've never given him one because I enjoy his tantrums when he rips his clothes far too much."

I grin, thinking about how angry the dragon gets when he half-shifts without warning. I can see the appeal—pissy Aubrey is pretty hot. "Okay, but can we get out of here? I think I'd like to continue the rest of our outing... somewhere less public."

"Going to put the rabbit back in the cage before we go back to the dance floor?" he asks, holding his hand out.

My lips curve. "Mmm... after I take care of something."

We navigate our way back to the club floor and I tug his hand over to the bar. Rennie gives me a suspicious look, but I shoot him a grin back and bat my lashes. When we're standing in front of the snooty flamingo again, her eyes widen as she takes in my ears, and she looks over at the gargoyle, who shrugs.

"Thanks for keeping our drinks cold," I say, picking both up and tossing them back, one after the other. The alcohol burns like a motherfucker, but I look the bird in the eye as if I do it all the time —telling her I'm not a bunny to be messed with. "Catch ya later, Lucinda."

With that, I pull my snickering boyfriend through the crowd, shaking my cottontail in victory as we find a spot in the crowd to get our groove on.

I'm going to call tonight's outing 'Kinks and Bad Bitch Unlocked', that's for damn sure.

Scoob

Chess

Chess

Since our family chat about the multitude of issues facing my angel, I've been in overdrive. I found a rolling board for the main living area in the Tower and I've been here every chance I get, laying out the mysteries we're trying to solve. I was ecstatic to create a huge transparent vellum cling for the back of the clear board, so there's a timeline at the top and a map of the school underneath. There are dates and times of the incidents so far ranging from the prom disaster to the most recent disappearances. Locations for all the problems, including the bullying shit, are marked with magnets holding a list of names of those involved.

This looks totally fucking professional and I'm super jazzed about finishing up the last part. I have space for columns listing unanswered questions, theories, and tasks for each of us. Right now, Aubrey and Renard are focused on the bullshit fake paper, so Felix is nosing around the staff. Most of them are terrified of him, so he can ask about all the dangers without worrying whether they'll respond. Fitz is helping Delores with more self-defense training and I'm supposed to create more clings of the mysterious pictures.

For once, I feel like a genuine part of the team because I can help. My skills and meticulous eye for detail are perfect for creating our workspace. No one threw me a bone; they want me to contribute. It makes my heart sing with happiness.

Of course, some of that is being able to connect with our angel physically. We haven't had Fitz join us yet, but the time is coming soon and my cheetah is practically vibrating with excitement. Being with the two people I cherish most, together, is almost a dream come true.

And Fitz and Dolly are equally eager.

I know because I've caught the hungry look in my tiger's eyes and the shy glances from the bunny. Neither of them has said anything to me, but I can smell them. We're very close and it makes me a little giddy. Maybe I should start another chat with the three of us so we can play? I bet Fitz would love that shit, and I know our girl would enjoy the naughtiness of it.

After all, what kind of future mate would I be if I didn't take care of the people I love?

Blinking, I put my hand over my mouth when that thought pops into my head. It's not as if I'm in danger of spilling the beans—no one but me has this period free. Fuck knows, Fitz and I have said those words plenty of times before, but I don't think he's said them to her and I know I haven't. But as I think about it, I know with all my heart that it's true, just as I knew when I fell for my consort. My angel is part of our forever now, and I can't wait to share her with the tiger I adore.

I let out a deep breath, thinking about how wonderful our night was New Year's Eve, and how supportive the rest of the guys were the next day. They ribbed me a little, which was expected, but no one made me feel silly for being so happy. When I mentioned the way she marked me, we all looked at one another for a moment before agreeing the class with Zhenga was totally necessary.

My face heats as I continue using the markers to list clues on the board. Having to attend her class in person to learn about the fables fated mate shit was embarrassing as hell. Even Fitz was hyper as hell afterward, so we all had a long talk about what happened to us with our bunny rabbit. Felix looked pained—I don't think he ever considered having a proper girlfriend again, much less a mate sent by the Fates. The two ancients exchanged a lot of 'eyebrow talk', which I'm familiar with enough to know it surprised them, too.

Something has been going on with those two since before my angel arrived and now it's spread to her, as well. I don't know what they're hiding or why they took her into their confidence, but even before Ren's date, I could see her gravitating towards them. Not just separately, either—together.

I ponder that for a moment, frowning as I try to imagine the two of them together like Felix and me, but it simply doesn't compute. My thought train must be on the wrong track—whatever they're hiding isn't a relationship. I have no fucking clue what it could be, but that doesn't seem likely when I try to spin it in my head.

My phone buzzes in my pocket, startling me out of my musings. Pulling it out of my pocket, I see a message from the gargoyle of the hour, asking me to meet him at the spot where we found the dead weasel. I have no idea why he'd want to meet there, though I guess we never went into that prey tunnel to check it out. Maybe doing a little Scooby-Doo will help us shake loose some connections between the poison, the dead kid, and the disappearances?

It definitely can't hurt to check it out.

Texting him back to say I'm on my way, I set all my shit aside and take off down the Tower steps. I'd do anything to keep our girl safe and if part of that is crawling through creepy, bug filled prey tunnels, I can take it.

I mean, Dolly uses them all the time, so they can't be that bad, right?

Right?

WRONG.

After I zoom across campus like a maniac, I find a perfectly composed gargoyle leaning against a tree. His expression is amused when I come to a halt in front of him. I run a hand through my tousled hair and shrug. "You said it was important."

"And it is, *mon ami*, but perhaps not a five alarm fire?" Chuckling, he shakes his head and gestures at the spot with the mass of brush covering the door. "It occurred to me we could explore down here and see if we find anything that connects to what Aubrey and Dolly have been researching in the archives."

I nod. "The thought crossed my mind as well. The whole dead body thing was distracting, and we lost track of what might be a source of clues while we dealt with the aftermath."

"Exactly!" he says, clapping me on the back. He bends down, brushing the debris off the door before he gives it a big yank. "Let's get to sleuthing, my friend."

I follow him down the rickety ladder, and when I get to the bottom, I pull my phone out to use as a flashlight. There's probably some way to light the tunnels outside of tech, but I don't see it yet. Not every prey species has excellent night vision, though, so we'll stumble on it, eventually. Squinting, I look at the rough-hewn walls, noticing there are drawings scratched into them. They don't appear to be anything more than old warnings about certain staff or students, so I don't think they mean much.

Except that prey staff feel scared enough that they have to leave one another cave drawings as warnings… which is awful.

Renard is examining a door ahead, so I walk over, tilting my head to look at it. The door doesn't have a handle or knob, instead it has a knocker shaped like an eagle. "This must be a secret storage area for things belonging to Shirdals. Much like some rooms in the Tower, it can only be opened if you know the specific pattern it requires. That will take more research—a fact that will give our librarian a giant woody, I'm sure."

"Do you think it has anything we need in it?" I wrinkle my nose as I look at the construction of the entrance, wondering if we could simply take the damn thing apart.

The gargoyle gives me a knowing look. "People do not put things behind locked doors that are not important, Chess. Whether it applies to our current situation, I can't say. However, it won't be surpassed by a mere drill. This has magic and from the feel, it's ancient magic."

He leans in to sniff the wood, looking very serious as he does so, and I frown. *What is he doing? And if we've all been raised that magic is gone from the shifter world, why do we keep bumping into it?* Everything about this adventure is curious, especially since none of this has been an issue in previous years on campus.

"Interesting," he murmurs. Ren turns and looks at me, his expression puzzled. "When *ma petite* and I were out, I felt a presence that concerned me. The scent of someone long dead and dusted floated through the air from a dark alley, but I did not want to investigate with her along. I thought perhaps I was imagining things because it's impossible for that person to be here, much less alive."

I know for a fact this is more than I've ever heard about the gargoyle's past and I'm afraid to ask who he believes has risen from the grave. I don't think he's ready to share the story yet and from the pained look on his face, it's not a happy tale. "This magic also feels like that?"

"Yes. But again, it may simply be someone with a similar lineage. There are those who are not dead, and this could be their signa-ture. We have no idea how long these tunnels or the doors have been here." Renard pauses and sighs. "I flew around the campus after a hunt, looking for signs of the person, and the familiar scent led me here. Another reason to check it out, *non?*"

I nod, chewing on my lower lip thoughtfully. Does that mean all of this is tied to Ren's past, not my angel? Or are we looking at this as one complete picture with a singular villain when there are many angles at play? That seems like something we should consider, so I tap his shoulder. "I realized we're assuming something connected these things to one another, but what if some things we connect, but others are a result rather than a part of the scheme?"

"Very good question, Chess. It is possible that the murder is not connected to the disappearances, but to something else entirely. It seemed unusual for one student to die while others vanish. If we also consider the different factions warring for control right now, that seems even more plausible."

We head down the corridor further, both of us keeping our eyes sharp for details. If we can find more clues, that might tell us why my friend is picking up traces of someone who should be long dead on our campus. I frown, sniffing a bit when we approach an atrium that has a lingering scent that feels familiar to me. I'm not sure where I've smelled this before—perhaps in town?

"You smell it, too? And you recognize it?" Renard's gaze is curious as he watches me circle the space.

"Yes. I can't place it, though. It's quite faint here and I don't know where I recall it from." I walk up to a pedestal in the middle of the room, studying its construction and the symbols carved into the marble. "I know a few of these—I've seen them on Bloodstone."

His brow furrows, and he bends, moving around the piece. "I see a few I know as well. Let's locate a torch and we will snap more photos for Aubrey."

While he searches the tunnel for its actual lighting system, I look at the murals on the walls. There's a lot of greenery, but when I touch it, the paint feels... off. Reaching behind me to the small of my back, I pull out the utility knife Felix insists we should always carry, despite having claws. Our Raj believes we are weapons, but it never hurts to have an option that won't damage our bodies.

I suppose he was right.

Using it to scrape carefully, I work to remove the lush leaves of a large tree. It's slow going, but Ren seems to have trouble figuring out how to get more light in here, anyway. A growl of triumph echoes in my throat when it reveals what looks to be an ocean illustration.

Why the hell paint over an ocean with trees?

I keep scraping little by little, but I only find more of the same. Huffing, I move to a new section of wall, hoping that will give me a better answer. Ren finally comes in with the torch, looking at me curiously.

"I didn't take you for a vandal, cheetah."

Snorting in response, I shake my head. "There's something under this and, like you said, no one covers shit up if it's not important."

"Then we'll find the equipment to reveal its secrets, Chess. With that knife, you're digging a hole to China with a spoon." His lips curve and he tilts his head. "Let's take our pictures and head back to the Tower. I bet our resident authenticator has some whizbang in his archives to x-ray or black light things."

Turning bright red, I nod. "That's probably a better plan."

"I'm not just here for my looks, Chess."

What's Up Danger?

Delores

If I thought the fall semester was exhausting, it did not prepare me for spring at all. If we thought our teachers were in a frenzy during the winter exams, the new semester is a flurry of time-consuming assignments. Finishing everything requires so much energy, I'm barely able to keep my eyes open.

I swear, they're trying to keep students studying behind closed doors twenty-four-seven.

I don't have a frame of reference, but Cori and Rufus are equally worn out. I spend most weeknights with them, buried in books, while munching on takeout and guzzling caffeine like addicts to stay awake. The theme of our dinner break tonight is all about venting our frustrations about being chained to our rooms like house-elves.

"What's the point of having five fucking boyfriends if I'm not able to, you know, do shit with them regularly?" I grumble, as I dip a crab Rangoon in sauce.

Rufus snorts, smacking his thigh. "Oh, Coco, our girl is growing up! She's complaining about not getting laid enough!"

The polar bear chortles in response, grabbing the container of vegetable lo mein. "Never mind that we're not getting any, either. I barely had time to chat with a hot chica in the library before having to bail with the book I was looking for."

"Oh, shit, Cori. Don't get caught making out with someone there or I'll never hear the end," I groan. "The big guy hates people defiling his library."

"Except you, right, Dollypop?" Rufus gives me a smirk as he picks a meat skewer clean suggestively.

I shake my head, eyes wide. "Even me. No hanky-panky in the library proper is a rule."

"Uh-huh. And what kind of hanky-panky is going on outside the library proper?" Cori snatches the crab from me with a knowing look.

My face flushes. "Not much. I mean, I've had sex with Fitz, Chess, and Rennie. The other two are still more hands-off than I'd like. I guess it takes time, but sometimes I wonder..."

My sex life is taking a massive hit from this academy lockdown.

"Girl, I applaud your demand for more dick. Too much is never enough." I shoot Rufus a look and he shrugs.

"Maybe it's the boredom talking. We're all locked up like handmaidens, and you have at least three guys on active duty, so I have to live vicariously."

"Rufus, you've run through five guys since Valentine's Day. You are not hurting," Cori chides. "I, however, am amid an epic dry spell."

I give her a sympathetic smile. Cori is always sassy sunshine, but she's obviously struggling to find someone to connect with this year. My spunky friend doesn't go into detail about her disappointment, but I wish I could find her someone to share the enormous amount of love she has to give. Unfortunately, I'm a walking disaster, and until I get all of my issues sorted, I feel like I'd be more of a hindrance than a help.

"Coco, we need to get out of this stuffy burg. We're far too fabulous for these plebs. Maybe we can see about the Apex exchange program?" Rufus says, yawning broadly. "That is, if we survive these fucking exams."

"Agreed. We need to get through this shit so we can graduate, and then the world is our oyster." I rise, walking over to the coffeemaker to make another giant tumbler. I won't be able to stay awake if I don't consume more caffeine.

"Make me one, too, Dolly," Cori sighs, as she opens a thick textbook and settles against her bean bag.

We're in for a long night.

THE MORNING OF MY FIRST EXAM, I STRETCH MY LIMBS AND RUB my hand over my face and shift uncomfortably.

When the nurses helped with my birth control, they also gave me the lowdown on how to take care of my various 'sex marks'. Bettina gave me some lotion called arnica to use, which made all of them titter like young girls. I might have to put some on my muscles today despite my pointed lack of hanky panky lately.

Paired with the grit in my eyes and the ache in my bones from days of hunching over laptops and books, my entire body is killing me.

That's not counting the hours of dance and vocal rehearsals...

"Okay, Dolly. You have four more days of this and then it's Spring Break. All you have to do is make it through four more days."

It sounds easy when I say it out loud, but I have no idea how I'm going to survive it.

Stumbling to my closet, I decide I don't give a fuck about the Apex dress code today. If some asswipe wants to give me demerits, more power to them—I'm wearing the PJ pants I stole from Rennie, Chess's worn tee shirt, and Fitz's hoodie.

And my goddamn bunny slippers. Fuck 'em if they can't take a joke.

I grin to myself as I toss my hair into two messy pigtails, grabbing my bag to head for Shifter Basics. Felix won't give a shit if I look like a trash panda, and Zhenga has been less acidic since the guys dropped by class that one time.

It almost feels like she's on my side. How weird is that?

My phone buzzes, and I realize my 'escort' has arrived. I jog down the steps to the front of the Tower, sliding my sunglasses on as I walk up to the impatient looking dragon.

"Here," Aubrey grunts, as he hands me a travel mug that smells like caffeinated heaven. His eyes slide over my attire and he quirks a brow. "That's not your uniform."

I snort, taking the tumbler and sipping it greedily. "I have no fucks left to give. I'm so tired."

His hands clench at his sides as I groan at the delicious drink. "Rennie's rebelliousness is rubbing off on you—I can't decide if that's a good thing or not."

"Don't be a grumpy old man! Being rebellious is fun." I tilt my head for a moment, studying his expression before I get a brilliant idea. "Give me one of your shirts and I'll wear it tomorrow. Is that better?"

The dragon shrugs, walking with me across campus toward the training ring. When we pass the library, he finally responds. "Fine. If you really want to."

Covering my mouth with my free hand, I try to stifle my giggle. "I'll come up after my sex ed exam. Maybe we can have everyone over and order take out? I have to go to bed early because of my dance midterm tomorrow, but I could hang out upstairs for a while. I… miss you guys—all of you."

Aubrey pauses, turning to look at me seriously. "It's very quiet without you. There's entirely too much brooding going on, and it's not only from our poetry-loving emo boy."

I frown, feeling my chest ache a little. I don't enjoy thinking my guys are having issues when I haven't been around to help. But then… no one has mentioned a problem until now, so…

Is it about me? Have they changed their mind about sharing and someone's mad?

"Don't get upset, bite size. We're okay, just lonely without you," he says hurriedly.

He stops walking and pulls me into a tight hug. I let out a sigh of relief. This physical affection is more Rennie's style, but I've been deprived lately, so if my cranky librarian wants to give me a cuddle, I'm here for it.

"Thank you. I really needed that." I lift my head, looking up at him. "I don't enjoy hearing you guys are upset, and I hate that I've been away so often. I promise I'll stay close during break."

Aubrey finally lets go of me, looking a little embarrassed by our public display. "I think everyone would enjoy having you back. Jinx misses you when you're locked up with the polar bear with the allergy."

"Rennie sends me pictures. I know that she's glued to you the most when I'm not available—you can't fool me."

He huffs, turning to continue stomping toward the training grounds, and I laugh. For someone with a fetish for cute things, he sure is touchy about it.

"You're going to be late, snacklet. I doubt the Raj will appreciate that.."

I mean, that's sort of the point, isn't it?

"I'll take my licks if it means I get to spend an extra few minutes with you." I pause for a moment, realizing something I hadn't had time to even consider. "Is the brooding why the chat has gone silent? I didn't think about it before, 'cause I've been buried in work, but everyone talks to me privately."

"We're trying to give you space to work, of course. But also, we've been assembling our pieces and trying to figure out how they connect while you're busy." Stopping again, he rubs the back of his head as he sighs. "Felix is worried more kids will go missing during the break. He and Fitz are trying to identify ones a bad guy would find appealing."

This time, I shrug and kick a rock across the grass. His statement worries me because I know Rufus and Cori have plans for me to hit the big city with them over the break. The guys are going to fucking lose it if they think I could disappear when I go out. "Truth for a truth? My friends want me to go to some events over break."

"Fuck," he mutters. "Felix is going to go ballistic. What kind of 'events' are we talking about?"

Sighing, I give him a crooked grin. "A festival concert for a couple of days."

"Dionysis' flask, nibblet! Could you have picked a worse idea?" He shakes his head, holding his hand out. "Do you have any idea how hard it will be to manage Fitz at a fucking festival, much less keep you safe?"

Taking it, I ponder for a second. "I figured that would be part of the fun."

MY second exam went late, my phone is dead, and I feel ready to drop. Consistent lack of sleep for the past two weeks is catching up with me, and I still have three more days of this shit. But I promised Aubrey I'd take a study break, and what kind of girlfriend would I be if I didn't stick to my word?

I trudge up the stairs of the Tower, furrowing my brow when I find no one home. Grabbing a soda from the fridge, I go down a couple of levels to Rennie's room.

At least I know where to find Jinx.

When I open the door, the kitten comes bounding out, and I smile and nuzzle her soft fur. Her little mews make my heart feel squishy, but I'm too damn exhausted to give her a proper petting. I look at her with an apologetic smile.

"Sorry, baby. I need to lie down. Hopefully, you'll be okay with that."

I walk into the gargoyle's bedroom, dropping my bag on the floor. Keeping Jinx curled in the crook of my arm, I walk over to his nest and flop into the huge recessed pile of blankets and pillows with a grateful moan. Every time I get to curl up in this giant pile, it feels like I'm lounging on a cloud and I love it.

I think I'll just lie here until the guys get home...

LOUD shouting wakes me, and Jinx scrambles off the bed as I struggle to sit up. My heart pounds and I tilt my head, trying to make out what's going on upstairs through the thick ceiling.

Oh, shit. I totally left my last exam without my escort.

Quickly rolling to my feet, I scurry out the door to the stairs, feeling terrible that I let my phone run out of battery without sending a message to the group chat. My last exam was sex ed, but I think it was supposed to be Rufus or Cori meeting me after class… although, it could have been Felix… *Shit, I don't know anymore.* An apology is ready on my lips, but half-way up, I pause, realizing the problem is something else entirely.

"I don't know how they got it up here without anyone seeing them, but a dead body on the balcony is unacceptable!"

At the word 'dead body', I leap up the remaining stairs and charge into the room. "There's a dead body up here? How did I miss that? I've been alone here for a while…"

Five sets of eyes turn to look at me, and this time, their gazes are full of fear.

Sabotage

Felix

Felix

"Henrietta, this shit is unacceptable!"

The diminutive avian shifter shrinks behind her desk in terror, but I don't care. Her handling of the mess on campus this year has been subpar at best and downright criminal at worst. She's molting feathers everywhere as she tries to control her flickering shift. I growl again, knowing we won't be able to get her to see reason if her animal is this panicked.

"What Felix is trying to convey," Aubrey begins, pausing when a hawk appears. The headmistress zooms around until she hits the glass of her window and shifts back while sliding down the wall. Our fiery friend sucks in a calming breath and tries again. "We have several problems that affect students and staff negatively. You must take action before Apex becomes a laughingstock."

I see where he's going—get her to worry about the academy as she'll fight for that so she isn't ousted.

Renard pushes off the wall, walking over to help the hawk up and into her chair. "I suggest we start with the most expedient matter,

Henny. This plagiarism claim stinks like day old fish on the Captain's dock."

"It's fucking bullshit. You didn't ask anyone to check it out before you sent that letter," Fitz snarls as he prowls to the desk and puts his hands on it to get in her face. "The florist and the briquette over there checked four separate plagiarism checkers—even human ones. I dug out a tree's worth of posts, referencing the scheme on the Apex boards. You let those bitchy twats and Professor Limp Dick snow you."

Our supposed boss looks at each of us for confirmation and sees how serious we are. She absolutely fucked up and even though we gave her time to figure it out, she ignored the signs. Now she's going to have to reverse the decision, apologize, and have Fitz wipe the boards. The students will be furious and you can bet your ass he's going to plant shit to keep better track of the bullies. Henny will regret cowing before the pack of slavering morons before this is over; my twin will accept nothing less than justice.

"I-I can fix this," she squawks as she looks over the proof Aubrey compiled. "Of course Miss Drew won't be expelled, but I don't know if we can do everything the plan you submitted suggests. The students have rights and…"

I'm about to open my mouth when Chess speaks, his eyes amber with the glow of his cheetah. "Henrietta, I had the pleasure of meeting the woman who gave birth to Miss Drew on New Year's Eve. While I'm a Khan and her viciousness doesn't concern me, do you wish to be on Lucille Drew's bad side? If you don't allow us to erase this incident from the records, it will reflect badly on their family name, and I'm sure Dolly will have to inform her mother."

Ho-leeey shit. Fucking the princess has made our meek sibling a secret bad ass.

Fitz beams like a proud parent and walks over to kiss the hell out of his consort. He doesn't give a single fuck. We're in a business meeting with our boss, but my twin showed his love with zero fear of judgment. I'm not sure how he turned out the way he did with our upbringing, but I'm a little jealous right now. He's certifiable, but somehow more emotionally healthy than any of us.

The cheetah beams like he's basking in the sun before he turns back to Henny. "What do you say?"

"No, no, Professor Khan. Informing Madame Lucille is unnecessary. I will need to have a conversation with Professor Abel about being more discerning when taking the word of one student against another. His intentions were good, I'm sure, but he failed to confirm the accusation before bringing it to me. That's not acceptable, and I will address it firmly."

The dragon snorts, blowing smoke rings across the room. "Somehow, I doubt that. However, if you agree to our terms, this incident can be kept between us."

Cutting my gaze to her, I stalk closer, letting the alpha pred out for a moment. "Agreed, but you will also get these nasty little bitches under control. I don't care how you do it, Henrietta Shirdal, but the dirty tricks like piss-filled dorm rooms, newspaper articles, and faked plagiarism *stop now*. If it doesn't, I promise you will also face the wrath of the Khan ambush."

"Truth," Fitz sing-songs. "Dear old Dad doesn't love Felix, but he'll be livid that someone blatantly disobeyed a directive to appease measly Council assholes."

Chess looks thoughtful before he adds, "Insubordination is a *death sentence* on Bloodstone."

That has the poor hawk shifter molting like crazy despite not being fully shifted. I have no idea what the hell her heritage is—not fully Shirdal for certain, which explains a lot—but she's damn near having a panic attack. I look at Renard, hoping he has enough control to discuss the rest of our requests with Henny before she passes out.

The gargoyle winks and walks over to pour her a glass of water from the pitcher on the sideboard. "Calm down, Henny. The tigers are only stating what could happen, not what is happening. Dramatics seem to be necessary in order for you to take us seriously this year."

His words make her hawk settle slightly, and the headmistress plops down into her chair to catch her breath. "Yes, of course. I deal with many demanding individuals and this isn't unusual. My… issues seem to be worse today than normal. The pressure from all the unrest is making me very high-strung."

How the hell can she tell the difference?

"We have other concerns," Renard says calmly. "You are aware we found another dead student in my private living space last week. Most of the students have left campus for break, outside of a few, so we are working to find the security breach."

"Finding another student harmed is terrible for the school. At least with disappearances, they occur off campus. We can't be blamed," Henrietta says as she fiddles with folders on her desk nervously.

That's what she's worried about? Bast's furry tail, that damn kid is dead!

"I doubt the parents see it that way, but the breach did not occur with my security. At least, not from an entry and exit standpoint." Ren looks at her, then at us, and sighs. "There are clearly outside forces getting on to campus. They have either found a weak point in the school perimeter or they are using magic. The body appeared at the top of my Tower with no record of any untoward activity on my system, Henrietta."

"Magic? That's a fairytale, Monsieur Laveaux. Shifter societies don't have magic anymore," Henny scoffs. "They must have gained access another way. Technology is fallible."

Aubrey arches a brow. "It is, especially with lax users, as we have on campus. However, between his tech and the band of prey at his command, I believe that did not happen this time."

Her face gets red and I push the water glass toward the flighty bird. "Breathe, Shirdal. We want permission to speak to the school security department, access to key logs, and every map they have of campus. The rest Fitz will get for us from older city archives."

"That.. doesn't sound like too much to ask." She finally settles, turning to her computer and opening her email to comply. "What else do you need?"

"An email to the National Library so I can research the poison from last spring more thoroughly," Aubrey adds. "A list of the students and families who left for spring break to verify arrivals at their homes via social media. And we need to know *immediately* if anyone does not return on time."

Nodding, our boss continues working as we talk. She almost looks relieved and I wonder if taking this on will put us in the line of fire instead of her. "Henrietta, you *cannot* tell the Council we are investigating. They are too powerful and if a member is involved, they will scramble to cover it up. More people could die."

Her face goes white this time. "But what will I tell them about progress?"

"Tell them they should send the Sibbies in," Fitz says with a snort. "It's what should have happened from the first corpse. Don't be dense."

"Madame Lucille was very adamant we avoid that at all costs."

"I'll bet she was," Chess mutters. "She's probably butt cheek implant deep in this fucking nightmare."

His meetings with our princess' mother definitely went poorly and I'm a little chuffed. He hasn't discussed it with us yet, just mentioned they were accosted at the restaurant and he handled it. I give him a sharp look, letting him know I want information after we finish with Henny.

"This is only the beginning of trouble here," Renard says as looks out the window. "I can feel it in my bones. We have not found a motive for any of the terrible things going on except for the childish heirs' pranks. The deaths and missing students are actions of a far more patient, calculating enemy—or enemies."

That statement hangs in the air for a moment, and we all stay silent as we consider it. It doesn't bode well for the princess, nor for any other student.

"Let's take this one step at a time, Rennie," Aubrey says as he rises from his chair. "Make sure we have everything we need before nightfall, Henrietta. We may be the only ones who care enough to save your chickenshit hide from what's coming."

On that churlish note, we leave the spare Shirdal heir quaking in her chair as we head home.

I'm Good

Felix

"This is a terrible idea," I mutter. "How did she convince all four of you perfectly intelligent shifters to take her and two of her friends to a fucking outdoor festival?"

My twin rolls his eyes, bouncing around the living room of the townhouse. "Because it's Spring Break, duh! Baby Girl wants to have fun like a normal girl and fuck if I'm going to deny her."

Chess shrugs, giving me an apologetic smile. "Sorry to overrule you, Felix, but Fitz is right. Campus is no safer than this place with bodies dropping. Dolly might as well have some fun before school starts up again."

Rubbing my hand over my face, I growl softly. While they have a point, I'm not sure the extra work on self-defense she's been doing with my twin is enough to feel secure. The annual Shifter Fantasy Festival in Cambridge draws a crowd from all over the country; I'm not comfortable having that many unknowns around the princess. The five of us are formidable opponents—if we can get to her fast enough. Knowing our girl, she'll make that a challenge every second we're there.

Besides, who the hell wants to camp out on the dirty fairground rather than sleep on Egyptian cotton?

"Don't act like a tiger caught by the toe, bro," Fitz says as he stuffs shit into a duffel. "Poetrypants even bought some sort of fancy glamping tent or some shit. He says we're partying in style to make the spicy lizard happy. This shit is his jam, you know."

My head turns to give my brother a look of complete bafflement. "What in the actual goddamn fuck is glamping?"

The asshole just starts howling with laughter, slapping his knee as he snickers. Chess is no more helpful because he's smirking like a dick, too.

I'm going to hate this shit; I just know it.

Maybe it's time for that spanking I keep threatening.

"OH, THEY'RE HERE!"

My eyes widen to giant saucers as a Mystery Machine looking fucking van decorated like a moving disco ball comes roaring up the drive to Apex. When it squeals to a stop in front of the enormous piles of crap everyone seems to be determined to bring, I have to pick my jaw up off of the ground. The princess claps her hands and bounces, which is all Chess, Ren, and Fitz need because they're whipped as hell.

A head full of rainbow colored curls pops out of the passenger window. "Girl, it's been too long!"

Why are teens so dramatic? They've only been gone for four damn days.

Aubrey looks skeptical of the van, but he's been all in on this shit because no one would go to these nightmare fuel events before the princess. He loads bag after bag of shit into the back of the honey badger's Magical Mystery Tour Van with a big grin. If I didn't know better, I'd think he was getting off on this.

Everyone I know has lost their ever-loving mind and I'm the only sane tiger in the asylum.

"I'm so excited! Ru-Ru, thanks for taking us all in your van. I didn't know you kept a car off-site," the princess says as she hops into the van with a grin.

The punk rocker gives her a smirk full of innuendo. "I don't share the Love Machine with just anyone, Queen D. But since your harem of hunks bought all the fab camping shit I suggested, I'm making my contribution."

'Love Machine?' Fucking hell.

I look around as I climb into the third row, hoping I'm not sitting anywhere that's been sprayed with closeted jock spooge. Aubrey and Ren huff laughs as they join me, letting Chess and Fitz flank our girl in the first row.

"Oh, don't worry your pretty face, Your Majesty," the cheerful polar bear says as she snickers. "I made sure we got this rolling mattress detailed before today. I'm not eager to stew in Ru-Ru's conquest juices, either."

Huffing, I roll my eyes at her. "I'll be fine for the next few days."

She and the badger laugh, making Dolly turn around and look at me with bright blue eyes I could drown in. "Thank you for coming. I know you've been reluctant for a bajillion good reasons, but I'm really looking forward to having fun with all the people I care about."

Her sincerity melts the crankiness right out of me and I take her hand, lifting it to my lips. "You're welcome, Princess."

I'm rewarded with a bright pink flush and three groans. When I arch a brow, my twin just smirks at me like an asshole. Leaning forward, I put him in a headlock and give him a noogie regardless of his howls of protest.

Take that, you little shit.

"Okayyyy, adults acting like children! Buckle up and keep your hands and arms inside the ride. We're off," Rufus says from the front. "ETA one hour and twenty minutes, followed by camp setup. I'm your tour guide for this lovely journey into EDM festivals, so sit down and behave."

Freya, save me. The horny badger is in charge.

Fuck my life.

After I helped Fitz set up the family sized monstrosity they picked out, I claimed a chair on the porch of our luxurious setup. Apparently, that sneaky French asshole had this collection of amenities delivered before we arrived. A group of sword swinging raccoons were here guarding it and summarily hopped in an Uber once we got settled.

Sipping my ice cold beer, I look at the other shifters running around like human hippies with yurts and tiny sport tents. Aubrey walks out to join me, sitting down in the extra large sized rocker on the other end of the deck. He has a scotch in what looks to be a very convincing plastic rocks glass. I salute him as my body relaxes.

"Our girl is in her friends' tent getting ready?" I ask as he sighs and watches the surrounding crowds with a tiny grin.

"Yes. She left outfits for each of us—I'm concerned she believes us to be her private Ken dolls."

The thought makes me snort, almost spitting my beer out. "Damn, I needed that, lizard. Good on you."

He grins and shrugs. "I have always wanted to attend something like this. Ren will always follow and the other two appreciate chaos in a way you do not. Snacklet wants us all to have a good time, so improving your mood is a priority, Raj."

"That's why we're so fancy, huh?"

The gargoyle saunters up, draping himself in the armchair next to Aubrey like he's part feline. "Oh, we're not accustomed to outdoor lives, either. But it's good to be the kings, *non?*"

I chuckle, shaking my head. "Any idea how we're keeping everyone safe in this giant, drugged up clusterfuck?"

They blink, tilting their heads at me eerily similarly. Finally, Aubrey speaks. "We're alpha tier, apex preds. Scent mark her and only the stupidest motherfuckers on the planet will even approach."

Well, shit. I suppose that's true for any horny college kid or random cradle robber.

"What about those dumb enough to intrude?" I ask, arching a brow.

"Fitz will kill them. I doubt we'd have to lift a finger," Chess says as he walks out. "Any of us could, but his ADHD is going to be off the charts once that music and light show starts."

The tiger in question comes running out of the crowd in front of us, and my jaw drops. He's drinking some weird pink concoction in a fishbowl with flashing lights and fruit and various shit sticking out of it. They adorned his limbs in enough glow bands to make him look like a 'My Little Pony'. Then someone painted his face and chest in neon paints around the weird strapped harness he's wearing instead of a shirt. The psychedelic shorts he's wearing are barely there and the look in his eyes is just as crazed as the pattern on his pants.

Turning my head slowly to look at my friends, I mutter, "Who let him bring pred-stasy?"

"No one, big bro! I'm making friends everywhere I go. Look at this baller fucking drink! It tastes like magical unicorns, like my baby girl!"

I can feel the hyperactivity vibrating off of him.

Holy Mother of eight-legged horses, this is a red level emergency.

Before I can tell the others, I see our young counterparts exiting the other tent. They dressed the bear in straps and tutus with high boots and sparkles. Her badger friend is wearing some sort of electric cowboy contraption that leaves way less to the imagination than I'm comfortable with. But the silence I can't seem to surmount is for our princess as she strides over.

Delores is barely covered, and it makes my tiger snarl possessively inside of me. Her outfit consists of a pink, shimmering two piece bikini with pastel rainbow flowers adorning the cups. Her bunny tail is out and under it, a matching light rainbow train of sparkling tulle trails to her feet. Holographic platform boots that meet pink thigh harnesses with bunny shaped rings adorn her legs. To top it off, she's sporting adorable ponytails, her bunny ears, and matching day-glo rabbit makeup.

She's a bunny shaped, glow-in-the-dark, fantasy lovers' wet dream.

"Holy fuck," Aubrey says in a reverent whisper.

Fitz turns and runs over to her with a whoop. "Baby Girl, you got Saucy McStuffyshirt to say 'fuck'! It's a festival miracle!"

"Fitzy, maybe tone down all the yelling? I feel like we're in a cheerleading movie," Chess says as he walks over to them. He leans in and pecks the princess on the cheek. "You look sexy as hell, Angel."

Her face lights up as she basks in the attention of my twin and his consort before she sashays over to the rest of us. Doing a small twirl, she looks at the ancients and me. "Is Fitz right? Do I look okay?"

Renard uncurls his body, stalking over to her before leaning in to whisper something in her ear. Our girl turns bright pink, smacking him lightly, and he laughs darkly. "Keep that in mind, *ma petite*."

I wait as she walks over to Aubrey, who seems to have lost his ability to speak entirely. Finally, she comes over to me and I tug her into my lap. "You're playing a very dangerous game, Princess. That's less clothing than you wear in the lake for class."

One of her ears wiggles at me and she shrugs. "I'm no one's victim, Felix—not anymore."

Arching a brow, I cup her cheek with my hand, pride shimmering in my eyes. "That's right, Princess. You're learning to take care of yourself and if that fails, you have all of us behind you."

"Thank you, Sir," she murmurs with a playful grin and I groan.

Of fucking course she did.

Popping off my lap, she bounces over to her friends, gesturing at everyone but my twin. "Now all of you get yourselves together before it gets dark. Come on, Fitz… join us while they get ready."

I watch my hyper, drunken, likely high brother take our girl's hand as they follow the bear and the badger into a writhing crowd of people.

"Fuck, we're whipped."

Chess shrugs and continues watching them leave. "I can't find it in me to care, Raj."

Pondering the outfit Dolly is wearing, I pause before I reply. "Truth, brother."

Seize the Day

Delores

Delores

Delores

"From the top!"

I give the honey badger an incredulous look as I pant, shifting from foot to foot while I stretch my calves. This rehearsal is one of the most intense workouts I've had in a long time.

Sure, we all danced for two days straight at the rave, but we were floating on clouds of Pink Flamingo Fishbowls and lusty predstasy. Or, Fitz was, because I'm not ready to try more than the alcoholic enhancements, no matter how many of my guys are there to back me up. Those three days were the most carefree I've felt in my entire life, and now I'm back at this damn school.

Dancing in black lights is much sexier than dodging bullies and letting my bestie torture every muscle in my body for hours on end. The level of regret I feel for revealing my acrobatic ability is bone deep at this point. I've done so many flips and handsprings since this morning that I may have scrambled my brains.

Rufus is a tinpot dictator with directing, and someone I'm currently sleeping with gave him control of the entire show.

"Ru-Ru, we need to take a break. I can't run tricks twenty times in a row; I'm going to pass out." I pair my statement with a pleading look, noting the other dancers and cast look ragged as well.

His face screws up, but Cori quickly intercedes. "This is going to be the best number the talent show has ever seen, but not if someone gets hurt while we rehearse."

That seems to register.

"Fine! Take ten, but make sure you're reviewing the counts. The leopards are all late at the beginning of the newspaper section. It's hold… 1,2,3,4… jump on 5,6… open 7,8! That's what rips the paper and starts the hardest section of the dance break. It has to be right!"

Walking over to him on my toes as I work the cramps out of my arches, I give my friend a stern look. "It's even more important that they pick up the fucking papers and throw them. If I hit one of those while I'm tumbling, I'll be lucky if I don't rocket off the stage."

Cori snorts. "I thought you were going to kick that gator's ass when she stepped into your coupé-jeté."

"We're lucky Dolly got Professor Sarabhai to extend extra credit to the dance students, or we wouldn't have enough people to do this performance justice," Rufus grumbles as he drops to a crouch with his scribbled notes.

Cori and I exchange a look. She's glowing like a rainbow goddess while I look like a pastel rat, but her part isn't nearly as active as mine. There were only two dancers who could tumble willing to work with us. The others are strictly *#TeamHeathers*, and I refuse to risk someone tripping me on purpose. My punk rock friend was determined to direct one of the hardest dance scenes from Broadway, so I'm covering a lot of the harder dance and gymnastics moves. It's exhausting and I have to rest for a while.

But it can't hurt to get in more cardio when there's a goddamn sociopath loose, right?

The polar bear plops onto the boards, and I follow her, wincing when my ass hits the ground. My muscles are screaming like they were by the end of the Festival. I may have misjudged how sore I am, and I'll be lucky to get up when we start up again. Rufus arches his brow, tilting his head like he's caught the scent of a tasty treat. Ducking my head to avoid his sharp gaze, I subtly shift my weight until I'm comfortable.

"Why, Dollypop, is there something wrong?" he coos. His grin is almost feral, and I realize I've triggered the one thing that will distract my friend from his tyrannical reign in the director's chair —sex.

More specifically, gossiping about sex.

"No," I reply, as I lean back on my arms to relieve the pressure on my achy backside. I try to keep my expression neutral, but I'm not sure it will work. He's going to know and I might die on the spot.

Looking between the two of us with her colorful curls bouncing, Cori frowns. "What am I missing, guys?"

His smirk deepens as he watches me squirm, but eventually, Rufus turns to the bear. "I'm calling bullshit on our little bunny. Either she's gotten very adventurous with her... back door or someone's been getting naughty with a paddle. Which is it, Dollybear?" I open my mouth to deny it, but he shakes his head. "Don't even try it; I've been around the trailer park long enough to recognize the signs, girl."

Fuck. I should have known I wouldn't be able to hide this from them.

A little voice in my head tells me I shouldn't be hiding it from my friends anyway, and I bite my lip. I'm still learning to share things, and though I'm not as embarrassed as I used to be, this was a novel experience. I don't want to look foolish, because for all I know, I did something wrong. However, if Cori and Rufus can talk me through it, maybe I can make it even hotter next time.

If there is a next time…

My ass throbs again, and I wiggle until I find a new position to ease the ache. "Um. I… no… the second thing."

Way to look like a hopeless newb, Dolly.

"Ohhhhh," Cori breathes. "That explains a lot, actually."

"Like what?" I wrinkle my nose, feeling a flush creep up my chest. I know they can see it in my skimpy dance clothes and it makes me feel even more ridiculous.

Rufus barks a laugh. "We're not judging you, babe. There's no shame in the game. If you both enjoy it, why not indulge? I sure as fuck do." He pauses and looks at Cori before turning back to me. "I'm only concerned you didn't get taken care of, and that's why you're squirming like a whore in church."

"You're going to need an ice pack. It will still help, even if it wasn't done right away. Let me send the stage manager after one," Cori says as she rolls to her feet. "Patrice!"

Nervousness floods my veins as I watch her stalk to the otter shifter, her hands gesticulating wildly as she gives her instructions. Rufus is observing me as he taps on his phone, and it's making me worry about my obvious lack of knowledge in this arena. He says they aren't judging me, but they look more frustrated than they're letting on. Every time I let go of my fears and get wild, I do something wrong and tick people off.

Maybe I'm cursed.

When she rejoins us, Cori reaches over and takes my hand. "Okay. Now that's settled, we need to tell you what else you should do after you ice it."

"Already on the Amazon, Coco. Medical ass lotion, arnica, and aloe are on the way." He clicks his screen off before addressing me. "Apply the lotion first after you shower. Once it has some time to sink in, you can use the arnica for bruises. The aloe is in case you do something more 'slappy' than 'thuddy' later on. It'll help with redness versus bruises."

I blink at his unusually serious tone, but I nod. "That's all after the ice?"

Cori squeezes my hand and grins. "Look, Dolly, we're all shifters. Sex activates the primal—the animals inside of us—and we all experiment with shit. They made our bodies take pain differently, and for some people, impact play is extremely pleasurable. You will not weird Rufus and me out by getting kinky with one or more of your guys."

"Fuck knows. They've all been around long enough to develop a catalog of kinks and shit," Rufus adds. "Who knows? Maybe you'll end up teaching us something."

"Teach you guys things?" I shake my head, not believing that for a second. "What in the hell could I teach you?"

"Girl, you've got all the drool-worthy dirties to play with," Rufus grins. "Tails, twins, older guys, wings, fangs, claws… and that's before we get to your fluffy little tail."

"Ooh!" Cori claps her hands. "I bet they like to chase. Do they chase you, Dolly?"

Panic grips me as I'm flooded with emotions surrounding my experiences with my men. My skin heats—both from arousal and embarrassment—and my friends look at one another and high-five with hoots of laughter.

"They totally do, Coco. Look at her face. The big bad boys like to hunt the pretty bunny."

"Rufus!" I hiss. He's talking at max volume, and Patrice is approaching with a variety of ice packs. Her expression changed the moment he said 'hunt' and if she runs her mouth, I'll be dealing with another bullshit slut-shaming media campaign.

"What?" he bats his lashes at me. When Patrice clears her throat behind him, he whips his head around to glare. "Gods, Patrice. Make some noise when you sneak up on people."

Cori takes the ice packs from her with an apologetic 'thank you', but she blessedly waits until the aquatic shifter is gone before handing it to me. "Sit on this while Rufus and I let the others know we're extending the lunch break. You need to sit on this for a few minutes before you get up and flip all over the place again."

I nod, positioning the ice gingerly. It's cold as hell, but the soft exterior of the gel pack she chose helps. "The floor is killing me. We need to get someone to make mats. Speaking of which, I still think we need to ask Chess if the set design students can help for their exams. Our number is more complex than we planned, and we're going to need so much time to get the choreography right."

"Even if the three of us are the only ones singing," Cori grouses. "I can't believe Professora Balena refused to offer extra credit to the vocal majors because 'only opera is true music'. Musicals are life."

The honey badger rolls his eyes, but he finally nods. "I hate giving up creative control, but you might be right, Dollypop. Spanks for the input."

My face flames and I kick a foot out at him, catching him in the knee. "Stahhhhp." He and Cori chortle like thirteen-year-old boys, and I huff in irritation.

"Seriously, Dolly. We really are here for you. I know you're taking that sex ed class with Zhenga, but from what I hear, it's taught from a data perspective. Ru-Ru and I can share personal experience," Cori says softly.

"Tips and tricks about vaginas and dicks; that's our superpower!"

Rubbing my hand over my face, I sigh in resignation. "I'm never living this down, am I? You two are gonna torture me about my sex life until the day I die."

"You're stuck with us forever," they say in unison.

Looking at their cheesy grins, I can't help thinking about how lucky it was that I poked my head into the theater last spring. I wouldn't have survived this year without them, and even when I'm struggling with my past trauma, they're patient and kind. Rufus and Cori are my 'ride or dies', and I wouldn't trade them for anything.

"You realize I'm a magnet for trouble, and people are always trying to kill me, right?" I say with a fond smile.

Rufus snorts as he pulls his phone out. "Hell, Dollybear, I have entire branches of my family tree trying to kill me. I call that a Tuesday. Your haters are cubs' play in comparison."

"I don't have enemies like Michael Corleone over there, but my orientation pisses a lot of douchebag jocks off. Last year Ru-Ru spent more time beating their asses than their meat."

My eyes widen, and I look at Cori in shock. "I didn't know that. You're always so… confident in who you are."

"Apex has always been shitty, Dolly. You're the target this year, but that's nothing new. The assholes pick new victims every year— though, I'll admit, your ex-BFFs took the bullshit to a whole new level." The polar bear shrugs and winks at me. "I learned to give them the finger and move on."

"Oh, you gave them the finger, all right…"

Cori and I kick him and he yelps. We look at one another and burst into giggles as he pouts and rubs his thighs ruefully.

"Watch the jewels, ladies. I'll have you know my balls are the hit of the Apex soccer team."

I arch a brow at him, feeling playful. "Yeah? I thought that was the sport where you can't use your hands."

"Exactly." He waggles his brows and we all dissolve into laughter again. An alarm buzzes on his watch, and the badger groans.

"Well, ladies, I hate to break up our gossip sesh, but it's time to sneak in a bite before we get back to work."

Cori holds out her hand, and I use it to pull myself to my feet. I'm still sore as hell, but at least the bruise isn't throbbing anymore. Giving her a grateful look, I pick up the ice pack and walk over to my bag to shove it inside.

I have the feeling I'll be needing this again—if I'm lucky.

I Want You

Aubrey

Being back to the normal grind after the amazing time we all had on Spring Break is annoying. I usually love being able to kick morons out of my library, but the time our little family had alone was much more satisfying.

Even Fitz tearing around the rave covered only in glitter and body paint, screaming "I Am The Walrus" was better than this shit.

Rubbing my eyes as I squeeze the sparkly tiger mochi Chess gave me, I chuckle at the memory. Felix was ready to murder his over-stimulated twin, but Rennie reminded him Fitz was tripping balls and would remember little to none of it. That made the future king practically salivate, so he and I chased the high tiger around snapping photos we plan on using later.

Dolly thought the whole thing was hysterical and let the naked cat give her piggyback rides throughout the grounds.

Who would have thought any of that even possible before last spring? Not me.

Being back in session has cut our time with her immensely, as she's swamped in school work and rehearsals for the talent show. It's my turn to take her on a date, but I haven't asked yet. My dragon and

I are in contention with each other more than we have been in centuries, and it's making everything difficult. He wants to claim her now and I can't decide where to have dinner.

My companion suggested that perhaps a solo outing with our girl, in a neutral setting, would help me find the Zen I worked so hard to achieve over the years. I don't believe one date will soothe the roiling turmoil in my gut, but he made his damned 'pleading face' and I finally gave in. The grouchy hermit routine bothers him, especially since he's allowed Dolly into the fortress around his heart. If I can find even a partial truce with my animal, it would make things a lot less stressful at home.

Unlike the others, I don't want to plan a fancy trip or send specific clothing for Delores to wear. It's not that I'm against a big production—in fact, I find the idea very appealing. However, for the first time, I would rather save my natural extravagance. At the moment, my mind and heart are too fraught to do it properly, and Dolly deserves my full attention while showing her how I feel.

Rather, how my dragon feels—which, at the moment, is far too feral for her to witness.

The sound of the archive's airlock opening interrupts my brooding, and I look up from my stacks of books on the table. "Ah. You're awake."

"As are you," Renard says, arching his brow. "Might I inquire when the next time you plan on sleeping might be?"

Rolling my eyes, I go back to examining the book that came in for authentication this week. "Don't be dramatic. I sleep fine in the spare room if I'm too tired to remain upright."

"Mmm. I suppose that's why you look like a giant, stubbly wreck, huh?" The gargoyle drops into the chair across from me, watching me through narrowed eyes.

"Pfft," is the only reply he gets as I cross-reference another book for verification.

His heavy sigh is tinged with frustration, and he pauses before speaking again. "Aubrey, for the love of Aed, go get ready for your date with Dolly. Stop being a grumpy old asshole. I've known you fifty times longer than anyone else. If you don't get your horned head out of your ass, you'll be sorry later, *mon ami.*"

Here comes the French; I've got him going now.

The dragon inside of me rumbles to life as the fire in my belly ignites. Rennie's lips curve and his eyes flash electric blue, instinctively responding to the challenge, but he doesn't shift one of his languid limbs—yet. My oldest companion knows I can't allow myself to damage the precious books in my hoard —not again—so he's keeping his own inner beast tightly leashed.

"I don't like being told what to do, Monsieur Laveaux," I snarl.

He's the only one I trust to tangle with my temper this way.

Rennie rolls to his feet gracefully, strolling to the door and pressing his finger on the pad to open it. "I suppose that's why I do it, Lord Draconis." That said, he strides out of the archives, and leaps into the elevator space, climbing up the walls like the theatrical sod he is.

Son of a bitch. Way to ruin a perfectly good brood, Rennie.

AFTER A NAP, A SHOWER, AND A GREAT DEAL OF PLAYFUL SNIPING later, I'm dressed for my trip to town with Dolly. It's a casual outing, so according to my in-house fashion guru, I shouldn't wear a jacket. Fussing with the collar of the light-colored oxford, I take one last glance in the mirror. I'm not vain, but I feel very exposed. It has been a long time since I've done something like this, and I don't want to fuck it up.

"You'll be fine," Renard calls from his cozy spot in the nest. "Stop overthinking it."

As if stopping my brain is an option.

"If you say so," I mutter, and head back into the room. Pulling my phone out, I realize I need to go down and meet our girl. Her friends are dropping her off at the Admin building on their way to work on sets for the talent show. The way Delores lit up when she talked about the piece she's performing was enough to make my heart squeeze. If nothing else, seeing her so happy is gratifying. Before break, she seemed ready to toss in the towel.

"Catch!"

I barely get my hand up in time to snatch the car keys as they come flying towards my face. The gargoyle grins at me, his expression full of faux innocence, and I roll my eyes at him. "Hilarious. I'm headed out now."

Trudging down the steps of the Tower, I consider how much things have changed since Christmas break.

The tone on campus is hushed—as if everyone is waiting for the next student to disappear without a trace. Henny asked the professors to load students up with work to keep them indoors studying, rather than sneaking around for parties and hook-ups. The meeting we had with her after the first day back revealed six more missing students, though none from families influential enough to cause a fuss. Much like the body that appeared on our balcony, despite security measures, not a trace remained of those who didn't return from their homes.

If someone can sneak into Renard's sanctuary to drop a body, is anywhere safe?

I doubt it. Rennie's aversion to technology doesn't stretch to our home. The Tower has a fully equipped alarm system with motion sensors we activate when we're out. After all, the two of us have more valuable artifacts than anyone else at Apex, and neither of us appreciates invasion of privacy. But this motherfucker didn't trip our system—they either climbed the sides or came from above.

Magic may not be the answer, as my lover thinks, but winged shifters could.

Dragons don't take kindly to people invading their homes, especially ones who aim to hurt their treasures.

And Dolly is my treasure, without a doubt.

Shaking my head, I push all of that away as I arrive at the Admin building. Renard's stupidly sleek Aston Martin parked in front— proving he really has the prey staff wrapped around his clawed little finger. I would have preferred we switch this roller skate out for one of his larger vehicles, but he stubbornly refused. That mischievous streak of his is going to be the death of me, especially if he ever gets Dolly to play along.

"Aubrey!"

Turning my head, I see the bunny in question waving as she walks up to me with the badger and polar bear. Her friends look like Sid Vicious and Nicki Minaj as they stroll up with my beaming date. They wear their eccentricity like a badge of honor, which I believe has given Dolly permission to be herself without judgment. I'd thank them, but the punky one is giving me a suspicious glare.

What in the name of Osiris did I do to him?

"Listen up, Prof," he says as they reach the car. "We brought Dollybear here for your little jaunt to town, but she'd better come back unscathed."

The polar bear bobs her curly head, rainbow hair flying as she points an accusatory finger. "Even when it's consensual, you're too old not to know how to take care of our girl. Don't make us hunt you down."

Dolly is turning as pink as the proverbial bunny's nose, and I'm left to gape at the two furious looking students escorting her. Not only are they threatening a professor, but they're serious as a heart attack, and I don't have a clue what they're talking about. I walk around the side of the car and open the door, so the girl in question can get in.

"I applaud your fierce defense of your friend, but I have absolutely no idea what the fuck you're talking about." I pause, letting my dragon slip into my gaze for a moment. The suggestion that we would hurt Delores woke him up, and I have to squeeze the squishy kitty in my pocket to help calm his irritation. "I would never allow harm to come to the nibblet, nor would I let her suffer any ills. Your staunch concern is misplaced, I fear."

Good job, Aubrey. You didn't even roast them alive for their insolence—nice.

Rennie would be proud of my measured, pragmatic approach. I wait for the badger to nod and then look at the colorful bear for her agreement. Once they both give their approval, I round the car and squeeze myself in. It's ridiculously small, and I'm not, so Dolly immediately dissolves into giggles. I scowl at her, even though I'm secretly enjoying the adorable sound of her joy, and peel out of the lot.

The quicker we arrive, the less time I have to spend crammed into this clown car.

"Aubrey! You drive like a maniac," she chides, giving me a stern look.

I arch a brow at her. "Buckle up, bite size. This is going to be a bumpy ride."

"You're telling me...," she mumbles sarcastically.

I don't respond until she complies. "If you're worried about my driving that much, we'll fly next time."

"It's a date."

Which is how I asked her on a second date as our first began.

"HOLY SHIT, I FORGOT—IT'S EASTER!" DOLLY EXCLAIMS AS WE park in the oddly packed lot.

I blink, looking around in shock. They filled the town square with decorations, vendor booths, and a myriad of activities that spill over onto Main Street. Scents waft on the breeze from food trucks, and a vast staging area fills the center of the park, its line extending the length of the path I'd hoped to privately stroll along.

How would I know we were walking into a writhing mass of appetizers and their spawn? I don't pay attention to weird human holidays based on zombie guru stories!

Rubbing the back of my head, I give her a sheepish look. "I didn't realize all of this was going on. If you'd prefer to go somewhere else, we can..."

"No!" Her face is shining with excitement as she watches the crowds. "I want to stay."

What?

"You want to… stay here? With all the… humans and… shifters?" I'm sure my face is a mask of confusion. She knows me, knows things I don't share with anyone but her and Rennie, so wanting to set me loose here is a surprise. Not to mention, despite living at Apex longer than anyone else, I wasn't aware they held events where we mixed with humans at all.

I suppose even I can learn something new.

Dolly claps her hands, her pastel hair bouncing on her bare shoulders. "Aubrey, this is an entire day where everyone is excited to see a bunny. Of course, I want to stay!"

She's so fucking adorable; I'm going to lose my shit.

I finally crack a smile, holding my hand out to her. She's so young and it takes so little to make her happy. Even if this will be like sticking bamboo shoots under my nails, I wouldn't deny her this joy. "Okay, lunchable. We'll walk among the sheep so I can learn what all the fuss is about."

"Yay!" Dolly launches herself across the cramped console, wrapping her arms around my neck and planting a smacking kiss on my lips.

Holding onto her waist, I struggle to keep the dragon at bay. "Who knew that's all it would take for you to initiate contact?"

She sniffs as she pulls away, shrugging a shoulder carelessly. "It wouldn't take much if you'd quit being so cranky all the time."

I know she doesn't fully understand how rare shifters like Rennie and I work with mating—almost no one does—but that's a secret for another time.

"I'm not cranky," I protest, as she leads me to a booth full of ridiculous looking tiny clothing. "I've been working late trying to gather the information you requested, so I'm tired."

Dolly picks up a sparkly purple collar with a bow on it and I realize this is a table of pet clothing, of all things. "This would look adorable on Jinx."

It's almost painful to admit she's right, so I grumble a bit while she loads up a small basket of items and hands it to the prey shifter manning the booth. Her grin only widens when I pay, but she takes the small pink bag and slides it onto her wrist. We walk past a few more booths, and I continue buying all the things she coos and gushes over.

It seems I have as much trouble saying 'no' to her as I do to Renard, and they both know it.

I watch her make her way around the town, noting the symbiotic interactions between the clueless humans and the shifters that live here. The spider shifter selling hammocks can make a fortune on something that costs her nothing but time, and the humans will pay a premium for a 'hand-crafted' item.

There don't seem to be any predators here, which is not surprising—young preds aren't known for control or subtlety.

When we make it to the middle of the square, she gives me an evil smirk, and it makes my eyes narrow in suspicion. I don't know what she's got planned, but it can't be good. No one close to me makes that expression unless they're getting ready to do something they know will piss me off. She tugs on my hand, practically vibrating with mischief as she pulls me over to… a line?

"We're going to get our picture taken with the Easter Bunny!" Dolly squeals as she leans into me and bats her lashes. "I want to frame it and put it in the Tower."

Hell no. Absolutely not. I'll never hear the end.

She must see the refusal brewing in my expression because she amps up the lash-batting and pulls a pout. "Please, Aubrey? Pretty please with sugar on top?"

I shake my head, warring with the part of me that craves cuteness. "No."

The pout gets bigger, and she widens her eyes. "Pretty, pretty please? I'll pop my ears out. Then we can both feel silly."

She's as big a cheater as my companion, and my eyes narrow. If I have to play along, I'm going to make her work for it. "Ears and tail. Plus, you have to do something silly in the photo—to make it fair, of course."

Her nose wrinkles, but she finally nods. "Okay. But I'm gonna stand here in your big hulking shadow while I shift, so no one sees me if I don't get it right."

I snort, moving to block her from the rest of the onlookers. "Go ahead, then."

Dolly clears her throat and squares her shoulders—which is even more adorable, because who does that before they shift? Finally, one fluffy angora bunny ear pops free, followed by another, and she gives me a bright smile. "I'm doing good, right?"

"Yes, you are bite size. But you forgot…"

She giggles and shakes her head, the floppy ears making her even cuter, and I have to squeeze the squishy cat in my pocket until it practically pops. "No, I didn't."

Frowning, I watch her spin, and I'll be damned if her fluffy cottontail isn't poking out the back of her black lace sundress as if they made it for it. My eyes travel up her body until they reach the choker she's wearing; the stone embedded in the locket looks a little familiar…

Motherfucker.

"That dirty rat. He gave you a piece of that damned talisman!"

Her fingers make a zipping motion over her lips, but I can see the smug look in her eyes. I know that's how Renard keeps his clothes from shredding, but he's purposely withheld the magic from me because he knows how much it annoys me. I'm going to make him pay for this betrayal, but for now, I have to get through this sensory overload.

The line moves and we chat as we wait, playing a surface-level version of two truths to pass the time. When we finally get to the stage, the partially shifted bunny bounces up to the human in the lumpy-looking rabbit suit. It's incredibly surreal to see these people queuing to take pictures with a giant fake animal. They'd lose their minds if they realized an actual shifter who turns into the same animal was in their midst.

Humans are the least aware species on the planet—it's an indisputable fact.

"Come on, you stuffy librarian! Get in the picture with me!"

Drat.

I trudge over to awkwardly stand near the weird rabbit man. Dolly rolls her eyes and leans over the costumed idiot to grab my shirt. Stumbling forward, I lean down and only glimpse her wicked grin before she's kissing me. I can vaguely hear the whirr of a lens clicking in the background, but my full and undivided attention is on the silky feel of her plush lips pressed against mine.

And that is how Aubrey ended up buying an overpriced picture of a bunny snacklet kissing a surprised dragon in front of a sweaty human in a fur suit.

MASQUERADE
Delores

"Ugh, take it from the top!" Rufus puts his head in his hands, his shoulders slumped in defeat.

Full tech rehearsals for the talent show have become our daily nightmare. The inability of the various arts disciplines to work as a team makes for constant friction, and Rufus' patience—thin as it is—is ready to snap. I don't blame him—unlike our number, the other acts from the dance and music departments are all solo performances, so every pred is the star in their own head. There are a few tolerable small preds, but most of our tantrums have come from a single source.

The Heathers.

My ex-besties have thrown together a Pred-mart version of the Cell Block Tango from Chicago. It's easily the worst thing I've ever seen, and I'd say that even if they weren't my nemeses. They're trussed up in LaPerla rather than lingerie designed to work on stage. When they're miked and moving, it's a shitshow of nip slips and plumber's cracks. Add to that their complete lack of rhythm, choreography resembling a bad strip tease, and singing so off-key it physically hurts, and you have a hot fucking mess.

I can't decide if this is all on purpose to ruin our show or if they're just this ignorant, but it's making Rufus lose the plot.

"Dollypop, can you please talk to that brainless twit in lighting about her timing? If they disrobe on stage, I'll fail this project and it's a huge chunk of my grade. I know the shifters in the audience won't give a fuck about nudity, but not being able to control my cast will be a black mark on my resume, no matter what."

I take pity on my friend, rising to walk back to the light board to talk to the owl running the spots and cans. She's a nervous little thing, and Rufus has been taking out his frustration with the Heathers on her all afternoon. Her wide eyes settle on me through thick-framed glasses, and I give her an encouraging smile.

"Does this..." I gesture at the blinking lights, switches, and buttons. "... have programming? Like, can you cover our butts by putting something together that you could activate with a push of a button if they screw up and pop a seam? If so, that would help everyone relax a little, I think."

Specifically, a high-strung honey badger on the verge of a mental breakdown.

The tech girl nods quickly, a grateful expression on her face. "Yes, yes! I can't believe I didn't think of that. I can set it to quickly activate and hide… inappropriate stage attire."

I suppose that's one way to put it. Full frontal nudity is another.

"Good. Please set it up, and also work with the sound guy to automate music to play when it cuts their mics. I appreciate it, truly. My friend isn't a bad guy—he's so stressed about his final grade that he's about to pull his hair out." She gives me a nod and a half smile, and I walk back to the row where my two friends are whispering.

When I join them, Cori throws an arm over my shoulders. "Dolly, it would probably be easier at this point just to kill the Heathers. Ru-Ru knows people who could do it."

A laugh bubbles out of me before I can stop it. "When they were trying to kill me, we ignored them, but when they butcher Kander & Ebb, it's time for them to die, huh?"

Rufus harrumphs as he looks at his set list, making scribbled notes in the margins about the various performers. The notes are hard to read and I get the impression that's probably for the best; they may not be kind. It's obvious the other performers didn't spend the past six weeks rehearsing for this show, and to say they are rough would downplay the situation. Cori's exam was based on the costumes for our group, so she's not as worried as he is.

"Excuse me… is anyone paying attention? My lighting is wrong again," Gold whines as she stomps over to the proscenium.

I arch a brow as I look at her, unwilling to even dignify her antics with a response. Gold and the other Heathers' mindless minions scared me when I first arrived because I was alone and had no support. Now that I have Rufus, Cori, and my guys, I can see how pathetic their games are. Their own followers would leave them in a second if they found a better meal ticket, and the power they believe they wield is far less than they assume.

Herr Director gives Gold a scathing look before he scoffs, "If you'd wear actual costumes, you wouldn't have to worry about being unflattering. Since you're determined to wear that…" he pauses and rolls his eyes. "… we don't have a choice."

"My father will—" Pink starts.

Cori whips her head around to glare at her, white fur shimmering over her form. "Look, you smelly trout. I am a good person—I do yoga, avoid red meat, and champion the little guys. But you and your friends are really testing my non-violent philosophy over here."

My gaze cuts to Rufus and he shakes his head. Apparently, we really don't want Cori to lose her whole peaceful warrior thing. If the bloodthirsty honey badger says it's bad, I'm going to assume it's terrible. He walks up behind her and puts a hand on her shoulder as she continues to stare down the plastics, and I mimic his actions on her opposite side.

The newest Heather goes to open her mouth, but Rufus bares his fangs. "Not the time to earn your stripes, McLachlan. Back in line with you." When the blonde slips back in line, he yells, "From the top! We're not allowing this mess on stage if you can't get your shit together."

The house lights go down as the music starts, and I instinctively tense. Cori squeezes my arm, and the tension seeps out of me. Ever since the whole 'body on the balcony' incident, I haven't complained about sticking close to my friends or the guys. Even though I feel like I'm getting better at protecting myself, I learned a harsh lesson about going anywhere without a buddy. There's no reason for my pride to get me killed.

As my eyes adjust to the darkness, I tilt my head and squint at the loge on stage right. My night vision isn't as good as the other preds, but I'm fairly certain there's someone up there. I don't know if they have on a cloak or a hoodie, but shadows obscure their entire form as if they're trying not to draw attention to themselves.

If this is someone's idea of a joke, it's not fucking funny.

Elbowing Cori, I whisper out of the corner of my mouth, "Don't look; don't react. There's some weirdo up on the balcony dressed like a fucking stalker. It could just be a creeper trying to catch a nip slip, but it could also be a psychopath."

Maybe even the campus psychopath...

To her credit, Cori remains calm as she covertly sneaks a peek before mimicking my tight-lipped hiss. "I see them. They don't look big enough to have taken down some victims—I mean, that tiger shark shifter was stacked, D. This idiot is probably one of the Heathers' petty posse trying to Ghostface you on the way out."

"My eyes are better than both of yours, ladies, and I promise that person would have to be venomous to have taken out the shark or the bear over winter break. I mean, unless they're a fucking ninja trained in Batman skills." Rufus' gaze is back on the Heathers as they pranced around the stage like idiots, so he must have seen enough.

I never went to watch them cheer back at Shifter Secondary. Lucille said nothing beyond 'the Pred Games are a waste of time and energy'.

Discreetly sliding my gaze back to the hooded observer, I murmur to my friends carefully. "What if there's more than one person doing all of this? Is that possible?"

"I don't know, Dolly. It would have to be someone who either works or attends the school. I'm not sure multiple strangers could run around the campus without being noticed," Cori replies.

Unless they're not strangers… and they live here.

Holy shit! What if they know about the prey tunnels?

A shiver runs through me. I've been using those tunnels all semester to get around safely—that is until Rennie requested I have a chaperone at all times. I haven't shared my knowledge of these routes with Rufus and Cori because I promised the prey staff that I wouldn't tell any students about them. But if someone has gotten their hands on the secret map app, or if they're prey themselves, they would have full access to all points on campus, from any direction.

This is awful. I have to tell the guys after rehearsal, but I don't know what they can do. We can't seal the tunnels off, because the prey staff need them to get around safely.

I slip one hand into each of my friends' as the realization hits that, little by little, the mysterious killer—or killers—has made it so nowhere on campus is safe. That's fairly impressive at a school full of the biggest, meanest predators on the planet. What kind of person has the skill and reach to do this? It can't simply be some run-of-mill sociopath—the body on the Tower balcony proved that.

Oh, shit! Does the dead kid in our Tower mean the killer has wings? I can't imagine them dragging the damn thing up eight flights of steep stone stairs.

Theories whirl in my head as Rufus focuses on huffing at the Heathers bumbling across the stage. If a potentially dangerous shadowy figure wasn't lurking in the wings, I'd be grateful for the distraction. But right now, all I can think about is who could have placed the corpse on our balcony. The victim was a medium-sized shifter, so smaller avians probably couldn't have achieved it, unless they had help.

That leaves bigger avians. I don't think I've met any climbing shifters here, so that's an unlikely option.

"Rufus!" I squeeze his hand. "Do we have shifters that climb at Apex? Like ones that could climb the Tower."

"Some of the big cats are excellent climbers, but I'm not sure about something as high as the Tower, especially since it's made of stone. If there was enough erosion to create claw holds, maybe, but I doubt it. It's really more likely someone would get in from the stairs or by flying. Why? Are you worried? I assumed your gargoyle has that place locked down."

His question makes me squirm. The guys asked me not to tell anyone—even my friends—that someone breached Renard's defenses. Aubrey was the one who brought me around to keeping the secret. He insisted that if only we knew, someone might reveal themselves by mentioning the body at the Tower. Since the other buildings on campus have been left alone, one slip in phrasing would give us a new lead on the killer.

I don't like keeping things from my friends, but I understand the strategy. It makes me feel like a jerk, though, and once this is over, I'm going to apologize immediately.

"Because I'm thinking about how the creeper watching us up there got in. The doors to the upper levels have codes when the theater isn't open, and we didn't open the balconies for this rehearsal yet."

"That's brilliant, Dolly," Cori whispers. "It could all be connected."

I nod resolutely. "Once the Heathers finally stop, we should break for dinner. I guarantee by the time we get up there, the asshole is gone, but maybe we can find clues to who—or what—it was."

"Like the Scoobies!" Rufus chortles. "Jinkies, Dolly, a clue!"

I roll my eyes and elbow him in the ribs. "Yeah, and most TV shows prove no one gets away without leaving some evidence. It couldn't hurt to snoop around in case they did."

Cori snickers, muttering, "That's it, no more true crime for you. You're not Sherlock Holmes."

That sends us all into giggles, and my tension evaporates again. At least now I have some actionable steps for when rehearsal is over. I'll need to talk to my boyfriends too. If we're going to survive the rest of the semester, we need an offensive plan—traveling in pairs will not cut it. I sigh, turning my attention back to the screeching dogs on stage. I'll have to watch this nonsense until Rufus calls a dinner break.

And that's when the body drops from a rope, bouncing in the air in the middle of the stage like the motherfucking Phantom of the Opera.

Circus
Felix

Surprisingly, Henny has been true to her word for the past two weeks since the break.

The plagiarism thing disappeared with a wishy-washy apology note. Those two-faced bullies snipe at her in class, but no gross or dangerous pranks have popped up while she's been rehearsing. We all take turns escorting her around campus, and she's begrudgingly allowed it. The second dead student and fourteen missing made it an easy sell.

It was like evil was on pause until the end of the year—until last night.

My tiger instincts knew better, but she didn't want us watching the practices, so it didn't spoil the show. The hanging Chad last night proved our princess isn't safe, nor are the rest of the preds who attend this school. We have to amp up investigating this shit now —follow leads to connect the students who disappeared or track down more herbologists about the poison. The living room in the Tower is full of 'mystery' boards, so we've got our hands full tracing every minuscule detail to find a motive.

Unfortunately, I don't think we'll get any further until we find out why this is happening now, and Renard agrees. No matter how we spin all the events on campus, they don't have a common thread except they started once our intrepid bunny arrived. The killer doesn't leave clues, and the gargoyle is still putting out discreet feelers regarding magic in our midst. But the danger is getting worse, and no one will bring in the SBI to get it under control.

I hate being unable to control shit.

Sighing, I fidget in my seat as we sip our illegal drinks in the fancy ass theater the Shirdals built as a monument to themselves. It's easy to forget this talent show horseshit is an annual event because I never attend. Fitz usually suffers through it to support Chess, but he takes his payment in spades afterwards. Our two winged grouches are stuffed into seats as well, and I guarantee those fuckers haven't come to this in the centuries they've been here. We're here to keep our girl safe, so despite the likelihood of this being shitty as hell, we're not going anywhere.

That's some fucking personal growth on all our parts—go team.

I chuckle at my internal joke and Fitz arches a brow at me. "Something funny, broski?"

"Don't call me that," I mutter. "But yes. I was thinking about how much all five of us have changed over the past year—in a good way."

Chess leans over my twin, giving me an amused smile. "Yet you haven't asked Angel out yet and you're the last one, Felix. Aren't you worried she thinks you got coerced into this arrangement? She's slowly gaining more and more confidence, but it seems fragile. The damage done to her in the past isn't fully healed."

Pondering that for a moment, I look at our rag-tag family. Fitz and Chess haven't been with her together—yet—but they're tighter than ever with one another and her. Aubrey and Ren seem to be cagier than normal, but they've found something to share with her as well. And she obviously adores them separately, despite all their ancient shifter quirks. I'm the only one who hasn't taken the opportunity to get to know the princess better in a private setting —and I don't just mean sex.

I'm falling behind because of fear and Khans don't do that—especially rightful kings.

"You're right," I whisper as the lights finally dim. "I'll ask her out after the show."

The dragon looks at me in amusement, shaking his head. "Seems like a good time, tiger. You've got the flowers and everything. Glad you figured out where we were herding you."

Blinking, I look down at the colorful bouquets of exotic flowers Renard assembled from his private garden. "This was a trap?"

"True story, bro. Jalepēno Jackass over there came up with the plan and we all contributed." Fitz frowns as the spotlight hits the stage. "Now, hush, so we can support Chessie and my baby girl."

I gape at him, shocked they shamelessly admitted conspiring against me—even my family! Did I really have my head that far up my ass? Scrubbing my hand over my face as an overture starts, I think about it and realize they're probably right. I'm not just 'taking it slow' with Delores; I'm keeping her at arm's length despite agreeing to this polycule.

That's not fair to either of us, and tonight, I'm going to change it.

Chess' hesitant description of last year's show didn't quite prepare me for the disaster masquerading as talent at this school. Mind, a few students had good singing skills, though not in the arts program, and a couple did a decent job on instruments. But the non-theater arts majors doing scenes or dance numbers with nothing more than rich kid egos have been excruciating.

Like the eyeball scarring bouncing of the princess' enemy squad as they emulate a movie they clearly didn't get the point of. So far they've butchered the music, fucked up basic dance, and are bounding out of their lingerie more than anything else. The fact that I can tell it's so terrible means the tricolored badger directing has to be losing his fucking mind.

My eyes cut to the balcony Fitz and I combed over last night, making sure there wasn't a shadowy presence lurking. Dolly finally admitted it after we grilled her about every second of the rehearsal, but she wasn't happy about it. She's been adamant we can't see her piece until tonight, but the last practice this morning made us all uneasy.

"Don't worry, Felix. I had security check on everyone who entered and close the doors for re-entry. We might have a problem if there's a fire, but otherwise, no creepers should be able to get in," Chess whispers.

"I still believe it should have been postponed after the body dropped." My hands tighten around the program as I look around, trying to scout the audience and ignore the caterwauling on stage. "Henrietta caved to those idiot moms, and it puts everyone at risk."

"Well, not everyone…"

I arch a brow at the cheetah. "How safe are the preds on campus who aren't here, since all the guards are here?"

"Shhh. You two will get us tossed out and I've been waiting to see what my baby girl has spent all her time perfecting," Fitz growls softly. "If I had to sit through this silicone peep show, I want to see our girl in all her glory."

He's not wrong.

"She's coming up soon," Chess murmurs. "I'm grading while I watch, so I have to know."

Letting out a deep breath, I watch the last bit of this never-ending nightmare, practically thanking the gods when it finally ends. There's a smattering of applause and more than a little laughter as the Heathers prance off-stage with smug smiles. My eyes narrow as I watch the new one who claims to have transferred from Bloodstone. Fitz and I know it's a lie; miscreants are sent there for life, not to return with a pardon.

This Mc Lachlan chick is yet another mystery I haven't had time to explore. While her allegiance with the other bullies is annoying, she hasn't proven dangerous—yet. We've got so many enemies and things to figure out on our boards that I've tabled her presence for the moment. When I have the patience to contact my father's assistants, I'll find out who the fuck she is and why she's here.

Besides spying on Fitz and I.

The lights dim again and when the spotlight comes up, the curtains pull back on a set made to look like New York City in the mid-1800s. Chess beams when I give him a thumbs up—I'd recognize his work on the sets anywhere. They dressed all the students in costumes that make them look like newsboys, facing away from us in their knickers, suspenders, caps. I'm pretty sure I see the princess, but without her trademark hair giving it away, the lighting makes it hard.

Then the song starts and I scoot forward in my chair.

Holy leapfrogging Hermes!

I think I can pick out the better dancers as they leap, slide, spin, and stomp over the stage to the forceful music. Fuck if I know much about this shit, but I can tell by the look on the badger's face —they're doing well. As they get closer to the edge of the stage, I can make out her polar bear friend as well. She definitely seems to carry some of the harder singing parts and her dancing is pretty damn good.

At least, I thought so until the princess comes striding out into the middle of the stage. She drops a paper and launches into a spin move that lasts so long people shoot out of their seats to applaud. When the noise dies down, the other players crowd around her playfully. My heart stops when they move away and she's gone.

What the hell, is there a trap…?

"Motherfucker, look at that!" Fitz says, pointing to a corner where our girl is standing cheekily. She winks when we look at her, then does a stupid amount of flips and gymnastics, landing just short of the edge of the stage. The crowd goes nuts again, and she does another run as three other girls join her in the feat. By the end, they've all landed in the middle again, dropped into a painful-looking split that makes my balls ache and the song is ending with a shout.

Aubrey is clapping so hard I think he's going to break his hands and Fitz is literally bouncing on his seat like it's a diving board. I give Chess a shocked look and he shrugs, mouthing, 'Told you so'.

He most certainly did not.

The audience continues going fucking banana pants as the group gets up and takes a bow, looking happy and excited for the praise. Dolly is in the middle, holding hands with her bear friend, her face so bright that it makes my chest ache. I wish everyone could see her shining like this, especially her asshole parents, because they'd definitely see the woman my friends fell for.

After a few minutes, the Broadway crew exits the stage and then returns with the other performers. People are still applauding for the musical performance, but at least the others can bask in the clapping as well. The Heather girls are standing on the back half of the stage. They're glaring daggers at the performers in the newsboy outfits that reveal absolutely nothing, but didn't need to.

Dolly's group had talent and hard work to prop them up, not nip slips and thongs.

Jerking my head at Fitz and the others, I climb over the seats in front of us, pushing my way through the crowd until I reach the stage. Delores comes running up, her eyes full of pride, and she drops to her knees to greet us.

"How did I do, Sir?"

I have to stifle a groan, making my twin snort, but I hand her the flowers Ren brought with a broad smile. "You were amazing, Princess. You stole the show."

"Hell yeah, she did! I want you to do all that crazy bendy shit in bed, baby girl. You've been holding out on me," Fitz says, as he growls at her playfully. "No more hiding freaky-deaky shit."

Her laugh makes me smile even more and I hold my hand out. "Do you have plans for an after-party or would you like to come home and have some takeout with us?"

"That doesn't count as a date!" Renard sing-songs from behind me.

Asshole.

"I've spent weeks with these guys getting this down. Let's order in and climb into the nest for a movie," Dolly says with a smile. "Do I get to pick?"

"Absolutely, angel," Chess says. "You deserve some serious pampering after that."

"Goody!" she shouts as she jumps to her feet and runs over to tell her friends. When she returns, her grin is almost splitting her face. "I hope you're ready to watch Dirty Dancing because nobody puts this bunny in a corner anymore."

Oh, fuck, what have we gotten ourselves into now?

FIGHTER
DELORES

THANKFULLY, THE TALENT SHOW WAS NOT AN ABSOLUTE TRAIN wreck. Cori and I would have had good grades anyway, but Rufus was almost unbearable near the end. The audience loved our song and dance, so I was happy, especially when I got to go home to snuggle with my guys.

It almost overshadowed the shock of Chad's body dangling from the rope in the middle of rehearsal—almost. That's been bothering me ever since. I can't help wondering why the killer dropped a dead body at rehearsal instead of during the actual show. It wasn't the optimal location to get attention and Chad's parents have money, but not enough to turn the tide to a proper investigation.

There were parents, donors, talent scouts, Apex faculty, and Council members at the actual show. You'd think that group would be a better audience for a dramatic statement. It's as if the shadowy figure in the wings was more concerned with scaring the students than the big wigs.

I'm not sure what to make of that.

Is this person hunting me? Are the dead people connected to my presence here at Apex?

That makes little sense, though. I didn't know most of the people who went missing; they were sophomores and upperclassmen. The only ones connected to me were the weasel and Chad. The first barely spoke to me and the second couldn't remember my name after twelve years of school together. Of course, the ominous note the former sent me was odd, but again, I hardly knew him.

I'm determined to figure out what the hell is going on at Apex before someone I care about gets hurt.

Aubrey and I have spent countless hours in his archives, but we haven't figured out where I recognize the damn drawings from. Fitz and Chess are tracking down every scrap of info we can find in various agency records to find a connection between the victims or their families. I even gave them the dossiers Clotilda made for me during the summer, when I was planning revenge. Her research was on the Council families, but I thought maybe it would help connect the dots somehow. Even Rennie is taking off occasionally to meet with people he won't tell any of us about— though it has yielded nothing so far.

We can't get our hands around the reason this started when I arrived or how kidnapping students is related.

In '*A History of the Honorable Academy of Apex Predators*', it mentions the 'Society' can access their powers through a vaguely described list of items. We haven't located any of them yet, but the drawings seem to be linked to their hiding spots. I've asked Ren and Aubrey several times if they recognize any of it, but they always redirect me. I assume there are reasons for their hesitancy, so I haven't pushed it. Our two truths game has allowed us to get to know each other better; but I understand certain subjects are sensitive. I'm not a hundred percent certain I want to push their boundaries that far yet.

Even though it might help us figure this out… before more corpses appear.

I hate that my presence has made everyone unsafe.

Regardless of the brave face I'm putting on, I don't want anyone to get hurt because of me. Solemnly gazing at my bathroom mirror, I wonder if I'm not worth the trouble I've already caused. Lucille would agree with that sentiment—she's told me how little value I have a million times. I know Rufus and Cori care about me, and the guys have opened up in their own ways, but I can't help wondering if I'm more of a burden than a bright spot.

My mother's criticism practically rings in my ears, as I brush my hair and brood.

As if I've summoned her, my phone rings, and I groan. When I see my mother's name on the screen, I press my forehead to the cool glass. I haven't heard from her in weeks, which gave me room to breathe. She'll have something disparaging to say about my performance at the talent show, though she couldn't be bothered to attend. The entire audience loved our performance, but Lucille will never be pleased with anything I do. With a sigh, I press the green button and wait for the snide barb in place of a greeting.

"Delores," she purrs. The sound makes my entire body tense— Lucille is good at toying with her food. "I'm so glad I caught you!"

She says it like I had a choice. If I hadn't answered, she would have sent Bruiser.

"Hello, mother. It's nice to hear from you. What can I do for you today?" It's easier to ask her what she wants as politely as possible at the beginning of her calls. Getting down to business means I don't have to endure as much drunken rambling dotted with random threats.

"Don't be like that, my daughter. I was so pleased to hear about your outstanding performances in the talent show. You made our family look poised and talented, according to my sources."

What the hell?

Suspicion floods my veins at her words. Lucille doesn't give compliments unless she wants something. Praise from my mother costs way more than I'm willing to pay, so I brace myself for what's coming. "I appreciate your kind words, mother. I rarely earn your praise. I am pleased that I represented our family well."

Her laugh is airy; she's transformed into her delightful socialite persona. "Oh. Delores, don't be so dramatic. I only wish for you to secure a husband who can provide for you in the manner to which you were raised. Our family name is respected, as you know. I want to protect it so you can wield its power in the future."

Well, this is new.

Her personality transplant makes me extremely skeptical. The real Lucille has to be laying in wait under the surface somewhere. I don't believe this pile of tripe for a second. She's made it unquestionably clear she didn't want the family name associated with me at all—that I will never take her place on the Council as heir. Whatever she's fishing for must be very important for her to make this much effort.

I'm not concerned about her finding me a husband. I've found my fated mates, and I don't need to worry about her political matchmaking. My hope for a future with them is rooted deep in my heart, and the seed blossoms a little more each day. I'd like to find time for a bit of naked time with the remaining grumpy kings, but that will happen when the time is right.

I believe it in my heart.

It occurs to me I've been ignoring Lucille as she droned on, and I blink in surprise. I never used to tune her out so easily. I was too scared she'd say something important, and I'd be punished for missing it. Shaking my head in amazement, I refocus on her voice, trying to pick up the thread of her conversation.

"...my sources tell me they've seen you in the company of several professors outside of class hours. Paired with news that you were 'claimed' by two Khans, it sounds like I should prepare for wedding bells?"

Wedding bells? Hera help me, what are her spies telling her, and how much do they know?

During her last call, Lucille fished for information about what shifters lived at Apex and how close I was to certain ones—namely Renard and Aubrey. She's never specifically asked about my dating life, except to tell me she'll basically have to sell me off. There's something going on here and I don't know what it is, but I have to be very careful how I approach her.

Lucille is many things, but stupid is not one of them—and she didn't raise a fool, either.

"I don't feel comfortable discussing my love life yet—everything is so new. I have made no commitments that would require a white dress, so don't worry. After everything with Todd, I'm not ready to be serious with any one person."

"Delores, don't make this so antagonistic! I'm your mother, and I want you to be happy," Lucille says, her voice dripping with saccharin sweetness.

Okay, what in the actual fuck is going on?

Lucille never speaks to me like this. She didn't even speak to me like this as a baby—or so I've been told by Mattie. In fact, I've never heard my mother speak to me in anything but acerbic tones with condescending looks that translate over the phone.

What is her game?

"I am happy, and even though we haven't defined our relationships the way you'd prefer, I have met men who treat me well. I've been on a few casual dates so far this semester. There's nothing else to tell, Lucille."

"Hmm" is all the answer I get.

I'm sure she wants the specifics, but until I know what her agenda is, I'm not giving up any details—even if only to lead her astray. She's a crafty old leopard, and can't be trusted. Information is currency to Lucille, and I've watched her use it to her advantage my entire life.

"Why did you call, Lucille? My grades are exemplary, and we're coming up on final exams soon. I'm sure the Administration staff will report back to you, so there's no need to follow up with me directly unless you're unsatisfied."

"Delores Diamond Drew, I am in no mood for your sass today!"

That sounds more like the Lucille I know and tolerate.

"All I want to know, daughter, is if you are happy and if you're spending time with people who are equivalent to your stature. I don't want to hear that you're dating another mangy hyena who will shame our family in the public arena."

Ah, there it is.

She's worried I'm dating someone who is beneath my station, even though it's perilous and by name only. All of my men would fit her criteria and then some, but for their exile—which doesn't matter to me in the slightest. "I hate indulging your elitism, mother, but my dates aren't from the wrong side of the tracks. I know that's probably surprising given my… what do you call it… disability?"

The sparkling laugh echoing over the line again tells me she switched back to the loving mother personality that I know she isn't. "Delores, this is why we fight. You don't know how to take my sense of humor."

Uh-huh.

"You realize Apex has more pressing issues than my sex life, right?" I reply, unable to keep the disgust from my tone. "There are sixteen missing students and a third dead body dropped from the rafters in the middle of my rehearsal. As a Council member, I'd think you'd care far more about dead kids than who I'm having dinner with."

"Of course I am aware, Delores. I'm not living in a cave, nor am I profoundly stupid. Don't insult me," Lucille growls, noticeably not claiming to care. The shift in her tone means she's done with the pretense; now I've questioned her authority, and she's angry.

That makes two of us.

"I wanted to make sure that I was keeping you informed," I purr, matching her fake sweetness, knowing it will rile her more, and not giving a fuck. "The campus is a very dangerous place, and the Council doesn't seem interested in helping us. Staff members have been doing most of the policing. The professors seem to have gone into homework overdrive to keep us locked in our rooms, but what little security there is here falls woefully short."

"This conversation has taken a turn, Delores, and I'm not interested in hearing you whine. It's time you learned to defend yourself, like a true predator, and remember that even the people closest to you may be a threat. You've been a pampered heir for far too long, and this little 'serial killer' issue is the perfect thing to force you to sharpen your instincts and take action. We can't have you ending up dead outside the Society tunnels like a lesser predator."

She wants me to go up against a serial killer? No wonder I'm so fucked in the head.

Sucking in a deep breath, I rein in my temper. It's not like it's a surprise that Lucille truly doesn't give a fuck if any of us die, as long as the school—and the families who fund it—look good. If I want to get her off the phone, I need to play nice. "I apologize, Lucille. I didn't intend to be disrespectful."

A delicate sniff, followed by a sigh, tells me I appeased her. "I only called you for a status report on your life, Delores, but it seems like you've developed an attitude problem. I've never heard you talk to me in this manner, and I don't appreciate it."

Fuck, now what am I going to say?

For unknown reasons, I decide to be honest. "I'm growing up, Lucille, and a lot has changed about me this year. I'm not the person I was when I came to Apex… under a death sentence."

She pauses for a minute, as if considering, and for a moment, I think I've gotten through to her. "Yes, I believe you have changed. I'm uncertain if it's for the better, but you have developed at least the beginning of a spine. You may have some Rostoff in you yet."

I know she considers that high praise, but given the rumors I've heard about her family, I'm not sure that's the direction I want to head. I thank her anyway, if only to get this painful conversation over with. "I appreciate the sentiment, mother. I will strive to be worthy of your family name, because I know it's what you always wanted for me."

Hopefully, that's what she needs to hear.

"Don't be ridiculous. I've never thought you would be worthy of my father's name, and your emergence proved me right. However, at the very least, you can be less of a daily embarrassment."

So much for that.

Seeing as I'm not free from this conversation yet, I grab my makeup bag and carry it out to the vanity so I can get ready while she babbles about the legacy of the Rostoffs. She's never spoken about her family this openly before, so I may as well soak in the intel. I haven't decided yet if I want to see if Rufus and Cori or my guys want to hang out, but I don't want to look like a hot mess express, either way. I toss my hair into a ponytail and apply light concealer as Lucille continues to extol the virtues of her father's business prowess.

"...my father's family has been dominant in the export business for over three hundred years, Delores. We are a formidable power in Eastern Asia, and unlike your father, we don't allow anyone to disrespect us. You are too weak to understand the strength a Rostoff woman has to embody to survive..."

"Yes, mother," I mutter, as I add blush and smoky eye shadow and pull out my black eyeliner pencil. Ringing the insides of my lash line with the kohl, I look in the mirror, expecting to see the damaged girl Lucille's moaning about.

Except…

Instead, I see a woman who had the confidence to completely remake herself into the person she wanted to be. From colorful hair to piercings and even the bad bunny tattoo on my butt, I made every choice. I'm startled to realize that I truly like what I see. It doesn't matter if the Heathers or Todd or even my mother think I'm worthless anymore—I know I'm not. I have friends and boyfriends who like me for who I really am, not the plastic doll others tried to mold for their purposes.

I've wasted so much of my time on those who don't deserve it.

The long-forgotten *'Fuck 'Em Up, Sis'* list shoved in my vanity drawer included my parents, but it was also full of those who wronged me at Shifter Secondary and Vom Prom. With a satisfied smirk, I realize I've defeated them all over the past year. I humiliated Gold and Todd in Shifter Studies. Pink failed with her little newspaper smear campaign, and the rest of them aren't even worth the energy it would take to exact revenge.

No, the only worthy opponent here is Lucille.

She's the one who didn't properly teach me about life as a shifter, or prepare me for the position she swore I would take as her heir. My mother didn't allow Mattie or anyone else to give me the tools to survive in our world—despite any claims otherwise.

I came to college without knowing my family history or even how other shifters behave. Everything that made me feel like an outsider at Apex wasn't simply because I was a bunny; I was so sheltered that I wouldn't have fit in even if I'd emerged as a predator. Lucille's goal was always to make me feel useless.

So I'd be easier to manipulate.

I pull my '*Fuck 'Em Up, Sis*' list out of the drawer so I can look it over. This is the list of a young, brokenhearted girl who was lost, scared, and alone—someone with no support system and a trampled self-esteem. Someone who could only think about enacting sweeping vengeance for the way she was treated, instead of calculating moves.

That's not who I am anymore.

Grinning to myself, I take the black eyeliner and cross everyone off the list… except Lucille. My mother wants to drone on about how a Rostoff woman has to be strong?

Well, she isn't ready for the one she created.

With that, I add winged liner to my look and a bright pink lipstick that matches my outfit. On a whim, I press my lips to the bottom of the paper, sealing it with a spiteful kiss. Deciding this saucy aesthetic will be my ongoing inspiration, I rummage around for tape so I can hang it on my mirror, as a visual reminder of my sharpened focus. I don't see any, but there is a pack of gum, so I pop in a stick and chew for a few moments as I listen to see if Lucille has taken a breath yet.

Nope, still droning on about her father. It's almost Oedipal, I fucking swear.

I spit the gum out and use the wad to stick the updated list to the glass, grinning at the image. It will remind me I am worthy of love and friendship, even if my bitchy mother doesn't agree. I will not let her abuse me anymore—we will play her games on my terms, as equal opponents.

Delores Diamond Drew has had enough. I'm a Rostoff now, bitch.

From now on, I'm going to do exactly what she suggested. I'm going to summon the inner strength to take control of my life, starting with figuring out how to keep more students from dying. If the Council and their lackeys won't protect us, then we have to do it ourselves. Hiding in the dorms isn't fixing anything, and I'm tired of running scared—like prey.

My lips curve as I pick up my phone, looking at it for a moment before I unceremoniously hang-up. Turning the ringer on silent, I drop it in the purse on my dresser, deciding once I figure out my plans, I won't look at it again for the rest of the night.

Lucille Rostoff may be the enemy, but she's no longer the boss of me.

A loud knock on my door has me freezing in place. For one frantic moment, I assume Lucille has somehow already sent Bruiser over here to punish me, but even she doesn't work that fast. Staying absolutely still, I sniff the air, trying to determine who is in the hallway before they can scent me in return. I refuse to let anyone intimidate me or steer me away from my newfound confidence or mission. No matter what challenges come my way, I will solve the mystery of what's going on at Apex Academy once and for all.

I may not be Nancy Drew, but I'd make a pretty decent Velma.

Wicked Ones

Chess

Shifting from foot to foot in excitement, I wait for my angel to answer the door. I've stumbled on something amazing and I can't wait to show her what I found.

To think, I wasn't sure about the transparent boards until Ren pointed out how versatile they were. Ducking my head, I smile as I think about how close our little family has gotten. Being an orphan wasn't easy, despite how well Felix and Fitz treated me, and having the support of all our friends is making me feel warm and accepted. Even Aubrey is getting a little less gruff, and I hope he'll trust me to come into his archives next.

With permission, unlike my mischievous consort.

My lips curl when I think about Aubrey's rampage after he found out Fitz rubbed his fucking nuts everywhere in the clean room. My angel paid her own price for her mistake by filing thousands of password change forms. The run he made Fitz take around campus to avoid being fried was damned funny and well deserved. Everyone but him knows better than to fuck with the dragon's lair.

Where is she?!

I pull my phone out, shooting a quick text to the guys to see who Dolly is with. She's not answering the door to her room, and I know she has free time right now. I want to show her a clue that I hope will lead us to some of the damn artifacts we need, but she's not around.

Now I'm worried.

My phone buzzes and I sigh in relief when Fitz tells me she's in the shower, according to her phone tracking. I'd be upset with him for violating her privacy, but she honestly loves that he does it. I don't get it, but then, I've lived with Fitz for my entire life. I definitely don't need him obsessing enough to install GPS or, god forbid, cameras.

Oh, shit. Does he have cameras in there?

I panic a little when I realize I can't put it past him, so I test the door to see if it's open. "Angel, it's me… I'm coming in!"

All I hear is music coming from the bathroom when I walk in, so I take my keys out of my pocket. Turning on the little penlight I bought after our trip into the tunnels, I flick it around to see if I catch the glint of a camera lens. I stroll around the room, checking various things for a hidden webcam until I come to a shelf that makes me blink.

What the actual fuck is this?

Amongst the shelf full of stuffed toys and pop culture figurines are three jars with… body parts suspended in them. Squinting as I move closer, I see one has three fingers that look male—if the fingernails are a tell. The next has an earring adorned ear that's clearly female, and the last has a furry claw that I can't figure out. The jars aren't labeled, but I have a good idea where this shit is coming from.

"Oh! Chessie!"

I whirl around to see my angel pad in, wrapped in a bright pink towel and adorably on the nose bunny slippers. Her hair is in a matching towel, wrapped in that weird turban style all women seem to be born knowing how to achieve. "Good afternoon, Angel. Have a nice relaxing steam?"

Her cheeks flush and I feel she did more than wash her hair, but I let it go. Dolly walks over to the dresser, pulling out lingerie and clothes as she winks at me. "Were you looking at my trophies?"

"Trophies?" I sputter.

Her lips curve as she heads for the bed, dropping the towel to give me a view of her soft, round ass. She bends to put on her underwear and I groan, adjusting myself carefully. "Yeah. Fitzy gives them to me. The fingers belong to dickwaffle Todd because he touched me without permission this summer."

My eyes widen. "He didn't…?"

"No, no. Fitzy was there, and he saved me, but as the big kitty." Dolly hooks her bra and spins it around—another miraculous woman's trick—then shrugs. "Nothing happened, I promise."

I frown for a moment. "And the ear?"

"That one I'm not sure about. He just said people need to learn to listen to both sides and put it on the shelf." Her grin widens as she tugs on her jeans. "The claw is from that fuckhead professor. Fitz says putting your meddling fingers where they don't belong is a lesson he won't forget."

Suddenly, I know where the ear came from. My consort is quietly avenging every wrong that's been done to our girl since she arrived. She'll be lucky if she doesn't get a hyena dick in a jar over the piss thing. I watch her pull her shirt on, looking for signs that she's uncomfortable with this, but she's all smiles.

By Odin's sparkly eyepatch, Fitz has someone just as ruthless and crazy as he is to love him.

This is why she doesn't give a shit that he stalks her; he's her protector and savior.

I get it now.

Walking over to her, I lift her hand, kissing her knuckles gently. I'm something completely different to her than Fitz is or than I am to him. We're complimentary pieces and when you add Felix, Aubrey, and Renard, it's a fearsome quint of shifters.

"I need to show you what I found, Angel." I grin broadly at her, tugging her to the door. "First, we need to go upstairs to the nest room. Then we'll go to the next place."

"Hold on!" she pulls back, giving me an excited look. "I need shoes for the second part, silly."

Oh, right.

"Okay, but be quick!"

AFTER I SHOWED DELORES THE WAY THE TRANSPARENCY OF THE drawings she was puzzling over fit perfectly against the actual map of Apex, she almost screamed.

"I knew it! I mean, I didn't know it, but I knew it was something familiar. The shape of the campus is the same, but the drawings might be… the tunnels underneath?"

I nod, grinning at her in excitement. "I thought so, too. This circular area close to the spot we found the weasel was where Ren and I explored. You saw the pictures, right?"

"Yes. Rennie said some runes were Celtic, which he knew, and Felix recognized the ones from Bloodstone like you," she says. "Aubrey saw some he knew, too."

"Exactly. I think we're looking for something to decode that stone, and the way these tunnels all pass under our home means we're part of this. I think the key we need is in the Tower."

"Oooooh, Chessie!" my angel squeals as she throws her arms around my neck. "I know where we should look. There's a big creepy room with stuff on the third floor. It's across from the kitchen. We can look there without a problem, but if we have to go higher, we'll need to talk to Rennie. Above the third floor is super restricted."

I arch a brow, and she motions like she's zipping her lips. "Okay, angel. Keep your secrets, but we should explore the first room you mentioned together."

"No duh!" Dolly grabs my hand, yanking me away from the boards and to the steps with a crazy grin. "Time to find some artifacts, Dr. Jones."

Oh, hell. I knew we shouldn't have watched that with her and Fitz.

I see bullwhips in our futures.

Looking around the hallway as she tugs me to the door, I ponder. Nothing really looks special, but when she opens the doors to our destination, that feeling changes.

This room has to be important.

"There's a lot of stuff in here that I figured was old junk," Dolly says as she walks in the opposite direction I do. "But if the drawing is an overlay map of the school and all roads lead to Jericho, then the key to the weird room you saw might be here."

I grin over my shoulder at her. "Have I mentioned how damn sexy your brain is, Angel?"

She winks at me playfully. "Back at you, my knight. All my guys have hot, nerdy brains, even Fitzy. People don't give him credit for it because of his… exuberance, but they just don't know how he works."

Running my fingers over the edge of a painting that's making my instincts flare, I think about her words. Then I remember his comment about Catch-22 and grin to myself. She's totally right; Fitz's intelligence got overshadowed by his behavior and neurodiversity. It took someone with patience and love to help him show that side of him without fear.

"You know, Angel, I've never seen him act this mature and put together before. I mean, outside of bringing you body parts and dressing like a cracked out unicorn at raves." I chuckle at the memory of my two loves running around drinking out of fish bowls with glazed eyes.

She bounds over with a weird-looking box and glittering eyes. "I like his gifts and passion for life. Plus, reading out loud to him is fun, too. We play games with it and he has really interesting points of view. Also, I think this is a puzzle box."

Way to bury the lead.

"Good job, Angel. I think this painting holds a clue, too. I'm not finding anything yet, but the dude in it?" She looks at me curiously as I take a deep breath. "The man in it is almost certainly the twins' great-great-great-grandfather."

Her eyes widen comically, and she gasps. "No fucking way!"

I nod, grimacing. "The current Raj took over when his mother retired to Thailand. People weren't thrilled because he was young with a poor reputation and his mother killed her mate to ascend the throne. She did because he was a paranoid psychopath with delusions of grandeur, but the ambush saw the markers of those illnesses again in her eldest son."

"Why did she retire, then?" Dolly asks, as I continue fiddling with the frame.

I sigh. "Remember, we weren't around. The rumor is he forced her to retire much younger than she preferred. Her home in Thailand is more of an exile than a retirement villa, if that's true. Felix planned to look into that when he took over."

Her eyes narrow. "Hence the application of a new, unapproved law that prevented him from ascending to his birthright." I nod and the loud snarl that echoes in her chest shocks me. "I'm coming for that motherfucker, too. Once I handle shit here, your adoptive father is on my new fucking list, Chess."

The ferocity radiating off my angel is enough to make me drop to my knees, my expression agape as I whisper. "By Odin's wrinkly balls, angel… you just alpha'd me to my knees. I can't even look at you."

"What?! How?! I'm not…" Her breathing escalates and I force my hand up to take hers, still keeping my head down. The touch calms her a little, and she finally speaks. "We can't let anyone outside of our family know until I figure this out. I'll have to work with Felix to make sure I can control it."

Her hold snaps and I nod when I can finally look up at her freely. "You're definitely right. No one can know a prey animal has this power. It would put you in even more danger."

She lets out a long breath, staring at the ceiling as she grumbles, "Could I be normal for one fucking day? Is that too much to ask?"

Laughing, I rise and pull her into my arms. "Normal is boring, angel. Now let's figure out the rest of this puzzle so we can tell the guys."

"Deal."

THRILLER
DELORES

AFTER MY ADVENTURE WITH CHESS, WE UPDATED ALL THE BOARDS in the Tower and everyone took extra assignments.

Aubrey took the painting of super great grandaddy Khan to the library to run tests on it while Felix agreed to work with me on the scary alpha thing. I couldn't replicate it for them—of course—but they believed Chess when he said he felt the push. Everyone but Fitz gave each other terrified looks as he described it, and I considered bopping them all in the nose.

Not comforting, assholes.

Time passed quickly between our detective work and focusing on my end of the year projects and exams. The threat of the killer is still a concern, but the Heathers aren't bothering me. Between my bullies' distraction and the workload, the rest of their minions have dropped their campaign of whispers down to sneers. People have approached me since the talent show video went viral, but they were fine with either joining the bullies or doing nothing to help until three weeks ago.

Barf. I'm not putting stock in their fickle loyalties.

One good thing came out of my fifteen minutes of fame: it made it much harder for Pink to use her dad's connections and her platform to fuck with me. That quieted the Apex boards down and I'm not constantly bothered by the dings of being tagged in nasty shit—for the moment.

Yellow seems to have fully ingratiated herself with the group, so she's following orders instead of trying to get attention. It wasn't hard to figure out she was behind the plagiarism bullshit. Cranky old Professor Cormac made her the Apex paper delivery person and even the asshole Abel is giving her a wide berth. It solidified her place with my ex-frenemies, but made her toxic waste to the staff.

Not that she seems to care.

It feels fantastic to be free of the constant buzzing for the last part of my freshman year, though. I'd much prefer to be working on the mystery, my classes, and my relationships. The Heathers are part of my past that won't let go because of their petty need for narcissistic supply. Each day I'm supported by people who actually care about someone other than themselves, and I get farther away from them and my psyche gets healthier.

I have better things to do with my life than play games with such vain, immature sociopaths.

While studying for final exams, Aubrey has been sending me tidbits from his research to look over whenever I take a break. We've been texting theories back and forth—including one that all the drawings are actually map overlays. We're not sure what the remaining three go to, but we think getting the painting and puzzle box to reveal their secrets will help.

Renard is the one who figured out we need to take everything to that atrium on the night of the Blood Moon at the end of this week. We decided not to risk waiting for the next one, which sent everyone scrambling for answers. I have to focus on working my cottontail off for my finals while they do their things. Lucille wasn't serious with her show of support and will lash out if I flunk because of searching secret tunnels.

My mother is up to her neck in this bullshit, just like it seems the twins' father might be. *What I don't know is why the Council is stealing or killing students…* But the 'how' has to relate to Lucille's slip about the 'Society tunnels'. Somewhere on campus, the damn things must be accessible from an outside entrance. That's how the killers and kidnappers are getting past security on the ground and in the air.

Felix is determined to find and plug that leak in the perimeter, so until he does, I'm not allowed to go anywhere without my escorts.

This is going to be a long, long week.

SIGHING, I TURN OFF THE SHOWER AND STEP OUT INTO MY STEAMY bathroom. I'm supposed to meet my 'escort' in a few minutes, so I have to dress for tonight's super-secret prowling activities quickly. Somehow, I doubt the rest of my guys will take this as seriously as Fitz intoned, but I'm going to humor him. Even if we don't find a damn thing with the ritual Aubrey finally found behind the painting, I'll keep the shining chain from the puzzle box. It's got two tiger charms on it and I think it's a Khan relic.

Now it's mine and I'll use it to remind myself I have a phony tiger king of Bloodstone to deal with later.

Pushing aside my fury for another day, I walk to my closet. The black leather catsuit Rufus helped me pick out fits like a glove. I lace up the thigh-high combat boots with a smile of satisfaction, knowing the glowing collar Rennie gave me will keep this from getting destroyed. Heading to the mirror, I pull my rainbow waves into a high ponytail, add some smoky, bunny-burglar eye makeup, and tuck my phone into the hidden pocket on my hip.

What else will I need? I hate to be unprepared.

Frowning, I reach into my top drawer and pull out the folding knife Fitz gave me, clipping it inside my bra. It's hidden by my boobalicious cleavage in the half-zipped suit. As Felix says, inside of thirty-four feet, I have an extra edge with a knife and combat skills. Outside of that, I can run my ass off until I find better ground.

Because of the twins, I'm ready for anything.

A sharp knock at my door startles me, but a sniff tells me it's my gargoyle patiently waiting like a shadow in the bright hallway. Renard would never just barge into my room like Fitz, even if it doesn't bother me at all when the tiger does it. His odd mix of courtly manners and hungry desire are such a contrast, and I can't help but feel my stomach tingling as I think about it.

"Coming!" I call as I tuck the brass knuckles Aubrey slipped me after our date in the opposite pocket. I've missed my guys while we all worked, and I'm hoping to reconnect in the nest tonight. Renard's low chuckle makes my core ache, and I grin as I throw the door open. "Ready to solve a mystery, big guy?"

He snorts, taking his eyes over the skin tight suit as his tail flicks up one of my legs slowly. "Someone's channeling Emma Peel tonight."

My lips curve as I do a little twirl, summoning the bunny tail I know they all love. "I look super stealthy, right?"

"Indeed, *ma petite*." His smirk deepens as his tail slides up my tummy. "What else is hiding under there?"

"Wouldn't you love to know?" I push up on my toes and kiss his lips lightly before giving his ass a light smack. His eyes widen and I giggle, feeling confident under his hungry gaze. "Let's go find the others before we get distracted."

Winking, I turn on my heel, putting a little sashay into my steps as I head down the hall to the elevator. I can feel his eyes on my ass, and a tremble of excitement races through me at the thought of finally getting some answers, so I can focus on luring the rest of my guys into admitting how they feel.

It's time for me to show these men who's really in charge.

Once we're gathered in the tunnels, I can feel the tension that won't seem to go away. The twins are worried about the connection to their father. Ren is fretting about the magic he can't confirm, and I'm panicking about Lucille. The only ones who haven't found a tie to their pasts yet are Chess and Aubrey, but it seems likely we're going to expose a vast network of rich assholes. That might include people they know soon enough.

Hera help us if we can't find this shit before our enemies do, because we have no idea why they want it.

"The Captain and his crew should be ready any moment, *ma petite*," Rennie murmurs as he leans in close.

I nod, swallowing hard as my eyes sweep over the room again. My men mean so much to me, and I don't want this to hurt any of them. I'll never forgive myself if it does. Re-centering myself, I focus on half-shifting to my bunny. It's getting easier every time, so when it happens, I'm less discombobulated than I have been in the past. I walk to the pedestal, putting my hand on it as my ears twitch.

This is it, Dolly—the moment of truth.

Ren walks over to me, looking pleased at the ears, tail, nose, and claws I'm sporting. "Are we ready to find out what this all means?"

Chess nods, reaching out to place his hand on top of mine. "Absolutely. I want to find the next clue and the next until we can keep our angel safe."

Felix does the same, then Fitz, then Aubrey, and Rennie smiles as he uses his tail for contact so he can hold the ritual notes. His voice is deep and smooth, not stumbling once over all the foreign words and text he has to read. When he finishes, we all wait, holding our breath for something to happen, but it doesn't.

I frown. This can't be—everything Aubrey and I found pointed to doing this on the Blood Moon, and here we are.

Yet not a damn thing is happening….

"What the fuck?" I mutter as I glare at the pedestal. "Work, you stupid ritual bullshit!"

"I'm not sure that's going to help," Chess says with a fond smile. "It's not like Aubrey when his Smackbook annoys him."

A disappointed expression crosses my gargoyle's face as he reviews the notes, and my anger bubbles to the surface, threatening to overflow. All of this research and frustration has been for nothing —I'll still be looking over my shoulder all next year. A deep growl of irritation escapes my throat, and even my tigers look surprised.

"Tell them to let it rip, Rennie!" I snarl. "It's obvious this needs a little more power. It's time for Plan B." The others give me a curious look, and I gesture to the walls, letting them know to get back.

Within seconds, a loud boom shakes the ground of the clearing, sending dirt and rocks cascading from the concealed doorway in the tree trunk. Once the dust settles, we find a bunch of dancing racoons in pirate hats pumping their tiny fists in front of a blasted out archway leading to the antechamber.

I can't help smiling at the picture they make, even though fury is still pumping through my veins like lava.

Is it weird to be so angry you can't speak and still be amused? Hell if I know, but I'm a big sloppy mess of emotions at the moment.

Turning to face my guys, I plaster on a cheerful grin. "Come on, guys. If being here on the right night didn't do it alone, we need more ideas."

When they give me matching defeated looks, I growl again. That changes the tenor of the room immediately and my brow furrows. "What?"

Fitz grins through dropped tiger fangs, his expression hungry as he replies, "Chess was right, baby girl. Your alpha is fucking spank. My cock is ready to rip out of my pants like the Hulk."

"You look like dinner," Rennie says as he grins slowly, walking around the pedestal with a predatory gleam in his eyes. "Doesn't she, Flames?"

"Dinner's off the table until we figure out what to do with this thing," I snark playfully. "But that doesn't mean I won't give chase later."

When I look over at Felix, he's partially shifted and something about it feels like we're headed in the right direction. Chess catches my look and suddenly, he's a cheetah. He leads the twins to the pedestal, so we're all touching it now. My dragon continues his reign of silence against the wall, and I chuckle. He throws up his hands when I pout, finally giving in without me having to ask.

Aubrey's scales shimmer in the moonlight as looks at the designs on the stone shining in the moonlight. He arches a brow at Rennie. "Maybe the Captain did us a bigger favor than making the chamber accessible. These runes, cuneiform, and symbols are lighting up with the moon's light. Try the words again, Rennie."

"You need to move a little to the left, tigers. Flames, you go right a bit. We're blocking a few of the designs," the gargoyle says.

Felix and Fitz retreat as one, and the dragon steps aside, his wings folded in. Unobstructed moonlight streams through the gap near the ceiling. It hits the stone altar and suddenly, the entire chamber is filled with a prism of colorful light.

Not just on the Blood Moon, but in the Blood Moon's light…

"Now what?" Felix says, looking at the designs on the walls in confusion. "It's like they're supposed to show us something, but all I see is these ugly murals."

Renard grins. "Get your phones out. Everyone use the panoramic setting and spin around the room taking pictures. We're all different heights and that might be important."

"Huh?" I ask curiously. "Why?"

"Because I think Chess needs to do what he did to the maps Flames found under this paint. One is this campus and the others might be the locations of more artifacts or info about the Society. These designs will help us figure shit out about where that might be and what to look for."

Felix tilts his head. "Why do you say that?"

"Because there are five major pred academies in the world, Baby Girl. If they stored some of this shit at Apex, what are the odds that the other maps are for Capital Prep, Académie des Crocs et des Griffes, Zhuǎnxíng U & M, and Bloodstone," Fitz says as he rolls his eyes. "Duh, eggheads. All the languages correspond to that area, don't they?"

Aubrey turns to me, looking like he's been smacked with a smelly fish. "What in the name of Athena's toga have you done to that tiger?"

Rolling my eyes, I stomp my foot. "You guys need to stop acting like I fixed Fitz. He's always been fine, and he's smart as hell. No one accommodated his neurodiversity before, so he stopped trying to prove himself. The next person to suggest I did anything but listen is getting my boot straight up their ass."

"They might like it, Baby Girl. Who knows?" Fitz gives me a smirk, but I can see the flush on his cheeks at my fervent defense. He knows his friends don't mean anything bad, but I'm damn tired of them doing what everyone used to do to me—talk like I'm too dumb to get shit when they didn't give me the right info to understand.

It's time they understand he's a person, too, and they're being assholes, even unintentionally.

Felix walks over and claps his hand on his twin's shoulder. "Sorry we underestimated you, bro. I could blame it on how we were brought up, but that's just an excuse. Every idiot in this room is smart enough to have made the connection if we'd paid attention better."

"It's all good," my tiger says hoarsely. He looks over at me, his eyes shining a little. "Should we get this show on the road now?"

I nod, grabbing my phone and starting my circular spin around the room. Each one of them follows suit, getting their pictures at every angle possible, so we miss nothing. I'm eager to place the maps and symbols when we get back—it may mean we have to take trips.

Lucille and Bruno never let me travel with them.

A large set of five lines at the very top of one wall makes my brow furrow, and I walk over to it. Under the light, circles and staffs in the mural seem to perfectly fit on them and my eyes widen.

"Shit! It's music!"

"What is bite size?" Aubrey rumbles, looking at me curiously.

Winking at him, I head to the wall, pushing up on my toes to zoom in on the snippet of music. "Find out if there are four more."

Each of them walks to a different section of the moonlight, calling out when they locate their bars of melody. The one I saw was in the Apex portion, so it must be something... *Oh!*

"Follow me!" I yell as I dash away from the atrium to the locked Shirdal door. When I get there, I rap the pattern of notes on the door and it pops open like it was just waiting for me.

Holy shit, that worked.

"Let's go on an adventure!" I grab Fitz's hand, tugging him toward the gaping doorway that opened. The rest of them grin, following us into what turns out to be another fucking tunnel rather than a room.

Humming the jaunty dwarf song under my breath as we follow the dimly lit path, I hear Felix whisper 'what the hell?' from the back of the group. I shake my head, leading the group through the darkened passageway towards a faint light in the distance. Fitz's hand is warm in mine, and my frustration from earlier fades as we get closer to unveiling the secrets of this place.

"Watch those wings, dragon," I frown as someone growls into the darkness.

"It wasn't me, Felix. Perhaps you ran into a sconce," the dragon harrumphs, but I feel a slight breeze as he readjusts his wings, anyway.

When we get to the end of the tunnel, we emerge in a clearing surrounded by thick forest. I have a vague idea of how far we walked and in what direction, but the space we're standing in is completely foreign to me.

Letting go of Fitz's hand, I walk to the center of what appears to be a circle made of unfamiliar symbols burned into the grass. Before I can open my mouth to ask Aubrey about the markings on the ground, Fitz lets out a snarl.

"Did any of you see that? It looked like someone wearing a fucking cloak, hiding in the trees."

Renard stalks to the edge of the circle, peering into the darkness suspiciously. "I did… and the smell is familiar…"

"Over here!" Felix yells, stomping in a completely different direction to glare at the thick foliage.

One by one, we all glimpse the figure, even as they seem to disappear and reappear at will. Throughout it all, I stand in the middle of the circle as my guys sniff and snarl at the edges of the clearing. Their backs are to me as they try to suss out exactly where the hooded stranger is and I'm trapped in the middle of their protective ring.

I feel a shiver start at the base of my spine as I consider the possibility there could be more than one—closing in on us. My ears twitch one after the other, flopping into my face limply, and I shake my head, annoyed to lose control of my shift again. I open my mouth to get their attention, but a sudden burst of light in the middle of my chest makes me shriek in pain.

What's happening to me?!

The sensation of a hard punch to the gut forces me to double over in pain, and when I can't stand any longer, I fall to my knees on the grass. Smells, sounds, and colors flood my vision, and I dig my claws into the earth as if to hold on. Panting, my head drops and I close my eyes to keep the vertigo from making me barf, wishing I could call for help.

My body feels like it's a roiling tempest. Darkness invades my brain, and my eyes pop open to look up at the round, full Blood Moon. Snowy white fur sprouts up in thick patches, poking out of the sleeves and neckline of my catsuit. I've never half-shifted this completely before and I have no idea what to do, especially since it comes with some sort of electricity shooting from my frame.

The weird lightning gets the attention of my men.

They spin to face me as I notice they're standing on five marked points in the circle. Before I can attempt to speak, something inside of me snaps. My eyes ache and burn and the fangs Felix loves to talk about drop in my mouth. I raise my hand, holding it out for help, but it's glowing like some sort of superhero origin story. They're all staring at me in shock.

Lucille was right. I'll be lucky if anyone wants an abomination like me.

My wail of pain echoes over the landscape and I clench my fists to stop the weird shit from escaping my hands. Unwilling to watch everything I care about crumble, I lick my elongated fangs and turn tail. Leaving my men behind, I run through the woods at top speed to escape my inevitable heartbreak.

I'm some sort of freak—the Heathers and everyone else were right.

No one will want me now that they know I'm cursed.

Run, Run, Run

Renard

A CHILL RUNS DOWN MY SPINE AS THE FIVE OF US WATCH OUR GIRL take off into the night. Everything that has happened tonight has me spiraling, as long-buried memories spring from the depths of my mind. Hooded figures, ancient magic, and taboo rituals are secrets I left behind when I was exiled to Apex. The resurgence of the past is making my gargoyle rage inside.

Why is this happening again?

"What in the name of Anubis just happened?" Aubrey mutters as he runs a hand through his hair. His sentiment echoes across the group as we look at one another in shock.

"The world is full of magical things, patiently waiting for our senses to grow sharper," I murmur under my breath.

"Poetry is not helpful," Felix mutters. "We need a plan."

Aubrey flexes his wings, scrutinizing the center of the circle from a healthy distance before squinting up at the moon. He looks at me, and when I nod, he turns to the felines with a grimace. "What Rennie is struggling to say is… he believes our girl isn't just a rabbit shifter. She's got magic in her blood."

"Bullshit. Magic users don't mix with shifters anymore," the tiger replies, crossing his arms over his chest. "Whatever… happened… is some kind of trick using science to fool us. This kind of shifty behavior is why shifters separated from magic users centuries ago."

A roar echoes off the treetops, and we all startle, turning to the most likely culprit in the group. When Fitz shrugs, we spin again, only to see Chess' spotted tail disappearing in the direction Delores ran.

Oh, fuck. His animal is pushing him to find its mate, even if they haven't completed a bond.

I sigh, noticing the talisman on my neck flaring in retort to Felix's statement. Aubrey is old enough to remember when magic users and shifters existed in harmony. He knows magic is no more dangerous than any other weapon, if wielded properly. "Magic is not why she went hopping off, Felix. Whatever happened tonight revealed a part of her she wasn't aware of and probably triggered her fear of rejection like the first night she shifted. Something bigger is at play than simple Council politics, but we can't waste any more time talking about it now."

"What do we do?" Fitz yells, throwing his hands up in the air. His eyes are wild as he looks at me, and I can see the fear for Chess and our girl flickering over his features.

"You two need to shift and hunt down the hooded figures. Aubrey and I will take to the skies and find Dolly." They protest, but I shake my head. "We can cover more ground quickly from above and there will be fewer obstacles to cloud our vision. Plus, your noses are infinitely better than ours."

Finally, the rightful Raj nods, seamlessly shifting to his tiger form. Fitz stalks over to Aubrey, poking him with a clawed hand. "Find her."

"We will. See if you can corner one and capture them alive—they may be the key to keeping Dolly safe," the dragon responds reassuringly. "I can't be sure if they are behind the murders, but they saw what happened here tonight, and we can't allow our girl to stay on their radar." Throwing his head back and howling in rage, the enforcer shifts and joins his brother as they head into the woods as one.

A sudden thought worries me. "Do you think Chess is attempting to corral Dolly on his own?" While I wait for the dragon to answer, I look around, then close my eyes and allow the shift to my true form to begin. I feel his eyes on me as he considers my question—Aubrey has always loved watching the pulse of magic flow over me when I fully shift.

The light from my talisman glows with the same electric blue as my eyes, crawling over my body until I'm completely enveloped in its power. Obsidian covers my skin and my normally lithe frame expands up and out until I tower over my friend. My wings and tail stretch, while my fangs and claws sharpen with the full effect of my transformation.

It feels good to let the beast out.

"If he did, he's in for a nasty surprise. We have no idea if our girl can retain higher brain functions fully shifted, much less if she has magic to wield," my companion finally replies as he follows my lead and transforms into an enormous blue dragon.

I nod, hoping Chess doesn't allow his emotions to lead him into doing something reckless. Since my exploration of the tunnels with the cheetah, he's been driven to help protect our girl and I worry it will override his common sense. He's not an alpha animal and can't react with both the animal and human sides of his mind.

"Are we saving our girl, or are you going to brood at the moon all night?" the dragon growls, small puffs of smoke escaping his nostrils. "The longer we wait, the further away she gets."

I chuckle softly at his prickliness. He's worried as fuck about her and has no idea how to handle it. "Alright, Flames. It's time to fly."

ENHANCED NIGHT VISION IS A BLESSING WHEN YOU'RE SEARCHING THE night for your missing magical rabbit girlfriend.

Aubrey and I have made several passes over the forest, and now we're headed towards the east side of campus where the training ring is located. I've had to coax my old friend out of simply burning the entire place down—despite the obvious drawbacks of that solution—at least four times. He's belching fire and billowing smoke like a volcano, and if the campus didn't know there was a dragon in their midst before, there's no mistaking it now.

My fear for her safety, and the safety of others, is all-consuming, but Aubrey needs my calm support right now.

Suddenly, a flash of white appears in the corner of my eye, and I adjust my course to get a better look. A column of flames rockets past the tip of my wing, and I whip my head around to glare at the infuriated dragon. "Careful! I saw something. Let's take a closer… without scaring her off."

I've barely finished speaking when Aubrey dives for the ground like a heat-seeking missile, and I groan under my breath. If it's not our girl, he's likely to fry whatever unfortunate shifter distracted him from his search. Flexing my wings into position, I angle myself toward the snowy fur, intent on hitting the ground before he wrecks havoc with his anger.

My landing isn't particularly graceful given my speed, but at least I'm close enough to intervene before he goes berserk. "Aubrey, we have to be calm; Dolly may be frenzied. She needs us to help her gain control of her animal brain, and you, *mon fougueux ami*, need to find your zen to help me follow this trail."

Sliding into a half-shift, he glances behind me before smirking. "You mean the trail of blood behind you?"

The scent finally registers and I turn in the direction he's staring. My hands tighten into fists as I see the haphazard drops and splatters leading across the field toward the Shird. I close my eyes for a brief second, taking my advice, then nod at Aubrey. Together, we follow the trail in hunting formation as more blood and... what looks like entrails... appear in our path.

"Troubling," the dragon rumbles softly.

"More like... curious..." I reply as the gore leads us through the patio area behind the arts building and towards the edge of the lake.

Aubrey snorts, his reptilian eyes full of the worry he's trying to get a handle on. "Curious? Aren't you concerned that Dolly's in trouble? Look at this fucking massacre, Rennie."

I think about it for a moment, realizing that as we've prowled along this trail, my worry for her safety has actually lessened. My concern for everyone else, however, is rising by the second. This trail of fluids and fleshy chunks is not our girl—it's someone who made the mistake of crossing her path. I just hope it wasn't anyone she'd regret ripping limb from limb when she emerges from whatever headspace she's in.

"No, actually. *Ma petite* has transformed into a shifter who can truly take care of herself from now on—once she learns to control it. The how and why this happened are vital to understanding the events of tonight. However, at the moment, our focus has to be on locating and helping her through what had to be a terrifying realization."

"Not to mention cleaning up this fucking mess," he grumbles. "Let's not forget the paperwork involved in an accidental death on campus, either."

Barking a laugh, I look over at my companion. "Nothing trumps your bone deep hatred of paperwork, does it, *mon ami*?"

He pauses for a moment, turning to look at me seriously. "Humor aside, Rennie, how do you propose we get a newly changed magical shifter to leave the primal hunger phase and come back to reality? It's not like we've ever met one. What are we going to do —tie her up until the moonlight fades?"

"As fun as that might be, I don't think shibari is the answer you always seem to think it is." He gives me a fangy grin and shrugs as I tilt my head. "For now, we need to figure out who these pieces belong to, subdue her, and strategize from there. I'm uncertain how strong the magic part will make her—we'll need to research that later—so let's proceed with caution."

"Got it. Identify leftovers, pin her down, and then decide how to calm her," Aubrey repeats as we move again.

The trail is heading towards the Tower, and I'm fairly sure that at least one shifter is dead, if not more, based on the detritus on the ground. Something in her brain, even as animalistic as it may be at the moment, sent her running towards our home. That bodes well for our mission to soothe her until she shifts back.

I hope.

Winding our way around the base of the Tower, we approach the courtyard carefully. Aubrey sucks in a breath, pausing as we take in the sight in front of us. I stop as well, muttering softly, "*Until at last, serene and proud, In all the splendor of her light, She walks the terraces of cloud, Supreme as Empress of the Night.*"

Standing in the center of the courtyard, bathed in moonlight, is a rainbow haired rabbit shifter. She's surrounded by swirling magic and holding the head of Professor Abel in her clawed hand.

Our girl whips her head towards us, ears twitching as she roars an unmistakable warning through elongated fangs. The sound makes my eyes flash and my tail flick, although not in agitation—my gargoyle likes it. A blast of smoke fills the air as my dragon companion chuckles to himself, despite the seriousness of our situation.

The white fur around Dolly's mouth is stained like a sociopathic clown did her lipstick. It doesn't take a genius to figure out why we've been dodging chunks of flesh as we tracked her down.

She stumbled on her least favorite professor and tore him to bits.

Shaking my head to dispel the primal urge to chase her until she submits, I slowly move towards our girl, keeping my voice level as I speak. *"Ma petite,* drop the head. You're done for the night."

"Tasmanian devils are stringy and tough anyway," Aubrey offers as he follows me. "And the hairballs are murder."

Her furry face twitches with what appears to be a fangy grin, but she doesn't let go of the gruesome trophy.

As I reach the edge of the courtyard, I try again. She seems to recognize us at least, as she's not attacking, and that's a point in our favor. "If you drop it, perhaps we can dance again? The moonlight is—"

A roar echoes off the stones of the surrounding buildings, and I have to bite back a sharp retort. I don't dare look away from the rabbit to see why Aubrey lost his temper, but as the blur of scales passes me, I know our luck just ran out. "You will calm down!"

The fully shifted dragon grabs her in his talons, and he pushes off the ground as his enormous wings propel them into the sky. Delores drops the head, and it bounces off the ground at my feet, causing me to grimace and back away.

So much for being the older, calmer shifters who can talk her down safely.

I watch the two of them soar high into the atmosphere. Moonlight glints off his midnight blue scales as he swoops and dives with her clutched against his chest. She must be fighting him—unsuccessfully—because though he throws his head back in pain and shoots fire across the starry sky, he doesn't drop her. I consider heading into the Tower so I can get the height needed to join them, but I can't take my eyes off of the scene unfolding above.

Another column of flames shoots through the air, and twin growls pierce the night as Aubrey lands on the roof of the Tower with a deafening thud. His form changes to a half-shift in a blink, and as I watch from the ground, the wererabbit does the same. My lips curve when my old friend yanks our girl closer and kisses the living shit out of her.

Well played.

Shifting back to human form as I walk towards the Tower entrance, I smirk at the raccoon guarding the door. "Have the Captain dispose of that..." I point at the head and then gesture at the trail we followed. "... and the rest of the mess immediately. Nothing we did tonight can be traced back to us."

The crew member salutes and takes off toward the lake to inform the others, and I step inside my home, wondering what the Khans found on their hunt. Though the danger of her true nature may be abated, Dolly still isn't safe until we find out more about what happened tonight.

Especially when everything in that circle felt so fucking familiar…

*If she's not really dead, we're in a **lot** of trouble.*

THUNDERSTRUCK
FELIX

IN OUR RUSH TO FIND THE HOODED FIGURES AND CHESS, FITZ AND I tear up the ground when we burst out of the forest. Huge paws slap the grass and tight muscles bulge as we leap through the air into the Shifter Training Circle. An unfamiliar scent greets me and I catch my twin's eyes as we prowl around the stone arena. He peels off, checking the perimeter while I stay out in the open.

There's something here, and it's angry.

Sitting in the middle of the battleground my family built, I let out a bone jarring roar as only a Raj can. Hopefully, it draws our enemy out of the shadows for a fair fight. If not, I'm going to hunt it down and rip the eyeballs out of its sockets.

No one threatens our girl on my watch.

The night is still, and I huff in frustration. Shifters and magic users split over the bullshit tactics of their kind—shit like attacking then hiding from the fight. As much as I don't want to admit the gargoyle is right, everything about the air in the circle feels *wrong*.

My brother's head pops around the corner of a bleacher section, shaking to let me know he, too, came up empty-handed. Tigers can't frown, but I would if I could. Joining him, I take a deep sniff of the weirdly sweet yet musky scent, then pad across the circle. I know my twin has my flank without words; it's part of our bond as Raj and enforcer. When I reach the outer edge again, I try to catch the smell, but it isn't there.

I may have to explore other senses—not that I know if I have them.

Walking out of the battle arena, I track the feeling of dread in the pit of my stomach. When it lessens, I change course, correcting until it gets worse. I don't know what the hell I'm doing exactly, but since I occasionally get a whiff of the prey I'm seeking, it must be working. We pass the Shird, stalking away from the lake and Tower towards the middle of campus. This is where we had the snowball fight and I realized Delores was meant to be in charge.

Of what, I don't know, but between her command of the team and using alpha power on Chess…

It's not hard to put together that she's not normal prey; the question tonight poses is what the hell is she then? Her longer bunny fangs, the claws, her half-shift—all of it pointed to something I've never even heard of. That was before she turned into a ball of blue bunny lightning in the moonlight.

Wait. There it is.

The aroma hits me again, and it's strong, so I take off across the wide expanse towards the Honeywell Admin building. When I round the side to face the freshwater lake, I'm too dumb founded to stay in my full animal form. Fitz skids to a stop, shifting to stand next to me as we look at the scene in shock.

An island has risen in the center of the water and on it is a group of hooded figures chanting. The blue light from before surrounds them as the sound gets louder and when one moves, it reveals Chess lying on the ground in their circle. Fitz lets out a snarl, but I put my hand over his mouth.

We can't give away our position or they'll come for us, too.

"We'll get him, brother. But right now, we have a tactical advantage." His eyes are murderous as he glares at me, and I know he's going to break free. "*Stay.*"

My twin gives me a look of betrayal when I use the alpha voice to keep him in place, but I can't have him running off half-cocked and bringing this shit on our heads. We don't know who or what these people are; if we push a fight, we will absolutely lose.

"*Pariatur, tenetur libero possimus.*"[1] The cloaked leader shouts as they raise a hand in the air. They're holding a crystal that looks familiar, but I can't place it. Acolytes echo the sentiment and the person continues. "*Lumine Sanguinis Luna, deos invocamus olim. Regnum terribile incohatum est cum regina a rege in exilium erit finis.*[2]"

Fitz wrenches my hand off of his mouth and leans in, hissing, "Do you understand a fucking word of this shit? It's like the TV show Chess likes with the brothers who hunt demons."

I shake my head, knowing he's right. "I don't speak Latin. This will be a job for the winged warriors."

"How?! It's not like we're going to remember and we don't have a secret phone pocket in our tiger skins, fuckhead."

My eyes narrow and I give him a look that backs him down for a moment. "The damn cameras, dummy. Ren put up more cameras on the building edges after the fucking Tower incident. I think they have sound."

"I fucking hope so or we're screwed because someone cheaped out." His chest rumbles with a growl, then he looks at me pleadingly. "We can't let them hurt him, Felix. It will kill me."

Grimacing, I turn back to the light show, trying to see what they might be doing with our adopted brother. He's not moving, but Fitz would feel if he was dead. So he's alive and knocked out— hopefully. "We won't let them kill him, brother. But we do need back-up. Where the hell are the others?"

"I don't know, but I'm going to kick their—" He stops talking when the chanting gets louder and Chess' body lifts into the air.

Fuck, fuck, fuck. Don't do this, you spell casting knob heads. I'll never get my brother back if his consort dies.

"*Dimitte vinctum, O Magna Horned Deus, Et Dea Mater. Hoc vase utere ut erumpere primo obice sic vivimus!*[3]"

With a cry of victory, the leader flings their hands out and a wave of power like I've never felt in my life hits the campus. Fitz and I are knocked to the ground when explosions trigger all over in a cascade of decimation. Reaching over, I grab my twin's arm as we desperately suck in air. The smell of smoke and fire is followed by loud alarms and screaming from every direction.

Where are Delores and the ancients? What happened to Chess?

"Not...not... dead," Fitz gasps as he squeezes my arm in return. "Have to... find him."

I blink, trying to move my limbs carefully. Fuck knows if we have concussions or internal injuries—we were too close to that blast. And Chess... Gritting my teeth, I gather all of my strength, knowing it's my time to be the real king. I force my tiger to emerge and stand on shaky legs until the world settles. There are people running in every direction; it's pure chaos.

I don't care. I'll get my brother's love or die trying.

With a roar of anger, I leap into the water and swim towards the fucked up island like my life depends on it. The hooded fuckers are gone, but our boy is lying there, still as a statue. It takes every ounce of energy I have to get to him, but I finally hit the shore. I'm exhausted, but I can't stop; I have to save him for Fitz and our family.

I suck in a deep breath, my lungs burning with effort, and let out my command in a roar that makes my throat raw. When my head drops, I watch as Chess' body flickers for a moment, then the forced shift takes over. His cheetah emerges, curling into a mewling ball. I don't know the extent of his injuries, but I let my legs give out and drape over him to protect his form while he tries to heal.

We lie there as the world around us goes to hell in a handbasket, my eyes half-closed as my heroics take their toll. The acrid smoke of fires burning hot on the land doesn't help me breathe easier, but I stay in place, guarding the sleeping cat with my life.

I'm about to give in to sleep myself when a much bigger, much angrier sound echoes off the land and makes the water around us tremble.

When I look up, there's our brave as fuck bunny and my brother riding a goddamned dragon who looks ready to level the entire place in one go. Renard is flying behind them, his electric blue gargoyle eyes alight with fury. They land with an earth shattering thud that bounces both Chess and me, and I finally close my eyes in relief.

"Good thing… you got… to ride… the dragon… before we died," I sputter at Fitz.

Then my eyes roll back in my head and everything goes black.

.

Download In Prey We Trust now!

GET A SECRET BONUS SCENE!

For a secret bonus scene that follows *Come Out & Prey, click the link below, sign up for my newsletter, and get your freebie.*

Get your bonus scene here!

REVIEWS, PRINT, AND MERCHANDISE

If you have enjoyed this story, please review it.
It helps other readers find my work,
which helps me as an indie author.

Thank you!

Reviews are appreciated on the following platforms:

TikTok
Instagram
Facebook
Bookbub
StoryGraph
Threads
Tome
Lemon8

To purchase print copies or merchandise, go to The Worlds of
Cassandra Featherstone

WORLD GUIDE & PRONUNCIATIONS

PEOPLE

Delores Diamond Drew (duh LOR es DIE mond Droo)

Lucille Rostoff Drew (loo SEAL ross TOV Droo)

Bruno Drew (Brew noh Droo)

Matilda/Mattie (mahTILduh/ mahTEE)

Bruiser (Brew ZER)

Heather Erickson (heh THUR AIR ick sun) aka Gold

Heather Barrington (heh THUR BEAR ing tun) aka Pink

Heather Honeywell (heh THUR hun EE wel) aka Silver

Heather Charles (heh THUR ch ARRL zuh) aka Purple

Todd (doosh BAHG)

Fitzgerald Khan/ Fitz (FIH TZ jair uhl duh/ FIH TZ KAH N)

Felix Khan (FEE licks KAH N)

Chess Khan (CHeh SS KAH N)

Aubrey Draconis (AW BREE Drah CON iss)

Renard Laveaux (Rey NAR d LA Voh)

Rufus (Roo fuss)

Cori (KOR E)

Bindi Sarabhai (Bin Dee Sair AH b HIGH)

Annabella Balena (aha NUH bell UH Bah LEY nuh)

Henrietta Shirdal (hen REE ett UH SHEER dahl)

Raina the Raccoon (REY nuh)

Clotilda (CLOH til duh)

Luc Growlvinchy (looKUH GR owl VAHN she)

Patrice (pah TREE ss)

Lucinda (loo SIN duh)

Betsy (behT see)

Bettina (beh TEE nuh)

Argyle (ar GUY uhl)

Clarice (clair EE suh)

Zhenga Leonidas (zen GUH lee oh nEYE diss)

Gregor (grey GORE)

Professor Abel (ay BUHL)

Professor Cormac (kore MAHK)

Minerva (min ER vuh)

Heather Mc Lachlan (heh THUR mac LOCK lan) Yellow

LOCATIONS

Apex Academy - college they attend

Drew Mansion- Delores' home

House of Growvinchy- designer fashion house she worked at

Cambridge- nearby large city

Gazelle Dorm- Delores' original room assignment

The Tower- where Renard lives (among others)

Khan Battle Arena- Pred Games & Shifter Training

Bloodstone Isle- Khans rule this island and reform school

The Jade Sceptre- Khan owned mid-tier restaurant

La Belle Epoque- French restaurant not owned by Khans

Honeywell Admissions Building- cafeteria in here

Shirdal/Shird- Arts building

Townhouse- Tiger ambush staff housing

Draconis Library- where Aubrey works and archives are

Prey Tunnels- run under campus for prey staff

Leonidas Gym

Shirdal Theater- where they perform

Le Joyau de la Couronne- fancy restaurant owned by Khans

Liquid Onyx- club in the city

Sneak Peek: Secrets of State U

Killer Queen

Morgana

Looking around the campus with a critical eye, it isn't hard to notice the differences between the campus of Swallowtail and State U. The major difference is age, of course, but even secondary schools overseas are unlike the blatant marketing machines that are American universities. State U doesn't resemble the colleges I've seen in American movies or on TV, though much of that is the Society's doing. However, banners, statues, plaques, signs, and even architecture are emblazoned with the school's motto—*Honoris. Veritas. Potentia*—as if constant reminders will enforce the virtues it extols. *That* differs from the places in Europe I attended or worked in.

"Getting used to the sales aspect of education here won't be your biggest challenge and you know it," I mutter to myself.

When the outcome of my trial led to a guilty sentence, I didn't expect the punishment they handed down. Instead of being jailed for the murder of my ex, they decreed I would replace him as the Dean at State U. I wasn't the only one who disagreed with my purgatory—the vote on the High Council was split down the middle until a mysterious figure cast a vote in favor of my exile. They summarily dismissed me from Swallowtail Academy and sent me home to pack my shit for a journey overseas to the nest of corruption created by the man I thought I would marry.

Not only am I the youngest Dean to ever hold the title, but I'm the only hybrid to head one of the Society's schools.

Placing me at the helm of the crown jewel of their American institutions made their unorthodox punishment even more bizarre, but I've never believed the group that guides our kind to be infallible. The irony of replacing the being responsible for all the university's current issues with the fiancee who killed him hasn't escaped me. It's like my penance for not blowing the whistle on him instead of taking my vengeance in blood.

They did not impress hard line elders with the eventual outcome, but that had to be expected. Some supernaturals don't believe in the young being given positions of power, especially when that young candidate is also a woman and a hybrid. Given that I believe Magnus had cronies at various levels of government he was paying off, some of them must be worried I'll expose them to prove I was right to remove him from this world. Either way, the assholes who are screaming I'll ruin their precious programs and reputation haven't shut up since I left the trial chamber.

Let them whine about their outdated, elitist standards. I'll show them.

I turn away from the greenery of the campus, leaving the balcony to take a seat at the enormous desk in my overly plush office. Knowing the way parents and donors behave in this country, I assume every inch of this space has been purchased not by the college, but by donors who had 'one little request' for my ex. Magnus Corona was well-known in academic circles for milking the wealthy Americans until they ran dry, but his lack of ethics couldn't go on forever. My greedy, demonic lover went on the lam after a series of scandals involving kickbacks, illegal sponsorships, sports, and sexual harassment. The last one is why I hunted him down and eventually watched the last breaths he took on this planet with vengeful glee.

I'll start looking for a decorator immediately. If it's not in the budget, my trust fund will cover it.

Like most lost ones, they left me on the doorstep of a very talented witch and her gargoyle mate. I never found my 'real' parents, but growing up on Swallowtail's campus was not a burden. It was different when my adoptive parents were professors there—three hundred years brings a lot of changes. When I graduated, I attended Oxford and came back to work there in administration because I miss the old buildings and libraries.

That's the gargoyle in me, I know.

My adoptive mother is blind—except for the gift of future sight. Being a beautiful, blind witch couldn't have been easy when she was teaching, but she met my father in college and they've been together ever since. When they graduated, they came back to Swallowtail to teach. Eventually, she became the head of the Witchcraft & Wizardry department at the Finishing School and my father was the chair of the Physical Education & Training program. Over the years, my mother's gifts made their investments and ventures fruitful enough to retire while they could still enjoy it. They live on a small island in the Mediterranean where supes of their caliber like to soak up the good life.

Once I get settled here, I might invite them to come tour the campus. My father would particularly enjoy the Gothic structure of the buildings; they were constructed to evoke the feeling of Oxford and he loves those old buildings. I give the picture of them on my cherry wood desk a half smile and sigh when I realize it's going to be a while before I can extend that invitation.

First, I have to figure out how to get this ship back on course. Loyalty divides the staff; the students are due to arrive in two weeks, and I have a lot of house cleaning to do within these hallowed walls. It's going to ruffle feathers to do the things that are necessary to keep our supernatural accreditation *and* our human sports certification. I'll have to let some staff go, shuffle departments and assignments, and bring in new people to monitor certain aspects of the college's accounting to satisfy all the requirements we need to meet by the end of the semester.

State U has never been forced to toe the line quite as closely as we must now, and that is all because of Magnus Corona's lack of scruples and inability to think without his dick.

Not that any of his adoring fans will believe it for a second—and that is the rock I'll have to push up the hill for the foreseeable future.

"They'll have to get on board or get the fuck out," I say as I compare the list of coaches, trainers, and support staff for the football team. "I don't have a choice and neither do they."

***

When I finally finish going over the massive budget for the major boys' teams, my brain is damn near fried. I cannot fathom how colleges here justify the expenditures of these programs compared to the paltry sums I saw on the balance sheets for academic programs. Americans truly have lost their focus with education, and it doesn't surprise me at all that Magnus could manipulate this to his advantage. There's so many discretionary funds and black holes in the books that I'll have to find someone much more numerically inclined than myself to help me wade through this shit.

It's almost like it left room for loopholes and nefarious deeds.

Pushing to my feet, I rise from the high-backed leather chair and slip my shoes back on. I've been at this for hours and because I don't have office staff, no one was there to remind me I should eat or take a break. I had to fire everyone who worked in Magnus' immediate circle—both out of principle and necessity. I can't prove they knew what he was doing, nor that any of them would try to harm me as retribution, but I'm also not stupid enough to let someone with loyalty to my ex pour my goddamn coffee.

Coffee.

The word makes my blood hum and I know it's time to find sustenance—particularly caffeine. I locate my phone on the massive desk and slip it into the pocket of my suit pants. My appearance has been a topic of gossip on campus since I arrived—social media is a terrible curse when you're in the spotlight, even if it's for the right reasons. I've seen staff and alumnae commenting on the 'uptight murdering bitch' strutting around campus dressed like someone from the *Addams Family* as if their vitriol isn't public when they post on Facebook.

My lips curve as I look down at the bespoke Tom Ford suit, Zegna tie, and Louboutin heels. Dressing the part has always been a theme of mine, but Magnus preferred the 'rumpled academic' look. He allowed the staff to run around looking like grad students and that will soon end. If they hate me for looking sharp compared to my frumpy ex, they're going to hate the new dress code when it rolls out in a week. I will not go as far as the Society schools did at home or in other countries, but I refuse to have the press haunting our grounds while taking pictures of grubby looking professors and coaches for their rags.

If this is the crown jewel, it needs more polishing than the High Council realizes.

Before I go out, I shake my purple and black curls out of the messy bun, letting my hair settle over my shoulders. A quick check with the selfie mode on my phone tells me my makeup doesn't need to be freshened—thank hell—so I close the camera and put on my sunglasses to keep my sensitive eyes from the waning sun.

I'll need the State U app to find a place that's out of the way. I open it and cringe—the damn thing is hideous in form and function. I make a mental note to interview app designers and web developers; the website has to be as poorly maintained as this bullshit. Yet again, I marvel at the level of incompetence men can show without consequence. It finally loads the map and I scroll around until I find a coffee shop on the edge of campus. I don't want to go to a break room or the food court—there will be far too many eyes on me and I'd like to relax.

Noting the landmarks around the shop, I walk out onto the balcony and touch the amulet at my neck. My wings spring free, sprouting through the suit without a single tear, and I leap into the air. Catching a wind shear, I glide to the far end of the commons, then bank to the right towards the arts building. They nestled the little beanery I identified between the theater and the gallery, so I pull my wings back so I descend slowly as I approach.

When I land, the magic of my mother's amulet helps me slip my appendages back in gracefully and walk towards the door without missing a beat. I open the door, take off my sunglasses, and stride in with confidence. I'm not here to throw my weight around, but I can't let anyone see me sweat, either. I look at the menu board before I lower my gaze to see the barista behind the counter.

Holy. Mother. Forking. Shit.

The guy behind the counter is beautiful, and I don't say that lightly. His long blond hair is pulled back in a ponytail, but somehow, it doesn't look douchey. Paired with his patrician features and thin silver framed lenses, he projects the air of a student, but not a new one. My guess is a grad or doctoral student and this is his side hustle. The muscled forearms and powerful hands tell me he's not just a bookworm, so I ponder what discipline this lithe, gorgeous supe is studying. When I finally drag my eyes back to his, the aqua color of his is mesmerizing.

"Can I take your order, ma'am?"

Yikes. That destroyed my brief fantasy.

"Um, yes, sorry. It's been a long day. I'd like a triple espresso and a club sandwich, please." I feel my cheeks heating not because I was staring—he's got to be used to it—but because I got caught checking out one of the students.

It's not forbidden at State U, but I am the murdering bitch with ice in her veins that's here to destroy everything the university stands for. Or, so the article in the *State U Review* said last night. There's no way this gorgeous coffee-serving man doesn't recognize me and I'm sure I'll get an earful about my evil ways once he's done making my order. In fact, I should continue watching to make sure he doesn't mess with my food for revenge.

Yeah, that's why I want to watch him.

"I don't blame you for coming here. It's not one of the campus hot spots. Mostly we get professors, arts kids, and the occasional normie who wants to hide from the masses."

I blink, realizing he's nailed my reason for choosing this shop without even trying. "I think it's rather cozy."

"You don't have to pretend, Dean LeCiel." His pretty eyes meet mine again and I feel that heat creeping up my spine. "I'm aware of how contentious your appointment was. It doesn't bother me, honestly. I've been a student through much of your ex's reign and since the music department was of little concern to him, I don't have any allegiance to the former administration."

Definitely a doctoral candidate. His thesis is probably massive.

Covering my mouth as the unintended double meaning of my words occurs to me, I wait until the urge to giggle like a teenager fades. It would be extremely unprofessional of me to comment on his... attributes... especially since that kind of bullshit helped bring Magnus down. Of course, that doesn't mean I'm not wondering now...

"Dean? Hello?" The hot barista is waving his hand as he looks at me curiously.

"I'm sorry to be so rude. I didn't catch your name?"

There we go. That sounded totally normal.

"People call me Slade," he replies with a slow smile.

That doesn't surprise me in the slightest, and I wonder if he might be part Fae. Not giving me his real name is part and parcel with them, and so is ethereal beauty. "You may call me Morgana when I am here. I think titles are dreadfully stuffy, but..."

"You have to set boundaries early because you have mutinies to deal with."

Frowning, I tilt my head. "You aren't reading me with magic, are you, Slade? Even during my ex's time, that kind of invasion of privacy wasn't allowed."

"No, no!" He stops making the sandwich and gives me a sheepish look. "I inferred it. I mean, I don't run with the undergrads or the popular crowds, but I hear things. It wasn't hard to figure out that you're at the hole in the wall shop so you don't have to be on stage while you eat or that you're going to make big changes because of all the charges against the former dean."

I nod, observing him. "I believe you, though I probably shouldn't. Betrayal hides in obvious places; I'm living proof of that."

His features look sharper as he smirks. "There are those of us who don't believe what you did was unjustified, Morgana. Living here at State U will provide you with plenty of evidence to give the Council that will mitigate your actions."

"That's both my desire and my deepest fear, Slade. There's only so much bad PR this place can take before the Council shuts it down and moves on."

A coffee cup and a plate with my sandwich slide across the counter as he murmurs, "You'll have to decide if that's what you want when the time comes."

"I know."

Read the first three episodes free on Kindle Vella: https.//hi. switchy.io/bloodontheice

Sneak Peek: Bloodthirsty

QUEEN BEE

They dim the lights in the club, and the spots click on as the curtain slides open.

It's a full house tonight in the little burlesque club off the Rue Pierre Montaine.

Chez Arc En Ciel is not well known compared to the *Moulin Rouge* or *Le Lido*, but the wealthy from both sides of the Seine gather here for shows four nights a week. If you pass the various layers of security checks to even be permitted to book a reservation, you also have to be able to afford the two thousand Euro per guest cover charge. If you don't eat or drink anything, that's all it will cost; however, that would get you blacklisted.

Intro music pumps through the speakers and I stand on my mark in the opening position. My cane is resting on the wooden boards of the stage by my front foot as I pretend to lean on it. Roars of applause echo through the room as our troupe of dancers catch the lights, sequins sparkling like diamonds when the stage lights rise. We're dressed in pinstriped black pant suits and fedoras to match the big band style opening to the song. As soon as the horn-filled intro finishes, the dance begins.

I follow the routine with precision, snapping and popping my hips to the beat as we spread out across the stage. You wouldn't know by the fake smile on my face that I'm scanning the crowd. Two fan kicks later, I've rotated past the proscenium, and I think I've found my mark. Twirling, I stop in the place I need to be for the bridge, singing along as if my life depends on it. It might, to be honest, because I need to sell my cover tonight, so no one notices me.

The Guillotine moves in the shadows, but tonight, she's in the spotlight.

My ass shakes as I dance my way through the song, swinging the prop cane I'd replaced with one of my design. You wouldn't know by looking at it, but it's not the painted balsa the other dancers have for a very specific reason. I need it to complete the mission that forced me to spend two months in Paris working my way into this job at *Chez Arc En Ciel*. If I can't strike tonight, the surveillance, counterintelligence, and time spent building this cover are wasted because my mark is leaving for Asia tomorrow.

Tonight, the Cobra dies for his sins.

The break of the song slows the music and the dancers pour into the crowd to wiggle around the rich assholes. It's choreographed, but it's also to advertise each girl for private dances in the lounges upstairs. We're not strippers—not that there's a damned thing wrong with a woman using her body to support herself—but we do bare more skin in the closed rooms. The *laissez-faire* attitude of the owners means as long as we kick them thirty percent of the fees for those dances, they don't care what any of the girls do in the rooms. I'd find it sleazy, but the girls who work here are highly skilled performers who choose to make thousands of dollars a night rather than peanuts in some ballet troupe or chorus line.

By the time I've flirted my way to the VIP tables, the Cobra is staring intently at all of us. Spotlights pin each one of us on the floor at the bass hits, and I swivel my hips as my free hand slides down to the secret spot on my jacket. In unison, we tear the jackets off to reveal rhinestone studded bras with straps criss-crossing our waists like shibari ropes. A lift of the fedora and pop of my hip, along with the beat, draws the fierce-looking brawler's eyes directly to me. I pout prettily and stalk towards his table with the swagger of a tiny dicked asshole that owns a monster truck.

His thin lips pull back over the famed curving fangs he had implanted. Dark, glittering eyes follow every move I make as I approach, and I pretend to whip my hair from side to side as I check for his guards. They're here somewhere, but I need them to be far away so I can beat my escape before they notice. When I get within inches, I tap his leg with my cane and spin around to shake my ass in his face. The grunt of approval makes me want to heave, but I turn, holding onto the prop with both hands. My feet click on the floor in a soft shoe step as I make 'fuck me' eyes at the dirty bastard. He leans back, his pants tented as he gestures towards his lap.

Fucking gross.

I don't care about his weapons trade or what happens when people get the shit he moves. I have no clue why I have to take him out. The reason they have sentenced him to death isn't part of my contract, and I'm nothing if not a dispassionate observer of the darkest parts of human desires. Twelve years at *l'Academie* ensured I care very little about anything that isn't directly related to my ability to complete my jobs.

Sighing, I dance closer and drop onto his rather unimpressive erection and wiggle. There's plenty of cloth between us to prevent him from doing anything I'd make a scene over, so I focus on the task at hand. I slip the cane behind his head, resting the wood against his neck as I tug him forward. The move reads as playfully bringing his face to my breasts, but at the last second, I click the release built into the custom weapon. One end slides open to reveal the razor sharp garotte and before he can say a word, I yank it through.

Faint gurgling is the only noise besides the end of the song, and I carefully slide the sides of the cane together. Climbing off the nasty fucker, I put my hands on his cheeks so I can pretend to flirt with him while I arrange the head so it looks as if he's leaning back in the booth. It needs to look realistic to allow me to return to the stage with the others. When I have it settled, I back away from the booth, blowing fake kisses as I walk backwards through the crowd. I almost collide with a dark-haired guy with his collar pulled high as I head for the stage, and I roll my eyes. Whatever celeb that is trying to keep their face away from the paps is doing a shitty job of it.

The entire troupe takes a few bows and shuffles off of stage left to the wings. I exhale a sigh of relief when the next group enters on the opposite side. I haven't heard shouting yet, so I don't think the Cobra's men realize he's down. Now I take this emetic pill, have a vomiting episode, and I'll get sent home.

That's when Arabella Montaigne, the burlesque dancer, will cease to exist, and Remy Arsine Benoït will re-emerge.

I smile to myself as I chew on the tablet that will have me retching my guts out in a few moments. This is a more complex extermination than I usually prefer, and I can't leave my normal calling card behind. The Cobra's head had to remain in the booth rather than get delivered to his home in a basket.

Such a shame, that. I quite enjoy the reactions my little gifts engender when they're discovered.

Walking into the dressing room, I carefully strip my costume off, putting all the pieces in my bag. Every item in the locker room that belongs to gets placed in the duffel carefully as I wait for the effects to hit me. It won't do to leave loose ends, even if my prints have never touched a single surface in this place. My gut roils and I turn, facing one of the other dancers as the vomit finally comes. Gracelia screams like she's being skinned when I hurl on her and it's everything I can do *not* to smirk through the chunks.

"C'est la merde!" she shouts, running for the showers as if she's on fire.

It takes less than a minute for the owner to send me home for the night. I walk out the back door of the building with everything just as the sirens scream.

Perfect timing, as always.

I jump into the first cab I can hail, directing him to the *Hôtel de Crillon*. Their suites are the ritziest in Paris, and it's my go-to hideout when I'm here. I used to only stay in the Bernstein Suite, but some rich fuckwad purchased it six months ago. If I could track them down and beat the hell out of them, I would, but I booked my schedule until late 2025. Assassins with my skill set and accuracy are getting harder to find. They forced the old guard into retirement because they refuse to adapt to the digital age. Too many cameras, crime labs, and hackers running about to do everything Cold War style.

The future of murder for hire is millennial, people. We're old enough to be stable, but young enough to be agile with new technology. Plus, most of them are broke AF from crooked ass student loans.

It's not an issue I have, but I've been in the business since I hit double digits. You don't survive *l'Academie des Invisibles* if you haven't killed someone before the end of primary school. It's unheard of.

I was eight the first time I used the weapon that would become my signature.

Shivering, I tap on the window of the cab and bitch the driver out. He's taking a longer route than necessary to raise my fare, and I'll have his guts for garters if he doesn't knock it the fuck off. A string of curses in French erupt from him when I voice the accusation, and I slam my palm on the window with enough force to crack the plexiglass barrier. He almost drives into another car, but when he regains control, he makes the requested adjustments to our route.

We arrived at the front entrance after a few more arguments and a traffic jam around the *Champs*. I throw the euros at him in disgust, memorizing the medallion number for later. He's not worth my time, but I have quite a few contacts who might be interested in blackmailing a cabbie in town. Getaway cars are cliche in the crime world now. Most ne'er-do-wells like myself find greater comfort in anonymous taxis or ride-share accounts hacked through the deep web accessed on burner phones. If your ride doesn't know you're a villain, there's no one to flip if law enforcement comes looking.

I never look the same for any job—ever.

I will not use Arabella Montaigne as a cover in the future, and once I move to the location of my next job, I'll ensure that she meets with a terrible fate. It's a lot more work to slowly kill off my alters once I've used them, but it's also why I've never even come close to being caught. The dancer with long wavy red hair, freckles, and big green eyes will never grace the streets of Paris again after I hop a plane. She will, however, get a minor story in the paper and an obituary when I decide how she tragically dies.

The Guillotine will rise from her ashes and be reborn.

Sneak Peek: Children of the Moon

PROLOGUE

Twenty-one years ago…

A powerful wave of apprehension hits me as we approach Claridon's house. Pausing at the edge of the forest, I wait until we can see what awaits us. The silence is deafening as we take in the wreckage of what was once the home of our dear friends.

They splintered the heavy cabin door in pieces littered around their yard like an explosion sent the shards flying. When the wind shifts, the foul stench of death and rot slams into us, making my wife gag. Lights are flickering ominously in the shattered windows and another scent—burnt food—catches the breeze as we approach.

"Cast protection before we reach the porch," I murmur.

"*Ego invoco deus ab mihi. Protego mihi ab hostili et malum.*[1]"

I nod solemnly, repeating her words to invoke our Goddess' watchful eyes on me as well. The scene in front of the house does not inspire confidence about what we will find inside.

The air is thick as we step onto the porch and another smell wafts towards us—blood. Its metallic tang invades our senses almost to the point of tasting copper on my tongue. Climbing over the debris, I look at the once cozy living area. Shredded cushions, torn drapes, stuffing, and other destroyed furnishings lie scattered around the room. When I bend to examine the destruction, I find coarse animal hairs embedded in the remnants. I pick some up to sense the aura of the creature it came from, but all I feel is death.

The bloody hoof prints puzzle me—I do not recognize them as belonging to any creature I'm familiar with. Whatever came to this house was not a normal shifter, nor was it a common magic user. The level of malice and lack of emotion concerns me. Its aura is like that of a necromancer or one of their creations.

I follow a set of heavy prints to the hallway leading to the dining area and kitchen. Swallowing hard, I prepare myself for the carnage I know will appear. The rotten food and decomposition scents are so bad I have to raise my shirt to cover my nose before I vomit.

It is certain our friends are dead; no one can lose the amount of blood that coats the surfaces and walls while staying alive.

"What made those claw marks? I've never seen such deep furrows," my wife whispers.

I shake my head, holding a finger to my lips to keep her quiet. I've never seen that type of mark, either, but we don't know if there's anyone still here. We must stay silent while we explore. The food on the stovetop is burned and has flies on it—that's the rotting smell. Wood is barely burning in the oven, just a few embers remaining, but it tells me our friends were caught unaware.

It means the malevolent being that attacked the wolves did it within the past few hours.

My heart stops when I remember their baby girl. Feray had to be here when it happened; it's the New Moon and both of her parents stay home during the start of the new lunar cycle.

"Freya, forgive me. I almost forgot the baby," I hiss at my wife.

Her eyes widen and her hand flies to her mouth. I see the tears forming as she thinks about what the condition of this place means for a defenseless infant. Together, we leave the kitchen, intent on heading back through the outer room to the stairs.

Just beyond the landing, we stumble over the body of Claridon. His corpse is mutilated, but I recognize those battered hands anywhere. He clearly put up a hell of a fight to keep the intruder from making it past him. Despite that, it ripped his chest open and his intestines are hanging out. Blood spatter decorates the once lovingly decorated walls, painting them vermillion and signaling his desperation to protect his family.

Swallowing again as I look at Imogen, I tilt my head at the trail of bloody hoof prints that lead to the nursery. We were here when they found out they were expecting, when they assembled the room, and even after Feray was born. Now the beauty of that memory has been sullied by the scene before us.

We have to be strong…

Once we're both ready, we follow the prints to the door of the baby wolf's room. The sight that greets us is horrific: it splayed Lyra out as if nailed to a cross and impaled her head on a post of the baby's crib. Blood is dripping down the whitewashed wood, making its way to the pink carpet. Dead eyes stare sightlessly at us as we hold our breath and enter. The injuries to our friend are a testament to how hard she fought to protect her child, though in the end, she also failed.

I don't want to see what this monster did to the baby we considered a sister to our child. Forcing myself to approach, I stare at the empty crib in astonishment. There's no sign of Feray, nor that it harmed her in this room. I whip my head around to look at my wife in shock.

Was this a kidnapping? Why would they kill everyone so brutally instead of simply sneaking in to snatch the baby?

My eyes dart around the room until I reach the closet. I stalk over, throwing the door wide. There's a pile of dirty linens and blankets in the bottom, which is unlike Lyra. She always kept everything tidy, so much so that we all teased her about it. Tossing the clothes over my shoulder, I dig down until I reach the floor. I call for light and my magic brightens the dark space enough for me to see a tiny seam at the baseboard.

Claridon was always paranoid, and I never understood why. We both lived simple lives in a small town of magic users and shifters, well outside the dangers of the big city. He was a master craftsman and Lyra ran a bakery; there was nothing to worry about. Humans were far away from our little town and the stench of corruption from the gangs and Councils doesn't exist in Silver Falls.

But I recognize a bolt hole when I see one, so I search frantically until I find the lever that will spring the door open. It takes several tries to successfully open the door—Claridon was top-notch at his trade—but when it swings out, I gasp.

There, wrapped in her father's shirt and Lyra's clothing, is Feray. She has the warding amulet Imogen made for her on her chest, and I realize that even while scared for their lives, Lyra and Claridon ensured the beast wouldn't find their child. Between the magic of our amulet and their scent swaddling her, the baby is hungry and tired, but safe.

I lift the tiny infant out of the hole gently, my eyes filling with tears. Her baby scent makes my heart hurt for my fallen friends and I clutch her to me tightly. It's our responsibility to take care of her now; I know that. Imogen nods when I look at her with a sad expression, then walks over to the dresser, opening a drawer. When she hands me the baby sling, I know she feels the same.

Once I secure Feray to my body, we make our way back to the stairs and head out of the house. It will need to be burned to keep that creature or anyone else from following the scent trail to our home. We don't want anyone to know Feray is alive; she will be safe with us as long as we continue to have her wear the amulet that suppresses her wolf.

Raising her with our daughter, in a new town, is the only way to keep her alive.

I didn't wake up this morning knowing I'd have to abandon my entire life and our home, but I know as surely as the sun will rise tomorrow what we must do to protect this baby. Looking down at her curiously, I ponder the situation again. A magical beast used as an assassin seems like overkill if their target was the infant. Slaughtering her family was also unnecessary—that thing could have slipped into her room and killed her before anyone knew it was there.

Lifting the magic on her amulet for a moment, I wait until Feray opens her eyes. That's when I realize why my friends put it on her. My wife walks up beside me and runs a finger over her cheek. Her red hair looks very much like mine and as long as we keep the magic refreshed for the spell, she will look as though she is our natural daughter.

"We must pack up and move immediately," Imogen says as we walk out. "The capital city is vast, and no one knows us there. That will allow us to raise her as our own—a sister to Fiadh."

"Yes," I murmur. "I will send a message to the local council to inform them we are moving. The death of our friends and their daughter are too much for us to bear here. You simply need to keep her secret in our home until we leave."

She nods. "What about the monster who did this? Who would send it to kill a baby, and why?"

"Someone who scared Claridon enough to make a secret bolt hole in the nursery and forced Lyra to ask us for that amulet. I don't know what they were up to, but obviously, it was much bigger than our tiny town."

Imogen frowns. "We made three amulets, love. Why weren't Lyra and Claridon wearing theirs?"

"I don't know, Gen. Whatever the reason was, they took theirs off and someone powerful hunted down their daughter. Nothing is what it seems here, but we must protect Feray. We will keep her wolf suppressed for as long as possible—up to her Ascension if we can. She'll grow up and if she's destined for something bigger, she'll be able to assume that mantle when she's ready."

Taking this baby on and keeping her secret violates our coven laws; we both know it. Hiding her means we will always be on the run—we need completely new identities when we flee to the capital. It's a lifetime commitment, but the look on my wife's face tells me she's certain this is the right thing to do.

I know without a doubt that being was pure evil, and it came with one purpose: *assassination.*

Tomorrow, we begin our lives on the lam with two babies—there is no other option .

Get   it   now: **https://books2read.com/
newmoonrisingCOM1**

Sneak Peek: Veiled Flame

Loser

Kat

The little blue icon on my app has been glaring at me all day, but I'm too damn nervous to open it. Everyone at Woodlawn High has been buzzing all day with their notifications and the squeals of joy and moans of despair were too much for me to take. My anxiety is through the roof—this is the moment I've been waiting for since middle school, but I can't seem to force myself to bite the billet and check.

Maybe it's because I don't have the support system most of my classmates have?

That's probably true, given I've always been a loner and I don't fit into any specific 'caste' here. It's hard to make friends when you get shuffled from foster home to foster home over the years. I've rarely stayed anywhere long enough to make a friend, much less a group of them.

I'm not delinquent or anything—the families I've been placed with just return me like a pair of pants that doesn't fit after a year or so. The caseworkers click their tongues sympathetically and hunt down a new placement, but I've never been given a reason *why* people don't want me around. One lady said I must be born under a bad sign and hell if I knew what that meant other than I'm not good enough to keep around.

It would be different, almost understandable, if I misbehaved or got bad grades. But I don't—I'm always in the top five percent of my class and I do everything I'm asked. I don't even lord my smarts over the other kids or adults. Being presentable and unassuming was something I adapted long ago to improve my probability of staying in a home long term.

Unfortunately, it never worked and though I should be a shoo-in for scholarships and acceptances galore, I can't bring myself to be rejected yet again.

So I wait for the last bell of the day, slinging my bag over my shoulder and trudging home to the latest in my temporary housing. I can't even contemplate looking at the possible heartache waiting for me in the college application system WHS insisted we use. The fear is too great and despite knowing I'll be on my own for good at the end of this year, I'm unable to risk the pain.

I hate being this way.

My court mandated therapist says it's some sort of attachment disorder that's common in foster kids, but I think that's bullshit. The problem isn't *me* not forming attachments; it's asshole adults not forming one to me. Being left at a safe haven in a fucking basket as a baby wasn't because *I* did anything wrong—again, fucking adults couldn't handle their commitments.

As usual, I arrive home to an empty house. There are two other kids who live here—Bryce and Blake—but they're at football practice. Of course, the Jamesons *love* them; they get to strut around at games because their strays are the stars of the team. I'm not mistreated, but I'm definitely an afterthought. Both of my 'parents' are still at work, so I drop my bag on the couch and head for the kitchen to get a snack:

Don't get me wrong. I *could* have been placed in far worse homes than any of the seven I've been in since elementary school. None of the ex-fosters starved, beat, molested, or abused me. They were all decent folks with jobs and houses that weren't hellholes, but they never liked me.

I have no idea why. I tried to be everything they wanted.

But when the end of each school year came, I was handed in like a textbook and off I went to some group home until the next contestant stepped up. It baffled everyone, not just me, but that's what happened every single time.

Sighing, I pull some fruit out of the fridge and grab a soda. I have homework to do and if I want to have time to work on my stories, I'll need to get it done before the house is full of people at dinner time. Bryce and Blake will have gotten messages about their applications, too, and I'd bet my pinkie toe those idiots got into some big sports school. Brett and Allison will be oozing happiness for them and I don't know if I'll be able to keep food down if I have to admit my failure when they ask.

Being eighteen sucks ass.

After I grab my books and tablet, I head down to the den. I have to give my current parents credit; they set up a very nice workspace for us to study in the converted basement. By the time they took me in, the Jamesons created a cozy room down here where the three of us could relax and do our work for school without being interrupted. It might have been more for the boys than me, but I appreciated it all the same. Desks, a couch, big chairs, and bookshelves fill the space, making it almost seem like our minilibrary. They even put a small fridge for drinks and snacks in case we had to be up late to cram.

It's my favorite place in the entire house and I spend most of my time here.

I sink into the huge armchair, putting my drink and snack on the side table. It only takes a few minutes to arrange myself in the soft cushions and I pause to tug my headphones out of my pocket. Music always soothes my jagged edges and I need it to stay focused on the bullshit AP Calculus I need to keep my average up in. My course load is heavy, but I applied to tough colleges. I wouldn't have a chance to get in, especially on a scholarship, if I wasn't taking equally challenging classes in comparison to all the prep school kids.

As always, the sounds of Vivaldi carry me away as I scrawl equations on my screen and before long, thoughts of the blue notification completely fade away.

"Kat!"

The shouts barely register as I continue working on the problem set, gnawing on my lower lip in concentration.

"Jesus fuck, where is she? I could eat a hippo!"

"Kat!"

Thumping followed by what could pass for a stampede of elephants jerks me out of my math filled trance when Bryce and Blake come down the stairs. They smell as bad as the aforementioned pachyderm's cage, so they must have rushed home right after practice. The blond twins glare at me as if I'm the offending element despite being sweaty and covered in dirt and grass stains.

This doesn't bode well.

Usually, they're tired and hungry after practices so I'm used to cranky ass boys, but tonight, there's a light to their faces. That had to mean they've gotten their letters and dinner will be a gush fest in honor of their perfection. I'm going to need all of my strength to fake smile and nod as Brett and Allison fawn over them.

I don't begrudge them their success—not really. They work hard and play even harder on the field. It's not their fault they're the American dream teens and I'm the nerdy basement troll no one wants. But it's awfully hard living in the shadow of their bright light, especially when I'm no less intelligent or talented.

"I'm finishing the AP Calc, guys. What do you want?"

They roll their eyes at me before Blake scoffs. "It's not due until Monday. You're so hyper."

Duh. I take anxiety meds, douchebag; of course I'm 'hyper.'

"I can only be who I am, Blake." That earns me a snort from Bryce and I know it's because he thinks that's the problem. "Is dinner ready?"

"Almost. Get upstairs and set the table so we can shower—Brett's orders." Blake grins smugly.

The two of them seem to always arrange it so chores get passed to me for some half-assed reason and this is no exception. Sighing, I put my stuff aside, fully intending to hide down here after the dinner mess is cleaned up. Likely by me, but like I said, I could definitely live in worse foster homes so I let it go. Doing some chores isn't worth risking the group home for the last few months of my high school career.

They take off running up the stairs and I wait for them to disappear before I follow suit. My phone is tucked in my pocket and I feel like it's a stone of shame I have to bear. I know once the adults make over the twins' success, they will remember me, and I'll be forced to find out what disappointment lies in wait for me. The dread weighs on me, but I head into the sunny kitchen and pick up the pre-prepared pile of plates, silverware, and napkins on the counter.

Allison looks up from the stove and gives me a half-smile, nodding as I take the dishes into the dining room. Like I said, no one is mean or horrid, they just seem…obligated. After a while, it makes it hard to waste time trying to be bright and sunny. Being reserved makes it a hell of a lot easier not to feel rebuffed when they don't pay attention to you regardless.

"Make sure you include champagne glasses for your dad and I!" she calls from the other room.

The twins definitely got acceptance somewhere big. Brett must have gotten the bubbly on the way home.

Once I set the table, I return to help Allison bring out the roast and sides. I'm a little amazed at her efficiency when it comes to getting the housework done while working full time, but I suppose it's something people with real parents get taught as they grow up. My home life has been so fractured that I haven't learned how to cook more than very basic shit from YouTube videos. That may be a problem after graduation, but I've never felt comfortable enough to ask Allison if she'd teach me. I'm sure she would try, but it doesn't feel right.

"How was school, Kat?"

I look over my shoulder, seeing Brett in the entry to the dining room. He's already changed from work and smiling, but I see the distraction in his eyes. He's waiting for the boys to come down. "It was fine. I've got a Calc test at the end of the week. I'll be studying a lot to get ready."

"Good, good. No matter what happens with applications, keeping your grades up will ensure no one pulls any offers," he says.

Those words aren't for me. They are for the two wet haired boys who just appeared behind him.

"Kat's too much of a geek to ever let her grades slip, Dad," Blake says as he pushes past his brother and drops into his usual chair at the table. "Grab me a Powerade since you're in the kitchen, mouse!"

Both Brett and Bryce stare at me and I turn around, heading to the fridge despite the fact that I was *not* closer than the other twin. Out of habit, I take two of the drinks and a soda for myself. I've been here long enough to know Bryce will send me back to get him one as well. It would feel like typical sibling stuff, but for some reason, I just *know* they do it to fuck with me. I have no idea why I feel that way, but trusting my gut has been the one thing that helped me get through all the upheaval in my life over the years. It's a good gauge for knowing when I'll get booted or if people are being earnest in their reactions.

The therapist says that's some sort of trauma induced early trigger warning shit, by the way.

After I hand out the drinks, I sit down on my side of the table and we wait for Allison to come out. Brett is at his seat at the far end of the table and the twins are punching each other as they look at something on their phones. I know where this is all going but I drop my gaze to the table, swallowing the coppery taste of fear as it courses through my body.

I'm going to be exposed and there's nothing I can do to stop it.

Read the first three episodes free on Kindle Vella: https://www. amazon.com/kindle-vella/story/B0BSTMB1X3

NOTES

SUDDENLY SEYMOUR

1. Come here
2. Perfect

THE GIRL WITH THE FLAXEN HAIR

1. Fangs and Claws Academy

EVERYBODY WANTS TO RULE THE WORLD

1. Good day

SONATA NO. 14 "MOONLIGHT"

1. My heart

HAIL TO THE KING

1. In blood, we are bound; In death, we are victorious.

ANGEL EYES

1. The Crown Jewel

THUNDERSTRUCK

1. Together, we free the bound.
2. By the light of the Blood Moon, we invoke the gods of old. The reign of terror that began when the princess was exiled by the King will end.
3. Release the bond, O Great Horned God and Goddess Mother. Use this vessel to break free the first barrier so we live again!

SNEAK PEEK: CHILDREN OF THE MOON

1. I call on the gods. I protect myself from enemies and evil

About Cassandra Featherstone

Cassandra Featherstone has channeled her lifelong passion for writing into a flourishing career, a journey that started when she first grasped a pencil as a gifted child with ADHD.

Her debut novel, born during the solitude of COVID lockdown in March 2020, draws on a tapestry of personal encounters and insights that resonate deeply with her readers.

An international bestseller, Cassandra has topped Amazon charts in categories such as LGBT Anthologies, LGBTQ+ Mystery, and Bisexual Romance, among others. Her works navigate the complexities of bullying, PTSD, body dysmorphia, mental health struggles, personal reinvention, and the empowerment of claiming one's own space. Importantly, Cassandra offers a thoughtful and respectful portrayal of LGBTQIA+ relationships, subtly reflecting her own connection with the community through her narratives.

Her literary repertoire spans sci-fi fantasy, urban fantasy, paranormal, and comedic genres in academy whychoose settings, with a strong commitment to portraying consensual, safe, and accurately depicted BDSM and kink lifestyles. Her books are an invitation to explore transformative stories that are both inclusive and engaging.

Often affectionately called 'The Muppet' for her wacky theater kid personality, she resides in the Midwest with her tech-savvy husband, their creatively inclined college student, a literary-minded dog, and four scheming cats.

READ MORE AT CASSANDRA'S WEBSITE OR HER FACEBOOK PAGE. SIGN UP FOR EXCLUSIVE CONTENT AND UPDATES HERE.

FIND HER ON ANY OF THE SOCIAL MEDIA BELOW AS SHE **LOVES** TO CHAT AND **NEVER** SLEEPS!

THE MISFIT PROTECTION PROGRAM SERIES

Road to the Hollow

Return to the Hollow

Home to the Hollow

Rejected in the Hollow

Revealed in the Hollow

Healing in the Hollow

Revenge in the Hollow

AUDIO OF THE MISFIT PROTECTION PROGRAM SERIES

Road to the Hollow

APEX ACADEMY CAPERS

Come Out and Prey

Let Us Prey

In Prey We Trust

Oh Holy Spite (3.5 novella)

Eat. Prey. Love.

Prey It By Ear

AUDIO OF THE APEX ACADEMY CAPERS SERIES

Come Out & Prey

Let Us Prey

In Prey We Trust

TRANSLATIONS OF THE APEX ACADEMY CAPERS SERIES

Come Out & Prey (German)

Let Us Prey (German)

In Prey Trust (German)

DISCORDIA UNIVERSITY

Veiled Flame (Book One)

Quiet Burn (Book Two)

SECRETS OF STATE U

Blood on the Ice (Book One)

Suspicions on the Stage (Book Two)

FAETAL ATTRACTION

Hell on Wheels (Book One)

Book Two Title TBA

VILLAINS & VIXENS

Bloodthirsty (Book One)

Ruthless (Book Two)

Wicked (Book Three)

AUDIO OF THE VILLAINS & VIXENS SERIES

Bloodthirsty

Ruthless

TRIANGLES & TRIBULATIONS

Hoist the Flag (PQ)

Yo-Ho Holes (Book One)

CHILDREN OF THE MOON-
WITH SERENITY RAYNE

New Moon Rising (Book One)

Waxing Crescent (Book Two)

Waxing Gibbous (Book Three)

Full Moon (Book Four)

Waning Gibbous (Book Five)

Waning Crescent (Book Six)

RISE OF THE RESISTANCE

Ream Exclusive Prequels

Hooked on a Feline (Book One)

Peacock Me Like A Hurricane

Book 3 TBA Title

REAM SERIALS

Secrets of State U

Discordia University

Denizens of the Dark

Faetal Attraction

Agents of the Ouroboros

Rise of the Resistance

F.E.A.R. Academy

ANTHOLOGIES

Unwritten

Shifters Unleashed

Jingle My Balls

Love is in the Air

Silent Night

Snowed In

All Hallows Eve

www.ingramcontent.com/pod-product-compliance
Lightning Source LLC
Chambersburg PA
CBHW061043210726
48294CB00001B/11